ALSO BY *Zoë Oldenbourg*

THE WORLD IS NOT ENOUGH

THE AWAKENED

THE CHAINS OF LOVE

DESTINY OF FIRE

MASSACRE AT MONTSÉGUR

Cities of the Flesh

Cities of the Flesh

OR THE STORY OF

Roger de Montbrun

by

ZOË OLDENBOURG

Translated from the French by
ANNE CARTER

NEW YORK

PANTHEON BOOKS

A Division of Random House

FIRST PRINTING

© Copyright, 1963, by Victor Gollancz Ltd.
All rights reserved under International and Pan-
American Copyright Conventions. Published in New
York by Pantheon Books, a division of Random House,
Inc., and simultaneously in Toronto, Canada, by Ran-
dom House of Canada, Limited.
Library of Congress Catalog Card Number: 63-13696
Manufactured in the United States of America.

Originally published in French under the title *Les
Cités Charnelles*
© 1961, by Éditions Gallimard

PART ONE

ONE

Write with a gilded pen, wrap the letter in a silken cloth, put it in a sandalwood box: will this make the words any richer? There are two identical keys to the box: one hanging on a chain round my neck, the other in paradise—on a red silk girdle, between two hard, firm fruits no bigger than small pomegranates. Blessed for ever is that man to whom God grants the joy of tasting them.

One warm, flushed evening, on a feast day, hawks were soaring and swooping like arrows in a fiery red sky while magpies and wood pigeons fluttered in terrified circles and the air rained blood. The ladies on their palfreys were strung out like a necklace of bright coloured gems against the brown and russet trees behind them. They sat waiting for their hawks, hands raised, each calling her own. One moved forward out of the line and cried aloud as a splash of red blood fell on the folds of her white cloak, directly over the heart.

The bird that had come to rest on her glove was not her own; she was still staring in surprise at the strange hawk's eyes and the red stain on her mantle when Roger de Montbrun came to her and held out his hand to take the creature. He said:

"My lady, I have never set eyes on you before, but my bird is quicker than myself. He recognised his mistress. All I have is yours."

From the moment their eyes met across the hawk's head and the two embroidered gloves they knew and loved one another. The woman seemed even more dazzled than the man, as though thunderstruck: her eyes were wild and burning, like a hawk's before it swoops on its prey.

"Where does this blood come from?" she asked. No wounded bird had been brought down within twenty paces of her.

"Till now my name has been Roger de Montbrun; from this day forth it shall be whatever you choose to call me."

The lady said: "Let me keep this hawk. I greatly fear mine is lost."

7

She stroked the bird's head against her chin and turned back to join the other ladies.

She wore a white cloak that fell in heavy folds over a green woollen dress, trimmed with black. She was tall, slender and straight, like a young man, and a blue silk scarf was wound about her hair. She was beautiful, though common eyes would not have thought her so, since she was dark-complexioned, with no touch of colour in her firm, smooth cheeks. Her eyes were long and grey in colour, like two small fishes: not blue or green, but a clear grey.

She had been married five years to a knight of Toulouse, had borne two children, and was known to be devoted heart and soul to the Catharist cause.

Now at that time the Cathars had attained the height of their strength and were everywhere respected: Rigueur's joy and pride were not, therefore, to be wondered at. (Though her true name was Gentian, Roger would never call her anything but Rigueur.) She was a proud and happy woman indeed, with a great gift of eloquence.

Yet it was not for her eloquence that he loved Rigueur, but for her grey eyes, her long slender neck, her lovely white teeth and many other things that a lover can tell over silently like his beads, from dawn to dark, though he cannot speak of them to a living soul. An unruly curl on his lady's temple, a mole on her cheek, a pink scar on her brown hand—these are secrets all can see. They are not hidden away in a box. A woman can be loved for the scent of her black-fringed gloves, for the great jade and silver buckle which clasps her cloak across her breast, for the thousand things that belong to her and to no other woman.

Rigueur painted her eyes with a brown salve and wore a necklace made of chased silver balls. She never wore more than a single ring: the one her husband had placed on her finger on their wedding day, a round emerald in a setting of red gold. Yet her husband was no longer a husband to her—not, at least, in the eyes of ordinary folk who believe that to be husband and wife means sleeping in the same bed.

Only common lovers can hate their mistresses' husbands. Moreover, hers was the husband any lover would have wished for his beloved, even though the man who could so neglect the loveliest of women must be held a little mad. His name was Bérenger: he was a good knight, one of the finest swordsmen in

8

the Count's domains. When they saw him scaling the walls in his black helmet, with the black surcoat over his armour, even the most faint-hearted felt impelled to follow him: and once he had gained a footing on the parapet there was no driving him back. His features, though scarred with burns, were not naturally ugly and still retained something of their charm. Even in his cups he kept a cool enough head to avoid wounding anyone by a thoughtless word. A considerable asset, this, after ten years of warfare, during which all men able to bear arms had changed sides not once only, but two or three times, willy-nilly.

It was not, therefore, surprising that Rigueur should love her husband. Roger too developed a strong friendship for the chivalrous knight. They often supped and slept side by side and talked together on many occasions. Bérenger was by five or six years the elder of the two, which made him about thirty-five when they first met. It was not difficult to win his friendship; no need of flattery or false pretences. He had such a deep knowledge of music and hunting, and all chivalrous skills, that a year spent in prison would not have seemed too long in his company.

Roger de Montbrun had seen something of the world: he had been one of the Count of Toulouse's personal followers. At eighteen he had been dubbed knight at the hand of Count Raymond himself. In those days, when the Count was still master of his own, life was good. Men spent more time in hunting than fighting, and could speak to friends and enemies alike with equal freedom. Even then, the Count was at war, either in Quercy or Provence, and he and his followers were always on the move, billeting themselves in the castle of this or that unruly baron; and there, while negotiations went forward, there would be more feasting and intrigue than exchange of blows, until often enough no one could decide who ought to pay the mercenaries their wages, they had been passed from hand to hand like dice in play. Gambling was such a popular pastime at the Count's court that even though the Synod had forbidden it abbots sometimes lost half of their benefices in this way. (Those who accuse the Count of disliking the clergy are quite wrong: he bore no ill-will except to his sworn enemies, and for this he cannot in all fairness be blamed.)

When Roger was twenty he saw his master flogged in the square outside the church of Saint-Gilles, stripped all but naked,

9

with a cord round his neck, before a crowd of bishops, abbots and barons. Milo, the Papal legate, went at his task with a will and scourged the firm, white back of the premier lord of Provence like a lay clerk scourging the back of a whore found drunk on Good Friday. He scourged him until the blood ran, and his lash was not silk or paper but birch rods, so that all might see he was not doing it for show. Certainly the Count did not think it was a show, nor did his friends, nor even the Archbishop of Narbonne or the Bishop of Carcassonne, both of whom turned away, red with shame and anger. (Pope Innocent, inspired not by the Holy Ghost but by evil counsellors, had been endeavouring for many years to remove the lawful bishops from their episcopal thrones and replace them by the Count's enemies; and the bishop he had caused to be elected at Toulouse was such a man that the Count would willingly have submitted to another flogging if at that price he could have been rid of him.)

Only a short time before this black day, the Count had been received in Paris and Aix-la-Chapelle with all the honours due to his rank, if not with altogether the friendship he deserved. He would have done better to use the money he spent on these journeys in bribing the Papal chancellor, for all the help he was to get from the King or the Emperor was not worth a basketful of nuts. Yet the King and the Count were closely related, sharing the same grandfather, King Louis VI of France. It is impossible to imagine the Count's generosity to King Philip and the loyal and open friendship he showed the King, and his son, and his son's wife (these two, later on, were to be much worse than the King). But among men of no faith, courtesy is taken for weakness.

In Paris and Aix, Roger had seen fine lords and lovely ladies, and painted and gilded churches, and he had learned a number of new songs, but he had learned very little about the war which was brewing. In Paris the younger knights were saying quite openly that the Pope was making a deal too much fuss over the murder of a single monk* and that even in France there were plenty of men who would have been better pleased to slit such a legate's throat than the Sultan of Egypt's. At Aix, there were German lords (some of whom spoke the Provençal dialect

* The Papal Legate, Peter of Castelnau, whose assassination at Saint-Gilles on 14th January, 1208, was the immediate cause of the Pope's call to arms. (Translator.)

fluently) ready to call the Pope a thief and a traitor, and clerks were composing scurrilous songs about the uses the Roman cardinals were making of German money. The Emperor considered the Count too much a friend to the King of France and gave him a neutral welcome.

Yet the Count had a gift for making himself loved: even when he was old and tired his charm of manner would have disarmed his worst enemies. His wife, the Countess Leonora, Infanta of Aragon, was still young in those days and so famed for her beauty that one glimpse of her golden hair and rosy cheeks would have made kings and emperors with a spark of chivalry in them pledge their realms to safeguard her inheritance. But because Count Raymond brought back nothing from his travels save smiles and kind words, he must needs endure a flogging for a sin he had not committed. (Such, at least, was the general opinion: that the Count had never ordered the murder and had suffered himself rather than betray a vassal.)

On that June morning at Saint-Gilles du Gard, the notorious red cross did not lie so heavily, compared with the hatred it was later to inspire. None the less, they were not so very many who donned it, barely a dozen in all, from among the Count's household and followers. Thus, Roger became a Crusader, in great pomp, amid the lighted candles and chanting choirs on the church square where the Count had been beaten: he had kneeled down and kissed the red fabric of the cross as he took it from the white hands of the legate who had trounced the Count so thoroughly.

The legate had given him his sword, blessed and consecrated, and he had to swear on this sword, just as his comrades had done before him, to defend the Church of Christ Jesus and the Catholic Faith, and to exterminate all the heretics he could find, and to serve the leaders of the Crusade with all his might. The Count had sworn all this and therefore his followers might do the same.

In order to win their master's favours, men will offer him their daughters or betray their brothers; there are even some who will tumble in the mud on purpose to make him laugh. Moreover, the Count had no lack of spirited jesters, witty and educated men he would not have parted with for a thousand silver marks, even to the King himself. He had them perform in the private

11

chamber of his palace on the evening after taking up the cross, while he was eating his first meal as a Crusader. They pinned red crosses on themselves, before and behind, and declared that the best means of ridding oneself of one's enemies was to become one's own enemy; and that the easiest way of avoiding hunger was to eat oneself. Then they put on grotesque mitres and chasubles and celebrated a parody of the Mass, passing the chalice of wine, miraculously replenished, from hand to hand. There was much laughter and the Count's chaplain, who had seen such things before, laughed too—for though the Count was a deeply pious man he was also, it must be admitted, very broad-minded. All those present, flushed with wine, laughed heartily, without constraint, thinking it was no bad thing to be a fool and able to make people laugh at things that were not funny at all. *It made no difference that the Count was not on good terms with the Viscount of Béziers, the Viscount was still his nephew and vassal, and a very gallant knight.*

There was talk of the 'forty days'. Come to me all you sinners, thieves, murderers and coiners, you need no longer fast, weep or mourn, for in forty days, not thirty-nine or forty-one, a man may win forgiveness. Jesus Christ was quite ignorant when he said that conversion must be for life: a revelation from the Holy Ghost has shown our Holy Father, Pope Innocent, that it is enough for a man to wear the cross for forty days to be absolved from all his sins.

In those days Roger was like most young men of twenty, if he thought at all it was of trivial things: seeing red every time a comrade looked askance at his hair, drawing his sword or dagger whenever a man spoke ill of Toulouse, racking his brains to decide whether this or that lady had really glanced at him, wondering if he had caught the pox from a girl who attracted his passing fancy, chewing his fingers with anger over the thought of a word left unsaid at the proper moment. When you are twenty both heaven and earth are hidden from you by your own face: a handsome face, not unattractive to women, but one it seems even better to keep for yourself, free to look straight ahead without seeking the eyes of any other.

His father, in Toulouse, was arranging a wealthy marriage for him at the time. Because of the Crusade, which Roger undertook only out of duty, the marriage did not take place. In Toulouse, more than in any other city, it is hard to please everyone. Maybe for one father-in-law lost there might be ten found. Roger was to remain for a long time with no other fortune than what he carried with him and the Count's gifts. The Count was still leading the life appropriate to his rank, and was surrounded by a suite large enough to people a small town, including his chaplains and clerks, notaries and scribes, his minstrels, jesters, barbers, astrologers, doctors, mistresses, cooks, huntsmen and falconers, as well as many humbler servants. But when he went to meet the crusading army at Valence he rode with only a small company, among his knights and their men as befitted a soldier in action.

A fine, hot day, a stark blue sky, all one blue like a huge piece of cloth, pierced by a single, great white-hot nail. The terrible white light flattened road and plain and river until everything seemed blanched and drained of colour. It was a journey like many others, the same trotting horses and the same songs on the road. The banners of Toulouse had not changed their colour.

There was feasting for two days outside Valence and in the city, where the Count took his place among the leaders of the Crusade with the honours due to his rank. By birth, fortune and knightly valour he was the greatest of all the barons there, and the Duke of Burgundy and the Count of Nevers were not fools enough to forget it. He brought only a small company, but his horsemen surpassed all others in the richness of their accoutrements and the splendour of their harness, shields and banners.

So they went from one feast to another, until it seemed as though the Count engendered feasting like flowers in springtime. There was music and kissing and toasts drunk in honour of all the kings in Christendom, not forgetting the Pope; there were carpets laid down in the streets and before the tents, and torchlight processions at night to the sound of trumpets and viols.

As for the crusading army, the Count's soldiers would not have been able to describe it, for accustomed as they were to war, they had seen nothing like it. They looked down on it from the walls of Valence wondering what was the use of this monster with its hundred thousand heads and this forest of banners with their scarlet crosses. The river Rhône was choked with barges

13

and lighters, roads and fields were like a seething ant heap as far as the horizon, and at night the plain was covered with camp fires until it looked like a starry sky. Those who remembered the passing of the crusading army on its way to Marseilles, twenty years earlier, swore that they had never seen such a gathering of men and horses in such a small space, there must have been more than ten thousand fighting men alone. It made a man giddy even to contemplate the amount of bread, wine, salt, and soup, and hay and oats all these could consume, and how much dung and urine they could produce. How could the commanders control this army, and what would they do with it once the campaign had begun? The Pope had made a fine mess of things with his forty days' indulgence!

Even now it was hard to understand how such an army could have made the journey from Lyons to Valence in ten days, and augured no good. Otherwise the knights and squires of the great barons, seen at close quarters, were no worse than any others, although it was hard enough to swallow the way they looked at you when they learned you were from Toulouse. The Count's orders were to avoid all quarrels and bloodshed on pain of death by hanging, seeing that in the marquisate of Provence, as in all other lands under the dominion of the Counts of Toulouse, every man fighting for the Catholic Faith was sacred by virtue of the sign of the cross which he wore. He must be treated as a guest and friend, even as a superior, because he was not simply the soldier of some terrestrial prince but of Holy Church. Honour and respect were the Crusaders' due, for they came to deliver the country from the plague of heresy.

(It should be said here that the Count had not brought his jesters with him but had surrounded himself with churchmen, as was befitting to a Crusader prince.)

It was better, therefore, not to mix with the Burgundians, or with the men from France or Champagne, except when duty made it necessary. Many of these men wore a rosary round their wrists, laughed only with twisted lips and looked at women with the forced distaste of men fasting. There was nothing surprising in this: the whole camp echoed with psalms and *Aves* and cries of: "As God wills!" and "For the Cross of Christ!" There was at least one priest to every ten men and one white friar to every hundred; while even in the whores' tents men were swearing by Christ Jesus and the Virgin Mary.

14

For the men of Toulouse it was an odd and testing experience to find themselves there, as allies, witnesses or merely hostages, and they were for ever wondering what the red cross was doing on the Count's garments. They stood firm as steel in maintaining—in all good faith—that their lord was the most Catholic of all the Crusading princes, since no man within living memory had yielded so much and promised so much of his possessions to the Church, nor consented of his own free will to make such sacrifices.

Roger de Montbrun was to have little time for reflection— either in those days or afterwards. In the first place, he was merely one knight among many in the Count's personal service, he had neither a company to command nor lands to defend, he was attached to the Count like a bell on a horse's bridle and all that was asked of him was good behaviour and unquestioning loyalty. Then it was not difficult to be loyal to the Count: there was never a more generous master. He would give away a ring from his finger or a cup from his table, for nothing, out of pure friendship and with such a graceful manner that he almost made you believe he was treating you as an equal (these gifts changed hands quickly, lost in gaming or betting). Riding at the head of the great army, among the procession of great barons, from Valence to Montpellier and from Montpellier to Béziers, Roger admired the arms of the Crusaders from the North, their horses and, most of all, their noble bearing. From Montpellier onwards they wore full armour, to show that they were at war, and as the least of the knights passed by, the townspeople cried out in amazement to see their helmets and coats of mail glittering in the sun and the bright, gay colours of their tunics, shields and harness. The great lords had gold and enamel on their helmets and pearls and coloured stones set in the hilts of their swords. There were shouts of: "In God's name!" and "For Christ Jesus!" and "Holy Cross!" and men brandished swords that had been blessed and blessed again, and sanctified with pieces of the True Cross imbedded, under glass, in the pommel. (Of these notorious pieces of the Cross, no bigger than wisps of straw, it was said that if they were all put together they would make not one cross but an entire forest. They were sold from Stockholm to Barcelona and from Paris to Jerusalem, to any man willing to pay ten marks, or even five.) Roger had no wood from the

Cross in his sword, he had instead a splinter of bone from St. Valerie's foot.

The bulk of the army—consisting of mercenaries, archers, siege engines, foot-soldiers, diocesan militia, pilgrims, the sick, the laggard and those who were simply brigands—had by-passed the city of Montpellier and were waiting for the cavalry to go by before resuming their march. In the presence of these swarms of men, collected together so senselessly, the question recurred: where could such an enterprise end? Who could ever feed them all for forty days? They could not rely on the land, livestock and reserves of food had all been stowed away safely in the towns and castles; yet surely the Count of Toulouse would not have to bear the cost, as part of his penance? In the meadows outside the city, the Crusaders' banners waved like poppies over a field of young corn, great and small, fringed with gold or made of heavy, unbleached linen, and the noise of singing and oaths was like a rumble of distant thunder. So many men crowded together without women, in mid-July, was not a pretty sight, and if they grew quarrelsome the blame lay with those who had brought them there. Moreover, they had brought them to fight, but who were they to fight against seeing that no commander would ever be rash enough to engage such a mighty army in the open field?

Indeed was there ever a war where the participants had less reason for fighting? The Pope had preached the Crusade against the Count, only to see the Count himself become a Crusader: a fact to make men laugh or cry as they felt inclined. But was the Viscount of Béziers, who was neither heretic, rebel nor excommunicate, to stand by and see his lands devastated when he had just made his submission to the Church with oaths, sureties and hostages? Surely men must be mad to wage war on those who offer peace? Had not the Viscount come in person, humbling himself much more than was necessary before the Abbot of Cîteaux and the legate, ready to swear anything rather than see such an army descend on his lands?

Certain it was that they meant to take the city of Béziers at all costs, even if they were to lose half of their soldiers in the process; certain too that they would have taken it in any case since the Viscount had the bulk of his forces at Carcassonne; the garrison of Béziers was scarcely larger than in time of peace

16

and the city in no condition to stand a siege. On the day the Crusaders planted their banners before Béziers the inhabitants were still digging ditches and there were not even any engines of war on the ramparts.

They would have taken it for certain in three or four weeks' siege because they had good siege engines and strong bands of sappers and engineers: men saw them at work at Carcassonne, and their Flemish and Swiss crossbowmen were worth a knight apiece. They would have taken it, and the commanders knew this perfectly well on the day they held council to decide what was to be done with the citizens, and how to distinguish the innocent from the guilty. Though Count Raymond was present at the council, sitting opposite the Abbot of Cîteaux (who was then his sworn enemy) in the legate's white tent, he was not there to say yea or nay but only because they had not dared not to invite him. Having pledged himself to serve God's soldiers with his counsel and to obey them in all things, he remained there, eyes closed and chin in hand, listening while they talked. He could do no less, neither could he do any more.

(It was not wise to approach him in those days, or to risk speaking one's mind to him: he was bitter and irritable as he had never been, and ready to say that he could count on no one but himself, that he no longer expected anything of his friends, vassals and servants, except to be left alone. He said, too, that at his age it was quite enough to be taken for a murderer thanks to over-zealous friends, and that thank God he had no need of anyone to defend his reputation; and that to defend his subjects and the liberties of his country it needed one head, not ten or twenty, and that one a head not battered from morning to night with useless recriminations. If he vented his bad temper on his own people, this was because he was compelled to be polite to others. In fact he did not dislike the Duke of Burgundy and the Count of Bar and deliberately showed them greater friendship than they deserved, the better to underline his contempt for the Abbot of Cîteaux—who was already, in name and in fact, the head of the army. The hatred which lay between him and the Abbot was the talk of the camp and every day supporters of one or the other had new stories to tell of double-edged remarks that had passed between the two men: the Abbot, like the Count, was known to have a formidable wit.)

If the Count had been able to influence the decisions of the

17

French commanders, by however little, then certainly he would have been greatly to blame for not having done so. But had he even ventured an opinion, the Abbot would have pointedly done the reverse; and since the barons could not agree among themselves they were dependent on the Abbot whether they liked it or not. It was decided, because the city had apparently made common cause with the heretics (and this was only apparent, since it was merely a false pretext invented by the Crusaders: a man is not a heretic for wishing to keep faith with his liege lord); because the consuls of the city had refused to deliver up their fellow citizens and so cover themselves with shame, all the citizens were to be treated as rebels and enemies of the Church. Even then they had to decide which citizens, and whether only the notabilities and known heretics were to be punished, or all men of an age to bear arms.

If the siege had only lasted for two or three weeks, nothing would have happened, and at least it would have been possible to reach an agreement about the fate of the defenders. Because in the event the attack was so furious that a tragedy occurred which would remain like a scarlet stain on the hearts of all those who were present for the rest of their lives.

It was such a tragedy that men dared not believe it, either the next day or a week later. There was still the same sky and nothing had changed: faces had not changed, or the voices of friends; men ate, drank and thought as before. But the life they had led before that day was dead and another life was beginning; thoughts went back constantly to the time when this thing had still not happened, and God knows why that time, troubled and tormented as it was, seemed as lovely as a lost childhood.

Because this thing had happened there, within the walls of Béziers between sunrise and sunset on that day of St. Mary Magdalene, it was madness for men to believe that the next day would be a day like any other, and that there were other places where this thing had never happened. What good are leaders who lose control of their men to such an extent? The next day they mount their horses again and go on their way, with arms and banners flying as before, singing *Te Deums*, and in a few hours they have already ridden far enough for the smoke of the burning city to be no more than a red and grey cloud on the horizon.

Those who came from Toulouse took no part in this, of

course. They were more blameless than the Viscount Raymond-Roger himself, because he had left the city to sustain the first shock while he made himself secure in Carcassonne. They took no part in it, having never wished or intended to take part in the attack. They had seen it, and to begin with what they had seen was little enough: the Duke of Burgundy's troops surging in to the attack, dragging ladders and rams. (They were not expecting a surprise attack that day, but to give the people their due they were at their posts at the first sound of the alarm and in their proper places; there was no panic or confusion or rounding up of stragglers.) The tocsin was ringing high up in the city, and already there was fighting on the ramparts and at the gates.

Then the tocsin turned into a knell, and in many heads that knell would toll for ever, it continued as long as an arm remained to ring it though its tolling was soon drowned in the tumult. There was no need to be at the foot of the wall to see that the attack was fierce and the garrison overrun; the Orb gate had been breached and the Crusaders' foot-soldiers were pouring through as though into a Church until on that side of the city there was no defence left to speak of. A thick hedge of scaling ladders had been run up against the east wall. A good half of the army was swarming up them, looking from a distance like so many thousands of wasps, and all were yelling: "For Christ Jesus!" and "Holy Cross!" until the clash of swords and the screams of wounded men and horses could no longer be heard. And still the knell tolled on.

Just when was it that they knew things were getting out of hand? The clamour from inside the city was not ceasing, it was getting louder, rising to such a tearing, piercing crescendo that the noise of fighting was lost in it like a roll of drums in a thunderstorm. The whole city was screaming in its death agony.

"*What is that noise? Has the sack begun already?*"

"*The sack? This is a massacre. They are seeking out the heretics.*" But how the devil were they to know them? The horsemen were milling about underneath the walls like straw blown by the wind, and now the Crusaders' banners had been raised over all the gates of the city.

It was a tough assault, by God, and well carried through.

The news spread like a wave through the camp, shouted from one to another. They are killing them all, they are killing them in the churches. Count Raymond summoned his brother Count

19

Baudouin, and the lords of Roquefeuil and Miramont, and putting spurs to his horse he set off with his guard in the hope of finding the Duke of Burgundy. The Duke was not yet inside the city but on the ramparts, surrounded by a dozen knights, giving orders in a curt voice, made hoarse with shouting.

"*Clear the gates! No one can get in!*"

"*By Our Lady*," said the Count, "*the city can't be left at the mercy of that rabble of soldiery for much longer. Think of the havoc!*"

The Duke, his face scarlet under the helmet with its golden circlet, was scanning the ramparts anxiously.

"*The Devil himself would be lost in this hell. The wisest course is to let the soldiers spend their fury on the heretic rabble, and then take care of the booty afterwards.*"

"*But you can see what they are doing. They'll slaughter half the city if they aren't brought to their senses!*"

"*Who's going to bring them to their senses? Things have reached a state now where even cowards are going berserk. Go and talk to the Abbot.*"

The Abbot was looking as fine as the flower of the French knights, mounted on a grey palfrey with his helmet gleaming with gold and a white mantle covering his broad shoulders over the coat of mail. He was surrounded by his clerks on horseback, carrying his shield and his white banner with the silver fringe. He stared at the Count and his men with an air of disdain, as much as to say: "Where have these creatures come from?" His face was terrifyingly hard and grim.

"*By God, my lord Abbot, are you deaf? Can you hear that din? What are you going to do? It is time to sound the recall.*"

The Abbot laughed harshly. "*It is always time with you, lord Count, and still you come an hour too late. Would you put out a fire by sounding the recall?*"

"*They are killing women and priests. A report of all this shall go to the Pope.*"

"*I myself shall make the report. Do you not see that this is no longer the work of men, but of God?*"

"*And what a God!*" The Count turned away, swearing like a carter. It was all he could do. The city was like a blazing building and it was impossible to get in or out. Those of the citizens who tried to escape were cut down by battle-axes at the gates, and the naked bodies of soldiers whose equipment was still usable were flung down from the walls into the moat.

20

And still the tumult grew, but the bell was no longer ringing. It lasted only five or six hours, but to anyone who ever heard such screaming each minute seemed as long as an hour and it was as though the sun stood still and the slaughter had been going on for days inside the city. Slaughter. Hundreds of lovely girls whom no one even paused to rape, the sick, not even dragged from their beds, and brave, stalwart men who defended themselves with hammers and pokers.

They killed the thieves in the prisons and the wealthy barricaded in their homes, old women and noble ladies who tried to buy their lives with their jewels, and beggars riddled with diseases and filthy sores, and little naked children who ran to hide themselves under benches. The work of killing was easiest in the churches: there was no need to search for the people, or hunt them down, they huddled there like sheep, too closely packed together to offer any resistance. They killed the priests and the sacristans and the little choirboys, harlots and women with child, boys and youths and mothers clutching three, four and five small children among the folds of their petticoats. They killed weavers and wheelwrights, butchers, bakers, smiths and merchants, street porters and notaries, washerwomen and seamstresses, even the dogs and the poultry and everything living they could find in the city except the horses. If any survived it was through no fault of the pilgrims, for they were everywhere, sniffing in every corner like hounds nosing out game.

It was all over long before evening, and when at last the horsemen were able to make their way into the city the rioters were roaming about among the corpses with swords and axes in their hands and their legs red with blood up to the knee, still hunting, hunting for something left to kill and finding nothing but here and there a newborn child hidden among the straw in a stable, or a wounded man too terrified to feign death.

Men-at-arms, tired out with killing, their swords sticking to their gloves and their tunics reddened until the crosses no longer showed, reeled through the streets, haggard eyed, and seemed on the point of falling on their own cavalry. Others were vomiting over the corpses and weeping, not out of pity but because they had come to the end of their strength, for many of these people were not professional soldiers and had never killed before in their lives.

In the streets around the churches and the city hall feasting was already in full swing, because these were the wealthy districts. The houses were filled with laughter and singing and clattering dishes, while from their windows hurtled everything from severed heads and limbs to saucepans, books, lamps, pillows and joints of meat. Lengths of heavy, brocaded silk, muslins and flowered hangings lay spread about the streets, and here and there among the dancing men was one wearing a woman's dress, encrusted with heavy, gold embroidery, a sable mantle or a consul's scarlet gown. They were more than half drunk and all of them were laughing, laughing until they fell down, their grotesque garments flapping like fools' motley under the bloody, grinning faces, burned black by the sun. Still more were running about stark naked, with strings of precious jewels round their necks, and babies' christening robes, smothered in gold lace, on their heads. Never was so much good wine spilled in so short a time: the roisterers were tapping the barrels and rolling them out into the street, on top of the corpses, until it became impossible to tell whether it was blood or wine that ran in the kennels. There was ten times more than they could drink and these were not the men to leave for others what they could not carry away themselves. They took only what was made of gold or silver and made a sport of wrecking all else, since it is not given to everyone to destroy in an hour enough wealth to pay an army for two years.

Their feasting was hard earned, and it was all the profit they gained from their conquest. By the time the cavalry reached the prosperous quarters of the town, the sack was already becoming a brawl, and the men too drunk to defend their loot when it was snatched away from them. (All the same, they revenged themselves richly by throwing blazing torches into the barns and woodyards, and arson was a trade they knew well. Trapped by the smoke and flames, the knights and their men were forced to escape from the houses they had lately occupied, leaving behind them sacks stuffed with jewels and gold plate, to try at least to save their horses.)

Their leaders rode grimly through the town, for it was not a pretty sight. It was very hot and they were weary. Even those who had not had time to fight felt exhausted by the din and the shouting, and the shock of having taken so strong a city in such a manner. No city had ever been taken like it before.

The air was heavy and stifling with the smell of blood, wine, sweat, vomit and excrement. Every man had the taste of blood in his mouth and there was not one who did not feel sticky all over. They had intended to move into the town, clear the houses and divide the plunder, but there was not even a place to sing vespers. The churches were all stuffed with corpses. The dead had to be cleared away with shovels to make room for the horses to pass.

They did what they could, but what could they do in a place choked with such a mass of raw and bleeding flesh that already it was beginning to stink, and which by the morrow would be unendurable? There was too much death, there was so much that the living felt ill at ease in the city. The dead were the stronger here, for once they were all together, all in agreement, friends and enemies, rich and poor, prisoner and judge, debtor and creditor. There was no longer love or hatred between them, no troubles or disputes over an ell of cloth or a light o' love. They were all together, united for ever at one stroke. A whole rich and powerful city turned into a place of death.

They lay there on the ground as if they were drunk, twisted into strange and obscene postures, draped over the stones by fountains whose water ran red, kneeling in doorways or peeping with their battered and faceless heads from windows. Only the rich had been stripped, and they exposed their naked flesh shamelessly, some fat, hairy, or wrinkled, others young and fresh, while the guts spilled out of their ripped-up bellies, and the pale, slender bodies of little children lay like white flowers in between the ragged poor.

Those whose faces could still be seen regarded the living with insane stares—with eyes that, whether they were fixed, blank, terrified or merely indifferent, still seemed to see. It seemed as though their eyes could see much more than the living ever would.

Meanwhile, the living stared about them without understanding, because it is possible to feel pity for one dead man or for ten, but twenty thousand . . . No human heart can hold pity enough for that. They were deafened by the noise and heat of the assault, and now that the bells had stopped ringing the only noise was the ordinary clamour made by soldiers quarrelling— which was still noise enough, though they seemed hardly to hear it. It was as if they were longing to hear the screaming and the knell again because henceforth all other sounds would be meaningless.

The dead were stronger than the living here; their blood

23

spread a sticky, shining carpet over the streets and streaked weird patterns across their bodies.

The men of Toulouse passed through the city also, not for plunder (none would have been left for them even if they had wanted it), but because their Count had his place among the leaders of the Crusade and whether he liked it or not he had to drain the cup and carry this red cross he had taken up to the end. He had not taken it up as a sign of battle and victory, but like a shield. He still wore it on his white silk tunic, over his suit of mail, and he did not blench as he passed by churches bulging with corpses and squares strewn with the heads of women and children. He looked and printed all this in his mind, already preparing his accusations with a controlled fury that burned like vitriol. There were things that had to be said, and while there was still a man to say them, a man against whom neither Pope nor kings could ever be contemptuous enough to close their doors, these things should be said, and said to the full—and by Our Lady it was a fool's errand! Speak to them until the day of Christ's coming and they would never lift so much as the tip of their little finger unless they stood to gain by it.

Theirs was a strange passion, and this pilgrimage would not count in their favour on the Day of Judgment. They were there, among the rest who, though they did not seem unduly proud and joyful, were at least able to think that here was a job well done and one that would be long remembered. They wore the same red cross on their breasts as the murderers did.

They counted for nothing there. But because they had to think of something, their first thought was: "*The Count knew what he was about, thank God. Our own cities will never suffer like this. If it is possible to escape at this price then every man in his senses should cover himself with four crosses, not just one.*"

This will not happen to us. We have had a lucky escape. Yet knowing this makes no difference, it changes nothing: what the eyes have beheld this day is a thing so hideous that it scarcely seems to matter if all other cities suffer the same agony. Now, in all the streets and all the churches, there is nothing to be seen but corpses. And still they were powerless. Though the people of Carcassès call us turncoats and traitors until the last Judgment they will never be able to say that Count Raymond's people took any part in this business, or that by words or deeds they could have prevented this tragedy from happening.

24

They did not have to dispose of the bodies, because by the same evening the city was in flames, and burning so fiercely that they had to leave hurriedly, abandoning much of the Crusaders' own equipment and many horses, as well as all the booty.

This was all that occurred. The army took the road again, as lightly as it had come, since there was no plunder to carry away and (for the moment at least) the captured city was no longer habitable.

It was not the Catholics who did this, or the knights, or the bishops and their clergy. It was not done by the men of France, or Champagne, or Burgundy or Provence; nor by the archers, or the engineers or those who supplied the army. As for the rioters who had been seen at work, there were not enough of them in the army to make an end of a whole city. Who then had done it? God. Only God can perform actions which are beyond the strength of men. God's hand must have been at work, since the affair was to carry such benefits to Christ's army. Certain it was that but for that day's madness the Crusaders would never have established themselves so firmly in the region. More castles submitted in a few days through the fear inspired by that day than the mightiest army could have taken in two years.

God.

Roger de Montbrun was not a great personage, nor was he a man better than other men, indeed he was rather worse than better, and in order to tell his story one must begin at the beginning. He was the eldest son of Pierre-Guillaume de Montbrun, a gentleman of Toulouse with considerable social ambitions and some importance in the city. He had little fortune but a great many friends, thanks to an ancient name and a great reputation for gallantry. In the house of his proud, quick tempered father Roger had grown up like a young dog being trained for the royal pack. He was active and steadfast, well versed in all those skills which can be taught by the whip: in letters, music, falconry, venery, heraldry, dancing and all feats of arms.

From his father and his father's friends he learned that it was a much less serious offence to break a leg hunting than to stumble in the middle of a dance; and that a man could gamble away his money, his mistress and his horse, but must never show that it grieved him. He learned, too, that a man could lie about serious matters but not for little things; that he could claim to be a lady's lover when he was not, but never if he was in truth. He might act as go-between for a friend or a subordinate in a

25

*love-affair, but never for a superior; and it was permissible to accept presents
from a man in a higher position than himself, but never from an inferior,
however wealthy. He must never change his friends, or render a service
to anyone who might be a friend of his friends' enemies.*

*Like most of his comrades, Roger came in the course of his service,
first as squire and later as a knight, to regard the Count as a sort of
adopted father. For Pierre-Guillaume de Montbrun he felt only the common kindness he owed to any man of his own family, and he in turn was
considered by his father purely as a colleague, a useful instrument to
increase the family fortune. But the Count was entirely disinterested,
knowing neither ambition nor jealousy; his was the greatest freedom of
all, the freedom from the tormenting desire to outshine others. For this
reason Roger felt himself closer to his master than to any other living
creature: and since his was not a vulgar spirit he served his lord without
flattery or calculation, without striving to put himself forward. He was
no more servile than the branch of an oak that has no need to question
its dependence on the tree.*

Roger had felt all the bitterness of this tie, deeper than any
blood tie, in those forty days of the Crusade. There were many,
even among the most loyal and respected knights, who, for all
their devotion to the house of Saint-Gilles, had drawn back
and found any number of excuses for not sharing his humiliation. Only his closest friends had joined the Crusaders (yet still
without taking the cross), Count Baudouin and a few poor knights
who hoped to gain favour with the Count by their action (and
whose efforts were not wasted). Wretches quaking for their
livelihood they were çalled, who dress as madmen because their
master has gone out of his mind with fear. God knows what more
cruel things were said, for bitterness of feeling ran high in those
days and tongues wagged fast. Even those who, later on, were to
eat out of Simon de Montfort's hand could say: We only did it
when we were forced to, we did not anticipate the need.

No, no one held a knife to your throats. Certainly Count
Raymond (whatever the Abbot and the other men of the legates'
clan who called him a bloody tyrant, a Herod, might say) was
not a man to hold a knife to any man's throat. He was capable
of bitter hatred, but his anger was brief; he never bore grudges
against those who served him and forgave easily.

For very shame they would say: *"It is we who are the wiser and
all the rest of you are mad to think that any defence against these people
is possible. Has no one told you that they are God's army?"*

26

During the siege of Carcassone the King of Aragon and some of the Viscount's knights had come into the tents of Toulouse, honestly believing that the Count could make the French commanders listen to him. *"We are all brothers,"* they said, *"and if there has been any disagreement between our master and you, or if, through youth and thoughtlessness, he has offended you, remember at least that he is your sister's son."*

The Count had no answer for them; yet there had been no disagreement that he could remember—and it was in his nature to bear a grudge. *"If he had listened to me . . ."* That is what the old always say of the young, and the knights must have been thinking: "He is trying to pull his chestnuts out of the fire and gain control of the Viscount's domains as the price of his treason." As though there were anything left to gain! The Crusaders had drowned in blood all question of right and betrayal, of friendship and enmity, of courage and cowardice.

They fought like madmen, dashing themselves in a howling tide against walls a hundred feet high and attacking with such fury that it seemed as though they meant to tear the towers down by main force: while over all the thunder of sling stones rose their deep-throated chanting of the *Veni Sancte Spiritus*. For every man of the besieged garrison they killed they lost ten of their own. These Frenchmen were fine soldiers, they were so proud and fierce in battle that every man, even down to the little squires with their chins as smooth as girls', advanced without flinching, without even a pause, under the hail of stones and arrows: they had sworn on the cross and on holy relics never to take one step backwards until the retreat was sounded. *The town would surely have been taken by assault or by surprise but for its walls, which were the stoutest and most strongly fortified in all Provence, and but for the man who held it. He was one of the noblest lords in all Catholic Christendom and no better knight had been born in that land for fifty years. If he had not been lured into an ambush and treacherously imprisoned by the Count of Nevers, Carcassonne could easily have held out until the end of the forty days.*

There were many, surely, who wished to God that they owed allegiance to the Viscount and not to Count Raymond. The Viscount's men stood on the walls and the high barbicans, paying no heed to the arrows and sling-stones as they toppled the ladders with their loads of swarming men down into the moat, and laughing and shouting as they shattered helmets with one

27

blow from a battle-axe. *"By God,"* they cried, *"your crosses shall not save you now, you shall all suffer the same fate!"* The rage in their hearts was such that even though they were enduring agonies from the heat and the stench of corpses, they might well have held out for another three weeks, but for the treachery which robbed them of the Viscount, and in the Crusaders' camp the shortage of food was so great, even then, that a loaf of bread was selling at two sous.

However, it was the Viscount's own fault for trusting in their word—he should have known what to expect from such enemies. Meanwhile, the men from Toulouse remained in their tents, lost in the middle of the vast camp, as big as three cities, and waited patiently for the forty days to come to an end. When a man is at the mercy of a dangerous lunatic he says what he is asked to say and does what he is asked to do; there is no shame in saying 'yes' in such circumstances, or in humouring the madman in order to extricate oneself without too much harm done.

The Crusaders were not mad, far from it. But after the things they had done on that day of Mary Magdalene there was madness in the air, because a knell that tolls for twenty thousand souls is not easy to forget. Such things do not happen in a Christian country, they have never happened before, and to the men who did them one can only doff one's hat and say: The stakes are too high. Keep your dice in your pocket.

It was God's work. The Abbot of Cîteaux proclaimed it in the city hall in Carcassonne, after the town had been captured and sacked, and there were monks and clergy in their hundreds to cry it through the tents and bivouacs. *It was God's work. Only He could have performed so much good labour in so short a time. You need not swell with pride in this deed, my lads, because this great triumph has been wrought by God alone as a reward for your zeal, your prayers and your sacrifice. Never before in any land, pagan or Christian, have such great things been accomplished: your children and your grandchildren will still talk of them. Your brothers who have perished as martyrs in this campaign are even now in paradise, their souls are white lights before the throne of God.*

They said this and much more, and thanks to the wine and grain found in the city the soldiers had double rations for two weeks, and had no more fighting to do. Cities were capitulating before the Crusaders' banners were even seen on the horizon, and sending out their magistrates and their bishops with hostages,

28

to say: *Welcome, lords. You come to deliver us from the Viscount's tyranny and the plague of heresy.*

The Count of Toulouse and his followers went back to their city, very sad and perplexed, to be taunted and derided by the very people who, eight years later, would weep for joy and kiss the ground where the Count's horse had trampled it.

Shame is quickly forgotten. Even now, after the flogging and the Crusade, hounded by the Bishop's threats and recriminations even in his own palace, the Count was still there, master of his own lands. But the Viscount Raymond-Roger lay chained in prison while a Frenchman ruled in his place and men swore fealty to him as if the Viscount were already dead. Any leader who puts his head in jeopardy when he himself is the head of his people is mad indeed, better that he should submit to any shame than leave his country headless.

Roger de Montbrun lived in this way for a long time, moving like a wandering Jew from city to city, from court to court, from palace to castle and from one feast of welcome to another of farewell. Paris, Troyes, Rome, Florence, and Paris again, and afterwards Toulouse, and Narbonne, and again Toulouse, then, after a year of fighting, Saragossa: and then, after the defeat and death of the King of Aragon and an interminable succession of abortive campaigns and fruitless negotiations, came exile in London, and later in Rome, and at last the great return through Spain and Provence: living for ten years, never more than six months in the same place, and more often a month or even a week.

There were about a dozen of the Count's suite—since a count must have a suite, so that if he cannot see familiar landscapes he can at least see familiar faces about him—who stayed with him to the end, through wind and weather, through all his travels, great and small. On the great journeys there would often be a whole court to go with him, because there were plenty who loved travelling. But when they were only a small company the journey was often a sore trial, always left to the same men. In the end these few ceased to complain and grew accustomed to one another. From rivals, the knights and soldiers of this permanent escort became true friends, sharing the same dangers, joys and fatigues, until they almost forgot that they had any other family and friends in Toulouse. Moreover, the Count had never lacked faithful friends and would never have forced them to go with him. But this passionate devotion became an obsession among them. "Leave my master in order to go home to my wife (or my parents)? Do you take me for a boor?"

29

So they wasted the best years of their lives for a man who cared for them in the same way as he did for his horse or his gloves.

Of course if Roger could have known, in that summer of the year 1209, that Rigueur, small and hard as a green nut, was serving her probation in the heretic convent at Foix, if he could have known this, he might perhaps have given his heart to the heretic faith. He was twenty, and his mind was blazing with horror at the great massacre and at the causeless humiliations they had suffered. It did no good to say over and over again: *"I was there. I saw it. I heard it. We heard them screaming for hours on end . . ."* How could he describe what he had seen? He had seen it, that was all. Should he swear vengeance? How, and on whom, was he to be revenged? After such a hideous deed one could only retire from the world. There were many who said this, but few who would actually do so, not because they wanted vengeance but because nothing seemed any use any more, and the earth seemed fouled for ever by the stench of corpses.

Men talked of it in the evenings, among friends, in the Count's tents. "It was done on the Abbot's orders", they said, or "on the Duke of Burgundy's", or: "No the soldiers got out of control and did it themselves." "No, they would never have dared unless they were under orders." "They misunderstood their orders " "It was madness, they got them drunk on purpose."

Yet however they looked at it no one could understand. But one thing they did understand: the Crusaders hated our country and our language so much that they would cheerfully kill us to the last man. For them it's all one whether we are heretics or Catholics, all they want is to hunt us all down and take our lands. They said other things too. "When the Pope hears of this he will take back his indulgences and excommunicate them. They have desecrated churches and slaughtered priests, and people can be excommunicated for less than that. When the King of France, the Emperor and the Pope come to hear of it, they will be covered with shame before all Christendom."

So they thought. They still did not know that the Pope had sentenced Catholics as well as heretics, that he had turned his anger against the whole land. They did not know this; and in those shameful days, while the Abbot of Cîteaux was offering thanks to God, they were thinking: "The Pope does not know of this yet. Tomorrow the Abbot will sing another tune."

When one is twenty even grief takes on the air of black festival. Roger tried to smother his grief by making up songs against the perfidy of churchmen with his friend Raymond-Jourdain de Cissac. They thought the Abbot was stark mad because he said: "This is God's work." But he was not mad.

When Pierre-Guillaume de Montbrun felt ill-used by his eldest son, he would say: "Still, at least you have red hair!" Indeed they both had—hair so red it hurt the eyes. It was even one thing which Roger did not dislike about his father. Yet Roger was handsome, despite his red thatch: his skin had a healthy tan, more red than gold, his long, black eyes looked lazily from under coppery brows, and he had a firm red mouth and long straight nose. The warm colouring and noble lines of his face made those who saw him forget the fashionable prejudice against red hair, and envy him for the flaunting crown, with its tints of fire and blood, which he bore so easily on a head carried high.

With such a face, Roger seemed born to be the lover of some lady with a proud and faithful heart. But in those days he knew nothing of love, he was not a creature endowed with feelings so much as a hot-blooded animal treating all women as his lawful prey. There are noble ladies who will glance at a man in church or in the street, and afterwards send a maidservant to ask whether he is willing to swear by God and the Virgin Mary that no one shall ever know, and of these Roger had known quite a few. There were even some, quite unknown, their faces veiled by a mask of white silk, who would await him in richly furnished houses where no one knew their name. (Roger's curiosity was so far aroused by one of these ladies, as young, fair and delicate as a princess, that he wished to meet her again. But the wish sprang from vanity, not love, for he believed her to be of very high birth, and he did not seek her long.) By the time he was twenty Roger had had more sweethearts than he could count, and yet was never weary of the sport. On his return to Toulouse, after the forty days of the Crusade, he and two of his companions (Raymond-Jourdain and Azémar de Miradoux, who was to be killed three years afterwards) lived for a whole week in a brothel, never leaving it, except to go out into the street before the open doorway, illuminated by torches from dawn to dusk, and fight. When his father sent a servant to fetch him out he told the man:

31

"Tell him I have not so much to do at home that I need put myself out. I have better work here. He and my uncles would do better to spend their time here too, because there is better work done here than any they do at home."

In those riotous days they went from one girl to the next, taking all the youngest and fairest, and then, for a change, two Moorish wenches, as black as coal, and when the revelling was over they left behind everything they had, down to their last rings and their baptismal crucifixes, even all the buttons off their clothes. (The crucifixes they bought back, later, at double their worth.) By the end of it all they were so glutted with all thought of women as to be almost ready to turn monks, and the sound of so much laughter and singing made them think it even more amusing to weep.

Pierre-Guillaume de Montbrun was not a man to own himself beaten by one failure. "As to that marriage," he would say, "we may be grateful to the Bellacs for breaking it off. Roger will find a better match."

Jourdain de Bellac, who was to have been Roger's father-in-law, adhered openly to the Cathars, and Pierre-Guillaume thought it likely that, for a few years at least, such men would not be very favourably received at court.

"Don't waste your time in trying to find me a bride," Roger told his father. "Bertrand will be eighteen soon and you had better look for a match for him. I think the Count will give me a wife before very long now."

"When you are my age you will realise that it is not easy to fly with one's own wings," said his father. "You can wait for ever for the Count to give you an heiress for your pretty face. Is he God, that he should love the poor better than the rich?"

Listening to his father and his uncles, Roger wished he was back in the brothel. These men had seen nothing, they did not know what they should think, and they were almost ready to proclaim a victory—not from any wish to flatter the Count (they were not born to flatter) but from their pride as citizens of Toulouse. They had been prudent and in the end the Pope himself would admit their right. The Crusaders' army had retired, the last remnants would be driven out before the spring, and the land of Toulouse would have proved its devotion to the Church without having to take up arms.

They had come through the Great Terror and had not been

32

smeared with blood, they were clean, quiet (despite their constant alarms), dull. As for the massacre: God had permitted that in order that the perfidy of the churchmen and the new bishops should be revealed at last. The Abbot of Cîteaux? He had long been known to covet the mitre and benefices belonging to the Archbishop of Narbonne, but this could not come about while the Count lived. The Viscount Raymond-Roger? He was young and had not known how to manage his affairs. It is not enough to be a good knight. *They killed women, and old men and little children.* War means killing. Richard of England with his bands of Navarrese had passed through Toulouse.

Roger's brother Bertrand told him: "You have dishonoured our family in order to keep yourself in the Count's good graces. I have never liked time-servers." Bertrand believed he had been sacrificed to his elder brother, and envied him, even though he loved him. He was a fervent believer in the Cathar Faith. He went to their sermons and saluted heretics openly in the street. His father teased him a little but was not displeased. Roger refused to lose his temper at the term "time-server". Bertrand was a child. Six months earlier he would have struck his brother for much less.

Bertrand was repainting the targets which they used for shooting practice. In the absence of a *salle d'armes* the young people had taken over the courtyard of the house, to such an effect that visitors could no longer find a place to stall their horses. One of the targets was made in the shape of a cross, the other bore a shield with a lion on it, the arms of Simon de Montfort, who was the new Viscount of Carcassonne.

"Have you seen him?"

"Who?"

"The Montfort."

"Only from a distance. He is past his first youth and does not seem to be a man of much humour."

"Is that so! He must have a sense of humour, surely, to style himself Viscount. The Count has a sense of humour, too, since they say he has offered to marry his son to de Montfort's daughter."

"People say many things. And when you have scored ten hits in that lion's eye, I suppose you will think you have wounded de Montfort himself."

Bertrand's thin face, with the redhead's fair skin, flushed suddenly to the colour of ripe strawberries. *"At any rate,"* he said, "*it is better than spending my days frolicking with whores.*"

His elder brother gave a derisive snort. "Then you haven't tried it!" he said. With that he left his brother, wondering why the boy should annoy him so. They all seemed to him now like the painted figures he saw on the walls of the Count's palace. It was in houses and courtyards just like these that dozens of men like his father, and dozens of boys like Bertrand, who used to joust at their painted targets, had been slain. Yet this little fool had never seen anything but pictures in his life. The picture would not become real until they split open his little blond skull with an axe. He would be real enough then: one hundred pounds of real dead flesh. Tell him, "*This I have seen, and it was horrible.*" But this one could tell no one.

(Rigueur was in her convent at that time, thank God, and knew nothing of all this, except that Satan had sent his army to destroy the faithful. She was very young then, and her spirit burned like a red-hot coal. With the exception of her parents, who were both devout believers, and the baptised Christians and the holy ladies of her convent, she had seen nothing of life. Later she would have her share of tragedy, for her father, who was a gallant fighter and a great hunter of Crusaders, was captured alive in the year following the battle of Muret and executed at Carcassonne. First they hacked off his right arm, then the left, then the left leg, then the right, tying off the arteries so that the blood would not flow too fast and the man die before the moment came to cut off his head. Yet bitterly as Rigueur wept for her father, she was to weep yet more for the evils that befell her country.)

It was better to be in the Count's service than in that of many others: there was little to worry about and the certainty of being on the side of right. Sickened by everything as he was after that ill-fated campaign, Roger clung to the Count as though his master had been God incarnate. He loved him. Perhaps, indeed, it was the only real love he had ever known (until the day he met Rigueur, that is). His friend Raymond-Jourdain de Cissac was rumoured to be the Count's son, and undoubtedly looked very like him. The Count was a greater lover of women than Solomon, though even so much less than the old Count, his father, had been, and there were many who could claim the kinship of a brother or a son and yet had no claims upon his inheritance. Besides, as only happens to the rich, people credited him with three times as many children as he really had.

Because of his resemblance to the Count, Raymond-Jourdain had his dagger always at the ready, seeing an allusion to his bastardy in everything. Nevertheless, this blood-kinship was a trivial thing beside the kinship of obedience, or rather of habit, which bound the little company of the Count's 'servants' into a strange kind of family, centred round, and utterly devoted to, a father for whose wishes and commands they must be ceaselessly on the watch, whose joys and sorrows they shared, whose opinions they discussed and whose tastes they knew as well as their own.

In the end, because he drove himself so hard, and for something which lay so close to the heart of every man in the region, they came almost to have no thoughts that were not his. They forgave him his curtness, his changing humours and the indifference which was growing as he grew more tired—he was well past fifty now, and looked sixty. During those years of travels and wars, of flight and return, he had endured so much humiliation that he had to summon up all his pride to keep his regal bearing and smile as graciously as a reigning prince at those who were treating him as a beggar. He was easily moved, ready to weep at small setbacks, with a tendency to self-pity and bemoaning his fate. It seemed to him that if right prevailed then God and the Devil, as well as kings and princes, should have only one desire: to preserve his son's inheritance. But when no one took any interest in his son, though he was young and charming, beyond complimenting his handsome face, the Count grew bitter and distrustful and vented his ill temper on his followers, blaming them one moment for being lukewarm in their affection, and the next for excessive zeal. If any of them, through their attachment to himself, seemed to neglect his son he would remark sharply that a count's son, even if he was only a child, had a right to the respect of his vassals, and that if any of them were too craven to believe that this child would one day be Count of Toulouse, they had only to go and swear fealty to Montfort.

But they did not blame him for his bitter words, for even in anger some princely courtesy or natural goodness prevented him from wounding anyone. Even when they were directed at a servant who had warmed his wine too much, his reprimands were much less those of a master than of a friend, astonished at

35

some clumsiness or lack of attention on the part of those he loved; and when he was angry it was simply as if the other were free to show anger in his turn. Yet it was true that no man ever marked better the distinction between those he considered his inferiors and those he could, in some way or other, think of as equals. His brother, who suffered all his life from the slights and annoyances inflicted on him by his elder brother, knew this better than anyone, and never was there so little friendship between sons of the same mother. For all that he had deserved it Count Baudouin was greatly to be pitied, for he died at a rope's end under his brother's eyes, and almost at his hands. Many men of lesser worth had been pardoned for their treachery, and that more than once.

In those courts where the Count was received increasingly as a poor relation, Roger learned chiefly to listen, and hold his tongue, or to say the proper thing; sometimes, too, he had to woo ladies in order to learn their husband's secrets, for those were the days when they still believed it possible to change the humour of kings by means of intrigue, and private influence, and with gifts and promises. They thought men would be found fool enough to let themselves be gulled by small profits into forgetting the greater. But even the King of Aragon, although he was a brother-in-law twice over, to the Count and to his son, had come into the land as a master rather than a friend. He had allowed one of his knights to insult the Count publicly, for offering advice which he would have done better to follow. (King Peter would not have suffered defeat and death if it had not been for his own folly and suspicion, and the fear of being told later that he owed his victory to Count Raymond's advice. He would not have the Count able to say afterwards: Brother, do not preen yourself, we won this victory together. . . .) But if the King paid a high price for his disloyalty, at least he was the only one who had not carried his disloyalty to its conclusion. Neither the Emperor nor the King of France lifted so much as a finger to help him, and King John of England did no more than send a body of soldiers and some money—and the money was all given back in gifts and banquets when the Count was forced into exile in London after he had been driven out of his own city by his bishop and Prince Louis of France.

Money passed from hand to hand so fast that the Count was continually being forced to borrow from some to pay others, until he was almost reduced to asking his followers to pawn their possessions in order to lend him the money he needed to pay them. Hatred of the French and the desire to see the Count regain his lands were so strong that his army served him on credit during his campaigns.

The war was not an easy one to wage. The citizens of Toulouse, Montauban, and Moissac, as well as those of the other cities that were still free, were more willing to provide him with men than with money (at that time, at least); the starving soldiery were pillaging the outlying districts of the city and after the torchlight processions and the tears of joy were over, folk in the liberated castles could be heard muttering that after all they had been better off under the Crusaders. Whether they were better off or not still remained to be seen, but soldiers will rape and plunder as well as fight, whether they wear the cross or not. So the men of the Crusaders' garrisons were flung down from the walls on to the pikes below and then finished off with scythes and pitchforks; and later, when the French recaptured the castles, they did the same things to the Count's soldiers and strung up garlands of hanged citizens along the walls. In the army quarrels broke out between the soldiers belonging to the Count of Toulouse and those who served the Count of Foix on the smallest provocation: if there was a victory neither could bear the other to claim the credit, and when they had suffered a defeat each blamed the other's cowardice and did their utmost to prove that this or that company had been the first to run.

They slaughtered cattle and set fire to buildings, and caused such misery in the countryside that more than one man wondered: "Is this what we are fighting for? To destroy our own property? Even the French could do no worse." Yet they knew that they could do worse, and so they fought on.

As in a nightmare, the enemy was beaten, he withdrew, went away, and then back he came again, fresher and more sprightly than ever in his gleaming armour with a new scarlet cross on his tunic and brand new weapons in his hands. Year after year. Men thought: They are not fighting over their own soil, their young men come here simply to display their gallantry, and look on it as a sport or an act of piety, or simply a chance to enrich themselves. But for us it means the life or death of our country.

Simon de Montfort is not their kinsman or their rightful lord, and yet if this goes on for much longer, these people will have

37

wrought such havoc for his benefit that the land will no longer be worth anything, even to Montfort himself.

(Though a man may have to fight, he is not compelled to enjoy the sight of blood, especially when he has seen too much of it, and Roger could admit this to Rigueur without shame. Some things are not pleasant to look back on, even for one who is neither a saint nor a weakling: a man whose guts you have just ripped out with your lance, clinging to the weapon and gazing up at you with the eyes of a stricken deer; and another with his skull smashed in by a mace, his furious young face vanishing suddenly into a mess of blood and bone and one eye hanging like a bubble over what was left of his mouth. Your first thought was to thank God you had got him first, and then afterwards you remembered that gleaming, grey eye staring at you, as though it could still see. It had to be like this, of course: "Him or me, and how much better that it should have been him." Six men in all he had killed in fair fight, six men, two of them knights, and all for the price of two gashes in his left thigh, one broken arm and a sword cut in the left side.

Suddenly you are rushing forward, uncontrollably, howling and yelling, ahead of the advance; sword against sword, slashing, feinting, attacking and parrying, a finer gamble than any other because of the vast stakes, and when seized by uncontrollable fear and anger you lay about you with all the strength of your arm. Then, when your enemy is dead, you strip the body, helped by your squires, and take his arms and his horse, hang his shield up outside your tent and make a present to a lady of the earrings and pins taken from the corpse's linen. The knight's name had been Gillebert de Rumilly, he came from Champagne and was a brave and chivalrous knight who had been first up the ladder on to the walls of Lavaur.)

God knew, the hatred one felt for them was in proportion to the evil they did. So it happened that when the soldiers made toys of their bodies—or of the pieces that were left of them—no one was surprised. During the great siege of Toulouse heads were fired back and forth instead of gun stones and men were no longer afraid to think that one day their own heads might suffer the same fate. And though women lost their wits when they recognised in these missiles the shattered remains of a husband or a brother's face or hair, that was the fortune of war. The poor women of Toulouse had seen so much that they were often worse than the men, and when a prisoner was delivered into their hands it was not pleasant to watch.

No one could ever say that victory was bought too dear. They would have damned themselves six times over in order to defeat the Crusaders, because to a man who has his health paradise, and hell too, are small matters compared to this world. Moreover, when the Church is cursed with an unjust Pope people care little for excommunication. This Pope had pledged himself to afford friendship and support to the Count in full council in Rome, and then had struck him in the back. In full council and in the name of all Christian bishops, Pope Innocent had treacherously proclaimed theft an act of piety, and killing Christians the road to heaven. By their intrigues he and the new bishops had wronged the whole Church, for in their courts the victims were condemned and the murderers rewarded. The Pope himself, in an attempt to save his face after such scandalous villainy, summoned the young Count Raymond to Rome and heaped fine words and caresses on him. But if he thought this Judas kiss would save him from God's judgment he was wrong, because six months later he was dead.

The Count—he was sixty now, and so bowed with fatigue, to say nothing of grief and anger, that he could barely stand upright —was of sufficiently high birth to speak to the Pope as man to man and tell him what he thought of his behaviour. It was all he could do. There was no friendship between them, but there was at least honour, and the Count was entitled to proper respect, if not to trust. Moreover, as a prince of the blood royal and legitimate heir to one of the greatest provinces in Christendom, the Count certainly had more right to his title than Pope Innocent to his, and it is easier to turn a horse into a mule than to make a common man of a count. While as for going into exile in a strange land to do penance, living on a pension granted out of charity, this was something that no one in their right senses could expect him to do.

He said none of this to the Pope in so many words; it would have been both useless and unwise, but he said as much and more about the bitterness he felt, his innocence and the betrayal of his trust, simply in the hope of making the Pope uncomfortable. In truth there was nothing more to hope for from the Pope: he could not have served Montfort better if he had been his cousin or his own brother. Even while he wept over the innocent blood that had been shed he was bestowing the county of Toulouse and all the Occitan lands on the murderer, in the belief, maybe, that lawful *seigneurs* can be elected like Popes, by graft and intrigue.

The Count left this den of thieves, this gilded prison that was the court of Rome, with his wife and friends, and his still numerous retinue, to find, he said, a retreat where he could end his days, since he had been forbidden to show his face in his own lands ever again. The Counts of Foix and Comminges and Roussillon went home again, reconciled to the Church, and with more anger than despair in their hearts.

Three months later, however, the Count and his son disembarked at Marseilles, with a following that would not have sufficed to take even the smallest castle, and gained effective control of all Provence in less time than it took to send a courier from Toulouse to Rome. They marched in triumph from Marseilles to Avignon and from Avignon to Beaucaire, accompanied by a vast new army which they had no need to pay, and loaded with so many gifts that they were able to give generous rewards to all their friends. It seemed as though the grief of seven years of war was wiped out in a few days and transmuted into a joy none believed had been purchased too dear. Inside the white walls of Avignon the squares were decked with flowers, and father and son were acclaimed with more blessings and adoration than statues of Christ and the Virgin Mary on Easter Sunday had ever been. The Pope died of rage when he heard of it, because that day made it clear that God is on the side of right and justice and that He is not to be taken in by trickery and deceit.

Then began the hard business of reconquering the province. It was hard, and joyous too, for now people knew that the act of investiture which had been given to Simon de Montfort by the King of France was nothing more than a piece of paper: he could lock it up in a steel chest, but it would make him no whit the richer.

TWO

ONE EVENING during a hunt—the eve of his thirtieth birth-day—Roger had met the woman of whom he said: *"She shall be my seigneur."* There are some blessed days when all the omens are good and when the game of chance becomes a solemn rite, a banquet spread in advance. It is a single moment of triumph, unlike anything that has gone before or will ever be again. That evening the light of the setting sun was redder, the shadows a deeper blue, the sound of the horns at once gayer and more melancholy; each cry was more piercing, each colour more intense, it was an evening when the heart was rent irrationally by an excess of joy. There was a splash of blood on her white cloak, directly over the heart, and the hawk had come to rest, as it was bound to, like some strange betrothal ring, warm, living and stained with blood.

It was the first big hunt for many years and, to those who had been hunting men, the innocent blood spilled without hatred, the birds' cries falling softly on the ear like forgotten music, the file of noble, gracious ladies, all the trappings of peace, meant more than repose: here the tents were erected and fires built for pleasure alone. They had forgotten that the forests were still full of game: fields are ravaged, cities destroyed, while in other forests, ten leagues distant, the enemy are blowing their horns and slaughtering our deer and partridges. Tomorrow they will be within their walls and we shall be outside—but men must live and in every war there comes a time of truce.

What is it the poor complain of? Our bright clothes and pure-bred horses? . . . But there would be no fruit without flowers, and without pleasure no heart for fighting.

My heart was captured in that hunt, borne away at sunset by a slender hand in a green glove. Two grey eyes captured it, and it was given and received by means of a splash of blood on a white cloak. When a man is seized by the madness of love, he becomes afraid, he wants to run away, out of sight of the eyes that have wounded him. Even the company of his closest friends seems sad and wearisome. That evening, by the camp fire, Roger felt something like regret for those eves of battle, and the carefree songs brought tears to his eyes. It is a hard thing to burn with love and see no chance of quenching the fire—yet how can a man hope to make a good impression when he is afraid?

His fear was so acute that he dared not ask who the lady in the white cloak was. He was afraid of learning that she was the loving, faithful mistress of some gallant knight; or a Spanish lady, one of the Countess' friends, who was only staying briefly in Toulouse; or a woman of loose reputation with a new lover every month (she did not look like it, but faces are deceptive and love even more so). All night long he burned with restless desire, telling himself that far from speaking of her, it would be better if he never saw her again.

All the same he wanted to talk about nothing else. In the morning he told himself: "Thank God and your parents for giving you a face that could not be thought ugly. There is no shame in loving when one has some hope of success." In wartime even the cruellest women become gentle, they no longer expect to be courted for ten years.

Roger was able to see, not the lady herself, but her husband, at Michaelmas, which the Count celebrated by a banquet in Toulouse. They were preparing for the winter campaign and Roger thought: "Unless I can speak to her before we leave I am likely to die unshriven." (His head was so full of her that no other woman held any attractions for him.) It is easier to reach a woman through her husband than through her father or brother, and Bérenger d'Aspremont was noted for his chivalrous nature.

He was in the Capitol Square, standing below the dais reserved for the barons of Toulouse, among the lords of Villeneuve, Miraval, Rabastens and other heretic *seigneurs* (he himself was a fervent believer and many people claimed that he had been secretly baptised). After the meal, when the older men were sitting down at the tables, while the ladies and young men made ready to dance, Roger was able to observe his rival. He was well built, with fine black eyes, and to tell the truth seemed the sort of man able to keep his wife for himself, but the skin of his face was all seamed and puckered where he had been badly burned during the siege. He sat at the draught board, his chin on his left hand, pondering his moves with calm good humour and never moving a piece without being certain he was right. But

42

although he was a good player it was at the game of draughts that he lost his wife. Roger de Montbrun had played the game in every court in the West and prided himself on knowing more than fifty plans of attack.

He allowed himself to be beaten none the less; but from draughts the two men went on to reminiscences of recent and past campaigns, and then to praising ladies. They got on so well that at last Roger was bold enough to beg the knight's assistance in an affair of love.

"It is an honour for any gentleman to serve Love as far as in him lies," answered Bérenger. Roger said that one of his friends was in love with a lady who lived in the knight's house, and was pining because he could only see her from a distance.

"My house is open to both of you," said Bérenger, "as it is to all friends of the Count. But as for the ladies' apartment, I can only introduce you; it will depend on you and your friend whether they ask you to come a second time." So, in order not to seem jealous, a man is compelled to let the wolf into his fold; but Roger cared so deeply for this woman's honour that he made up his mind not to make use of any messengers or confidants.

He saw the lady a second time. He was trembling in case he should not know her again or find her beautiful. He knew now that her name was Gentian de Montgeil, she came of a Cathar family, and her mother had taken the veil and lived at Montségur; her father had been a notorious slayer of Crusaders and priests. Her husband, Bérenger d'Aspremont, was rich and belonged to a noble family. Of his wife much good (or ill, according to the speaker) was recounted: she was known to be a true believer in the Cathar faith, she held love and lovers in contempt, spoke her mind on all subjects, saluted ordained Christians in the street and, it was said, had the intention of withdrawing to a convent. Until now Roger had never attempted to woo a woman of this type, he had been content to honour them from a distance.

To his friend, Raymond-Jourdain de Cissac, Roger avowed that he had lost his heart to Bérenger's cousin, the lovely Béatrix de Roques.

"You must pretend to be in love with her," he told him, "because I don't want my secret to be discovered."

"What an idea! Do you think I need employment? Do you

43

want me to bring my own sweetheart's anger on my head for the little time we have left in Toulouse?"

"For the little time we have left in Toulouse, do you want me to lose my only chance? If I don't see her I shall die."

Raymond was closer than a brother to Roger and there was never any jealousy or ill-feeling between them. He agreed to the proposal and Roger wrote a letter for him, aimed at reassuring the sweetheart in question.

The Aspremont mansion had been badly damaged during the war and only recently, to some extent, repaired. Only a part of the façade had been newly painted, but turrets and windows bore the marks of fresh brickwork. Inside, the tapestries were missing and rough sketches of animals and foliage had been drawn in charcoal on the white-washed walls. Weapons and suits of chain mail were lying about on benches, and brightly painted shields stood drying in the hearth. In their own apartment, which was pervaded by a smell of wax and balsam, the ladies were grouped on low chests and cushions around a high-backed chair on which sat a thin, old woman in black. They were listening to the mistress of the house, who was standing before a lectern reading aloud. Her voice was strong and clear, and as intent as a child's: anyone listening could feel her joy and pride in reading such splendid words.

The exultant voice was explaining why it was against reason to believe that Christ had ever become flesh, and expounding the contradictions and pitfalls to which such a doctrine must inevitably lead. Her head was tilted slightly forward on the long neck as she read and her face flushed by a rosy glow reflected from the pages of the book. She raised her head and saw her visitors and invited them to sit down. For an instant Roger saw her eyes dilate and the grey pupils deepen to black.

She continued her reading, and now her voice was trembling and shaking with happy, suppressed laughter. When he saw how beautiful she was, Roger felt afraid: it seemed as though his secret must be exposed at once. What other woman could compare with this wonderfully strange, elegant creature who propounded her refutations of the doctrine of two natures with all the ardour of a woman talking to her lover.

There were five ladies in the room, besides a dozen or so maidservants and waiting women: Lady d'Aspremont, Lady de Roques and her mother, Lady de Miraval, and Bérenger's sister,

44

Lady de Bermond, and her daughter, Agnes. They were all looking at the silent old lady in black, with the air of novices watching a bishop. (These pious heretics showed an amazing devotion towards their ministers, far greater than anything seen among the Catholics.) The book's title was: *A complete and definitive refutation of certain pernicious doctrines concerning the so-called double nature of Our Lord Jesus Christ and His supposed incarnation in flesh. A work aimed at combating superstition and assisting the numerous ignorant persons seduced by the false arguments of the priests of Rome.* The treatise was the work of a heretic from Lombardy named John of Cremona, and had not long been translated into the Occitan dialect. There were only two copies of the work in Toulouse, and it could not be kept for long in any one house. Roger and Raymond-Jourdain had therefore to listen to the reading of this pious work for nearly an hour more, little though they approved of its contents. The woman reading had a lovely voice and her cheeks were aflame.

"Oh God!" Roger was thinking. "What is this prison I am in? This wonderful prison. I shall never win her favours—I shall die first."

He studied the younger women in the room, trying to find one of whom he could make an ally. By some chance, which he attributed to his own lucky star, he saw that one girl had red hair. She was sitting on the floor plaiting a fringe; and when Roger caught her eye they exchanged a secret smile of amusement.

The girl's name was Arnaude and she lived with her parents in the district known as Saint-Cyprien. All the time he stayed in Toulouse, Roger thought about Arnaude like a lover thinking of his sweetheart, so precious does everything that can help him to his lady seem to a lover. In order to go and watch for the girl on the Old Bridge he would leave his friends in the middle of a meal, neglect the Count's service and forget to go and visit his father. Time was short: the army was to take the field again in November, and hardly a week went by without the Count receiving letters asking for help, while from the towns round about refugees were already pouring into the city for shelter— so many by now there was no room left to accommodate the numbers of ragged and injured poor. It was worse than ever in winter. Ruined houses were hastily roofed over with wood and canvas which caught fire at the slightest breath of wind and many children died that year in the sea of mud around the ruins and along the ramparts. The town was more crowded than during the siege, with all the people coming in from the surrounding countryside; however fast the population was depleted, it was renewed again even more quickly. Of those who had lived in Toulouse before the Crusade, half had disappeared and more people died of cold and disease than were killed in the war.

When men have seen too much misery they come to hate it. As Roger rode through the ruined streets he cursed the red-headed girl for making him come to such wretched places to find her. Barges were creeping down the yellow river below the bridge; a grey smoke was rising from the devastated outskirts of the city, and the beggars, huddling in the cold rain like rows of onions under the parapets of the bridge, did not even hold out their hands to him. Builders went by hauling carts full of sand and stones. Then Arnaude appeared, walking quickly and muffled up to the eyes in her cape.

"Hey, there! Aren't you afraid of robbers, going out alone like that?" Arnaude laughed. She liked him, because his hair was red like her own.

"Be patient," he told her, "we shall soon be rid of the brigands." The girl sighed.

The army was to leave any day now and Roger was still thinking: "I must have my wish before I go." Yet he had not spoken a single word to the woman who was robbing him of his sleep and appetite. He saw her only occasionally, and then always in Raymond-Jourdain's company. How could he let her know of his love when he was doing all he could to conceal it? He knew her no better now than on the first day. Less, indeed, for his desire was so intense that he dared not look at her. It is difficult even for a man who is not naturally timid to converse agreeably when his voice is husky and his eyes heavy with passion.

Bérenger was not a jealous or suspicious man. Raymond-Jourdain remarked that he was like putty in his wife's hands. Under her influence Bérenger never went to church, sheltered heretics openly, attended their sermons ceremoniously with his entire household, and altogether compromised himself to a much greater degree than his religion demanded. His wife encouraged him with all the ardour of her sex, but Bérenger's friends condemned the woman's natural enthusiasm much less than her husband's weakness.

46

In any case the war had still not been won, and who could say whether those too zealous in the heretic cause were not digging their own graves? Roger found himself blamed in some quarters for his friendship with a man who clung so insolently to his faith. In time of war, courage becomes a measure of friendship, and the Crusaders themselves respected Bérenger and said that the capture of such a man was worth a castle.

They set out to hunt the Crusaders as though on a wolf hunt, in small groups, and their luck was bad. The de Berzy brothers were short of men and not risking their soldiers unnecessarily, besides which they knew the country too well to let themselves be taken by surprise. The men of Toulouse found their trail marked by burned villages, men hanged from the trees and wells full of carrion. Those who set out determined to bring back Foucaut de Berzy's head on the end of their lance, returned crestfallen, saying: "We'll be able to dig them out after Christmas." The good people of Toulouse took every prisoner who was brought in for Foucaut, the citizens collected in the streets and women were shouting.

"Listen, good people. The young Count has sworn to capture Foucaut and his brother Jean after Christmas, and there will be no pardon for them, even if Amaury de Montfort offers the city of Béziers for their ransom!"

A week before Christmas, Roger met Arnaude on the Old Bridge. This time he had to speak to her at all costs because the ladies of the Aspremont household were to set out on a pilgrimage to the fortress of Montségur the next day and would remain there until Lent. The girl told him her mistress would never read love letters and added that she, Arnaude, was not the kind of girl who would be persuaded to play the part of a go-between for money.

"I swear to you," said Roger, "that you will gain great honour by serving the truest and sincerest love ever born in the heart of man. I am baring my secret to you because I know you are wise and courteous. We leave after Christmas for a new campaign and if anything should happen to me I want my lady at least to know my mind."

"God forgive you for saying such things!"

"You can well believe I shall fight with a better heart," said Roger, "if I know that my lady has at least read my letter."

He said a good deal more in the same vein and in the end the girl took the letter and hid it among her petticoats.

47

"Ah, I have always been told that my red hair would get me into trouble. Now here I am doing something I don't like in the least simply out of friendship for you. I shall never be able to look my lady in the face without blushing, as long as I live."

All that day Roger was like a man wondering whether he is to be executed in the morning. He was so restless that his friends thought he must have been bewitched and turned into two people. One moment he was in the Narbonnese castle, the next at his father's house, the next in church, and then riding outside the city walls, spurring his horse as though a dozen of the enemy were at his heels, and he had no sooner returned to the castle than he remembered some urgent business at his armourer's. These movements were not intended to hide his real game but were simply an effort to escape the sense of vertigo which was spreading red and green spots before his eyes. At his father's house he felt thirsty and drank two cups of wine, only to find that he felt thirstier than ever. At last even Pierre-Guillaume, who was not in the habit of questioning his son, said to him:

"Roger, if you have done anything which you think may bring trouble on yourself and all of us, you can share it with us."

"Do you think I have killed someone?" Roger demanded. He left the house, in a fine temper, but returned twice more in the course of the day. He had been drinking, much more than usual, but this was not normal drunkenness: he felt perfectly clear-headed and to prove it he flung his knife squarely into the centre of the silver cross on his father's crest. The old man failed to appreciate the joke and told him to go and find his targets elsewhere.

There or elsewhere he suffered the same torment. His wretchedness was so great that he almost forgot the reason for it. When he remembered it was worse than before. "Oh God, what have I done? Was there any need for such haste? She will hate me."

But since he was no coward, the next day he made up his mind to pay a courtesy visit to the Aspremont ladies, who were to set out on their journey that morning. The horses were standing ready in the courtyard and two servants were busy with the covered, two-wheeled cart which was to carry the children and their nurse as well as the baggage. The ladies, already wrapped in their furred cloaks, were saying goodbye to their friends in the hall. A cold wind blew in through the open doorway, making the flames dance in the hearth.

48

Lady d'Aspremont was standing by the fire fastening her cloak with trembling hands, and Roger knew from their trembling that she had seen him come in.

Until that day the mere sight of him had been enough to make her as happy as though she had just drunk some wine, just enough to make her want to laugh for no reason. But that day her happiness—because she *was* happy—gave her no joy, and Roger could feel that she was suffering as much as himself. He went to her and asked if his hawk was still alive. The lady did not look at him, her cheeks were brick red and her eyes wide open, as though she had to force herself not to shut them. Roger had never been so close to her before and he could see the tiny lines on her lips, and count the hairs in her eyebrows, and he smelled the warm, harsh odour of her skin, mingled with the scent of musk and new fur.

She said: *"Have no fear for your bird. I am fond of him and allow him to want for nothing."*

Roger knew her well enough by now to know that these words held no double meaning, and that she was really thinking of the bird. He was surprised to find himself able to speak almost in his natural voice.

"Some people might say: 'I wish I were that falcon', or that glove, or that brooch. How sad it is to be constantly obliged to speak in metaphors."

She tensed and jerked up her head so that the half-fastened cape slipped from her shoulders and fell at her feet, but Roger's eyes were fixed so intently on her face that he did not even think to pick it up. Gentian was still gazing into the fire. She gave a deep sigh, like a sob. *"I wish I were the wind and the rain, I wish I were a crow in the fields."*

"I want your permission to speak with you," Roger said. But from the warmth in his tone he might rather have been saying: "Do not leave me to die", or "I want to hold you naked in my arms", or other things more passionate still. Gentian shivered and turned to face him, but she did not look at him, and her wide grey eyes were empty of anger, scorn, vanity or fear; she was like a traveller who has stumbled upon Merlin's magic cave, listening to the chiming of his golden bells.

Then Roger picked up the cloak which had fallen to the ground and placed it round the woman's shoulders, and in that short moment it seemed to him that all his life had been spent in doing

49

nothing else but that—that nothing else existed beyond the need to hold and protect her, to wrap her in a thousand furred cloaks after a thousand never-ending nights of love.

She said: "*Leave me in peace until I come home again.*"

He would readily have sworn to leave her in peace all her life if she wished, and never to leave her in peace again for a day or an hour. In love, the words yes or no, lies or truth, have no meaning. Gentian walked across the room, unsmiling, to where the other ladies were talking together by the door, a tall and slender figure, her small head drawn backwards by the heavy mass of her hair, bound up with a red silk scarf.

Good manners demanded that Roger now join the men of the house to escort the ladies some three leagues on their journey, as far as Auterive, where the men halted. Lady de Miraval, the eldest of the three ladies—and a woman accustomed to getting her own way—asked her cousin Bérenger not to tire his horses any further since this was a day on which women preferred to be left to their devotions, undisturbed by the presence of men. Without dismounting the travellers passed the parting cup from hand to hand. Then the ladies continued their journey, followed, ten paces behind, by Bérenger's old squire and four men-at-arms.

Bérenger turned back to Toulouse with his nephews, his brother-in-law and Roger. The wind was cold and dry and there was a layer of white ice in the puddles in the rutted roads. "If only the roads were still safe," Bérenger grumbled. "These women think things are back to normal, as they were before the Crusade. Since my cousin Alfaïs has been living there I am no more master in my own house than when I was a lad of twenty." (This venerable lady, who had formerly been very rich, had lost her son and son-in-law, and also her house, during the war and therefore Bérenger felt obliged to treat her with the same respect as a mother.)

Roger swore to himself that no one capable of bearing ill-will towards Bérenger d'Aspremont should ever know the secret of his love. Bérenger was a simple, honourable man and to wrong him was to dishonour oneself.

The same evening Roger met Arnaude in the square outside the Narbonnese castle. She was watching for him and this time he begged so hard that she agreed to mount pillion behind him. The girl generously lent herself to love's service and stayed with Roger for hours in the house of a friend of his, a cloth merchant who had lent him a room for the night on many previous occasions.

She brought him a letter from Lady d'Aspremont. *"You deserve a reprimand,"* the letter ran, *"since you have done something you should not have done in making use of a servant, not your own, at the risk of compromising her in my eyes and me in hers. But I should blame Love for this, rather than you. Know that I am not angry with the girl. You know how to respect women, and therefore you will not think ill of me, whatever I do."*

Ah, thought Roger, I should have learned more from another messenger. This girl is merely an ignorant serving wench, what can she tell me? They were lying on the big bed and Roger had placed the lighted candle in its sconce on the cover between the girl and himself—not to avoid temptation, but to reassure the girl.

She had small, black eyes and a snub nose covered in freckles, and on this particular night excitement made her quite pretty. She said: "I've never been involved in anything like this before. Promise me you will do no harm to my lady."

"How could I? I am entirely at her mercy. What did she say to you?"

"This is exactly what she said: 'Since you have been so silly, you shall be my messenger. And may God punish you if you dare think ill of me.'"

Roger's first question was to ask if the lady loved her husband, and Arnaude told him: *"Yes, very much. But they do not sleep in the same bed."* (God be praised! I was sure of it.)

"She has children, though?"

"This is only since my lord Bérenger received baptism, after he was wounded."

"Do you mean his wound made him unable to satisfy women?"

"Oh, yes! You know how badly his face is scarred."

"Was it only his face that was damaged?"

"No, his shoulder too, and his arm. It was before the assault on the Old Bridge. The skin was all torn off his face. He roared like a flayed ox."

"What about the lady?"

"She said he must receive baptism if he asked for it. She was so unhappy that she refused to eat or wash, and she sat and watched by his bed all night, so that it was pity to see her."

Arnaude added that it was a shame, and it might have been

51

the lady's face that was scarred and not Lord Bérenger's. (She had recovered her beauty again after the birth of little Raymonde, she was no longer as thin as she had been, and she had taken to wearing coloured gowns again, and painting her eyes, but for all that he would not look at her. Instead it was she who looked at him as though he were the handsomest man in Toulouse.)

"God! That's not the most cheerful thing you could tell me."

"She wanted so much to do him honour that she used to follow him everywhere so that people should not say his wound had lost him the love of women. She learned the court dances as well, and the latest songs (because she does not come from these parts) so that my lord Bérenger shall not say she holds the customs of Toulouse in contempt."

"Does she love him so much, then? This is a right sad message she sends me. Or can it be that you are lying, to protect your master's interests?"

"Oh, no! I am no liar! I am telling you what everyone in the house knows. And I have seen her at sermons, and in Lady de Miraval's house before her marriage (because I used to be with my lord Bérenger's sister), and she was not happy to be married, you know, everyone said so. She wanted to remain unmarried and devote herself to God. Then, afterwards, my lord Bérenger went away to Aragon—because he would not serve Count Simon de Montfort. My lady was pregnant, and about to be brought to bed when the Crusaders came and brought such misery on us, and there was fighting in the streets. That was when my father was killed: he was trampled down by the horses in the Place Saint-Étienne. My lady Gentian comforted me and held me in her arms (I was very young then, not much more than a child). She told me: 'They cut off my father's arms and legs, and after that they cut off his head. If people were to die of grief there would be no one left to drive out the French.' She said: 'We must not let them despise us and say that all we can do is weep. You are old enough to throw stones and carry buckets of boiling water!' During the siege she worked like a man on the ramparts. My lord Bérenger was here during the siege as well, you know, and she made her peace with him (because in those days he was in love with her, even though she was not very pretty and was ready to drop from weariness all day long, with all the wounded to be cared for and the alarms at night and the shooting). All the jewels and splendid fabrics

52

in the house had been sold for Count Simon's taxes: you saw for yourself how the ladies were dressed during the siege. My lord Bérenger said: 'When we have beaten them, I will buy you more necklaces and silks and girdles and rings and everything, and you shall be honoured as you deserve!' But she told him she wanted none of these things. All the same he kept his word, and a year after Count Simon's death, when he had won back his lands in Carcassès, he came back to Toulouse with three cart loads of plunder taken from the Crusaders. 'Here,' he said, 'our own shall be served first, and first of all the soldiers' pay. The greatest honours go to the best soldier: my wife is not a native of Toulouse, but she has a heart as brave as the bravest.' There was more than one lady would have loved him then for all his scarred face, because he was happy and confident again; and he honoured my lady Gentian in every way, except in one only."

"Tell me if you think she still loves him."

"Ah, have I got second sight? She did not send me here on his account."

"Did she say nothing about me?"

"When I gave her your letter, she was afraid to read it. She sent me away. Then in the evening she called me to her, and she looked as though she had seen the Devil. She told me: 'Since this is how matters stand you shall see that I need never fear scandal. We have been through so much that a little danger like this seems a joke.' And then she gave me the letter."

The second candle was guttering, its wick sunk into the melted wax spilling over the rim of the candlestick. Roger lit a third candle, saying as he did so:

"We shall have to stay here all night."

He saw that the girl was trembling and asked if she were cold. She told him she was only tired. He had made her talk until she was almost ill with exhaustion, interrogating her like a judge and forcing her to keep awake. He wanted to know what sort of things the lady liked, who were her friends, whether she was fond of her children, whether she prayed often, and what gem she had chosen for her emblem. He asked if she seemed pleased with her new hawk, whether she ever mentioned him, and in what tone she did so, what songs she liked to sing when she was alone with her friends, and what was her favourite spice. Was she ever angry, and was she given to weeping? (In answer

53

to this question he learned that she wept so little that at one time people had suspected her of being a witch, but this was before her marriage, in the days when she used to see visions. She was so little given to weeping that even on the day when she went out to search for the body of her brother, Renaud, killed in the assault on the Old Bridge, she was dry-eyed.) Who was the person she loved most in the world?

"She has not told me that."

"Can't you guess from her behaviour?"

"She loves everyone, except enemies and traitors. She is even kind to animals, and strokes them and speaks softly to them."

"Is she jealous of her husband?"

"Oh, no, because he hasn't a mistress. I think they tell one another all their thoughts."

"Ah, you cruel girl! Has she sent you here on purpose to torment me?"

At that moment he very nearly hated the girl and would cheerfully have sent her packing if she had not been the only person he could talk to about his lady. All the things he was so intent on finding out exasperated him more than lies because he was not learning them from the lady's own lips. If many lovers are content to communicate through messengers like this, it must be because they do not know what true love is.

Because his love was even then riding over icy roads wrapped in a cloak of fox fur, Roger felt exhausted and aching. Two months he must stifle thus, stifling under the weight of what, for want of another name, is called love, but which is more like the pressure of a huge mountain growing in your body—understand that who may. A creature smaller and slighter than yourself becomes a weight to crush the whole earth.

He discovered his utter loneliness, he who had never been alone in all his thirty years, who saw life like a king's court, a battlefield, a brothel, a procession or a fairground—as a succession of places where to be alone was unthinkable. The loneliness he was experiencing now was like Adam's before woman had sprung from his side; surely the most painful state a man can be in. He was like Adam, weighed down by the life in his cumbersome new flesh and a brain whose only use to him was for naming hundreds of animals, wondering why God had put such a need to talk inside him when there was nobody to talk to.

There were things he wanted, things he needed to say to this

54

woman that he felt could never have been said before. Certainly he himself had never imagined anything like them. He had to tell her the truth, it welled up in him inexhaustibly, heavy as gold and warm as blood.

Early in the morning he and Arnaude went down into the street, still dark and empty, but already wakening to the cries of water carriers and sellers of wood. In the kitchen they found an old woman flinging sticks on to the fire under the cooking-pot. She said something as they passed, which was not a blessing, and Arnaude flushed and hid her face. When they were outside she said:

"I won't come on your horse again. I'll go by myself. That is the first time in my life anyone has called me such a dreadful name."

Roger said goodbye to her and went for a walk along the city walls. He was thinking of the sadness of true love, which the ancients likened to a naked child, a helpless creature in spite of his cruel arrows. Once a man is fairly hit he draws on himself only mockery and suspicion, and if he takes a single step towards the object of his love he finds himself in situations as vulgar as they are ridiculous.

How was it, he wondered, that in ancient times lovers were capable of loving truly and never revealing their secret to a soul? It was enough for them to watch their beloved from afar and sing her praises so obliquely that even she herself might die in ignorance of ever having been loved. Roger did not feel capable of so great a love, being as eager to receive as to give, but for this he blamed the harsh times in which he lived. A heart must be at peace to burn with a hopeless passion, but what man can love in peace when he thinks that, if things go badly for their side, his beloved is in danger of being raped by some drunken soldier? Or when he himself might be scarred or maimed tomorrow by an unlucky shot? Will he then deny himself the right to hope for the greatest happiness of all? Undeniably, there is something splendid about having loved for twenty years in silence, but three months is another matter.

Before he set eyes on this woman, Roger had never realised such passionate tenderness was possible. He was caught in his own madness, like a bird in the mating season, lost to everything except the desire to find his mate. He seemed to see her at every street corner.

55

"I wish I were the wind and the rain . . ." Wonderful words, they would make wind and rain seem as gentle as a loving caress, abandoning one's body to the crows of the field nothing to be feared. Let the winter rain be to me like a message from her! Why should I reproach her for her past loves? Is there anything more noble than a woman showing her love for a scarred man? (Oh, my darling, when my face, too, is scarred . . . Love is like that: you believe you will never obtain your heart's desire and at the same time you move in as though you had been living with the woman you love for ten years. You even imagine what you will tell her on your deathbed—if God grants us so long a life. "You are still lovelier in age than you were in the days when we first loved one another! I have never been false to you." Meanwhile, you have to go on a mission to Carcassonne, knowing that, fifty leagues away, she is praying God to save her from temptation.)

Roger arrived in Carcassonne four days before Christmas, with the Lords of Roquefeuil and Miramont. They were there to arrange an exchange of prisoners, involving three knights of Toulouse whom the young Count had sworn to have freed before Christmas. Roger and his companions therefore spent the feast in the French camp where they heard some splendid Masses: the Archbishop of Narbonne in person had come to do honour to Count Amaury de Montfort (to whom he still gave the title Count of Toulouse). Amaury gave the three newly released knights fresh clothes, horses and silver cups, and they drank wine in the great hall decked with the shields of France, Champagne and Normandy, together with the two Frenchmen who had been released like themselves. Roger could only put his anxieties in a box and turn the key. (There are some lovers who go everywhere with a long face and a black scarf tied round their left arms, to show how desperately in love and faithful they are, knowing that ladies always come to hear of such things in the end. But Roger de Montbrun was the kind of man who looks silly with a long face, perhaps because of his flamboyant hair. He was still handsome enough to make even the strictest ladies turn to look at him, though he seemed framed more for vanity and pleasure than for love. He dressed well, too, his shirts were always white, his doublet of scarlet silk was trimmed at neck and sleeves with leather braid studded with gold, and his belt

56

of Cordova leather was worth the price of a horse. He had been about the world for ten years and knew that fine clothes make a man seem wealthy, even when people know he is not. His long experience of court life made him a man easily entrusted with diplomatic missions, since he was honourable, not easily corrupted and known for a good Catholic.)

The emissaries of the Count of Toulouse maintained an appearance of goodwill towards Count Amaury's French knights, but with some reserve, saying by implication: "We cannot blame you, because we know that you serve an unjust cause out of loyalty to your master." When one of the Crusaders stood up in their presence and raised his goblet to proclaim the health of Amaury, Count of Toulouse, they remained proudly seated, half-smiling, half-displeased, indicating to their hosts that courtesy forbade them to take up this challenge. Amaury—a fair, stalwart young man with a placid face—then proposed the health of his noble cousin Raymond, *Marquis of Provence*, upon which Raymond de Roquefeuil and the other knights rose and said that they could not drink this health, since although the person was to their liking, the title was not. At this several of the older knights also rose to their feet, protesting that they would not be flouted thus in their own city by men in revolt against God's Church. They added that Count Amaury was being altogether too tolerant and allowing himself to be taken advantage of. But Amaury and his uncle, Guy de Montfort (a brave and prudent knight), pacified their followers by reminding them of the three knights and ten sergeants-at-arms still held prisoner by Raymond at Montauban, who had been living in great misery since October on account of their unpaid ransoms.

The cathedral was all decked out with flags and oriflammes, and the golden vessels and sconces and red crosses on the banners seemed on fire in the blaze of thousands of candles. The Archbishop himself officiated, assisted by the Bishops of Carcassonne and Béziers, and when he pronounced the *Gloria* in ringing tones, the choirs and the voices of the faithful responded in a triumphant roar. The power of the hymns and the splendour of the crosses and banners, glittering in the light of a thousand candle flames, made the victory for which they prayed seem almost within their grasp.

Kneeling beside the pillars at the back of the nave, as befitted men who could not approach God's Table, the men of Toulouse prayed with more bitterness than religious fervour. Lord Jesus, must our eyes behold Your pure Body consecrated by such hands as these? This man has become primate of the Occitan lands at the price of his countrymen's blood; at Béziers, and in other places, he has spilled other blood than the blood of the Mass. Shimmering with gold in the midst of all the shimmering lights, the Archbishop was bending down towards the men kneeling on the altar steps, kneeling there with their hair smooth and shining and their long pleated gowns trimmed with squirrel fur and caught in with belts of gold. Honour to the first of Christ's soldiers, to the sacred army of God! At their head was Amaury de Montfort, with his uncle Guy, and his brother, and Guy, the Marshal of the Faith, and Lambert, and Foucaut— Foucaut too!—and Robert . . . All of them gathered together for the Christmas truce and come here to plead with the Lord to grant them a long-overdue victory in the coming year.

To all of them the Archbishop held out his blue-veined hand, adorned with the amethyst ring, and offered the white Host, purer and more holy than the Virgin's body. To all, each one of whom had killed and been responsible for the killing of more men, women and children in that land than he had soldiers in his pay on the day he joined the Crusade. Blessed be God's mercy which can so wipe out the stain of innocent blood.

After the third Mass on Christmas morning, Count Raymond's men went to the monastery of the white friars where the Archbishop and his court had taken up their residence. He was to set off the next day on his way to Narbonne and, from there, go on to Montpellier, where he would take horse for Marseilles to embark for Italy. In spite of his great age he was continually on the move, and those who had business with him did not moulder in antechambers, but had to pursue him like a seller of stolen game.

Raymond de Roquefeuil, Jourdain de Miramont, and Roger de Montbrun waited their turn in the convent parlour after they had begged the favour of paying their respects to Monseigneur Arnaud. This favour was not granted to them until midday, and even then they could think themselves lucky to have been admitted, since being under sentence of excommunication they were not entitled to it. But the Archbishop, who could be courteous when he wished, received them in his private chamber, alone but for his secretary and three white friars.

Seated on a cushioned chair framed in red hangings, his strong, tanned face crowned with a circle of white hair and his big frame enveloped in a flowing, white robe, he was still handsome, despite the weary, deepset eyes beneath heavy, brown lids. Raymond de Roquefeuil (who was not far off the Archbishop's age and had known him for fifty years) spoke of the great joy which he and his companions felt at seeing Monseigneur Arnaud again and being able to bring him Count Raymond's greetings and filial duty. Faithfully remembering the Lord Archbishop's patience towards him, the Count humbly begged him to accept these Christmas gifts of a copy of St. Augustine's *City of God*, illuminated and bound by the Brothers of the hospital of St. John at Toulouse, and a set of draughts, in ivory, ebony and gold, of Moorish workmanship. These gifts were little enough but they served to show the Count's affection for the Lord Archbishop.

One of the monks held up the gifts for the Archbishop to see, and when he had studied them with eyes which, beneath their apparent disdain, still gleamed with a young man's greed, he remarked that Count Raymond must imagine he had nothing to do with his time, but that indeed he hoped one day to be able to reread the works of St. Augustine in a volume so pleasantly inscribed and reverently adorned.

"As for the Count's affection," he added, "he would do better to prove that to me by deeds rather than by gifts. I have watched his behaviour for twenty years past, and it is not hard for a man to be generous when he has enriched himself with the Church's possessions."

Raymond de Roquefeuil said that the Count had long repented of his past faults, and had never asked anything beyond the right to justify himself fully and prove his attachment to Holy Church. If Monseigneur Arnaud could use his influence with the Holy Father to get the Count and his son readmitted to the communion of the faithful, peace would swiftly be re-established in the land and the Church of God restored to the privileges and honour she enjoyed everywhere before the war.

"This is not the first time I have listened to such arguments," said the Archbishop. "Can the Church receive back into her bosom a man she has already absolved three times over and who has always hurried straight back into his errors?"

"My lord knows very well," said Raymond de Roquefeuil,

59

"what are the true feelings of our lord the Count; and he knows too that it is with tears and groans that Count Raymond and the young Count have resolved to act as they have, and that they would never have dared contest the Council's decisions or act against the wishes of our Holy Father the Pope in their own interests, even if it was a matter of saving their lives. But having in mind only the interests of their subjects, for whom they are responsible before God, and the peace of the land, they returned in answer to the people's entreaties, like good shepherds who will not leave their sheep to be preyed on by mercenaries.

"My lord cannot be unaware of the pride and cruelty of the late Count Simon (whom God, we must hope, has received into His paradise), and although in his paternal goodness Monseigneur Arnaud has taken up Count Amaury's cause—seeing that he is a young, inexperienced orphan—he should know that the sons often follow in their fathers' footsteps and that a foreigner is more likely to prove ungrateful than a fellow countryman. Brave and chivalrous as Count Amaury is, he will never be able to wear the coronet of Toulouse without arousing great resentment among the people, and endless troubles which are bound to injure the cause of Holy Church whose servant he professes to be."

"It does not become me," said the Archbishop, "to judge the decisions of our beloved Reverend Father, just as it does not become the members of the body to command the head. In the twenty-six years your master has been Count of Toulouse he has made us so many promises that ten clerks might spend three days in writing them down and never finish, but he has not raised a finger against the heretics: he would find that hard to deny."

"Let my lord consider," said Jourdain de Miramont, "that he is reproaching our master with past faults. Moreover, our master, Count Raymond, though he has done nothing to be ashamed of, has voluntarily renounced his rights and titles and become merely the first subject of his beloved son. Let my lord rather reflect that, as good guardians of the lands they hold by God's grace and by right, the Count and his son have always done their best to avoid trouble and discord; and that Count Raymond, wishing to be a father to his subjects and not a judge, has at all times hoped to bring back to reason those who have strayed by gentleness, persuasion and good example rather than by fear of punishment. You cannot make even a horse or a dog love you by beating it."

"He has indeed set a fine example," said the Archbishop, abruptly crossing his legs. "An example that plenty have followed: that of robbing monasteries and setting fire to churches."

"My lord, count the number of churches burned in the last ten years for which others beside the Count are to blame. It is our enemies, my lord, who see heretics everywhere, even among the clergy. If there are still some strayed souls, in Toulouse or elsewhere, the reason for it certainly lies in the unduly severe penalties which the Count's enemies have wrested from our Holy Father the Pope. It is no wonder the Church is ill-respected in our country and that people say Count Raymond must be mad to remain faithful to a Church that treats him in this fashion. If he is excommunicated, when he has adhered firmly to the true faith all his life, how can his subjects help believing that there is nothing to be gained by serving the Church? After all the hardships and violence their country has suffered how can our knights fight for a Church that seems to be like a mother to their enemies and a cruel stepmother to themselves?"

The Archbishop said that there was no simple solution to the business, that the Count's attitude seemed to be: "Give me everything and then afterwards I will concede half of it", and that Raymond knew only too well that once reconciled to the Church he would be master of the whole country from Agen to Avignon in three weeks, and it was not yet certain that the Church would get any advantage from it. However, if the counts would give firm guarantees of their good faith and were willing to promise to leave Count Amaury in possession of the Viscounty of Carcassonne and bind themselves not to make war any more, it would be possible to re-examine their case. The three knights were delighted with this speech and decided that the Archbishop was a very just and sensible man. (They did not forget his great quarrel with Simon de Montfort, nor the solemn excommunication which he had caused to be pronounced on Count Simon from every church in Narbonne.)

Watching him, Roger de Montbrun thought of the Abbot in the coat of mail who, eleven years earlier, had refused to stop the massacre. When a man can be useful to us we approve of him, and cover his bloodstained hands with white gloves. Roger found himself thinking of the Archbishop with sincere and heart-felt goodwill, and praying God to grant him long life.

61

In this elusive war, with its constantly changing face, yesterday's enemy turned into a friend and love and hate blended into one another. From the convent the three men went to Count Simon's tomb in the church of St. Nazaire. They were accompanied by four French knights, courteous gentlemen whom they had met before in Simon's tents during various truces. All of them, the Frenchmen and the men of Toulouse, spoke of the late Count Simon as a gallant knight.

He lay there, in the crypt where thirty white candles burned day and night, beneath a great marble slab on which his portrait was carved in relief and painted in gold and silver, azure and scarlet. He lay there, beneath the stone, surrounded by banners, with his shattered head and his chilled body stuffed with herbs and unguents: Judas Maccabaeus, St. Stephen, protector of the weak, defender of the faith, soldier of Christ, Count of Toulouse.

He had entered into heaven without confession or absolution, with his bloody, faceless head and the red cross of a Crusader. "Here is Your soldier, Lord, who has never spared his body in Your service. Here are his grey hairs and what is left of his teeth and chin. Here is Your mercenary, Lord, come to claim his promised hire." "Go back, go back to earth, Count Simon, go and find My Pope, to declare you blessed, My bishops to sing your praises, My soldiers, your brothers, to build you a splendid tomb: as you have served Me you shall be honoured, but for those who die in mortal sin, even God Himself can do nothing."

"You who laughed and sang for joy on the walls of Toulouse to see him slain . . ."

"You who revenged his death by slaughtering women and children at Marmande . . ."

"You who could only run and shelter inside your walls when he was alive."

"You who received our castles and our daughters from his hands when he was alive."

"You who hacked our best friends to pieces and flayed them alive."

"You who peopled our land with men without eyes, without hands and feet, with violated women and bastard children."

"Remember Roger des Essarts and Guillaume de Contres and Simon the Saxon——"

"Remember Amaury de Montréal and his sister, the noble lady Guiraude, and the King of Aragon."

So many things to say that were left unsaid, thoughts that

62

through too much brooding had come to hold more weariness than hatred, so many words, worn out, like old but unforgotten songs, that no one has time to sing any more because their heads are full of new ones.

Ten years the war had been going on; soon this corpse, embalmed and sealed in its three coffins, would be two years old, and already decomposition had gone so far that even his memory was no more than dust. His friends had barely been left the time to weep. As they went out into the street, where the cold rain ran in muddy torrents down the housefronts decorated for the holiday, the seven knights discussed that year's harvest, the cost of weapons and the French king's health, and the inconveniences of such a protracted war. In a month, they might meet again, face to face on a castle wall, or in some mountain pass, and there there would be no more talk, it would be a case of which of them would be the first to bury a foot of steel in the other's belly.

These Frenchmen were fine-looking men, tanned, weatherbeaten and seamed with scars, with lithe bodies and piercing eyes: fine soldiers truly, each one worth a company. They had seven, eight or ten years of campaigning behind them, and had become old, hardened, sharpened, and polished like pebbles; they were weary but never beaten, and they bore deep in their eyes their mourning for dead friends and brothers. Hatred between soldiers is short-lived; they are all comrades in death without sacraments, all vowed to mortal sin as monks are to God, by loyalty and obedience.

One of the four Frenchmen, whose name was Manassé de Bury, invited Roger to visit his home (this was in fact a jeweller's house which he had occupied ever since being driven out of his castle near Saissac). His wife was the heiress to a domain near Senouillac, and they had three young children. She was a heavily built, dark-haired woman, with a bad complexion, and several months pregnant. She seemed uncomfortable in Roger's presence and sat with lowered eyes.

"You see," said Manassé de Bury, "what contempt the King and the Pope hold us in: we have the whole country on our hands, thanks to them, and yet they send us neither men nor money. After all we have borne for the faith of Christ Jesus, they treat us as if we had come here to enrich ourselves at other people's expense. It is nine years, already, since I have seen my own

63

country, my estate is mortgaged down to the last vine, and God knows if I shall ever see it again."

"I imagine," Roger said, "it might not be very polite of me to wish you a speedy return home. If Count Amaury makes peace with our own Count, won't your children's inheritance be assured?"

Manassé, a man of about forty, with fair hair and a brown face, looked with a troubled expression at his wife who was holding a wan little girl in a sky blue dress on her knee.

"Thank God," he said, "they have a right to their inheritance. But we live in times when there is no longer any respect for the laws and my wife has no lack of cousins able to contest her marriage. Yet she will not be the one to say she was forced."

The lady looked at him with tired eyes that held more love than sadness. "The bitch!" Roger thought.

But he did not blame Manassé de Bury: every man tries to increase his fortune and to keep it, especially when he pays for it with his own blood—and Manassé was a brave knight.

"It is a sin," Roger said, "for Catholics to make war among themselves like this, for lands and castles. Does the Pope believe we can wipe out heresy when we are already having trouble enough to defend our own property?"

Manassé shrugged and his small grey eyes were grave and thoughtful. "That is what all your people say. And—God knows I do not wish to offend you—you tell us so often there are no heretics among you that in the end we believe you all are."

"By the belly of St. Peter," said Roger scornfully, "have you not yet seen that all these troubles began with scheming priests who set fire to the house to get rid of the cockroaches? So many on our side and your own have fallen because of their pride and avarice that over a million Catholics have been killed for one dead heretic. Let Count Amaury try and keep his inheritance if he can, but he need not treat us as heretics to do so."

The Frenchman warmed his hands at the brazier glowing on a tripod in the middle of the room; the little girl had moved close to him and was playing with the sheath of his dagger which hung from his waist. He stroked her hair, carelessly, as one caresses an animal.

"To listen to you," he said bitterly, "we have brought this heresy among you. Better ask my wife, and she will tell you what she knows."

Roger glanced sharply at the lady: the Frenchman had no

business to know what she knew. The man was a boor to bring his wife into the argument in this way. But he said politely: "You have reassured me. Your wife cannot have told you any ill of her country and I was wrong to take your reproaches in bad part. But," he added, "I am surprised that, with such a gracious advocate at your side, you do not place a greater trust in our country. You can judge the worth of our ladies by your own wife. It is a point of honour with us to deserve the esteem of our ladies."

Glad to talk of something other than war, Manassé de Bury began praising the ladies of Toulouse for their beauty.

"How many of our village girls has he raped," Roger wondered, "to gain his knowledge?" The thought gave him almost no bitterness, he knew too well what a soldier's life was like, and knew that if he himself should he ever find himself in that man's country . . . "They have lived like lords and we have not been able to stop them. How many of our own have served them, and fought less well than they did?"

Aloud he said: "Our ladies prize feats of arms very highly, but they value true nobility and delicacy of heart and soul even more. That is why we think little of those among us who rail against the heretics and want to rob them and throw them in prison: it is unchivalrous conduct, and men will only be converted by love and gentleness."

"I can scarcely see you converting one particular heretic whom I had burned by love and gentleness," said Manassé. "He was infernally tough, and left to himself he would have converted half my garrison. There is only one weapon against people like that."

Roger took his leave of the knight, promising to intercede for two of his men who were still prisoners and too poor to pay their ransom.

"They are local boys from home," said Manassé, "but since I was robbed of my domain at Senouillac I have barely enough to live on myself. I'll do as much for you, one day." (Pray God, thought Roger, you never have occasion to thank me! And seeing how green and soft and lovely you seem to think your Île-de-France, why don't you go back there and take your little bastards with you.)

A month later the young Count and his knights rode back into Toulouse with vizors up, banners waving in the wind, and drums and trumpets blaring throughout the city. The campaign had been short and fierce, and the men in such haste to get back home that they had wasted no time in repairing the dents in their armour: they arrived as they were, with cloven shields, battered helmets and tunics ripped to shreds, black with blood and dust. Every knight was greeted by shouts of joy from the crowd as he entered the city gate, while the criers announcing their names were lost under the roll of drums. Honour to Toulouse!

They brought back prizes with them: two half-naked men bound so securely to their horses that they could barely move their shoulders, led by foot-soldiers, and their faces and bodies black with the stains of battle. Erect, bloody and silent, their dark, anxious eyes staring into space, they were escorted by ten men with pikes at the ready. *"Hands off, good people. Have no fear, the Count will give you justice."*

The two brothers were very alike, both had the same heavy chin, haughty mouth and bull-like forehead; they did not appear to realise that for once they were the victims and not the executioners. Roger, who had helped to capture them, thought now: "God, why is my lady not in Toulouse? She would have taken part in this rejoicing." The de Berzy brothers were hated in Toulouse and the country round as no other knight of the Crusade had ever been (with the exception of Simon de Montfort). The Count had sworn that now he would treat them not as prisoners but as criminals. *"You have escaped once, Foucaut, this time you are going to pay!"*

The scaffold was raised high in the Capitol Square and the drums were beaten. The crowd gathered for the spectacle. They cheered the executioner: the blood that was to flow that day was noble. So Jean and Foucaut drained the cup they had presented to so many others: they too had to make the sign of the cross and kneel before the block. Their severed heads were stuck on pikes and carried through the town.

God grant us many such days, there is no time to lose. In the winter we are the stronger, but with spring there will be fresh pilgrims. The Bishops of Reims and Rouen and Clermont have promised troops and archers, and knights will come in great numbers from Flanders and Champagne. May they have no fortresses left to defend by the time they come, but only castles to besiege.

Roger rested in his father's house after the labours of the

66

campaign, for his body had been so sorely punished that the whole of his right side, from thigh to armpit, was one great bruise, all grazed and bleeding. His brother Bertrand told him: "Lucky you have a Toledo hauberk. With mine you wouldn't have got off so lightly!" (Bertrand was a gallant lad, but jealous. He had fought so well during the siege that the young Count had knighted him. But he lacked the money for a knight's armour.)

Roger felt like an intruder in his father's house. Pierre-Guillaume, his red hair fading to a dirty pink colour, was already thinking of his soul—he was not a heretic, but he was wavering, saying that they set an example by their saintly lives. Roger, on the other hand, was a sincere Catholic, who said his prayers and honoured the churches. Bertrand, now married and a father, was the actual master of the house.

"I suppose," Roger suggested, "you couldn't manage to identify yourself less closely with the Cathars? Our city is already a notorious haven for heretics. Faith is a matter of the heart, why shout it from the rooftops?"

"I have not been taught to veer with the wind. At least I am lucky enough to pray freely, *our* bishops do not excommunicate people, or go about preaching war on their flock. But you are like a dog fawning on his master for smiles and caresses."

"Can I claim rewards for myself, when the Count has not enough to pay his soldiers? If you are scared I may rook you of your share of our inheritance, why didn't you take a rich wife?"

(Bertrand had married a girl with only a small dowry, and one, moreover, not of noble blood: the daughter of a Jewish lawyer converted to the Cathar faith. This man had once been very rich, but had lost all his property during the troubles caused by Bishop Foulques' Brotherhood, when his house had been looted and burned. But the girl was pretty and Bertrand had been too besotted about her to care for anything. In order to be able to marry him, she had renounced the Jewish faith and been baptised, but both of them were fervent Cathar believers. By this lady, whose name was Rachel Abrahamide, Bertrand had already two sons. On account of these little boys, old Pierre-Guillaume had become inordinately fond of his younger son and wanted to make over a larger portion of the family inheritance to him than to the elder. Roger did not mind, but Bertrand believed he was jealous.)

"I haven't taken a rich wife," he said, "but at least I have

67

given our father grandsons. While you, the eldest son, haven't been able to get enough out of the Count to have our house repaired. *I* have never been a courtier! But as for you—you do the job and don't profit from it."

The argument between the two brothers was growing so heated that the lovely Rachel came and begged her husband to stop quarrelling with his elder brother who was a very gallant and chivalrous knight. (She was a gentle creature who loved nothing so much as peace in the house.) Bertrand, who considered his brother much more handsome than himself (which was true enough), said nothing, but became gloomy and depressed. Because Roger was a Catholic and a bachelor, Bertrand was convinced he must be a sink of iniquity. Roger hardly dared smile at his sister-in-law, though he was very fond of her.

It was not a cold winter, but it was wet, and winds that were warm and chill by turns battled in the streets, thrusting in between the houses, making their frames creak and the plaster drop from the walls. Rain seeped into the patched-up houses and in others, partially rebuilt but still unroofed, the new beams rotted. Yet in spite of this the whole city echoed with the sound of hammers and singing workmen; horses and mules trotted through the rain, down narrow streets littered with rubbish, to their watering places. In the business quarters, the shops were open again, protected by wooden screens, and filled with fabrics from the East, dishes and all kinds of metalwork from Spain and Africa, skins, hides, furs, glassware, woollen stuffs—nearly everything, in fact, that was to be had before the siege. The armourers were the great kings of the moment: they had no need to go out into the street to attract customers.

It was in his armourer's shop, where he had taken his coat of mail for repair, that Roger encountered his beloved in person. She was dressed in a long, grey cloak with a little hat made of marten's fur, soaking wet, on her head, and accompanied by a maidservant and two tall, thin, swarthy men. She was talking excitedly, arguing about the price of a coat of mail which she said was not true Toledo work and weighed a good three pounds more than it should.

Roger had not thought about her for some days; and seeing her again he knew at once that this love was as true as God. His joy was so strong that he felt like a man who has always believed himself an orphan when suddenly brought face to face

68

with his mother—although it was not as a mother that he loved this woman. His first impulse was to run to her and take her in his arms. The madness which rules lovers made him forget in an instant even the fear of displeasing her. He went up to her with unconcealed delight, beaming like a man let out of prison, and said that he had never wanted anything so much as the pleasure of seeing her again.

She did not smile. She seemed unaffected and her eyes were grave as she answered:

"I am not sorry to see you again, either."

"Don't think I sought you out on purpose, at least," said Roger.

She looked him straight in the eyes. "Neither have I sought you out."

The lady's two brothers were haggling with the armourer, swearing by the Holy Ghost, by their beards (they wore short, square beards after the fashion of the mountain men), and by the pupils of their eyes that they had never paid so much for shirts made of such inferior steel, and that at Saragossa not even a mere sergeant would touch such goods. . . . This was untrue and they were obviously eager to conclude the bargain. Master Guillaume, the armourer, tugged impatiently at his grey locks and remarked that the gentleman would have done better to equip themselves in Saragossa, or Foix or wherever it was they came from, since he was not accustomed to having his wares insulted in this way.

"Come then, Sicart," said the lady. "We shall find better further on."

The armourer said that for Lady d'Aspremont he would be willing to lower his price by three Toulouse sous, but not one penny more.

Gentian said to her brothers: "This knight is a friend of Bérenger's, and therefore is yours too."

Roger submitted to an exchange of kisses smelling of garlic and old leather, and the two men uttered suitable praises of Count Raymond's valour. They themselves were in the Count of Foix's service. They bore as much resemblance to their sister as rusty swords to a brand new blade, being dark skinned with dirt in the creases of cheeks and eyelids, men still young but worn out by a life of hardship, their short leather jerkins greasy and torn and their long legs encased in grey leggings criss-crossed by a network of black laces. Their deepset eyes, under heavy, straight brows, shone with the cheerful brutality which is the mark of the professional soldier.

The lady glanced at them affectionately. "Two of my four brothers have been killed by the Crusaders," she said, "so we have to love each other twice as much. May God save you, sir knight, from such an acquaintance with the woes of the flesh."

Roger talked of the death of the de Berzy brothers, of his own travels and the things he had seen in the French camp, and mentioned the goodwill the Archbishop had shown towards the Counts of Toulouse.

"Amaury will not hold out much longer if the sentence of ex-communication is lifted," he said.

The lady and her brothers stared at him in horrified amazement: to them the Archbishop was the Devil incarnate.

"I would prefer to have nothing but misfortune all my life," said the lady, "than that any good should come to us through such a man. That would be too high a price to pay for peace."

"No price is too high," said Roger.

She looked at him without anger, with a thoughtful surprise. "I am sorry to hear you say that," she remarked.

"The greatest favour I could wish *the Abbot of Cîteaux*," said Sicart, the elder of the two brothers, "is a rope round his neck. We want nothing from him—except that he shall not die before justice is done."

It had begun to rain heavily and they were compelled to take shelter under a birdseller's awning where the screams of parrots and peacocks and the gruff cooing of pigeons made such a din that they could scarcely hear themselves speak. A cart passed, flinging up muddy water from the puddles, and Roger put his cloak round the lady to protect her from the splashes.

"I should not like to disagree with you about anything," he almost shouted in her ear. "When can I speak to you for long enough to explain what I mean?"

She was silent, she seemed feverish, her nostrils were dilated and her breast rose and fell as though she needed air. Roger saw how much thinner she was since their last meeting and how much her face had sharpened. He said to her:

"I have never found you lovelier. But your cheeks look so thin that I am afraid you may be wearing yourself out by fasting too severely."

She smiled serenely. "I have never been afraid of fasting. It is not that which has made me thinner."

"Tell me how I may try to see you alone."

She did not answer and said nothing more to him until they reached her house. Her brothers talked of an expedition against Carcassonne: if the counts surrounded the city now, it would not hold out until fresh Crusaders arrived. . . . My most noble lady, we still have not done with talk of war.

That same evening, Roger met Arnaude outside his father's house. She said nothing, but gave him a letter. He urged her to come inside and wait while he read it and wrote an answer. She said: "For God's sake don't be long!" As though it was a simple matter to ask a lover to be brief.

Gentian wrote: "From certain things you said, I see that on many things we do not think alike. I do not blame you for this and shall never ask you to alter your opinions for love of me; neither will I ever change my own. If you wish to see me alone, know that this depends on my will alone, and that I know no other prison than honour. However, you have my permission to speak of your desire to my noble cousin by marriage, the Lady Alfaïs de Miraval. She is courtly, discreet and well versed in the art of love. Do not mention my name, but explain your position to her and tell her everything you know. I am sure there is no better counsel I can give you: the lady in question is of a noble and upright heart, she will give you no advice that is inconsistent with honour."

". . . My lady, must a stranger be the judge of something which I would not confide in my best friend? I will do it, since you wish it so, and if (as I greatly fear) this lady's decision is not as I desire, I will submit to it. But you are compelling me to run a risk so great that it almost makes me lose my reason, for how can I convince someone who has more cause to hate than to love me? Consider that, if she is indeed wise, she may guess it concerns you! Consider that we are at war, consider that my duty may send me into another land tomorrow. If I must submit to your will, then I would not believe that you are imposing this test on me to mock me, or to free yourself from my attentions. You should judge by my discretion that the love I feel for you is true and faithful, and that for the honour of sleeping with you I would forsake, not simply my family and friends, but even my eternal salvation. . . ."

Roger wrote at least three times as much as this, telling Arnaude all the time: "Wait a little longer, I've almost finished." Then afterwards he regretted what he had written. He did not have to reply. The need to speak to this woman, even in a letter, had robbed him of all common sense. Surely a man must be mad to start pouring out to a lady things he should tell no one but himself? Can any woman esteem a man who does not keep his anxieties and distrust to himself?

How is it possible to prove one's love when there is no time? Their departure was fixed for the second week in Lent; and even when all other matters have come to seem trivial, they cannot be neglected without incurring the disapproval of friends. Roger de Montbrun decided to resort to drastic measures and, from that day on, he ceased to shave his beard, dressed in the short, black robe of a penitent, went only on foot in the streets of Toulouse and every morning walked from the castle to the church of La Daurade carrying a ten-inch lighted candle. Everywhere he went, even at the Count's table, he refused to eat, drink or take part in dancing or gaming. In fact he made it clear to all and sundry that he was in love and unhappy in love. Furthermore, he told his friends that he would continue in this mode of life, even when travelling or with the army in the field, until he obtained justice from the lady who scorned him without cause.

After Mass on the morning of Easter Sunday, he despatched Raymond-Jourdain de Cissac and his brother-in-law, Jacques de Miradoux (who was related to the Miravals by marriage), to see the noble Lady Alfaïs, who was spending the day with the Countess's ladies in the Narbonnese castle. He sent the lady a Christmas rose, wrapped in silk threaded with gold, and Raymond-Jourdain told her that it was the gift of a man in great affliction who entreated her graciously to act as arbiter for him in an affair of love. Lady de Miraval was a proud woman, and even though ruined and in mourning for her son and son-in-law, she still arrayed herself in gold-embroidered veils and gowns encrusted with jewels for her appearances at court. She sat in the Countess's chambers, among the ladies of Roquefeuil, of Verfeil and Alfar, on her own chair under a purple canopy, with her daughter and the young Aspremont ladies and her daughter-in-law, Braïda de Miraval, standing or seated on cushions on the floor around her. She received the two emissaries graciously, saying that she was ready to serve as arbiter in any honourable matter that could enhance the glory of women and of love, because the brutalities of war should not make men forget the laws of chivalry. She therefore invited Sir Roger de Montbrun to call upon herself and two other ladies whom she would beg to be present also, with three men of noble blood who were prepared to stand surety for him.

Thus, Roger found himself the same evening standing his trial in one of the Countess's private apartments. Seven white candles burned on a gilded hearse before the high-backed settle on which the three ladies were sitting. Roger came just as he was, with his two weeks' beard and a face he had no need to whiten in order to make it look pale and drawn. He and his three friends kneeled before the ladies and promised to conceal nothing of the truth except the names of the persons involved.

Roger put his case as clearly as he could without giving away the lady's name. Lady de Miraval listened, leaning forward with her chin in her hand and studying the suppliant with shrewd, grey eyes in which from time to time there flickered a tiny spark of intense curiosity. She was not an old woman—little past fifty—and her figure, moulded by a purple and black striped dress, was straight and slim, while her thin lips were set in a faint smile, imperious but kind.

"Is it right," she asked, "to complain in this way of a lady you have known for such a short time?"

"My lady, you know that time means nothing to lovers. You know too that in war our time is not ours to use as we would."

"And do you not know that the first duty of a lover is patience?"

"I do know. But nature and reason compel every man to seek the remedy for his hurt."

"Nature is a harlot," said the lady, "and reason a blind and vicious horse, dragging us down evil ways. If you seek vulgar pleasures in love you will draw on yourself the contempt of all women."

"God forbid!" said Roger. "I can promise you that no lady, however proud, would not be honoured to be the object of such a faithful love as mine."

"Are your friends ready to confirm that you have never committed yourself to serve another lady, either in Toulouse or anywhere else?"

73

"They are. Two of them have been my companions from childhood and know everything about me. You may question them freely."

"Although I regard the habit of swearing as wrong," said the lady, "you have my permission to swear by whatever sacred object you please. Since if it is true that, without making use of any magic or deceit, you have managed to attach to yourself the heart of a virtuous lady (and this, at least, is what your story suggests), it is possible that you may be worthy of it. But the noble ladies of Roquelure and Giremont, and your own friends, are my witnesses that if ever a lady becomes the subject of scandal on your account you will be for ever dishonoured and may never again show your face at banquets or tourneys, since no woman worthy of the name will acknowledge you. Any man who pledges himself to Love's service must perform it with diligence, humility and discretion."

After he had sworn the required oaths and kissed the lady's slender, beringed hand in its violet-coloured glove, Roger was admitted to the dignity of a lover. On the first Saturday in Lent, he shaved, bathed and changed his clothes, and passed his time in gazing at the sun, listening to the bells and praying in church for quite other things than the forgiveness of his sins. Early that morning Arnaude had brought him a letter, which ran as follows:

"Since the judgment has gone in your favour, it is proper for me to allow you to speak with me. You are leaving in three days' time and I must not leave you to play blind man's buff any longer. You shall say what you have to say to me tomorrow at the crossroad marked by three stones on our domain of Belvèze. I shall tell you my mind also."

They met in a pine wood, close to a crossroads where stood a stele built of three stones carved with crosses. The sky was pale grey, there was a warm wind and the horses' hooves splashed through puddles of water. Gentian wore a dress of grey cloth and a red scarf wound about her hair.

They brought their horses to a halt near the abandoned watch-tower of Belvèze, partly gutted by fire and inhabited only by crows. There, without dismounting and heedless of the fine rain driving into their faces, they talked like people drinking after a long walk, thirstily and thinking of nothing. Roger said that he had lived for thirty years knowing nothing of life, that the only thing which was real was to see his beloved and speak to her freely, without her he was so lonely he did not know what

74

to do with himself. She said that her life had not been lacking either in joys or sorrows, and that she was free. She feared nothing. She would not lie.

"I would not want you to have to lie on my account," Roger told her. She gave a proud smile. "No one compelled me to come here. I did not ask you to keep our meeting secret for my own sake."

"I know that, it was for your husband."

"I have a greater affection for him than for my brothers. Even though my heart is given to another, I will not wrong him."

"Ah, must you remind me of that affection?" said Roger. "I know it will torment me all my life."

She said: "If you love me, you must love him. I know you love him already."

"Is there anyone I would not love if it brought me nearer to you?"

He told her how he had won Arnaude's confidence, and how he had picked her out because of her red hair. She looked up at him, studying the bright, rust-coloured curls falling over his brow from beneath the edge of his black fur hat, and broke into shouts of laughter, gay, arrogant laughter that went on and on, she laughed and laughed as though it gave her a never-ending joy. Roger had never felt so much pleasure in hearing anyone laugh at him.

"God!" he said. "You have a good laugh."

She stopped for a moment, then started laughing again, better than ever, but less noisily, with a guttural, cooing sound, so wild and tender that Roger burst out laughing in his turn; and suddenly there was a beating of wings as the startled crows flew up around the tower with a joyous cawing, and Gentian's horse reared and shook his mane and gave a shrill whinny.

They set spurs to their mounts and galloped away, leaping over the scorched undergrowth and the young, green pines. They rode aimlessly for a good half-league before finding themselves back at the same tower, and with difficulty reined in their horses, which were trembling and glistening with sweat. The tower, with its broken door and cracked, smoke-blackened stones, was not a pretty sight, but to Roger the pale, late sunlight falling on its topmost stones seemed to give it a holiday air. "It would do no harm to put this tower in order again," he said.

The young woman shook her head. "They say it brings bad

75

luck. Last year three Crusaders barricaded themselves inside and they were such good shots that every one of their arrows killed a man. They preferred to be burned alive rather than come out."

"God keep their souls," said Roger. "I shall never speak ill of this building."

"Let us go," said Gentian. "Look, our horses are hungry and thirsty and trembling with weariness, and we could stay here like this for three days and it would still seem less than three hours. I feel strong enough to tire out a dozen horses."

Roger said: "The force of love inside me is so strong that I could climb to the top of this tower as easily as if it were a ladder—and when you are no longer here I shall feel like a man of sixty. How is it that you have this power to give me life and take it away?"

"It is the power of the Devil of the flesh."

"If that were all," Roger said thoughtfully, "I should not be the last person to know it, because few men have been possessed by the Devil of the flesh as I have been. There is nothing to boast of in that, but I ought not to hide it either. I think I must have had three hundred women in my life, and maybe even more than that."

"Do I not know?" she said, and her voice held more kindness than censure. "I really believe I do know you, but that was not the Devil I meant."

"When can I make you my mistress?" he asked. "In love all else is pride, vanity and false-seeming."

She stiffened and pulled hard on the reins, making her horse plunge until Roger had to grasp the bridle to control it. He looked into the woman's face, close to his own, above the creature's plaited mane, and saw that she was tense and quivering as though she could see all the stones in the tower crashing down on her, and yet there was no fear in her eyes, only an immense surprise. Almost fainting from the brutal desire he felt for her, Roger let go of the bridle and the lady's horse bounded forward. She set it galloping down the muddy path towards the stream and then followed a long chase through the undergrowth and the fallow fields. They met again by a steep-sided gully whose slopes were covered with thorn bushes and dry branches, while down below a dark trickle of water crept among rotten leaves and mossy stones.

76

"*Men died down there, too,*" she said. She turned towards Roger, and there was a fierce joy in her face. "*I will show you that I do not fear the Devil. He is like a small, wretched animal that I can crush in my hand.*" Then they went back, each going their separate way, without so much as a kiss, but determined to let Love have his way with them. He possessed them both with an equal strength.

Unhappily, even the most legitimate love can be forced to feed on crusts and beg its bread at street corners. During the preparations for departure they had barely time to exchange more than a few words in the hall of the Aspremont mansion, cluttered with boxes and baggage; barely time to smile from a distance, riding through the Capitol Square. Gentian d'Aspremont was happy in those days, with a hard, dazzling happiness that made her sing out loud as she packed chests with clothes and sewed embroidery on the men's armour. Servants were stitching and embroidering banners and repairing the horsehair plumes on horses' trappings: once again the house was transformed into a workshop and knights who came to pay their respects to the ladies before leaving had hard work to make themselves heard above the uproar of singing, laughter and screaming children to whom no one paid any attention. Before leaving the city Roger went out of his way to pass by La Daurade and call at Bérenger d'Aspremont's house. Bérenger welcomed him joyfully and offered him a brimming goblet of Corinthian wine, saying:

"May you find this campaign, like this goblet, full of honour, happiness and good fortune. I hope to see you in my tents before Montréal."

"I hope to see you in mine and to offer you a cup of wine in return for this, not so good, perhaps, but given with the same goodwill. May you too have honour and profit from this war."

"*Amen!*" said Bérenger. "All of us are seeking the same profit and God will not withhold it from us for much longer."

Roger went upstairs to pay his respects to the ladies and found the Lords of Roquefeuil and Lantar with them, and also a Cathar deacon, an old man, as thin and withered as a parched tree. He was not preaching, he was telling the two men how they could find him in the camp if ever they should be grievously wounded. All those present were listening to him in silence, standing as erect and solemn as if they were watching a priest

77

consecrating the Host. On this occasion Roger, like the others, prostrated himself three times before the heretic. He did not know what made him do it: whether it was the thought that he might be killed, or to please the lady. She came to him and, taking his hand, drew him over to the window.

"Are you not a perjurer?" she said. "Haven't you sinned gravely against your faith?"

He said: "To please you I would do much more."

She looked him straight in the eyes with an air of grave kindness which she reserved for him alone. "You are a light and frivolous man," she said. "We of our faith do not try to deceive God."

"I am not such a fool as to think God can be so easily deceived. Many people lie, even when they believe they are speaking the truth."

"You swore to me that you would always speak the truth."

"With you I could not utter a false word, even though I said the sun was black."

She studied him for a moment, her expression candid and thoughtful. "It may be true, it is black," she said slowly.

"When can I prove my love to you by something other than words?"

She drew herself up to her full height, her nose almost touching his face, and her eyes darkened suddenly, burning him. "I want to hold you inside me, and keep you there and nowhere else for ever! Haven't I seen arrows and sling-stones too?"

He felt tears rising suddenly into his eyes from the pain in his whole body because he could not hold her close to him, and what he felt was no common desire but a tenderness that neither words nor looks could express. "As true as God lives," he said, "nothing will happen to me so long as you want me."

They met again, quite frequently, in the course of the army's manœuvres, and at court banquets in between battles. They learned, too, to talk together as though continuing the same conversation from one meeting to the next: they remembered every word spoken, answering quite naturally a question asked a week before, and taking up a sentence where they had been forced to break off and leave it hanging in mid-air. But since they could still find no way of being alone together they remained chaste until harvest time (all previous loves seemed to them like

78

a dream, having no part in their lives, and they felt virginal, like two creatures who had never known sexual union). Moreover, as they were both repelled by the thought of sharing their secret with a stranger, they could see no means of coming together.

Then, two leagues from Belvèze, in the domain of his brother-in-law and friend, Bernard de Montrabé, Roger had a tent erected in the woods beside the banks of the river Sausse. It was a white tent painted all over with golden arrows and surmounted by a green canopy, and he spent on it all the money that was due to him right up to Christmas—although he had to rejoin the Count's army three days after the feast of SS. Peter and Paul and had only twelve days left to find a way of borrowing the money. If even the poorest of men is prepared to spend a year's income on a mere wedding, how much more would a man do for a beloved mistress? Roger bought brand new silken carpets, red candles decorated with crosses painted in gold, striped cushions, a silver cup and even a cage full of singing birds. He had everything carried on muleback to the oak wood where the tent was set up in a clearing of long grass, already turning yellow, among the foxgloves and great stones, black with lichen. (This was perfect madness. He left only three men to guard the tent and even they had orders to depart at the first signal from him. Fortunately, there were no armed bands in the vicinity at that time.)

"I don't know who your lady is," Roger's brother-in-law told him, "but I cannot help envying you for the way you honour her. She must love you very deeply."

"Understand," Roger said, "that she scorns me and will never come here. I have had this tent put up in her honour so that I can stay here and think of her whenever I please, for as much time as we have left for walking about freely without armour."

When she was twenty-seven, on the evening of a hunt, the evening she lost her hawk, Gentian de Montgeil met the Devil.

She was a soul forewarned, tempered by prayer and grief. How could she have failed to know him at first glance? He had come to find her, led to her by a strange bird, because the beasts obey their master's will. He came to her on his black horse, through the rays of a red sun, at that twilight hour when the whole world changes colour and glows with the temptations of hell. He was dressed in red, with red hair and a high-coloured face in which the black eyes, set under coppery brows, gleamed a still deeper black in the light of the setting sun. The extreme beauty of this face hurt the eyes: how can such beings dare to show themselves among men?

He came to her and spoke to her, and told her she belonged to him; he told her his name, which was that of a knight in the Count's retinue, and all he said might have seemed merely ordinary courtesy. But she knew this was dissimulation.

She kept the bird which had brought her this strange evil on her glove, and never thought to ask her friends who the red knight was. She was not one of those inquisitive women, given to asking questions such as: what is that man's fortune? Is he of good repute? Is he married, or pledged to the service of some lady? It matters little what hood a hawk wears, or what chain fastens him. These things will not change the colour of a single feather.

The blinding beauty of fallen angels, the weak angels damned by the lures of the flesh—this is a beauty which glows like an immense red beacon, like a great golden lamp filled with incandescent fire; and whoever encounters it on earth in the person of a human creature is possessed by it for ever. That night, in the tent where the Miraval ladies were sleeping, Gentian clasped the frail, warm bird to her for a long time, rubbing it against her bare throat and breast, while the strange bird shivered in its sleep and thrust its imprisoned head against her body. Gentian loved animals, and this one was not wild, and seemed to feel itself at home. Whose hands had caressed these feathers yesterday? "The hands I have not seen. I saw only hunting gloves made of red leather."

"I shall speak to no one of what I have seen," she thought, "they would only say it was love-sickness, the feeling any woman has when she sees a fine-looking man. How can this man walk about quite openly in Toulouse with that archangel's head without setting fire to the heart of every woman who looks at him? Must I be distracted and out of this world never to have heard people talking of such a bird of paradise? Or is it simply a vision, and have I alone eyes to see him?"

Who could she talk to? Gentian had a husband, though he had not been one for two years, but he was still a friend with whom she shared all her thoughts. He often came to her in their house in Toulouse to play with the children. Their little daughter was learning to talk and he would teach her words and try to make her repeat the lyrics of songs. When she saw him come into her apartments, two days after her return from this momentous hunt, she thought: "God! How can I tell him? Surely we shall both blush for it."

He came and sat on the floor beside the bench on which she was sitting and drew little Raymonde on to his knees, brushing the long fair curls off the child's face with his big hands, calloused from the steel gauntlets, and puffing in her face to make her laugh. Gentian wondered: "What is the matter with me? I feel as though I were drunk. What is it? Even my children seem different—as though all the colour had drained away from them."

She had to tell him. But how? *"Bérenger, two days ago I saw the most marvellous thing in the world." "Bérenger, there is a man in Toulouse, at the Count's court, more wonderful than all the angels in heaven."* How can one say a thing like that to a man who has once been handsome and has not forgotten it. All your brilliance, Bérenger, and your youth, devoured by boiling oil! (As though, even as he was before his injury, there could be any comparison between them! Ah, these eyes have looked on so many lovely things and so much that is ugly, yet never have I seen anything like this.)

It was a temptation of the Devil, and the bird is the Devil's messenger: is it likely that a creature with such perfection of features should come straight up to you, should choose you, out of all others? It was the red light in the sky that evening which made my eyes deceive me.

Bérenger saw that she was preoccupied and asked whether she had a fever. Because she would not lie to him, she stood up and asked him to go with her into the window embrasure where they could not be overheard. Inside the room the children were shouting and her women chatting over their spinning, and the Lady Béatrix was bending over her lectern reading aloud.

"What is it you have to say to me? You look terrified."

"Terrified? Oh, no!"

(A year earlier, a little while after the birth of Raymonde, they had spent a night alone together in their tent. It was a night of sorrow and shame for both of them and one they could not easily forget. They had decided then not to tempt the Devil again, since nature herself was against their marriage. That night Bérenger had said: *If ever you fall in love, may I be called a dog if I speak a single word of reproach to you.* Later, he had repeated the same words in cold blood. But possibly he thought she would

81

never fall in love, because the life she led, her piety, and the care of the children and the house, made it unlikely that she would have time to think of love. Yet an instant is enough for the lightning to strike.)

He asked: "What is it you wish to speak to me about?"

In that moment she knew that the Devil was forcing her to remain silent, she was dumb. As in a dream, she wanted to speak, but her lips would not move. She left the room and ran on to the enclosed balcony, thinking the fresh air would bring back her powers of speech. She leaned on the balustrade, looking down into the courtyard where grooms were leading in visitors' horses. "None of these horses belongs to him," she thought, and realised that she knew exactly what his horse was like: the way its mane fell, the blaze on its forehead, the colour of the reins and the tassels on the harness. It was a four-year-old black stallion. It had become supremely important to her to see that horse there, in that courtyard. It was not there and never would be (without a miracle, at least).

Once possessed by this kind of madness there is no course but to fight. Either from timidity or respect for the conventions, even the most ordinary women will do it. Surely, then, a tried spirit, forged through so many nights of prayers, should be able to laugh at such thoughts? "Alas for me! Marriage has ruined me. I knew there could be no dipping in the tip of a finger, or even a whole hand, and then drawing back."

"The harvest is ripe, your whole field is aflame, you opened a door to the Devil on the day you gave a man your hand, and he was bound to come for you." Yet it was not the idea of sensual pleasure which terrified her, but the thought: "This man will never love you, he is too beautiful, too perfect."

Not for an instant—yes, a child of fifteen would have had more sense—not for an instant did it occur to her that this man's heart might be less beautiful than his body. Because of this, she said nothing to Bérenger, though he had followed her out on to the balcony, asking if she felt ill. Ill, great God, yes! At that moment all her old affection for him was dead, she thought that he was empty, superficial, even crass. (This was nonsense: she knew she would suffer death for him and he for her.) *What kind of a man is he, that he can't look the truth in the face? If I could not tell him about this, it is because he cannot bear to hear it.*

Before her marriage she habitually spoke the truth to everyone

82

on all subjects. Bluntly—for her nature was blunt. By becoming a mother she had lost this gift of hardness. What was the use of wounding? Men are weaker than we are.

If ever I have to pass through such a test, Bérenger, you shall know nothing of it. May I never be able to say that you have offended me in word or deed, for God knows I do not deserve it! But the best of men has unworthy thoughts of us.

In a week, in three weeks, they were under arms again, the house still cluttered with debris and scaffolding, the repairs never finished and the workmen unpaid so that they could pay the soldiers. But for Lady de Miraval, even the ladies' own apartments would have begun to look like an armourer's shop. She, however, clung firmly to the old customs, saying that there had been a deal too much talk of war in the last ten years, and that in the intervals of fighting men needed to see other things besides coats of mail. She insisted on the young ladies' making themselves look attractive and not neglecting the graces of their sex, and herself set a courageous example. This she did for her daughter, Béatrix, three years a widow and sick with grief.

Béatrix dressed in silk gowns and silver necklaces, read devotional books, sang songs and embroidered dresses for her little girl. "Be cheerful and beautiful for the child's sake," her mother told her, "so that she need not be ashamed of you!" Béatrix obeyed her mother meekly. But little Marquezia, brought up among Bérenger's children, almost came to believe that she was Gentian's daughter. (Gentian, admittedly, seemed to prefer the orphan to her own children: this was her nature. She forced herself to be stern towards her own flesh and blood through fear of loving them too much.)

Between campaigns, then, life in the Aspremont household was fairly peaceful, almost gay. And peace and gaiety worked on Gentian like a charm: a cheerful song, a child's laughter or a torchlight procession warmed her whole being. She might never have known suffering. One died and was reborn each day. Tomorrow the fighting would begin again: there would be the red and yellow woods, the blackened fields, the grey sky, the burned villages, the camp set up before some castle and the siege engines brought into position. As yet the Crusaders would have no shortage of crossbow bolts or cannon balls. They were not keen on being taken alive.

(Béatrix's story was this: her husband, Raymond de Roques, had been brought back to the Aspremont mansion during the siege with his head smashed to pieces by a missile and wrapped in his bloodstained tunic. They had laid him down on the table and Béatrix had said: "I want to see." There was a pulp of shattered bone, teeth, sinews, blood and brains with the broken halves of the metal face-piece still buried in it. Only the partially undamaged helmet showed that this had been a head. Béatrix put her hand out and touched the pink and white skull and gory locks. The blood was already congealing. That day Gentian had lost the child she had not known she was carrying: the sight of so much blood had brought the blood gushing from her own body and the pain in her belly made her lose consciousness. Two days later, she was up again and sped back to the ramparts. A dozen times she narrowly escaped having her own head crushed. She might have been drunk. She wanted to meet that faceless death face to face.)

. . . How frail a thing is a man's face; a single stone in the right place is enough. They are good marksmen and they aim at the head to avenge Count Simon's head—I may never see his face again. I shall have nothing left but the grey hawk, the grey hawk that came and took me. My hands will never have touched that red hair.

She felt changed, as though by a baptism in reverse: she was aware of her body as she had never been aware of or known it before. Every part of her, from the pit of her stomach to the pores in her skin, had become living and vulnerable, soft and eager: if she put some fruit into her mouth, she felt its caress on her lips; when she kissed her little girl, she wanted to bite her, and she thrilled so much at the sight of one of her women who had red hair that she wanted to laugh aloud. "Either I will get over this, or I shall go mad," she told herself, and she did not care because her desire to see this man again was too strong to let her think of anything else. Then, one fine day, Bérenger brought this knight and one of his friends into the house, and at that she knew he really loved her. For months he did not give himself away by a word or a look, he merely came and paid his respects to the ladies and then retired, leaving with them his friend, a pale, brown-haired young man bearing a strong resemblance to the old Count.

(How did she know this indifference was feigned, that he only

84

avoided her because of his deep love for her, she who considered herself no lovelier than others and knew nothing of his life? It was as if he burned with a fire which only she could see; in those days her trust in him was boundless and she saw the proof of his love in everything he did.)

On the day Arnaude brought her the letter, she was frightened by the fierce joy which shook her body. This letter was no bolder or more eloquent than many others, but Gentian seemed to feel the whole man, the weight of his hand and of his heart, in every word. Other men's desire had left her with a sense of outrage: not thinking herself beautiful, she knew she was desired more than she should be. "It must be true," she reflected, "that love is madness. I hardly know this man, he is not even one of my friends, and yet I am not thinking of myself, or of my own joy or pain, I am thinking only of his wretchedness and of how I can help him to his desire. If I were God or the Devil, I should carry his beloved to him by magic to give him the happiness of making her his own."

Certainly she never, for an instant, tried to combat her malady by prayer, because from the day when she realised beyond all possible doubt that she desired a man with a physical passion, she had known that her prayers could no longer be pure and whole-hearted and would be an offence to God. Her faith had not weakened, but now it had become speechless. She carried out her normal religious obligations with the stern impassivity of a servant watching over a treasure which does not belong to him and which he has no right to covet. None the less, when her friends set out on their pilgrimage to Montségur she went with them, wondering as she left whether she would ever return to Toulouse. Perhaps, she thought, it would be better if I died and he forgot me. (This journey and the prolonged separation it involved seemed to her as cruel as death: she knew now that only death could prevent her from giving herself entirely to a love which must place a soul for ever beyond the reach of Truth.)

Festivals are commonly public celebrations, with music and feasting, almsgiving and kisses of peace, but how should this festival be celebrated when there were only the two guests and no friends and maidens bearing torches? You do not set all the bells in the town ringing to proclaim that a lady loves you with

85

a true love. But perhaps up in the sky where angels who belong neither to God nor the Devil dwell among rosy clouds, golden bells may be chiming merrily to celebrate the union of true lovers.

The delights of love may lawfully be shared with a woman whose heart is pure and sincere.

Yet honour demanded that this should be a solitary feast, a feast of which no one must know, not even Arnaude, though she had brought the lady's answer. It was a short letter.

As you have shown your regard for me up to the present, I owe you the same regard. Since you ask me for a reply, tomorrow I hunt alone and you will find no one but myself at the Crusaders' tower. But I wish to encounter no face but your own throughout the day until sunset.

The morning dawned hot and crickets were chirping beside the burnt-out tower. Afraid of not being the first to arrive, Roger left his brother-in-law's house at sunrise and waited for a long time, watching the shadows of the dead trees growing gradually shorter and swinging round to the right across the yellowed grass and the grey earth of the path. Gentian arrived alone, her face unveiled and her eyes shining like those of a man nerving himself for a hard fight. They rode through the forest without speaking, both of them grave and ill at ease. Then the white tent came into view through the trees and when she saw the gilded arrows and green silk awning Gentian blinked in astonishment. The hangings were drawn back from the doorway and through the opening could be seen a hearse bearing seven red candles, a broad, low bed with a coverlet of striped silk and a cage full of birds.

While Roger watered the horses the lady walked up and down in front of the tent whistling in amazement.

"Roger," she said at last, with undisguised merriment, "I really believe you must be a man quite given over to vanity and the lusts of the eyes! If you have really bought all this rather than borrowing it, you will be forced to sell it all again in a week, at half it cost you."

"Never in this world," he said, laughing (no amount of teasing from her could make him angry). "All this belongs to you. I shall not touch it until the Day of Judgment."

Her eyes were twinkling as she said: "I hope you will rise again surrounded by such lovely things. You can use them to bribe St. Peter to unlock the gates of paradise." It was good to laugh with her! Yet the two of them had not come'there for laughter.

He said: "My love, this house is yours to do as you like with. Inside is all that is needful to eat, drink and repose yourself. If you do not wish me to enter it with you, I will stay by the door and be your guard. You have proved your trust in me so fully that I have no right to ask for more."

"Do you think I will take you at your word?" she said.

They went into the tent and Roger struck a spark to light the candles. Rosy points of light started from rugs, goblets, and birdcage, and long, flickering shadows multiplied themselves on the white canvas.

"Is it not lovely?" Roger asked. "I know it is very little, but everything seems to me a hundred times more lovely when I look at you. If this day you vouchsafe me one kiss, all the treasures in the Pope's palace would not suffice. . . ."

Gentian was suddenly grave. "Do as you will," she said. "Ask this kiss of me and I will not refuse you."

He went down on one knee and she bent over him and put her hands on his shoulders. For a long moment they looked at one another, he straining upwards, she leaning down and trembling so much that she had to support her weight on him in order not to sink to her knees also. Knowing the gift of the lips to be almost the last, they had held back so long for fear of arousing a desire too strong for them. Finally, he reached the quivering mouth that struggled instinctively to elude him, biting and gnawing as though he were feeding on it, and then, rising slowly, he took her whole body, hips and shoulders, breasts and thighs, into his arms; all the warmth and weight and supple strength of her young body, barely hidden by the folds of her gown.

How should love be given and received? In this feast the mind has no part, it belongs to the body, which seeks its own joys. The headlong rush of a few minutes takes one to the goal that has been desired, longed for and contemplated for months and months as the fulfilment of every conceivable happiness. The candles had hardly burned down and the shadow of the tall pine tree on the roof of the tent had not moved three inches. In his small cage, hung high up on the tent pole, a black merlin was endlessly piping the opening bars of a love-song. How many times? Thousands.

The vast forgetfulness of all shame, all fear, of everything beyond this sensual drive, could have lasted for hours or only as long as the scream of ecstasy that alarmed the caged birds.

87

From the first moments of mutual violence they had both known that from now on the hunger they felt for one another could only grow.

For a long time they did not speak, any more than animals speak, they simply gazed and clung, coiling and uncoiling, coming together again, like a pair of dancers or fighters slowly circling and measuring one another before they attack. Attack and defence were both past, leaving only the need to become part of each other, to know one another, not simply with their eyes, their minds or their hands, but with all the length and breadth and weight and warmth and strength of their whole bodies, bodies as yet still hidden, silent and secret, in which is the greatest wealth of true lovers.

For anyone can love a face, but the body is an animal, mindless and vulnerable, and it takes a great love to accept it to the end, to surrender it freely. (This nakedness that neither I myself, nor my friends and bedfellows, have ever beheld except unthinkingly, by accident, and that even my husband was only able to see by force and despite myself, because I have always been shamed by it—here it is, given up to eyes that do not wound, enfolded in another body whose nakedness does not offend my sight—surely this man must be possessed of the Devil if he can transmute a natural, physical act into so great a joy? It is the Devil I serve now, he is my friend and I can see only goodness in him.) She lay there—slender and brown as a boy but for her breasts and the slimness of her waist, spreadeagled on the green and white striped coverlet like a great St. Andrew's cross, brown and rose and yellowish white. Her body was firm and warm, with nipples like long, brown buds and black hair in a plait not easily undone; it was fresh and untouched, she had lived barely six months of her life with a man as other women do. "Could he really leave you like that? May God bless him for it: I should never have been able to."

"But he is not like you," she said. "He is changeable." He looked at her wonderingly.

"Truly," he said, "it wanted your goodness and the understanding that comes from love to see that I am not changeable. You are the first person who has ever said it."

She thought: "If he were the worst of men my love would still make him seem good to me. I shall never believe any slander of him."

88

Of the three hundred women he had held in his arms, his body retained no trace; yet caresses of another kind had left their mark on that body. Long, smooth white scars and stars of puckered flesh adorned both arms, his left thigh and his right side, and Gentian had seen enough wounds to know the cost in pain of ornaments of this kind to impress the ladies—though Roger was not a man to boast of them.

"So much blood," she said thoughtfully, running her finger over the great scars. "You have lost so much blood. How many cups would it fill?"

He frowned. "I suppose they have put their mark on us. God! What a dreary existence! We live like hired mercenaries."

She nodded slowly. "Roger, you are a perfect weathercock, you don't know what you love or what you hate."

"I do. I know very well. What do you mean by that?"

She did not answer, she seemed abstracted, faintly surprised, as though she were pondering some awkward problem.

"You love me," she said at last, "and yet you have kept on you an object which I shall never love, and that, out of respect for the thing itself, you should not have kept. See, it has stamped itself on my shoulder, like a seal on wax."

She looked at the pale, clear mark which the chased silver crucifix had made on her skin.

"Why didn't I think of it?" Roger said, and pulling the silken cord over his head he tossed the cross on to the carpet at the base of the candle-holder.

"Did I ask you to do that?" Gentian said, shocked. "Is that how you treat an object you hold sacred?"

"Ah, I have pawned it and bought it back so often that it must have lain in much worse places than that. Besides which," he added reflectively, "my chest is not a particularly hallowed place, either."

"Why do you say that? To me it is better than angels' wings. Should I have become your lover if I had not known you to be better than other men?"

"How can I ever understand that?" said Roger. "Apart for the true love I bear to you I don't believe I have any great merit."

"As I know you now, I should refuse to believe my eyes if I saw you perform an evil action. There is no evil in you, except that you serve Satan. But I serve him even better than you."

That was like her, he knew: she was convinced that it was

89

impossible to take a step without serving Satan. It may have pained her once but it did so no longer. She was a happy woman, grave and happy.

She was fearfully calm. Solemn and withdrawn, like a fortune teller melting wax over a candle in order to read the future. She was looking at her left hand, lying on the purple and green stripes of the coverlet, as though she were seeing it for the first time.

"I thought I should die of loving you too much," she said.

"Now," Roger said softly, "it is life and death between us, it is as though we were welded together. But for the war I should spend my life watching at your door. We shall have to die of thirst nine days out of ten. Shall I see you during the campaign?"

She told him that love was a powerful demon who was now in their service and that he would be able to bring them together though three walls kept them apart. And he would close the eyes of those who should not know.

This was the day he gave her the name, Rigueur, which he was to keep for her all his life: he gave it to her out of gratitude, just because she no longer had any rigour for him, only a boundless goodness. At sunset he took her back to the burnt-out tower. Both of them were silent, so tired out with loving that they could scarcely hold the reins, and sad because with their clothes on again it seemed as though they were compelled to wear a disguise.

Before they left the tent Roger had himself plaited his beloved's hair and woven into it the black silk cord he used to fasten the neck of his shirt. This was the only thing of his that she would consent to take. And because red was thenceforth to be their secret colour, she gave Roger half of her red scarf.

With the help of the Devil, Gentian d'Aspremont was able to go hunting at Belvèze twice more before the campaign began, accompanied by two grooms and the Lady Béatrix—because Béatrix guessed her secret. She wandered far in pursuit of her hawk and was herself taken by the hunter who lay in wait for her—or, more accurately, she was plucked by a greedy and impatient sparrow-hawk and eaten alive a thousand times over without being any the worse for it. Love's pleasures are not a game, and whoever tastes them once loses his soul to them. *"Béatrix, speak to me no more of prayer and salvation for I revel in my damnation."*

90

"You will get over it," said Béatrix. "I have known the same temptation and I would have given anything to have had it longer. May God keep the man you love alive for you."

Nevertheless it saddened her to watch her friend growing silent and thoughtful: at night, in the bed they shared, Gentian scarcely said a word to her, and lay stiffly with her hands behind her head and her eyes wide open. She could not speak, because her thoughts were those that cannot be spoken without betraying love. She was thinking of the warmth of the forest, of a path bordered with moss and deep pink heather—and of laughter and tears and tender words and a moist body covered with freckles and scars and random hairs—the strange, secret companion of a handsome head crowned with red curls. She was thinking of two long brown eyes that were so eloquent, and trying to understand all that she read in those eyes: so much goodness and wisdom and strength and much more besides. . . .

In those first days they thought much more of the joys of the flesh than of love itself. They were starved and it seemed to them as though, in the short time they were alone, they would never be satisfied. In the city they hardly managed to say more than a few words to one another when Roger called at the Aspremont house, playing the difficult game of friendship with her husband. (He was jealous at this time, and bitterly unable to forget the tenderness his beloved had once felt for this man.)

They were separated so often in the first months of their liaison that the unnatural existence nearly drove both of them out of their minds. In time of war a man is not free to follow his beloved like a shadow, either openly or in secret. Throughout the whole campaign, which lasted for two months, Roger tasted the full delights of love only three times in all, by gaining admittance to his beloved's tent disguised as a water-carrier while the servant on guard happened to be asleep. (Out of the twenty times he kept watch in this way, the ruse succeeded only three, and that must have been due to the good offices of God or the Devil, because there was great risk of being surprised. The nurse slept in the tent with the two young children, and sentinels passed by regularly on their rounds, calling to one another and waking the guards. The camp slept uneasily, fearful of spies and marauders, enemies creeping up in disguise to attack the tents with swords hidden under their clothes—and this enemy who comes in the night to steal caresses has no use for his sword if he is taken: though he were to kill ten men, still one cannot kill shame.)

True love can find happiness even in adversity, and although they were compelled to make love fearfully and in silence, the lovers had great joy. The time came when Roger pressed his face to his mistress' side and wept. "One more hour of life, two at the most," he thought. He watched in the tiny, glimmering red flame from the night light, while she fell asleep, her pale, delicate head thrown back on to the loose mesh of black hair, and her wide, dark mouth curved into a weary, victorious smile. "No man," he thought, "ever had so much love from such a woman." And out of impatience and to see her eyes again he woke her. She looked up at him with grave surprise out of pupils drowned in shadow, and then shivered forlornly.

"What, so soon. . . ?"

"No," he told her. "It is hardly time for matins yet." And it seemed as if they were together again for a week. Afraid of falling asleep, Roger put his hand on the lamp whenever he felt his eyes closing.

Love must be groomed like an animal and trained in the hard school of Privation, Constraint and Self-control if it is to survive, for honour is to a woman like the sun to the vine.

Rigueur often thought of death in those days: she could not look at a knife or a sword without considering cutting her own throat. "For lovers who love one another truly, there is no other safety. When I was young I so longed to keep my virginity that I thought a man's kiss would sear my flesh like a red hot iron. And now I am burned all over until there is not a single clear place on my body and I feel no pain, only joy. If I have not died of it already, it is because I know I cannot live long."

"In that case why do you fear for my life so much?"

"That is weakness," she said. "Ought we not to be able to offer each other death?"

In fact, though Roger thought them strange, these were words of wisdom, but he was not to realise it until long afterwards. The young, however much they may have suffered, still believe that tomorrow will bring happiness. Courage, we have almost won through, courage, we have not fought in vain! *"Rigueur, we shall live to see a new spring-time in our land."*

It was a fine, clear autumn and as a relaxation from the fatigues of campaigning the young Count arranged a hunting party in the course of which the lovers were able to have long talks together. Roger rode that day between Gentian d'Aspremont and her friend Hélis de Roquevidal. The two young women had no taste for hunting, saying that enough murders were committed in the land already and they were not inclined to shed innocent blood. They rode slowly along remote paths, their spears at rest, gathering branches of oak and ash whose autumn colours they thought the richest, as they passed, while their grooms followed behind. The Lady d'Aspremont was talking of sin and salvation. "Strictly speaking," she said, "there is only one sin: birth, and only one salvation: death. Not the death of the flesh that comes to every living creature but the true death of which the Lord spoke to Nicodemus. Truly it is easier to return to one's mother's womb and be born again than to die that death. But you Catholics live by a heathen law that says this second birth can be brought about by magic, with a little water and a few words of Latin recited over an unconscious child. According to you, your priests have the power of transforming evil into good by the sign of the cross and a few prayers, and some oil and water, and all kinds of carnal rites that commit neither the soul nor the body to anything. Is such a faith worthy of Jesus Christ?"

"Hasn't the Church tried to extend the blessed charity of Jesus Christ to every living soul by adapting her laws to meet the infirmities of our nature? He wanted all the sheep to be saved."

"And so they will be," said Rigueur, "but not by trickery and deceit. They shall all experience the passion of spiritual death and rebirth, some in one year, some in a hundred and some in a thousand. But by bringing sin and salvation down to a human level the heathens, in their short-sightedness, are destroying countless souls: does not your Pope, being a man, believe he has the right to save and to damn souls? Are not Catholics in our own land excommunicated for having acted rightly? And if the Count dies tomorrow, they will say he is damned, not on account of his real sins, great as they are, but because of his good deeds."

"If ever that tragedy occurs," Roger exclaimed, "the Pope will be damned first, for God's mercy is greater than that of the Church! God has permitted the wolves to enter the fold in the guise of shepherds in order to test our faith!"

"But you still believe," queried the Lady Hélis, "that they have the power to ordain priests, grant sinners absolution, and

93

change the common food of the belly into the flesh and blood of Jesus Christ? Would God have given such power to wolves in the guise of shepherds?"

"We must believe," Roger said reluctantly, "that if they have such power it is God who has given it to them. There being two orders in creation, that of Nature and of Grace, we must therefore deem Grace the prime order—as, by way of example, if our Count were an evil man he would still be our liege lord. It is the same with the Pope: I can hate his character and still honour his holy function."

Rigueur shook her head, remarking that such reasoning was over-subtle and Jesus Christ had never taught anything of the kind. In this world it was certainly necessary to obey the laws of the land, just as it was necessary to eat and drink in order to nourish the body, but that God existed beyond all such considerations. In the same way, she said, "according to the laws of this world, a woman is not expected to bring calumny on her husband by publicly avowing her love for another, but this is an obligation which has nothing to do with faith. And Catholics have made lawful marriage into something sacred when more often than not people marry out of greed, carnal desire, obedience to their parents, or simple pride. A marriage blessed by your priests is sacred and a union not blessed by them, though it springs from the purest love, is described in words it would not be proper to repeat. A child born in wedlock is a gift of God, while a child born without their blessing is held to be the fruit of the Devil. How much good sense is there in all that? Isn't it rather an unlawful confusion of things human and things divine? Jesus Christ never said that people living in a state of carnal indulgence could be saved."

Roger had no effective counter to this argument in which he felt personally involved. "Those are hard words," he said, somewhat uneasily, "and they would be melancholy hearing for any man who loved you."

"I do not hide my feelings from those who love me any more than from those who do not. The reason I mention it at all is to show you that your priests are mistaken in thinking that man's body and will were created by God. In reality they are the work of a cunning and powerful craftsman who did not form them for the service of God."

"I should tell you," said Roger, "that I love a lady so perfect that the mere sight of her is enough to convince me that our bodies are the work of God."

She gave a challenging laugh. "Isn't the owl the loveliest of creatures in the eyes of her mate?" He could feel the excitement through her lighthearted words. "Our eyes are made to see beauty in this world, since they were created for this world. See how beautiful the forest is now, yet all this is nothing but decay! See how beautiful are the crows and vultures wheeling in the sky above the branches, yet they feed on carrion! Your lady is no different, her body is rottenness and conceals all manner of impurities."

(Later Roger was to learn that at the time she was carrying his child. She had been reluctant to tell him since she knew enough medicine to extricate herself quickly from a situation which might damage her honour. On her return to Toulouse she was seriously ill for two weeks and Roger did not see her; he was told she was suffering from verdigris poisoning.

Telling him about it afterwards, she said: *"It was worse than dying a dozen times over, but I was happy in a way because this illness has left me free from the curse of women for ever. I shall bear no more children."*

Roger had to admit that this was a considerable blessing indeed, but a cruel blessing. Lovers who share their beloved with another man beget children in complete security and watch them grow up attached to a father who takes them for his legitimate heirs; true, this is a pleasure not unmixed with anguish, but it is one with which many men are content. But this happiness is nothing to the joy which is denied them, of possessing alone the key to their garden and not having to smile by day at a man who outrages you by night. In short, every man makes the best of his situation. "To tell the truth, my sweet, I would have preferred to help you invent a hundred schemes for going into hiding for as long as was necessary. A son of yours would have been like an angel from heaven to me." Roger genuinely mourned for this child, as though it had lived and was dead. Moreover it is possible that he might never have known of it but for an incident which came close to shattering his union with Rigueur for ever.)

She had told him this painful story, concealing nothing, admitting all the disgust she had felt for herself and for her body. *"Roger, the reason I am telling you this today (after concealing it from you for six months) is to make you realise that I shall never be a wife to you. And so that you may never wish for Bérenger's death nor hope to have legitimate heirs by me."*

"Do you think," said Roger, "that I am capable of turning against you for such a thing? I have forgiven you without even thinking about it. I can't tell you how much I regret it. But you are putting me to so severe a test that I am ready to believe you are weary of our love."

"Ah, would to God I were, and you too. Today or in a year. Is Love made for old men with white hair? You know I am not telling you this through want of love." This had been the subject of bitter enough discussions between the lovers for two weeks past, because Roger was to all intents and purposes about to marry. Rigueur said that for his family's as much as his own sake he ought not to refuse the match. Pierre-Guillaume de Montbrun was very set on it. Roger's friends commented:

"We are at war. Shall it be said that you are afraid of the dangers and responsibilities of a *seigneurie*?" In fact Roger was not afraid, on the contrary he wanted them more than he would admit.

On their return from the Easter campaign, the young Count Raymond had summoned him to his privy chamber.

"Roger, I have spoken to you many times of the friendship and goodwill I bear you, but thanking men with words is minstrels' work. And although I have plied that trade before now, without possessing either the talent or the title for it, I am beginning to tire of it, and so are my knights, though out of respect for my father they will say nothing of it to me. It is high time I bestowed on you the fortune you deserve."

Roger answered that his lord the Count's esteem was reward enough for him (while privately reflecting that the Count was indeed slow in recognising his merits).

"The lady in question," the young Count went on, "is the heiress of the manor of Layrac in the Toulousain. As you know, the male line died out with Bertrand de Layrac and his sons, who perished at the siege of Penne. Simon de Montfort gave the daughter in marriage to the eldest son of Herbert de Vitry. However, as she was only six years old at the time, the marriage was never consummated. The young man was killed last year, at Montréal, and you know the manner in which the girl regained her freedom. Now the vassals of the domain, which is a fair size, are begging me to give the girl a husband from among my knights, a man who can hold and defend her lands. That is why I thought of you."

Roger replied that he was greatly honoured but that he was the lover of one of the loveliest ladies in Toulouse and therefore did not wish to commit himself to marriage. The Count said such scruples were all very well in the old chivalrous times but that with a fine fortune at his disposal Roger would be able to make himself proportionately more worthy of his lady.

"I am in love, myself," he said, "and it never occurs to my mistress to complain of my marriage." (Indeed since he had been married when he was fifteen she would have been wrong to do so.)

At this Roger let his heart speak out in all sincerity, or very nearly, saying that it was enough for him to have served his liege lord to the best of his ability.

"I am already thirty-one," he said, "and the last ten years have seemed like twice that number in all our lives. I am hardly seeking my own fortune. If you need a man to hold the domain of Layrac, I am ready to obey you, but there are others who will do as well. For myself, it is enough to know that I was your first choice."

The young man took his vassal's refusal for mere formal politeness, and in this he was not entirely wrong. He pressed the matter by saying that the Crusaders had done a good deal of damage to the domain and that he had to ensure the safety of his lands by entrusting them to men able to hold them.

Roger said neither yes or no, which in itself almost amounted to saying yes. When he had talked the matter over with Rigueur he was sorry he had not refused. (They were meeting two or three times a week now, at the house of the same merchant who had lent Roger a room before, on the day he took Arnaude there. It was not easy, and Rigueur had to wear a veil and change cloaks with that very Arnaude who waited for her on these occasions, hidden behind a pillar in the church of St. Étienne. Lovers are like alcoholics: once the habit has become a necessity, they care very little about the manner in which they obtain their desires. Moreover they were both still young and hot-blooded and kept perfect faith with one another.)

The news that her lover was to be obliged to take a wife came as such a shock to Rigueur that for a good five minutes she could say nothing at all. Her cheeks and lips turned grey and her eyes dilated. She sat like a statue on the edge of the bed, her hands clasped in her lap, looking as rigid as though she had not moved for hours, as though she would never move again until the Day of Judgment. Faced with this reaction, Roger, who had neither wit nor skill when he spoke to her, could only sit beside her, dumb as a carp, wishing himself dead and buried. At last he told her that if he had to watch her like that for another minute he would slit his throat with his dagger. She said: "I am making you suffer terribly. I don't know what is the matter with me."

He swore he wanted no other bride and that one day, if God allowed, he would make her his lawful wife.

"Do not touch me today," she said, "leave me to think about this."

The next day she wrote him a note telling him not to reject the maid of Layrac. *For in times such as these men ought to protect women and a noble house should not remain without an heir, nor a valiant man without lands to defend. In three days I will see you and tell you my mind.*

During those three days Roger endured martyrdom. The pain he had read in his lady's face burned in his blood, he could think of nothing else, and he suffered the more because at bottom he had already made up his mind to accept the proffered marriage. After all, he told himself: "It is one of the best manors in the Count's domains: once the vines are replanted, it will make you a rich man in a few years. And Bertrand de Layrac was one of the best knights of his time."

That was true. The old knight had been killed on the walls of Penne, together with his two sons, because he would not retreat when the machine he was defending caught fire. He hacked away the blazing beams with his axe and flung them down on his assailants, and hoisted Brabançons as tall as himself into the air with his giant strength and smashed them against the wall like clay pots. After his death the Crusader Herbert de Vitry had marched on Layrac and was met with crossbow fire. Once the place was taken he had avenged the insult. Bertrand's grandson, a boy of thirteen, was hanged with the rest, and the girl, Guillelme, married off to Herbert's eldest son. She was six years old, and they left her to live with her nurse in the castle garrets. Herbert de Vitry held the castle and lands for eight years.

98

When he heard of his son's death (he was killed before the walls of Montréal), Herbert summoned his younger son from France with all speed. The Count's armies were actually besieging Layrac when Herbert de Vitry had the marriage solemnised in the castle chapel in the middle of the battle, with himself, the bridegroom and the witnesses all armed, with mud and blood on their armour. The girl refused to say 'I will' (she was truly of the blood of the Layracs) but Herbert said that the husband's consent was enough. Afterwards the men hastened back to the ramparts where they were sorely needed. A few hours later the castle was taken and Herbert de Vitry (a very valiant knight) broke through the ranks of Toulouse and escaped through the great gate with ten of his men. They were pursued relentlessly across the fields of Layrac, fighting one against four, and one of the horsemen carried off the maid on his saddle bow. She screamed out: "Help, friends, help! I am the heiress of Layrac!" She was taken to the camp of Toulouse, trembling and laughing for joy, her hair and her clothes drenched in the blood of the Crusader who had been hewn down by axe blows on top of her.

After the campaign, which took place at Eastertide, Guillelme de Layrac was escorted to the Narbonnese castle and presented to the Countesses of Toulouse, and the chief vassals of her domain—Jean-Rigaud de Marcillac, Ratier de Villemur and Pierre-Aimery de Magnanac—went with her. There, before the Countesses and the young Count and the barons of Toulouse, Guillelme asked to give her oath of allegiance on the Gospels and swore that she had never been violated, and that her second marriage was null and void since she had not consented to it either in her heart or by word of mouth. Her nurse and the vassals swore likewise. Afterwards the girl flung herself at the Countesses' feet and asked them to grant her aid and protection; she was dressed in a blue silken cloak and taken to live in the Narbonnese castle as one of the Countesses' maids of honour. The young Count promised the vassals of Layrac to provide their lady with a lawful husband.

Roger had seen her for the first time on that day. She was not particularly beautiful, in spite of the long hair the colour of ripe oats, falling over her shoulders: she had a pale face, marred by acne, and a stubborn little brow; her blue eyes, under strongly marked eyebrows, were bright and hard. She was clearly not a young lady reared among orchards and painted chambers, and

99

she was still very young, not more than fifteen. (Later on she was to develop into a handsome woman.) The girl sat among the ranks of the Count's vassals in the audience chamber, surrounded by her three old soldiers; looking serious and a little bored and gnawing her small, full lips.

The wedding took place in the same audience chamber, and the old Count himself had consented to join the couple's hands. (This he did out of friendship for Roger, taking on himself the role of a father to the heiress of Layrac.) When she set her eyes on her future husband, Guillelme gave a little laugh, like a short, piercing whinny, and hid her face in her sleeve—her manners were still those of a child. (Much later she was to say that she had never seen a man with such red hair, and this was why she laughed; but it was because, from that first day, she thought him handsome, too.) But in the first years of their marriage, there was no love between them. On the very day of their betrothal, Roger took the girl aside and told her he had long been in love with a woman of his own age and did not believe he could change; but that he considered an alliance with the house of Layrac a great honour, and would be a protector and friend for its lady and do all he could to be revenged on her enemies. To this she replied that she cared nothing for love and indeed hoped never to know it. "Though I have taken a husband, it is only for the sake of our lands and so that our line shall not die out; otherwise, I should have preferred never to marry." Girls of fifteen say these things in their ignorance. Guillelme was as virginal as it is possible to be, and of this Roger was to have proof.

The marriage of Guillelme de Layrac to Roger de Montbrun, knight, was celebrated, as befitted a wartime wedding, before the Capitol to the sound of drums and trumpets. The bride and groom, dressed in red robes and crowned with flowers, presented themselves before the consuls, bringing their offerings; and among the men in the wedding procession one in every three was in armour, because the young Count was anxious to retake Puylaurens before the coming of the Crusaders (who were expected by Ascension Day). As a special favour the couple also received a nuptial blessing in the sacristy of St. Sernin. (Roger was not at that time expressly excommunicated, but only no more nor less so than any citizen of Toulouse.) Later Herbert de Vitry was to register a complaint to the See of Narbonne accusing Guillelme de Layrac of bigamy and adultery.

The heiress of Layrac went back to her castle on her new husband's arm, escorted by her armed vassals and Roger's soldiers, happy in the restored honour of her house. In the fields of Layrac nothing grew but poppies and couch grass and of the great vineyards half were reduced to fallow land, strewn with the broken stumps of the vines. Peasants streamed out from the villages on to the road to watch their lady riding past under the banners of Toulouse, although they had no gifts to offer her but field flowers and wild strawberries. Roger had nothing to bring them either, except hope.

In the castle he sat with Guillelme on Bertrand de Layrac's high-backed chair and caused the shield of Montbrun to be hung up beside that of Layrac, and all the men of noble blood in the domain came and knelt before him to swear fealty, Jean-Rigaud de Marcillac at their head. Roger bound himself to them by a solemn oath, and with handshakes and kisses on the mouth, so that they became his men and he their lord; and with his hand on Guillelme's he swore henceforth to hold the honour and the lives of the men of Layrac as dear as his own life and honour; and to respect the customs of Layrac as those of his own house. He promised, too, not to exact from the lands of Layrac, for purposes of war, more than a third part of the revenue from the vines, the tolls from the bridge, and the corn, wood and wool, which third the men of Layrac were bound to yield up to him unquestioningly as long as the war should last.

These were promises in the air: the domain was so ruined that there could be no question of corn, or wool, or even of logs of wood. Herbert de Vitry had deforested the entire right bank of the River Tarn as far as Villemur to such an extent that they had rather to think of replanting. It was decided to double the tolls and enrol all able bodied men on the domain in the work of rebuilding and carrying stones, until the season of the grape harvest. The castle had been badly damaged in the last battle. Herbert de Vitry had not escaped empty handed and no money was left in the coffers. However there was still some fine plate, cloth, candlewax, some good wine and bales of wool. Roger distributed a proper amount of all this to his vassals; and Guillelme walked about the great hall with its broken windows and smoke-blackened walls laughing aloud, embracing the vassals' wives and saying:

"God be thanked! God be thanked! They won't come back

again. You should have seen the way they honoured me in Toulouse."

Poor innocent, she believed the manner in which she had regained her liberty had placed her among the ranks of the bravest. (When she cried out "Help! Help!" during the battle the man who was carrying her off had used her as a shield; she had escaped without a scratch and claimed to have been saved by a miracle.) Her vassals, who had served the Crusaders rather than abandon the castle, regarded her affectionately. "She will give us a fine heir," they said. "She has old Bertrand's blood in her veins!" Guillelme was well built, tall and strong for her age. Her only defect was a shrill rather hoarse voice, which she had had ever since the day she saw her brother and the men of the garrison hanged.

". . . *You know what happened to pretty little Ferrande, seigneur Roger? You see those hooks in the great chimney—they hung her up there, two months ago. Herbert's squire, Girard, had made her his mistress. She was up on the tower, at the top of that staircase, sending signals to our army—and when they caught her they had their pleasure of her in turn, here in this room, after the morning meal; and afterwards they hung her up in the hearth, like an ox, and made up the fire. All roasted alive, and there were some who ate of it. . . . They were so mad with rage because they saw they could not hold out any longer. The Vitry and his son went out on to the ramparts after the false marriage they made me go through, and I was so frightened they would rape me that I clung to the chaplain and hugged him in my arms as if he had been my nurse. And then you should have heard the noise when the fire reached the chapel! Because our army was already inside the great court, and de Vitry shouted out: 'By the guts of the Virgin, take the girl! Christ's blood! Charge through the great gate!' The girl was me.*" She was talking very fast, her cheeks flaming. She added that she would prefer to live with the knight's family in Toulouse.

"*Jean-Rigaud saw everything they did,*" she said, "*and daren't say a word. He was too scared, because they had locked up his eldest son in the dungeon underneath the keep. And when de Vitry was drinking he would order Jean-Rigaud's wife: 'Fill my cup'. He forced Ratier de Villemur's daughter to sleep with him, and she went and hanged herself on the big apple tree at the bottom of the orchard. Ratier fled to Toulouse after that. And Jean-Rigaud had the key of the secret passage, and would never give it up to anyone in case any harm came to his son. Because he had sworn not to reveal the hiding place to anyone but the lawful seigneur of the*

domain. That was what he said as an excuse. I was not a true seigneur,
I was a child. On feast days de Vitry made me come to his table, and
told me that I was as good as his daughter, and all my own people were
miscreants and traitors and once the war was over he would have me
brought up in the Catholic faith. And I was so frightened of him that
last year I vomited up the wine he had made me drink all over the table;
and he slapped me and called me a slut, and said I must be pregnant.
I wanted to kill myself that day. I was so silly I thought it might be
true."

"You shall not live here," said Roger, "until you have forgotten all this. When there is no trace of the Crusaders left in
the land, and the castle has been repaired and the vines replanted,
you shall come back here as *châtelaine*, and we shall hold banquets in the orchard and dances in this room."

When he had inspected the château of Layrac from top to
bottom, received the accounts of the domain and the secret of
the underground passage from Jean-Rigaud, given orders for the
rebuilding of the walls, and taken his share of the weapons and
valuables, as part payment of his wife's dowry, Roger returned to
Toulouse, whence he was to rejoin the Count's army. Not until
then did he celebrate his marriage feast, modestly enough in his
father's house, for there was little time or money to spare.

The wives of Jean-Rigaud de Marcillac and Ratier de Villemur and Guillelme's aunt on her mother's side assisted Rachel de
Montbrun to prepare the nuptial chamber. Guillelme was put
to bed in the great white bed, dressed in her dead mother's
wedding shift and adorned with flowers gathered in the orchard
at Layrac; and her maids lighted the oil lamp beside the bed.
Then Roger left the feast, while his father and friends drank a
silent toast in his honour.

Theirs was a solemn marriage night, like a vigil under arms,
and the good soil was found intact, and was duly tilled and the
seed sown, though the couple took no more joy in the work than
labourers at work in the fields. In the morning Guillelme asked
whether she had done everything she should, and whether she
had really conceived. Roger looked at the sheets, strewn with
faded flowers and smeared with blood, and at the young girl's
legs, smooth and straight with no bony angularities. . . . He did
not know how to answer her, he felt such sadness, because a man
in love does not see things as they are, there is a coloured glass
before his eyes. A taste of wormwood in his mouth, and bells

ringing in his head. Every word he has to utter, every action he has to perform becomes a painful task. Truly a ludicrous situation, and one never to be admitted to anyone. To think that love can make a man of past thirty as nervous as a maid who has lost her virginity! And an altogether sensible and proper course of action appears the most irresponsible folly. "Good God, how could I ever run such a risk? A man's native ambition can drive him into betraying his love."

(Yet she had said: *"Roger, you ought to do this, for love of me, because if you refuse won't people say this girl has some hidden blemish which they were compelled to tell you of?"*—"By God, and so she has! Who knows whether her marriage to de Vitry's son isn't valid?" *"For shame! You yourself do not believe that. Never let Bertrand de Layrac's granddaughter be held in contempt for such a reason."* She was unnecessarily generous, and ready to defend the cause of any woman widowed or orphaned. "If I take a wife will it not be betraying you?" She had answered that that was a small grief and she had known greater—a discouraging piece of information in itself. She had said that she cared little for herself and that he, Roger, was worrying his head unnecessarily over trifles.)

At this time, then, she was at Belvèze supervising the harvesting in Bérenger's place, since he was in the Carcassès hunting out bands of brigands on lands of his which had been lately reconquered. Roger had to see her that day because the Counts were already encamped before Minerve, and it would never do to arrive too late, and find himself blamed for his absence if they had been driven back. Oh, the foolishness of women, saying one thing today and tomorrow the reverse! She, who never lied, had not been afraid of lying to hurt herself. Had anyone asked that of her? Is it necessary to go to any lengths to drive a man mad when he already has enough troubles to worry him? (Roger still did not know her then as he was to know her later, and deeply though he loved her he sometimes felt impatient and angry to such a degree that he came near to leaving her.) He found her at the edge of a field in front of the manor house of Belvèze, helping her women load hay on to a cart (there were few men, that summer, as there would be also in the summers that followed. . . .) She was standing beside the ditch, in a dress of light grey stuff, open at the neck, with her hair falling down her back; a white veil was tied round her head and her face was red and dripping with sweat. The three small children—her own

104

son and daughter and little fair-haired Marquezia, Lady Béatrix'
little girl, were running round her, tumbling in the hay like
young puppies. The sun was so hot that the meadow and the
long, low house set among old apple trees, with the hill behind it,
seemed bleached grey and white, and the sky was periwinkle
blue; the scent of hay was breathtakingly sweet and strong. All
this—it was the day following his inauspicious marriage night—
affected Roger with such a mixture of tenderness and exasperation that he would have needed very little encouragement to take
Rigueur in his arms then and there, in front of the haymakers
and the three children, and smother her with kisses. For her
part, when she saw him she gave a cry and drew back. *"Ah, God!
What are you doing here? You have your house and I have mine."*
He knew from the expression on her face that she would not
speak to him, either that day or the next, and that she detested
him to a point where she could not bear the sight of him. Rather
than add to her displeasure, he went away, feeling as though his
heart and brain had been changed into leaden weights.

*His anguish made him incapable of thought. Another man would
have reasoned: if she is angry it means that she is a prey to jealousy, and
that is a proof of love. This did in fact occur to him, but it made no
difference. Better not to be loved than to expose oneself to such misery:
it reduces the most sensitive of men to the level of a village idiot, hardly
able to tell his left hand from his right.*

Accordingly, Roger betook himself to the camp of the Counts
of Foix and Toulouse, who were investing Minerve, seeing that
he still retained enough of his common sense to command his
men, and to greet the vassals of Layrac, who were waiting for
him at the crossroads at Verfeil, without gaping like a carp in
his grief. He said to them: *"Friends, with God's help we shall have
justice on Herbert de Vitry in this campaign."* But in his heart, he
felt no hatred for this same Herbert, only an immense self-
loathing (and why the devil had the Crusader not managed to
keep possession of the girl? Stupid thought: Layrac was a fine
château and would be easily put to rights).

In the camp which had been set up outside Minerve, the
drums rolled continuously, as they buried the dead, without
candles or psalm-singing: so many people were dying from
dysentery and the polluted water that there was talk of breaking
camp. On the other side of the fortifications the Crusaders were
also digging fresh graves every day, but they did not raise the

white flag. Crows and vultures screamed and flapped their wings over the flayed carcasses of horses in the moat. In the hot June weather the stench was so strong that the sentries were relieved every hour; the camp was infested with fat black flies which attacked eyes and mouths and swarmed over the meat as though it had been carrion. Many horses perished, splendid animals, bought for high prices in Spain and Provence. The men's morale was so low that even the Aragonese mercenaries— six feet tall and as broad as oxen—were flagging, squatting close beside the tents in the hope of finding a patch of shade. Inevitably, men began to talk of plague although this was simply ordinary dysentery. To keep their spirits up they told each other: "The other side are in a worse plight still; they'll surrender in a few days."

But they did not surrender, and Guy de Montfort's banner with the silver lion was raised again each morning, the fringe blackened and the red dye fading in the sun. A few arrows hummed in the air, rarely crossing the palisades. There was no truce but no assault either, owing to the shortage of men well enough to fight; even so, it was every knight's dream to see old Guy's grizzled head on the point of his lance. (This Guy was a hard, cruel man and all of them had dead to avenge on him.) The young Count had it proclaimed throughout the camp that if Guy de Montfort should ever be captured he was not to be killed but put in irons and released for a good ransom, because he was the best knight in France after his brother, the late Count Simon. He also sent his heralds out along the palisades to call out to the defenders that whoever would yield himself up should have his life and his valuables safe. "*For God and your honour, yield! You are deceived, good people. The war you are waging is evil and will bring you no profit!*" Those on the other side called back: "*For the cross of Christ Jesus and Montfort! Next year we shall be in Toulouse and your false Count in London or Saragossa!*" Guy de Montfort escaped capture again on this occasion (he was never captured or defeated, except by the arrow which pierced his head five years later), but the two Counts liberated more than thirty castles that summer in the valleys of the Minervois.

They prospered so well that Roger returned to Toulouse bringing with him a big cart full of booty—grain, weapons, fine leather and cloth and a box of women's jewellery—and took to his bed for a week, worn out by dysentery and the fever which

106

had resulted from a wound in his arm. It was Rachel who nursed him: Guillelme had little knowledge of medicine and scarcely seemed to remember that she was married. From Rachel, Roger learned that the girl was pregnant, and thought to himself: "Thank God, I have done my duty there."

He had pursued Herbert de Vitry and his banner of a black arrow on a red ground all the way along the valley of the river Agout, from Lavaur to Labarède. There the Frenchman had joined up with a troop of Crusaders from Normandy who were getting ready to return home. The ensuing battle was unequal. Roger had only twenty horsemen with him, four of whom were vassals of Layrac who had sworn to take Herbert and his son. They were forced to withdraw into the tower of Labarède and Roger had it proclaimed from the top of the tower that he challenged Herbert de Vitry to single combat, and flung down his glove, wrapped round a stone. Herbert rode out to the battlements in person and took up the glove on the end of his lance, crying out that he had never been afraid of brigands and had good hopes of dragging the usurper (by which he meant Roger de Montbrun) at his horse's tail; Jean-Rigaud de Marcillac and Ratier de Villemur, he added, should be flayed alive for the atrocities they had indulged in at Layrac after his departure (this was true: they had not let off lightly such Crusaders as they found on the domain). Roger was actually discussing the terms of the combat when Jean-Rigaud, who was standing beside him, seized a crossbow and took aim. Herbert de Vitry put up his shield before the bolt slammed into it, splitting it almost in two. Whereupon the Frenchman withdrew, saying he would never fight with traitors.

"Tell me, Jean-Rigaud, were you trying to rob me of my man just at the very moment when he was speaking to me without suspicion? That was ill done towards me." "*It is clear you have never suffered from him*," said the old squire. Roger was to have more than one opportunity of learning what the men of Layrac had suffered from Herbert de Vitry. But from that day on there was no friendship between himself and Jean-Rigaud. He could take no good news to Guillelme, and he would long remember the insult he had suffered at Labarède because of his vassal's action. When vengeance is the concern of the whole country, it has been said that every knight must have his share of wrongs to avenge—and Roger inherited the wrongs of Jean-Rigaud and

Ratier de Villemur and the family of Layrac. Guillelme was a chatterbox, for all her cracked voice, and it was not easy to forget why her voice was like that.

For his own troubles Roger had only himself to blame: moreover the Aspremont household was in mourning for the death of one of Bérenger's nephews and because of this the ladies were receiving no male visitors. He was unable to see Rigueur again until after the Count's death, on the day of the nativity of the Virgin. He met her at the gate of the Hospitallers' cemetery in the company of the Lady Béatrix who had come to weep on her husband's tomb. Roger himself was praying beside another tomb, or, more accurately, beside a stone coffin standing outside the cemetery, in the monastery garden. The two young women were dressed in dark gowns and carrying baskets full of bread for the beggars. Roger said daringly to Lady d'Aspremont that it was of little use to give bread to the poor, which anyone can give, and at the same time refuse alms which you alone can grant. He added that he was more to be pitied than others in the great grief into which his master's death had plunged him, since the person who might have consoled him for his loss spurned him cruelly.

Rigueur took a piece of bread from her basket, broke it, offered one half to Roger and bit into the other herself. Her cheeks were burning and her eyes grave and frightened, as though what she was eating were poisoned. The next day Roger received, through Arnaude, a letter which ran: *Know that every day I curse nature for making me a woman. When I see you so bitterly afflicted I no longer have the power to resist your desires and my own. Satan has damned me by setting me on fire with love for a man neither false nor cowardly and I can more easily be my own enemy than yours. I should have died of my jealousy. To recapture our past happiness I would walk over blazing coals.*

Indeed she had been walking on blazing coals ever since the day of Roger's marriage. She had desired this marriage, thinking that by it she could free herself from him and him from her, but the fire that burned in her was too fierce and she had become a prey to seven demons instead of only one.

. . . Perhaps their love could have lasted for ten, or fifteen, years. A married couple, who see one another every day, may tire of their love, but for lovers, when they are constantly separated yet keep themselves as faithful as by a marriage vow,

108

life is so hard that they have no time to grow tired—they are perpetually famished, and the interminable failures and frustrations of their situation leave them anxious, jealous and impatient. Refusing to eat is not a sensible way to try and kill hunger. Nevertheless, from bitter mourning, and urgent tasks, and from lawful attachments, strength must be stolen to satisfy a passion which in the eyes of the world seems at once noble and shameful: what it is in the eyes of lovers, God alone knows.

An old beam can be replaced by a new—but one man by another man? Even the dogs in his empty room mourn for him and refuse to eat. Old? . . . Ah, when a young man dies one weeps out of pity for him, but at an old man's passing, the weeping is for oneself, and for the long years during which one's affection for him was able to grow and ripen slowly.

Old, and the more precious on that account, like the old trees whose spreading branches cover a whole village; the charm of an old man who has thought and suffered too much touches more deeply than a young man's. He led the life of a wealthy burgher, dressing simply and going about the streets of Toulouse on his white horse with no other escort than one squire riding ahead and another following, and his secretary to take down letters, because he would write anywhere, even when paying a visit or on a journey. He was as pleased as a young man when the townspeople crowded round his horse and the women lifted up their children for him to touch with his glove. It was not that he was jealous of his son, but he was afraid of being set on one side. Old, he was not really old, little more than sixty-five, and his spirit was more alert than ever; but his body was so worn out that he was always wrapped in furs, even in high summer, and his strength was exhausted by a ride of three leagues outside the city.

His death was almost unexpected. Watching him sinking, his followers thought that this man, frail as a cobweb, would last in that condition for years, simply by virtue of the unwearying courtesy which forced him to smile graciously even through a grimace of pain. Moreover, his was the saddest of all deaths because, watched over, bewept and lamented as he was, and surrounded by friends, the presence of the one Friend he needed in the hour of death was denied him.

The knell was rung throughout the city on the direct order of the young Count, and there was no solemn funeral. In the death-chamber the two bereaved Countesses, two mourning infantas, dressed in black after the fashion of Aragon, stood beside the old body which there had been no priest to wash clean of its stains by his prayers. They stared with their black-rimmed eyes at the man they had followed for so many years,

109

*through humiliation and defeat, exile and return, until his dubious victory
had placed them, most Catholic of princesses, under the ban of excommunication. What last respects can a widow pay to her husband when she is
forbidden to pray for him? He died like an animal, for all the magnificent
bed with its scarlet curtains worked with the cross of Toulouse, for all
the odour of perfumes and wax candles; women were sobbing and men
wringing their hands and tearing their hair, while the bells tolled from
one end of the city to the other; why must shame and anger be added to
grief? There was not a man in Toulouse that day who did not feel the
dishonour inflicted by the Church on the first citizen of the land like a spit in
the face. Dead, the Church had reduced the most respected man in Toulouse
to mere carrion. Not a single psalm would be sung, not a prayer said,
not in St. Sernin, nor St. Étienne, nor La Daurade, nor La Dalbade, it
was as though Raymond de Saint-Gilles, Count of Toulouse, had never
been: offer no candles, no prayers for his soul, the rotten branch has
been lopped from the vine, cast into the fire and burned.*

*The body lay in state in the castle hall, on a black pall with no cross,
surrounded by torches, and the vigil was kept without priests or prayers.
While in the city, the Count's enemies—especially among the clergy—
held their heads high and repeated ugly stories about the excommunicated
man's last moments, claiming that he had been cruelly tormented by
devils who struck him in the face (which was false). They said that such
a death was the just reward of his countless adulteries, his cupidity and
blasphemies. God is no respecter of persons or titles, they said, Cain had
died the death of Cain, the fratricide had descended into hell, to the
hempen cord which had broken his brother's neck.*

*Long and patiently the Prior of the Hospitallers of Toulouse and the
castle chaplains comforted the young Count, in so far was permitted them
(bearing in mind the orphan's piety and his great grief). They told him the
Holy Father would certainly relax his edict before long and then, after an
official rehabilitation by the court of Rome, all the Catholics in Toulouse
would be permitted to have Masses sung for the dead man's soul, and his
body could receive proper burial. To all this the young man said nothing,
he only turned away his head to hide his tears; grief had made him intolerant
and among his friends he continually referred to the clergy of Toulouse as
traitors, saying that he would never forgive them because they had had no
pity for his father's sufferings. "They do not trust me," he would say
"because churchmen are like wolves: feed them, fatten them; they will
still slink off back to the forest."*

*The young Count received fresh oaths of allegiance from all his
vassals, and promised them (verbally, not in writing) to respect the faith*

and customs of each of them as his father had done, and to sign no treaties without the consent of the barons and the consuls of the free cities. The old Count of Foix and his son, who never left his side, told him that he would never maintain his authority unless he guaranteed all his subjects equality before the law as regards their religion. "We have already won such important victories," they said, "that it would be foolish to stop half-way." (They belonged to the heretic faction and were themselves known as true believers.) The young man began, as his father had done before him, by making promises to everybody, but lacking his father's experience he was not over skilful at the game, and thought of nothing but war.

He took such joy in fighting that it was no wonder he was never defeated; for five years already he had carried his banners from castle to castle, hearing himself cheered as he rode by, sword raised and face uncovered, to the sound of trumpets. Everywhere he was worshipped like the archangel Michael in person. He wore shining armour, and ladies strewed carpets of flowers in front of his horse's hooves, while every victory brought new songs and torchlight banquets in which he was always the leader of the dancing and the laughter and in inventing new games to play; never in any land did a man conquer the hearts of more noble ladies (a melancholy thing for the Countess, who was, moreover, older than himself and, since the birth of her daughter, sterile.)

Seeing him so full of life and burning for the task ahead of him the most cautious said: "Neither God nor the Devil could stand against this child, he has brought good fortune back to us, he will wrest his pardon from the Pope as he wrested victory from Montfort." Many among the Crusaders themselves were saying: "He is the lawful seigneur, it would be right to swear allegiance to him, if only he were not under sentence of excommunication."

But for the Church and the calumny of the bishops, he would have been able to reconquer and hold all the Occitan lands.

111

THE SUMMER WAS so short they scarcely noticed its coming. It happened in this way: one fine day a wave of joy broke through the whole country, spreading from village to village and from city to castle, lighting hundreds of torches—the last blaze of so many that had gone before. They thought: "It is all over, at last we can begin to live", and they had really believed it. Months went by, several months, a whole summer, a winter, another summer and another winter. That was all. They had not even begun to live, they were still getting ready for it. It was not even a respite, only a mad fever of hope, so short that it was forgotten immediately. And yet, God knows, how sweet it was!

Two years free from war, with no Crusaders in Carcassonne. Not a single Crusader, not a single French banner, and the bells were ringing as the young Viscount, Raymond Trencavel, returned to his father's palace in Carcassonne; the bishops were deposed and shut themselves up in Montpellier and dared not come out, and the soldiers were free to put their armour away in their chests and have their houses repaired. They thought they had won peace.

Although nothing was yet the same as before, this was only a beginning. They needed time to breathe, for the vines to put fresh shoots, and the castles to be rebuilt and the debts paid. . . . There had been so much hatred and weeping in fifteen years of war, so much to forgive and forget, such great hopes, that plenty of the young felt almost old, and plenty of those who were young no longer found their shattered youth again, they did not remember to hate the enemy or to love the dead, they were living in the present and throwing to the winds the little that was left in their coffers. . . .

The peace might perhaps have lasted for another ten years, may be even more, but for the Church.

The old Count's body still lay in its unsealed coffin out in the wind and rain, in the garden by the cemetery which he could not enter. There was no bishop in Toulouse, no processions, no Masses sung, and it was easier to find a heretic minister for the dying than a Catholic priest. People grew accustomed to the silent burials, to the permission to inter their dead granted as a favour—not everyone has the misfortune to be born a Count, and even declared heretics had a right to their six feet of Christian earth;

moreover, funeral feasts kept their former solemnity despite the lack of priests or prayers. Weddings were gayer than ever as, after a hurried blessing in the sacristy, the newly married couples went before the consuls with their offerings, to the music of viols and citterns. (There was a veritable spate of marriages in those years, because many people had waited for the end of the war, or of the interdict: now the war was over and the interdict threatened to continue. With the permission of the absent Bishop, the priests were granting dispensations, in order to avoid the scandal of open concubinage.)

It was a time of great prosperity for the heretics. Although the Count (who was powerless in the matter) had forbidden it, they had reopened their houses, even in Toulouse itself, and were teaching openly in the lands of his more powerful vassals, from Mirepoix as far as the Albigeois. They were the effective masters of the country: the seigneurs obeyed them in everything and gave them all the lands, houses and money they could afford.

Men do not know how to recognise happiness when they have it: for many people these were the best years of their lives and they did not know it until afterwards. They were busy thinking: "God! We are utterly ruined; the land is so poor. When shall we return to the life we lived before the Crusade?"

Roger de Montbrun, too, had plenty of time to think of all this later, more time, in fact, than he could have wished for. In those days he spent half his life on horseback and was beginning to tire of travelling: after thirty-five a man thickens and feels the weight of his body. No matter, believing one is free of a hauberk for a good spell of time is a piece of luck in itself (though the time was short, and God! to think that they were going to find the war too short next!). Riding in the Count's escort, riding the roads of the Agenais and the Ariégeois, riding to great hunts and tourneys; riding through ravaged countryside, towns swarming with masons and full of wooden scaffolding, roads thick with travellers on foot and on horseback, and convoys of merchants . . . the whole country was on the move, either travelling or simply wandering, and although brigands were as numerous as during the Crusades, at least they knew that cities would not be held to ransom or the harvests burned.

Riding from morning to night—as though they were still hurrying to catch up with lost time—and stopping for two or three days at a time in Toulouse. This was necessary because

Roger's father was growing old and complained of being neglected. At each visit Roger would bring him partridges, quails and pots of red pepper and ginger.

Ever since his elder son had made a good marriage and sired a son, Pierre-Guillaume had shown signs of favouring him more than Bertrand. Like everything else, his fondness found expression in ill-temper: according to him, his sons were boors, so debased by war that they were no longer capable of civilised conversation. He himself read many good books, or made Rachel read them aloud to him. Roger listened patiently to his father, then, on occasion, came to take Rachel's place at the chess board because the old man, in the intervals of meditating on his salvation, prided himself on being one of the best chess-players in Toulouse; this was no longer the case and his son had his work cut out to let him win. The old man would look at him with melancholy, faintly mocking, contempt. ("You think I can't see through your little game?") All the same he was pleased to be the winner.

Rachel, who was as good as gold, bore with her father-in-law so patiently that one would have thought she had no concerns beyond the old man's welfare. Yet she had seven children and the house to run, because they were not rich and Bertrand was never at home. He divided his time between the Capitol and the house run by the heretics in that part of the city, sometimes even travelling outside the city, always busy about some secret or half-secret mission; and although he spent himself unsparingly in the service of his Church he had little time to think of heavenly matters. His father was fond of saying to him: "*Martha, Martha, thou art careful and troubled about many things. . . .*" In fact he considered him foolhardy and feared the persecutions might still return (in this he was not mistaken, although at the time they took his fears for an old man's ramblings, which indeed was all they were).

Roger settled his wife, Guillelme de Layrac, in the same house, with two maidservants and a nurse. She had a room of her own which her husband had had attractively decorated with paintings of hunting scenes. This Guillelme was a strange girl: her eyes gave nothing away, there was never any telling what she was thinking; she was neither reserved nor friendly, and treated her in-laws with calm courtesy—although only Rachel had been able to win her affection. Roger thought perhaps she doted on her child too much to think of anything else. The child, a little

114

boy, had a sweet face but a sickly body; at three years old he waddled about like a duck on his crooked little legs. He was a quick, laughing child, and when Guillelme showed him the pink, doll-like figure with the red hair and long brown eyes, Roger felt distinctly proud of having a son. He loved his heir more than he cared to admit and sometimes reflected that this child was Rigueur's son, too, desired by her and conceived in one night of love and anguish; and that young Guillelme had borne the fruit which belonged to another, like the robin bringing up the young of the cuckoo. . . . Guillelme was growing pretty and Roger was glad to avoid her on account of her youth and her blue eyes. (In three years Rigueur had trained him so well that he dared not permit himself the slightest lapse; since he could not have hidden anything from her even had he wished to. She never even asked him questions; he told her everything, right down to his shifts to escape his creditors. This marriage, which she had almost forced him to accept, had brought her such suffering that twice Roger seriously considered killing his wife.)

Pierre-Guillaume de Montbrun never recovered from the fact that he had failed to be elected a consul; now that he was over sixty-five and weakened by a stomach disease, he no longer hoped to hold the rank in the city which was his due. He vacillated constantly between his two sons, undecided which of them to favour above the other; he considered them both lacking in address, and that neither possessed the proper virtues to lead a man to the consulship. Roger's ambitions were petty and limited, he was content merely to hold the Count's stirrup; Bertrand had more stuff but less judgment: and a man must be able to manage both sides, or at least appear to, if he was to be fit to hold public office. Bertrand, moreover, had married a woman of no fortune, so, since Roger's marriage, their father had come to rely increasingly on his elder son and tried to make him understand that he was no longer of an age to be writing love songs and scouring the country like a knight errant.

"I am reproached by all my friends," he would say, "because you are never seen at the Capitol and show such great contempt for public affairs." Roger had no contempt for public affairs, but a close acquaintance with too many kings and princes had led him to consider in his heart of hearts that a consul of Toulouse had very little influence over the affairs of the land. Besides which a good love-song can often make a man's reputation at court,

115

and lend weight to his words (since it is often more important to be well thought of than to be wise and discreet). Furthermore, his songs were not bad—though he did not compose the music to them himself, but simply the words—and they were sung as far away as Champagne and Aragon. In them he praised Rigueur's beauty and her virtues to the skies, and it is a well-known fact that any man with the reputation of a faithful lover is highly esteemed by his peers. (Rigueur accused her lover of worldly vanity on this score; she was right, and yet he wrote mainly for the pleasure of making up words to describe her, and singing songs in which each word was like a secret between them—in fact Rigueur never dared sing these songs at all because the lines in which he spoke of the lady's cruelty and harshness invariably made her blush. There were things they meant to say, but for these there are no words for lovers to use, since men, in their ignorance, have found only crude and ugly words for them. What paeons of victory may echo in a lover's complaint, only he knows who made the song.)

To read their songs one might well believe that lovers in ancient times had nothing else to think about but love. Where are the ladies who spend their days talking of love, and their nights in giving and receiving kisses in a secret chamber, guarded by one trusted friend? Happy the knights who could devote themselves to love from morning to night, dreaming of it in stillness and giving themselves up entirely to their unbridled folly. Roger pined fretfully at Layrac, where he was supervising the work of rebuilding the keep and making good the ramparts, and soon managed to annoy his vassals, who considered him too proud; he could not tell them he was in love, and that a faithful lover is like a drunkard in a house where there is no wine. His persistent love for a woman belonging neither to his own faction nor his faith was to lose him many people's friendship in those years, and lead him to neglect new friends he might have made.

In that first year of peace, Rigueur spent nearly four months in her own country, staying in her brothers' house, between Termes and Foix. She passed her days, and sometimes her nights, wandering on the mountainside, on horseback and alone since she had taken no man or maidservant with her; and recaptured her impoverished childhood in the lanes she had rambled through as a child gathering wild strawberries.

Roger spent three-quarters of his time in the Sault district that summer, living alone in an abandoned tower a quarter of a league from the house of Montgeil; on his arrival he would haul up his red scarf to the dead branch of an old oak tree. Rigueur could see it from the top of her house; she had eyes which, in the common phrase, can pierce through a brick wall. She could see an ant at fifty paces and pick out a thousand stars in the sky that no ordinary eye could distinguish. When she saw the signal she would go down to the stables for her horse and her brothers never asked her where she was going. (They were gallant men who respected their sister's freedom; after leading a vagabond existence for fifteen years, they had seen so much that they would have asked no questions of an angel if one had come down from the sky to preach to them. These pious men considered murder, pillage and blasphemy as mere peccadilloes, and their sister could have given herself to a dozen lovers without offending them. *"God judges no one."* It was a long time since they had judged themselves. Later, Roger was to realise how great was the wisdom of these men as simple as peasants and as tough as mercenaries.)

Rigueur would set off alone, in her grey woollen dress with her hair knotted up in the other half of the red scarf that fluttered from the oak branch; the cloth was so worn that she had to mend it continually, but she clung to it in memory of that winter's day when she had seen Roger in her home, after she had received his first letter. Roger had chosen the colour for her because of that day, this bright, soft red, like a ripe cherry—because of the same silk scarf which, on that winter's day, covered her hair and and gave to her pale face the brilliance of alabaster.

In the tower, they had to sleep on hay and cook their meat on a fire of brushwood on the threshold; bats lodged in the rafters and swallows beneath all that remained of the thatched roof. There was no window, it was always cool and dark inside, which was a good thing, for the days were so hot that they could have cooked barley cakes on the stones of the threshold. The water from the spring crept out a drop at a time and it took an hour to fill a pitcher.

The little tower stood on the edge of a slope, surrounded by oaks and nut trees, which continued down to the bottom of the valley, like an immense green fleece, with rooks and kites soaring above. Now and then Roger brought down a hare or a grouse (when a man does not mean to be the guest of the people of the country he does well to carry a bow and arrows on his saddle bow). Rigueur did not like this, and he had to pluck or skin the game himself; she, who boasted of the way she had flung stones on to the heads of the Crusaders during the siege, suffered at the idea of shedding animal blood and ate scarcely any meat. To please her lover she would sometimes consent to taste some of the tenderest morsels, because they had not much to eat during their days of peace: water, dried barley cakes, pepper and garlic, strawberries, and mushrooms grilled over a wood fire.

Roger had never believed a man could be so rich: he was like a potter moulding his clay, like a hunter plucking his prize, taking freely, from top to toe, with both hands, the loveliest thing in all creation. With both hands, both arms and both lips, all is yours, take and eat, you shall not go hungry today or tomorrow; no one will drive you out at dawn; you can go to the end of your desire. There were days and nights, tranquil awakenings, and mornings when they could sleep in the sun on the warm moss and thyme, and hear nothing but the sound of crickets and the long, harsh cry of the kites. This was a shepherd's happiness, a common joy the humblest might possess, but with a woman of such high heart, lead is transmuted into pure gold: in her he found such great peace that he would gladly have spent his whole life thus.

She was not like other ladies made to lie on beds of swansdown with silken covers, eating only quails and thrushes and veiling their faces whenever the sun touched the tips of their noses: in his youth, Roger had loved several of these, believing a woman's worth can be measured by her fragility and the delicacy of her perfumes. Rigueur had the stamina of a horse and was as agile as a mountain goat; at thirty-two she still possessed the quick, lithe grace of a young girl. She had never been able to school herself to the languid movements proper to noble ladies; she laughed out loud like a man, talked energetically, walked fast, and her long, slim hand had a grip of iron.

For more than four years, Roger had possessed her as often as decency and discretion would permit (since even among lovers who practise true fidelity—and they are few—those who receive a full pardon as much as twice a week are rare indeed), and these too-brief hours of joy had only roused his hunger further. But now, instead of being satisfied, as in the nature of things he should have been, he became more and more involved.

Like an apprentice, finding the perfection of his art only with time and trouble, he was for ever discovering new merits in his beloved.

He explored her tirelessly, from the beating of her heart to the smell of her skin, and the flecks in her eyes to the tiny callouses on her palms, and still sought for more; and sometimes, far from her, he would feel a rush of impatience because he could not recall the exact colour or placing of a particular beauty spot (she had hundreds of them, and he used to call them, not in the best of taste, the stars in his sky). Altogether, he was convinced that no man of his age had ever been such a slave to love. Whenever he was with her in the woods, walking through the pink heather and the warm grass quivering with the whirr of the cicadas, he thought of Toulouse and of his own domain like a peasant thinking of his toil. With her alone he felt a free man.

That summer they talked together for longer and with greater honesty than many people manage to do in fifty years. Roger had never known there were so many things a man could need to say—and when he was away from her, even when he was surrounded by friends, his head was always full of thoughts he had to tell Rigueur: sometimes he could bear it no longer and would make some excuse to slip away and have his horse saddled up. It seemed to him as though he had never known her until that summer. She loved him truly then, without either distrust, sadness or regret. And the knowledge that he was in truth the only man who could please her bound Roger so closely to his mistress that he felt a stranger wherever she was absent. At that time she hoped to convert him to her own faith, believing that he possessed more natural virtues than Zacchaeus, the Magdalene or the centurion. (Later, to be sure, she would change her mind, after he had done that thing for which she could never forgive him: later, she would say that she had always known he was the Devil.)

When the grape harvest was over, a letter from Lady de Miraval summoned her back to Toulouse. This letter ran:

Beloved cousin and dearest child, it is not fitting that you should remain so long with your brothers. I do not tell you this on account of your children, or of my granddaughter Marquezia, who are old enough not to let the unhappiness they feel at your absence appear indiscreetly; nor on behalf of my cousin and your husband, Bérenger, who would never go against your wishes in any way; nor for my daughter Béatrix, who takes your place in the house uncomplainingly, finding in it a distraction from her melancholy. But for my own sake, my dear child, and for the sadness I feel at your absence, I beg you to return to the hotel d'Aspremont; for if you delay any longer I shall have to believe that it is my old woman's temper and my manner of speaking to the servants which have vexed you to such an extent that you prefer to live with your brothers. Surely, my dear child, everyone knows that you are the first lady of the house, and all our pride, and were never treated as a stranger by us? And that in my widowhood and bereavement, and despite my former repute, I lay claim to no greater honour than the friendship of my cousin Bérenger and yourself? Do not, I beg you, wrong me by allowing the world and our friends to believe that you wish to yield up to me a first place which I have neither the right nor the desire to claim. . . .

Rigueur read this letter to Roger and said: "My noble cousin is a woman who knows what she wants and knows how to get it. My brothers will accompany me to Toulouse tomorrow."

"When will you return here so that we may have our freedom again?"

"Next spring, perhaps, but do not hope for it too much. I owe a great deal to this woman, Roger, although in the past she has unwittingly done me much harm: she has been like a mother to me. She would never have written me such a letter if she had not thought I was gravely wronging their house. So we must submit."

Roger realised that this life could not last for long. The summer was coming to an end. The woods were red and brown, the burns swollen with rain, and in the mornings a white frost lay on the grass like silver down. *"Rigueur, if our friendship has not now become more solid than this stone, I shall never be able to believe in any friendship more."* She laid her hand on the worn and polished white stone, hollowed in the centre, which formed the threshold.

"I believe it is solid," she said. "God will judge."

Rigueur's brothers, small landowners, so poor they had not even shirts to wear under their jerkins, went with her to Toulouse. They were struggling to put their ruined domain to rights and, having only five servants altogether, they worked by turns as labourers, as masons, or cultivating the vines, and went out hunting when they had the time. Sicart, the eldest, was already close on forty and hoping to get married the following year: he was betrothed to the daughter of one of the joint *seigneurs* of

Bélesta and was going to Toulouse to choose the piece of silk he wanted to give her as a wedding present (the two brothers did not possess the price of a button and the money was lent by Bérenger).

Roger saw the two men again at the Aspremont house and took care not to tell them that he was as well acquainted with their land as with his own. They had aged since the meeting on the eve of the Montréal campaign, and grown darker and thinner. For them peace brought as much hardship as war, and they said that even in their father's time there was hardly enough to eat in the district, while now the land was in such a state that it would take ten years to clear it and make it productive.

"To say nothing of the deer and wild boar ruining the little we have left, and the hail which beat down the vines a week ago . . ."

Imbert, the younger, laughed as he described how, on the eve of the storm, they had hauled up the last bucket of water from the well and sprinkled it over the courtyard and kitchen garden to bring water from the heavens.

"And when it came everyone was saying: It would have been better if things had stayed quietly as they were. We know what we ask, but we never know what we are going to get."

Sicart, the one with the broken teeth, had long, grey eyes like Rigueur's. Ten days' dirt lay on his cheeks and the black hair falling over his brows and ears was as shaggy as a goat's. In spite of the lines drawn by a fatigue that had become second nature to him, he looked a happy man. He had had enough of war, he said, and much preferred to go hungry in his own house and be dependent on no man. Then he went on to describe the progress made by the Cathar faith in his own region and the splendid gatherings present to hear the sermons at Chalabre and Mirepoix and below the rock of Montségur. "The war has not been the disaster we believed it," he said, "but rather an advantage, because God, foreseeing this test, has raised up among us such a man as Monseigneur Guilhabert, to say nothing of all the other Christians strong in word and deed. God would never have sent them to us but for this deluge which has broken over us. The Church has never seen lights of such brilliance, and all the efforts of Babylon have turned to her own confusion. . . ."

This manner of speech sounded strange enough in the mouth

of a man who, encountered on a deserted road, would have struck terror into the stoutest heart; his voice was rough and his mountain accent aggravated still further by the loss of his front teeth, and he gave the impression of repeating phrases learned by heart, like a priest who knows no Latin. Yet his eyes were shining with the calm intensity of a people so fanatically pious that they would walk over hot coals rather than enter a Catholic church.

That day Roger accompanied Bérenger and his two brothers-in-law to the new heretic seminary in Toulouse to hear a sermon preached by the Deacon Vigoros. The famous deacon did not bely his name; he possessed a vigorous voice and his words were full of fire, while he explained so clearly that the only way to gain salvation was by baptism and laying on of hands and the renunciation of all earthly thoughts that, listening to him, Roger felt practically determined to ask for the Consolamentum on his deathbed. (*Yet he never once entertained this thought consciously, as a serious decision, nor was he even tempted to; it was simply an idea that happened to cross his mind. Of that he was positive.*)

When he had exchanged kisses with the other heretics present and acknowledged the reverences of the faithful, the deacon retired to the upper room for the blessing of the bread, whither only about twenty of the faithful were permitted to follow him. Among these was Bérenger and also—somewhat to Roger's surprise—Bertrand de Montbrun and his father-in-law, Isaac Abrahamide. The two brothers greeted one another like strangers as they passed, exchanging a glance of that involuntary irony which men of the same blood and differing opinions have for one another. Roger's glance said: "*Climb to the top of a tree: it will not make you any taller.*" Bertrand's: "*Are there no concerts or dances in Toulouse, that you come here for amusement?*" On the way home the two lords of Montgeil paid tribute to the beauty of Toulouse. Never, they said, had so many fine houses been rebuilt, and such an extent of walls and battlements erected, in so short a time: there could be no comparison with the state of the city four years earlier. New buildings were everywhere, and even the old houses were unrecognisable beneath new paint. To think that on this very spot there was once a ruined house they had used as a quarry for gun-stones during the siege—one would never believe it was the same place. Look, there are windows with glass panes and turrets of parti-coloured brick! Can you see finer work in

122

Paris or Avignon? Though they were not natives of Toulouse, the two brothers had a pride in the city, resulting from their part in the siege seven years earlier; moreover, they had left their own flesh and blood there: their brother Renaud, killed in the assault on the Old Bridge.

People were beginning to forget that they had still not made their peace with the Church. This Pope will die, they thought, and the new one will put everything right again, because it is unnatural to leave a Christian country under an interdict and exclude a Catholic prince from the communion of the faithful for a political quarrel. The Archbishop of Narbonne thought so, and regretting his past errors, under the stimulus of age and the approach of Judgment, he was now as merciful towards the son as he had been severe to the father. He said too that the old customs, however imperfect, were more valuable than new laws imposed by foreigners. The young Count talked with him for a long time, in the palace where Monseigneur Arnaud resided in Montpellier, with the other bishops. Monseigneur Arnaud told him that, being on the point of appearing before his Judge, he was still in full possession of his faculties and prayed night and day for the salvation of the Occitan Church. His heart bled to see the Lord's vine in this land ravaged by noisome foxes (he meant the heretics), battered by hailstorms and threatened by rapacious brigands on every side. It was not hard to guess who these rapacious brigands were: a considerable quarrel was growing up between the old Archbishop and the bishops belonging to the French faction, in the course of which Monseigneur Arnaud was accusing the Bishop of Toulouse, Monseigneur Foulques, of sacrificing the interests of the Church to his private ambition, and likening the Bishop of Agde to a rusty weathercock, always pointing in the same direction and crying, "Toulouse! Toulouse!" all the time, as though Toulouse were the den of a man-eating lion. The lion, as they well knew, was elsewhere: never invite the wolf into your house to drive out the rats, never make an ally of one stronger than yourself. Louis would not come as the servant of the Church, but as her master.

Furthermore, the detestable innovations which the Holy Father, in his excessive indulgence, tolerated in Rome, said the Archbishop, would soon deprive the Order of Cîteaux of all but the right to say "Amen", while the disputatious beggars would command the ears of kings and Pope alike; already their seminaries were springing up like mushrooms all over Christendom, and although people called them "the dogs of the Lord", making a bad play on their name, "Dominicani", this was hardly a thing they could be proud of, for was it seemly to compare monks and priests to unclean beasts? They glory wrongfully in their poverty, in the belief that in this way they are aping the heretics. Hardly any of the heretics are converted, instead they cause trouble among the Catholics by bringing the ancient orders into disrepute and sowing discord in the monasteries. By encouraging these innovations, the Bishop of Toulouse has done harm to his Order, now the brand he used against God's enemies will burn his own hand.

The Archbishop did not have to bewail for long the neglect of his services and those of his Order: at the beginning of the second year of peace, he died, to the great grief of many Catholic citizens of Toulouse who prayed whole-heartedly for his soul's salvation. (It stood in some need of it.) He was to have pleaded the Count's cause with the council and they had founded great hopes on him. Besides which, the Archbishop elected in his place was worse for the region than Achitophel himself, being so devoted to the King of France that he was rumoured to be in his pay. Had Louis been the Pope in person, the Archbishop could have served him no better.

The trumpets were blaring gaily as the young Count left the city at the head of a troop of noble barons and notables. The splendid cavalcade wound its way through the streets of the city to the gate by the Old Bridge; and on the eve of his departure the young Count had given a great banquet in honour of the Count of Foix and the Viscount of Carcassonne, and had distributed meat and wine and copper coins to the poor of the city. He was the kind of man who could drown his cares in gaiety and said that fortune loves those who keep their heads held high. Though he was going to demand justice for his cause, he had no intention of presenting himself before the council in the guise of a repentant sinner, seeing that his cause was good, even the best that might be, that of God and the right. More-over, with the help of his clerks and notaries he had drawn up such a document in support of his case that he said neither calumny nor intrigue could fault it, and he swore to carry out his oath and see justice done to his father.

Those who went with him were well aware that right is nothing without good advocates, and that the men who should have taken the role of advocates would rather be their accusers; so that the matter would be deferred once again and they were spending money to little purpose.

The previous evening Bérenger d'Aspremont had said: "What manner of return should I wish you? You know the Count's mind better than I." (Those of his party, very few of whom were admitted to accompany the Count, looked forward to this council with great apprehension; they feared that at Bourges, among the smooth-tongued bishops and churchmen, the young Count might pledge himself to dispossess the heretics of their goods, without consulting the barons and commons.) Roger told him the Count would do nothing without the agreement of the barons and the Count of Foix, but that they must not put the horse before the cart—the Count being the cart and the bishops the great, powerful, uncertain-tempered horses. "It is our misfortune to have lost our archbishop just at the very moment when we had such great need of him."

At this, Bérenger and his two sisters' husbands, and Lady de Miraval, all protested violently, saying that this was blasphemy and such a man was never to be regretted.

"God is just," said Lady Alfaïs, *"and He has not permitted that villain to escape eternal damnation by buying himself off with a good deed at the end of his days. God is not to be deceived and He does not let the rotten tree bear good fruit."*

"Would to heaven, then, my lady, that God were less just and more merciful! He has deprived us of the staff on which we thought to lean. We no longer have a single bishop to take our part, with the exception of Monseigneur Guillaume-Raymond of Carcassonne, and he has been legally deposed for fifteen years and will scarcely dare to appear at the council."

Bérenger seemed unusually bitter and troubled. "Ah," he said, "there are some things one may believe to be true and yet prefer to leave unsaid. Do you think I fear for my property? I tell you, I would sell everything, even my wedding ring, if gifts would make us free of Amaury! And if they find they have not despoiled us enough, we shall be only too happy to pay, since it seems that in a Christian country we can be compelled to purchase with gold what is ours by right."

"You know very well," said Roger, "the Count would never wrong any of his subjects."

The Count had made up his mind to swear whatever was asked of him against the heretics, so long as the sentence of excommunication was lifted and the King able to accept his homage. It was said: To make a promise is not to keep it. The bishops knew that truth better than anyone and published everywhere that the promises of the son were worth no more than those of the father. But at this council, the Count had no promises to make, and the money so laboriously scraped together for the journey was thrown away to no purpose: neither Amaury de Montfort nor Raymond of Toulouse said a single word worth saying there. They were asked to submit themselves to the justice of the Church.

A fine tale to tell the ladies of Toulouse: they took us for babes who haven't yet learned to talk. And no doubt those who say the Count behaved foolishly in leaving Bourges before the end of the talks are quite right, since an arrow in the chest is still preferable to one in the back. (Besides, the enemy who meets you face to face may hesitate at the last minute and not fire.) He is young, and made more for battle than for argument and debate, and if you had seen all that great assembly in robes of purple and scarlet, with mitres and gilded crosses, and heard the haughty fashion in which the legate and the Archbishop of Bourges spoke, you yourself would have said that there is no more to be gained with such men by speaking than by holding one's peace. Perhaps, too, by speaking the Count might have committed himself to things he would have regretted later and the whole country with him. What more had we to wait for? Another council? If Amaury's rights were confirmed once again, had we anything left to promise the Church in return for the chance to make another appeal?

"Much good your wealthy marriage has done you," said Pierre-Guillaume de Montbrun. "You mortgage your lands in the Count's service, and for the privilege of lording it among his entourage, and now you have not even the means 'to pay your soldiers. Do you take your bailiff for a magician, do you think he finds gold pieces under his horse's tail?"

Roger listened and shrugged his shoulders. His father always made out the evil to be greater than it was; he did not think his family profited enough from his son's fortune.

"Father, you know quite well that ravaged lands do not begin to yield a profit in a year or two. We must be patient. You know I do not frequent gaming dens, and I keep no concubines! I am more niggardly with myself than with others."

Guillelme, who was just eighteen, understood nothing of her husband's affairs and thought he was preventing her from leading the life which was her right. She had, as became her position, fine clothes and two women to wait on her; but money was

126

lacking for the small luxury articles a woman needs, and she complained that she no longer dared go into a shop because the merchants would give her no more credit; and added that she had no doubt Roger behaved more generously to the woman he praised in his songs. Roger thought it pointless to tell her his lady would take no presents from him. From Bourges, he had brought back a small dagger, its hilt studded with celandines, for Guillelme. She said: "Do you think I am going to set up as a cutler, then? This is the fourth knife you have brought me."

He had forgotten and did not care to admit it.

"My dear, I cannot find one handsome enough for you."

"I did not think," she said, "that considering the dowry I brought you, you would treat me with less regard than a gentleman ought to have for his mistresses."

How could he explain things to her? She was young, and at that age people think only of themselves.

"My dear, it is barely two years since we were still at war and it has not been easy for us to drive out Amaury and his people and re-establish order in the land; and if men had not fought for your lands and for other lands you would be the wife of a Crusader today. I earned your dowry, too, with my blood. Be patient, in three or four years from now I shall build you a house in Toulouse where you can live in style and entertain your friends."

She was watching him and beneath her pale blue veil her blue eyes were now sulky and suspicious. Once again Roger thought how pretty she was and that it was a shame that, for reasons of honour, and also because of the risk of a bastard, she could benefit no one with her beauty.

She was a good mother to the child, always kissing and cuddling him, and he never left her arms except when asleep. Who knows, perhaps she would have liked other children? At her age it became hard to lead a life of chastity. Sometimes she seemed to regret that she saw her husband so rarely.

"*Be patient, my dear. When our affairs are in a better condition . . .*"

What affairs? In those days they were living on hope, the great affair was to see the Count confirmed in his rights and reconciled to the Church. While that affair remained in suspense it seemed as though nothing else could be undertaken, for the Crusaders had gone, and gone completely, though in Rome and in France they were still preaching the Crusade. But this Crusade without Crusaders made only fools laugh.

The time of peace was over, and still they did not know it. They did not know that their misfortunes were not finished but to come. In fact it was in consequence of this very Council of Bourges that it all began. The Council's judgment was announced in Toulouse, where it was read publicly from all the church steps, and copies were made to be sent to all the free cities and read to all citizens in the domains of Toulouse and of Foix and the viscounty of Carcassonne. It was stated that, by decree of the Council, the noble Raymond, son of Raymond de Saint-Gilles, formerly Count of Toulouse, and Roger-Bernard, son of Raymond-Roger, Count of Foix, and the noble Raymond, son of Raymond-Roger, usurper of the title Viscount of Béziers and Carcassonne, were solemnly excommunicated (as though they had not been for nine years already) and declared guilty of heresy, rebellion against the Church and the King of France, and unworthy of all clemency; and the sentence fell on all free persons among their followers or dwelling in their domains who continued to serve them in defiance of the Church's express commands; furthermore, the aforementioned counts and viscounts, and all persons obdurately continuing to serve them despite the commands of the Church, were declared heretics and rebels and legally and lawfully deprived of all property and lands. In addition, the viscounty of Carcassonne and the county of Toulouse were to be yielded up to their master and legitimate overlord who had been robbed of them by violence and rebellion in violation of the Peace Treaty signed by Raymond, formerly Count of Toulouse, at the Lateran Council of 1215, and approved by the Holy Father, Pope Innocent III of blessed memory.

It was likewise stated that Count Amaury, son of Simon de Montfort, Count of Toulouse and Viscount of Carcassonne, in gratitude for the aid rendered him on many occasions by King Louis of France, and for the goodness which the said King, his liege lord, had always shown him, paid homage to King Louis for his lands of Toulouse and the Carcassès, Razès and Albigeois, and yielded up to him, fully and absolutely, on behalf of himself and his heirs, all rights he possessed over the said lands; in consequence of which the said lands were the direct dependencies of King Louis of France and had no other lord and master than the said King. As for those lands seized by the aforementioned counts and viscount from their seigneurs, friends and relations of the Count de Montfort, the King pledged himself to confirm these lords in their domains and receive their homage for them.

In the council chamber of the Narbonnese castle, the news was received in a fitting manner, without useless protests and lamentations. Things were otherwise at the Capitol, where the citizens were more quickly roused to anger than the nobles, and there were daggers drawn, curses and shouts of treason, and threats to the Bishop's supporters. The consuls sent criers throughout the town to inform the people that the judgment of the Council of Bourges was neither definitive nor formal, and that an appeal would be made to the court of Rome. The Count, for his part, issued a similar proclamation, declaring that his good faith had been abused in the matter, and that he would fight to the death of his last soldier, even to his own death, rather than accept such a judgment. For a few days the city remained in a state of ferment, all Catholics of the Bishop's party, and the clergy in particular, were compelled to barricade themselves into their houses and there were broken windows and doorways piled with filth and rubbish. People in the streets were telling one another: "We know what we want, but we never know what we shall get. Now we have got rid of Amaury, this is the moment to claim a victory. Louis has become Count of Toulouse by the workings of the Holy Ghost."

They laughed and cried over it and then forgot all about it. The most confident said: "Louis has already fled from Toulouse once, he will not go poking in the wasps' nest now that all the country is in the Count's hands." *While every week during Lent, abbots and clerics were arriving in Toulouse, some sent by Monseigneur Foulques, others by the Archbishop of Narbonne, and others again from the Holy See, bringing threatening letters and pronouncements inciting Catholics to desert the Count's cause. They talked of the indulgences the Holy Father would dispense to all men joining the Crusade, and of the great fervour which the French people felt for God's cause in the Occitan lands; they said that in the spring the King would come with all his chivalry and the French bishops with their well-equipped soldiery, burning to avenge the insults to Christ Jesus perpetrated by the people of Toulouse.*

It was in vain that the Count and the consuls forbade them to speak in public. Some of these men, belonging to the new order of the Preaching Friars, retorted that they were under no obligation to obey excommunicated persons, that the King of France and Bishop Foulques were the only lords of those lands, and that they would gladly suffer martyrdom rather than allow anything to prevent them from telling the truth to the people. They compared themselves to the prophets Amos and Jeremiah, putting ashes on their heads and imploring the citizens to repent and save themselves from being massacred as the inhabitants of Béziers and Marmande

129

*had been. In Toulouse this manner of speech provoked anger and jeers.
But in the countryside and small manor houses, people listened to them,
wondering whether these prophets of doom were not better informed than
their own lords and bailiffs. The lords of the manor said they would
rather see a horde of mad dogs on their land than a single Preaching Friar.
They spoke so violently that their false charity seduced no one except
credulous old women and feather-brained youngsters; but their continuous
fulminations and threats did succeed in inspiring terror: fresh wounds
are bound to bleed when they are scratched. (No one as yet could foresee
what these men were to become later on, or the great power they were to
acquire as a result of their hypocritical austerity and the favour of the
Pope. Many people took them for true servants of God and only deplored
the violence of their language.)*

*To think that men believed they were free to live at last! Lord, if this
be a punishment, at least let us know for what crime! Are our accusers
better men than us?*

"You see, Roger, you see: who is destroying us, who is betraying us? It is not just one pope, nor just one or two bishops—
all those who serve this Church have the same features, the
features of Antichrist. Can you still believe they are clothed
in the Holy Ghost?"

"Unhappily for us, they are! Is there anyone who would have
borne their injustice if they were not? We are forced to endure
them because of the sacred ministry entrusted to them. And do
not think they are all betraying us to our enemies, because it is
not the side which roars the loudest which ultimately wins. By
our patience we shall obtain our pardon in the end."

"Ah, you have a rattling tambourine on your shoulders
instead of a head! You cannot think straight, you always say
yes and no at the same time!" Rigueur was as restless that winter
as a swallow before a storm, she would not stay two days in the
same place, but would ride from one convent to another and
return to Toulouse only to set off again the next day.

*"Do not ask me where I am going, my friend, my business is of no great
importance, but I have no right to speak of it except to people of our faith.
Hard times are coming for our Church, this time we shall not be taken
unprepared."*

Never before had Roger realised how strong was her attachment to her Church, because hers was one of those generous
natures which are fanned into passionate flame by the approach

of danger. She busied herself taking up collections and seeking out Catholic ladies in order to convert them, or at least induce them to assist her Church. If she also helped in preparing places of refuge and secret meeting places against the possible renewal of the persecutions, she said nothing of it, but it was certainly this which formed her chief concern. She was always saying: "This time we shall not be caught unprepared."

She had little time left to devote to love and, even when she was alone with her lover, talked mostly about the foolishness of the Catholics and the frivolity of men who thought of nothing but repainting their houses and choosing jewels for their mistresses. (In this she was both judge and plaintiff, because Bérenger had fallen in love some months previously, and she felt humiliated for him.—Although, God knew! if every man in the land was to wait for the return of the old times before thinking of love, they all stood a good chance of being bent and hoary before that day came! The girl was pretty but empty-headed; and even Bérenger's friends had given him to understand that it did not become a man of his age and rank to take a girl picked up in a stew for his concubine. He retorted that the fault was not the girl's but that of her parents who had taken insufficient care of her, and that it was enough for him if she remained faithful in the future. Rigueur said: "I ought not to distress myself, since I can see he is happy." Happy he certainly was, to a degree which made him seem handsome again in spite of his burned face. Whenever he was not in the presence of ladies he would boast eagerly of his sweetheart's grace and the hidden beauties of her young body, as fresh as spring flowers. It would not be fair to say he did not think of the war, he thought of it, like everyone else. But with the carelessness of a man whom success follows, he always said: "We have beaten them so many times; what have we to fear? They will not stay long." He was one of those who feared a bad peace much more than a good war.)

It seemed as though in ten or even twenty years' time they would still be arguing about the number of Crusaders the next spring would bring; that they were condemned to go on digging fortifications and scouring the already devastated countryside to fill castle granaries for the rest of their lives. Everyone, from the Count down to the smallest landowner, the poorest citizen, was determined to stand firm; everyone was saying: "Better to die than see them invade our homes again. We have borne enough." But there was great wretchedness, and with the cold weather came even worse hunger, and hunger is a bad counsellor. The peasants were slaughtering their cattle in defiance of the stewards' orders. "What does it matter?" they said. "In the spring the Crusaders will take everything."

Once more folk abandoned their lands and went to stand in long queues outside the convent doors and the city halls and beg their bread. The price of bread and beans rose higher every day, while the foreign merchants shut their shops and hired armed bands to carry their wares out of the country. Weapons and all military equipment cost twice as much as in the previous year; the mercenaries were growing discontented and their captains carried their complaints right into the Counts' palaces, threatening to lead their men away if their wages were not paid up to six months in advance. The money had to be found. All those who had lands to protect and troops to arm suddenly found themselves transformed into hunted beasts, running from town to country, from one banker to another, in the hope of picking up a few more crowns. The bankers would lend nothing without sureties, especially in the Carcassès and the other territories belonging to the Viscount. "What is the value of land that will be a royal domain or some Crusader's fief by tomorrow?" they said. In this they were right.

Roger de Montbrun rode round his domain of Layrac, from one village to another, accompanied by Jean-Rigaud de Marcillac, and wherever he stopped the poor crowded round him like flies, the women holding up infants as skinny as plucked fledglings. He ordered the distribution of a soup made of bran and beans, and had the reserves of corn, barley and oats loaded on to mules and carried off. He told them: *"Be patient, good people, for the love of Christ! We are not taking this from you for our own greed, but for the service of our lord the Count and our country's freedom."* But because he himself was well fed and mounted on a good horse, and clad in a cloak lined with otter skin, the poor people envied him, and murmured: "See what becomes of our corn."

Roger held a council in the château of Layrac to which he summoned all the vassals and yeomen farmers. There were five or six good swords amongst them. The men were dressed in woollen gowns, patched and cleaned for the occasion, and they stood, blowing gloomily on their fingers—the room was very cold because the windows had not yet been mended—and talked in low voices among themselves. Finally, Jean-Rigaud de

Marcillac said to Roger: "*We fought, at Penne and Layrac, to defend our liberties, and we lost there much of our wealth, to say nothing of our men. Not even the Crusaders would demand what you are demanding.*"

"I am not demanding, gentlemen, I am asking! I may have given my word to come to your aid and protect these lands, but I must have the means to do it. Every man must contribute something in the face of a common danger."

Once more they consulted among themselves and Jean-Rigaud said: "We are your vassals and those of the Lady Guillelme, but we have made neither oaths nor promises to the Count of Toulouse. You are his man and you are taking our goods to use in his service, yet it may be that the Crusaders will come here while you are campaigning thirty leagues away, with your men and ours."

"If ever they come here," said Roger, "I will ask leave of the Count and come to defend Layrac, and I shall bring enough men to hold it, so long as the walls and the moats are well fortified."

They listened to him grimly, scratching their chins. In that instant he felt a sudden spasm of vertigo; because he sensed that none of these men believed one word of what he was saying, nor of what they were saying themselves, that he himself did not believe his own words. Like *Paters* and *Aves* which have been repeated a hundred times over, their words no longer bore any relation to their thoughts; they were all lying, or rather they were speaking from habit, although they had in fact nothing to say. They believed so little in this war that they might have been concerned with some fable of the days of King Arthur—as though there had never been any fighting in the land and it were fated to a thousand years of peace. The inhabitants had suffered so much that now they could no longer believe it. They were living in a dream.

Roger departed once more, taking with him the corn and silver wrung so painfully from men who no longer placed any trust in him. In Toulouse the news was not good: at court men were loudly condemning the conduct of certain powerful barons, among them Héracle de Montlaur and Pierre-Bermond de Sauve, the Count's brother-in-law, who had gone to Paris to offer submission to the King and swear fealty to him for their lands. Men jeered at them and said: "*See the sheep, in such a hurry to be sheared and flayed they are running up to the butcher and bleating for joy.*"

133

The Count seemed more sad than angry: the King was raising an army the like of which had never been seen before, even in the First Crusade—the troops belonging to the Count of Champagne alone were stronger than all Count Raymond's. Were they going to be outnumbered by one to ten? There was no question of fighting a pitched battle, but at least they hoped the castles might hold out. The barracks were full of volunteers who had flocked to enrol in the militia, but these were not professional soldiers, and they had already seen enough of troops getting themselves massacred and doing nobody any good by it, at Muret. Everyone was singing songs directed against Rome and against King Louis and the Legate, thinking at the same time: "Please God, let the Pope die, or the King die! The Pope is old, the King is weak in health. Please God, let the English land in Normandy, or the Emperor invest the marches of Champagne and the Île-de-France!" They were living on crazy hopes, and meanwhile it was spring and famine stalked the countryside and every man was wondering whether there would be a harvest that summer.

At Easter, Roger was able to meet Rigueur outside the château of Belpech, on the road to Foix. She was travelling to Mirepoix to take part in a retreat with her friends Béatrix de Miraval and Hélis de Roquevidal. It was cold and the wind, burrowing underneath the womens' cloaks, made them billow and flap like banners. They looked up at the black sky and said: "God! We shall have such a downpour on the road to Mazerolles!"

Out of consideration for the two lovers, Lady d'Aspremont's companions went on ahead, leaving them to ride alone, side by side, a hundred paces behind.

"Why did you not come to Toulouse last week?" Rigueur was saying. "Now I shall not see you before Ascension Day."

"Don't talk to me of Ascension Day, or Pentecost," said Roger. "I prefer not to think of what is to come."

"If you, the warriors, do not think of it, then who will? Are you, too, losing your nerve? After what we have endured, is there anything left in the world which should still frighten us?"

"It is not fear," he said. "Merely that my men are demanding a hundred marks for three months' service. Among my vassals I can find scarce a dozen men who will make good soldiers."

"In Toulouse during the siege, women and children fought

134

like soldiers! Scythes and pitchforks are as good as lances when the men are not cowards."

"My life, I talk of nothing but this from morning to night—as though it would make the King of France any richer or poorer. And I have lived without you for three weeks now. You know well enough how hard that is for me."

"I waited for you. And now I shall not see you again for two months."

"To us any meadow or wood would be finer than a gilded chamber. You need not fear the cold; at the mere sight of you I burn fiercely enough to melt an icefield."

She gave a deep sigh. "If you love me do not speak to me of such things. I am on my way to holy places and it is not fitting for any woman to enter them unless she has kept herself pure since the new moon. There are some customs we must respect if we do not wish to become like animals." Her lips were trembling as she spoke. "In times like these, especially, Roger—if only you had the will to ask those who can to pray for you."

"I do not believe," he said, "that there is any saint to whose service I would not willingly vow myself if they could only help us. It seems that God is too high and far away to care for our rights."

"No. The God of this world knows well what he is doing, and those who serve him are powerful and successful in all things. The God you serve is the Devil, and you are amazed that he cares little for our rights!"

He had never seen her attack his own faith so fiercely before, but he did not blame her. He felt depressed and irritable at having made a journey of thirty leagues out of his way only to find the door of his garden locked against him: these are things which happen only to true lovers. It is cruel to insist upon one's rights when a woman refuses for reasons of piety.

Roger accompanied the ladies as far as Mazerolles, where a great public meeting was to take place, at which the Deacon Raymond de Mirepoix was preaching in the castle courtyard because the hall was not large enough to contain all the congregation. The heaviest of the downpour was over, but it was still drizzling. The Deacon was standing on a small wooden platform, under a white awning, on which the lords of the castle and a number of venerable ladies in black veils and habits had also placed themselves, sitting on benches and bales of straw. Four knights stood, bareheaded, at the four corners of the dais, with spears in their hands, and a good third of the men present in the courtyard were soldiers, who were entitled to the best places. On that day, Roger felt such an intense desire to understand the ways of God that he wondered whether he were not like Saul persecuting the Christians (although he had never persecuted anyone). He listened and prayed with the rest, and whatever else he lacked, it was certainly not fervour.

As he spoke, the Deacon raised his arms to heaven, and uttered loud cries and sobs, like a man possessed by the Spirit, saying that the sins of the time were great and the want and wretchedness greater still, and that it was permissible, even pleasing to God, to resist the Church's enemies with force when all other methods of turning away their wrath had been tried and failed. . . .

"For they have received admonishments, and warnings and humble supplications, and gold and sureties have been offered them. To avoid bloodshed your liege lords were ready to grant them much more than right and justice demanded. And they have listened only to the voice of their own hatred and covetousness. Brothers, they are more impious than infidels and more covetous than publicans, but Christ has not bidden us answer their hatred with hatred. Not with hatred but with steadfastness; not with hatred but with courage, for verily I say unto you that by yielding to the wicked out of cowardice we injure them as much as ourselves, and damn their souls at the same time as our own! You will not be responsible for their deaths in a state of sin; the fault is theirs, and that of their leaders and their prime master, the Prince of this world!"

The holy man preached for a long time, exhorting the faithful in this vein. He told them that Babylon was now making her last attempt and preparing for her final assault, and compared the the army that would soon be ready to fall like a dragon on the Occitan lands, to destroy the Church of God, to the colossus with feet of clay. The golden head, he told them, was the French King's splendid chivalry; the torso and arms of silver—they were the power and cunning of the bishops; the copper lions—they were the cruelty and boldness of the professional soldiers; but the whole was supported on legs of clay and feet of mud: hatred, dissension, impiety, lasciviousness, sloth and the innumerable other impurities which corrupt armies that wage an unjust war. *". . . Brothers, if you stand firm in the knowledge of this, you will be stronger than any numbers!"*

136

"God!" thought Roger, "that our bishops and priests could preach thus! But the best of them can only lower their eyes and say nothing, and they cannot even comfort us with the sacraments."

His hair was soaked with rain and the cold water was trickling down his face and mingling with the hot tears. He was weeping because others were weeping, and because a too-great pity was tightening his throat, pity for the land they would not leave in peace and for all those who wanted to live and were not permitted to. Like the other knights, he prostrated himself three times before the Deacon Raymond, and asked him to pray for him. *"May God make a good Christian of me and bring me to a good end."* His heart was afire. What does it matter? he thought. We say this or that, so they will only let us pray at last. (He was never to be sorry for this, because he had really done it from no contempt of the Catholic faith, but simply out of the great sadness in his heart.)

In the evening he took his leave of Rigueur, who looked paler and more solemn than usual, and made her promise to come to Toulouse after Low Sunday. (He would have done better never to have extracted this promise from her, but one can never foresee everything.) He left Mazerolles in the company of Guiraud de Laurac and Guillaume de Belpech, two very gallant knights who, moreover, had served under Montfort in their youth, but were none the less fervent heretics. Both of them were going to Toulouse on business (since they held a part of their lands from the Count of Toulouse). They seemed worried and morose, and from the previous day's sermon retained only a kind of melancholy resignation: one cannot hear such sermons every day.

"What can we do? We have two months before us at the most, by the end of May we shall have them at our gates." "Carcassonne will not hold out long," they said, "nor will Béziers. Viscount Raymond does not know how to enforce his commands and all the Catholics in the city of Carcassonne are going to beg for pardon, because they say it is still better to be the French King's subjects than food for the crows."

"There is no denying they are right," said Roger, "but the Viscount should not allow them to speak out."

"He is lucky if he is allowed to speak himself: he is eighteen and his tutors are arguing over who shall rule in his place.

137

While the consuls swear by the King's peace alone, because they say Louis is a gallant and pious prince and they will suffer less from him than they will under the Viscount." The three men shouted with laughter, and Roger said the good people were two years behind the times and thought they were still in the days of Amaury.

"Do not laugh," said Guillaume de Belpech. "On the day Louis enters the city there will be more informers outside his chancellery than beggars outside the church of Saint-Nazaire. Louis sets great store by being reputed mild and kindly."

"No man was ever crueller," said Guiraud. "Not at least among those who wear a crown: even as a youth, did he not wish to raze the whole city of Toulouse to the ground? And we know the things he permitted at Marmande during his second campaign, where no one had betrayed or offended him (and his father, the good King Philip, was still alive then). Now that he is King himself, what fear can stop him?"

"Not the fear of God, certainly," said Guillaume, "nor the fear of dishonouring himself in the eyes of ladies, because he is well known to be led by the Queen, and the Queen is entirely devoted to the Preaching Friars."

"It is not surprising," put in Roger," that they preach so well. When the King comes he will give them back the lands they acquired from Count Simon. Because of his advanced age, the Pope has allowed himself to be seduced by their false charity. They are fanning the fire in order to regain their stolen lands, and the saint they pray to is Louis of France. God grant that by tomorrow we do not have to pray to the same saint!"

All three men were speaking as though the Crusaders were already in the land, dividing up their spoils. Peace was lost, and freedom depended entirely on the sword's point; they felt as though they had gone back ten or fifteen years, without having grown any younger.

No one who does not know what fear of the French is can understand.

What had happened? Three months later, when the King was laying waste the district of Carcassès and occupying town after town without a blow struck, they were no longer afraid. Bishops, castellans and consuls marched out of the great gates in procession, to meet the Crusaders, carrying the keys of their city on a golden cushion. The King did not even

138

have to have the old banners taken down before he could replace them with his own; he held celebrations in the city hall and heard Mass in the cathedral. Then they were no longer afraid. They watched the Crusaders move in, and were content to shut the shops and hide their wives and daughters, and say: "God, here they are again!" They had been used to this for a long time. They were not afraid; they wept.

Three months later, after the fall of Avignon, when they had fully understood that once again the country was to drink the same cup, they were to welcome the King in such a fashion that he could no longer inspire fear; then he had no enemies other than those who were fighting, and those he never saw face to face. But that Eastertide, when the great army was still preparing to march, fear had fallen on the land, like a cloud so thick that it seemed they would never again see the sun. People did their work, bought and sold; they married, buried their dead, and talked of the cold weather and the harvest to come; but their thoughts were on none of these things, because fear was there, present and alive in all their eyes, like some hidden disease.

The bravest shouted it aloud; the more fearful said: "They will never come here." The others thought: "Pray that the consuls and barons are not fools enough to defend the city." In Toulouse itself, the citizens walked in the Capitol Square with lowered eyes, and gathered outside the Narbonnese castle, murmuring: "Does the Count seek our deaths?" But the Count had it proclaimed everywhere that the French would never take so much as one acre of land in his city, and that if need be he would garrison it with all his barons and knights, and would send for two thousand soldiers from Aragon and Gascony; and he would summon the King of England and the German Emperor to his aid, to drive out the French and send them back to their own country before the autumn. He himself rode bareheaded through the city, without either heralds or drums, and as the crowd surged up to him, clinging to his stirrups and to his horse's reins, he said to them:

"See how you have been betrayed by your bishop and by my cousin Louis, who should be our liege lord, and yet comes to steal our goods and our lives. I shall never betray you, I give you my oath; they shall not touch one single horse of yours, not one thread of your garments. Toulouse shall be defended, even if I have to pledge my own wife and daughter to pay the soldiers!"

By speeches of this kind, he put fresh heart in many of the people, since they could see he was not saying it to mislead the world, but was blazing, like white hot iron, with anger and passion.

But although the ordinary people listened to him joyfully, his own knights shook their heads and said: "Would to God the old Count were still alive! He knew better how to deal with the French." The young Count was already twenty-nine, but his father's friends still looked on him as a child.

How can a man fight when he can no longer count on anyone in the country, save the nobles and mercenaries? Moreover, the knights had their own lands to protect, and the mercenaries would not fight for nothing. How is it possible to fight with a few thousand soldiers pitted against tens of thousands? Because, apart from the Count's own army, they had nothing to speak of. Every man answered: "We cannot desert our own lands." Even the Count of Foix.

Fight? However they made up their minds to it, there were some days when they felt like men trying to put out a forest fire with a bucket of water. (This was not altogether true, but in those days all men, or nearly all, thought thus. Their heads were afire with terror of the French.) After Easter, therefore, Roger returned to Layrac with his wife to prepare the castle's defences and renew the oaths of allegiance of those men who were to follow the Count's army. Guillelme brought gifts for the vassals' wives; she herself was dressed in gold necklaces and had a circlet on her head covered with tiny pearls, because Roger had told her: "Make yourself look pretty, so that they will be glad to defend your inheritance." Pretty she certainly was, pretty enough to seduce a Preaching Friar, and the vassals' wives and daughters prepared a splendid feast for her in the castle hall at Layrac and decorated the table and Guillelme's chair with snowdrops and violets. They were never tired of embracing her and telling her they would never forget her grace and sweetness.

With the men it was different. They held a council in the evening, at which Roger and Guillelme, though they sat on high-backed chairs, on a raised dais, felt lower than the earth. Their vassals reproached them bitterly for sacrificing them in Count Raymond's quarrel. For them, there could be no question of defending the castle, since their lord himself was leaving on campaign instead of staying with his own people.

"You have my word," said Roger. "As soon as I have arranged my own affairs, I shall send my wife to you with fifty good soldiers and my son with her. You may judge for yourselves whether, knowing they are here, I shall not do everything to come to your rescue in the event of a siege."

Jean-Rigaud de Marcillac answered that this was not a

sufficient surety and that it was even an added danger. "We know Herbert de Vitry well enough," he said. "And if he finds your wife in the castle he will not have much difficulty in annulling the marriage. His second son is still living. You would be delivering us into his hands."

Roger was red with vexation, and Guillelme biting her knuckles. "There are a good thirty nobles among you," said Roger, "including youths, and I will send you some hired men. You don't really believe that Louis will turn up here with a thousand knights, siege engines and engineers, all to take the château of Layrac?"

"If he wants to take it he will send what is necessary. No man in his right mind has any desire to imitate the gallantry of the people of Béziers. Moreover, at Béziers the Crusaders had no dead to avenge." (Six years previously the heads of a dozen Crusaders had been smashed between the hammer and anvil in the Layrac forge, and there were plenty of men in the country who regretted it now.)

"Sirs, for God's sake, let us not sing the Dead Mass for a man who is only sick, let us rather seek a good doctor. Do you believe that, after the things Herbert de Vitry's men suffered here, you run any smaller risk in yielding up the castle than in defending it?"

"It is not right," persisted Jean-Rigaud, "that you should put the Count's interests before those of your own domain, after taking our men and our goods. The Crusaders would not do as much."

At this Guillelme rose and said she would not be insulted in this fashion, and moreover all the world knew she had suffered more from the Crusaders than Jean-Rigaud. She added that she was quite ready to challenge them and her husband would defend her against those who insulted her. The girl's brave words and cracked voice shamed the men of Layrac, and Roger felt some gratitude to his wife for it. After this incident peace was restored and Roger received the oaths of the seven men who were to follow him to the army and promised to do all that was needful to avert a siege of the castle.

"*Well, sweetheart, I think we shall have to bear with it. After all, it will make the King no richer or poorer.*"

They were on the road to Montauban, chilled, miserable, and spurring their horses more from anger than haste. The dawn

141

light was pale and misty and Guillelme was continually turning round to make sure the two soldiers of their escort were still following them, because she was afraid of brigands.

"Must I sign too?"

"I fear so, my dear. My signature is not valid without yours. If anyone ever reproaches you for it, you can say that I forced you."

"I will write whatever they like," she said, "so long as they do not make me swear fealty."

She was crying, sniffing occasionally, and her small, pale face was swollen with sleep until it looked almost the face of a child.

When they reached Montauban, the couple went to the house of a cousin of Roger's, Pierre de Montbrun, who was a canon of the church of Notre-Dame. (Pierre had studied law and letters and Roger frequently consulted him on matters of business.)

"It is the most sensible course to take," said the canon, "but I do not advise you to go to Montpellier, your friends will take it badly and, as you are from Toulouse, you are not obliged to go. The best thing is to write a letter addressed to the King, as many lords who hold land in the same district have done. Whether or not you receive an answer, you can always prove that the letter was written two weeks after Easter, before the Crusaders' army had begun to march."

The two cousins pondered for a long time over the wording of the letter, and then summoned a clerk, to whom Pierre began dictating in Latin.

In his letter Roger declared that he, Roger de Montbrun, Lord of Layrac, *in full agreement with his wife, Guillelme, Lady of Layrac, having always been a good Catholic and devoted in his heart to his gracious majesty, King Louis of France, having always held the perversion of heresy in abhorrence, and ardently desiring for his country the peace, justice and prosperity which only his Royal Majesty, the well-beloved lord Louis could impose on the land; and furthermore deploring the vexations and injustices which the Catholic Church had continually suffered through the insolence and the blameworthy complaisance of the Count of Toulouse, and bitterly repenting the errors into which, in consequence of his youth and folly, he had formerly allowed himself to be led, of taking arms against the Christ's soldiers contrary to the Church's edict, accordingly submitted his land, goods and person entirely to the mercy of His Majesty, King Louis, and desired henceforth to have no other liege lord than the said most wise and merciful king, and swore to be faithful to him and promised to serve him as best he might in all his wars and against all enemies of the crown.*

Whereupon, Roger de Montbrun, Lord of Layrac, humbly entreated His Majesty to forgive his past faults and dispose as he wished of his goods and lands, in anticipation of the lifting of the sentence of excommunication justly pronounced against him, Roger, by the Holy Fathers of the Council of Bourges. He further begged the King in his goodness to consider that he, Roger, had borne arms against the Christ's soldiers only under constraint and perforce, since he could bring numerous witnesses to prove that he had always been a Catholic in thought, word and deed. And he offered fervent prayers for the triumph of His Majesty, Louis of France, for the re-establishment of peace and the complete extinction of the poisonous hydra of heresy which had caused so much evil in all the lands of the langue d'oc.

Pierre re-read this letter aloud, translating as he did so, and Roger frowned, wondering whether the tone of the epistle was sufficiently polite and submissive. Others must surely have done better.

"Pierre," he said, "I think we are fairly bad clerks, you and I. These compliments are as warm as vows extracted under torture."

"It is the signature that matters, Roger."

"You are right," said Roger, gritting his teeth. "I only hope I shall have plenty of new sins to crave pardon for before I need this letter."

"You will not have the time," said Pierre. He did not believe the country could hold out for another three weeks. He himself was terrified, for he had been living under threat of a trial for heresy for several months and each day he expected to receive a formal indictment. And yet he had done nothing to be ashamed of.

"Frankly, Roger," he went on, "is there any man these days who could not be taken for a heretic or a heretic sympathiser? One would have to be a Carthusian. You laymen are left in peace, but life is becoming impossible for clerics, especially since the King has joined the Crusade. We are accused of treachery on both sides. I am accused of tolerating heresy because I baptise the children of heretics, when they are nobles and belong to great families."

"It's a fine thing," Roger said, "to see them accusing priests of heresy for giving baptism to children now! One of these days they will probably compel us to walk upside down."

143

"Aren't you doing just that at this very moment? What were you telling the Bishop's chancellery a little while ago?"

Once their letter was duly rolled up and deposited in a box, the two cousins and Guillelme went to the Bishop's palace to request an audience with the Bishop's deputy. They met there many other excommunicated lords who had come to give proof of their good intentions (certain of them were notorious heretics and famed as such for a long time). Roger spoke privately to the deputy's chief clerk, and gave him three marks for the poor; he allowed himself to be questioned closely on the purity of his faith and proved that he had not strayed from Catholic orthodoxy on any point; then, showing his letter, he said that being only a simple knight he did not possess the skill to express adequately his true feelings, but that he wished to submit himself to the King's mercy.

"Your letter," the clerk told him, "will be passed on to the royal chancellery before the King leaves Paris. My lord Archbishop of Narbonne is greatly rejoiced to see so many noble knights showing their fidelity to the Church." ("Ah, that Archbishop," thought Roger, "would have done better to get himself elected elsewhere! Much cause he has for rejoicing.")

He said: "My wife and I are ready to sign this paper before witnesses and affix our seal to it. I have given orders that no man on my land is to obstruct the passage of the King's army (if it comes there) so long as their goods and persons are respected."

The clerk advised him to stay in his castle himself to see that this order was carried out.

"That," said Roger, "I cannot do. I have my aged father, my brother and my whole family in Toulouse. The Count is hasty tempered and if I default he may take vengeance on them." (Scarcely a credible excuse, and no one, in fact, credited it.)

Pierre de Montbrun and two knights of Montauban served as witnesses to the signature, Roger inscribed his name and Guillelme added hers in small, faltering characters and then broke the pen in two, threw it on the ground and stamped on it. (Such an action on the part of a woman shocked no one, rather the reverse.) The couple walked for a long time with the young canon under the arcade in the main square, conversing with other knights who had come to Montauban for the same purpose or in order to recruit soldiers. The same hidden terror lurked in all their eyes, the same dazed expression. "Can this really be about to begin again, and we cannot avert it?"

"*Obviously the King will not let go so easily: look at the expense he has been to, while his father never lifted a finger to help Montfort. He is levying a tithe on clergy and lay clerks, just as in the time of the Crusade against Saladin.*" Bitterly humorous, they said: "He must think we are strong."

"My poor sweet child, our troubles are not over yet. I cannot let you rest, because we must be in Toulouse tomorrow."

Guillelme wrung her hands and wailed: "Ah, may the men who receive that letter come to a bad end. May they have no joy in any life." (She was a heretic, as her parents had been, and believed that souls lived more than one life.)

"Why torment yourself so? The bravest men may be compelled to employ a shield." It was a feeble enough excuse.

"I know one lady," Roger said to Pierre de Montbrun, "who will not praise what I have done here."

"Have we come to the point of courting a lady's praise?" asked the canon. "Who can still think of the praise of women when it is a matter of famine, and men dying and foreign soldiers in our houses?"

But because Roger knew that Rigueur was to spend that week in Toulouse he thought of nothing but the means to see her again, for he had no grief or shame or trouble that he could face squarely until he had shared it with her. And, God knows, he expected reproaches; he knew, too, that he would not have much difficulty in justifying himself, since in none of this was he to blame.

On his return to Toulouse, he sent his servant to Arnaude, who was now married and living on the outskirts of the city. He wrote: *My life, I do not wish you learn from others what I would rather tell you myself. Though I have had to take measures to safeguard my lands and the men who have sworn fealty to me, I need not blush for it more than others, because you know that I am not the only one. If you can come to the place where we usually meet tomorrow, put two candles in your window. I will pass your house this evening. (If you put out three candles, I shall know it is for the day after tomorrow.) Do not delay for the love of God, for I am nigh on a dead man, with all the troubles that are heaped on us, and I cannot live again until I see you. Would that I could hold you always in my arms, day and night, like a holy relic to guard me against all evil! Know that I can neither eat nor sleep until we meet again.*

145

Passing the Aspremont mansion that evening, he did not see either two or three candles in the window of the turret where Rigueur dwelt; there was no light at all. This put him in a considerable difficulty, since this was not the moment to present himself at the house in person. Bérenger, and all the men of his party, took a severe view of the 'turncoats' as they called those who had made their submission to the King. Thus, for two days Roger had no news of his mistress, and had indeed scant time to seek for news. He had to find money and arms and harness. This was no small matter because all articles of equipment had doubled in price.

When he made his appearance in the knights' hall of the Narbonnese palace, the Count came up to him and said with a bitter smile:

"Well, Roger, it seems that you love peace and wish with all your heart for Louis's victory?"

"My lord," Roger told him, "Roger de Montbrun must not be confused with the Lord of Layrac."

The Count looked at him in astonishment and laughed again, with real amusement this time. "What's this new song? Maybe you think I have been drinking and am seeing double?"

"My lord, you are well aware of the kind of victory I wish them. But it is allowable for any man to try and protect his possessions if he can."

The Count said: "If I permitted myself to bear grudges, I don't imagine I should have twenty friends left among those who owe me fealty. Let us say no more about it. Tell me rather, without falsehood, exactly what can I count on for the aid you owe me?"

"On all I have: myself and four knights fully equipped, with six men apiece, and a company of fifty Navarrese besides."

This was a great deal to promise, but in that moment Roger would have pledged his wife and son to recall the pain he had caused the young Count. From the castle he went straight to his father's house to find Guillelme.

"My dear, I have promised the Count twice the number of Navarrese I have, and at present I have not even enough money to pay those I have. I must pledge what gold or precious stones you possess; you know what the cost of soldiers is today."

Guillelme had some fine jewels in her coffer, inherited from

146

her mother. She was attached to them, because her nurse had taken great trouble to hide them during the time of Herbert de Vitry, and had made her consider them as little short of relics. She went to get the chest and almost flung it on to the table, saying: *"Take them! But I know from the way you manage your affairs that I shall never see them again."*

He slapped her, without malice, as though correcting a child— he was himself unreasonably vexed and agitated.

"Aren't you ashamed? When the burgher's daughters are coming to throw their last remaining trinkets and earrings in a heap before the Capitol so that the Count shall have the wherewithal to defend the city? Your grandfather and your father and your uncles gave up something more than gold necklaces for our country."

Guillelme stood with her hand pressed to her scarlet cheek, watching him with wide-open, tear-filled eyes. Roger felt such a surge of pity and desire that he was within an ace of taking her in his arms and persuading her to give him a second heir. That he did not was due to lack of time. He had to pledge the jewels that very day in order to be able to recruit the Navarrese he had in mind. Among the moneylenders the price of gold was dropping every day; they said that in the case of pillage or requisition they would lose both the money and the pledge.

"If I have called her Rigueur hitherto," Roger wondered, "should I call her Douceur now? How can she refuse me a sign of life at such a time?" Was it surprising that she should be angry? That evening he received a message at last. His valet brought him an oak box which he said had been brought by a young woman with red hair. In the box Roger found some ashes mingled with the remains of the black silk cord that Rigueur had worn for five years woven in her left plait. The cord had been cut into small pieces, an inch or so long. It was not necessary to be a soothsayer to read the message: this meant rupture, according to the rules, for women rarely write at such moments lest they should provide an excuse for an answer.

Only this is a method which, however good when it concerns a transient affair, should not be permitted between true lovers. Great God, to have hurt her is already hard enough—to have hurt her and be unable to comfort her is too much! He stared at the fragments of his cord, trying to imagine how she must have felt, to cut it to pieces like that—how angry or how sad—

147

she who loved that black lacing so much that not once in five years had she forgotten to plait it into her hair. They had never given one another rich gifts, only the paltry presents that poor children exchange at the time of their first love. The hawk had died the summer of Amaury's departure and Rigueur had had him embalmed and his little, shrivelled heart, as small as a walnut, sewn into a silken bag which she wore on a silver chain.

"Rigueur, if we only had the time to lacerate ourselves in this way, if I could still spend cunning and patience to find a way of speaking with you. If we had the time, beloved, I would willingly spend six months besieging your house again to prove the tenderness I feel for you. But where shall we be in six months? The King will march on us in May, and before midsummer our fields and vines will be burning. I have so much business to put in order before I leave for the campaign that I cannot stay more than two days together in Toulouse."

Lord, when these troubles began I was twenty. Now I am thirty-seven. That is all the difference. They come as they did before, bringing with them their crowd of pilgrims, and they too are seventeen years older than they were at the time of Béziers. They are coming back to us with a fresh army, and for every man of theirs we have slain in fifteen years of war they bring back three. Those who have never seen them do not know what they were like before, these splendid knights, with their gaily coloured banners and their arms shining so brightly that all the way from Valence to Avignon the road looked like a city street on a great feast day—or what the foot-soldiers were like, swarming over the fields, or the boats, and the gaily-decked barges that spread right across the river Rhône until one could not see the end of them.

We set out, armed, equipped and ready, our banners raised and the trumpets and clarions sounding before us and on the city walls. There were no bells ringing and our priests did not give us their blessings, or else blessed us in secret: we have done without prayers and psalms for so long now! The Crusaders were outside Avignon, their camp larger than the great city which lay beside the river, and for every one of our men they had twenty. (Thank God the people of Avignon have not broken their word, but have stood firm for us. It takes very little to inspire fresh courage.) We did not set out to drive them away from before the city, but only to let them know they cannot leave their camp or ravage the countryside, and that we fear them where they are ten to one but not otherwise.

It is not war that makes us afraid: we have waged that for long enough,
God be thanked. It has become a habit. In time of peace—and God knows
that was short, we have said how short time and again—in time of peace
we wake up at night wondering: "Where shall we go tomorrow? When
will the siege be? From which quarter the attack?" Nothing. No one to
attack. We have cares enough to fill the day, but Lord, how small a thing
they are beside the trouble of risking one's skin. And now it is all beginning
again, and with our armour we must put on the terrible knowledge of war,
and even that is not so hard to bear, for our bodies have grown accustomed
to it. What we fear is not the war, it is fighting for a cause that all of
Christendom seems to take for a bad cause, when it is the best and most
righteous of all. Who will not say: "The heretics are right"? It is not
a pope or two, or a dozen bishops, it is the entire Church (with the
exception of a few wise and pious priests who are declared guilty of
heresy as soon as they open their mouths), the entire Church is abused by
the calumny our enemies heap on us. Even the Count of Champagne who
has always been our friend and does not love the King, even he is taking
the Cross with his knights and planting his banners before a free city which
has done him no wrong. We shall never have popes or bishops who are
different. The Church has been sold to Louis of France. Our Mother
sold, our Judge sold.

They were expecting war but no war came; they were expecting fear
such as had never been seen in the land before: and midsummer came and
went, and the feast of the Assumption, and still the great army was
encamped before Avignon, and in Provence and the Carcassès people were
beginning to say: "The King would do well to have a house built beside
the Rhône and bring his wife and children there, because if he has sworn
not to move until he has taken the city he will stay there until Christmas,
until Easter, until the end of his days." In fact the Count of Champagne
and the Count of Brittany had gone away at the end of the forty days for
which they were pledged to stay, and many other barons greatly desired
to do the same. They said: "If he takes himself for Simon de Montfort
let him be quick and show what he can do, because when he has no soldiers
left, like Simon, it is to be feared that the citizens of Avignon may
speedily shut him up in their dungeons to punish his perfidy." There was
much laughter at this, and as for those foraging for supplies for the army,
they captured them alive and hanged them from oaks and olive trees along
the roads. Though the Count's men did good work that summer, most of
it was mercenaries' work: plundering convoys and massacring small
bodies of men, causing fires near the enemy camp and poisoning wells
and springs. When they did manage to lure a hundred or more men-at-arms

*away from their camp by crossbow-fire, they would retire, in order to
draw them as far as possible—sometimes the Crusaders would hurl
themselves in pursuit and never return—or only in small pieces. The
crosses in the camp cemetery stretched as far as the eye could see, and so
many Crusaders died of the heat and disease that men were saying: "See,
the whole magnificent army will melt away like snow in sunshine."
They laughed at that, and cities and counts sent delegations to the King,
thinking: "If he fails to take Avignon, what can we lose?" Because the
bishops and abbots, and the Archbishop of Narbonne in particular, were
still saying:* "This siege has given him sorrow and bitterness
already, that is plain. He has lost the Count of Namur and plenty
of other barons, and the behaviour of Count Raymond's soldiers
is putting him in a towering rage. Either he must take the city
or, if his patience runs out, he must request a dispensation freeing
himself from his vow and raise the siege, but in either case look
for no mercy from him. No other city, not even Carcassonne or
Béziers, is likely to hold out as Avignon has done."

*Those who had laughed hitherto were no longer laughing on the day
the French broke their word and took and occupied Avignon, under the
pretence of a truce (because rumour had it that the city never formally
capitulated), and truth to tell they had scant time for weeping either.
Throughout the Caracassès there was rejoicing in the King's honour,
the bells were ringing and people climbing on to the walls and decorating
the streets. Any who still talked of resistance were stoned and dragged
through the streets, their faces smeared with blood and spittle. "Traitors
you are for seeking all our deaths, it is a pity your Bishop and your Viscount
had time to escape!" The most benign lord had only to enter Carcassonne,
he would not find there a single face without a smile, because when
their lives are at stake men will go to any lengths, and they will smile
for fear more readily than for love. The King rode into Béziers, and
Carcassonne, and into Pamiers and Castelnaudary, and Beaucaire and
Pylaurens, and was honoured and feasted and hardly condescended to
stop and receive their homage. The seneschals did this for him.*

*As for his soldiers, the meadows along the road were strewn with their
corpses until even the vultures were sated, because never was an army
more weary or in worse condition. The men were abandoning their
engines and cases of munitions because they had not the strength left to
carry them, and the Count's soldiers were dogging their heels picking off
men, horses and mules with their arrows. This army looked more menacing
from a distance than at close quarters, because in reality, for all its size
and strength, it was so riddled with fever and dysentery that the knights*

were scarcely able to sit their horses, and neither was it an easy matter for them to live off the country, except in the towns, and only the great barons entered these. It was pitiful to watch them dragging their equipment through the October rain, bent double and forcing the pace—they knew only too well what awaited the stragglers.

The signal for surrender echoed through every castle and the lily banners were flying over keep and city hall: for how long? Even if half that great army had been sick, there would still have been enough of them to make a pitched battle unthinkable, and the veteran Crusaders had not come to go away empty-handed. Then, just when everyone expected the King to march on Toulouse, and when the Count was already preparing the city walls to stand a siege, the wind changed once more: the army turned back when it was almost within sight of the city, so suddenly that the people of Toulouse asked themselves whether this was a trick or a miracle sent from God. The news that the King was ill had been reported and embroidered on so often at every crossroads, during the previous six months, that now no one believed it any longer.

But this time he was well and truly ill. The conquered cities through which he passed on his way north saw him go by in a litter hung with blue silk adorned with golden lilies, with gilded lances at each corner, drawn by six white horses. From time to time he would lift up the blue-fringed curtain to reveal his face, thin and quince yellow, with a melancholy smile quivering below pale, grey-rimmed eyes. Ah! Bon voyage, *Prince Louis, King Louis, go and tell them at home how it profits a man to listen to the evil counsel of priests, and try to steal his kinsman's lawful heritage!*

He had no time to go and tell them at home: at Montpensier, in the Auvergne, when he was scarcely out of the Occitan lands, he died, and his friends carried home his embalmed body, sewn up in an oxhide, in his litter, hung now with black cloth and preceded by a cortège of bishops and white friars chanting psalms.

The good news crossed the mountains a few days after the feast of All Saints, and in Toulouse everyone was singing: "The King is dead! The King is dead! We shall have joy and honour again!" *There was no singing in the cities which had surrendered to the French, but the soldiers of the garrisons Louis had left behind dared not risk walking the streets alone at night. Everyone was saying:* "God is just, we shall not have to endure them long. He has shown clearly where reason and justice lie in this affair. The little kinglet is not yet twelve, by the time he begins to show his claws we shall be so strong that we need not fear him."

When he had made fresh treaties of alliance with the Count of Foix, Count Raymond carried on the war on the castles, just as in Amaury's day. It was a hard winter. Neither Simon nor Amaury had ever maintained so many troops in the Occitan lands during the winter, and the veteran Crusaders had many atrocities to avenge on the lands they had reconquered.

The Preaching Brothers and the soldiers of Christ redoubled their efforts, and combed the cities in search of heretics. "Do not lift your heads, you vipers' spawn," they said. "In the spring an army will come from France that shall be mightier still, for do you think the French will leave their King and so many noble barons unavenged? Our Holy Father, Pope Gregory, will allow you a time of grace, until Easter, but if you have not driven out your excommunicate and heretic seigneurs in that time, you shall perish with them!" Such friendship existed between the Frenchmen and the Church that, in defiance of custom, the seneschals of France were themselves, upon royal authority, fulfilling the office of ecclesiastical judges. In Narbonne, the King's men, with the seneschal Humbert at their head, led to the stake the heretic Bishop of Carcassonne, Monseigneur Pierre Izarn, an old man so wise and holy that the Catholics themselves honoured him. This was an unspeakable outrage to all the heretics of the land, not merely those of the Carcassès, because the love they bore their bishops was something beyond the understanding of any Catholic. Moreover, it is not acting as a good Catholic to make the Catholic faith the object of ever-growing hatred, and if the Pope had been better informed he would not have tried pouring vinegar into open wounds in this fashion. But it was common knowledge what kind of men surrounded the Pope and with what slanderous tales about the heretics in the Occitan lands they filled his ears. He was even more severe on them than his predecessors, as events were soon to show.

It was beneath the walls of Auterive—to which the Count had once more been laying siege for the past two weeks—that Roger was at last able to see again the woman who, for more than a year, had refused to speak to him. It was the month of May, between Easter and Pentecost, at the beginning of the bad season. (People no longer reckoned the seasons by the sun and the heat of the weather, but by the number of Crusaders.) During the winter they recovered ground, and in the summer were more than likely to lose all they had regained. The French besieged inside Auterive, emboldened by arrogance and optimism, had attempted a sortie, because they could no longer get supplies through by water and had no wish to be reduced to eating their horses. In what was, admittedly, a hazardous enterprise, they had none the less succeeded in causing some damage in the Count's camp and winning back to the castle. It was on the evening of this sortie that Roger and his men reached the camp, in company with Guillaume de Belpech who was also bringing a small force of men. When they were still some distance away they had been able to see that fighting was going on, because the French had set one of the siege engines on fire, as well as part of the reserve of fodder.

The machine was burning fiercely and for a hundred yards around the heat was almost too great to allow tents, beams and ladders to be carried out of range of the fire, while the screams of the many burned and injured men could be heard all over the camp. Roger and Guillaume de Belpech expected to be met with cries of joy, but they were lucky not to be received by a flight of arrows instead, because in the half-light they had been mistaken for Humbert de Beaujeu's Crusaders coming to relieve the castle.

"You blind moles! Don't you know the colour of the cross of Toulouse when you see it now?"

"Reinforcements! You should have been here this morning. You're just in time to count the dead."

"Are there many killed?"

"We shall know soon enough—Bernard de Cissac has just been carried off with six inches of steel in his belly."

Without waiting to pay his respects to the Count, Roger hurried straight to his friend's tents; there he was told that Raymond-Jourdain was in the hospital tent, north of the dyke, where his brother had been taken.

In the big tent, bodies were lying one upon another, two lighted torches spluttered and smoked, and the air was thick and heavy and smelled of fresh blood; black flies were settling on pale flesh gleaming with sweat and striated with blood. Attendants pushed past, carrying bowls of water and pitchers of oil, and it was impossible to hear oneself speak for the screams and curses.

"Is Raymond-Jourdain here?"

"He went away—his brother was asking for a priest."

"In God's name, where is Bernard? It's impossible to recognise anyone in here." Roger picked his way between the bodies, his

153

feet slipping on blood, to where the wounded man lay. With his face grey and pinched, and blood trickling from his mouth, Bernard was not easily recognisable; he was still breathing harshly, but the staring eyes saw nothing. It was all over, and the priest would not come in time. Roger stood there, looking at the dying man, too stunned to think of prayer, or tears—this was a man he had known for twenty years, not a friend, but one of those comrades for whom in a tight spot he would automatically risk his life.

He was still kneeling by the body, searching for one last glimmer in the eyes that were already dimming like misted steel, and two steps away from him a woman was talking to one of the wounded. Her voice, strong and almost joyous, was the voice he had been pining for eighteen months to hear. He turned to look at the woman, who was down on one knee beside a tall, bare-chested youth whose face was smeared with blood, and stroking his hair. She was saying: "How can you believe you are finished, friend? . . . You know very well that we are all brothers now, the same flesh and blood, from Count Raymond down to the humblest fighting man! Your brothers will *never* desert you."

The boy was listening to her gravely; the hand below his bandaged arm was purple and the arm itself red and swollen, but his eyes were fixed on the woman's face with the calm, trustful gaze of a child listening to his mother. "I am a weaver," he said, "employed by the silk weavers of Toulouse. If I lose my arm I shall have to beg for my living."

She said: "So long as there are rich men in Toulouse you will never have to beg; you will be paid the salary you deserve. And people will say: 'There goes Guiraud. He used to be a silk weaver but he gave his arm, not for silver, like a hired soldier, but for love of his city.' " She spoke with a warmth and serious-ness that compelled those who heard her to take her words for Gospel truth. She believed them so fervently herself. Her thin, drawn face, pouring with sweat, shone with a grave tenderness that was wholly innocent and fraternal.

She raised her head, and half rose, tensing her body as if to ward off a violent blow, then moved one hand to her throat. "Ah, brother," she said to the wounded man, "look what has happened: I can see a friend of whom I have had no news for a long time."

"Wounded?" asked Guiraud.

"No, a visitor."

"God be thanked."

Close by a man was screaming. His head and the upper part of his body had been scalded. Suddenly Gentian's strength seemed to desert her; she wiped her hand across her forehead, stood up and, holding up the folds of her grey skirt, its hem soaked with mud and blood, walked towards the entrance to the tent.

Outside, the scene was brilliantly lit up by the light from the still-blazing tower, and the campfires where the soldiers, famished after a hard day's fighting, were roasting sheep and kids. Five hundred feet above them, on the castle walls, more fires were burning. The air was cold and patches of black starry sky showed through the drifting smoke. Gentian sat down on some balks of wood piled by the entrance to the hospital tent and wiped her brow with her hand and her hand on her skirt: she was drenched with sweat and shivering and everything seemed to be sticky and clinging to her.

"You'll catch cold," Roger told her. "Take my cloak." She wrapped the heavy woollen cloak round her thankfully.

"Is he dead?" she said.

"Who?"

"The friend you came to see."

"Yes."

"He's better off than some," she said, still without looking at him. "Much better. There will be plenty who suffer agonies only to die in the end." Her teeth were chattering.

"This is the first time you have spoken to me since the day I parted from you at Mazcrolles."

"I am not so petty that I can think of myself in the midst of death and mourning."

"I have never done anything to hurt you, Rigueur."

She was looking straight in front of her, and her eyes were wide open, dry and burning.

"Do not speak to me of that. You have hurt me, *me* more than anyone, because no one else cares what you may do, providing you do not touch their property."

"You know I have not had two weeks rest in over a year. What do you blame me for?"

"You are not the only one. You can't help fighting. Leave it at that, I am too tired to talk about it."

155

"You are accusing me of doing something for which even the Count himself has never blamed me."

"I am not accusing you. The wolf behaves like a wolf, the fox like a fox, the vulture like a vulture—to each his own nature, there is no crime in that. I had thought your nature was different."

"If you had allowed me to explain the why and wherefore of it, you would not have condemned me."

She shook her head impatiently. "What for? . . . Words cost so little!"

Just then three soldiers approached carrying torches, leading the way for two dark-robed men whose grave, upright carriage betrayed their calling at first sight. Rigueur stood up quickly, dropping the cloak on to the pile of timber, and prostrated herself reverently before them; then she followed the little procession into the tent.

A minute later Raymond-Jourdain appeared with one of the Count's chaplains. The priest was carrying the chalice, covered with a square of black silk, and was trying not to run; he was red and breathless, his hair soaking wet, and his white habit stained with blood and vomit. Raymond-Jourdain showed no surprise at seeing his friend. There were black rings round his eyes and his mouth was sagging. He said: "Are we in time?" Roger did not answer, and gripped the other's shoulders with both hands.

There were no sung Masses or *Requiems*, but the priests would say a short prayer out of kindness. Labourers dug the graves behind the tents, those of the Catholics on one side and those of the heretics on the other; there were eighteen in all. A tolling bell and a melancholy chanting could be heard from the castle, where the defenders were burying their own dead. A white flag had been raised as a sign of truce, but in the besiegers' camp, carpenters and joiners were already at work once more, since the siege tower must be repaired as quickly as possible. The Crusaders, drawn to the ramparts by the sound of hammering and axe blows, shouted that this was a breach of the truce and called the workmen heretics and blasphemers. Permission was given them to descend into the moat to look for the bodies of their friends, because the smell of carrion was attracting flies.

Roger found Bérenger d'Aspremont weary, suffering from fever and boils on every part of his body, but still courageous. "If God wills, we shall rid the country of them before next

156

spring. When we have recaptured Auterive, the way will be open to Pamiers; when they have nothing left but Carcassonne, the Queen will finally have to summon them back to France." Queen Blanche received scant respect among the Count's knights, fair and noble lady though she was. They credited her with all the vices of Jezebel, and because she had made peace with the Count of Champagne, they said she had bought it at the price of her body (which was not improbable, considering that Count Thibaut was young and courteous, and famed for his love songs). "This lady," they said, "is shamefully disgracing her high lineage in order to obey the counsel of an evil priest: by making war on her mother's own nephew she is dishonouring herself. It is not love of God, or of the Church, which has brought her to this, but much rather the love of a man who in this infamous fashion is serving the Church. Because the cardinal-deacon is well known for his handsome face and pretty manners."

"When we have recaptured Auterive," they said, "only the knights, and those squires who are of noble family, shall have their lives spared. What would our men and the burghers say, if we spared the prisoners?" Bérenger was one of those who disliked seeing prisoners slaughtered and he said: "What is the good of taking their lives, when it is quite enough to cut off their right hands? They too have wives and mothers." (Roger was to be amazed on more than one occasion by the innate gentleness of the man, though in battle he fought with greater fury than others.) "Not so: a man who is mutilated seeks someone to avenge him, one who is dead is soon forgotten."

These Frenchmen were proud soldiers, almost as brutal as the Basques. When they took a prisoner they would dismember him alive on the castle walls, in full view of the whole camp, crying out: "*Thus we shall deal with every one of you!*" The camp was not so far off that they could not see or hear. ". . . Rigueur, why do you stay and watch such a thing? Do you not see enough blood as it is?" She was standing at the entrance to her tent, deathly pale, and upright as a waxen taper.

"I shall never see enough to understand. Why should it frighten me? They did it to my father. It is compassion, not cruelty, that makes me watch." She was sad that evening, as though dazed, and unable to eat or to attend to the injured. Roger went to her in her tent, since he no longer made any

157

attempt to hide his longing to see her, and it occurred to no one to suspect them.

She had grown thinner and harder. She still wore the same dress of heavy, dark grey wool, with a small, white veil held in place by a plain, black ribbon, instead of a coif. Her finger nails were raw and blistered permanently now, and her grey eyes, heavily underlined by chestnut-coloured shadows, were bright spots in her tanned face.

"Rigueur, you have changed. You are driving yourself too hard."

"I have been brought up to hardship from a child. It is because of you that I have changed."

"I did not think," Roger said, "you had time to think of me."

"Do you take me for some wanton creature? I have loved you as no one ever loved before. You men are not circumscribed by modesty or custom, and can bear such griefs more easily."

"You understand nothing of this, Rigueur. To console me, I would have to have a woman who resembled you in every way: who had your voice, your thoughts, and your heart. Tell me where I can find her?"

A little smile lifted the corners of her lips, austere but without anger. "Don't look for her. No woman with my thoughts and my heart would forgive you for your offence against her."

"Let me speak to you, let me justify myself in your eyes!"

"Ah, Roger," she said, shaking her head and brushing her hand across her brow. "I have found excuses for you myself. I have pleaded your cause against myself like an old lawyer. And I lost the case. Listen, I am going to tell you something. A certain knight loved a lady with a loyal passion (the lady's name, you should know; it is not I). Then, one fine day, he slapped this lady in public, and spat on her, and called her the most vile names. What would you say such a man deserved?"

"To be shunned."

"Not so, because he told his judges that he had never ceased to be faithful and had acted only under compulsion and necessity; indeed, further, that he had done it with the intention of serving the lady's own best interests. I don't know whether the judges would condemn him, but the lady considered herself soiled for ever."

Roger said softly: "Your story is not true."

"Yes it is, because the knight further claimed that several

158

other lovers of this lady behaved in the same way, and remained her faithful servants. As a result, the judges acquitted him, thinking that the lady no doubt deserved such treatment."

"Rigueur, who are these judges? Who has the right to judge us?"

She sat still, her head thrown back and her hands clasped round her knees; and she spoke, fiercely, her lips trembling and her voice choked with tears. "Roger, what is this? If we have the right to do and say anything at all, then what are we fighting for? Should our men watch our bishops burned and then go and hear sermons in secret? Should the Count sell his best friends, while promising them protection against his own stewards? You say '*I lied only with my tongue, not in my heart*'—but how are we different from the beasts if what our tongues say has no meaning?"

"When will you stop tormenting me? I could not do otherwise."

She sighed, stood up, and bade her old serving woman draw a cup of wine. "Drink," she said, "you shall not go away fasting, for all that."

"After you, my lady."

She took the cup and he could see her lips were quivering as she drank a sip and wiped her mouth with the back of her hand. "It is odd," she said, in an altered voice, "how it hurt me when you called me my lady. Roger, if I have hurt you, it was out of love."

"What kind of love? You used to say once that you would drink molten lead rather than hurt me."

She spoke to the old woman. "Go, Guiraude. Leave us. I will call you later." The old woman bowed and went out. Rigueur sat down on the coffer, her chin on her clasped hands, thinking.

"You see," she said, "Bérenger would never have done the thing you did. And he too would have told me: 'I could not behave otherwise'. The upright man can never be anything but upright, the false man anything but false."

He shrugged. "Haven't you known me for a long time? What kind of love is that, to turn away from me at the first lapse?"

She said: "Roger, you are the Devil, I have always known it. From the moment I first saw you. The Devil is not the wickedness of horns and fangs, but the weakness of the flesh. Lust, covetousness and vanity. I was a woman without a husband,

159

and easily seduced. The Devil tempted me with your handsome face, because I was too proud of my own virtue."

"The Devil could also be a want of charity," said Roger, because such harsh words gave him the sensation of being wounded in the thing he held dearest.

She drew herself up, and her eyes were shining as though this reproach gave her more pleasure than pain. "What do you say to me?" she asked, her voice quivering with defiance. "I am well aware I lack charity, and always have done. I am possessed by more devils than you, but at least I can call them by their proper names."

"That hardly makes any difference to me. Are you going to punish me all your life for a fault I committed against my will?"

"I have punished myself more than I have punished you," she said. "Leave me now, for never again shall I be able to believe a word you tell me."

There were several women in the camp, attending on the heretic ministers and caring for the sick and wounded, and such was the respect in which they were held, even by men most lost to God, that it was not even necessary for them to have an armed escort when they walked by the common soldiers' bivouacs. The best loved of them all, because of her courage and her cheerful eloquence, was Gentian d'Aspremont. Her usual companions were Hélis de Roquevidal and the lovely Saurine, Bérenger's mistress. (This despite the fact that Saurine was very young and the mother of a six month old baby; but Gentian did not wish it said of her husband: "He takes the wench with him for his pleasure and to attend on his personal wants." Saurine must occupy the position suitable to the mistress of a man of good repute. For her part, the girl revered Gentian and imitated her in all things.)

As dusk fell the ladies would assemble in a thicket beside a tall oak tree which had been struck by lightning. There, the reverend Gaucelm, an old minister, now bent and hoary, who was famed for his gift of healing, would conduct prayers with the help of two other ordained heretics. Only a dozen or so of the knights attended the sermons, but there was always a crowd of common soldiers, who were superstitious fellows and believed that prayer would help them to escape the Crusaders' missiles. Some of the camp followers came too, standing a little apart, and divided from the men by a barrier of stakes, and the ladies often had considerable trouble from them because there are no more turbulent and troublesome creatures than women of this type. It was because she was talking to one of these women that Gentian one day found herself involved in an argument with one of the Count's personal clerks, a canon named Jean de Marcenac, who reproached her for seeking to turn simple souls away from the true faith. She told him: "You are a kingdom divided against itself, since you must betray either your Church, or your country and your liege lord. As you have not gone over to the Crusader's camp you must mean well in your heart, and you are like the son who tells his Father: 'I will not go', yet obeys none the less."

Jean de Marcenac replied that he would not stand by while a woman who was not even an ordained heretic herself accused him of heresy.

The next day, while the knights were holding council in his tent, the Count beckoned Bérenger d'Aspremont to his side, and said to him: "Bérenger, you have a wife who does you great credit."

Bérenger was well aware what this meant, and answered: "That is true, my lord. Moreover you are aware of the district and the parentage she comes of."

"Never," said the Count, "will I prevent any man of my country from living according to his faith."

"So we all hope, my lord, with all our hearts."

"Never," the Count reiterated, "will I permit myself to reproach a lady, even if she were to do or say something which might wrong me."

"My lord, if there is a man or woman amongst us who could wrong you, it would be through ignorance or misunderstanding. You know that we would willingly give our lives for you and for your rights."

"I should not," said the Count, "wish it to be said in the camp, and among those close to me, that a man in my service is a traitor to the Catholic faith."

"My lord," Bérenger said bitterly, "the Pope says it so loudly, and the legate and the bishops, too, and all the Frenchmen with them, that it is hardly surprising if even amongst ourselves there are people simple enough to believe it. I am not a Catholic, but if I were I should feel greatly distressed."

"Then you should understand," the Count said coldly, "that

161

I too am distressed. And I wish there to be only love and friendship among those who serve me, let them be Catholics or heretics as they please, or Jews or Greeks, because that is God's business, not mine."

After this call to order, Bérenger was obliged to go and find his wife in her tent, and advise her to make herself less conspicuous. He repeated what the Count had said to him, word for word. She said: "I have shown no lack of love or friendship for anyone. The clerk provoked me, and I spoke nothing but good words in answer to him. Is it freedom to forbid people to speak their minds?"

"My dear, if things were going badly for the Count, they would be less polite about their manner of forbidding you."

"Ah! We are fighting," she said, "what else do they want of us? Are we fighting so that we may all be taken for Catholics?"

"We are fighting to protect his inheritance," said Bérenger.

She stood bracing herself against the tent pole, her head down, twisting her hands.

"Bérenger, one day he will sell us for the sake of peace."

"That is an ugly thing to say."

"I don't like to see you lying to yourself when you know perfectly well no Catholic is ever to be relied on. The best of them already think of themselves as Galahads and Percivals if they only half betray us."

"My dear, the Count has no one to betray. He has promised us on his father's coffin that he will not wrong us."

"As if you did not know what a promise means in these days! It is a deal. Promises can be made to everyone, but as for keeping them, that is a matter of waiting for the best offer."

Bérenger sank wearily on to the bales of straw at the entrance to the tent and hid his face in his hands. "You are a hard woman, you always have been. You know quite well what my opinion is. Am I a child? But let me tell you that even if he should betray us I will bear him no grudge, because for me a vow has never been something to be bought and sold. We have fought for so long at his side, and stormed so many castles and liberated so many cities, that he is like our father and our son to us."

"Why," Gentian was thinking, "can I not comb his hair for him, and bring him water to wash his face and hands! Only his mistress has the right to serve him, and I, even out of simple, fraternal affection, would not dare lay hands on him, so far have

I lost the habit!" Yet this roughly awakened tenderness for a man she no longer wished to make love to her troubled her. She thought: "*What ill fortune has made the only man who was ever close to me in heart and mind take this sudden aversion to my body? Was this, then, a sign destined to show me that I shall never find joy in the marriage according to the flesh? A cruel sign, and a bitter trial it has condemned me to!*" She moved and sat down next to Bérenger, humbly, and began questioning him about his health, about his young child, whom he kept in the tent close to him, with Saurine and the nurse—being unable to have the two eldest with him in the course of this campaign he had become greatly attached to the youngest. "The boy is always laughing during the day and cries all night," he said. "But I think he is getting used to the noise, the sound of shooting no longer frightens him. We will have to change his nurse when we have taken the castle, because this one wants milk."

Gentian listened and nodded, resigned, like a grandmother, and at the same time troubled: how great is the longing inside us to clasp to our breasts these little bundles of warm tender flesh! There was a pain in her bosom and she pressed her two hands to her breasts. Breasts which could not die, which still hungered for bites and kisses. A hunger exacerbated by tenderness and compassion, until she died in anguish at the thought: "Tomorrow, the next day, will be the battle; we know what they do to prisoners, and I shall never conquer this fear inside me. . . . Knowing him so close, my whole body burns as though he were a child I carried in my womb." She forgot Bérenger and his friends, it seemed to her as though in all the camp only one man was vulnerable, one alone, her own flesh. "This life is too hard for me," she said. "*I think this is the last time I shall follow the army with you. I do nothing but cause trouble for you and I am exposed to too many temptations.*"

Bérenger looked at her in surprise. He had never heard her complain. He thought she must be ill, because her cheeks were burning and her eyes big and darkly shadowed. He said to her: "God keep you, I will not force you to this life. When we have taken the castle, I shall give you an escort to conduct you to Toulouse or Mirepoix, or wherever you please."

The day before the assault on the castle, the Count had a great procession round the camp with all his knights on horseback, wearing surcoats of embroidered silk over their armour. Flags were waving, helmets adorned with fresh plumes and lances with coloured ribbons and ladies' sleeves. The Count forbade all games of chance on that day, and had the whores placed in an enclosure which they were not allowed to leave until the attack was over; and it was decided that no wine should be permitted to the men except at daybreak, in a double ration with the morning meal. *"Let those who want to, pray, and the others remain quiet, for if we do not march into the place tomorrow we shall have to leave, or else dig trenches all round our camp, because Humbert de Beaujeu is sending a thousand men from Carcassonne to relieve Auterive."*

On the walls, the defenders were raising a new assault tower thirty feet high, with mangonels of such long range that all that part of the camp within their angle of fire had to be hurriedly evacuated. To get a better view of the preparations for the combat, the ladies had climbed up to the Count's tents, which were in such a position as to command a view of the entire camp at one glance, ditches, palisades, and the defences on the ramparts.

"I think that wooden tower, over there, looks dangerous," said Lady d'Aspremont, "and will surely cause us trouble in the attack on the gate." The other ladies—they were fifteen in all, several among them old and wise and expert in the art of warfare —began discussing the best method of taking this tower, since it did not look easy to set it on fire.

"—And how can it be attacked without movable towers or a covered gallery? It is so well guarded that it would be folly to hope to take it by using ladders and close fighting." These remarks, it may be said, were not falling on deaf ears. The knights who had accompanied the ladies were listening to their comments without enthusiasm, because they were well aware they lacked arms and men for a properly managed assault. Roger, therefore, went up to Lady d'Aspremont and asked her: *"Do you wish me to swear that I will either be the first to capture that tower, with six of my men, or die in the attempt?"*

"Not with six men, or with twenty," she said. "I desire no vows."

He wanted to tell her that she was as beautiful as a king's sword, and that there was not a man in the camp but would willingly have sworn such an oath, not to please her, but to do her honour. He was amazed at the art and cunning women had in changing their faces at the same time as their clothes and by painting their eyes and their cheeks. That day, dressed in a gown of heavy silk with an almond green cloak flung over her shoulder and silver bands encircling her head and neck, she was more than beautiful. Only the day before he had seen her so pale and tired! That evening all the ladies had dressed in their best, and adorned themselves to delight the eyes, so that the men would be proud of them and say: "How could we fail to fight well? The others have no such noble women in their land."

. . . How much more proud, and more cruelly touched, must be the man who could say: "Others see only the rind of this lovely thing, but I know the taste of it; where they behold silken folds and an embroidered girdle, I see her soft skin and those infinitely precious hidden graces which a woman would rather die than reveal to a man, unless she loves him. . . ." The better she is decked and guarded by her garments, the greater is the wish to have her defenceless. Her warmth, her softness, her smell, her savour, all these things which belong to one person alone, can so much wealth be allowed to waste in idleness?

"I have scant hope of pleasing you, my lady, but I will make this vow here and now, so that, if God wills, you may be praised through me." As he spoke, Roger knelt and placed his hand on a clump of dry grass at the lady's feet. "I swear, on this earth, which your feet have touched, before these ladies here and these noble gentlemen, may I be called a coward if tomorrow I do not take at least three mangonels on that tower, with two squires and four Basque soldiers to second me!"

As he spoke in a loud voice, Lady de Miramont, the eldest of the ladies present, moved towards them with her friends and said: "This is a severe vow, but one which merits consideration. Since the Lord of Layrac wishes it so, we shall choose a courtly arbiter to follow the combat and say whether the vow has been well kept, or, if not, whether some impediment has intervened for which the knight is not to blame."

"Four Basques," said Lady de Cissac, "do not seem to me to be enough, and the Lord of Layrac would not be failing in his promise if he took seven."

Engagements of this nature are quickly made on the eve of a hard battle, and two knights—Bernard de Portal and Pons d'Arsac—approached to say that all the honour of such an enterprise should not go to the Lord of Layrac, but that the two of them, also, with four men apiece, would swear to capture the other mangonels (four in all) and the arbiter should only have to decide who first set foot on the tower. They pledged themselves, for the honour of their ladies and of all the ladies present, and for Jesus Christ, not to descend from the wall until the castle had been taken. *"Amen,"* said Roger. "For Toulouse and Jesus Christ. There is no man in our camp who does not fight for Jesus Christ." (The two knights were heretics and considered Catholics only a little above mercenaries.)

Gentian had not said a word, either of approval or censure. Her long hands, in the black gloves, were clasped tightly against her breast, and her face was drawn and bloodless.

That evening, after prayers, it was she who sought out Roger and said to him: "What are you doing? I hate you."

"What wrong have I done you?"

"You know very well. Must I pray God for you to be a coward?"

"Why, Rigueur? I have a good chance of success. You don't know my Navarrese; with plenty of drink inside them, those lads will leap into a flaming cauldron."

"That position is so well defended," she said, "you will be killed before you have fixed your ladder."

Roger congratulated himself on the success of his manœuvre (this was the first time he had ever felt a wish to make her suffer) but out of habit he endeavoured to reassure her, saying that it was nothing, that the defenders were manning their machines only with sick men while the bulk of their chivalry would bear down on the west wall. . . .

They had left the path and were walking among sparse trees beside the wooden palisade. They had been forgotten in the fever of this battle eve. In the distance they could see the fires on the ramparts, the pale blurs of the tents, the camp fires scattered over the plain and the lines of wooden towers and palisades standing out in the moonlight as black shadows against the grey earth. Torches were moving about between the tents while up above, on the towers, the defenders were exchanging signals. Behind the ditch on the other side of the palisade, crickets were chirping in the grass on a cleared slope where only a few thorn bushes and partly broken saplings had been left standing.

They passed a sentry who called out: "Who goes there?" Roger gave the password, and the man responded with a short,

deep laugh, like a horse neighing. Rigueur said: "We are mad.
It is late and you need a good eight hours' sleep."

"I shall not sleep unless I am with you. Rigueur, will you let
me fight without admitting me to your friendship once more?"

Her voice breaking, as though in a scream, she said: "What
friendship!"

Another sentry passed them, calling: "Greetings! May you
have profit and pleasure!" "Thanks," Roger answered. "I wish
you as much for tomorrow."

A white, three-quarters moon was gliding slowly above the
castle among small clouds like a flock of white sheep. Towards
the ramparts, a huge glowing fire was still burning in the camp
forge, and from it came the sound of a hammer striking the
anvil.

A goat, fastened to a stake, was browsing near a pair of
enormous haystacks. Behind the stacks loomed piles of felled tree
trunks, ready to be made into palisades and siege engines and
smelling of fresh earth and resin. It was dark in the shadow of
the trunks and the ground was covered with sawdust and wood
shavings. Roger said *"Here"*, and spread his cloak on the ground.

And at that moment he seemed to feel no love or mercy, only
mingled desire and a furious need to hurt. He was thinking:
*"I'll make you sorry for what you did to me, I'll make you weep and
laugh for joy, I'll make you say so many things that you will never
recover from this night, whatever may happen to me tomorrow. . . ."*

But he had no sooner touched her, no sooner discovered again
the taste of her mouth and the warmth of her lips, than all his
anger was forgotten; it was as though a dyke had burst in his
heart, carrying him away in a warm torrent—his throat was full
of sobs and so many tears that no woman ever wept more. The
moon had gone down long ago, and still they were not asleep,
they had so much lost time to make up for. They did not even
speak of the morrow, it was as though they were to die before
the dawn.

The sky was white and in the beleaguered city the bells were
ringing for early Mass, and the air was freezing. Dew was
mingled with sweat in their hair, dew on their clothes and on the
bark of the trees; and in the pale light faces were invisible but
for the blue of eyes and the shadow of a mouth. They heard the
sentries' voices and the cries of water carriers, and the neighing

of the beasts as they were watered and trumpets sounding the call to the morning meal. It was then that one longed for sleep, then one would have given one's life for an hour's sleep. This is what is called happiness. To be hungry, thirsty, sleepy and to think: "God! Nothing is more beautiful than those felled tree trunks and this brown woollen cloak, except this small pale head with the black hair." (There was not one chance in three of escaping alive, and it is on such mornings, such clear, cruel mornings, the smallest crop of dew makes a man's heart feel like a holiday, especially when he comes fresh from a sweetheart's arms!) "My life, it is time. My men must be waiting for me."

"I shall hardly have seen your face again."

"This evening," he said, "we shall be inside the castle in the great hall of the keep, and you will be at the ladies' table, with silver chandeliers to light you."

She was slowly lacing up the cord which fastened the two sides of her gown. "Why didn't you kill me, last night? I wish the Count would change his mind and sound the retreat."

He thought: "Surely she is the best of women, abandoning all pride in her fear for my body."

The tents were growing whiter, here and there pale fires were lit, and the camp was swarming with horses and men; while long files of soldiers were already dragging ladders and rams and faggots of wood towards the moat.

"We shall be seen," said Roger. "Let us part here."

"Roger, I did not allow you an hour's sleep last night."

"What do I want with sleep?" He shrugged, he felt like singing. "Let them up there," he said, turning his head towards the castle, "spend their night sleeping or praying, since they have nothing better to do. But we have a better comfort. When the sun touches that tower above the moat, I shall be up there already, just as I am: you will know my men by their red shirts."

Roger was relying much more on his men than on himself, because he was not, in all honesty, feeling in a state to accomplish prodigies of valour. While his armour was being put on him he studied the four Basques whom their Captain had selected for him: they were the best age, neither young nor old—about thirty—with ten years' campaigning experience in Aragon and the Carcassès; tall, broad-chested, with legs like chapel pillars; plying the hook and the mace with the speed of jugglers. "*A silver piece for each man, over and above his wages! If you don't deserve it today you'll never need it again.*" The men laughed; their captain had made them just sufficiently drunk. Roger drank a cup himself before setting out to join his comrades in front of Count Raymond's tents.

The knights of Toulouse, on horseback, with shields raised and banners waving, advanced towards the ramparts, the Count at their head, to the roll of drums. The Count of Foix's men attacked near the bridge, waiting for the Count of Toulouse to give the signal before launching their attack on the breach made by the machines' firing (the wall hereabouts being so badly damaged that the Crusaders had to keep half their forces there). Up on the ramparts the mangonels were still holding their fire, and the Count said: "A good sign, my friends, they are short of ammunition. *For Christ and the Virgin! Let each man think of his sins.*" He raised his sword and the trumpets sounded, while a cry rang through the ranks of soldiers like a gust of wind; one after another the knights lowered their lances before the Count and the altar on which reposed the relic of St. James, and moved away to ride to their battle stations.

. . . Roger and his squires leaped down from their horses ten paces from the moat where the Basques were waiting for them, clad in red, with leather helmets, and their studded maces over their shoulders. All along the ditch, teams of sappers, protected by mobile screens made of wood soaked in water, were turning wooden faggots and barrowloads of earth into the muddy water. A few arrows whistled past and one of the men assigned to the ladders fell, struck in the eye, nearly toppling his comrades. And the battle began. The mangonels were now firing to such purpose that the Count had about twenty Aragonese hurried up with one of the rams to act as a target to draw the fire, and allow the ladders to be put in place.

Roger made for the ditch with his two squires and the Navarrese; who were singing as they marched, in their outlandish tongue, some sweet and mournful song which brought tears to the eyes. Heaved upwards by twenty men, the ladder rose, tottered backwards, then crashed against the wooden sides of the tower with all the force of its hooks. Arrows were whistling round them. Roger yelled: "No time to lose, lads!" and climbed up first, holding his shield above his head. (The swifter Basques were much better at this job, but custom demanded that the leader go

169

first. And after climbing quickly, in full armour with the additional weight of a shield and a thirty-pound battle-axe, a man reached the top somewhat out of breath.)

Moreover, in order to keep the ladder against the supports, and avoid being flung off, you had to work with the axe until your arms were near breaking and your hands skinned. Once a footing had been gained on the wall, the problem became not to go straight over the other side, since there was such howling and shouting for every man who gained a footing that he had ten grapnels and ten swords about him at once.

The Navarrese were already closing in on the mangonel tower, roaring and bellowing, with arrows sticking out of their helmets, and their maces dancing at arm's length so fast that each man seemed to have not merely one but two. (There was nothing to match the strength and fury of these men: the French feared them so greatly that they flayed them alive when they could and used their skins to protect their engines.) For a knight this was a bad moment, because he would have to fight against ten, men leaving their posts and rushing at him, each eager for the honour of finishing him off and getting his armour. His axe must fly left and right, before and behind, with both arms, commending himself to God. "*Yield, dog of a heretic, unless you want your friends to get a present of your head by noon!*"

When it is a case of saving his skin every man becomes as valiant as Roland and Oliver, because after the promise he had made Roger was denied the right of surrender. Setting his back against the timbers of the tower, he wielded his axe like a butcher gone mad, thinking: "Lord, if I get out of this alive I'll become a Carthusian monk!" He could not see for the sweat running into his eyes, and he could feel his axe losing speed: later he learned that a pike thrust had slashed his right arm, but at the time he had not realised this. He only saw the two halberds which menaced him draw disturbingly nearer, recoiled and lost his footing.

The next day the Counts raised camp and fell back on Toulouse: Humbert de Beaujeu was bringing up reinforcements and the army was in danger of being caught between two fires. The knights were beginning to say: "This is foolishness, we shall never win back an inch of land from them. God grant we can keep what we have left." They blamed the Count for over-carelessness. Humbert de Beaujeu arrived with fire raisers and

Aragonese, pillaging towns and firing vineyards; it was more profitable to harry him in small bands than to waste time laying siege to a castle. Two knights and a fair number of soldiers had been killed during the attack.

Roger never saw any of his Navarrese except one again. He himself, taken out of the moat with superficial wounds, could sit his horse more or less, and supervised the preparations for departure and the embarcation of his gear. The empty, wrecked camp looked like a turned up anthill in which the last ants were still scurrying about dragging eggs twice as big as themselves —sacks, chests and bales of hay were piled up on the river bank, and thickened to a solid mass near the barges, where the haulers were shouting that there was enough to sink their boats and they had never carried such cargoes.

The Count went by road in a splendid cavalcade, with his gaily caparisoned horses, banners flapping in the wind, and drums beating. The nobles moved off in their turn, in long convoys, some through the fields and some by the water meadows, while bands of soldiers followed the river bank shouting and singing. The camp was struck in the tired but happy chaos usually associated with a fairground; terrified cattle trotted between the convoys of carts, jostling the beggars and stragglers. The barges slowly left their moorings, to the hoarse, measured cries of the boatmen. They quitted the castle of Auterive as though there had never been any question of taking it; they were going to find a camping ground elsewhere.

"And, God, how quickly the greatest happiness and the greatest dangers are forgotten! Only yesterday morning . . . yesterday morning, before noon, I was enduring such anguish that with all my heart I would have changed places with a leper, and no sooner was I out of the ditch than I was not even pleased: my whole body cut and bruised and shaken, and an inordinate rage in my heart, into the bargain. Why did we start the assault if it was only to sound the recall at noon? The losses are not great, but, small loss by small loss, it begins to add up." Roger mourned bitterly for Guillaume, his second squire, and the three Basques, killed so stupidly—and but for the vow he had made he would never have considered mounting the wall at such a bad place.

Stupidly dead, a swift, agile squire, still young, and Navarrese such as were no longer to be found in the land, wasted, thrown away for two mangonels that were not likely to do us much harm anyway, seeing that we were already almost out of range. . . . Small success, small failure, and on the march once more; and the day before everything had seemed so important that they might have thought themselves laying siege to Carcassonne instead of Auterive, and thus it was every time. They worked themselves into a fury, as they had been doing for ten years, for eighteen years, and there was no end to it.

Roger reflected also that he had not gained his point with Rigueur, and that he would still have to plead for a long time— she is like a city, he thought, which has opened its gates under threats; and whoever enters such a city sees his banners thrown down as soon as his back is turned. There is barely time to go in and out, and we no longer have the time for such combats. All he could see was an occasional glimpse of her green cloak appearing round a bend in the road, among the string of riders travelling under the Aspremont banner. Raymond-Jourdain de Cissac rode up to him and asked after his wound; his eyes were red and his face swollen, and his perpetual rather weary smile was wearier and sadder than ever. He was taking his brother's body back to Toulouse. "We are lucky," he said. "We can bury our dead on our own land; unlike them. What wouldn't I give to be able to fight on their land one day!"

The Count of Foix departed to fight in his own lands, where he had accounts to settle with Guy de Montfort, and Count Raymond continued in the direction of the Albigeois, because there were several great castles in that province which had sent secret delegations to him in his camp with letters from stewards and castellans: "We will deliver the place up to you with the garrison and with the names of all traitors, so long as you have a strong enough army to man our outer walls." As far as promising went, the Count was always promising: the army was not large and the common mercenaries badly paid; it was safer to take them to the Albigeois rather than allow them to revictual themselves in the country round Toulouse. The army advanced in slow stages, dispersing on the journey like beads dropped from a rosary: some departed to visit their own lands, others hunted after Crusaders at the hazard of chance encounters. There were occasions when the Count found his entire escort consisted of only ten knights, and his regiment of Aragonese, who had been following him for so long that they were more devoted than men sworn to his service.

The Count was encamped near Lombers when messengers arrived bringing the news of Labécède. He was so afflicted by it that he did not leave his tent for the whole of that day, since he said the people of Labécède would not have held out for so long if they had not been expecting the aid he had promised them; and because the siege was so hard, the reprisals were hard too— all able bodied men, burghers and soldiers alike, died by the rope or the sword. "My friends," the Count said, "if they do such things in order to make those who wish to keep faith turn away from me, how shall we last out until the winter?" The barons of the Count's suite—heretics and Catholics alike—agreed that a fresh letter must be written to the Pope. "To my immeasurable distress and the deep grief of my heart," wrote the Count, "I find myself compelled to bear arms against the soldiers of my lord and cousin Louis, the ninth of that name, in order to safeguard the lives and property of my subjects. God forbid that I should believe my cousin Queen Blanche, and my cousin the King, who is an innocent child, capable of condoning such actions! May those who keep them in ignorance receive the just payment for their treachery! May it please His Holiness, our beloved Father Gregory, in his paternal goodness, to examine this matter and see whether it is just for Catholics to suffer martyrdom in their thousands on account of a few cursed heretics, of whom, but for this war, their lawful *seigneurs* would long ago have purged the land. . . ."

The Pope received many such letters, brought by messengers who did not come via the See of Narbonne: the letters reached Rome safely, and the Papal palace, but were certainly not delivered into the Pope's hands, since he was surrounded by declared enemies of the Count of Toulouse.

At Lombers, Roger received a letter from his wife in Toulouse. Guillelme did not write well, never having received instruction in courtly manners, but to say what she had to say, she was as competent as any other.

To my dear and well-beloved lord and husband, Roger de Montbrun and Layrac, greetings and success in all his undertakings. Dearest Lord, today I received news of Layrac, from Jourdain-Jean de Villemur, who came here expressly to beg me to intercede with you regarding a matter with which you are as well acquainted as I. The knights who hold the castle can no longer exist without you, given the fact that they have closed

173

their gates to Herbert de Vitry who has come with twenty men-at-arms and burned the corn in the mills outside the village of Magnanac; furthermore, this same Herbert has carried a complaint against you to the King's seneschal in the city of Albi and denounced you as guilty of heresy, and doubly traitor to the King because you made a false submission last year, and made your men swear fealty to the seneschal, while you yourself, far from seeking to obtain the raising of the sentence of excommunication pronounced against you, aggravated your perfidy by bearing arms against Christ's army.

Whereupon, Jean-Rigaud de Marcillac, who holds the castle of Layrac in your place, made answer by letter to the seneschal that you were guilty of no fault but were utterly devoted to the King and the Church; and that if you were constrained to bear arms in the Count's forces, it was in dissimulation and the better to help undo the said Count's evil designs. The seneschal refused to believe this, at least unless you presented yourself in person at Albi to do homage into the King's own hands (in the person of the seneschal) and stayed at Layrac without leaving it, or unless you left him (the seneschal) a suitable hostage at Albi. Failing which, he will denounce you as a traitor to the See of Montauban, and send Herbert de Vitry, with such men as he needs, to occupy the castle of Layrac in the name of the king; and he adds that since you and I are excommunicated and deprived of all rights to hold the said lands, there shall be no injustice in giving these lands to Herbert de Vitry in fief.

It is for you to decide what you should do, and whether you can find a way of preserving our rights. Know, further, that our son Pierre is well and his legs are straighter now, and that he talks as well as a child of his age can talk, and rather better; and that our son Raymond is also well, although he has had a milk fever for three days. And if God wills, we shall have a boy or a girl at Christmas and it is for this reason that I am unable to come and see you myself to discuss our affairs. Know, too, that your father and brother and your nephews are well, except that they are grieved by the bad news we receive more often than is pleasant. But we are all in good heart.

Your very loving and devoted servant and companion, Guillelme de Layrac.

Roger wept with fury when he received this letter, and going to find the Count in the orchard, where he was resting at the entrance to his tent, showed him the letter without a word. The Count frowned over it quizzically (Guillelme's writing was not of the most beautiful) and summoned his clerk to read the missive aloud to him. When the clerk had finished, Roger asked: "What should I do, my lord?"

"Go back to Toulouse," said the Count with a faint smile, "and bear your wife my congratulations on the good news she tells you: two sons already and a third child at Christmas! You are luckier than I."

"Do not make light of it, my lord. You know Herbert de Vitry, and evidently the seneschal knows him too, since by this threat he thinks he has me. Lands and castles may be retaken, but the dead can never be brought to life. This man has good reasons for desiring vengeance, and I cannot force my vassals to leave their lands with their wives and children, because I have not the wherewithal to support them."

"Do as you think best, Roger. You will not be the first, or the only one."

Roger reddened and drew himself up.

"I would rather give them my son!"

"Do not lose your temper; I did not mean to wound you. You ask my advice, but I can see no further ahead than you."

"My lord, if you were to come to Layrac yourself, even for one day, it would give the men there such joy that they would use their own guts for bowstrings rather than yield up the place!"

The Count smiled his gay, sardonic smile. "I am not Jesus Christ, to change my body into as many Hosts as the numbers of the faithful (may God forgive me the bad joke!) and I am already doing my best to be everywhere at once. When we have rid the country of the French, I shall not forget one of the men who have lost goods or relatives in our cause. My debt will be great; but still, should I be the worst of ingrates, if we win, no one shall have cause to be sorry for having served me!"

Roger said he would take steps to deal with the matter, kissed the Count's hand and withdrew. He set out for Carcassonne, intending to stop at Senouillac and visit the knight Manassé de Bury, who had regained his wife's heritage and held the castle for the past year.

As luck would have it, Manassé was at home. Roger found him on the ramparts busy supervising building operations. He gave Roger a smile of amusement and understanding: six years earlier he himself had been in very much the same situation as Roger, and could not be certain he would not be again. War is a perpetual see-saw. Then, Roger had arranged the release of two of his men without payment of ransom. "You see," Manassé said, indicating the burghers who were hauling sacks and barrels full of soil on to the mound, "how odd our task is. Today we are digging ditches, tomorrow we may have to fill them in and set to levelling the walls. Whatever a man does in this accursed land he is always in the wrong. We will never be able to recover our losses with the reinforcements the Queen is sending us!"

He took his visitor and his squire down to the castle hall, where the lady received them graciously. Her fair-haired young daughter—now nearly as tall as her mother—was standing beside her, blushing violently with her eyes on the ground. "Would you believe it," Manassé said laughingly, "she still remembers you! She was only just seven when she saw you at Carcassonne."

"That's hardly surprising, with my hair. And now she has become almost as lovely as her lady mother!" (Roger was not altogether pleased to meet young girls who remembered him too well: he was reaching the age when people begin to say of a man: "He must have been very handsome in his youth!")

"—I know," Manassé was saying, "I know how it is, it is not easy for you to break with your lawful lord."

"To be frank with you, sir knight, I am well aware that we shall never have peace with the Count. And I would prefer to hold my lands directly from the seneschal and not have to ruin myself in a war which does nobody any good. But see for yourself whether I can go to Albi with my vassals now and swear fealty to the seneschal in person? Because among his knights there is one, Herbert de Vitry, who I hope was never a friend of yours, since if he is your friend, it is useless my talking to you any longer."

"A friend?" Manassé said frowning. "No. But he is not my enemy either."

Thereupon, Roger launched into a passionate denunciation of Herbert de Vitry as a disgrace to French chivalry, the Church, the King, and all Christendom, and added that with men of his type there would never be peace and that as a result of this man's intrigues he, Roger, now found himself regarded with suspicion by the seneschal. Moreover this Herbert was such a treacherous knave that he, Roger, would never set foot in Albi so long as he remained in the seneschal's entourage. "The seneschal," he said, "had better not try and drive those *seigneurs* who are French and Catholic in their hearts too far, because though we love the King it is for the love of peace, not so that he can send our personal

176

enemies to ravage our lands, and be protected from our vengeance by the cross they wear! As true as God was born of a Virgin I shall never make my submission in a camp where my enemies are held in such high esteem!"

By the end Manassé de Bury could no longer understand what service was being asked of him, and Roger had talked so fiercely of his devotion to the King that in the end he almost believed in it himself. Finally, Manassé, convinced of his good faith, promised to intercede with the seneschal and make Herbert de Vitry keep quiet. Roger, for his part, promised to go to Toulouse and have a chest containing six pounds of silver pieces sent to Herbert de Vitry in good coin of Toulouse and thirty pieces of gold and a chestnut horse to Manassé de Bury. Then he took his leave, wondering desperately what he had left to sell. It had never been in his nature to plunder, except for the honest spoils won in battle.

"Séverin, my friend," he said to his squire, "if our bodies were worth as much to others as to ourselves, I would cut off my ears, and the flesh from my buttocks and the fat from my belly, for apart from that I have nothing left to give!"

Séverin, a taciturn lad, sighed and said nothing. (Roger had had him in his service for only six months, but he was already fond of him. He was twenty-five, broad-shouldered, keen-eyed, and, best of all, with a mild, even temper that was as calm under a hail of arrows as round a camp fire. They had still many joys and sorrows to share together and were never to be parted, except for reasons beyond their own control.)

At Toulouse, Roger was met with tears from Guillelme and reproaches from his father: it was not done to promise money when you had not got it, and the people of the Albigeois and the Crusaders seemed to think that Toulouse possessed the treasures of Golconda. Roger went off to seek his brother's father-in-law, Master Isaac Abrahamide, a man so wise and charitable that he was respected by the Jews of the city, despite his heresy. "Master Isaac, my very good lord, if you can't manage to get a loan on credit from your friends there will be nothing left for me but to hang myself on the first oak tree on the road to Montauban! I have drawn all I can from my lands; while the war lasts they will bring in nothing. In the spring we shall take enough goods from the Frenchmen for my share in the booty to be large enough to pay off my debt."

177

Master Isaac stroked his long grey curls thoughtfully and looked at Roger, his black eyes shining with sympathy between their brown lashes. "If it were Toulouse, sir knight, they would lend ten times as much on credit, at a low rate of interest, but Layrac is a long way off and there are no Jews in that part of the country."

"I will give them my eldest son as security. May I never see him again if my debt is not paid by Easter!"

"Would you have the heart," the old man exclaimed, "to part a young child from his mother for worldly considerations?"

"Master Isaac, this is only a matter of months. By Easter I shall have nothing more to fear from the seneschal, and he himself will be only too glad if the Count lets him depart with his arms and baggage."

"Do you really believe that?" asked the old man gently.

"I would rather die than not believe it!"

Master Isaac nodded his head slowly in the manner of the Jews. He was smiling sadly and his eyes were sad: he was one of those heretics who saw sin everywhere: what good is it to lose one's peace of mind by exchanging Lucifer for Beelzebub? Even if we have the King and Bishop Foulques in Toulouse, will we be a whit the further from God? These are only human affairs. (Later, the old man was to see that there was a vast difference between Beelzebub and Lucifer.)

"What have you done?" Pierre-Guillaume said to him. "How can you decide such a thing without consulting me? I can appreciate how a child old enough to understand can be given as a pledge, but Pierre is too young, he will pine!"

"You know very well I have no son old enough to understand, so what is the use of talking about it? He will have his nurse with him."

"You will let a child as delicate as he is," said the old man, "go and live with strangers?"

"Don't worry," Roger said bitterly, "he will be well looked after, would these people want to lose their money?"

Guillelme wept. Not too much, it must be admitted, because she was thinking more of her husband's interests than the child's happiness. "They will let me see him," she said. "I shall go every day, if I have to cross the city on foot!" Pierre was the prettiest child Roger had ever seen: his complexion was pale coral pink and his hair a red gold, so bright and delicate that in the twilight

178

it seemed to shine like a soft flame. Every feature of his face was already so perfectly formed that he resembled a handsome boy of fifteen in miniature. He was a lively child and would make Rachel and his grandfather laugh by repeating whatever they said. While his nurse was packing his tiny frocks and his dolls and wooden horses in a chest, he hung round her anxiously: "Why are you taking them all away from me? I haven't been a bad boy. I don't want you to hide my soldiers. I want to give them their dinner."

Roger took him on his knee and kissed him, but the child wrinkled up his nose and said: "You smell of wine." (This was true, and Roger was not often drunk. That day he had drunk until his head ached.)

"—Roger, how long will you leave the child with these Jews? Will we be any richer at Easter?"

"In the first city we liberate there will be booty enough from the property of traitors. If it is not Easter it will be Pentecost."

That night, Roger was at last able to rest in Guillelme's bed, though rest only in a manner of speaking. During the year and a half they had been living together Guillelme had fallen in love, somewhat more in love than was altogether proper for a lawful wife, though this was not entirely her fault. (And a pretty piece of folly it was to play at love with Guillelme, though to begin with he had been sincerely and even passionately involved.) "Ah! Would to God I was your concubine and could go with you everywhere and take care of you! . . . Who brushes your hair, and massages your body when you are campaigning? . . ."

"You know perfectly well that I am faithful to you," he told her. "Haven't we other things to worry about?"

"Roger, if that lady took you back again, I should die."

He had been fool enough one fine May night, when her pretty, soft white flesh had made him lose his head, to tell her more than he need have done about Rigueur: things a man says and forgets five minutes later, women remember all their lives.

But it is man's nature to like pepper and ginger better than fresh milk, to like rare, precious things, with a bitter taste, that burn like fire in the belly. (This, Rigueur, is to tell you that there is a long way between man and the beasts: you have a strange idea of people if you think the first little girl that comes along can make a man forget the woman he truly desires. If this were so there would be no more love on earth than apples on an olive tree.)

179

"If she took you back again I should die."

"Guillelme, let me tell you many people have said the same thing to me when I was young, and they are not dead, but have found faithful and courteous lovers."

"May God deny me salvation if I do the same! I shall still be faithful to you even when you are old. (What answer was there to that? That one is not too old at thirty-seven to feel the pangs of love? She, who was so proud of her lovely youth.)

"Roger, you haven't tried to see her, speak to her——?"

"No, I swear to you I have not." So, one swears falsehoods, not from cowardice or self-interest, but simply because it would do no good to do otherwise. But by the Virgin, it is better to take ten concubines than to be ensnared by a lawful wife whom one cannot dismiss, who bears children with red curtains in the windows and torches blazing before the house!

"When will you come to Toulouse again?"

"When the Count sees fit, my sweet. When he has driven the French back as far as Carcassonne many turncoats will tell him: "Our hearts have always been in your cause" and he will thank them for it without even a frown. But may he never have to thank me in that fashion!"

Roger met Manassé de Bury at Castres, and talked to him at considerable length of his wish to live at peace with the seneschal.

"I have seen him," said Manassé, "and he gave me his word not to put Herbert de Vitry in possession of the castle. But if for any reason it is not possible for you to come in person and pledge your lands to the King, he insists on sending twenty of his men to garrison the place in the King's name, and that your vassals must treat them properly and disobey them in nothing which may assist in its defence."

"*Amen*," said Roger. "I will give orders accordingly. And I assume that my men at Layrac will be treated as friends and not as enemies." Privately, he promised himself to make the twenty soldiers he was allowing to take possession of his property in this way pay dearly for the humiliation: they should wish they too had passed between the hammer and the anvil, like their comrades of seven years past. Only, pray God, let us drive the seneschal out of the Albigeois before Easter!

Lord God, is it permitted to hate like this—a hatred that is an ache in the heart and an ache in the belly, a hatred that takes the breath away? What have we done to them that they should come and suck our life's blood like this, year after year, every spring and every summer—with their northern speech and their red crosses and the way they eternally call themselves God's soldiers when they are pillaging houses and raping our women. When will they leave us alone? Is this a war? By the rights of war we had defeated them, and yet here they are claiming that anyone who resists them is a traitor and a thief. The Pope has decreed from his lofty seat that to be a good Catholic you must stand still and have your throat slit like a sheep.

Liars and thieves, may none of you ever see your own homes again! To our misfortune, we let them go, with their tails between their legs, without men or money, taking as their only treasure Count Simon's dead body. Amaury and his uncle Guy, and Guy de Lévis and Lambert de Thury and the rest, each one of whom deserved to be torn limb from limb and bone from bone, so that every village they devastated might keep a piece as a relic! We allowed them to depart, honourably, believing their shame to be punishment enough; and now here they are back again, telling us that we were the ones who stole from them the property they had first stolen from us. This time we shall not let one of them go, and when they are put to flight we shall lie in wait for them in the mountain passes! And those who surrender shall save their lives but not their limbs. We will not leave them one inch of our land, if we have to fight for another ten years.

Though we have to live and die under excommunication, we still prefer the enmity of such popes and bishops to their blessings.

"Suppose it were possible to fall as deep in hatred as in love, how many tortures should I not make that man suffer? When he lay sleeping in my arms it would have been easy for me to slit his throat with my dagger. But in those days I would have borne a thousand tortures myself to keep him safe. How could I not have known he was the serpent?"

"Ah! Béatrix," Gentian said aloud, "you were a bad counsellor to me! Did he offer you presents? Or were you jealous of my good name?"

Béatrix said: "You have always been violent in your speech."

"Unfortunately it is only in speech! He did not give you presents but can you swear you did not cherish a secret tenderness for him that made you plead his cause?"

181

"You are losing your memory. When did I plead his cause?"

"Didn't you say just what was needed to make me give way to my madness?"

"Indeed, you were mad," said Béatrix, "and anything that was said to you made your madness worse."

"Know that I do not blame you," said Gentian. "But my madness seems so great that I can't prevent myself from believing all those around me were afflicted by the same madness. Madmen see pieces of gold in the stones of the road, and take mules and cows for angels with shining wings, because they have lost control of their eyes. I was like that, and my affliction lasted several years."

The two women were at Mirepoix to celebrate Easter; but this was an Easter of war and the men attended sermons fully armed while on the city walls soldiers were busy strengthening fortifications and repairing mangonels. From the top of the towers they could look out over the burning countryside and at any moment expected to see the banners of the cross appear on the road from Pamiers.

Béatrix was pressed against the wooden parapet peering through an arrow slit, and trying to guess the source of the smoke which was spreading along the horizon. "They can't be far away," she said. "No, surely it is madness to hate one who is on our side."

"He is not of our faith, Béatrix. Once I thought we were all brothers. Now, I know that those people are worse than the Crusaders, because they protect us so long as it is in their interests and betray us when there is profit in betraying us."

"You are a child," said Béatrix, with her bitter-sweet smile, "if you think there are many men who don't think of their own profit above all else! But if we treat the Catholics like children of the Devil, they will betray us with less regret."

"They can do it, and gladly for me! And set us free of this spirit of prostitution. We have walked by devious paths, and we have loved our customs above our faith. We pray to God and we listen to the Word of the Lord, but the God we worship in our daily lives is Jehovah. Béatrix, is that not enough to drive one mad?"

"There is so much to drive one mad," said Béatrix, "that I shall not stay long in this world. As soon as the war is over I shall ask Monseigneur Guilhabert for permission to enter the community of Mirepoix on probation. It will be hard for me to leave you. But it is harder still to watch you living at my side tormented incessantly by the Devil. For over a year now, your friendship has been more bitter than wormwood to me."

Gentian studied her friend for a long time, with an effort, as though her eyes had to pierce through a thick veil in order to see her. She was literally enveloped in a veil of a suffering which cut her off from the world.

"I am sick with shame and anger," she said. "If I were silent the stones would speak. I mean, if I were silent my madness would burst out of me in some more unseemly manner."

During the sermon, Gentian stood among the other noble ladies and listened eagerly to the commentaries on Holy Writ. The Deacon delivering the address was speaking of the Vine, and of the branches which remain on the Vine, and those which are rejected and burned because they bear no fruit. "Lord, I have not remained in you, they have not let me remain in you, I wanted to but they would not let me. I was not a withered branch, I was torn away by force! I have been flung into the fire and burned. Lord, you seek out the strayed ewe, but what do you do for the burned shoot? I burn brighter and longer than the dry branches, my sap is still living and cries out in me . . . *Lord Jesus do not answer my prayer, Lord Jesus, do not hear my voice, Lord Jesus, ignore my agony, Lord Jesus, have no pity on me!*

"Lord Jesus, you know nothing of evil, do not let me soil your Name by a false prayer. For verily, I know nothing of you, except that I am cut off from you.

"I have committed no sin, for does the bird sin in flying? Satan created me with powerful wings and I have flown high and far in his red sky. Surely now I should step forward in the midst of this assembly and say: *'First let each one of us declare the manner in which he serves Satan!'* We are liars. We dare not reveal our bodies' nakedness, but that of our souls is much more dreadful, and before God himself souls hide themselves in garments of iron! I want to shout aloud my deepest desires and throw them from me, so that they may destroy themselves in the gaze of the Spirit like ashes dispersed by the wind."

But, as one stone in a building cannot begin to move by itself, so you are not free to follow your impulse, and Satan devours your soul in secret, for he is apt to deceive men and to flee the light which kills him he has invented shame.

"I was broken by my own folly, because I violated nature's law in me, not through God's grace but by my own will! And I could say to all the noble women of my country: I have done no wrong to Love. I have not taken my love in aversion through false modesty, pride, or fear of censure. Know, ladies, that my heart was so true I would have cried my love in the face of the world if the man had been what he should have been!

("He committed an ugly deed in the eyes of men, and I dared to judge him. I should have said: 'Everything he does is good.' He came back to me when he wanted to and bought me as one buys a prostitute, and did not even pay in advance, no, more than that, he used me, and went away without paying the price.)

"Can any lady answer this question? When a lover promises to accomplish an impossible deed or die, should he be blamed if he does not die? How happy I was when I learned he had escaped unharmed! But love is a madness, and that is why my love has turned to hate. You played me too cruel a trick, my friend, if you truly loved you would not have permitted yourself such a ruse.

"Am I an animal to be trained by fear? Tell me, all ladies in love, whether it is lawful to give oneself to a traitor and a liar? Wretched woman, you thought you had deceived Satan! He has fooled you easily enough. In your ignorance you took for true love what was merely the whim of a man without honour.

"He gave me no other proofs of love than one would bestow on a prostitute. He merely employed the words and manners suitable to a prostitute of my rank.

"Woman, who, since before the fall, has prostituted herself to the serpent, is a lamp of luxury, even in her virgin innocence. That is why she is despised; this man has known five hundred women and is unmarked by it, and he will know a hundred more, yet for him it will be a matter of little consequence. But you, with one man only, and deeply in love, you have prostituted yourself."

So, by fasting and austere meditation, Gentian passed through her trial and purgation. Once having made herself a promise to conquer an irrational passion she endeavoured to exaggerate her hatred, disgust and her desires in order to kill them by very weariness.

"My daughter," her mistress had said to her in her convent,

at the time when she was still very young and terrified by the horrors of war, "if you feel thoughts within you which frighten you, and you cannot drive them out by fasting, beware above all else of combating them by prayer, as the infidels do, for you know nothing of God, and fear and evil will take root in your soul in God's name. Rather meditate on the object of your fears, make it an obligation and wear it out with thought, until it becomes a food without savour. This is a dangerous test, but less dangerous than that which lies in forcibly repressing the natural imagination." Gentian had hardened her soul to visions of massacre and burning and had learned in this way not to tremble at the sight of blood and the screams of the sick. But in her youth she had never been touched by lustful thoughts: such things filled her with a horror before which her soul was dumb. Then Bérenger had taken her and made her love him when she would not have done, as if in a dream. But the dream was short. Amid the crash of bullets, and the screaming, in blood, fire and mourning, love had passed over her like a cavalry charge on a tournament field.

(Then, she had thought it was over. His face was red and swollen, seamed with scars; the eyebrows and lashes were beginning to grow again, and new black hairs sprouting on his chin, appearing at random on the flushed, uneven skin, and he looked at himself in a little steel mirror, his eyelids twitching. "God be praised. He has removed temptation from me! We shall never again be husband and wife."

"Did I say that, Bérenger? The day you shall be pleased to come back to me, I shall think it great happiness."

"I no longer have my own face. I shall never again be able to touch you without thinking you are remembering me as I used to be." He managed to hide his suffering pride and, by his graciousness, gaiety, and contempt of danger, make people forget his former features. Besides, his character had not changed, he was still the same frank, straightforward man, but Gentian knew that now it was as though he had been turned into two people, that he was playing at being himself, like a king concentrating on playing the King's part in a mystery play. So, with the years, he found peace of mind once more. But his wife was his secret wound, because he could no longer sleep with her; it was stronger than his will.)

How did this come to pass? How can a love so tender have

turned into hate? "I have not hated the man who cast me off, I hate him who still loves me!" Gentian thought. "From the day when I tried to tear myself free of a tie which gave me no more joy, I have known that I should never succeed without bitter suffering. Many women, when life separates them from their lover, give way to the temptation of more guilty delights than debauchery, and pass their nights revelling in the phantom caresses of him they love. I was like that, because I was possessed by a desire for lust as fierce as the most burning thirst. If I did not hate him, surely I should have loved him? If I loved him, surely I should have sought to satisfy him in all things? There was one night when he proved to me that I was nothing; he had only to wish and I became the thing he wished, I spoke the words he wished, I returned his caresses as he wished, and I was no more than a part of his own body; endowed with the semblance of thought in order that his pleasure should be the greater.

"That night, I had no more respect for him, only a single prayer in my heart: *Let all the world perish and he not die!*

"But he did not know that Eve's cunning is greater than the serpent's: I have made bitterness out of what was a nameless delight, and I have conquered the body by the body. For this bitter root I chew between my teeth every time a loving thought comes into my heart, this root burns my mouth and my throat until I all but faint from the bitter taste. At first I took a perverse pleasure in it, and at night I would feed on this bitterness, as though on the softest gift of love. But at last I grew tired of its noisome flavour and had to force my hands to put the dry stalk into my mouth and to bite on it. Sweet is Bitter and Bitter Sweet, and all the sensations of the flesh are nought, and there is neither good nor evil in human affections. Now, surely, his kiss would be so bitter to me that I should choke with disgust?

"Oh, corrupt and inconsistent being, proud serpent of the flesh that you are, are you not thinking: 'I have not deserved this?' What man has ever deserved anything? Did you deserve to be an idol in my eyes? You deserved neither my love nor my hatred, any more than I deserve anything myself. I have hurt you, because among the hundred faces of your heart there is one of tenderness too, but why should I be so afraid of hurting you? Your eyes are blind and see only the world you yourself have forged for yourself, and in this world I am the woman who hurts you; can I do otherwise?

186

". . . But there is really no reason, no reason at all, my friend, no reason why I should prefer you to anyone else. . . ."

On her return to Toulouse for the winter, Gentian began to eat again and recovered her strength, and she gave herself more and more to the care of the house and the children. She thought: "I am thirty-five and I am still alive. It is time I learned modesty and humbleness."

But a little before All Souls she had to face a new, cruel temptation, in the house of Hugues de Roaix, which was at the time the principal heretic house in Toulouse (although, out of regard for the Count, heretic meetings were, to some extent, clandestine: the faithful were informed of sermons and public prayers by word of mouth, and the ceremonies did not take place in the hall but in the cellar, which had been specially arranged for this purpose). There, among the ladies of the faithful, Gentian encountered Rachel de Montbrun, accompanied by her eldest daughter, Hersen, and her sister-in-law, Guillelme de Layrac. The Lady Rachel, who was famed for her piety and goodly life, had a place in the front rank of the faithful, immediately behind the baptised Christians, and Gentian and Béatrix should also have taken their places in the front row. Guillelme was immediately behind her sister-in-law and when Gentian saw her she clutched her friend's arm and said: "*I can't go on, let us stay here.*"

"In God's name, let us go to our places, do you wish to demean us?"

"I feel," whispered Gentian, "as though some force is holding me back." This was perfectly true, for no sooner did she take one step forward than she started backwards violently, and, rather than disturb the prayers (the minister who was to officiate was already advancing towards the little stone rostrum to recite the words of the public confession), she stayed where she was, among the bourgeoises in their grey stuff dresses. She could not pray, because every now and then the Lady of Layrac's hard, blue gaze would rest on her, over the lowered heads of the women reciting the responses. "How wretched to be tall! I stand higher than all of them and she can see me. Why does she turn her head like a weathercock?"

"This is frightful," she whispered to Béatrix, "it is as though she were devouring my very bowels."

"Who?"

"Guillelme de Layrac."

Gentian left the Roaix mansion after the kiss of peace, without greeting any of the ladies present, since in order to speak to them she would have had to walk past the place where Lady de Layrac was standing.

"What devil has got into you?" said Béatrix, when they were once more in the street. It was raining, the torches were guttering in the wind, and despite the lateness of the hour the three servants who were escorting them had to clear a way through the loiterers gathered outside the mansion. "Make way for the noble ladies! Hasn't the curfew sounded long since?" Pierre de Roquelaure, a knight who was coming out of the Roaix mansion with his sons, offered to accompany the ladies as far as their house; he had a large lantern and his sons were well armed. The rain was spurting from the gutters and running in torrents in the kennels. The yellow light from Pierre de Roquelaure's lantern swept the house fronts with their barred windows and small carved niches in the walls filled with the figures of saints. When they reached the Aspremont mansion the two women were drenched and hurried to the hearth in the downstairs chamber where the fire still glimmered under the ashes. The servants were already in bed, and Saurine, Bérenger's mistress, was sitting up alone by a table which she had laid with bread, salt and olives. (Food was scarce in Toulouse that year, and masters and servants alike consoled themselves with remarking that fasting was pleasing to God.)

"There you are," said Saurine, her eyes bright with weariness. "Have you seen a horrid vision?" Gentian said she did not know, but she ate nothing, and drank only one cup of wine. In her room, she said to Béatrix: "*There is a devil in that woman.*"

"Not in that woman but in you. You are not yet cured, whatever you may say, and it is jealousy which torments you."

Gentian held her bare arm over the candle. "How long would you like me to burn like this? Look, my arm isn't even trembling. With this pain racking my body I can still talk to you: the devil I saw did not come from myself, but from that woman! It is she who is jealous of me, because of a superficial man who gave away my secret to her."

Béatrix seized the candle and put it on the floor—the skin on her friend's arm was already inflamed—and said: "When will you reach the end of this madness? You are a prey to a lying devil. Give way to lust, then, since that is your nature."

"Don't you know that temptation is the measure of our strength?" Gentian was clenching and flexing her fingers, and she tensed as her bowels writhed with the pain. "These antidotes: the irons, the fire and the bitter herbs—didn't they talk to us enough about them in the convent?—are excellent for the ordinary temptations of the body. Henceforth I shall know no other lusts. But the devil has left me and gone elsewhere, and today I have seen him."

"When," Béatrix asked bitterly, "will you learn indifference? There is no road to Truth for one who is perpetually jigging like a bell round the Devil's neck."

Gentian blew out the candle and, instead of getting into bed, lay down, just as she was, in her shift, on the tiled floor and stayed there without moving, as stiff and straight as a corpse, her bare arms stretched out as though crucified, staring upwards. She invariably slept with her head pointing north and her feet south, while one arm was to the east and the other to the west, in order to annihilate herself the more completely and become one with the invisible force which regulates the movement of the stars—complying with the eternal need to seek for some semblance of order, even in chaos: and in this position she managed to quiet her vain thoughts. On this particular night, the pain from her burned arm kept her from sleeping and made her see showers of sparks against the black vault of the ceiling.

She thought: "That woman does not know yet what a force of hatred is in her. She has a weak spirit, but her heart is strong, and she will suffer a hard passion!"

"—and this is my beloved Béatrix's wisdom: goodness, charity and compassion. Because she is cold and feels no desires, she does not know what kind of charity and compassion a man wants from us. I began to hate him from over-much love, and he did not hate me. Now that hatred has entered into this innocent creature.

"If he could forget me and love her, then I too should love them both, and all would be peace, friendship and love . . ."

. . . How they fought for another year, a winter and a summer, from the Toulousain to the Carcassès, from the land of Foix to Rouergue, from one town to another, from plain to mountain, without even taking the time to set up camp, attacking and fleeing and not always sure who

189

was attacking and who fleeing, how they fought all summer, seeing the broad ribbons of smoke stretch left and right in the landscape of Toulouse, how they fought, with what tears of rage and what lust for vengeance, God should know, God who loves justice and honour!

Bishop Foulques rode, cross in hand, through the ranks of the Crusaders, surrounded by clerks and abbots, exhorting the soldiers: "Let not one vine be left standing, not one apple tree, not one olive tree! Let there be not one ear of corn, not one ear of barley, oats or rye; may the fields burn until there is nothing left, not so much as would fill the paunch of an ox! Let all the cattle you find be slaughtered; let there be done with it as the Israelites did with the cattle of the Amalekites. You have not come here to fill your own pockets, but in the service of our Holy Mother Church." Monseigneur Foulques revenged himself on the lands of his own diocese for the insult he had suffered: since he was no longer able to collect the taxes himself, the Count should have nothing either. Has God ever said men should justly die of hunger for having driven out their bishop?

Never before had the land known such devastation, not even in Simon's time. The whole countryside, from Toulouse as far as Auterive, and on to the Carcassès and then to Muret, was razed so utterly that a sheep would not have found grazing there, and poor folk were leaving the district by barge and raft on the Garonne, and on foot along the roads, dragging their carts by hand because there was no longer anything left to feed a donkey, and soon they had eaten the donkeys, mules and goats and even the dogs. Many children and old people died on the roads, because there were already so many beggars in the cities that disease was becoming rife in the streets and the burghers were forced to barricade themselves inside their houses. People camped in the fields around the monasteries and the monks gave them what they had: huge cauldrons of soup made with barley or bran hauled out on wheelbarrows; and where there was one bowl between three people, they were well off, because the monasteries were not rich either that summer, and the whole of the Pope's wealth would not have sufficed to feed so many mouths. And when there is famine in harvest time, what will be winter bring?

In the Counts' camp, admittedly, there was bread and corn to eat, and plenty of pepper and salt; and the soldiers were rightly served first. But so many beggars followed the army that they could not be got rid of by prayers or threats; and through them dysentery infected the camp—until even among the knights' followers one man in three was sick.

From Toulouse, the consuls sent an endless stream of messengers to the Count: "Most beloved lord, Are we, who have remained faithful to you, to suffer more cruelly than traitors and turncoats? The price is already so high in the city that good craftsmen can scarcely afford one loaf a week, because the reserves in the mills and granaries are only enough for a month at the very most. Even in Count Simon's time we did not experience famine such as we shall have this winter, if you do not come to the aid of your city! . . ." "My lord, would you, in your great goodness, draw off the seneschal's troops towards the mountains so that we may still save what is left of the vineyards round about La Salvetat! May it please your Grace to consider that if the wine trade is ruined for ten years the city will never recover from it, because all the markets will be taken from us by Moissac and Carcassonne!" But though it is easy to draw off small, isolated bodies of troops, the whole of the seneschal's army, firmly entrenched in their camp, or manœuvring with a solid bodyguard of crossbowmen to protect their flank and rear, is another matter; it is folly to attack them in the open field and risk losing the entire army at one blow.

It is easy to say we can fight as long as we have soldiers left. The whole land is not made up of soldiers. There is no great gain if the soldiers hold out alone, while famine spreads from the country into the cities. Though many people, especially among the burghers, believed this, the Counts did not think so. They were receiving good news from their spies in Paris and Carcassonne: Queen Blanche was so tired of this war that she was writing to the Pope, entreating him to relieve her of her vow to pursue the Crusade, upon consideration of her son's extreme youth, the cares laid upon her by the affairs of the realm and the difficulty she was experiencing in raising the money necessary to maintain such a strong army in the Midi while gaining nothing except losses of men and equipment. The seneschal, Humbert de Beaujeu, did not obtain a quarter of the reinforcements he demanded. "This year," the Count kept saying, "will be the last, we shall recapture Carcassonne by next spring."

If the whole country had thought thus, the peace treaty would never have been signed. But many people saw only the immediate danger and did not think of what tomorrow might bring. For that matter, Olivier de Termes and Centulle d'Astarac behaved like madmen in making their submission to the Queen for fear of seeing the famine spread to their lands. The Count made no comment, either good or bad, on their conduct, and thought rather more bad than good of it, because both he and the Count of Foix and their knights were beginning to get the reputation of gravediggers in the country. People said: "They can always find money to pay their hired soldiers, and their horses eat oats when women and children have to feed on acorns."

191

(And how the devil can one make war if one cannot feed horses and pay men? One can sell clothes and jewels, but weapons cost what they do cost—and one is compelled to enrich the armourers of Toledo or Marseilles instead of giving bread to the poor. If that was a sin, God punished it indeed, but of all the sins they had to regret in their old age, that was certainly far from the most shameful!)

You left at dawn at the gallop to harry an advanced post of the Crusaders, falling upon them in a din and clangor of metal striking fiercely against metal, of clattering sabots and the screaming of horses and men in mortal terror, with thick clouds of dust obscuring everything. And after the dust came the smoke, and red tongues of fire leaping and spreading through the undergrowth and the flash of casques and waving lances and the shining flanks of plunging horses, magnificent wounded horses rearing to their full height to come crashing down on a mêlée of men's bodies, shields and broken lances.

They raced across woods and meadows, friends or enemies, attacking, parrying blows, playing the game like young men at a tourney; and in the evening comrades met again in camp, bruised, exhausted, their eyes shining with the brutal joy of having a few more dead to their account and their own limbs still whole. As for comrades lost, God keep their souls—there was little weeping for them, the living said: "Tomorrow we shall revenge them." At nightfall they lighted torches and the soldiers went round the camp singing and brawling; every evening they celebrated victory, not for anything very much, just to flout the other side. While in the knights' tent the cup passed from hand to hand and musicians played on viols and sang songs in honour of Toulouse, and of absent ladies whose hearts were worth more than the joys of paradise.

The strange thing was that these days were like a holiday, filled with frank and loyal friendship, and wild hope—so great was the poverty of the land, and so racked with anguish all thought of the morrow, that every man was thinking: *"Vive Toulouse!* May this stand to our credit in heaven. When nothing is left to lose, there is everything to be gained."

(In those days, Roger formed a strong tie of friendship with Bérenger d'Aspremont; they slept in the same tent and rode side by side into battle and on the road. All evil bears its own

192

remedy within it, and the thing which most often sunders men can engender a sincere and heartfelt friendship, because it is natural that two men attached to the same woman should have some hidden similarity of temperament in common which draws them together.) Among friends, in the tents or in the *salle d'armes*, they talked of God, of women, of music or venery, with more warmth than ever, and planned alliances between children still in their cradles or as yet unborn. Men who, two years earlier, had barely greeted one another in the street were ready to open the veins in their wrists and mingle their blood.

"Let us swear that never will any one of us desert the Counts' camp! Let us all swear together never to accept a shameful peace. May he who first speaks of a peace harmful to his brothers be disgraced and despised of all ladies!" They swore with all their hearts, encouraged by the wine, for they were drinking heavily. The labourer is worthy of his hire. There was not a knight in the camp who did not think: "So long as we hold out, nothing is lost; if we can only hold them in check for two or three years more, we shall win back Carcassone and Narbonne, Beaucaire and Avignon!"

There were no longer Catholics and heretics: if they spoke of religion at all it was mildly, and courteously, as men speak of a true love. . . . One August evening when it was too warm to sleep inside the tents, Roger had gone with Bérenger down to the river where rushes grew behind the old willows that overhung the water as though to drink. A few horses were grazing on the still green grass in a coppice of nut trees; black fish were darting and gliding in the clear water and the evening star shone ever more brightly as the colours faded from the sky. The chirping of crickets and croaking of frogs covered the hum of the camp. On the far bank some wild ducks were bathing with a great splashing and flapping of wings, and it did not even occur to the men to fire at them.

Roger said that he would never believe the world and all the good and lovely things his eyes could see could be the work of the Devil. It was quite possible that the Devil, in order to spoil God's work, had created evil things such as reptiles, flies and lice, as well as poisonous herbs and diseases. But he could never have been capable of producing lovely, perfect things, even something as simple as a humble wild flower.

Bérenger said that this was all appearance, and that the Devil, being the first-born son of God and originally the most

193

beautiful of all the angels, still retained the idea of and the desire for heavenly beauty, and was always struggling to produce its faithful likeness; but he never succeeded. Scarcely had one of his works attained the appearance of beauty than it changed and withered, since all that seems to us lasting is no more so than the flower of the field, and the duration of the sun itself is no longer than a blink in the eye of eternity.

From these banal considerations, they went on to talk of the nature of Jesus Christ, since Roger could never bring himself to agree with the heretics on this point. He swore he had weighed the pros and cons a thousand times in his heart and discussed them with priests and very wise heretics, and was completely convinced of the truth of Catholic doctrine. St. Paul himself said that if Jesus only rose again figuratively speaking, his preaching would be in vain; and if Jesus Christ rose again in the flesh, then he must have lived in the flesh; and if he had not really suffered, and really died, and if he had not really been a man, he could not have really loved mankind. "This," Bérenger said, "comes of a mistake in the interpretation of what the Scriptures mean by 'man', because this is not the animal flesh, similar to that of beasts, but the Spirit, fraudulently lured into the carnal world, but which has nothing to do with this world. Thus, Our Lord Jesus Christ was, in this world, that soul of pure light which shines in darkness and has never illumined a gross and perishable form."

"Yet, is it not written that he wept and suffered hunger and thirst? Surely this is as though God wished to lead us into error? How could God try to deceive?"

"Out of pity for our gross nature and to undo the Devil's wiles he showed himself to men in an aspect which they could apprehend. Just as he spoke in parables to those who could not understand, so he made a kind of living parable of his apparent body. But those who have the gift of spiritual life have no need of the support of the flesh."

"May I ask you frankly, friend, whether you have received the gift of spiritual life, or are you only speaking from what you have learned from sermons?"

"That," said Bérenger, "I cannot rightly tell you, for I had my time of grace when I received baptism, and my sins have once more darkened my life. And to be completely frank with you, I slept with a woman eight months after receiving the Spirit, and those eight months seemed far from short to me! And so long as this war lasts, many people will be compelled to expose themselves to the sin of homicide to defend our Church. But afterwards, if I am still alive and am considered worthy of renewing my vows, I may be able to discuss these things with you with real knowledge."

It was getting dark and the water was slapping between the reeds with a melancholy sound, owls hooting in the wood, and the mind and heart turned naturally to serious thoughts, as a way of atoning, at small cost, for the day's sins. That evening, watching Bérenger's severe profile etched in black against the dark blue sky, with his tangled curls and long, knotted neck, Roger wondered whether he had not wronged this man who was his friend. (And yet, if all men knew the actions and secret thoughts of others and believed themselves obliged to exact vengeance, what a carnage our life would be! Since my love for this man is firm and true I have nothing to reproach myself with on his account; never shall I feel either the wish or the intention of hurting him.)

The astonishing thing was that between two days' journeying, in a tent, or the guardroom of some castle, one still found strength to compose songs in one's head and commit them to memory. Passing through Toulouse, one wrote them down on paper and set them to some music. There was no other way of telling your thoughts *to* a woman who refused to see you and to read your letters (it was not even certain that she would hear the song). No one who has not known the wretchedness of being deserted by a woman who once loved him deeply can understand: the memories of a too-warm tenderness poison your soul, you say to yourself: "This thing is not possible, she must have gone mad." Then, as soon as you have a moment to spare, the sickness takes hold of you again.

> In a field the other day
> I saw a gentle shepherd lad
> Weeping and playing on his pipe
> A mournful song.
> My shepherdess has left me
> And I must die.
> The wolf has taken her white lambs
> And she cannot forgive me
> Because I could not protect them.

195

I tell you, pretty shepherd,
That she is false
For true love cares not
For wolves or lambs.
The summer sun has never
Refused to shine
To punish the olive trees
For growing crooked.

Seek rather, friend,
To find the slanderers,
The traitors and thieves
Who have stolen your good name.
But if your shepherdess
Had a loyal heart
Never would she,
For wolves or lambs,
Nor houses, fields or woods,
Have deprived you
Of her love.

Besides this moral pastoral tale, Roger wrote another song, in
a more bitter tone, which was sung at court throughout the feast
of Pentecost; this was much talked of, because it seemed extremely bold, and many ladies judged it disrespectful, and
expressed the opinion that a lover had no right to speak so
bluntly. The song ran more or less as follows:

I love, perforce, her Rigour and her Hate
Since she has such a cruel heart
That I can never hope to win it.
But I remember one summer evening,
On the eve of a fierce battle:
That evening the look in her eyes
Was not (by St. Foy and St. Valerie)
Either hard or cold, but full of goodness.

But she is like the cruel rich man
Who from the poor man turns his eyes
In case he should give alms.
She is like the child at play
Plucking alive the bird it has caught.

If for too much loving one must be punished
Who would still serve Love?
And if I must love one who hates me beyond reason
Surely I am like the madman
Eating sand and stones.

To return so much love with hate
Is neither Rigour, Cruelty nor Severity!
In any other lady but the most perfect
I should be allowed to say
Her Rigour is Pride and Folly.

But never may such words
Escape my lips.

The allusion to the look full of goodness, especially, was considered indiscreet and Bérengère de Ribemont, Raymond-
Jourdain's (secret) sweetheart, declared that a man who boasted
thus of a lady's favours might very well deserve to be hated.
Roger told her: "All is permitted to him who has nothing more
to lose, for truly it would be difficult for me to make myself
more hated. But I could present my case before any tribunal you
wish and show that I have done nothing to deserve such treatment."

The more he blamed the woman who had treated him so
cruelly the more he desired to see her again. He wrote to the
Lady Béatrix, letters full of humility, begging her to intercede
for him, but received no other response than this: *Do not importune
me. I have a sincere esteem for you, but it would be betraying my friend
to speak to her of that which she wishes to forget.*

Is it permissible to lie in wait for a lady in an empty street
and carry her off by force in order to be able to speak to her?
Roger had no talent for such measures and would have preferred never to be forgiven than to commit such an offence
against Rigueur. But he was beginning to indulge, like a youth,
in dreams of fires or bloody affrays that might permit him to
come to his beloved and carry her off, swooning and defenceless,
on his horse. How wretched is a man when he can see no other
way but this to approach his love! Better to seek a new love or
have no love at all, but how can a man forget a love so deep?

He was mortally tired because of all the troubles which were
raining on his head: debts, loans falling due, soldiers threatening

to leave, famine at Layrac, his father complaining, his vassals complaining, his son ill, excommunication and re-excommunication by the Bishop of Montauban (as though a man who had already been excommunicated for twelve years could be any more so!). This time, there could be no possible doubt: the domain of Layrac was so thoroughly devastated that not one vine was left alive, and they were utterly ruined. For how many years, God only knew. What was the good of having taken such pains to save folks' lives only to have them die of hunger? This was done in the name of breaking the pride of the men of Toulouse, for is it easy to make war hearing yourself accused of drinking the blood of your own vassals? "And Rigueur as good as declares that all our troubles come from those of us who serve Satan!"

Roger was trying to explain this to Lady de Miraval, who was at the Narbonnese castle for the Christmas celebrations. There was much talk of peace at that time, and it was said that Queen Blanche so strongly desired the end of the war that she was willing to be the first to send messengers to try and find some formula of agreement. What she wanted, it was said, was to obtain the Count's daughter in marriage for her second son, but this meant there was a danger of the country reverting to this son if the Count had no other legitimate heirs. "Is that a good or a bad thing? We may well hope that the young prince [he was only nine] might one day become a gallant and courteous knight and sincerely devoted to the manners of Toulouse."

"You, sir knight," said Lady de Miraval, "are not one of those who give the Count bad advice, but you are more concerned for his interests than for honour and justice."

"My lady, we have struggled so long for our freedom that it would be hard for us to accept an unsatisfactory peace. But words of this kind are worth only as much as the paper they are written on."

"You are too scornful," said the old lady, "of written words."

"My lady, I beseech you, do not remind me of an action which I committed against my will and which, I should tell you, damned me in the eyes of the person I esteemed most in the world! Do you believe it is possible to stop loving for such a reason?"

"Everything is permitted to a loyal and sincere woman," said the lady with her little dry but kindly smile. "She is the only

198

judge. A woman's duty is to remind men of honour's laws."

"Ah, my lady, the laws of honour have not been laid down by God nor revealed in the Holy Scriptures! Each man acts according to his own lights; and I do not think I have been lacking in honour."

. . . Since you complain of me so bitterly, and accuse me indiscreetly of Pride and Folly in your songs, I must prove to you that my conduct has been irreproachable towards you.

Do you think the desire for a chaste life can be a sign of pride and folly? Is a woman forbidden to feel such a desire?

Of any woman who gives herself up unrestrainedly to licentiousness it is said: she is a woman without honour. And of one who repulses men it is said: the devil is in her. I am unable to justify myself to you, who know that in your arms I tasted joy. You say to yourself: She must be either full of pride or mad to renounce such a joy.

I have gained nothing by avoiding you: I have suffered more. Do you think that I have followed your example and consoled myself in the arms of a young and pleasing lover?

You know my most secret thoughts. How can I justify myself to you without appearing a liar? I have desired chastity greatly; not as a sick person desires health but as a man fighting desires victory, since only the chaste are true and whole men.

Do not think that I want any glory for myself. Do not think that age and trials have weakened my spirit and that I am avoiding you in order to find peace. What peace is there for me? It is you, you who have peace (if this sad state merits the name), since it seems that you no longer avoid the lusts of the flesh, though there is no love there.

If only you, too, were able to free yourself from the demon of the flesh and be a free man! That freedom is the beginning of Knowledge. Can any man wish to be blind? Is it pride, to wish not to be blind?

We were not created for joy, but for Truth.

I have not made you better or truer. You had one heart for me and one heart for others.

I wanted to live many lives. God has made me see that I had only one, at least in this body. I have honoured and prostituted it at the same time, by serving the Church and serving a man, aspiring simultaneously to prayer and to caresses! Destroying myself continuously, the most wretched of all creatures!

It is written: "Pluck out thy right eye, and cut off thy right arm." Can such words have been spoken in vain? Does God desire our damnation?

199

If the carnal love which binds a man to a woman and a woman to a man was not the greatest of evils, it ought to be the greatest good : in fact it is impossible for it to be neither one nor the other, because our souls are too powerfully engaged in it.

But since people who are most lost to God hide themselves in order to commit it, then truly there can be no possible doubt it must be a great evil. And if it is evil, then love deceives us cruelly by making us see it as good.

I do not want to be deceived, for no living person has the right to desire to be deceived.

If only you had any friendship for me! But all you have is the lust of the flesh, and the eyes, and you are tormented by your pride. As for myself I have no pride; and if I am mad, I do not believe that I can be cured of this madness for which you reproach me.

Roger did not receive this long letter until the eve of his departure for France: when the letter was two months old. It had been written when the Aspremont family was leaving Toulouse for Montferrand in the Carcassès—at the time when they were having to fight for their corn, barley and fodder, and Bérenger hoped to revictual his own people at the spear's point on the land which had been recaptured from him by the Crusaders. Rigueur had entrusted the letter to Arnaude but, failing to find the knight in Toulouse, Arnaude gave the letter to her brother, who took it to Layrac, only to learn that Roger was in Provence. However, the letter brought the young man bad luck, for he fell ill on the journey and died in a hamlet near Castres, but before he died he passed the letter on to a mason's apprentice, promising him the knight would reward him handsomely. The apprentice lost the letter in a game of hazard, at Béziers, and the fellow from Béziers, a Spanish soldier, sold it in turn to a tapster in an inn for a flask of wine. In the hope of earning a noble, the tapster travelled all the way to Toulouse and finally found the man to whom the letter was addressed. Roger received it, its little leather bag stained with grease and wine, crumpled but intact. He read and re-read it and still failed to understand properly what his mistress was demanding of him: it was so long since he had expected a message from her, and his mind was on other things.

After the first impulsive moment of delight (at reading words which she had written) he wondered: "Why so many words, only to say that one does not love? What is the use of this letter if I am certain not to see her again before the summer?" Later on he was to read this strange letter again, pondering on the inconsistency of women: was this a good way to quench a man's passion—by reminding him of the joys of past love and the dangers of the bonds of the flesh? Ladies love to deck themselves in their chastity in order to enhance their value in the eyes of men, but Rigueur was not like that. She desired purity with a true ardour, and "By the Virgin!" thought Roger, "she should be praised for that if only I did not love her so much!

"If I have to become one of those lovers who are content with the heart (for many are), if I must renounce for ever the sweetest of liberties (and God knows I am no longer one of those who think of nothing but getting into bed the moment they see a woman, but have we ever talked more freely than on the days when we could give ourselves to one another?), if I have to renounce the most legitimate union that ever was (a union which was no mere whim but endured for years!), then I may as well let my beard grow and become a Templar, I may as well imagine I am past sixty already! When we have come back," he thought, "once the peace treaty has been signed——"

Everyone was talking so much about this peace treaty, about which the negotiations were to take place at Meaux in Champagne, that in fact no one knew any longer what to expect from it. Everyone was saying: "They are asking too much, we shall be binding ourselves hand and foot." But they thought perhaps the Count would be able to talk to the Queen and make her understand that there was nothing to be gained by shaving people too closely. Roger, who was one of the Count's suite, was so harried by his friends of the heretical party that he felt like a man entrusted with property which he is not sure of being able to keep safely. He knew, too, for a fact, that he could never change anything, either by argument or by intrigue—not he nor anyone else: all those who were going with the Count, knights or consuls, were men of good reputation, and held in high honour in Toulouse; but at Meaux, because they were enemies of the King and the excommunicants, they would carry no more weight than water carriers.

Pierre-Guillaume de Montbrun's comment was: "If we had to fight so hard and ruin the country to achieve a treaty like this! It would have been better to leave Amaury in possession of all the land he held, from Castres to Narbonne!" It would have been better. Old men talk of the happenings of five years ago as if they had taken place last week; and in those five years they had lived a whole lifetime; men had known so much joy, and hope, desolation, hatred, and weariness, that the time of Amaury was already becoming a legend. . . . The things they could or could not have done in that time!—and it was ten years ago, and then twenty.

Twenty years of war.

"Father, we should have got on very well with Amaury but for the bishops! And now, if we don't manage to win them over they will stab us in the back again."

"The Count thinks he can win them over by flattery, but it is a little late for that! Look: the day Bishop Foulques comes back to Toulouse, our house will be among his first targets, with the reputation that Bertrand has got himself! At my age, should I have to bother myself with fortifications and barricades and join in street fights?"

"If it comes to that, Bertrand and I will take care of it. Better peace with the Bishop inside our walls than war with the Bishop loose in the countryside. After the harm he has done us this summer what worse could he do?"

"You," said the old man peevishly, "are you a child? You are always asking what worse they can do. You keep saying: we have seen the worst. You have been saying it for twenty years and things are not going any better for it."

"The Count," said Bertrand, "has always favoured the Catholics more than the heretics, but which have served him best? He prefers to win back those who have betrayed him than to keep those who serve him."

"Nothing final has been concluded," said Roger, "nothing has happened yet." Nothing had happened indeed! When poor folk were dying of hunger in the fields and on the roads and children were dropping dead in the streets in the middle of the city just as in time of siege.

That year many people woke each morning and wondered: Surely I have been dreaming? Will it be just the same as before, or is it finished for good? How shall we come out of it this time?

Lord, the day we lose the Count there will be nothing left for us but to tie a stone round our necks and jump into the Garonne!

—Lord, we have not been defeated, yet we have been treated like men coming to beg for mercy in a shift and bare feet. When two men agree to make peace after a fair fight, is it just for one to take all the other's property and strike him into the bargain? Such an unchristian peace, and one so contrary to all custom, has not been seen in the memory of any knight or burgher.

May God forgive those who say: this peace is better than the war. Can one say: it is better to be hanged on an oak than an olive tree? In practice, there is nothing to choose between them, and if some people have a preference for the foliage of one or the other, that is their business. Supposing it to be true that they could no longer carry on the war (and this was a fact: empty granaries, empty coffers, and an army cannot hold out when the people fear famine more than the enemy.) Even supposing they could not make war much longer, certainly they could not make peace either—not this peace—and in fact they had not made it, others had done so, and they could only fold their arms and say *amen*.

Was it necessary to spend so much money, to gather together so many noble knights and wealthy burghers, and make such a long journey, if the only favour they were to be granted was the favour of being put in prison? Oh, the stupidity of actually coming to give themselves up as hostages! Surely they might have known that once the Count was at Meaux, and lodged in the city keep, he would be no more free to depart again than if he had been put in a dungeon, because if he had had the audacity to offer such an insult to the archbishops, bishops, legates and abbots, as well as to the Count of Champagne and the Queen herself, he would never have been able to justify himself to the rest of Christendom, and his cause would have been lost before it was even tried.

But tried it was not, in any case, because the Archbishop of Sens made a long speech, and so did the legate and the constable (who was the late Simon's brother-in-law), and they were all agreed in saying that Raymond de Saint-Gilles, formerly Count of Toulouse, had never from his earliest youth done anything but follow his father's deplorable example and cause endless troubles in the realm. Through his fault the land of the *langue d'oc* had been given over to fire and slaughter for more than ten years, monasteries had been pillaged and Christ's soldiers and the King's pitilessly massacred, and because of his culpable tolerance heresy flourished in the land and heretics swarmed there like worms on a dead body while, through the fault of the said Raymond, the Catholic faith was publicly abused and despised.

Furthermore, Raymond and the Count of Foix, with all the knights and barons and all the free cities who served the said counts, had for ten years incessantly undermined and disobeyed the most just and kindly authority of the King of France, the only lawful lord of those lands of which Raymond had possessed himself by rebellion and deceit. If therefore, in her goodness and compassion for her relative, the Queen consented to allow Raymond to enjoy the county of Toulouse, and take his daughter to be given in marriage to a son of France, this was a favour which the said Raymond had by no means deserved, and of which he must render himself worthy by his future behaviour.

They talked to such good effect that in the end the Count himself almost came to believe them and he returned to his apartments, after the long sessions in the great hall of the Bishop's palace, so exhausted that it was pity to see him. "What are we doing here, my friends? We are no more than the straw models set up for targets in a fairground." Splendid targets indeed, nicely painted and adorned, and easy to hit! The Count stood his ground gallantly, saying that he had always been a Catholic and ardently desired the downfall of the heretics, and aspired to serve the Queen and the young King as an obedient and faithful vassal, and that the heretics in his own lands were no more numerous than in Artois and the Nivernais. They answered him, with evidence in support of their case, that there were declared heretics among his own knights, and among the chief citizens of Toulouse, while the heretic seminaries were more prosperous and respected than those of the Catholics, heretic ministers were publicly saluted in the streets and even preached in the churches, and much more in the same vein. Can a man under sentence of excommunication tell prelates they lie? Especially when they were not lying.

"If such things occur in my country, I will have an inquiry made into it and can then re-establish order. And if the Church in her compassion declares that the sins of the fathers should not be visited on the sons, is it right that Catholics should suffer on account of their fellow citizens who are heretics, when these are neither their own friends nor relatives? Should we tear out the wheat with the tares? I desire," the Count went on, "to prove the purity of my faith by making my confession to my lord Archbishop of Sens or my lord Archbishop of Meaux, or to any other prelate present in this assembly. Moreover, all the knights, barons and consuls here present with me are ready to swear whatever oaths may be asked of them to prove that they were never, any more than I myself, in collusion with the heretics."

They answered him, with perfect justification, that since he and his friends had long been excommunicated and excluded from the communion of the faithful, they could neither make confession nor swear any vows; and that as long as they remained unabsolved by the Church the council could take no account of their declarations, beyond the purely suppositious and theoretical, so that it would do them more good to allow honourable and impartial witnesses whose words could not be doubted to speak for them.

"My very reverend and beloved Fathers and lords, if my word and the words of my friends have no value, why has my noble and honoured cousin, Queen Blanche, summoned me here, and given into my hand a letter, sanctioned by her, containing offers of peace? If I had been—which God forbid!—guilty of heresy, would Her Majesty the Queen have deigned to discuss peace terms with me, relying on my word of honour? If my word is without value so long as my innocence is unrecognised, what use is it to ask me to give sureties before becoming reconciled to the Church?"

The legate gave him to understand that it was by furnishing convincing proof of his submission and absolute obedience that he could earn the Church's pardon. The Count followed the debates, listening to the Archbishop of Narbonne, the Bishop of Toulouse, the Bishop of Carcassonne, the Abbot of Fontfroide and the Abbot of Belleperche one after another raising interminable lists of his crimes against the Church and the King of France. He listened with his chin in his hand and a taut smile on his face; very pale, his hair drenched with sweat, and so exhausted that several times his friends thought him on the point of fainting. And from time to time his eyes widened with terror. That night he held council in his bedroom. What was to be done? "You must find a pretext for going away," said his knights, "leaving us behind as hostages, then you can submit the matter to Parliament and the barons: there has never been any mention in the preliminary negotiations for peace of pulling down the walls of Toulouse and giving up the Narbonnese castle. How can you possibly sign such a peace without consulting the country?"

"Ah! Why don't they assassinate me at one blow, instead of roasting me over a slow fire! They will never let me go away, they will find some excuse for accusing me of open rebellion and arresting me. If I declare myself their enemy now, the truce is broken and I am in their lands."

He was really afraid of this, he was even afraid for his life, to the point of refusing all nourishment not prepared by his own cooks. He said: "To get out of here I will sign any paper they like to offer me. Once in Toulouse again, we will decide what can best be done to repair the damage."

Among themselves the barons said it was a great pity the Count was not as good an advocate as he was gallant knight, but had he possessed the eloquence of St. John Chrysostom there was little he could have said to people already determined in advance not to listen to him, because everything the Count could say in his own defence reflected badly on either the Queen, the bishops, the seneschal or the crusading barons, so that his mouth was effectually closed, unless he chose to plead against himself. This in fact he did, thinking he would at least earn the good graces of the French prelates and could make up for it afterwards. He spent all night dictating speeches, surrounded by his barons and clerks; it was open to anyone to put in a telling word, or a more subtle argument. . . . But it was all for nothing, because it always happened, as though by express design, that there was too little time in the sessions to hear the speeches of the men of Toulouse. "It seems to me," said the Count, "that I have a very good case for persuading my friends."

He still retained a tiny spark, however pale and flickering, of his old gaiety, and even in the Council Chamber, to which the men of Toulouse were only admitted after prayers were over, he still found the strength to turn to his followers to mimic the expression of some prelate or other, or wink one eye to underline some ridiculous metaphor in his judges' perorations.

"Let us drink to our return my friends, and forget all the rest! We are like fish out of water in this accursed country: all our flapping is to no purpose."

206

He was still hoping that his cousin would show some kindness towards him, if only in permitting him one heart to heart talk with her. Unfortunately, despite all his entreaties, he was not allowed to speak to the Queen; she herself, incited no doubt by evil counsellors, avoided an interview which might have evoked some tenderness in her. She was a woman and knew the Count, being younger than herself and deep in misfortune, would not stint either his tears or reproaches, or his appeals to the voice of consanguinity. The men of Toulouse saw her only once: in the square before Notre-Dame, decked out as stiffly as a statue in ermine and her widow's weeds, and seated on a gilded throne beside her young son.

It was a splendid sight: so many fine carpets, gold-fringed canopies and richly-dressed lords and ladies had not been seen, even on a feast day in St. Sernin's Square in old Count Raymond's time. The day was Maundy Thursday and the bells were ringing from every church in Paris. Burghers and artisans were crowding in serried ranks all along the quays beside the Seine, and people were perched on gutters on the roofs of houses on the bridge, and on the roofs of the mansions surrounding the square. The crowd jostled behind the wooden barriers, guarded by soldiers, and women and children were shouting joyously: "*God save King Louis!*" The King was a pretty, fair-haired child, tall and well-developed for his fourteen years, though still a little thin. His serious eyes returned continually to his mother.

The stage set up before the cathedral was covered with rich carpets and cloth of gold, the royal dais, the thrones, the lectern and table on which the treaty was to be signed glittered in the sunshine, with brilliant colours, glass cabochons and gilded studs, until the whole thing resembled an enormous shrine. The good people had every reason to climb up to the roofs and press round the barriers. The Cardinal-deacon, in his long red gown and red hat, stood up on the platform and blessed the crowd.

The Count climbed the steps, carpeted in Persian rugs, all alone, dressed in his dark red gown and black cloak, his only ornament the gold chain round his neck, as befitted a man doing penance. His friends, waiting in the square below and divided from the French barons by an empty space at least fifty feet wide, felt not unlike the goats, set on the left hand at the Judgment Day, while the sheep stand on the right hand of the Lord. If only the oldest or the most noble of them could have been permitted to mount the platform, so that the Count might have had a friendly hand to clasp! But the barons of Toulouse were held in such miserable esteem in Paris that the Count himself was barely allowed to approach the King's person. Not but what the entire pageant had been arranged with the sole purpose of making him climb those steps.

The legate's clerk read aloud the treaty reconciling the Count to the Church, with calm deliberation. *"I, Raymond, Count of Toulouse. . . ."* The Count, sitting on a wooden stool, on the King's left, with his legs crossed and his chin in his hand, listened abstractedly, as though the affair did not concern him.

The church of Notre-Dame may have been beautiful but the men of Toulouse did not sing its praises as they went inside: no place on earth had ever seemed to them more hideous. Notwithstanding, this was the first time for eleven years that they had been permitted to enter a church as true Christians to hear the Mass. The choirs sang the acts of grace. Slowly, assisted by two clerks, the Count disrobed, removing first his mantle, then his gown, then his shirt and his shoes, and knelt before the altar wearing nothing but his breeches and his body crucifix. Anyone who claims that there is nothing degrading in this, that on the contrary there is honour in humbling oneself before God and the Church, did not see the thing as they saw it. A rope around his neck, naked and bleeding from the rods, the Count was shivering so violently that those standing ten paces away could hear his teeth chattering.

They may as well say that Jesus Christ was not scourged in scorn and derision! And may Jesus Christ, sitting on the right hand of God the Father, remember the rods which struck His own most precious body! He was beaten that day before His altar and by His own servants in the body of a man who had done nothing to deserve this outrage.

When the legate had finished the scourging and had placed his stole over the penitent's head, the Count laughed—or, as some said, wept, because there are times when it is hard to tell sobs from laughter. Besides, he had plenty to laugh at: one may weep to have been robbed by thieves, but when the thieves call themselves benefactors into the bargain, it is wiser to laugh. That same evening, confined in the Louvre, the Count said: *"Let us rejoice and give thanks to the Lord, now that we are good Christians at last."*

As though they would not have preferred to live for another ten years under the curse of excommunication rather than hear Holy Mass in that way. Ah! it was to the Pope and the court of Rome they should have gone and not budged from the spot until their pardon was granted. They had obtained the King of France's pardon, not the Pope's, and God knows, they had little need to trouble themselves about that pardon.

For one who had known the prisons of Toulouse, the Louvre would have seemed a paradise only lacking in angels—good cheer, feather beds, wide windows, painted and vaulted chambers and in the evening wax candles to give as much light as anyone could desire. They could be served by their own servants, wash, shave and be cupped, they could play at dice, too, and listen to music. After a month in that prison the skinniest beggar would have become as big and fat as a Benedictine monk. But anger and impatience are worse than poisons, and they felt more inclined to bite their nails than crack nuts.

Five months in that prison was not really so long or so hard to endure. And yet a hundred times a day Roger told himself that he would rather have been hanged, caught leprosy, gone begging in the streets—all in all, being a prison, it was still a hard prison. Yes, all things considered, it was worse than the other kind. Worse, even twenty years later, with the knowledge of experience, he would still think that.

There was good company. That was true. The best that could be, for a man of Toulouse: not a man but was noble, wealthy, and famed for his courage or constancy. Sad company, when you know that so many honourable men of great reputation are held in prison out of scorn of their country. God knows, they thought, if the Count had left us as hostages, even in a much poorer castle, we should have held it an honour. . . . It is the knowledge that he himself is held as a hostage, in contempt of the treaty, that makes this prison so hard to swallow.

"They need not have gone as far as that." It was easy to say. There were seven or eight of them from Toulouse who had been part of the Count's household from their childhood: Guillaume de Roquefeuil, Bernard de Villeneuve, Bernard de Rabastens, men who, like Roger, had developed the habit of speaking of the Count as 'we'. They were more humiliated than the rest and stuck together, careful not to talk too much of what was in their hearts. In the days that followed the great hammer blow no one dared complain for fear of letting a despair which could only delight their country's enemies burst out too fiercely. They were there, at the court: Monseigneur Foulques, and Monseigneur Pierre-Amiel, and the relatives of Simon de Montfort who had not forgotten that missile hurled eleven years earlier from the ramparts of Toulouse. The Easter celebrations were in full swing. The bells of the hundred churches of Paris were chiming, reaching right up to the walls of the Louvre, and echoing in their heads, and bringing back past joys to the heart. From the paved streets rose the sound of chanting as the priests led the holy images in procession. For the men of Toulouse that Easter Sunday was a day of sin, not of grace, because in their great bitterness they thought: "It is our grief which makes them rejoice; they are like Pilate and Caiaphas boasting of having sacrificed the Lamb of God. They have made a courtroom of their cathedral church, and their priests have not been ashamed to perform the office of the Roman soldiers." Such thoughts were blasphemy, but those who are cast down by force are easily inclined to glorify themselves. Each word of the Easter Mass seemed to them charged with a secret meaning. May our turn come, one day, Lord, to raise the dead with You, our turn to say: "Hell, where is thy victory?"

What can we tell to our friends, who said, on the day of our departure: "May God bless and keep you"? Or to those who said: "May God grant the Count wins a better peace"? The city will endure on the signed order of her own *seigneur* what she would not suffer at the hands of Simon. May those who wanted peace be happy, because the Count was certainly the last person to desire it, and why should he have desired it? Was it he, or his children, who were dying of starvation? He would always have found enough to feed and clothe himself and his family, just as in time of peace, nor was it on the advice of his knights or barons, because he could have carried on the war for ten years, scouring the countryside like a hired mercenary, and taking for the war what little wealth the poor had left. He was driven to make peace out of pity for his people.

Because he was young and tender hearted, he was susceptible to pity. *"It is a poor pity that, in dealing with today's evils, forgets those of tomorrow. One more year, one year and everything would have been won back.*" One more year, two years, how many times had they said that?

To think that many sincere Catholics had waited impatiently for that day for twelve years—although after twelve years they no longer knew what to do with it—twelve years, years of sleepless nights, years of sick and feverish days, living with the one thought: the sacraments. The Body of Christ. Did they think that was a small thing?

The forgiveness of sins. (Sins there had been, more sins than in normal times.) The important thing was to make a discreet confession, or one might be refused absolution. (Otherwise one would be taken quite wrongly for a heretic.)

"... *Your brother.*"

"I have never been on friendly terms with my brother. I have always loathed his faith."

"*Do you pledge yourself before God to pursue by all means in your power all those you know to be contaminated by the heretical leprosy and denounce them to the Church and the secular authorities, including your brother?*" (God! Why do they always throw my brother in my face. He must surely have compromised himself worse than I thought!)

"I pledge myself, Father." ('That was no lie: one merely added the mental reservation: "by all means which honour permits" and reflected that there is no call to 'denounce' as heretics people who are already known to be so.) All the same, it was not a good confession, and after an equivocal confession Holy Communion itself has a bitter taste. "*Domine non sum dignus.* DOMINE NON SUM DIGNUS." *Non sum dignus*, unworthy, Lord, the most unworthy of all, have pity. Have pity on a sinner who receives You while his heart is consumed by damnable passions.

Lord, I promise this day by Your most pure Body which condescends to approach my lips that when I am old I will retire to a monastery and forgive them all with all my heart.

Lord, You who can distinguish the just from the unjust, why do You allow Your servants to say that murder is a sin for us and not for our enemies? If it is Your will that this war should end before our dead have been avenged, and that we should be delivered up to our enemies in order that innocents shall no longer die of starvation, take account of our great patience, Lord, and let our enemies not lead us into temptation.

Once we are back in our own lands, we shall tell our men: thank God for the sons you have left and for the fields which have not yet been ravaged. Beget new sons to take the place of the dead, replant the vines and the trees. A vine takes five years to grow to maturity, an apple tree ten, and a son twenty. If God wills, you will not have them destroyed again. And though you are poorer than before, thank God you are not poorer still.

Pierre, my own son, is of an age to leave the women's quarters. If he ever leaves them now, it will be for the cloister, and perhaps it is better that way. May he never wear any other helmet than the one I have promised him so many times and never given him (do men think of children's toys when they are at war?). When I go back to Toulouse I will get it for him. He won't wear it often: he suffers from enough headaches already. Why do they say that if he had not lived among strangers for five years he would not have fallen ill? Perhaps it may not even be true? For money. I have sacrificed my child in order to buy a man with nothing to his credit but his fame as a killer. It is true, Lord, all the world knows it: de Vitry was our enemy, he came to pluck out men's eyes, cut off their noses, and rip up their bellies with his pike. I sent him away from Layrac to go and play that game on some other domain in our land. The war is over, who will call him to account now?

The war is over, Rigueur. But not for you. You will say: "We have been betrayed. We must not give in."

PART TWO

ONE

Peace.

To listen to the sermons that were pronounced from the pulpits one would have said there could be nothing lovelier than this peace, a flowering of spring in autumn, and a blaze of summer sunshine in the middle of the wet season—the citizens of Toulouse were filled with such joy that they could scarcely believe their eyes and ears: churches were open, the holy office celebrated with a pomp worthy of the time of Count Raymond's grandfather, there were endless processions and pealing of bells, and then the arrival of the Cardinal-deacon, Legate of Gaul, who did not scorn to honour the repentant city with his presence—the priests had good reason to describe this joy from their pulpits, since but for them no one would have observed it.

Nevertheless, crowds gathered in the squares and outside the churches crying: "Long live the Count! Long live the peace! Long live the Legate! Long live the King!", not because they felt any particular desire to shout this, but because they had to shout something. An old man with hair as white as snow was to be seen walking through the city from the Bishop's prisons to the Pré-du-Comte, with a tall candle in his hand, numerous clerics and cantors going before and behind him, and an escort of soldiers armed with pikes. On the paper mitre set on his aged head these words were painted in red:

Ecce Guillelmus
Apostolicus
Haereticorum. . .

People watched him pass and said to one another: "What new lie are they going to make up? Who has ever heard tell of a heretic pope?" The old man walked firmly, his eyes on the ground; his toothless mouth was mumbling prayers. The soldiers made him mount a pile of faggots and fastened him to the stake with chains. He looked round at the crowd with a sad, astonished gaze, then sighed and closed his eyes. Soon the meadow and the nearby houses echoed with his howling, like a beast in pain.

It was nine o'clock in the morning and Roger was at table in his father's house. The meal was almost over when an apologetic

215

servant came to find Pierre-Guillaume de Montbrun and told him that there were some people downstairs who refused to wait. "They are clerks from the Bishop's palace," he said, "with an armed guard." The old *seigneur* said: "What have I to do with the Bishop's clerks? I don't owe them any money."

"They say it is something to do with my lord Bertrand."

"Tell them the Lord Bertrand will call and see them when he has the time."

"Father," said Bertrand, "do not lose your temper and let them come up. Please God we have not more troubles to fear than merely being disturbed in the middle of a meal!"

Pierre-Guillaume ordered the bowl of water to be passed round for washing their hands, and stood up, leaning on his sons' shoulders. When he was settled in his armchair near the window, he instructed the visitors to be shown up. The women withdrew, while Roger and Bertrand stationed themselves on either side of his chair.

The elder of the clerks bowed before the old man and drew from his sleeve two scrolls of paper sealed with the Bishop's arms. "We are instructed," he said, "to give these writs into the recipients' own hands in the presence of witnesses. Is the noble Bertrand de Montbrun in this house?"

"What's this, Master Imbert?" said Bertrand. "Have you gone blind?"

"This paper," the clerk went on, imperturbably, "is to be given in person to Bertrand de Montbrun, before witnesses capable of testifying to his identity."

"Enough!" said Pierre-Guillaume, testily, "you shaven-headed upstart, who are you to mock at us in this way? Give me that paper and get out of here as fast as you can and don't wait for a tip."

"Father!" said Bertrand. He stepped a pace forward and held out his hand.

"Is the woman Rachel Abrahamide, daughter of Isaac Abrahamide the Jew, and wife of Bertrand de Montbrun, in this house?" asked the clerk once more.

"You might at least have said, *the noble lady!*" cried Bertrand. "What do you want with her?"

"We have to give this paper into her own hand." Bertrand went very red, but ordered the manservant who was clearing the table to go and find the Lady Rachel.

216

"What's this?" said his father. "Are you going to let yourself be insulted in this way? You disturb your wife to please a pair of rats from the chancellery?"

"Father, for God's sake, let us take these accursed papers and let these people go. You can chide me afterwards."

Bertrand and Rachel found themselves summoned—upon pain of bodily constraint—to appear at the Bishop's chancellery two days after receipt of the sealed letter, to answer for crimes against the faith; this in accordance with new ordinances promulgated at Toulouse by his eminence Roman, the Cardinal-deacon, Legate of Gaul.

Bertrand was beside himself. "This is your peace!" he told his brother. "A fine life we have awaiting us! You'll see—all our property will be sequestrated and our children will have no recourse but to become masons or stone-cutters."

Rachel was weeping. She was a very lovely woman of thirty-five, plump, white-skinned, with black hair and eyes, eyebrows and lashes; her face was attractive even through her tears.

"So this is my punishment, Lord. Why did I bring so many children into this world? I shall die a hundred deaths a day if I have to watch them go hungry!"

"Sister," said Roger, "while I am Lord of Layrac we shall not want for bread. And perhaps if I speak of this to the Count, he may be able to intercede with the Bishop. If they confiscated the houses of all citizens guilty of heresy, half the people in Toulouse would be reduced to sleeping in the open air."

Bertrand glanced at him sourly. "It's all very well for you to boast, *you* have never been 'guilty', otherwise you would know the Bishop's court is unlikely to confuse me with 'half the people in Toulouse'!"

"Roger is quite right," said their father. "You will demand that they produce evidence, and your counsel will be able to show that your accusers are your personal enemies—once their evidence has been impugned, what other charges can be brought against you? That you have attended sermons? Anyone who says they saw you there must have been there themselves. If they are heretics their evidence is invalid; if they are Catholics you will say that you are just as much as they."

Bertrand listened to his father, his nostrils dilated and lips tight, as much as to say: "Have you nearly finished?" He was a nervous, excitable man, always ready to put up his hackles, like

217

a dog at the sight of a wolf. He was pacing round the room saying over and over again: "But why Rachel? Good God, why Rachel? The husband can answer for the wife. They can prove nothing against her. Rachel, my dear, have you done anything while I have been away that you have hidden from me?"

"Nothing," said Rachel. "Nothing, my dear, I assure you." Roger thought—wrongly in all probability—that she dared not speak out in his presence. He bowed to his father and left the room in an extremely bad temper.

He went to seek out the Count in his new residence—a handsome mansion near the Serdane gate—intending to make a considerable fuss. The Count was not seeing anyone, and there were numerous petitioners with similar complaints to Roger's. They waited, walking in the great square courtyard, under the rose-coloured balconies from which hung cages of brightly coloured birds. "When can we see him?" "He is hearing second Mass in his private chapel." "The Mass should have been over a long time ago." "He is giving an audience to the Abbot of Belleperche."

"Has he at least been informed of the names of those against whom charges have been brought?" "The matter does not concern his tribunals, so why should he know the names?"

"Have so many charges ever been brought against honest citizens in a single day? It is for the Count to intervene and avoid trouble. Surely he can ask the Bishop to proceed in order and only investigate the most urgent cases."

"As though the consuls had not said that to the Bishop's deputy time and again in the past week? They were answered that where heresy is concerned all cases are urgent."

Roger betook himself to the Bishop's palace, where he had a friend, one of the chapter canons, named Raymond de Cahuzac. He was not able to speak to him in private and had to shout to make himself heard above the crowd thronging the passages.

"Roger, put yourself in my place! I can do nothing for you."

"Do you know anything about his case?"

"How can I know? There are more than a hundred accused and nearly two thousand witnesses."

"But who are his accusers?"

"Roger, my advice is, tell him to answer yes to everything they say to him. They will authorise him to do penance."

At the Bishop's palace, Roger learned that families such as the Roquevidals, the Miravals, the Aspremonts, the Maurands and other notorious but powerful heretics had received no summonses, and was vexed for his brother's sake. Then he reflected: "So much the better: it shows they can't feel as strong as they claim to be."

As he was leaving the Bishop's palace, he met Master Isaac, with two of his Jewish friends. They too had been summoned, and were coming to ask for explanations.

"Sir knight, believe an old lawyer, this business has been specifically arranged by the Cardinal-Legate in order to demonstrate the excellence of their new laws. As soon as he has left Toulouse the prosecutions will be suspended and we shall be able to get the cases deferred, at least for those who can put down bail."

"Do you really believe," said Roger, "that there is any risk of a trial?"

"How do we know? I have never been afraid of prosecution, sir knight. I am old and my wife is dead. But it will be hard for the young ones. What miserable wretches can have testified against us? And I was fool enough to believe I had no enemies." He added that it would not be easy to find lawyers to defend them. Such a large number of accused would have called for the co-operation of every lawyer in Toulouse, and those he had already consulted said: "If we figure in the defence of heretics, we can never plead before the ecclesiastical courts; the judges will find all our clients guilty."

When he had walked a long way and talked to a great many people without any success, Roger went to the Aspremont mansion. He was no longer invited to visit the ladies of the house, but he hoped to meet Rigueur there by chance; in his misery he felt overcome by the urgent need to see her, even if he could not speak to her.

Bérenger was busy with preparations for departure. In the great hall servants were taking the armour down from the walls and packing household goods into boxes. Roger asked: "Are you leaving Toulouse for long then?"

"God knows. Life is cheaper in the country, and we shall be sure of firewood, and fish and game on the spot." Bérenger was not so much sad as busy and excited. A defiant light shone in his eyes. With him was his son Ricord, now—at fifteen—nearly as tall as his father and as handsome as his father must have been at the same age: black curls, pink cheeks and fire in his eyes. Roger searched the boy's face for his beloved's features but, except for the stubborn, almost ruthless, set of the bold mouth, nothing reminded him of Rigueur.

"Don't think I am leaving the city through fear of an indictment," Bérenger said, "because if I do in fact fear that, it is not for myself. It is not I who will be dishonoured, but the man who has promised never to desert us whatever happened. Now see: he gives me to understand, and some of my friends as well, that we would do better not to show ourselves in Toulouse, and to allow ourselves to be forgotten, as far as that is possible. It's a nice thing if, after we have served him with our blood and our money and—God knows!—with all our will and our love, we get nothing from him but the right to be forgotten!"

"How can you blame him? His hands are tied."

"I am not blaming him. When he came back to Toulouse, I swore fealty to him like everyone else. I went to do penance and kiss the Bishop's ring like everyone else. I promised to respect the Catholic faith and pursue heretics, and everything else that was necessary, and to which he pledged us without our consent. But that is the very last oath I shall ever swear in my life, and from today onwards I shall do as I think best and no longer be dependent on anyone."

"Do you imagine," said Roger, "he won't take up arms again as soon as the opportunity arises?"

"Possibly," said Bérenger thoughtfully. "Possibly. On that day I shall be at his side as an ally, but not as a vassal. And I shall serve him in everything that is for the good of the country and our Church, but in nothing else. He can take that as said."

"Have you told him that?" asked Roger.

"Yes. And he answered me: 'I have no right to ask any more of you.' He promised me aid and support in everything within his power, and added: 'For the moment at least, that is not promising you very much.' "

Bérenger looked round at the empty walls from which the paintings were already flaking away. "I may be forced to sell this house," he said. "And I shan't even get a good price for it, because who can buy houses like this just now? But in these times it is better to be able to carry your possessions with you."

Roger was not able to speak to Lady d'Aspremont that day; he only saw her from the courtyard, leaning on the balustrade of the covered balcony. She was resting her chin on her clasped hands and her expression was stern and sad. When she saw Roger, she frowned and turned away, her nostrils quivering as though she wanted to cry. Roger was deeply distressed by this and tugged sharply on his horse's reins, making the animal rear up, just beside the balcony on which the lady stood, and Rigueur started backwards as though she expected to see horse and rider leap on to the balcony. Roger got the animal under control and raised his right hand in a salute. Rigueur did not return his greeting, and hurried away along the balcony and into the house without turning round.

Seeing her close by and alone, Roger felt disturbed, and the image of the face he loved engraved itself on his mind, effacing all other memories and everything he saw around him. He knew she was unhappy and, with a lover's obstinacy, persisted in believing that he alone could comfort her. Moreover he thought that because she had run from him she must surely still love him. But he was not to see or speak to her again for years except as a stranger and in the presence of others.

In the heretic convent at Mirepoix, Lady Béatrix said farewell to her mother and daughter, and to Gentian.

"Leave me, my darlings. You were a temptation to me in this world, and now may I only see you again on the day when I am dead to this world and born again in the Spirit! When the Church deems me worthy of this, then come and share my feast; I have pined so long for the candles which shall burn that day. Forgive her who leaves you in a day of bitterness and grief. I have been a burden to you, dearest Mother. Surely you ought to rejoice because you will no longer have to bear with my lamentations every day?"

Lady de Miraval blessed her daughter and placed a lingering kiss on her forehead and eyes. "Ah, Béatrix, it should have been I who turned to God first, but I no longer have the heart to hold you back. May you find in God the happiness which has departed from us. I shall be so lonely in our house."

There was great unhappiness among all the heretic families, whether noble or bourgeois, and although the men managed to preserve their equanimity, the women were mourning as though for an only son. That autumn many widows and young girls left their homes to go and live a hermit's life, and there was strife in more than one home, because wives, who were not bound by the necessities of war and vows of fealty, reproached their husbands with their failure to defend their country's laws. But Bérenger d'Aspremont was not one of those who could be reproached for

221

this: the day peace was proclaimed in Toulouse he swore, on the heads of his children, on his sword, and on the candle burning before the Gospel—swore that he would never submit to such laws, and would live according to his own faith, which he would defend against the Count if necessary, even if he were to lose his life and his property in so doing.

He made Ricord, his legitimate son, and his two bastards, swear the same oath, and ordered them to take off the crosses they wore beneath their clothes, according to custom, and place them on the floor at the base of the great candle holder. "May this sign protect us as it has protected us hitherto! And may those who worship it hear the Mass as they please, since their Pope has given them permission: they have won their faith, let them keep it! As God is our witness, we have served the Count better than the Catholics." There were tears in his eyes and he was biting his lips to keep them from trembling. Gentian came to him and put her hands on his cheeks and kissed him solemnly on the lips, as a woman gives the kiss of peace to another woman.

"Never," she said, "shall we forget the shame we have suffered because we fought so hard! Bad cess to all those who do not think as you do!"

"That would be wishing harm to too many people, my lady," said Bérenger, "but God bless you for having shown me your esteem! May neither I nor any of the men here present ever deserve a noble lady's censure."

After this, the women had retired to their own apartments to weep and bemoan their fate; and it was then that Béatrix declared that she no longer had the courage to remain in the world. Her daughter was already past thirteen and betrothed to Ricord d'Aspremont whom she had loved like a brother from her cradle; and her mother was strong enough in her faith to support her absence. "If, after so much blood and tears and anguish, this peace is all we have managed to win, my friends, it must be in vain to oppose Satan in any way but by prayer and the grace of the Holy Spirit. Let them know that their new laws shall never make us afraid, and the love of our faith has never been greater in this land! They have no power to take our joy from us."

Lady de Miraval wept and wrung her hands; and little Marquezia, a sweet, gentle girl, wept too, silently in bed, biting her arms so as not to wake her companions.

Gentian's eyes were dry and her face red; she could not sit still

but paced savagely back and forth in her room like a caged beast
—she, who was always so agile, banging her head against door
frames and knocking over stools. Her body was on fire with a
grief she had no words to express—she could only repeat the
same vain words over and over again, going over the same arguments all day long, the same arguments that had been repeated
for twenty years in hamlets, cities and castles, which the whole
land was pleading in vain before God. If there was only a judge
in heaven or on earth who would hear us! And the litany was
beating again inside her head:

*All fortified castles surrendered, the walls of Toulouse pulled down,
our Count's castle held by the French, so much to be paid to the churches
and abbeys in indemnities; our fields burned and our vines uprooted, and
the Count's heritage to be bequeathed to the King, contrary to all justice—
and in return, in return for all this, could they not at least leave us our faith?
We have been despoiled, but at least let us not be dishonoured, our men not
forced to swear to betray their brothers, and ourselves not sold by the hands
of those in whom we trusted. If it was even a matter of saving their own
lives, or the Count's—but there they are reconciled to their Church and
absolved, the peace is sworn, our cities delivered up, and the stranger's
garrisons hold our castles while we are forbidden to keep soldiers, and in
return for such a peace they have sold us, and the Christian who wants to
live according to his faith is called a thief and a murderer! We are compelled to support foreign garrisons at the expense of people dying of
starvation, and even at the cost of this humiliation the Count could not win
the right to be master in his own house!*

*So that the poor people may no longer die on the roads, so that no more
men shall be hanged on oak trees at the crossroads, so that the harvests
may not be burned each summer and the vines may bear fruit—uh! we
shall have our corn and our vines so that we can pay them their tithes, and
our enemies will leave us in peace so that we can make them rich! Simon
de Montfort never demanded as much even in open war. That woman is
the Great Whore herself, the Devil's concubine!* Ah! What was the use
of not lamenting out loud when there were no other words in the
heart or in the head, no other words! *Our own leaders have abandoned us, the good Count of Foix who could have spoken for us was not
admitted to the Council!*

What use is it now to weep for fathers, brothers, husbands and
sons! Happy the dead, they have never known they were fighting
to bring the peace of the French and the priests. In her fierce
grief, Gentian thought of Roger de Montbrun as an enemy; she

223

felt soiled because she had loved him deeply. The memory of him was like a spit in the face to her, and even her former loving hate made her ashamed. She thought she could never bear the sight of him again. Fear of temptation? Would to God it were! She was drunk with a wine so bitter that she would have found comfort even in lustful thoughts. But to see this creature, once so handsome, and be ashamed of him and for him—and she had seen him, from her balcony, on his black horse; and he wore the same tender expression he used to wear. He would not put on his hauberk again, never again would he raise his banner, never again would he charge into battle crying: "For Toulouse and Christ Jesus!"

They have given in to the law of the conqueror, they are no longer men. Let them go to confession and communion, the interdict has been lifted, the churches are open! The Mass will never be celebrated on our lands at Belvèze, and our men will never swear fealty to Foulques or Marseilles. He has burned our fields and slaughtered our cattle and now he comes to claim his tithe; see, Roger, we are good Catholics, ours is a Catholic country again, and our Count is forgiven and reconciled to the Church, but we are not!

After leaving Béatrix at Mirepoix, Lady de Miraval and Gentian went back to Toulouse, to the Aspremont mansion, which Bérenger had left a month before. The lovely house was empty and silent: no horses in the stables or hawks in the mews— and to think they had gone to so much trouble to put fresh plaster and paint on the walls, and adorn the balcony with a carved balustrade! Water was seeping down the walls through cracks that had been poorly plastered over and rust eating into the window bars, as autumn drew on the house was decaying for lack of men.

"It will be better for you and Bérenger if I stay in Toulouse, my dear child, no one will touch the house while I live. One day your son and Marquezia will take possession of it again and watch their children grow up in it. This peace is not written in the book of God, nor sealed with the seal of angels."

"*Amen*, my lady. We must believe so, and that this shame will pass like a fever. It takes more courage to live in the world now than for the rigours of a convent."

Gentian, who had always believed she had courage enough for three lives, now found herself so broken that even a single life

seemed too long. She was thirty-seven, and not yet old, but for a
woman this is the age for self-forgetfulness. "My life has been lived
so badly, all upside down: love after marriage, marriage after
the convent, and now in maturity a confusion scarcely pardonable
in a young person. Ah! When I was young I had such a sure
judgment and such a burning faith. We have lost our soul in this
war, we have lived from one battle to the next, desiring victory
more than truth. The pearl of great price has been sold for a
thousand pearls of wood and brass.

"Oh, the cruel weariness of a heart that once believed it was
strong enough to conquer the world in itself. What does my life,
good or bad, matter when we have suffered for nothing, hated for
nothing and thrown the bread of the poor to the winds by promising them more than we can perform? The widows, the orphans,
the maimed may spit on us, for first robbing and then abandoning
them. They will say: 'The Christian faith has brought us misery'."

In that first winter of peace, Gentian had lapsed into such a
state of wretchedness that Bérenger asked her whether she was not
longing to go back to Mirepoix to join Lady Béatrix. "To be
perfectly frank with you," he said, "you are making our children
and servants unhappy by your own great sadness, and they would
rather lose you and know that you are in a place where your
heart is at peace."

"Do you find me inattentive to my duties?" said Gentian.

She was not inattentive to them, but worked harder than any
servant, the first up, and the last to bed, lighting fires, kneading
dough, dipping candles, and mending clothes, with the furious
energy of a well-paid worker. But she talked little and sang even
less, and when she smiled at her children or at Marquezia, the
smile seemed to cost her a great effort, as though she were lifting
a fifty-pound weight.

"I do not desire anyone to love me," she said, "or that my
sadness should hurt anyone; because it is of little consequence
whether I am glad or sorry. I should be no happier anywhere in
the world than I am here." Bérenger was sheltering two very
venerable Christians in his house at Belvèze, Guiraud de Montauban and his companion. Gentian was devoted to them and often
sat in their room with her mending or her loom and listened to
them in silence. "Monseigneur Guiraud is a holy man," Bérenger
said, "but you would hear better sermons at Mirepoix, and would
not be burdened with the cares of a household."

225

"You have not understood me: it is the children and yourself who hold me here. Bear with my sadness patiently, because it will pass as everything in this world passes."

Bérenger, who had been living with the lovely Saurine Mercier for the past five years, felt some bitterness and resentment for his lawful wife, though he would not admit it because he had a sincere esteem for her. (Later on, many years of troubles shared together were to lead to a deep love between them, much stronger than the indulgent fondness which frequently unites a husband and wife in their old age. But at the present time, since Bérenger was unable either to love or hate his wife, he told himself that they had become a burden to one another.)

"Bérenger," Gentian went on, "perhaps if you had married a different woman you would still be in Toulouse; you would have practised the faith in secret as many others do, and still be in possession of your lands at Montferrand. I am well aware that your friends blame me for having driven you to compromise yourself more than you need."

"No one, my lady, has ever made me do anything against my wishes, not even you. It seems to me that on the contrary, it is you who are regretting my foolishness for the children's sake. Because when they were small you spoke out boldly, but now they are grown up, you want honour and wealth for them. And that is my fault: while the war lasted I was among the foremost citizens of Toulouse and took my place in the Count's palace with my good fame as a heretic written all over my face."

"That is the reason I shall never leave you, unless you force me to!" said Gentian. "Do you really think I am pining for Béatrix, or for the man I once loved? Don't you know that your value is a thousand times greater in my eyes?"

How can one finally destroy such an inward grief?

Laughing and singing with a raging tooth-ache, lighting fires with hands covered with chilblains, reading when your head aches fit to burst—to all this Gentian had been broken in from her youth. She knew the intoxication of vanquishing the flesh: in her convent she had been reproved time and again for her excessive ardour. But why? The soul knows its own way, flesh that is violent needs violent outlets and has nothing to do with gentleness and proportion. By preaching moderation to me, she thought, they allowed me to fall into all the errors of this age, and my struggle is no longer against the flesh, but to gladden a heart full of sadness, and a heart that has good reason to be sad. Never was sadness more justified!

Nothing: not solemn meditation, or reading pious works, the sight of the children's pretty faces, or hard work, toiling for those one loves, prayers or the holy discourse of men of God; not the taste of wine nor the warmth of the hearth nor the soft breeze over the blackened fields where the crows fly, not even the memory of faces once loved (through having loved too much she was even sated with that joy), nor the hope of better days—none of these things could help her to kill a sadness which burned in her veins and the marrow of her bones. She was haunted by a cruel vision: a vast painted canvas surrounded her, glowing with colour and a succession of ever-changing pictures. The colours would fade and die away, and the background of the canvas become covered with bright pinpoints of light; then the colours would return, the white, then the pink, and the blue, and the pictures begin to move again in a simulacrum of living beings and inanimate objects, faces sweet to behold, smiling or sad, but all beloved. But this was only a veil, lighter and finer than a silken marriage veil, cold and lifeless, so fragile that one blink could dispel it, and behind it there was only the endless night.

How, behind the diabolical brilliance of the painted cloth, to find the heart's road through the black night. She could hear them weeping and groaning, but there there were, gyrating on the shining screen, their painted images smiling or grieving for the appearance of pain or pleasure. Oh, she thought, that I could become an appearance of joy for you, my beloved, that, from my dark night to yours, my love might cross this dead canvas to warm you.

Béatrix has chosen the easy way.

My son is as tall as I am; he is fifteen; his moustache is beginning to grow and his voice is breaking, and he blushes and loses his temper a dozen times a day. He has his own horse and bow, and is beginning to raise his voice in front of men, and talk of faith. He knows nothing of the country's troubles, small tragedies make his blood boil, like a quarrel with a comrade, an unmerited reproof or an unsuccessful hunt. He suffers as much as a man. Children do not talk much to their mother, boys especially. In the evening he comes to kneel and be kissed on the forehead. Looking straight into my eyes. He has Bérenger's black eyes, Bérenger's mouth, and an open, unthinking smile, the smile of

227

the little boy he used to be. His mother is a refuge, simple, safe, and he demands nothing of her. The girls, Raymonde and Marquezia, are both tougher and softer, more capricious too, they were not brought up for a life of hard work; their dresses are getting too short and their shoes too small, they always think they are starving, they have attacks of wild laughter and burst into tears, always about nothing; and at night, in bed, they tell each other stories about death, tortures and ghosts. Marquezia is fourteen, and she is beginning to look grave, and stop singing and running in front of the boys, and to look at Ricord with fear and suspicion because one day they will have to sleep in the same bed, and it is not easy for girls to reconcile themselves to that thought. Time goes so quickly when one is no longer young. God, thought Gentian, so quickly, they grow up so quickly, and what kind of life can they look forward to if the laws do not change? . . . Poverty is nothing so long as they only leave us alone. (She had a foreboding that one day they would have to leave the country for the sake of their faith.)

At the beginning of Lent, in the first year of the new peace, a troop of ten men at arms, escorting a priest and a clerk from Toulouse, stopped at the intersection of the roads between Belvèze and Rouffiac—the sentinel challenged them from his post high up in the watchtower, and told them they should go no further for the land belonged to the knight Bérenger d'Aspremont. "We know that without your telling us," said the priest, "and it is precisely this land that we have come to visit." At this the soldier blew a blast on his horn. Half a league further on the troop came upon Bérenger in person with his son, his brother-in-law and his servants, all armed for a boar hunt. "If you did not know that this land belongs to me," said Bérenger, "you know it now. What is your business here with spears and halberds?"

The priest drew a paper from the wallet fastened to his saddle bow and held it out to Bérenger; who glanced at it abstractedly, then tore it into pieces.

"You must know," he said, "that I am concealing no heretics on my lands. And if there were any on my lands and I was pleased to give them up, I should do so of my own accord. Go back whence you came."

The priest said he had been sent by the lord Bishop and that the men-at-arms belonged to the Bishop's guard. He added that they had full powers to seek out heretics on any land and in any house where they thought to find them, and that any person opposing this search placed himself in a position of open rebellion.

Bérenger repeated: "Go back whence you came. There are more than twenty of us and you are only thirteen, or, for practical purposes, ten. Risk your lives for such a paltry affair, if you like."

"Do not take this in bad part, sir knight, no wrong shall be done to your goods or your people. We are empowered to have your woods and your house subjected to a search."

The hunters raised their lances and Bérenger moved forward along the road, forcing the priest's horse back. "If you care whether you see Toulouse again, you will not go one step further."

He brought his lance up against the horse's chest, and Ricord, his son, tickled the priest's chin with the end of his bow. The frightened priest hardly dared turn and look at his men-at-arms.

"Ricord," said his father shortly, "lower your bow."

"It was only a joke, father."

"This is a man, not a dog. Let them go in peace, we will escort them as far as the crossroads."

"A report of all this shall go to the Bishop and to the Count," said the priest.

"No doubt," said Bérenger contemptuously. "It is your job to make reports. Only, I advise you not to meddle with soldiers in future, you may fall in with folk less patient than myself."

(It was after this incident that Bérenger met Roger de Montbrun at Cabaret, and Roger made him an offer that was one day to bring him a good deal of trouble, because Bérenger was beginning to fear for the safety of the Christians he was sheltering in his house. Roger possessed an impregnable hiding place deep in the cellars of his castle, the secret of which was known only to himself and Jean-Rigaud de Marcillac. Admittedly Bérenger had long been familiar with the anxieties which beset husbands who are no longer living with their wives, but he had not suspected Roger, or had suspected him less than other knights —friends or relations— endowed with handsome faces and good reputations. It never occurred to him that his wife would have taken a sincere Catholic as her lover. He had therefore accepted the offer made that day without further thought, and it was without further thought too that the offer had been made. But not understanding the loyal friendship existing between one man and another, Gentian took

229

offence at the idea that her husband might one day accept such a service from the man she had secretly loved. She thought: "God grant that he never has to render us this service!")

For this man she felt now the same grievous compassion that burned in her heart for her children and friends. And when she remembered Roger, this compassion was more vivid still, because, of all the faces painted on the cloth, with the illusion of flesh, his face was the richest in false colours and the most fleeting. And when she thought about him, and about that first evening when she had been conquered by one single glance, she understood how a new veil had been stretched before her on that day. Through this veil of light and colour, she had long looked at everything around her—and it had all been nothing but a dream, right up till the day when an ugly and cowardly act had awakened her. . . .

For a long time yet Gentian lived in the anguish of spiritual dryness, seeing always before her the gaping void behind the appearances which the lies of her fleshly eyes presented to her. Then one night of sadness and torment she found peace again, one hot August night—beside the well in the little inner court in the house at Belvèze. Two days before, Ricord had received his first real wound during a nocturnal attack in St. John's wood. A troop of the seneschal's men from Castres had fallen on the faithful gathered in a clearing for public prayers.

They had been driven off, with some dead on both sides; the people at Belvèze were strengthening the palisades and clearing the moat, and two signal fires were lit at the crossroads. Ricord had been brought back to the house with a spearhead in his left thigh and a knife wound in his chest. In the early hours of the morning they had buried the bailiff of Belvèze—a cousin of Bérenger's—in the orchard, and his dog was howling and crying over the grave; neither kicks nor caresses would silence him. In the house the women were weeping and mending their men's surcoats and carrying the sacks of corn and barley piled in the barn down to the cellars, for fear of another surprise attack. Gentian had spent two days and nights at the child's bedside, without closing her eyes or taking any food, and had gone out into the courtyard for a moment's rest and prayer. He was no longer in pain, he was sleeping.

It was a hot night, the stone walls and the stone coping of the well were still warm after the hot day and it was airless in the courtyard. The sky was as black as ink and the sound of muffled voices and children crying drifted out through the open door and windows under the overhanging gallery. A lamp was burning in Ricord's room. In the distance the dog was still crying in a shrill, pitiful whine as though he were being tortured. Gentian leaned heavily against the trunk of the old lilac tree that grew near the well and wiped her sweat-streaked face with her sleeve; everything seemed to exude the warm, bitter smell of sweat and her clothes were soaked and her hands moist with it—the child's sweat mingled with her own. Her own cheeks were burning with the child's fever, and her bosom ached from her child's moans and his hoarse breathing. He was only sixteen and so terrified by the terrible pain that he writhed like an animal caught in a trap.

He was no longer in pain. He was asleep. It was not a serious wound, and he would get many more (she had seen enough crushed, burned, gashed and purulent flesh to know that these were merely good wholesome wounds and a healthy, youthful fever that would abate with sleep. But the moans of her own flesh were burning in her bowels and she could no longer think of anything). It seemed to Gentian that the fever was attacking the very stones and the tree and the dry earth of the courtyard, that the broad heavy leaves of the lilac were sighing in pain, and the black overcast sky filling with the howling of the dog and returning it like an echo. Muffled thunder was rolling in the distance, then coming closer, and Gentian saw what looked like an immense siege tower, hauled up a rocky slope by a thousand men pulling on the ropes—it was coming closer, and the din would be fearful when it was upon her!

The pitcher beside the well was empty and hot, and Gentian let it down to draw some water; the water was low and a little coolness rose from the depths of the well, with a musty smell. By the time she had heard the splash of water and drawn up the pitcher, heavy warm drops were beginning to fall slowly about her, one trickled down her forehead, others fell on her hand and drummed softly on the lilac leaves.

It was not raining heavily, but in big, sparse drops; as though it were possible to hear each separate drop fall and to count them all. Gentian lifted her head and the rain fell into her eyes; it seemed to her that because she herself could not weep, the sky

231

was weeping for her. Instead of washing the sweat from her face, the rain itself was slowly changing into sweat. The hot stones were drinking up the rain. Inside the house, the voices had fallen silent. The black sky was shaken by distant thunder. The dog was weeping and wailing in his own language—there is such vast misery in the soul of an animal. One or two days more and he would die.

Lord, here before my eyes is my children's life: a giddy abyss of pain and ignorance that makes me faint to contemplate. Here before my eyes is my own life, and my husband's and those of my friends and of all the men, living or dead, that I have ever beheld —pain, folly, vanity and oblivion. When we are nothing but dust, the rain will still fall on the stones of this well as it is falling to-day. . . . The flesh of my flesh has already been exposed to the weapons of death, and my own can protect it no longer. Lord, the beast cries out in ourselves, the beast is weeping and will not be consoled. Oh, that my body could become like the root of man-dragora that takes into itself the sickness and pain of all who touch it. A light breath of wind made the lilac shiver and at the same instant a tremendous flash of lightning in the shape of a cross rent the black sky above the courtyard. For a moment Gentian saw the well and the gallery and the covered balcony smothered in its trellis of virginia creeper, and the great jars below the gutters, etched in white light, much brighter than sun-light, and then there was blackness again, as though she had gone blind; the crash of thunder burst on her head and it was as though the house were crashing about her ears shattered by a hundred-thousand-pound rock. Gentian leaped like an arrow and was in Ricord's room before she knew where she was running to. She clenched both her hands on the boy's shoulders to stop him leaping up. "Sleep, it is nothing, it is over."

In the wavering light from the small lamp the youth opened his eyes wide with terror. "Mother, I'm not going to die?"

"No, never! You are better now, go to sleep. It is only thunder."

The rain was now beating down in the courtyard with a noise like the sound of thousands of scythes being whetted, and blows hammered on the metal plate of the main door as the men returned from their nightly rounds; someone ran to open it, and the lanterns guttered in the rain.

Bérenger came into the injured boy's room, streaming wet and panting, his hair plastered to his forehead. Gentian and Saurine were watching by the bed, exhausted by the heat and feverish themselves, but happy because the child had fallen back into a healthy sleep.

"Thank God," Bérenger said quietly. "I was afraid for the house, but it struck the big poplar tree. There is nothing to fear, no one will come on a night like this!" He did not take his eyes off the sleeping child, and they were shining with a calm, tender happiness. Gentian knew, then, that what she felt in her heart at that moment was joy.

Then such a continuous uproar broke over the roof and in the courtyard that Gentian thought of nothing but holding her son's hand and stroking his brow, as though by her caresses she could prevent him waking up. The whole household was up and about, and they could hear the children crying at being woken up and the girls' excited shrieks; the horses were whinnying and banging their hoofs against the partitions of their stalls. "This is the end, and we shall have no more vines for another year. No fruit either. Hailstones as big as cherries and we'll be lucky if half the tiles aren't broken." It was not even necessary to say it, it was in all their minds.

At dawn the whole family, vassals and servants, gathered round the table in the great hall, and the reverend Guiraud and his companion said prayers; and the dawn rose on a day of peace. Round white hailstones glittered on walls and window sills, in the great court and the inner court, and began to melt; while in the orchard the apple and pear trees were as naked as in midwinter.

Two years later, a fortnight before midsummer in the year 1233, Bérenger d'Aspremont's entire household was in a ferment of activity: good clothes were taken out of chests and cleaned, and the bride's trousseau packed into a red, painted box and installed in a new cart. And so it was that Bérenger appeared again in his native city, in which he had not set foot for three years.

He crossed the old bridge and traversed the streets of his own neighbourhood, with his family, his vassals and squires, the ladies riding pillion behind the men and the men with their spears resting on their saddle bows. Many people recognised the Lord of Aspremont and raised their hats in a joyful greeting

233

because they thought he was restored at last to the Count's favour. At the Aspremont mansion, Lady de Miraval welcomed the travellers, weeping for joy. "Now God grants me the favour of blessing my grandchild and seeing her settled in life, and I can die in peace."

This was a formal speech and her joy was also formal; never had Lady Alfaïs had less reason to be at peace. "Take care to mount a good guard," she said, "and barricade the windows, there is such unrest in the city that we may expect anything; and above all, Bérenger, don't go walking about the city unarmed or without an escort. I have done what I can so far to avoid your case coming to a trial, but when they know you are in Toulouse they may take advantage of the opportunity."

"I dare hope," said Bérenger, "that the Count will not send his provost and constables to fetch me."

He went to the church of La Daurade, where Guillaume-Bérenger de Ribemont, a cousin of his mother's, was vicar. The old priest was not a heretic (though his enemies said so) but he was attempting in all good faith to establish peace between the heretics and Catholics. He received Bérenger in his sacristy and began by heaping reproaches on him.

"Is it not written," he said, "'blessed are the peacemakers'? You, who pride yourself on knowing the Scriptures, how can you forget those holy words? Here you are resisting, by force of arms, with open defiance and bitter speeches, an established power which, even if it seems bad to you, is none the less a test of your patience imposed by God. Many people who profess your faith do it with humility and discretion, and by so doing they conform to the precepts of charity at least."

"My dear cousin, for a long time I believed that was a practicable way. I do not blame those who submit on the surface. If I am defending my liberties on my own land by force of arms, it is not for pleasure."

"Bérenger, you have come to see me in order to ask me to marry your son according to the laws of the Catholic Church. And because I baptised these two children myself, I will do it. But, God knows, I should have liked to be able to do it with a lighter heart. Don't you know all that our honoured cousin Alfaïs has had to pay to the Bishop's clerks (by selling objects she held dear) in order to ensure that no one took up your case? Now the records will be placed in the hands of the Preaching Friars;

234

you know what they are and you know they are neither to be intimidated nor bought; moreover, they are truly not peace-loving folk. No doubt I shall also be accused of having blessed a sacrilegious union between two people resolved in advance not to respect the Catholic faith."

"You are looking too far ahead, my dear cousin. What can they accuse you of? Can there be anything improper in blessing the union of two baptised children? If the customs of the land considered marriages valid without the blessing of the priests of Rome, then maybe I should not have asked this service of you. But my son will (I hope) have to take his place among the knights of Toulouse, and I must have him married properly. Children won't wait until peace is re-established before they grow up."

For a week, the Aspremont mansion was filled from morning to night with visitors and their squires and horses, just as in the days before the peace. In the great hall, where the arms of Aspremont, Montgeil, Miraval and de Roques hung on the four main pillars, Bérenger presented his son to his friends. The bride, who was not to appear in public before the wedding day, dwelt upstairs in her grandmother's apartments, surrounded by young girls of noble family whose mothers had sent them to stay a few days in the Aspremont house as a compliment to Gentian and Lady de Miraval. They were short of beds, the carpets were worn and faded and Gentian was able to serve nothing in the way of refreshments beyond olives, almonds and honey cakes, but this did not prevent the girls from spending their days in laughter and singing. Gentian and Saurine received the ladies in the chamber destined for the bridal couple, displaying the trousseau (quite presentable, because Lady Alfaïs had had all Lady Béatrix' dresses and shifts made over and put all her remaining jewels into the dower chest). The old ladies talked of long-ago weddings, and those who were not so old made an effort not to talk about their troubles—they were so plagued by lack of money that even the most noble ladies were becoming as conscious of the price of bread, and the dates their debts would fall due, as any middle-class housewives.

On the Saturday before St. John's day, the Aspremont ladies received a visit from Rachel de Montbrun and her sister-in-law; and it was with a sincere joy in vanquishing an evil passion that Gentian (who had once felt an unreasoning hatred for the woman) now took Guillelme's hand and kissed her, and seated her on a cushioned chest beside Bérenger's sister. Guillelme's smile was somewhat strained, her blue eyes were hard and set and she avoided looking directly at anyone. Rachel was talking of the mingled joy and sorrow that any mother is bound to feel when her eldest son is married: her own was twenty already and she was hoping to receive a daughter-in-law in her own house before long. She sighed as she said this, and nodded her head, making her long silver and jade earrings quiver under her lilac-coloured muslin veil. They all knew that Lady Rachel was having difficulty in finding brides for her sons, since for three years she and her husband had been living on provisional liberty.

"I am not yet at the point where I have to face that worry," said Guillelme in her cracked voice. At this, Raymonde de Bermond, Bérenger's sister, told her: "Why, you are so young that you could be taken for a bride yourself."

She did not look her age; she was insolently elegant, but the heavy and brooding look in her eyes made it difficult to laugh and chatter in her presence. When Saurine offered her a bowl of toasted almonds and nuts, she made a sudden movement to avoid touching Saurine's foot with her own, and affected not to see the proffered bowl. Now Saurine was a proud woman and finding herself treated in this way she blushed and went to sit down on the window sill next to Gentian.

"I see, Lady d'Aspremont," said Guillelme, next, "that in your house you practise a greater charity even than Jesus Christ's, for it is written that he permitted persons of ill repute to enter his presence, but it is not written that he entrusted them with the care of running his house."

There was an embarrassed silence, and Gentian, not wishing to have Saurine insulted, answered with a forced smile: "Are you referring to me, my lady? I can see that you meant it as a joke, but my wits are too slow to understand you."

"I do not care," said Guillelme, rising, "if you choose to mock me. You are much older and wiser than I, but yet I know you have a great fondness for the colour red, which is not in your coat of arms. I have heard so much talk of your wisdom that I should not be surprised if anyone told me you had cast the evil eye on my son."

"Sister!" exclaimed Rachel, imploringly. "Sister, do not shame us with such idle talk!" But Guillelme was scarcely in a

236

state to listen to her; she was looking at the scandalised ladies, her eyes hard and bleak, like a hunted beast's, and her small red lips were trembling. With a terse gesture she wrapped her cloak round her and left the room, brushing aside Rachel, who attempted to follow. Seeing Rachel's evident distress, the ladies began talking of other things. They knew that Guillelme de Montbrun fretted about her sickly son and accused her husband and many other people of having caused his illness.

"My poor sister-in-law has known too much suffering," said Rachel, "and she is too young to be wise."

"Don't we all know what a mother suffers on her children's account?" said Gentian. "You must tell her that I am not angry with her." (She sincerely meant this, but her heart was heavy: she had a feeling that such an exchange in the bridal chamber, practically on the eve of the wedding, presaged bad luck. *"The colour red,"* she thought, *"if she said that with the intention of hurting me, surely I shall see our little dove's red gown bring her bad luck? It is my fault that the colour red in a man's hair has not brought her happiness. . . . Suffering breeds suffering and it steals among us by unknown paths, passing from one to another like a sickness."*)

"The poor woman," said Raymonde de Bermond, once Rachel had gone away. "She looks fifty; and she was still so lovely before that business of their becoming reconciled to the Church! Now she lives in a state of constant anxiety, and if her husband is home an hour late she sees him cast into prison."

"Do they both go to Mass?" asked Gentian thoughtfully. "A man like Bertrand de Montbrun!"

"What else can he do? He has eight children. His life is hell."

Gentian could well believe it: Bertrand de Montbrun would have got up from his deathbed to carry a message or organise a collection.

"Ah! I wish," she said, "I wish these celebrations were already over and we could go back to our domain; I shall never be able to live here until the Count has imposed his will on these lackeys of the Pope! How much longer will he let them go on insulting him?"

"Is this the moment to think about such things?" said Raymonde. "In two days' time you will be making the marriage bed in this very room. Let us keep our thoughts on cheerful things, as far as possible."

"We have come here for a celebration, and our men are

237

keeping watch at the street corner with swords in their hands."

That evening, Gentian went to the young girls' chamber to visit the bride and found her pale and tired, with dark circles round her eyes, and trying bravely to look happy.

"My darling child, what is it? Are you thinking of your mother?"

"No, no," said Marquezia, "it is the heat. I stayed too long on the balcony. It is terribly hot in the city."

"Be patient a little longer, darling. Tomorrow you will be left alone in this room, to rest and pray, before your ladies prepare your bath. Look, your pretty hair is all wet with perspiration."

"Mother, don't worry, I think all girls must be excited on the day before they are married."

Later, Gentian was to blame herself for not having talked to the child for longer, and for having left her in that hot room, its air heavy with perfume, full of gay, silly young girls crowding close to the barred window and whispering and laughing all night long. Lady Alfaïs had said: "Let her enjoy herself with her friends for just this one night longer. I will take her into my room tomorrow." Marquezia dared not admit that she hardly felt in the mood to enjoy herself.

When an illness comes so suddenly people's minds turn first to poison, then to witchcraft. Yet Lady de Miraval said tearfully that she had let no suspicious person come near the girl, and would herself answer for the food served to the young ladies. But the illness struck so suddenly and terribly on that marriage eve that one might have thought the Aspremont house was on fire. The panic that reigned there was so great that thieves could have walked in and stolen the master's armour and no one would have noticed. Bérenger had called in two women skilled in medicine and even a male healer, despite his reluctance to allow a girl to be tended by a man. William of Carmaux, the healer, was a Christian well known in the city for his skill and sanctity, and he told Lady de Miraval: "Abandon the vain hopes of the flesh, and think of preparing the invalid to receive baptism while she is still partly conscious. It is only a matter of hours now."

Marquezia lay in her grandmother's great curtained bed, screaming and crying, her hands tearing at her hair which was dripping with cold water. "*Mother, mother, take away my head, I can't bear it!*" Leeches made a strange black crown round her little red, mottled forehead. The two women doctors wrapped her naked body in cold cloths and made her drink potions which she swallowed only to throw them up immediately on the sheets.

"Monseigneur, you have just pronounced my death sentence," said Lady de Miraval, bowing before the minister. "But for God's sake do what is necessary; we will obey you in all things."

"Speak to the girl, and have fresh leeches put about her head to relieve the pain while it is still not too late. I will go and find my companion and the Book. Pray God I return in time!" Bérenger sent an escort of four men-at-arms with the holy man because the news had spread through the neighbourhood and gapers were already collecting in front of the house, saying: "*What a misfortune for Lady de Miraval! The young lady is at death's door, and they may not even have time to give her a heretic baptism.*" The girl was uttering such piercing screams that they could be heard even in the street.

Ricord, very pale, his eyes red and burning, was pacing back and forth in the courtyard, every now and then beating on the door of the staircase leading to the upper rooms. An old servant's scared face appeared on the other side of the little barred judas window. "Master Ricord, for God's sake don't make so much noise, you know I can't let you go up."

"Guilleberte, I shall break the door down! I shall kill myself, right here in front of you, with this knife."

"Monsieur Ricord, when the holy men have come you will be allowed up; she is not ready yet."

"I want to see her before that, Guilleberte! I want to see her before that!" His friends dragged him away.

"Ricord, what is the good? What is the good now? Have a drink and prepare yourself, will you be seen at her baptism with your hair all sticking up on end and your shirt undone?"

"Ah! She doesn't care, my poor darling," thought Ricord. "She doesn't care whether she sees me with my hair combed or untidy! Not once has she called my name, she only calls her mother." (He loved his betrothed dearly, and with a tenderness that amazed his parents for he was a tough lad.)

Visitors crowded into the hall but the blow was so sudden they could find nothing to say to the master of the house. All of them felt this blow fate had launched in the face of one of their number like a personal injury, as though God or the Devil were making it known that a man who remains true to his faith has no

239

longer even the right to see his children happy. Poison? Bérenger had no personal enemies, and Lady de Miraval was respected by the Catholics who were most devoted to the Bishop.

"Bérenger, don't be so dejected. Who knows whether this is not a sign of favour? Perhaps this child was destined to die a virgin?" Bérenger answered these trite expressions of comfort with a pathetic smile, bitter and abstracted. "Yes, yes, my friends. I must think so. If only I had been able to have her mother brought here . . . it will be a terrible grief to her, my friends!" The sick girl was still screaming, and servants were running as far as the street corner to watch for the arrival of the holy men. A crowd had already gathered in front of the house, and the chains had been taken away from the end of the street to allow the passage of a hay cart. Bérenger's brother-in-law, Bernard de Bermond, had given orders to the men-at-arms to stand by in case the Bishop should send some of his own people. When at last the ministers arrived one of the soldiers who had escorted them came to say in Bérenger's ear: "We have done our best, but I believe we were followed." Bérenger shrugged. "Who would dare violate this house on such a day?"

Dressed in a white shift with a wet cloth wrapped round her head, the sick girl was sitting on the bed, leaning back against a heap of cushions; and her clouded eyes stared sightlessly at the candle flames burning around the bed. The family and visitors stood close together for the room was small; and the women were biting their lips and fingers in order not to cry aloud. The ministers recited the prayers and exhortations as fast as the rule would permit, because time was short and they were not even sure the girl could hear them.

Gentian and Lady de Miraval sat on the bed on either side of the dying girl, holding her hands to prevent her from struggling.

"Little dove, just one more minute, only a minute! . . . Listen, listen carefully to what the minister is saying. Repeat it after him, remember now, try and say it. . . . My darling! . . . Our Father, our Father!" The girl moaned and repeated: "Our Father."

"Which art in heaven. Make an effort, darling." They shook her and urged her, with the desperate obstinacy of mothers saying to a sick child: "Be good now, one more swallow, you must." And under the pressure of their firm, loving arms the disease gave way, for a few seconds, and the panting, terrified

240

girl drew herself up in a last effort, not to pray, not to listen, but to obey, since obedience was necessary.

In the hall the friends and relations took their leave, bowing silently before the two ministers, who were pale and troubled themselves, since they did not offer consolation to such youthful invalids every day.

"Brother," Guillaume de Carmaux told Bérenger, "weep, since nature demands it, but harbour no unchristian thoughts. I know this disease, and it comes neither from poison nor any human ill will. May the Holy Spirit comfort and strengthen this maiden's soul! There is nothing more we can do for her."

"Thank you for your good counsel, Monseigneur," said Bérenger. His mouth was trembling so that he could hardly speak. "I think . . . I think you had better go out by the back way. My men will guide you. I have had the neighbours warned."

Lady de Miraval came down, and gave the two ministers a sandalwood box in which she had placed the necklaces and bracelets that had been intended for her granddaughter. "Her inheritance is not large, Monseigneur Guillaume, but permit me, for love of her, to give it into your keeping. May the Church make it bear fruit in the service of God's poor! And may the Lord forgive a woman's foolish vanity which kept these miserable gold trinkets and coloured stones to deck the body of her beloved child! Now I who watched her sufferings am the poorest of the poor. Tell me how long this will be!" She drew herself up to her full height, and swallowed, sniffing, while the tears trickled down her thin dry cheeks and she did not even trouble to wipe them away.

The ministers had gone when Guillaume-Bérenger de Ribemont, accompanied by a deacon and two clerks, came and knocked at the door of his cousin's house. Bérenger gave orders for the vicar to be admitted, but not the three other men.

"Bérenger," the priest said to him, "you are behaving like a fool. You leave my assistants at the door, and everyone will say that you have thrown them out. It is already said in the neighbourhood that your relative has received consolation from heretic ministers, and the Bishop does not treat such matters lightly. She has been baptised; she must have Christian burial."

Bérenger looked at the old priest, his eyes blinking and swollen with tears, apparently wondering what was the matter. "Cousin, you can see . . . there is enough noise being made about this poor child already. I know what you are suggesting: the sacraments of the Church, after Christian baptism, and before witnesses. I know you are acting from charitable motives, but I do not play with sacred matters in this way. Do not be anxious about her burial, I shall allow no one to touch her body."

"God help you, Bérenger. I myself ran no small risks and dangers in coming here, you know well enough that I am accused of too much tolerance."

"My dear cousin, there are occasions when tolerance becomes falsehood. If you cleave to your faith, then obey your superiors. According to your laws we are all quite rightly excommunicated and vile, you should have nothing to do with us."

The vicar withdrew and returned to the presbytery of La Daurade as discreetly as he could. In the evening a delegation from the Bishop's palace appeared at the Aspremont house, to make enquiries into the matter of a suspicious death. Marquezia's sufferings were already at an end and the women were crying and wailing while those whose duty it was to prepare the dead washed the frail corpse and combed and dried the lovely fair hair.

The Dean of the Bishop's chapter had come in person, accompanied by two brothers from the Dominican friary and half a dozen armed men, led by one of the city provosts. The men-at-arms on guard at the door said they had orders not to admit anyone, because the house was in deep mourning. "You should be aware," said the Dean, "that this order does not apply to us: we are here in the name of the Count and of the Bishop."

Bérenger's nephews hurried to their uncle, saying: "Must we be ready to fight?"

"Have you gone out of your minds? Are we on our own lands? The Count is master here." He gave orders that Lady de Miraval and Lady d'Aspremont were to be warned, walked to the door and himself drew back the bolts. His relatives and his men stood behind him. He saw the Dean in his white habit and the two monks in their white robes and black cloaks, standing, stiffly erect, two paces away from the door. And the Dean's clerk stepped forward first and asked whether it were true that a woman had died in the house without benefit of the sacraments of the Church. He bade the knight Bérenger d'Aspremont to allow the very reverend Dean and the Brothers James and Sicart of the Order of St. Dominic to enter his house in order to proceed to an enquiry on the spot.

"Are ye come out as against a thief, with swords and with staves . . . ?"
said Bérenger, slowly, staring at the provost and the men-at-arms with a dazed expression. "Forgive me, my lords, for quoting holy writ, as though I were mad enough to compare myself to our Saviour. My house has just been visited by a grief so cruel that it is not surprising I am out of my mind. If you have obliged the Count's provost to accompany you, that is your right, the new laws of our land permit you to do so. But know that I am the Count's man and a free citizen of Toulouse, and I am no criminal; I do not deserve to have my house violated on such a day."

"If you wish," said the Dean of the chapter, a big, stout old man with a pale face, "the soldiers will remain outside. But permit us to enter, because on this we have formal orders."

Bérenger allowed the three monks and the clerk to enter just as Lady de Miraval, supported by Gentian and by Raymonde de Bermond, made her entrance into the hall through the inner door surmounted by the Aspremont arms. The old lady had dressed herself once more in her black garments and had veiled her face with a long white veil, and she advanced with very slow steps, her hands crossed on her breast and hidden in her sleeves. "*I* am going to speak to them, Bérenger," she said. "Gentian, my dear, lift my veil so that I can look at them properly." She stopped in front of the Dean, who bowed to her respectfully, saying that he was grieved to see such trials inflicted on her by God. The two Dominicans remained stiff and straight as statues.

"Have I not heard it said, my lord Dean, that Monseigneur Raymond, our Bishop, sends you expressly to convey to me his sympathy in my bereavement?"

"My lady, my lord the Bishop does indeed condole with you, but he is greatly grieved by a rumour which is abroad in the city: it is said that you allowed your granddaughter to die in a state of sin, by depriving her of the succour of religion."

Lady de Miraval drew herself up and closed her eyes, while tears rolled down her withered, chalk-white cheeks.

"Tell Raymond de Falgar that I am sixty-five years old and that now my line has died out with that child. Tell him that his own mother, who was a worthy and noble lady, also knew the grief of losing her children. You will come back another day."

The Dean told her there was nothing improper about the presence of religious men in a house of mourning and that he and

243

his companions were quite ready to join with the family in praying for the soul of the deceased, if they could be certain she had died in the Catholic religion.

"She died in the Catholic faith and furnished with the sacraments of the Church of Rome," said the old lady impassively. "Will you doubt my word?"

"We do not doubt it, my lady, but my lord Bishop has given us orders to proceed to an enquiry."

"Speak. I will answer you."

"Witnesses claim to have seen no priest enter this house with the exception of Dom Guillaume-Bérenger de Ribemont, vicar of La Daurade, who remained only a few minutes."

"Were you unaware that a priest from Montauban, a worthy, holy man named Guiraud Tournier, has been a guest in my house for the past week? It was he who administered extreme unction, and he who is watching and praying beside her at this moment."

"We did not know that, my lady. Allow us to go up and speak with him and receive his corroboration."

"It is not decent to disturb the repose of the dead for questions and enquiries. You do not come as friends and I shall not permit you to go up."

"Be good enough to call the priest you speak of down here, so that we may question him."

"He is at this moment praying for the repose of my child's soul and you expect me to disturb him for such a trivial reason? This has already been a hard enough day for me, gentlemen, I beseech you to leave me now. I warn you that you will only go up there over my dead body."

The three monks looked at one another in silence, bowed to the old lady and withdrew. Before leaving, the Dean said to Bérenger: "After the welcome we have received, you had better not look for indulgence from my lord Bishop. As far as we, and the whole city, are concerned, your relative died in the hands of heretics. I have not had the house searched by soldiers, as I had every right to. But know that the house will be watched, and that the soldiers will be ordered to arrest any suspicious person seen leaving it."

"I am not fool enough," said Bérenger, "to allow people to be arrested whom I do not wish to see arrested. Go in peace, gentlemen, you have my word: there is no heretic in my house at this moment."

At dawn the next day, Marquezia's body was wrapped in white veils and linen sheets and laid on a silken rug. The women wept for a long time, kissing her pale face with the blue lips and eyelids. The golden hair arranged in soft waves down her grey cheeks was lovelier than ever.

"Ah! Let me say farewell to my child's child, let me touch her delicate hands, her little, pure breasts! This is your wedding, my little one, this is your feast and the great joy we had prepared for you! Now my torch is put out, my flower plucked; see, it is I myself who am in the tomb, my tree shall bear no more fruit! My granddaughter, you lie there with your lovely grey eyes, you who have eyes no more, while I have eyes to see a sight so cruel! Why have I not the strength to pluck them out with my nails—my eyes that were made to see such a sight? . . ."

"My dear cousin, my friend," begged Gentian, "it is time for the men to say their farewells so that we can cover her up." Lady Alfaïs was clawing her cheeks and tearing out small locks of her grey hair, and she continued to moan while the men of the family knelt, one after another, before the body lying on the table. Then the dead girl's face was covered again, the body rolled in the rug and wrapped in canvas, and Bérenger, Ricord, Bernard de Bermond, first bowing to touch the strange burden with their forehead, lifted and carried it slowly into the courtyard and placed it in the cart. The women began to sob so loudly when they saw this that passers-by in the streets ran to knock at the doors and windows to ask whether some new misfortune had occurred.

Bérenger d'Aspremont and his people mounted their horses and the gateway was opened to its full width. Two knights from the Count's palace who were approaching the house at that moment were astonished to see Bérenger d'Aspremont himself in the saddle, and dressed for travelling. "Count Raymond has sent us to say he still loves you and condoles with you with all his heart on your bereavement. And he would have certainly come himself had he not been detained by urgent business."

"Thank you, my friends, and thank the Count also that he still deigns to remember an old servant. I was subjected to such an outrage yesterday in my own house that I prefer to leave the city before the interment of my relative; because, whatever you can say, I know that I am not safe in Toulouse. Even if there are people in this city sufficiently lost to God to seek to profane the

245

body of an innocent maiden, I dare to hope they will not come and snatch her from her aged grandmother, because I am well aware that I am the one suspected by our country's enemies and it is my downfall they are seeking by provoking this enquiry into her death."

"Rest assured, Bérenger, the Count neither knew of this nor wished it and he will do everything to see that this affair has no repercussions."

"That, my friends, time will show. For the present, I must go to Mirepoix to carry the tragic news to the girl's mother, and observe proper mourning, without being harassed by legal actions at variance with our customs."

The knights bade him goodbye, somewhat coldly because they regarded this precipitate departure as a deliberate insult to the Count's person. Before leaving, Bérenger had sent a hasty note by a serving man to Roger de Montbrun. It said: *"If the offer you made me at Cabaret three years ago is still open, I should be glad to accept it. Come and see me at Belvèze after the feast of SS. Peter and Paul, and if the bargain no longer suits you I shall not blame you, because what was worth a hundred nobles three years ago is not worth ten today."*

Marquezia made her last journey on a cart drawn by two mules, hidden under bundles of clothes, pitchers of wine and sacks of beans. There had not been time to embalm her—the heart and intestines had been removed and the body placed in a bath of astringent herbs; in the hot June weather she could last four days at most, and the roads to Mirepoix were very crowded, so that a big cart could not make fast progress. They travelled by night, beneath a sky so glittering with stars that it seemed light even when there was no moon; shooting stars were falling over the barley fields on all sides, and were so frequent that they soon ceased to notice them.

"Ah! Those are souls falling from heaven. May the Lord spare our lost child that anguish!" Gentian was riding beside the cart, her heart leaping painfully at every bump in the road, as though she could see the stones bruising the child's body.

The funeral cortège stopped near a watering place for sheep at the edge of a field to allow the animals to drink. The women dismounted, exhausted, and lay down on the grass verge, and they unhitched the mules to let them graze. Ricord went to the cart and lay down in the dark close to the wheels, pressing his head against the broad wooden spokes. "Dead is my wedding night,

246

dead my desire, her warm lips, her warm cheeks changed into ice-cold wax, her sweet warm smell changed into a smell of rotten fruit.

"You are up there, above me, lying wrapped in carpets and veils that by now are sticking to your flesh, which is already turning brown, you are up there, smothered in sacks and cloths, as heavy as lead, stiff as a board—they took you from me, our enemies were jealous of my happiness, they would not have my father able to celebrate his son's wedding. They did this to you, they did it to me: I don't love you now, you are only a corpse, but may God deny me salvation if I do not avenge you! And if I do not smash the skulls of those who send you travelling the roads wrapped up in sacking like a deer slain by poachers, and spill their brains for seeking to take your body and drag it through the streets and burn it."

"Ricord, Ricord, are you asleep?"

The boy did not move. His father left him, saying: "Let him rest a few minutes more. My dear, I wish we need never get there. What shall we say to our cousin Béatrix?"

"God will give her strength: she is already almost through her purification. Soon she will be able to pray for us."

"You will tell her . . . you will tell her not to uncover the face, you will tell her not to touch the cerements. You will explain to her why we could not embalm her."

"Bérenger, do you believe she will really be safe at Mirepoix? The way things are going, in two years they will be making posthumous investigations down there, just as they are in Toulouse."

"My dear, in such matters the shame lies on them, not on us."

"No. Oh, no! those who endure the shame suffer more; how can we bear the thought that they might touch her body? Better to bury her in a wood among the mountains."

"After all," Bérenger said thoughtfully, "the ashes of so many men have been scattered to the winds in our country that I am beginning to believe that is better than a Catholic burial."

"How sternly you speak," said Gentian, putting both her hands on his shoulders. "You have more courage than I. Bérenger, do you believe we shall avoid a trial for much longer?"

"I no longer know," the man said, bitterly. "I believe that I shall not show my face in Toulouse again, now, unless they succeed in dragging me there with chains on my hands and feet."

At Pamiers, just as the cortège was about to cross the bridge, the leader of the men-at-arms guarding the crossing said to Bérenger: "Sir knight, I have had orders from Toulouse concerning you. I cannot let you pass."

"But tell me, my friend, if there was a warrant out for my arrest, surely I should be the first to know of it? You have always let me pass before, and I have never forgotten to tip you."

"We have information that among your baggage you are transporting the body of a woman who died in a state of heresy. You will have to wait while I inform the seneschal's provost."

Bérenger looked him straight in the eyes: "It is no use, my lad. Tell me how much you want and then we'll see."

"Two silver marks."

Bérenger took his purse and flung a silver piece at the man's feet. "Here, take one, and that's plenty. With what the Christians who cross this bridge give you, you've nothing to complain of." The man picked up the coin and stepped back a pace: "May God damn me, sir knight, if I have ever done such a thing!"

"He'll damn you right enough. If anyone questions you, you will swear you have searched our baggage. And that I told you we buried the woman in question in a field near Auterive."

At Layrac, where he appeared alone, having first conducted his new guests to the cellars and opened the door of the secret passage for them, Roger settled into the tower, which he had made his private chamber, and gave orders for Jean-Rigaud de Marcillac to be sent for. The old squire appeared, dressed in his best clothes and looking gloomier than ever.

"When you finally condescend to honour the castle with your presence," he said, "it is without warning and with such a small following that anyone might think you were doing it on purpose to take by surprise those who were stealing or damaging your property."

"That was not in my mind," said Roger. "Tell me, Jean-Rigaud, have you heard that there are any heretics on our domain?"

"Even if there were it would be without your knowledge. But I have heard nothing of it."

"If ever you do hear anything of it, you are not obliged to tell me."

Roger saw the old man's narrow, green eyes clear, and his

face lose some of its tenseness. "Would you know something then? To tell the truth, Lord Roger, we have heard nothing, since the peace, but many people regret it very much."

"What is the good of beating about the bush like this? The fact of the matter is that I have given my word that if ever a heretic is found on my domain, no man of mine shall dare to betray him. And if there are any among the men-at-arms who wish harm to the heretics, you will make them understand that if they ever dare make me go back on my word they will earn a hempen cord from me. Furthermore, you will give me their names so that I know who to blame in case anything should go wrong."

"Willingly," said Jean-Rigaud with a broad smile, that was at once jovial and harsh. "Because if we are covered by your word in this, we shall know how to deal with traitors."

Roger chewed his pen and wrote the names which Jean-Rigaud dictated to him, one after the other, on a sheet of paper.

"Tell me, Lord Roger," the old man said suddenly, "it is not my business, but you must feel very strong and well protected. I don't know what they say about it in Toulouse but here some very peculiar stories are being told about the new laws we shall have soon. The priest at Magnanac preaches sermons an hour long, telling people that before long everybody who will not go and confess themselves to the Bishop's new deputies will be put in prison."

"Indeed! And what if no one goes?"

"Many will go," said the old man, with a contemptuous smile. "The priest knows things about some of them, and to the others he says: '*If they learn that there are people in this part of the country who flout the faith, the King will send soldiers to burn the fields.*' This is to tell you that your hempen cord is a good thing, but, all the same, nothing had better be known of it in Toulouse."

"There has never been any greater friendship between you and me than was strictly necessary," said Roger. "But you must know that I will cover you entirely for anything you do to ensure that no one besides myself makes laws in my domain."

Jean-Rigaud thanked him and took his leave. He had his own reasons for not loving Roger: a year previously, on the evening of harvest home, one of his sons' wives had gone bathing in the moonlight with the Lord of Layrac. Moreover, Roger always showed a stony countenance to the old man, in order to give him no grounds for believing he wished to buy his silence.

Left alone, Roger wondered whether he had been foolish,

because he could guarantee the safety of the secret hiding place, but heretics were not accustomed to dwelling in caves like Carthusian monks and he would have to be stronger than the Devil to keep them from going out and preaching. Jean-Rigaud was to be relied on, he had been a heretic believer from his youth, and the two ministers had promised not to reveal the secret of the underground passage to any of their friends—they too, by virtue of their reverend calling, were men of their word.

After receiving Bérenger's letter, he had waited impatiently for the day of SS. Peter and Paul, telling himself that he would do much more to prove his friendship for a man who deserved it so much and who had been struck by such unmerited ill-fortune. Then, upon reflection, it had occurred to him that such a proof of good faith might perhaps restore, at least to some extent, Rigueur's trust in him—and that in any case it was no bad thing to give heretics the idea that they could rely on irreproachable Catholics and on members of the Count's very entourage. (The heretics were beginning to look on the Count with some suspicion, after the laws which he had proclaimed the previous year, and this was increased by another action, ugly enough certainly, and even shameful—and though the fault lay with Bishop Raymond, the Count was none the less compromised in the eyes of many people, and not all of them heretics. By pledging himself to both sides at once a man becomes suspect to everyone.)

Hiding two heretics who were known and hunted all over the country was no bad deed—seeing that, if these men were caught, they were certain to be roasted alive, a fate which, in all conscience, one could not wish to one's worst enemies; moreover, they were very worthy old men, and respected by Rigueur to such an extent that, for all her pride, she would kiss their hands and feet. One had only to see the way she looked at them to realise that she loved them sincerely. There was no question: they were gentle, kindly men, as the heretic ministers usually were, and they were loved for that reason—and even an old ruffian like Jean-Rigaud began to smile joyfully whenever he heard them speak. God give him joy of it! It would do him no harm to listen to sermons.

. . . But then, plague take the old robber, now he was wearing a good, green dyed gown, but at the time when I was begging him, him and his, to give me money, he purposely put on an old, patched and faded tunic. He is angry with me, because of his son's wife. . . . Not very pretty; but there was something about the way she held her head, about her trim, slender waist, about her smile, something which reminded me of Rigueur, otherwise, he thought, I should never have looked for anything with a noble vassal. But how could he explain that to Jean-Rigaud?

Rigueur. It was the same every time he saw her again: he racked his brains to say something that would touch her heart, and he could no longer find the right tone to write to her. He merely wasted paper to no purpose. That day he had finally decided to send a letter to her, because he thought: "It was really for her sake that I undertook something which could bring trouble on me. . . ."

And I am doing it, Rigueur, without hesitation, because you must know that I would give my life rather than betray your trust. Yet it seems to me that I have nothing more to hope for now.

In the name of the pure, frank and loyal friendship that existed between us, I implore you to be honest with me, because it is better to wrench the steel out of the wound sharply than to leave it there to fester. There is not one man you meet whom I do not suspect, even while I hope I am mistaken. There are even some days when I am ready to direct my hatred against Bérenger himself. . . . I would not for anything in the world believe such a thing, because I hold him dearer than a brother.

How can I believe that you, who were made for love, could be capable of dismissing a lover who did not displease you (quite the reverse), unless you had another love in your heart? Do you think I cannot remember? Is a chaste life, such as you desire, possible in this age? No, on the contrary, I think a woman who has forgotten her first lover is quite ready to love a second. And if another lover gives you greater joy, I am surprised that you are still alive!

Can you say: it is over, our time is past? May God blast the jealous friends who have made you believe so! I feel no older than on the day when I saw you for the first time—laugh if you like, because this is the right moment to say: Look in your knife blade if you have no mirror! Shall I tell you that there are other people in whose eyes I do not look old or ugly? If you deign to remember, I am not yet forty-five, and you know that Guiraud de Sorges loved the Viscountess de Sazerac passionately when they were both nearly fifty, and no one blamed them.

Remember, too, all the songs I have written for you, which have been sung by people of no mean birth who have envied my lady for being loved as she was—and remember all the words of love we have spoken, mouth, against mouth, more closely intertwined with one another than hands joined

251

in prayer! Remember the sufferings you have endured on my account, or rather on nature's which has deprived me of the joy of ever having a child by you (because you know I did regret it), and you know too that I have never said a word of reproach to you for it, and have loved you all the more because you were like a tree that is always in flower but will never bear fruit. You should remember this too, that no being in the world has known you as I have known you and that no one knows me as you know me. Why will you not deign to remember, my life, the many days, the many months, when we fought side by side for the same cause, our whole country's cause, thinking only of the next day's victory? And because we have not conquered, because we have been wronged and humiliated, will you deny a friendship that has never failed you?

Rigueur, I have such a hunger to speak to you that not even in the first days of our love have I pined so for your company. Do you really believe that my life is full of joys? You know well that it is not.

Without your trust, I am like a man lost in a strange land, because it is true that there are other things which are dear to me (you know well what they are), but they have nothing to do with my body. For myself I desire only one consolation, and only one honour, and that is not my soul's salvation.

. . . How can a man permit himself to write such letters, six years after the complete rupture? Unless he is a fool he should not. Or maybe, through thinking of cities lost and recaptured and lost again, he comes to believe it is the same with women? Nothing is ever lost; one can regain all. From his youth, Roger had clung to this idea: that life was impossible without the hope of regaining all.

Now his youth was gone, and only a shadow of his beauty remained (enough to please, however, but at past forty does a man look for easy victories?). The woman he was hoping to win back was not really beautiful or desirable, and he had little time for loving. Moreover he had a nineteen-year-old mistress. But he would need two lives if he were to love another woman as he had loved Rigueur. *She was so dear to me*, he thought, *that my head was full of anxieties for a week or more at the merest hint of sadness in her eyes; until I had seen her again. . . . I had no other joy but to see her happy.*

Roger's squire, Séverin, brought his master's letter back to him, with the seal unbroken, and with it, a word in answer written on the back of an old letter to Bérenger from his uncle because they had no more paper at Belvèze. *I have not refused to read your message*, wrote Rigueur, *in order to hurt you. Nor do I fear*

252

any temptation. Why do you play this useless game? I do not think of you with hatred. But if you were a man of any sense, you ought to forget a woman who can no longer be anything to you. And but for your pride and self-love you would already have forgotten her. God grant you other loves that may bring you greater joy, both to you and to your beloved!

As he read this letter, Roger was tempted to believe that Rigueur was right. Seeing things through her eyes, finding wisdom even in the words which should give a lover most pain—true love has these aberrations, these generous impulses. At such moments one thinks: "Am I a fool? Why didn't I think of what she says here for myself? A useless game? Of course it is. Pride and self-love? Evidently. But God of Gods, if it were only possible to see her, and see her again, to learn of her griefs and anxieties from her own lips. Ah! And how much rather learn of her joys. Joys that can mean little rejoicing for me."

Who are the friends Bérenger entertains in his house most frequently? Which of them sends his servants every day, or every other day, to ask some favour or offer a share in his spoils after a hunt? Dull-witted men are consumed with jealousy and say: "I have been passed over for a rival of lesser worth"—as though women were not the only judges of our worth. Moreover, a jealous man falls into the ridiculous error of believing he is to be preferred above all others, and stupidly shuts his eyes to his own faults, which he should know better than anyone. Therefore, for a year, Roger fought against jealousy, but he did not enjoy the idea that Rigueur was allowing another man than himself to sleep in her arms. Or might be, because he did not know for sure. But he had his reasons for believing it, since, though he met Rigueur at the most only two or three times a year, still he had eyes.

He had noticed it a year ago, or rather more than a year, at Easter the previous year, when he had seen her in the great hall of the castle of Fanjeaux. She was with her son and the young girl who was engaged to her son (she who was later to die so suddenly) and the ladies of Fanjeaux. He had managed to speak a few words with her, commonplaces like: Look, the April moon again, pray God it does not mean our vines will suffer. She had looked straight at him—it was the first time she had done so—with grave kindness. She had told him then that if she had to go on thinking about cold and hail and drought she would never stop tormenting herself, and that she had learned not to worry about tomorrow.

253

She had not grown more beautiful, and was dressed so simply that but for her great reputation for wisdom she would have done Bérenger no credit. She had only one small necklace of chased silver over her old green dress—that green dress, how well Roger remembered it! from the hem to the eyelet holes and the seam at the waist; it was the same dress, worn threadbare, but hardly faded. More faithful than its wearer, this dress of hers reawakened desires that had been long forgotten. What had changed? How could it be put into words? Her frank, open expression, the freedom that could be felt in her slightest movement, everything, to someone who knew what to look for, pointed to a woman happy in love.

She was not like that in the first years after the break between them, then her eyes had been hard and dark-rimmed, her features drawn—as though she were struggling against what she called the demon. And would she have looked at me with such tranquil kindness, he wondered, if a new love had not made her forget our past joys? Who is the man? A man of her own party and her own faith. (Because if she were capable of such kindness for a Catholic, how much greater should be her affection for a lover who shares her beliefs?)

In short, it is hard to love a woman tenderly and at the same time to silence all pride and resentment in oneself. How one longs at times to presume on the common man's licensed brutality that can break out in threats and insults and challenge its rivals to blows. But a courtly man is disgraced the moment he dares speak ill of a rival, or even tries to find out his name. . . . Which one, out of all Bérenger's friends and relations? Bérenger himself, perhaps. (This idea was the most unpleasant of all: that a man of his courtly manners could so abuse a husband's rights, and take advantage of legal ties to take back the wife he had neglected for so long—but all things are possible. Love is not a game of chess, one can win at it by cheating.)

Because he is a poor man, worried and hunted, because he is fighting as best he can to live according to his faith—God forgive her, why did she have to say so often that she no longer loved him? And I felt such friendship for that man! How many people, in their madness, imagine a husband is not a rival.

The country was suffering ten times more from the Church than it ever had from the heretics, because the Pope had

254

introduced new statutes in Toulouse and in the other dioceses of the Land of Oc which were so severe, and contrary to all custom, that even the staunchest Catholics were shocked. It was understandable that the inquisition into heresy should be entrusted to the Preaching Friars, because they were better versed in such matters than the lay clergy. But it was not legitimate to take authority for the inquisition out of the Bishop's hands, because the assertion that a simple monk could be more competent in religious matters than a bishop was surely heresy in itself: it was against common sense as well as Catholic doctrine. But Pope Gregory was so blinded, owing to his great age, that he had allowed himself to be outwitted by the Preaching Friars: he held the new Order's founder for one of God's saints, and was conducting an investigation with the object of canonising a man who had done more harm than good in the region of Carcassonne and the diocese of Toulouse (he had converted few folk, and sown much hatred between Catholics and heretics).

In Toulouse, the process of canonisation of Brother Dominic Gusman was talked of with some surprise; but this was undeniably a great honour for the Dominicans of Toulouse, who, thanks to the munificence of the late Monseigneur Foulques and the zeal of the Catholics of Toulouse, might with some justice claim that this was the home of their Order. Moreover, the Dominican friary had become a busier place than the Capitol since they had taken charge of the prosecutions for heresy, because they were summoning not ten suspects a day, but fifty or a hundred. As for the matter of witnesses, half the town, very nearly, had become implicated, because they had invented a curious procedure whereby witnesses testified in secret, and the judges promised not to reveal their names either to the accused or to anyone else, no more nor less than if they were speaking under the seal of confession. People said: "It will be secret baptisms next, and secret weddings, and consuls and bishops being elected secretly. We'll see some fine trials with secret witnesses! Will people be seen coming in to confound the accused with hoods over their heads and disguised voices?" "At this rate," the burghers of Toulouse were saying, "every man who owes money, or whose wife is too pretty, or who has a bad reputation, will become a heretic."

After yet another altercation with his brother— because Bertrand had become worse than a mad dog since he had been deprived of the right to leave the city—Roger departed for

Layrac, in considerable anxiety, wondering whether his domains had not been subjected to a search in his absence. Jean-Rigaud told him: "There is a rumour that Guiraud de Montauban and his companion are somewhere in the vicinity."

"Frankly, Jean-Rigaud, have you seen him, or is this only a rumour?"

"To tell you the truth, Lord Roger, I have seen them and heard them preach, in the wood of the Two Hanged Men. If they are in the country with your connivance, then you have done something that will earn you forgiveness for many of your sins on your death bed. I haven't heard Christians preach so well since the Crusade."

"Do you know," Roger asked, "where they are living?"

"Myself, no. And if there are folk who do know it they say nothing. Besides, I'd as lief not know. I have too many children and grandchildren, and too much to worry about, to get myself mixed up with hiding heretics."

In those days many people were turning to the heretic faith who would never have considered it before, because the heretics preached well, and helped the poor, while the people the Pope had sent to combat them, 'preachers' though they were, hardly seemed animated by Christian charity, and moreover their behaviour in Toulouse and other cities in exhuming the dead of honourable families and dragging the corpses through the streets and casting them into the flames was profoundly shocking. Furthermore there was no way of interceding for people kept in prison, since the inquisitors refused point blank even to see the friends and relations of suspected persons.

Then at last the blow struck which Roger had been dreading for three years. One day when he was at Layrac arranging a boar hunt, his father's old servant arrived from Toulouse, breathless and almost in tears: Master Bertrand and the Lady Rachel had been taken away by force the previous day by the armed guard of the Preaching Brothers and were now in the Dominican friary in Toulouse. Pierre-Guillaume, he added, had been taken ill with shock. (With some reason, indeed, and although Roger did not fall ill—it was hardly the moment for that—he was as shattered by the blow as if he had been struck on the head by a mace. Sinister rumours were abroad concerning the Brother Inquisitors: they were said to resort to torture when they wanted to obtain important admissions; and Roger knew enough of his brother's conduct to imagine that they might expect such admissions from him. At such times the call of the blood is stronger than the memory of quarrels and misunderstandings, because, to give him his due, Roger was neither jealous nor resentful.)

He therefore arrived in Toulouse the very next morning and went straight to the Count's house, and requested an immediate audience. The Count was playing chess with Monseigneur Raymond himself, since the Bishop played the part of the Count's intimate friend and adviser. Roger bowed very low to the Bishop, as was proper, and said: "Most dear and noble lords, do not be surprised at my lack of ceremony, because you see before you a man bewildered by grief who comes to demand justice or mercy. An insult has been offered to my house from which I fear my aged father will never recover, and my lord Count well knows that my father has always served your father and grandfather faithfully. Yet now, in his old age, he has been robbed of his comfort and support. I would like to think that you have not been informed of this matter, or else you would have been able to prevent it."

Monseigneur Raymond de Falgar answered that where heresy was concerned the Preaching Friars had full powers to seize the persons of those under warrant of arrest, and that neither the Bishop nor the Count could do anything.

"This, my lord," said Roger, "is contrary to all the customs of Toulouse, because we are all free men and, though we have sworn fealty to the Count and to yourself, we have not given our oaths to the Preaching Friars. If my brother and sister-in-law are charged with heresy, they depend on your justice, and we want no foreign justice in such matters."

At this the Bishop answered: "You may perhaps remember that I have myself donned the habit of the Order of the Blessed Dominic."

"My lord, if the office of the inquisition were entrusted to such a man as yourself we should have nothing to complain of! But the persons designated for this office by the Holy Father are judging us not as fathers but as enemies. My brother was reconciled to the Church three years ago and more, and has not missed one single Mass since, while everything that they have been told about him is only the gossip of people who accuse him so as to avoid having to implicate their own friends."

"Roger," the Count said, "I will see what we can do; go and tell

257

your father from me that I will do everything in my power to get your brother released on bail."

"My lord, that is not the answer my father expects! I shall not dare to enter his presence unless I bring my brother back to him. I swear to you that he is as good a Catholic today as I am. And you know that my father and I and all our family have always honoured the Catholic faith, and it is not just that you should allow such shame to be visited upon us! Consider that I have been in your father's household from my youth, consider that I have known you since the time you wore short gowns and did not come up to my shoulder! Your father, the late Count Raymond, was better than a father to me. You know, too, that I have not spared my money or my blood in your service, and I have never been one of those who demanded lands and pensions from you in return for helping to defend your heritage. I would rather go to prison myself than submit to the indignity of seeing my brother imprisoned and have it said that after twenty-five years of loyal service to the Count I am held in such small esteem that I cannot even protect my own family."

"Roger," said the Count, losing patience, "it is said often enough that I myself cannot protect my friends and yet I am a greater personage than you. Ask my lord Bishop whether I have the power to have whomsoever I will freed."

Roger knew this perfectly well, and he was in fact talking mostly out of his anger and unhappiness, because after a night on horseback he was too tired to control himself.

"Ah, my lord, I do know, and this is the cause of my complaint, not to you, may God protect you, but to my lord Bishop and our dearly beloved Father Gregory, and the Virgin Mary and Jesus Christ! If I don't obtain justice for my brother and sister-in-law now, I shall go to the court of Rome myself and throw myself at the Pope's feet to plead their cause, because I maintain that they are good Catholics and unjustly accused!"

After the second Mass, Roger went to the Dominican friary, accompanied by his uncle and Raymond-Jourdain de Cissac. Brother Guillaume Arnaud's first secretary received them and told him it was not permitted to see the prisoners before the end of the interrogations. Roger and his uncle pleaded for a long time, drawing attention to Bertrand's birth and good reputation, his father's health, the children's sorrow at being parted from their mother, to everything, in short, that people do put forward in such cases.

"Not to mention, Brother," said Roger, "the fact that very often people who refuse to say certain things when they are asked will do it more readily if they are urged by their family and friends."

"That is true," said the monk. "Follow me as far as the cloister gate and perhaps you may see him for a minute. You will be able to tell your father that we are not in the habit of ill-treating prisoners."

They were both there, clinging to the diamond-patterned iron grating. They looked pale, and their eyes were puffy from lack of sleep, their clothes in shreds and thick with lime dust. Under the purple veil which gave a violet tinge to her cheeks, Rachel's face was like the resigned, grief-stricken visage of a *mater dolorosa*, and her lovely mouth drooped in a fixed, melancholy smile. Bertrand, for his part, seemed utterly terrified. His usually smooth and sanguine complexion was marred by vivid blotches, his thick chestnut hair resembled a field beaten down by a hailstorm, and between his eyelids the pupils shifted incessantly to and fro as though he could not fasten them on any precise object.

"Roger, it is no use speaking for me. But if you can get Rachel transferred to prison—I'm not saying it's bad here, tell father, and we have nothing to complain of—but you know yourself she has done nothing, that it's because of her father and me." He was talking in a hoarse, feverish voice with a passion quite unlike a husband's natural anxiety for his wife. Roger had never seen a man disfigured by fear to this extent, and this fear penetrated his own heart like a knife because he believed his brother to be the bravest of men.

"In any case, she has told them all she knows . . ." Bertrand went on. "There is nothing more she could say even if she wanted to."

"Father is very ill," said Roger. (He was thinking of the monk standing beside him, close beside his shoulder, listening to Bertrand's words.) "There are remedies which only Rachel knows." Bertrand reddened, hesitated, then appeared to understand.

"No," he said. "No. No other remedies besides the sage potion and the lime flower compresses. Jacques' nurse knows that: three times a day and three hot bricks at his feet."

"That's enough," said the monk, laying his hand on Roger's arm. "Come."

Bertrand pressed himself against the grille and gripped it with

259

both hands, with a childish gesture, as though he hoped to squeeze through the bars and keep his brother there a minute more.

"Bertrand, I will do all I can."

"Come," said the monk again, "if you stay longer you will make his case worse."

"Bertrand, I shall not let this matter rest."

"Don't have anything to do with it," cried Bertrand.

"I shall wear out the monastery steps with my knees."

"I told you not to have anything to do with it, you have nothing to do with me. You have always been given over to our country's enemies!"

The monk who had let Roger into the cloister asked who was Jacques' nurse; Roger said at random that this was one of the family's old servants. "Try and find out her name, and come and tell us, it might help us in our enquiries."

Despite his repugnance Roger had to have recourse to Guillelme's good offices to ask where he could find Jacques' nurse to convey the message to her?

"This nurse," Guillelme told him, "is a goldsmith in the neighbourhood of Saint-Sernin, named Jacques Nourrissier. I'll go there tomorrow, on pretence of selling my topaz ring. And the less you know about this matter the better."

"Would you be afraid," asked Roger, "that I might bring trouble on myself?" (He knew that in her present mood she would wish all possible harm to him.)

"I am not afraid for you," she replied, "but in case, by your ignorance or clumsiness, you might compromise other people."

Pierre-Guillaume asked, "Well, have you seen him? How is he?"

"He told me to tell you that he had nothing to complain of."

"You boys," said the old man, "both of you take me for an imbecile, you keep everything from me. I am asking you, how was he? Had they beaten him?"

"I don't think so," said Roger. "He didn't look bad."

That evening, after vespers, he went again to see the Count and found him entertaining ambassadors from the King of Aragon and the Count of Provence at his table. The Count rose from the table, excusing himself to his guests, and said: "I am pleased to see you, Roger, but your grief is like an arrow in my heart because I am powerless to give you any help."

"My lord, you are too patient. How can you tolerate your

sworn enemies in your own city? These people are neither Catholics nor friends of the Pope."

"I shall not tolerate them long, Roger."

"Long enough, my lord, for me to be in danger of losing my brother."

"I promise you," said the Count, "that he shall not be burned."

Roger went back to the Dominican friary once more; it was in darkness, all the doors were shut, and no light could be seen from the outside except in the first-floor windows. The soldiers on guard outside the main door intercepted him. He told them: "If you are of Toulouse, my lads, I'm sorry for you, because the day this building goes up in flames no one will ask you whether you are good Catholics." He finished up at last at the house of Raymond-Jourdain, who was entertaining friends that day in honour of his eldest son's forthcoming marriage. The guests were drinking and singing in the vaulted, torchlit hall. Roger asked permission to join the feast. After the first cup of wine his mind began to wander and he climbed up on to the table, saying: "My friends, our enemies have achieved this miracle through the workings of the Holy Ghost: this wine we are drinking is truly the blood of our brothers. Let us drink no more until the day we can dip our goblets in the blood of our enemies: that will be wine fit for us to drink!"

This speech was received with enthusiasm and other members of the company got up to say that with God's help that was a wine they all hoped to drink, and each would fill his goblet to the brim. But meanwhile, in spite of this pious wish, many a cup of the good wines of Toulouse and Bordeaux was emptied all the same. Raymond-Jourdain climbed on to the table in his turn and said that he would willingly give his goods and his life for the Count and the Catholic Church, and he vowed himself to combat heresy to his last breath. "This new heresy, my friends, which is worse than the other, the heresy of those accursed men who say that men must be killed and country and friends betrayed in the name of Jesus Christ! Never did Jesus Christ or the Holy Church ever command such things! And may every man who says it is lawful to do evil the better to serve Jesus Christ be called a heretic. The holy Apostles themselves suffered torture, but it has never been said that they tortured pagans who refused to be converted. They bore witness by their own blood and not by other people's. But these accursed men are disgracing the Church and

261

bringing the Catholic faith into disrepute by their damnable statutes."

Then all the knights gathered round the table swore to toil with all their might for the reinstatement of the old laws and not to acknowledge the Dominicans as the legal judges in matters of heresy. "Because if the Pope is abused by evil counsel, and so destroys with his own hands the respect due to the dignity of bishops, it is up to the faithful to remind him of the true doctrine of the Church, which neither Pope nor emperor can change. One does not take the crook out of the shepherd's hands to put it into those of his dog."

One swears such oaths when one's head is fired with wine, but as for keeping them, that is another story. Roger emptied three goblets and then fell asleep. He woke up in Raymond-Jourdain's bed; it was daylight and his friend was shaking him and saying: "Get up, it is time to go to Mass. It is Sunday, no one must think you are avoiding Mass on purpose."

"Oh, my head is full of lead! I could sleep for another twenty-four hours and then for a week. What Mass? They are putting my brother on the rack now, for the Mass."

Nevertheless, he dressed himself, poured cold water over his head and went to church.

Bertrand was not on the rack yet, but the interrogations to which he had been subjected for two days had left him so tired that he was beginning to lose consciousness of what he was saying. He had not slept for two nights, and as soon as his eyes closed and his head dropped forward, two gaolers would shake him, and if he did not wake up they slapped him until he revived. A yard or two away was a man in a white robe and a black cloak (it was not always the same man) who kept asking him questions. Bertrand answered: "I don't know, let me go to sleep."

"You will sleep when you have answered."

"I have told you everything." But he had told them nothing in fact. They had interrogated him alone, then confronted him with his father-in-law, who said nothing either, except some pious speeches exhorting the judges to charity. In the end they told him the Holy Office abhorred unnecessary cruelty, and that as it was easier to make a woman talk than a man the judges considered it wiser to subject his wife to the torture first, because her obstinacy would certainly be easier to overcome.

Bertrand woke up thoroughly at this, and turned so red that his gaolers feared he was going to have a seizure. He said: "I swear to you by Jesus Christ that my wife knows nothing."

"We know your religion holds the use of oaths in contempt and that believers are licensed to swear as many false oaths as they like."

Bertrand said: "I am not a heretic. I know nothing of what you are asking me."

He was taken down to the cellars, where he found Rachel and his father-in-law sitting on a bench by the wall, half dead with sleep. Chains and an iron collar were stapled into the big central pillar which supported the ceiling arch. Two men with bare arms and unshaven faces seized Rachel's hands and ordered her to take off all her clothes above the waist. Bertrand turned to those who had brought him (among them, a monk and the clerk who took down the confessions) and said to them: "You are Churchmen, will you dare do violence to a woman's modesty?" He was told in answer that, having to interrogate women, the judges were compelled to treat them the same as men, and that where serious crimes were concerned there was no difference between the sexes. But Rachel screamed and struggled and the two men had to rip off her clothes by force, tearing her dress and her shift. Two gaolers held Bertrand's arms fast, but they were not needed; he showed no signs of moving. Old Master Isaac stayed motionless on his bench, his elbows on his knees and his face hidden in his hands.

To tell the truth, Rachel's poor, slack white flesh would not have tempted either monk or layman; but she was a pathetic and indecent sight, with her deeply wrinkled skin and her heavy breasts, brown at the tips, hanging like flaccid bags. They chained her with her face pressed against the pillar and her arms drawn upwards by the chains, and the executioner's assistant took his whip made of ox-tendons.

"Are you going to watch your wife beaten?" the monk asked Bertrand.

"She knows nothing. She will tell you nothing."

At the third stroke, Rachel screamed. The whip hissed and the woman's back was soon a mass of long weals from which the blood oozed. Bertrand leaped up suddenly and cried out: "Rachel, my dove, if they killed you before my eyes, I should still not speak. Hate me or love me as your heart dictates." The old man was

263

crouching with his head on his knees, stopping his ears with both hands; but Bertrand watched, keenly, the smile tightening his lips growing ever more taut.

The woman was screaming very loudly and her back was already flayed when the judge's deputy raised his hand and gave the order to release the sufferer. As soon as she was free of the chains she began pulling up her tattered garments to cover her breasts and shoulders. Her husband and father were led away so that she could give her testimony freely and without fear.

Red and shivering, Rachel was straightening her disordered garments; they made her sit down at a small table next to the scribe. Her teeth were chattering so loudly that she could not speak.

They read her indictment over to her once more: the woman Rachel Abrahamide, wife of the noble Bertrand de Montbrun, had in her youth been perverted by her father and induced to confess to the errors of the heretics known as Cathars or Albigensians; but deceitfully and in derision of the Catholic faith she had asked for Holy Baptism and been received into the Church and baptised, receiving at her baptism the name Rigaude, which name she consistently refused to use; she had then contracted a Catholic marriage with the above-mentioned Bertrand; but like the dog returning to its vomit she had not only continued to attend the heretic sermons and services, but had, moreover, secretly accompanied her mother to the Synagogue, as though one single apostasy and one single perversity were not enough for her. After having confessed her errors and become reconciled to the Church she had fallen back time after time into her former errors and had been present at administration of the Consolamentum to the dying and had saluted heretics according to the perverse custom of their faith—continuing all the while to attend church and receive the holy sacrament in sacrilegious fashion. For these deeds, duly attested by witnesses, she deserved excommunication, and should be handed over to the secular arm, unless she fully and entirely repented of her sins; in which case the Church would extend its mercy to her and keep her in its bosom so that she could do penance for her sins.

Rachel said that she repented of everything and that she was not a heretic; but that it was a great sin on the part of her judges to force such a shame on a woman as to compel her to undress before the eyes of her husband and father, that such things should not be allowed, and that never in all her life would she forget the insult which she had endured. She wept as she said this and kept on trying to put her clothes in order with trembling hands.

They asked her to tell what she knew of her husband's affairs. "Would you," said the judge, "wish to protect a man who has allowed you to be so treated and showed such indifference to your plight?"

Rachel said she knew nothing and that her husband did nothing beyond helping the poor and praying to God. It was true, she said, that she had attended sermons and public prayers and had seen many people there, but the learned judges must be well informed about these meetings and the people who attended them already from those who had denounced her.

"Do not try to evade the issue: if your repentance is sincere what we know or do not know is not important. What matters is that you should confess all your sins and omit nothing."

Rachel lifted her eyes in terror to the judge and the scribe, and clutched the clasp of her cloak nervously to her throat. In her present state, bareheaded (she had lost her veil in the struggle and dared not ask permission to look for it), with her hair undone and hanging loose, her dress awry, and her back burning, sticky and painful, she felt she had become a repulsive object, so repulsive that even she herself no longer blamed these men for torturing her, for very little more she would have begged their forgiveness. She was a delicate, sensitive woman and hitherto never permitted herself an unbecoming word or gesture. She said: "I swear to you that my repentance is sincere. As God is my witness, I am sincere."

They told her that from the moment she refused to tell the truth about the enemies of the faith there was no sincerity in her words. "I know nothing," she said, bursting into sobs, "I went to the sermons because everybody went. That is all."

"In whose house?"

"In several houses. I don't know any more. My husband took me; I don't know the names of all the faithful."

The judge informed her that the interrogation was only suspended, not terminated, and that by refusing to speak she was liable to find herself fastened to the pillar again and chastised like a hardened criminal. Thereupon, Rachel dropped her head in her hands and wept, pitiful little choked sobs, like a child. She wept and wept and was unable to stop. The judge took pity on

265

her and said: "What is the use? We shall get nothing from this woman. We will continue the interrogation tomorrow."

Bertrand and his father-in-law however were subjected to lengthy floggings several times that day, because confessions of great importance were expected from .hem. Moreover, they were not easy suspects to question because the old man was very weak and fainted after three strokes of the lash—they cut him down, and threw water in his face until he came to himself and sighed: "Ah! Lord, it has pleased you to deliver me into the hands of the infidel!" or "Lord, Lord, how they are putting my old flesh to the test!" but as far as confessions went, he admitted nothing, saying: "May God keep me from committing so great a sin! What have I to fear? Take my life, I am almost dead already."

Bertrand de Montbrun, on the other hand, was one of those wiry, energetic men who grit their teeth and stiffen under the lash and start singing so as not to scream. He told them: "Keep at it until tomorrow, until Christmas, if you like! I am a soldier and do you think to frighten me with your whip?" But since he had as good as had no sleep or food for three days, he began to laugh hysterically and his whole body was trembling when they unfastened him from the stake. This led the Inquisitor presiding to say: "This man is at the end of his strength, it would be cruel to continue."

The judge and his secretary argued for a long time between themselves as to the method by which they should proceed with this obdurate prisoner. A night's rest, they thought, would allow him to recover his strength so that he would be in a fit state to endure the question extraordinary. They could not count on the old man, he fainted much too quickly. "I warrant you," the Inquisitor said, "that this man will not talk, either tomorrow or the day after. For this type of man there is nothing but the dungeons."

"The dungeons? You are well aware that in a month's time his confessions will be of no value. We must strike while the iron is hot, and his case has been allowed to drag on too long already. How much fear will the Inquisition's justice inspire if we cannot manage to make him talk?"

It should be said here that Bertrand de Montbrun was thought to be the treasurer and collector of funds for all the heretics in the Saint-Sernin district; and he was presumed to know the hiding-places of several heretics who were concealed in the city (his passionate determination not to speak proved as much). It was a shocking thing to lay hands on such a man at a time when the Church's cause was already heavily compromised in Toulouse, and when insults were being publicly heaped on the Preaching Friars at every crossroad—to lay hands on such a man and find out nothing was to prove the Count and the Church's enemies right. They would be bound to assume that the man had been wrongfully accused, and everything the Inquisition said about the heretics was false.

But Bertrand did not speak under the water torture or the boot; he merely managed to injure his tongue because he bit it so hard, after which he was really incapable of talking. He had to be treated first and was then put in a dungeon in the Alemans prison, in the hope that he might talk later.

Old Isaac Abrahamide, from whom no confessions could be extracted beyond his invincible devotion to the heretic faith, was not handed over to the secular arm, despite his refusal to recant. It was feared that because of his age, his patriarchal appearance and his great reputation for charity, his execution might provoke unrest in the city, since it was getting near Christmas and the city was full of pilgrims and people from the outlying countryside; the streets, seminaries, churches and even the houses of the citizens were crammed with people just as in fair time. Furthermore, the Jews of Toulouse, while they abhorred Master Isaac's heresy, respected the old man for his wisdom and sagacity, and the Count let the Preachers understand that this was not the moment to offend the Jews because he needed money for the Christmas festivities and alms-giving. Isaac Abrahamide therefore profited from the indulgence of the Church, which still hoped to overcome his obduracy, and was imprisoned in a very respectable cell, where there was a window and a bed. But he died, after two months, of a chest infection.

In spite of all his efforts, Roger was able to learn nothing of his brother's fate, except that he was in the Alemans. Rachel, who was confined along with some other women in a communal cell, knew nothing either. People began to talk of Bertrand as though he were dead. One day, Guillaume de Roquevidal (who was much more of a heretic than he admitted or that anyone believed) told Roger: "If your father is the kind to be proud that sons of his have died bravely for their country, he should be happier still because you will never know the men your brother has saved and how many evils he has managed to prevent! We know that he has not breathed a word of the secrets which were entrusted to him."

"And why," Roger said bitterly, "had such secrets been entrusted to him?" And he thought: My brother has given himself up for this accursed faith, for this faith which is the cause of all our troubles, like a hired mercenary who is paid to go and get himself killed. What likelihood is there that they will ever let him out of prison?

In order to avert any risk of forfeiting his mansion, old Pierre-Guillaume went to the Dominican friary and accused himself of culpable tolerance towards the heretics and asked the Holy Office for a penance in proportion to his sins. He swore, too, that he had always disliked his younger son's behaviour, and had disinherited him, and that there was no longer so much as a wooden dish belonging to Bertrand in the house. Because he was a knight, old and respected in his neighbourhood, they did not question him too closely, and he escaped with the obligation to feed one pauper in his house for five years. But of Bertrand he could learn nothing, they merely told him his trial was not yet at an end.

All through Lent and after Easter, so many cases were tried in Toulouse that folk began to wonder how the Dominicans found any time left to pray to God—surely they must have pressed half their Brothers into service to assist the Inquisitors to interrogate so many people? Moreover the Pope sent them preachers of the Order from Italy, to reinforce them in the struggle they were waging: Brother Roland of Cremona spoke so forcibly from the pulpit to the effect that the people of Toulouse were all corrupted by the leprosy of heresy that it resulted in innumerable complaints to the Bishop, because neither nobles or burghers cared to let themselves be insulted by foreigners in their own city. After Eastertide, when they exhumed large numbers of convicted dead bodies, no Dominican could show himself in the street without being mobbed and sometimes hit by stones and drenched with dirty water. (It was at this time that the trial of Bérenger d'Aspremont and his family took place and Bérenger, his wife, and his son and daughter were condemned to the stake as obdurate heretics. They had left their domains six months before and were living in the Sault district, in the house of Gentian's brothers.) It was a common enough joke that the Dominicans burned many

268

people on paper and that this was a great saving of firewood, because nobles and burghers could be delivered up to the flames by the dozen in this way, while all the time they were known to be living peacefully in the south, welcomed by the great lords and honoured by their friends.

But enough people were really burned to make the inhabitants of Toulouse realise that times had changed completely. At great festivals and times of grace heretics were burned by fives and tens, whereas formerly not one had been burned a year (except in the first years of Bishop Foulques). More than half these ordained Christians, men and women, were well known in Toulouse, and seeing them dragged through the streets in this way, with paper mitres on their heads, and people singing songs of joy; seeing them bound in the centre of heaps of faggots on the Pré-du Comte; and seeing them, aged and venerable as they were, dancing and screaming like devils among the bright red flames, many believers of Toulouse lost heart; and many people became Catholics in this way, thinking wretchedly: "The Devil is the stronger in any case."

With the Count's approval the consuls of Toulouse had it published and proclaimed at every crossroads that it was neither right nor lawful for people to go to the Dominican friary and accuse themselves and others, and that the Inquisitors were usurping a power which the Pope had never given them, and before long the Pope would hear of it, and would indict them and they would be driven from the city. But Bishop Raymond had it proclaimed that by this action the consuls were falling into heresy and that they themselves would be called to account at law as guilty of protecting heretics. There was much talk in public and private against the Dominicans, but even those who talked still joined the queue at the monastery gate waiting for hours for their turn to make a confession. Such was the fear inspired by these men because of their statute authorising secret witnesses.

Ah! Did the Pope know what he was doing when he entrusted such great power to madmen? Truly, they were mad, and totally ignorant of all justice, their justice would even have been laughable if it had not led to such terrible consequences and brought such harm to innocent people. Never, in any land, had justice been seen so contrary to the laws.

At the beginning of Lent, Roger tried to procure Rachel's

release from prison, at least for a time; they needed her at home, he said, because her two youngest children, aged eight and six, were ill. He was answered that there were servants in the Montbrun household, and that persons under sentence were not allowed out of prison except in case of necessity, while the words 'perpetual imprisonment' were to be taken literally and he must not attempt to make a mockery of the laws.

Rachel was living in a clean room, where each woman had her own place for sewing and embroidery; they were able to heat food that was brought to them over a brazier, and could look through the window into the prison courtyard. One of them possessed a cittern, and they would often sing in chorus, but their only reading was the *Hours of the Virgin*.

"Don't think the children are really ill, Rachel. I only said that in the hope of getting you released." Rachel, looking thinner and older, still retained her old, sweet, pretty woman's smile.

"They have been good to me, Roger, tell father and my poor children that, be sure to tell them, I am not lying. . . . I hope they do not move me to another room, I ask nothing better than to stay here. I am calmer now. I need no longer torment myself on my father's account, thank God, and as for Bertrand . . ." here she looked up at the ceiling, with a vague smile, "you see, dear brother, I dream sometimes that he comes to me at night and tells me: 'It is fitting I should drink this cup. . . . Every day that I live, I am heaping coals of fire on their heads.' That is how he speaks to me from the cell where he is, and I know his words are true. And it frightens me, Roger, because I have no thoughts of vengeance."

"Is there no way of finding out, by paying the gaolers?"

She laughed gently: "You are still the same Roger! Always the same question. Find out! Better to buy my daughters new dresses. Find out! He is twenty feet underground, licking the walls of his cell and drinking his own urine, because they only send his pitcher down to him twice a week, he told me that too."

In the third week of Lent, Roger and old Pierre-Guillaume followed little Pierre's coffin to the church of Saint-Sernin with torches and funeral hymns. The coffin was almost as long as a man's, all white and covered with a cloth embroidered with silver thread, but the thing that lay inside was a tiny body with red hair, already rotten in its lifetime, the mouth and eyelids covered with yellow crust. His grandfather said: "God has released him from his sufferings." But Roger was deathly sad because he had hoped for a miracle, right up to the very last day; they had made so many vows, burned candles, called in so many doctors and sorcerers. Now that torment was over, finished for ever, there would be no more stinking sores, no more ointments, no more amulets; there was an end of the timid moans, like a hurt dog's, and the long, hunted looks, so full of hope, and the small, weary smiles. ". . . *Mother says it's because of you that I'm sick.*" Mother. She was his mother, of course. She stood at the foot of the coffin, before the tall, white candles, as pale as a candle herself, her blue eyes staring and her mouth set; she even forgot to mourn, she did not scratch her cheeks, she only clenched both hands, twisting them together as if she would break her fingers. To Roger, she said: "I shall not forget that it was you who killed him. I know, they told me: those Jews gave him a slow poison." She had clung to this insane belief for years now.

"How can you say that to me, at a moment like this?"

"Should I pity you, when you did not stay by him for three months of the year? Should I pity you, when you have cared less for me than for your dog?"

"Would you have me love you, when you hate me?"

"I have not always hated you. It is for that I cannot forgive myself; I have not always hated you." The couple no longer spoke to one another after the funeral, and did their best to avoid meeting.

"The day has not yet come." People who were living in the mountains, either in Corbières, Roussillon, Cerdagne or the county of Foix, did not find the time so long: their life had not changed very much. When people talked of the 'king' there, it was the King of Aragon they meant, and the heretics preached there so often and so well that they felt more free than in the days before the Crusade. This was not surprising, because many of them had come south to escape persecution and their convents contained more postulants than ever before. There were twice as many preachers living in this one area alone as in all the rest of the land of Oc. Olivier de Termes, though he kept several priests in his castle for the sake of appearances, welcomed the heretic bishops and deacons with great honour. Altogether, this

271

was a land where men could breathe freely; they understood why folk said: "The day has not yet come." They had too much to lose in a war (supposing they were beaten) and not so much to win. Olivier de Termes did not like to be reminded that, the year before the peace, he had made his submission to the French, while the Count fought on; now he said that none of the French king's troops should ever penetrate his lands as a friend. For this reason he had hundreds of noble men in his service who asked only a small wage and lived as best they could, some on charity, some by robbery, while they waited for the day when they could win back their own lands.

"If excommunication were what the priests say it is," thought Roger (the sight of this splendid and noble assembly, in which there was not one man, from one end of the hundred-foot-long hall to the other, but was renowned for his valour, made him laugh inwardly), "if excommunication were what they say it is, the roof of this hall ought to tumble of its own accord and crush such numbers of people destined for hell fire! Yet their faces have a healthier colour and their eyes are brighter than those of the Catholics living in Toulouse."

". . . Friends, let there be no jealousy or suspicion between us, let each believe as he likes and serve whom he likes, provided only it is a lawful overlord and not the foreigner. Fealty sworn to the Seneschal and the Bishop is like all oaths extracted by force: if it is violated, the shame lies with those who demanded the oath. But faith sworn to a lawful *seigneur*, either on this side of the mountains or the other, is a faith so binding that any man who violates it of his own free will should be declared unworthy of the esteem of ladies! When the day comes, let us all have our weapons ready, and let none of us have a father to bury or a son to marry on that day! Let no one say: 'Shall I ruin my lands to help my neighbour regain his?' Because the way our enemies are behaving to us, no one can be sure of keeping his lands. While half the country is in the hands of foreigners, there can be no freedom or safety for anyone."

They knew that well enough. And there were plenty of men, too, who would joyfully have surrendered their part in Paradise for the chance to fight again. Will it be next year? Or in two years' time? We are not getting any younger, and for want of anything better our young men are fighting against the Moors in Spain and forgetting their own land—and if only King James would not sacrifice the cause of his brothers and his vassals to the Pope! If only he had the courage to defend his own people, as his father, good King Peter, had, the courage to defend his own people without asking them what language they use to pray to God!"

In the courtyard of the castle of Termes, Roger met the two Montgeil brothers, whom he had already caught sight of from a distance in the hall, sitting in honourable places next to the former lords of Mirepoix, and he had to admit that he admired them, because he would never have dared to show such arrogance if he had been clad as they were. They were all but in rags, their legs and arms bare and blackened by exposure, until they looked like Africans, their coats patched with all colours, and their scabbards so worn that the leather hung from them in tatters. They had not grown any younger, either. With his hair faded to pepper and salt, and grey beard, Sicart looked like a man of sixty; but he held himself erect and his eyes, the colour of muddy water, shone from between hard, brown lids, crinkled with laughter lines.

"The last time we met, sir knight," he said, "I was preparing for my wedding, if you remember. Now, I am married, indeed, but to a different sweetheart, a sweetheart whose heart is so great that she gives it to a thousand men without becoming any the poorer!" Roger asked if this sweetheart was the profession of arms or love of his country. Sicart opened his great gaping mouth with its chapped lips and laughed, then he said that although those were good sweethearts, there was a better still, and she was the Lady Poverty, who made a man fear nothing and desire nothing for himself. "It is nearly eight years now," he said, "since I quitted the good lady who was willing to have me, all ragged and worn as I was, and she has never married, but is now praying for all of us in a convent at Montségur. No one will ever weep for us, except perhaps our mother, who is such a holy lady that she weeps for all who suffer. We shall have a long time yet to fight."

"Pray God, it is not so!" said Roger. "When the land is free, all those who have fought for their lawful masters will be reinstated in their lands and rights."

"Bah!" said Sicart. "Soon I shall be fifty, and Imbert is not young, either. What have we to do with lands and rights? Do we even know what they are any more? We have lost everything except our faith."

Roger asked the two men whether Bérenger and his family were well.

"What!" said Imbert. "But he is here, haven't you seen him? I thought you were friends."

"Indeed we are," said Roger, "but for a secret reason, for which he is not to blame, I must not meet him."

. . . There were so many pilgrims going to Montségur that veritable processions were winding along the valley roads between Termes and Lavelanet; peasants and artisans strode along the verge, on foot, with staves in their hands, and packs on their backs, taking it in turns to sing psalms. There were mule carts piled with sacks, tools, bolts of wool, strings of onions, garlic and dried fruit, and pottery and stoneware vessels, belonging to the many merchants and numerous other wealthy believers among the crowd who were bringing offerings. That summer, in weapons alone, there were offerings of more than fifteen cases of crossbow bolts, twenty English crossbows, as many bows, fifty lances and ten good shirts of mail. (It was rumoured that the castle was to be besieged and townspeople were clubbing together, by streets and neighbourhoods, to subscribe what they could.)

The village was poorly fortified, because the place was quiet, and very retired, and was bursting at the seams with hovels, shops, barns and stables spreading over the slopes and meadows well outside the walls. A new hospital had been built not long before at the entrance to the town, flanked by two huge barns which served as dormitories for the pilgrims. Sick people were brought here from all over the region and some even came from the Albigeois and Rouergue, so great was the fame of Montségur. It was a common saying among the people that folk who received the Consolamentum in the castle, or even at the foot of the great rock, would be sure of obtaining forgiveness whatever their sins had been. For this reason the cemetery at Montségur was very nearly as big as the one at Carcassonne. Most of the graves in it were fresh, and there were no Catholic crosses to be seen on the monuments and gravestones; instead they were carved with the square cross of the heretics and an occasional dove with outstretched wings.

In the long, narrow streets of the town, male and female Christians in their black habits walked about just as in former times, and permitted people to venerate them openly in the street.

The greatest preachers in the land honoured this place with their presence and stayed there as long as two months at a time.

Bérenger and his family were lodged in a house which they shared with the families of Congost and Bélesta, because it was no easy matter to find accommodation in Montségur in feast time, and men were continually bringing their friends, some from the region of Toulouse and others from Spain. People were camping in the streets, in attics and kitchens, until the place looked like a city under siege, or the shrine of St. James of Compostella on the day before Easter—except that there was no sound of bells to be heard, and no brothels or tumblers: here no one came on pilgrimage from habit, and all festivals were as austere as Good Friday.

"And if it is therein she finds her greatest joy," Roger thought, "then I too should find my joy there, because I must believe it is by her piety that my rival has won her back." However, he dared not join the processions of pilgrims climbing by the long looping road up to the castle which towered on its vast rock like some great rose-coloured eagle in its eyrie. (Roger, in common with most of the local people, believed strange things of this castle: he thought that it was enough to enter it to become a heretic believer on the spot. In fact this had actually happened to several Catholics who were thought to be firm in their faith.)

Outside the hospital, by the town gate, Roger met Béatrix de Miraval, accompanied by two ladies dressed in lay clothes who were carrying baskets of provisions for the sick. Béatrix, as became her new status, was dressed and veiled in black, and her pale, transparent face looked as young as though she were still thirty; her blue eyes were radiant and her features as delicate and clear-cut as those of a figure carved in alabaster. Remembering the kindness the noble lady had shown him in former times, Roger prostrated himself reverently, and Béatrix blessed him, in a sad, sweet voice, holding over him her long, thin hand, as slender as a child's. One of the women who accompanied her was Gentian d'Aspremont. She greeted Roger with a friendly nod before going into the hospital. Roger sat down on the stone step to think because he felt as though for seven years his head had been doing nothing but spin round in circles like a mill wheel, without producing one single thought he could adhere to for more than two days.

"And why," he wondered, "must the only creature in the

275

world whom I cannot do without live apart from me and treat me like a stranger? Since we have eyes and ears why does absence not bring forgetfulness? Absence is a greater crime than falsehood, abuse, blows or treachery. I am a coward if I do not get speech with her, because only cowards deny themselves what they know to be good for them.

"How can I follow her, and speak to her? She is in there, close by, I have only to enter the house where she is lodging, and I shall surely be welcomed as a friend. When she goes out into the street, surrounded by her companions, to visit the house of prayer, she is still straight and slim, and walks quickly in her worn, darned, green dress. I do not even know now the colour of her long hair, knotted so severely at the nape of her neck, and hidden under the white kerchief bound tightly round her head; perhaps it has turned white on her temples now that she is past forty? She is an austere woman, so free from the defects of her sex that, though still lovely, she never courts admiration, and looks at men as a man might look. Was there ever a glance so simple and direct? Her big mouth is as cool and serene as a child's.

"An old but unforgotten love has strange impulses," Roger thought. "If I were to learn that she had found peace in the arms of Bérenger or some other man, I believe I should cling to her with a fierce and bitter passion, and should be ready to try to bring her back to me by any means. It is not her beauty I covet (she is not so lovely now as she once was), but her will and her mind. And can she yield up her mind to me without yielding her body too? It is nearly always so between a man and a woman; and how gross an error is the belief that a man seeks in this way to make himself the master of his beloved! It is not so, for love inverts the law of the sexes. At the time when we were one single flesh I was entirely subject to her will."

Roger plucked up courage to confront Lady d'Aspremont beside the well in the town square. She was talking to the ladies of Bélesta and Frémiac, who were related to her; these ladies regarded the intruder with polite surprise, not wishing to make him conscious of his untimely intrusion. Roger said that he would not have presumed to interrupt a conversation uninvited in this way, but that he had a secret message to convey to Lady d'Aspremont; the person who had given him the message was hunted and in great danger and had entrusted him with secrets which no one but Lady d'Aspremont must know. Gentian turned pale. Roger guessed immediately that she was thinking of the reverend Guiraud de Montauban, though he had not been thinking particularly of him when he made up the story. Her voice was cracked with feeling as she said: "Come. Why didn't you tell me sooner?"

Roger followed the lady into the inner courtyard of the house where she lived, and sat down beside her on a bench underneath the arcaded gallery. The courtyard was small, cluttered with faggots of wood, jars and gardening tools, and four youths were sitting on the ground polishing scythes and weapons and singing in chorus.

"Well," said Rigueur. "Speak. No one is listening." He could feel her impatience and anxiety, and wanted to sink into the ground, to make up some impromptu tale of a search, of mortal sickness, a cry for help, traitors to be punished, anything, any lie that might preserve Rigueur's trust in him for a few more seconds. Certainly a lad of eighteen would have behaved more intelligently. He kept his eyes lowered, hunting for the words in which to admit his ruse. She had already guessed everything.

"There is no truth in what you told me," she remarked slowly. "You merely wanted to speak to me, didn't you?"

"It is true," he said, "I thought that that was the best way to make you listen to me. I was too eager to speak to you."

She gave a deep sigh—whether of relief or contempt he did not know. "Well," she said, not angrily but with a kind of resigned good nature, "since you must lie, and can't help lying, I shall have to listen to you. Can I let you go on believing that I hate you, or fear you? I do not hate you. Why do you try to take advantage of me, as though I were your enemy?"

"You are my enemy, Rigueur, since you return my letters unopened. What is it you imagine? That I want to possess you by force? You have refused for so long now to tell me frankly what is in your heart."

She said simply: "I did fear you at one time. Now I am quite willing to talk to you."

He listened to the firm, warm voice, as a musician listens with a practised ear to the tone of a cittern, trying to discern some imperceptible flaw in it. How painful it is to speak like a stranger to someone who was once so close! Someone, indeed, who was closer than any other. Moreover, by talking of his own wretchedness

277

he was not trying to soften her heart, and bask in sweet but commonplace expressions of comfort. "Rigueur," he said, "do you really not remember? How I used to be able to read your eyes, and you mine, how we were ready to endure anything rather than displease one another! Must I think of you as dead and buried when I can see you there before my eyes, and your body has changed so little that the way you shrug your shoulders and tighten your lips is still familiar to me? It is not easy for me to realise that your heart is different now. For pity's sake, at least tell me if it is another man's caresses which have made you forget mine so completely? Should it be Bérenger, or one of his friends, you know that I love you too much to wish him any harm."

She was looking straight in front of her, leaning forward with her chin on her clasped hands, apparently deep in thought. Once again Roger was struck by the supreme liberty of this woman's every movement. She was not cold, she was not distant, but the great warmth which emanated from her was a fire which warmed rich and poor, friend or stranger, without distinction. He thought: "No, I was mad, she has kept herself chaste ever since the morning I left her under the walls of Auterive", but what lover does not imagine such things?

She said: "How strange it is. How you torment yourself about futile things. You are made miserable by the thought that another man possesses me? What madness is this? Our bodies have been parted for so long. You live with other women; and you do not even desire me any longer. What right have you to ask me a question which even Bérenger, my lawful husband, has never had the effrontery to ask me?"

"Then I must believe that if you love anyone," Roger said, "it is not he."

"Ah! That is all you have grasped of what I have been saying," said Rigueur, and her voice was both weary and kind. "Why do you speak to me of such things? If you only knew! I have become more indifferent to them than a prostitute. The act you speak of —I could watch anybody perform it before my very eyes and feel neither pain nor pleasure. While as for abandoning myself to it! How could I, and who should make me? I wrote to you once that I desired a chaste life: do you think I was lying?"

"Do not be offended, Rigueur. Our desires alter, and our ideas with them. I have never considered love a sin."

"No doubt," Rigueur said thoughtfully, "in the sense that is understood by common people it is not one. Am I timorous? Who would have prevented me from writing to you, had I so wished, and knowing the joys of love with you? Knowing your nature to be chivalrous, could I have anticipated a refusal? Why should I have looked for lesser joys when I was free to know the greatest? No, the reason I did not want this was because my desires were drawing me elsewhere.

"Your thoughts do not surprise me: you have known me well and you say to yourself: 'Words are one thing and the urge of the blood another.' But I believe my blood has changed. Thoughts which used to trouble me have become like an old garment which I no longer need, and I have felt my blood run more freely, my bones become firmer, and my whole body more substantial. How can I explain it to you, Roger? If our veins and sinews could only speak, how much wiser we should be about life! So many wonderful thoughts, too subtle for our language, are revealed to us merely in a single oak leaf, if we only knew how to look! Even now, you have come to find me because of an image of pleasure which remains imprinted on your memory, but what do you know of the life which is in yourself and in me?"

"I love you," said Roger, "but much less for the memory of our past joys than for your own virtues. At this moment, more than ever. Because I understand what I should have understood long ago: that you are as though dead to love. It was so hard for me to believe this that I preferred to think that you loved another. As you are now you can no longer even understand my thoughts. Yet in spite of this your voice and your face are dearer to me than those of any other living creature."

At this, Rigueur turned to look at him directly, not attempting to meet his glance, but studying his whole face with grave attention. It was as if she were trying to read or divine something, some secret which was important to both of them—and in her lead-coloured pupils Roger could see her thoughts, eager and burning, close to love yet which were not love. He knew then that she was no woman for him (not at least according to the general conception of women), that she was a unique creature destined to be for him the object of enduring fidelity. He had only to hear this woman speak to appreciate the measure of vanity in his own thoughts and his own desires. And this, not because she was better than himself (though she was), but because for him, and for him alone, she was worth more than the being called 'self'.

"Ah! Roger," she said, at last, "if my virtues merited such affection, what a perfect woman I should be. You would be much to be pitied if you had never met a creature more worthy of your constancy. What you call my virtues are only an illusion created by the weakness of your own flesh. But for true virtue, the virtue which ought to be loved, you have no liking."

Taken aback by this unexpected reproof, Roger said that he revered virtuous people whatever their faith. Whereupon Rigueur answered that such reverence was not love; and that at his age he should have enough sense not to take splinters of light on water for true gold.

"And you, Rigueur, have you reached that point already?"

"Surely, if I did not love those who are better than myself, I should be like a mindless beast. Roger, Roger, there was a time when I believed you a thousand times better than myself! See, as I look at you now, I can see in your face a reflection of the virtues I saw in it then. However hard I look I can see no evil in you. And yet, you are, just as I am myself, a corrupt being, loaded with sin. Why should we cling so to appearances fashioned by our own eyes and our own thoughts? Do not think I despise you; what I feel for you is friendship."

"What kind of friendship, Rigueur? The same friendship you feel for all men, or a greater?"

She said she did not know, and that he ought not to think of it because it was of no importance. "Here is a picture of the heart," she said. "This water butt, under the gutter: the water in it grows stagnant, leaves and straws fall into it, it rains, and the butt fills up with water in autumn and with ice in winter, then the ice melts and it overflows; people use the water and it fills up again—and why do we let the mud and ooze stagnate in the bottom? I do not love my heart, why should you love yours so much? The only thing worthy of our love is not in ourselves."

"Will you tell me you do not love Bérenger and your children and the Lady Béatrix?"

"How could I help loving them? In our lifetime we are slaves of the flesh. But the love we feel for the Church is like the longing for light. May God grant all of us this longing!"

"Do you believe you have it already?"

"I do believe it," she said calmly. "I hope so."

"Rigueur, how could I fail to honour you for the way you love your faith? But were you a Jew or an infidel I should have loved you just as much. With you alone I have known peace. And whatever you may say, I have not deserved to lose you, and have done so because I was seeking other people's advantage rather than my own."

"That is an illusion of the flesh, Roger. You never look beyond appearances in anything, and that is why you are always disappointed. You persist in seeing something good in me, though I am nothing. Yet what have we lost but the joy which swine can taste as well as we?"

"It gives me such pleasure, Rigueur," Roger said, watching her eagerly, as though he wanted to sate himself with feeding on the woman's face, "it gives me such pleasure to hear your voice that it does not really matter to me whether what you are saying is cruel or kind. But God forgive you, you cannot know how cruel it is!"

She stood up and began walking slowly under the arcaded gallery; and Roger followed her, as if he were under a spell, like the enchanter Merlin. They halted at the door of the downstairs room, already full of people, from which came a warm smell of barley soup mingled with other smells of damp leather and sweat. It was getting dark. Men were coming in through the gateway, leading their horses by the bridles, to ask if there was room left in the stables. A young man came out of the room carrying a lighted torch and went to put it in the metal ring fastened to one of the pillars. A strange yellow light fought with the bluish twilight for possession of the courtyard.

"Are you going?" said Rigueur.

"Yes, I have to go back to the Count in Provence."

"The Count spends all his time in idle wars," she said, "winning plunder and glory. Roger, if you loved me, you would not want to speak to me, but to those whom I love more than myself. I am weary of my physical being, and only wish I could hate myself! But when I talk to you of the things I love, you always come back to my body. Truly, you are cunning and skilful with everyone except with me."

As she said this, she took Roger by the hand and led him into the lower room.

"Here," she said, "in this house, you will see only people to whom you should not speak, beginning with Bérenger and myself. It will be held against you one day."

281

"Who will not have such sins held against them? Rigueur, how can you expect me to go over to your Church? I leave tomorrow. All the troubles which are raining down on me leave me hardly time to breathe; and I think I shall have more peace in the Count's army in the field than in Toulouse! To the poor, poverty is no crime, but to those who have been rich it is a great crime, because there are many people who look to me for more than I am able to give. Where shall I find the time for prayer and meditation?"

She turned to him, her nostrils quivering and her eyes burning with a golden fire. "Are you then blind? It takes only an instant to see where good is and where evil!"

He thought at that moment that he would only have to say 'yes' in order to regain this woman's love for ever. And he knew, too, that he would not say it. She looked at him sadly.

"You have never thought of your soul, always of worldly interests which will do nothing to bring you to salvation."

The air in the long, narrow room was heavy with smoke from the torches, because the owners of the house could not buy candles. There were no cloths on the tables laid for the meal, and no other ornament but shields on the walls. The men and women, too, who were crowded in between the walls and the benches, waiting for the coming of the mistress of the house before starting grace, were as poorly dressed as labourers—only a dagger, a belt or a worn fur cap recalled that these people had once worn better clothes, since everything worth more than ten deniers had been sold or pawned. They had nothing left but their pride and their good manners.

"Rigueur, you have children. What kind of a life are you giving them? Bérenger used to have other ambitions."

"Are you afraid they will be cold and hungry? They will not be the only ones, or the poorest. I have no regrets."

He thought: "What a burning sincerity she has! Perhaps she is unconsciously consumed by a chaste passion for some holy man of her Church? It is a thing which frequently happens to pious women. Surely it should make me happy that it is her real friendship for me makes her desire my conversion so?"

He did not speak to her again before leaving, except to ask her permission to write to her. She said: "Roger, take care lest God should open your eyes when it is too late."

282

"Rigueur, I might perhaps have promised another woman more than I promise you, but I have never lied to you. I believe I shall live and die in the same faith, and God knows it is not for the happiness it has brought us that I cleave to it."

At the morning meal she had graciously given him a handful of fresh strawberries which she had taken with her own hand from the big dish. Roger kept the sharp, bitter-sweet taste of these strawberries in his mouth for a long time, and their scent in the palm of his hand. Oh, my darling, you are as good as earth, hard as the wood of the olive tree, hot as red peppers, and simple as the smell of strawberries. "Only a fool can love a person who wrongs him," thought Roger, "but I love in her her contempt for love and the passionate ardour of her faith. Should I love her if she had a different face? Ah, if I could only talk with her every day, or once a week at least!"

Meanwhile, it was neither every day nor every week, but every three months at best. Other joys and other sorrows drive out the memory of love, as one forgets a treasure buried in a foreign land.

Of all the wars the Count of Toulouse waged beyond the Rhône after the peace, this was the happiest, because this time the Emperor Frederick received the Count's homage for the Marquisate of Provence in person, and solemnly invested him with the title of Marquis, which the Count had inherited from his ancestors; and so the knights of Toulouse were full of joy as they rode along the coast, with their banners waving and their helmets newly painted, and then down into the valley of the Po to join the good Emperor's army, and decided that time was not wasted in fighting for him.

"Rigueur, my life, you may perhaps know that our Count has been invested with the Marquisate by the Emperor, and that thus, beyond all possible doubt, he will regain his inheritance, and we shall not have fought for three years in Provence for nothing! Therefore it is right that we should spare neither our horses nor our lances in the Emperor's service. You must know, also, that when we captured Viterbe, the day before yesterday, your servant was not among the last to enter the city, nor shall his colours be the last to deck the towers of the city hall today.

"Do not say, my dear, that we are going too far to seek a glory that would better become us in our own land; one must sow in order to reap, and these are good seeds. . . ."

Ah, but the corn was to be cut in ear. It was no good arming themselves with patience, prudence, boldness and cunning: the seeds were good, but

there were too many tares mingled with the grain. They would have for-
gotten anything for the joy of those days. Can any man bear to live without
joy?

Life was not happy in Toulouse. Since his return from Provence, Roger had found himself compelled to remain in his
father's house six days of the week, because old Pierre-Guillaume
was so broken in health that he demanded his son's presence all
the time. "It is enough," he said, "that you are abroad or in the
field for half the year, and the house lacks a master, because no
one obeys me any more." Bertrand's eldest sons were living openly
with servant girls, and piling up heavy debts; the children were
giving up hope of ever seeing their mother again and were growing lazy and insolent. Moreover, Guillelme had no wish to take
Rachel's place and keep the house in a proper manner.

She had, besides, good reason for not leaving her own room, as
she was more than five months' pregnant. She did not even take
the trouble to hide her pregnancy, and sometimes went down to
the kitchens with no cloak round her shoulders and her robe
stretched to bursting point across her belly and bosom. Meeting
her on the stairs one day, Roger followed her to her room and
asked her not to disgrace him publicly by letting herself be seen
in this condition. She met his eyes with a hard smile; she was still
lovely despite her pallor and her blotched complexion. She said:
"I believe I am known to be a married woman."

"All the same you surely don't expect me to have the church
bells rung for this child? You will go to your nurse at Villemur
to have the child, and in such a manner that no one knows
anything."

"What right have you to demand this?" she said. "For more
than five years you have treated me like a horse you have cast
aside."

"Be sure that if things were otherwise I should have avenged
my honour."

"For the lands I brought you in my dowry," said Guillelme,
and though her eyes were still hard her cracked voice was almost
pleading, "will you not do me this service?"

Not being in a patient mood that day, Roger flung in her face
a torrent of abuse the like of which she had never heard in her
life, and went out of the room slamming the door. He knew it was
cowardly to insult a woman already humiliated, but at that time

284

there was only hatred and contempt between himself and Guillelme, and he had only too many reasons for his evil temper. His father, while claiming to be dependent on him, was continually loading him with bitter words, cursing God for leaving him the worst of his two sons as a support in his old age.

"How is it," he would say, "that you have not yet managed to arrange Rachel's release? How can a house remain thus without a mistress? Other women with small children and eight servants to supervise (not to mention myself, because I no longer count for anything), have been released on bail. Let Bertrand pay his debt, since that is how he has wished it, but make them understand that we have already been punished enough! How can they deprive me, at my age, of a daughter-in-law who has served me for twenty-two years! . . ."

Roger returned from his visits to Rachel deathly sad because he was convinced that she was going mad. She herself was aware of this and refused to see her children because, she said: "Let them remember me as I was before." Bertrand, she no longer even mentioned, except to say that he was still alive (in fact, no one was certain of this). Most of the time she talked of the miracles of the Virgin, and claimed to be sincerely converted to the Catholic faith. *"When they permit us to receive the most pure body of the Lord, my joy is so great that when the chalice comes to me I seem to see a great light all made of angels' wings! I bless my prison for this joy."* They were pious words but she laughed as she said them, laughed as though they were some charming pleasantry which should delight her hearers. She asked Roger to bring her satin and gold thread so that she could embroider altar cloths. *"Money? What is money where the glory of the Lord is concerned? Nothing is costly enough. For I have been granted the grace of uttering God's praises, I who have lived all my life in the leprosy of error."* It was pitiful to listen to her, but Roger could only nod; she seemed sincere. Rachel's companions, burghers' wives committed for heresy, were fond of her and pitied her; one day one of them asked Roger what tortures his sister-in-law had been subjected to, thinking Rachel herself must be lying since a few strokes of the lash could never have reduced her to this state.

"Yes, indeed, father, she is very well. She makes no complaint. No, she is not thinner, quite the reverse . . . she is almost the same as she used to be."

"Then why are you looking like that? Roger, if I do not see her

285

again before I die the sin will be yours. If you were a good son you would pledge everything you have to pay her bail."

"Ha! What is the use of my telling you! If I took them all the gold of the Templars they would still tell me that no bail is adequate for offences of this nature."

The old man shook his head obstinately, and said: "It is because you do not offer them enough." He still did not understand that it was easier to melt a stone in water than to bribe the Inquisitors. "And besides," he went on, "you have not even managed to train your own wife to have some respect for me. She does not trouble herself to come and greet me more than once a week."

"Parbleu! She does well. She has nothing to gain by showing herself."

"Ah!" said the old man, with an expression of disgust, "shameless jade. At least Bertrand knew how to manage the household. And what, may I ask, are you going to do with the bastard?"

Roger did not know. The author of this unwanted present was Bertrand's third son, Azémar, a lad of seventeen; he could not be blamed too severely.

A few days before Christmas, Roger was surprised to see a clerk from the Seminary of the Preaching Friars knock on the door of the Montbrun house; the clerk brought a letter sealed with the arms of the Holy Office. He said it was intended for Roger de Montbrun, knight, son of Pierre-Guillaume de'Montbrun, and was to be given into his own hand in the presence of witnesses.

It was a formal writ, summoning the said Roger to present himself at the Dominican convent, before the Inquisitor, Brother Peter Seila, to answer for offences against the faith.

When he received the summons in the ground floor hall in the presence of his nephews, Roger's first thought was to say: "Above all, don't tell my father of this, he will worry over nothing." Then he went up to Guillelme. "See this letter," he said. "I don't know whether I expected it, but I see that I am caught in a trap. If I refuse to appear I can only leave Toulouse for good."

"Take refuge in Layrac," said Guillelme with her little mirthless smile. He shrugged. It was good advice, but people often rush into the jaws of the wolf through fear for their families.

"I don't know what they can prove against me," he said. "But I should think I am good for three years in the Holy Land, if not five, and it is possible that they will keep me prisoner for a few days. For goodness' sake do what you can to keep my father ignorant of this: tell him I am at Layrac. And write to Jean-Rigaud that I have been charged and that he must take what steps he can in consequence."

Guillelme was watching him, her eyes calm and set, and strangely bright; her round belly quivered gently under the blue silk of her dress, drawn smooth as a goldbeater's skin, and she laid her hand on it and sighed.

"There you are," said Roger, smiling faintly, with a mockery he did not feel, almost with resignation, "free of me at the right moment. They will probably not grant me any respite and in two months I shall be on the boat; and then you can make me the father of a legitimate offspring which will have cost me no labour. As they say: one can never have enough of a good thing." At that moment he really was full of kindness and goodwill towards his wife, and all his former resentment seemed to him petty.

The set, hard gaze of her blue eyes made him uneasy, but he thought: "Perhaps she is too ashamed of her condition to speak."

"There, there," he said, "don't stare at me as though I were a werewolf. I shan't run away, you have nothing to fear. And if by any unlucky chance they do send me to Acre or Constantinople, Guillaume will look after the house in my absence, and I will bid him respect you as his own mother. In any case, no one can accuse you of anything that I know of?"

"That is true," she said, "they have nothing to accuse me of."

"Ah! That expression of hers," thought Roger. "Like a wooden statue."

In the evening he went to consult his friends the Cissacs, who told him not on any account to leave the city, since he had no reason to proclaim his guilt when he had the means to clear himself.

"Ah! I should have gone to them of my own accord, and not waited to be summoned," said Roger. "What good has it done me never missing a Mass on Sunday or communion on feast days, and having gone to vespers and compline whenever I was able? As far as they are concerned the only people who are good Catholics are those who go and accuse themselves of crimes against the faith."

"They want to hold a great Inquisition for the Christmas

festival," said Raymond-Jourdain, "and they must have a few penitents who look more impressive than journeymen weavers and candlemakers. They have summoned Raymond Rolland, Rolland the consul's cousin, as well."

"Ah! Am I going to have to allow myself to be publicly flogged in the cathedral and thank them for having imposed a penance on me, as though I had sinned against the faith? In the old days they only prosecuted the believers."

Raymond-Jourdain comforted his friend as well as he could but did not promise to go with him to the Dominican friary. He was not afraid, he said, but his son had taken a wife from a family suspected of heresy.

"Between ourselves, Raymond, did you go to them at Easter, during the period of grace?"

"No, not I, but my wife went. She had little to confess and I thought it was best. We paid a fine."

That night Roger could not sleep; he woke his squire and asked him to light the candle and help him shave and dress. The wind was howling like a pack of wolves down the passage. Tiles were falling and the storm made the shutters rattle on their hinges. What was Bertrand doing, did he know even if the weather outside was good or bad?

"Séverin, you will leave early tomorrow so as to be at Layrac before nightfall. I am very much afraid I may not be able to get there myself this Christmas, but as for the presents, Jean-Rigaud will have to distribute them in my place; my wife is not in a state to travel either."

Séverin said nothing and went on shaving his master's chin, but his hand was shaking. This led to a slight scratch on Roger's left cheek and he said: "If you want to cut my throat, don't worry." He was on edge and the blood on his face seemed to him a bad omen.

He felt as restless as on the eve of a battle, and a battle in which he knew he was in a bad position, and wondered beforehand which way he should run in case of defeat, and if flight would be easy. . . . There was that business of the Christians at Layrac and, even if his connivance was not proven, the offence of tolerance was flagrant. They would say to him: "You visit your domain for more than three months every year, and yet you do not know this and that?"

"Well, yes, I did not know. They know I am too staunch a Catholic to tell me." (Surely everyone said that? That was the trouble, no one knew anything.) "But tolerance is not harbouring and this was not even tolerance: I knew nothing about it. I knew nothing."

"You have been seen saluting heretics."

"Who has seen me? Slanders. It is all slander, because I am known for a good Catholic and someone wants to ruin me."

Before dawn that morning Roger went up to see his father and told him that he was summoned to Layrac on urgent business, and would probably stay there for Christmas.

"Alas! Do you really mean to entrust the running of the house to a lad like Guillaume, and at Christmas too?"

"Father, I would not go if I could help it." The old man looked at his son anxiously, his head sunk into the greasy cushions of the big bed.

"Bad news, Roger?"

"No, but the matter cannot wait. Guillelme will explain. Perhaps I may even be back before Christmas."

He kissed the old man's hand and went down to the courtyard where Séverin was waiting for him with the horses.

The Circles of Hell

O R

Four or five prisons and numerous interrogations—
not to mention judgments

I

Roger duly presented himself at the Dominican friary, accompanied by his friend the canon, Raymond de Cahuzac, and the latter's brother-in-law, Izarn Péricart. This man was a lawyer and had come not to defend but merely to advise, though for all the advice he gave he might just as well have been a waggoner. "What do you expect?" he said. "In cases like this we are wasting our Latin; there are no prosecutors, witnesses, spectators, investigators or advocates to speak of, only the scribe who takes down the questions and answers, and they are making a mockery of it by calling it a trial. Advocates would only be listened to if they pleaded against their clients, and that is not our business." However, he counselled Roger to speak first, and to admit to all the faults he could. "I should be a fool to do that," said Roger. "I might easily mention things they did not know."

He waited his turn with the other people charged. There were a dozen of these, poor folk who had brought their wives and young children with them in the hope of softening their judges' hearts, no doubt, and obtaining a speedy release. The monastery courtyard was like a street corner on a market day, because women of the people are not easily subdued; they chattered and wailed and yelled at their children, and when the lay Brothers threatened to put them out they said they asked for nothing better than to go away and take their husbands with them. However, no one did go away and Roger, who had attended Low Mass at St. Sernin, was still full of pious thoughts and self-confidence when he was called for. His friends followed him into the audience chamber, where Brother Peter Seila sat enthroned on the judge's chair, behind a table covered by a white cloth; two monks stood beside him and a third was sitting at a desk shuffling some papers. The room was white and bare, even the capitols were unpainted, and there was a single black crucifix, a few candlesticks, and a plain, black and white stone floor. Besides this, there was a stool for the prisoner, set four paces away from the table.

Brother Peter Seila did not look up, but one of his assistants informed Roger de Montbrun, knight, that he had been summoned to appear alone and that the presence of the men with him was not required. If these persons had come to stand surety for him their names would be taken and they would be interviewed at the proper time if it was necessary. They were requested to withdraw.

Roger was left alone, feeling faintly ridiculous in the presence of the monks, in their off-white robes covered with plain, black cloaks. He was the only splash of colour in the room. He remembered to remove his hat of marten-fur and his gloves, in deference to the clergy, threw his cloak across his left shoulder and sat down on the stool in the tranquil attitude of one waiting to be questioned. In actual fact, Brother Peter frightened him: he was said to be gifted with the miraculous power of unmasking lies. He was a gaunt, bowed old man, with a bald head and a mouth so wrinkled that he seemed to have no lips at all.

After the usual questions, Roger said that his conscience was clear and the charges brought against him must rest on false testimony, but that to answer them he would have to know what he was accused of.

Then, instead of questioning him, they asked him to speak himself, and earn his judges' clemency by his own, voluntary confessions. Roger said that, not being guilty, he had nothing to confess.

The judge's chief assistant leafed through a bundle of papers lying on the table in front of him. "There are fifty-eight independent witnesses," he said, "all testifying that you are a secret adherent of the heretic unbelief. Do you think you have fifty-eight deadly enemies?"

Roger flinched at the words 'fifty-eight' and said cautiously: "Perhaps these people are heretics who wish me harm on account of my faith?"

"Are you, then, acquainted with so many heretics?"

"People might have mentioned my name without being acquainted with me."

"Is it possible that you were totally unaware of your brother's perfidy?"

"To be perfectly honest with you, Reverend Brother, I did know that he kept company with heretics; there was no love lost between us for that very reason."

"Was it not your duty to come to us and tell us all you knew?"

Roger shrugged. "What I knew, the whole city knew just as well."

"If every citizen reasoned in this way," said Brother Peter very slowly, "no heretic would ever be denounced to the court."

"You are well aware," said Roger, lowering his eyes, "that my brother did not lack accusers. Was it my place to accuse him?"

"When a house is on fire, it is up to the neighbours to try and put out the flames, not people of a different district. As a good Catholic you should have been the first to warn us."

"If I have been at fault in this, I ask your pardon, Brother. But I believe I have sinned only through ignorance."

"If you and your brother were not on good terms, why should he have tried to divert suspicion from you, and claim that you were a good Catholic?"

Roger bit his lip, and was hard put to it to keep the tears out of his eyes. "You can believe him. My brother never lies."

"Have you not just furnished us with proof of your bad faith? If you hold such a good opinion of your brother you must have an understanding with him."

"I do not hold a good opinion of him, I merely said that he was not lying. Would you have believed him if he had accused me? Or would you have said: 'If this man is accusing his brother, the brother must be a good Catholic'? I am guilty either way, because if he had told you any ill of me you would certainly have believed him."

The judge's assistant—Brother Alberic de Montpellier—said that the accused was wrong to lose his temper and cast aspersions on the justice of the Church, which, in the persons of the Brothers of the Holy Office, was only trying to diagnose his malady the better to be able to cure it.

"My very reverend Brothers," said Roger, "if ever, at any time in my life, I have been sick of this malady, I hope not merely to be cured of it, but also punished as a traitor to the faith! But God, who sees all our doings, knows that I am without reproach and that I have never denied the Catholic faith, either with my lips or in my inmost heart."

He was still waiting to be questioned about particular persons and actions, but his judges persisted in asking him apparently pointless questions, in an attempt to prove to him that he was heretic at heart. He must, they said, confess to the things of which he was accused of his own accord, because they knew the whole truth about his crimes, and in their pity for him they wished to bring him to a sincere confession: by this means alone could he deserve the clemency of the Church. Roger continued to answer that he did not know he was guilty of anything, that he was the victim of slanders and in order to refute the accusations brought against him properly he must know what he was accused of. This curious interrogation continued for several hours, and Roger was amazed to find a man like Brother Peter, Inquisitor of the Dioceses of Toulouse, Montauban, Rodez, Comminges and Foix, wasting his time in this way in convicting of heresy a man who could only be accused of minor offences. He thought: "Decidedly these men lack sense, or else they have been misinformed." There were three of them questioning him—Brother Peter himself, Brother Alberic and Brother Guillaume Maréchal; the two last being men still young, with thick brown hair forming a coronet round the gleaming caps of their tonsures, and the expressions of schoolmasters trying to catch out a bad pupil in some misdemeanour. As a consequence of finding all his answers given the most unexpected interpretations, Roger was beginning to lose his self-possession.

He wondered how long these men had been teasing him like this: he was hungry and sleepy, especially sleepy, less on account of the bad night he had passed than because of the three monotonous voices harrying him with idle questions. . . . Would he have persisted in admitting nothing if he were not conscious of his guilt? Did he have so little confidence in his judges that he believed them incapable of discerning the truth? If he believed he was the victim of slanders why did he not name the persons he suspected of wishing him harm? How, living in a land that was rotten with heresy, could he possibly be unaware of the heretics' schemes? Such ignorance was tantamount to complicity, because a good Catholic should eagerly seek out all he could learn about crimes against the faith. . . . Was it not known that notorious heretics were numbered among his best friends?

"Who?"

. . . He ought to know that himself, if he named no one it must be because he suspected all his friends of being crypto-heretics. Which of his friends could he warrant to be completely orthodox? All his friends? That was hardly likely. In the end Roger dared not mention any name, for fear of hearing them say: "If you tell us that so and so is a good Catholic, it is because you are trying to conceal his perfidy from us."

It was getting dark when they finally granted him a moment's respite. A lay Brother and a guard conducted him to a cell where he was able to lie down on a stone bed and close his eyes. He told himself: "If we can't eat, let's try and sleep." But when they came to fetch him again a quarter of an hour later, he thought: "So what. I have had to go without food or sleep for longer than this before now."

The three men were there again with their scribe. "No," Roger said. "No. If you keep me here till tomorrow morning I can tell you no more than I know."

"Do you believe, then, that the Holy Office is capable of demanding anything but the truth from you?" At this Roger almost lost patience and crossed his legs with a movement so abrupt that his hat and gloves fell to the ground.

"Brothers, how can I answer you? Tell me I wanted to kill our Holy Father the Pope, if you like, but at least let me try and prove to you that it is not true! Can any man defend himself if he does not know what he is accused of?"

"You say you are a good Catholic, and you talk of 'defending' yourself, when the Church has found you guilty? Will you say she has not accused you in good faith?"

"My dear Brothers, the most saintly of men can be led into error by the evil in men's hearts. Our doctrine has never taught anything different. Does it not teach us that only Jesus Christ and the Blessed Virgin Mary have been wholly pure and without sin?"

"This is an excellent proof of your perfidy," said Brother Alberic. "Have you not just given us to understand that Jesus Christ and the Virgin Mary did not partake of human nature?"

"I did not say that!" cried Roger indignantly.

"I said: you gave us to understand."

"Must I say that Jesus Christ and the Virgin were capable of error?" Roger felt himself slipping and in his anger about to say

294

more than he should, and he struggled desperately against raising his voice. "I have never believed the heretic teaching about Jesus Christ!"

"But you admit to having attended sermons?"

"Have I admitted it? Before the peace I went once or twice. I did not think I was sinning by so doing."

"But you know that the Church holds it a sin."

"Brothers, if this is my sin, you would have to live a thousand years in order to spend as long interrogating all who have committed the same sin. I went with a tranquil heart, knowing myself firm in my faith, just as one might go to hear a singer or a mountebank. I even thought I was doing well in finding out about the errors of the heretics so that I might the better be able to combat them. Do you not do as much yourselves?"

"Are you accusing us of attending heretic sermons?"

"Certainly not! But you do try and find out about their doctrines in order to refute them."

"If you had been properly instructed in the faith you would know that laymen cannot be armed, as we are, against the poisons of error, and it is not permitted them to absorb such poisons at will, because the power of studying and refuting these errors belongs only to men of the Church. By arrogating such power unto yourself you render yourself liable to a charge of heresy."

"I am not arrogating any power unto myself. But the heretics claim to be Christians and I wished to convince myself that their claims were false."

"In other words: you do not believe the Church when she tells you that they are heretics?"

"Of course I believe her! I am only confessing my own ignorance."

"And yet," said Brother Alberic, "we know that you long maintained a carnal liaison with the noble lady Gentian de Montgeil, wife of the knight Bérenger d'Aspremont, at present excommunicated and sentenced in her absence; and the said Gentian is known to be, of all the heretic believers in Toulouse, the most attached to the heretic perversity."

Roger gave an abrupt start and tensed.

"What an abominable slander! The lady you speak of is a model of chastity."

"You must care very little for your faith to speak thus of a declared heretic."

"She may perhaps be a believer, as you say. But I have never had carnal intercourse with her, and I am not permitted to let a woman's honour remain under suspicion."

"We need not lower ourselves to these false scruples of worldly honour. In fact, five independent witnesses have confirmed your guilty relations with this woman."

Roger asked in exasperation if he was being tried for adultery and whether matters of social behaviour were also within the province of the reverend tribunal. Whereupon Brother Alberic answered that insolence of this kind could only serve to compromise him further. "It is a notorious and proven fact that the said Gentian de Montgeil is known to be a devil in cunning, and that by her venomous tongue she has succeeded in seducing her husband and other persons reputed to be Catholic. It is hard, then, to believe that she has not succeeded in corrupting a man bound to her by ties which in this present age are generally considered so strong."

"Do you find it hard to believe, then, that a man should refuse to deny his faith for a woman's persuasion?"

"So this woman has tried to convert you to her faith?"

"I did not say that. This is all a story made up by scandal-mongers."

"So," Brother Alberic continued, "if you were not driven by profane passion, how do you explain your friendship with the knight Bérenger d'Aspremont, who for fifteen years has lived openly according to the heretic faith and is even said to have received baptism? Will you have the audacity to tell us you were unaware of his perfidy?"

"How can I have been unaware of it? I hoped to see him return to a better way of thinking."

"Did you not tell us that you had no heretic friends?"

"He is no longer my friend."

"But formerly, as a Catholic yourself and knowing him for what he was, you called him your friend?"

"I hoped, as I told you, to bring him back to the true faith by pious discourse."

"Your pious discourse had very little effect. Did he never try to convert you to his unbelief?"

"If he did, he was wasting his time. Do you then think so little of the Catholic faith? You seem to think that one only has to talk to a heretic to be corrupted immediately."

"This trifling is scarcely to the point," said Brother Peter. "We are judging you on your conduct, not on your words."

"My conduct!" said Roger. "So far you have not said anything to me about my conduct. I have attended heretic sermons and I am quite willing to pay a suitable penance."

"Several witnesses," said Brother Guillaume, "have seen you prostrate yourself before heretics."

"That is not true. Call these witnesses and let them say it to my face. And let them say when and how they were able to see me."

At this point the interrogation came to an end, and Roger was taken back to the same cell; it was dark and cold. A bare stone bed, a small square window with bars in the shape of a cross. Nothing to eat. At the foot of the bed was a pitcher of water, and Roger drank deeply until sated. He was not even tired any more, or rather was too tired to be able to sleep. It was no use racking his brains to think what they wanted of him, he could see nothing in front of his eyes but the heads of the three monks, they multiplied, swelled enormously, repeated themselves and melted into one another, and it seemed as though they were still asking him: "Haven't you just given us proof of your perfidy. . .?" "Lord, do they really take me for a heretic, or are they mocking me?" In spite of himself he believed these men were gifted with the power to read souls; it was their job. Therefore, he imagined that they knew he was telling the truth but wanted at all costs to convict him of heresy, the better to enable themselves to discredit the followers of the Count of Toulouse. "Ah, God," he thought, "Bertrand! Bertrand! This is all because of Bertrand and his obduracy! Can a noble and a man close to the court have compromised himself in this way? That was a thing which happened to burghers, and it was his father-in-law who drew him into it. . . . Bertrand, my brother, where are you now?" Despite his cold and hunger, Roger fell asleep at last, a dreamless sleep, as heavy as death. He woke to the sound of bells and monks chanting.

This chant sounded so sweet that for an instant Roger lay there in a dream: he was already old, and retired to a convent to do penance; this was his cell and he had slept too heavily and missed an office; his Brothers were down there, in the church, chanting the *Salve Regina*. He was ashamed of having slept too long, but glad to pray. To pray for ever in peace, because he could scarcely hear chanting without longing for the peace of prayer. This stone

297

bed, fasting and prayer. But Rigueur? To end his life without seeing Rigueur again. . . ?

He leaped to his feet, wide awake, rubbed his numbed legs, drank the water that was left in his pitcher and paced up and down for a long time between the window and the door, almost longing for the time for the interrogation. "Hunger, brothers, breaks us down after two or three days, but on the first day a hollow stomach is rather an advantage. Good soldiers fight on an empty stomach." He therefore appeared before the reverend tribunal with his clothes somewhat crumpled and his chin covered with a reddish stubble, but a smile on his lips.

Unfortunately his good spirits did not last long. By dint of finding the same questions repeated incessantly he was soon in the same state as on the previous day, and more wretched still because hunger was making his head ache. At the end of an hour, Brother Peter asked him: "Isn't it true that you handed over to the heretics the key of the secret passage underneath your castle of Layrac and that you have lodged two heretics there with the intention of infecting with heresy the domain you hold from your wife?"

Now Roger had been quite prepared to find himself accused on account of the heretics at Layrac, but not of the secret passage. His confidence wavered, he flushed violently, and sat gaping for a few seconds, unable to answer. Then he regained control of himself and asked harshly: "Who told you that?"

"The witness's name is of little importance. Is it true or not?"

"Yes, Brothers, the witness's name is very important indeed! You have that evidence from my wife!"

"We cannot reveal the witness's name but you yourself admit having confided this secret to your wife. Will you continue to try and deny it?"

"I most certainly do deny it!" said Roger. "There is not one word of truth in all this, Brothers. The whole story is a pure invention of my wife."

"Three witnesses have spoken to us about the secret passage underneath the castle."

"I do not know who these witnesses are. It is true that such a passage once existed at Layrac, but to my knowledge its entrance was blocked by a rockfall, thirty years ago, in the time of Otho-Jean de Layrac; part of the cellars collapsed while the ramparts were being rebuilt and the rubble was never cleared away. I

298

have never found any further trace of either the passage or the door."

"If this passage does not exist, why do you accuse your wife?"

"Because she was just about the only person to believe in it, and she kept the key of it in her chest; her nurse had woven God knows what stories round it for her. No other person would have mentioned the key."

"I was under the impression," said Brother Peter scornfully, "that we were not trying your wife, here, but yourself."

"Reverend Brother, is it for the Church's court to give credence to the fantasies of a loose woman who, to hide her own shame, is attempting to rid herself of her lawful husband? If you accept the testimony of such witnesses, you must be prepared to find me blacker than the devils of hell, because if she has been able to commit such an evil deed as to come and denounce me, it can have cost her no more to make up the worst slanders against me!"

"So, the fact that she came to bear witness to the truth in a matter of faith is an evil deed in your eyes?"

"Do not mock me, Brothers! What name should a woman be called who betrays her husband thus? And if, of the two of us, one is guilty of heresy, it is not I, since she herself has been a heretic believer from her youth."

"Once again," said Brother Peter, "do not try to avoid my question. You must see that you have betrayed yourself."

"No. It is she who has betrayed herself. Because there is no secret passage, and I challenge you to find even a trace of one if you search the cellars of Layrac until next Easter."

"We do know, indeed, that this passage is practically impossible to find and that only two men know of it: yourself and Jean-Rigaud de Marcillac, your chief vassal and steward."

"Well then, go and ask Jean-Rigaud," said Roger, at the end of his patience, and he thought: "She would have to involve the poor old fellow in this."

"How long have these heretics been on your domain?"

Roger gave a weary, contemptuous smile. "Ask your witnesses that. No doubt they will know better than I."

"Are there heretics on your domain at the present time?"

"How should I know? I have never heard any talk of heretics living on my domain."

"Roger de Montbrun, you are doing yourself no good by playing with us like this. We are not so simple as to be unaware that in accusing your wife you have made your own admission. You are concealing the heretic Guiraud de Montauban and his companion underneath your castle. If you refuse to help us capture them, we have authority to consider you an obdurate heretic, and expel you from the communion of the Church."

"Do you believe that if I really had done this thing, I would be fool enough not to have sent a warning to these heretics on the day I received my indictment? In two days they would have had ample time to escape."

"In that case you run no risk by guiding us to the place and showing us the entrance to the secret hiding place."

"I would willingly do so if such a hiding place existed."

It went on like this until vespers; so that by the end Roger was wondering whether it was worth persisting in his denials, because the famous secret passage must have been empty since the previous day at the latest; the Christians were not fools. ". . . and what about the crosses carved on the walls, and the candle stubs, and the remains of the fire . . . flagrant proofs. Good. So then one says: 'I have sinned and I repent. I did it for five hundred crowns, or under threats. . . .' And what if one of the old men were sick and unable to walk? Or if they had not been warned?"

That night, having had nothing to eat still and little to drink, Roger began to lose heart. He was so furious at his own stupidity that he started beating himself about the head. Ah! so many men compromise themselves stupidly because they think they are strong enough to be above the law. But once under lock and key, their only tools are their arms and legs, just like the meanest beggar of the streets.

In the morning, when the gaoler came to fetch him, Roger announced that he was ill and asked for food. Receiving no other response than a command to get up and go down, he obeyed, but repeated his request in the presence of his judges, asking them whether they meant to torture him by starvation. "I am an obedient son of the Church," he said, "and I am determined to do your will in all things. But I warn you that this is not the way you will make me speak."

"So you admit you have something to say?"

"I admit nothing. But I want to be treated properly."

300

"It is not your place to pronounce judgments on the way you are treated by the Church's court."

"My dear and reverend Brothers, is it proper, when I have to answer questions which concern my soul's salvation, that I should be tormented by such a petty inconvenience as the belly's hunger? And that when I look at you I should see—craving your pardon—loaves of bread in place of your faces? I beseech you, give the order to have a pauper's meal served me, such as you give to beggars every day in your charity."

He was answered that his request would be considered at the proper time. Did he persist in his denial of the evidence and his refusal to help the court?

"I want to help with all my heart, but you are knocking on the wrong door. I know nothing." They told him that in cases of such flagrant obduracy the court was authorised to resort to extraordinary means to force the accused to speak the truth.

"I shall gladly submit myself to that test," said Roger, "and I am ready to request it myself, if by that means I can prove my innocence. Weakened as I am, there is little likelihood that I should persist in remaining silent under torture if I were really guilty."

He followed the gaoler and the Brothers Alberic and Guillaume into the small, low room where stubborn cases were examined. The room resembled a smith's forge or a carpenter's workshop, there were boards, whips of all sizes, iron bars and rings, pulleys, ropes, and a huge fireplace where a half naked man with a deeply tanned skin was drawing up a big log fire with a pair of bellows. In fact the Brothers of the Holy Office of the Inquisition, though they were obliged by their functions to arm themselves with this apparatus, were reluctant to use it; they were less well equipped than the smallest rural court of civil justice. Except in extremely urgent cases they did not go beyond straightforward flagellation.

Brother Alberic conjured the accused not to force his judges to have recourse to methods which the Church reprehended and only tolerated by virtue of judiciary procedure. "Brothers, if you do not wish to believe my word, then you must have recourse to other evidence. God, who gives to innocents the strength not to weaken under the test, will judge."

As he uttered these words which the reverend Brothers must have heard many times already, Roger forced himself to continue smiling, but his hands and knees were trembling, less from fear than from excitement—a body that has had no food for over two days is hard to control. He took off his clothes as quickly as he could, his fingers struggling with the laces and pins. The shame of revealing his naked body to men fully-clothed had seized such violent hold on him that despite himself he felt some comradeship for the executioner with his bare arms and legs and his shirt open in front down to the navel. But the executioner did not have the same white, indecently tender skin, with occasional patches of pink, and faint down, and marks left by clothes, as a man who wore a shirt winter and summer. To think that this body had been an object of pride to more than one noble lady!

Pain. Roger was almost sure of that. Starving or not he had met it before, and this was nothing to fear; there was no risk to his life because ecclesiastical torture frightened no one but townsmen, those not broken to the odd profession of exposing one's body to missiles and lances. *They will never go far enough, they are only monks.* But, great God, this was no pleasure trip! At every stroke of the lash, laid on powerfully on chest or belly, Roger thought his last hour had come; he no longer knew whether it was better to tense or relax his muscles, and he was so firmly fastened by wrists and ankles that he could do little more than vibrate rhythmically, like a stretched cord.

He had bitten his lips until his mouth was full of blood, and then swallowed the blood as he tried to get his breath back after every stroke, because, thank God, the torturer had to take his time striking. How much longer? God ... "Mercy!" he screamed. The executioner stopped, and Brother Alberic approached the sufferer and asked whether he had anything to confess. Roger did not answer, he was thinking of one thing only: how to prolong the respite for as long as possible. Confessions? He was not even thinking of them. Even less than before. One does not endure such pain purely as a waste of time. Did he persist in his obduracy? He closed his eyes and drew in a breath of air, cautiously because his chest and belly felt as though they were all one raw wound. "I know nothing," he said. "As God is my witness, I know nothing. Nothing more than I have told you."

"Are you ready to endure another thirty strokes of the lash?"

"Ask your doctor that. You have to guarantee to keep me alive. I have no wish to risk succumbing and dying without the sacraments."

"I can promise you," said Brother Alberic, "no man has died of this treatment yet, even after a hundred lashes."

"Then I am ready. But I know nothing."

"You don't know whether or not you are a heretic believer?"

"I have never been that."

At the tenth stroke he lost consciousness, and they had to cut him down and revive him with cold water. They laid him on a mattress, because the doctor monk who was present at the torture said: "This man needs some nourishment first, or I will no longer answer for his life."

"Ah!" Roger thought. "I would do anything for that man! I would give him half I possessed if I could!" The monk was a small man, with a gentle, delicate face, and hands as light as feathers.

That day Roger de Montbrun was entitled to a mattress and a blanket, and a pillow under his head, and a hot brick at his feet; and to a compassionate stare from the lay Brother who held his head in his hand while he drank. Human justice acts in strange ways; it rewards a man when by his stubbornness he has rendered himself unworthy of forgiveness. Was this simple charity or to make him fit to endure the torture again? The young lay Brother had beautiful, dog-like eyes, a kind mouth, wide and serious, his sturdy body gave off a healthy odour of sweat, and a smell of freshly-laundered cloth.

Of the pain he had endured he retained only a cruel, burning sensation on the skin of his belly, and a dreadful weariness; he would not have lifted a finger if the building had been on fire. . . . They certainly knew their job with a whip. There was nothing worse, except red-hot irons on an infected wound—how had Bertrand endured the lash?

After vespers, a man came into the cell carrying a candle. It was the doctor. In the yellow light of the flame his face looked gaunt and sad; deep black shadows circled his bright eyes.

"Brother, for pity's sake, do you know whether my interrogation is finished?"

"I know nothing of that, my friend. I am only here to minister to the body, I am not privy to the secrets of the tribunal."

"Yet you must know what they accuse me of?"

"I have no need to know. I am here to serve you according to the poor lights which God has permitted me to acquire."

"Will my case be serious?"

303

"No. It is a passing weakness, due to hunger. Beatings of this sort are not prejudicial to health."

"I am glad to hear you say so, Brother," said Roger, with some asperity. "If that is so the reverend Brothers of the tribunal will be able to make me suffer the same treatment many times without endangering my health!"

"No, because the pain itself is so great that no one can endure it for long. In practice one can scarcely proceed to more than fifty lashes, and you had forty."

"Indeed! Brother Alberic mentioned a hundred lashes."

"He is not a doctor," said the monk, evasively. "Perhaps he wanted to test your resolution. But I never let them go beyond fifty lashes, or fifty-five at the most."

Strange as it was, the man's conversation brought a measure of comfort: he was so calm that he might have been talking of some ordinary sickness.

"Brother, you reassure me greatly as to my body, but it is for my soul that I shall need a doctor. You are a monk of our holy religion, will you deny me the comforting words you owe to every man in trouble?"

The monk lowered his eyes. "I am not supposed to know anything of your case."

Roger looked thoughtfully at his swollen wrists, which were badly bruised and bleeding. "Are women chained in the same way, also?" he asked. "It is enough to break the tendons. Brother, it is a hard thing to be alone, and that is why your holy tribunal is so little loved in the land: you make a man answer to you alone, with no friends or lawyers to speak for him. He has nothing but his own word and that word is considered of no account."

"Every man is alone before God. Can't you understand that, in your position? The Church in her mercy places you face to face with yourself in your lifetime, and brings you before a tribunal which is undoubtedly much less severe than that of the Last Judgment will be."

"I would like to believe it," remarked Roger, frowning, because he was having difficulty in collecting his thoughts, "but tell me, honestly: can I incur a major penalty for a minor offence? I have committed no offence beyond my close ties with several persons who are notorious heretics."

"The Brother Inquisitor judges hearts, not offences. He does not judge according to the justice of men, corrupted by the

304

manners of the age. I know nothing of your case, but it is possible that you are guilty without knowing it."

"In that case," Roger objected, "what use is the torture? You can beat a donkey until tomorrow but you won't teach it to talk."

"A man may be led to self-knowledge by excessive pain or fear. Why do you compare yourself to a donkey? God sends us trials to purify us."

"I have committed thousands of sins, Brother, but not the one with which I am charged."

"Perhaps the fact that you sought the friendship of heretics is already an acquiescence in heresy?" said the doctor gently.

Roger felt so tired and bewildered that he was conscious of something approaching a need to confide in this man.

"Ah! Brother," he exclaimed. "You wear a monk's habit, it is easy for you to talk! For twelve years we were excommunicated for the sake of our country. What province do you come from?"

"I am from Toulouse."

"So, we are fellow-countrymen. Then you should know what our city has suffered and how much the Catholics in Toulouse have been slandered and maltreated. It was not easy for us to adhere to the Bishop's party when the Bishop was selling us to the Crusaders. Monseigneur Foulques was a man endowed with great virtues and a sublime intelligence, but he lacked a father's heart for his flock!"

"When rebellious children are justly chastised by their father, they believe that father does not love them. Monseigneur Foulques showed exemplary patience towards you; time and again he granted you his forgiveness and you threw stones at him when he passed by in the street! The Blessed Dominic wept tears of blood over your obduracy, and he wept much more over the craven and lukewarm Catholics than over those wretched lost souls. For it is said: 'If you were but hot or cold . . .!' I was still young in those days and our Order was a mere handful of devoted men, inspired by a passionate grief at the scorn in which our faith was held in this land. And the Blessed—I mean, St. Dominic—comforted us, and renewed our courage by his steadfastness. For twenty-five years we fought on, in pain, toil and works of charity, while bad Catholics were sacrificing their faith to vainglory and worldly honour. Who else is it but men like you—if you really are a Catholic—who have brought discredit on the Church? Did

305

not the late Count Raymond have the audacity to invite Monseigneur Foulques to attend a heretic sermon one day? He himself attended them, in scorn of the faith, and pillaged the Church's property. And you used the name of Catholic like a screen, only good enough to hide your unbelief!"

Roger listened attentively to this discourse, struck not so much by the words as by the expression of sincere anguish which transfigured the monk's fragile features. The night and his own loneliness made him feel a kind of affection for the man.

"See," he said, and there was no bitterness in his voice, rather a feverish eagerness, as though he were trying to convince a friend, "see how unjust you are though you do not know it. You are judging the matter in the way your own party sees it; all those who do not belong to your party are traitors to the faith. It is natural for a man to think as his friends think, and each believes that he is right. But I can tell you that the reason many laymen seem lukewarm in their faith is because they are occupied by other business, business which is lawful even in the eyes of the Church."

"For every man," said the monk, "God should be the first served. Other business is only lawful in so far as it does not oblige us to disobey the Church. What use is your worldly vanity to you at the moment? God has delivered you up to judges who have no regard either to your birth or your fortunes. You are poor and naked now, poorer than the poorest peasant on your lands, you who used to take the bread from widows and orphans and barter it for weapons, or for the money to supply your pleasures. It is good that for once the Church should place herself above the justice of men, and chastise crimes that go unpunished but which are often the worst; that she should punish pride and culpable toleration as severely as adultery and stealing."

"Those are wise and pious words," Roger said thoughtfully. "I would like to believe that I have deserved this penance by my sins, and that it is so much gained from my time in purgatory. But I have been wrongfully accused."

"You are a Catholic," said the monk, with a calm smile which scarcely altered the pale, delicate outline of his lips, "and yet you can complain of being wrongfully accused? What is the sign you wear on a silver chain next to your body? Is that a vain ornament, a talisman such as folk carry out of superstition? He who died for you on the Cross was wrongfully accused, and He was condemned. Knowing that, which of us can say he is wrongfully accused?"

Roger blinked, wondering what more he had to answer for. He thought of the lashes he would probably receive the next day and told himself that, without mentioning Jesus Christ, there were plenty of men more innocent than himself who had endured harsher treatment.

"What's this?" he said. "Is it the Church's business to impose such a burden on us? Or to say: What does it matter whether or not this man committed the crime, he can never be wrongfully accused?"

"Truly, the will of the Church is not that of men but of God. You must realise that everything which seems to you hard to accept in the Church's actions is merely the effect of your ignorance of the infinite mystery of divine love."

On these pious words the doctor rose, bowed to his patient and went out, taking with him the nearly burnt-out candle. Left alone in the darkness, Roger wondered whether or not he was sorry the man had gone. He thought: "What is the matter? One or the other of us must be mad. We said nothing that was not good sense, and yet . . ."

Sleep would not come. He had slept for most of the day, stupefied by wine and food, and the worst of his fatigue had gone. "That man," Roger thought, "undoubtedly leads a chaste life and spends his nights in prayer and his days healing the sick.

"Men like him adhered to the Bishop's party during the war, as many others did who were neither monks nor clerks. Now they are the stronger, and they are having their revenge."

The strange thing was that Roger never for one minute believed that the man had come with the purpose of extracting secrets from him without suspicion or to sap his courage. Such is the power of night and pain; the soul is naked and any man who talks to you is a friend. As he was then, sitting on a stool by the bed, with his candle at his feet, and his thin, delicate hands clasped on the folds of his heavy woollen robe, he was resting from the day's labours; letting his heart speak, talking much more than the rule allowed. It was their job to be hard on laymen, and on soldiers especially.

"In the state I am in, should I be worrying about a man who means nothing to me. . .? Nothing? He has done me no mean service because I know that if they never go beyond fifty lashes

I am fairly certain to hold out. How can their thoughts be healthy when they live without women? That man is not much older than I am. The world is upside down when secular authority and great powers are entrusted to monks: one might as well entrust the task of making pottery to blacksmiths. It's hardly surprising things go awry. Judging hearts? The Devil they do! Brothers, to the Day of Judgment, the heart is supposed to be such a subtle commodity that it cannot be weighed in the balance or measured with an ell. Would you hang all men who have not good hearts?

"Then what else was it he said," thought Roger, "that disturbed me so much? 'Poor, naked and alone.' Alone. Alone before God? Every man is always alone before God, and at the day of his death . . . as though they had to put the whole world in prison! Alone for how long? And why are they attacking Catholics? Bertrand was not alone. (*You will never know what men your brother has saved. . . .*') Lord Jesus, must I believe these men are Your Church? If they believe it, they are much mistaken. But if they really believe it, what is to prevent them keeping me here until I have paid to the last obol?"

By dawn on the fourth day Roger felt as though he had been imprisoned for weeks, and was much less wise about his case than he had been at the moment when he faced his judges for the first time. He was beginning to realise that these men were free to make him live like this for a year if they liked. Count, consuls and bishops were without jurisdiction over the place where he now found himself. To whom could he appeal? He was given no writing materials and the gaoler would not listen either to entreaties or promises.

When he was led into the audience chamber, he saw the same three faces whose mere memory already sickened him. He was in a foul temper and enquired how the tribunal of the Holy Office could afford to waste their time in this way. Was Toulouse such a strongly Catholic city that they could find no other heretics to judge besides himself and did their entire work really consist in exhuming the dead and picking quarrels with Catholics who were guilty of having friends? Brother Peter's only answer was to ask him whether he was prepared to endure flagellation once again, or whether he preferred to confess voluntarily to his offences against the faith.

Roger found the flogging much crueller than on the previous day since the whip was falling on skin already agonisingly tender.

He yelled like a flayed ox but, knowing that after fifty strokes the torment would be over, he never even thought of crying mercy. "If they stop now," he told himself, "I shall never have the courage to bear it when they start again." Then, once he had swallowed his cruel medicine, he found himself lying on the bench, his chest heaving, his head on fire, and his heart beating spasmodically, almost sorry he had held out so long.

"Talk? What about? For pity's sake, am I in a state to talk?"

"Are the heretics in the hiding place you know of or not?"

"How should I know?"

"So, you have allowed them to use the hiding place?"

"No, the hiding place does not exist."

"We know that you conveyed a message from your brother to one Jacques Nourrissier, a goldsmith and a heretic believer who has fled the city. What do you know of this message?"

Roger felt his strength returning, thanks to the fresh anger which overwhelmed him. "Ask the good woman who gave you the information. She carried the message."

"So, you did convey it."

"I wanted to do my brother a service. I knew nothing of the message, my wife knew more than I."

"That is an admission," said Brother Alberic. "Will you repeat it in the courtroom?"

"Yes." He dressed, or rather allowed himself to be dressed, since he was bent double with pain. He walked like a man drunk, bitterly shamed at being the one man who had been flogged among others who were sound.

Yes. He had indeed repeated his brother's words about 'Jacques' nurse' to his wife, Guillelme de Layrac. She had said: "I will take this message myself." She knew that it concerned Jacques Nourrissier. If his wife was not to be penalised why was the court taking action against him?

He was not there to ask questions, he was told. Would he agree to reveal the secret passage in the castle to his judges and thereby clear himself of a charge which he claimed was false? Roger thought: "I shall gain nothing by confessing; whatever I say will be used as evidence against me."

"You are making a mountain out of an old wives' tale. Write to the Diocese of Montauban and let them summon Jean-Rigaud de Marcillac. He will tell you the same as I do."

"Which could prove nothing beyond the fact that you are

acting in collusion. Are you trying to divert our suspicions on to him?"

This question came like a slap in the face to Roger, and he very nearly said: "*I have told him nothing about it.*"

"How in collusion? We are not friends. That is well known."

"He is said to have been a heretic believer for a long time."

"I know nothing about that. I have not heard it said."

"You would not defend him if he were not your friend."

"I am not in the habit of telling lies about my enemies."

"Are we to believe that you would entrust the management of your domain to an enemy?"

"It was his right, according to the customs of Layrac. We are bound by oath."

"Knowing him a believer, like yourself, why should you have concealed the presence of the heretics from him?"

"That is an insult!" said Roger; and it touched him so keenly that his mouth filled with angry saliva. "May I be struck dead on the spot if I have ever been a believer."

"Yet you have been to Termes, and from there you went all the way to Montségur, which is well known to be a den of heretics and the place they hold most sacred."

"Yes. But I did not go up to the castle."

"What was your object in going there?"

"I wanted," said Roger, looking away, "to see a woman I loved and thought to find there."

"You are a good forty-five years old," said Brother Alberic, with an incredulous smile, "and you expect us to believe that you undertake such journeys for motives as frivolous as that?"

"Believe it or not. Do people only travel for serious reasons?"

"Is it not true that in your contempt for the Catholic faith you maintain contact with traitors who aim to recapture their confiscated domains in the Carcassès from their lawful owners? Are you not said to be in the pay of the former Viscount of Béziers?"

"In his pay. . .? Merciful God! The Viscount has not even the wherewithal to pay his own men. It is well known that I have always served our lord Count Raymond faithfully."

"Would it be on his orders that you went to Montségur?"

"*Here we are at last,*" Roger thought, "*the masks are off. If they go on I shall pretend to faint. After the thrashing I had just now, that would not be surprising.*" But far from fainting he drew himself up, keen self-pity lending him new strength.

"Brothers," he said, "for God's sake do not play this game with me any longer! Out of respect for our Holy Church, which commands us to obey you, I have borne being treated as no man of my rank should be treated. If my innocence does not seem to you sufficiently proven, you can take all the skin off my body—assuming your rule permits it—and you will find out nothing more! What I have admitted, I stand by. If I have wronged the Church through pity for my brother, I should be punished, but I deserve only a minor penance.

"But as for saying what you are trying to make me say, that I have been a heretic and protector of heretics, I swear to you by Christ Jesus and the Virgin Mary and all the saints that I am innocent. Never will I be craven enough to admit to lies against myself and against my honour as a Catholic!"

Seeing the accused so deeply angered and rebellious, Brother Peter declared that the tribunal considered guilt adequately proven, and that Roger de Montbrun would do himself no good by his continued obstinacy, since in this case the tribunal was empowered to excommunicate him and hand him over to the secular arm as an unrepentant heretic.

"I am not afraid of that," said Roger, fixing on the old man a gaze full of scorn and anger. "I am not yet so stupid as to let myself be caught in that trap. The tree is not yet grown that will be a stake for me, and to burn me there are not the faggots nor the men willing to obey you in all Toulouse."

Brother Peter raised one long, bony hand and said: "I declare this interrogation adjourned for further investigation. Let the accused be removed, since his presence is no longer required."

Roger almost found himself funny; these men took no more notice of his protestations than of a fly buzzing. He, who in height was as tall as they were, whose voice was as loud as theirs (louder even, because he was talking with some passion), who was probably older in years than the judge's two assistants—he who had been listened to with courtesy by counts and princes—was now so small a thing before these men that his words did not even reach their ears.

To make them listen to him, he had to say: "Yes, I did this or that, I saw such and such a person do this or that." They had no ears for anything else. He smiled scornfully, to no purpose: the smile of a village idiot would have been more intelligent. In the presence of these men the only thing was to maintain a wooden countenance, the slightest frown became an impropriety.

They read his depositions over to him in Latin. He did not understand it all and did not care whether he understood. He was thinking: "These men know what they are doing. A man who has just been flogged does not have all his wits about him. Were it not for their gravity of office, how they would be laughing at me!" Yet when the moment came to sign, he hesitated: "What penalty," he asked, "can I incur for the admissions I have made?"

"The tribunal of the Holy Office is not a draper's shop. The Church's clemency is in proportion to the sincerity of the repentance."

"Can I open my chest then, and show you my heart, to prove that my repentance is sincere?"

"We are the only judges of your sincerity," said Brother Peter. Roger signed with a shaking hand, wondering what pit he was digging under his feet by doing so.

The judges spent a long time deliberating over the case of Roger de Montbrun. Brother Guillaume said that in his opinion the man was sincere and guilty chiefly of toleration. Moreover, the witnesses were unreliable: to all appearances the accused was at daggers drawn with his wife, and it was always wise to treat women's testimony with a degree of suspicion, especially that of lawful wives.

"This man is a cunning fox," said Brother Alberic. "We have been tricked before now by great heretic believers who feign piety. Ordained heretics educate their believers in a spirit of consummate hypocrisy. Of the two brothers, this one may well be the worse. Is it reasonable to believe that the two men have not been acting in collusion? No doubt the elder's piety was a device aimed at protecting his family from prosecution."

Brother Guillaume leafed through the file, re-reading the witnesses' evidence. "Many people, beginning with the woman Guillelme de Layrac, agree that the two brothers did not get on well together, and that Bertrand de Montbrun openly reproached his brother for his adherence to the Church party."

"Precisely, Brother Guillaume. He reproached him too much. Being what he was he could hardly do otherwise, and it was a crude enough trick. Moreover, hasn't Roger de Montbrun been the lover of a woman only too well known for a mischievous heretic? In this age can any man resist a woman's influence?

Everything we know about this creature confirms our belief that she would never have granted her favours to a man who was not of her own faith."

At this point Brother Guillaume smiled involuntarily, and said that, although he knew little of the nature of women, in his view this person might very well have picked out the accused for reasons which had nothing to do with his faith. If the accused was not sincere, he would not have appeared before the tribunal, he would have been more likely to attempt to escape.

"Another trick; men of his kind do not admit their guilt. They proclaim their innocence to the end, in order to embarrass their judges. Haven't witnesses heard the accused utter hideous threats against our Order and our tribunal? He is said to have been driven to despair by his brother's arrest—is such grief really probable in a jealous and embittered brother who should rather, it seems, have rejoiced at the arrest? Brothers who hate one another are well known not to do it by halves."

"If," said Brother Guillaume, "this man had been what we think, his leaders would never have allowed him to (to put it bluntly) fling himself into the jaws of the wolf. Do not forget that his brother was taken by surprise and brought here under guard. Therefore, even if he has been a heretic agent, he can never have been a believer himself. They would not have entrusted him with the care of sheltering such a man as Guiraud de Montauban, and it is possible that his wife has, in fact, made up this story, knowing that the heretic Guiraud de Montauban was really in the vicinity of Layrac."

"The actual sin, Brother Guillaume, is less serious than the refusal to admit it. I admit that, without being a heretic, a bad Catholic can give shelter to heretics, either from cupidity (the heretics bribe even magistrates with gold), or for some worldly interest. This man knows very well that a sincere confession will earn him a less severe punishment, and yet he remains silent. It is a well-known fact that any man who persists too stubbornly in silence is a man with much to hide."

"How can we know? Five minutes after submitting to a flogging he can find enough strength to beat about the bush and defy us to our faces. Even if he is a heretic at heart, it appears difficult to make him admit it."

"Is that surprising?" said Brother Alberic bitterly. "He is still at the time of the fat kine. These people do not enrich themselves

313

with the goods of the poor for nothing; their bodies are vigorous, their hearts swollen with pride and their heads fertile in cunning. It requires a long patience to bring such people to humility and the fear of God."

After hearing what his two assistants had to say, Brother Peter decided to have the accused, Roger de Montbrun, transferred to the city prison after nightfall, and there placed in an underground cell for a month or so. The said Roger had amply deserved this penance for his sins. "Moreover, if his heart is really rotten with heresy, the poison will act more violently in solitude and despair, and the offence be more easily disclosed."

Thus began for Roger de Montbrun the penance he had merited for the sins of his life.

Guillaume and Jean-Bernard de Montbrun went to the Dominican priory every Saturday to attend the clerk's office of the court and sign their names on the list recording their presence in the city. In this Christmas week they were given to understand that since the man who had gone surety for them, and had put down their bail, had himself been imprisoned on suspicion of heresy, they must find another surety or go to prison. The two young men went straight to Raymond-Jourdain de Cissac and were received by the master of the house in a room smelling of fresh paint and plaster. Servants were washing down the tiled floor and scouring dishes and pans with ashes. Raymond-Jourdain was just back from a hunting expedition and out in the courtyard men were skinning deer and boar carcasses.

"There will be no feasting in our house this year, sir knight," said Guillaume, "and God knows whether we shall not soon be reduced to eating at other people's tables. Our uncle's bail is forfeit and we have come to you as beggars."

"It is too great a sum," Raymond-Jourdain said, "for me to be able to raise it in three days. Come with me to the Count."

The Count was in the great court, with all his knights around him, dressed and ready to attend second Mass. He took Raymond-Jourdain and the two youths aside and told them that in his opinion Roger was an egregious fool to let himself fall into the hands of the Preaching Friars, since he should have known that they would find Jesus Christ himself guilty of heresy, while he, the Count, was powerless to help anyone escape before the end of the investigations. He added that he would advance the sum demanded in bail, but that Raymond-Jourdain must stand surety himself and not mention the Count's name. Guillaume and Jean-Bernard could do nothing more but go to Mass at St. Sernin, their parish church, which they had to attend on pain of imprisonment. Afterwards they wandered about the cold streets, crowded with carts loaded with firewood and sheep being driven to the slaughter, for a long time in the driving rain. It was four years since they had been allowed to leave Toulouse, for so much as a hunting expedition. They were free to walk along the city walls, on the bridge and through the squares, seeing the woods change colour, the Garonne rise, the fields turn black and green and yellow—at twenty, liberty on bail is a torment one would not wish one's worst enemy.

On their return to the Montbrun house the two young men went to see Guillelme. "You must apply to the Bishop's court for an order releasing you from our uncle's guardianship," they said, "otherwise you will not be able to sign any papers concerning Layrac."

"I have no papers to sign."

"You will have," said Guillaume. "You will have to mortgage the big vineyards and the oak wood."

"Do you imagine," she said, "that you can bribe Roger's judges like that? You know very well they are not men to be bought."

"You will do as we say, sweet aunt, and ask no questions. Furthermore, sweet aunt, if we need any witnesses we shall find a dozen. And not against Azémar. We shall say that you prostituted yourself to a mason who has gone away, and that we are within our rights to desire no bastards in our family."

"You will be hanged," she said, but there was a haggard look in her eyes.

"As well be hanged as lead this life much longer. Give us the key of your chamber. We shall bring the lawyer here."

"Ah! What does it matter?" she said scornfully. "Take the key and steal whatever you can from me."

On the evening of the same day, Pierre-Guillaume summoned his grandsons and asked them: "Have you any news of Roger yet?"

"What news? If he had written it would have been to you."

"Do not mock me any longer, my poor children. Do you think I didn't realise where he was going the day he left? They will do the same to him as they have done to Bertrand."

315

"Who could have been treacherous enough to tell you the truth, sir? Our uncle told us we were to hide everything from you until the day his case was judged." The old man closed his eyes. "He said that? Who does he take me for? Lord God, have I deserved this? They will do to him what they have done to Bertrand. Of all the sons I had, only these two were left me." "Father dear, Uncle Roger will easily clear himself."

"They have taken him from me," said the old man, "but they will never dare touch *me*. Tomorrow I shall make a new will naming Roger's sons my sole heirs. You must not all be thrown out into the street after my death, supposing Roger were convicted. . . . My sons will have been the death of me. Both of them always restless and plotting, they never would stay quiet. Now, at their age, to be thrown into prison! The Preachers have a grudge against every man in Toulouse who is not a traitor. God keep you, Guillaume, from ever saying a word against them in public."

"We kiss their feet," said Guillaume, and his eyes were burning with hatred, "and thank them for putting our father in prison, in their great mercy."

"I shall curse you," said the old man. "I shall curse you both if you ever dare bring such a disaster on my old age. You are prisoners on parole."

The two young men shared their plans with their eldest sister Hersen and their younger brother Azémar. As soon as Guillelme had signed the papers, they intended to take the money and all four of them would leave the city. They would buy horses at Muret and go on from there as far as Mirepoix, where they would not lack friends. The girl, Hersen, hesitated on account of their grandfather and the younger children, as well as Raymond-Jourdain de Cissac who was standing surety for them and therefore likely to be in trouble. "Trouble? What about us? What worse trouble is there than living walled up alive like this?"

"*Walled up alive*, Guillaume? When our father and our uncle really are, and our mother in prison?"

"They are old. Why should we waste our lives?"

"Uncle Roger," said the girl, "has done nothing but good for us. If we run away, so short a time after his arrest, won't they believe we were his accomplices in some matter of faith? He gave himself up of his own accord to avoid causing us any harm."

316

"Hersen, one day poets can sing of me: 'The valiant and chival-rous Guillaume showed great respect for his parents, and his grandfather, and his uncle and his brothers and sisters! Such great respect that he never rode a horse, never bore arms and never did anything for his country except go to Mass and kiss the hands of his father's executioner!' This is a song that has been running in my head for long enough. I am twenty-two and Bernard twenty-one, soon we shall be old. Stay if you like, and we will go without you."

Two weeks later the four young people were on the road to Pamiers.

The underground cell was a kind of well, as deep as the height of three men. There was an opening at the top covered by a grating, giving on to a dark passage down which a man passed from time to time carrying a lantern. At these times the grating would be illuminated and shafts of light came down the inclined surface of the wall, without ever reaching the bottom.

Between two passages of the lantern, Roger discovered by experiment that he could count up to a thousand nine or ten times, indicating an interval of more than two hours.

The hunger and thirst were not the worst thing. Measuring time by the gnawing of his stomach and the passing of the light, Roger finally calculated that he was given food almost every day. What happened was that the grating was raised and a basket lowered on a rope, with a piece of bread and a pitcher of water, which had to be exchanged for the empty pitcher. The rope was too thin to bear a man's weight, so another means of escape must be sought. But what? The floor was not paved with flags but with stones a foot thick. The opening which served to drain away refuse was too narrow to allow the passage of more than an arm, and to judge from the stench which rose from it could not lead far: Roger was forced to cover it with straw. Even the straw was moist and sticky and could not have been changed for a long time. From whoever had preceded him in the cell, Roger inherited armies of famished vermin and on the first day, tired and broken as he was from his beatings, these creatures nearly drove him mad with despair. There were tiny ticks in the straw, and big fat lice, as well as fleas, and they were such a tough breed that it was use-less to shake himself, or jump up and down or slap his head and body. He had to accustom his fingers to feel the brutes in order

317

to squash them, and cut them in two with his nails—he got the big lice first, but catching the rest was a more delicate task.

For two days Roger concentrated so hard on this unaccustomed form of chase that he had little time to think of anything else (hitherto, even on the hardest campaigns, he had always found means to wash himself and shake out his shirts and other clothes, so that he had never experienced lice, or even fleas, as more than passing guests: now he envied the poor folk whose skins were better protected against these intimate foes).

Whenever he fell asleep, the lice would crawl over his mouth and eyelids, and when he stunned them with a slap, they would begin their march again almost at once. He killed hundreds of them. They were hard to get at underneath his clothes, and it was too cold to undress. Each time the basket came down, Roger shouted that he wanted clean straw, and that the old must be taken up. The invisible gaoler did not answer. When the prisoner held on to the basket for too long, he would tug at it impatiently, but still he never said a word. "*Well, comrade, are you deaf or dumb?*" (Perhaps he was?) Roger did his utmost to make him speak by calling him foul names and anticipating the ghastly fate awaiting his mother in the next world; but if he were not deaf the man must have heard it all before from others.

So, the war against the lice continued for three, four, five days, and then a kind of armed truce was established. To begin with Roger was sure he had killed many of them, and those that were left were either less vicious or he was getting used to them; and his fatigue was becoming more important. He submitted patiently to their biting and only returned to his task in fits and starts. Then hunger became more pressing and more acute, and Roger endured agonies of torture by impatience: every time the lantern passed he hoped, against all reason, to see the light stop and the grating open to let the basket through. "Supposing I have slept for a long time," he thought, because sometimes he fell into a sound dreamless sleep, so heavy that when he opened his eyes and saw the vague, grey shape of the barred opening he wondered wherever he could be. "In prison? But who has imprisoned me? In what battle?" Then the memory of his last few days above ground would come back to him. He had heard men speak and had answered them—proud men who believed themselves different from himself because it was their right to judge him.

But he was as strong as they, because he had a tongue to speak and eyes to see them. Now he was deaf, dumb and blind.

Oh, reverend Brothers, what wise men you are. How well you stop your ears against any words you do not wish to hear. Now you are deaf and I am dumb, I am deaf and my gaoler is dumb, I am deaf although my ears are tuned to such a pitch that I can hear footsteps echoing up there in the gallery twenty paces away. I can hear my own breath, and sniffing, and the rumbling of my bowels, and the rustle of the straw every time I move—what a punishment for a man, to be reduced to hearing no sound but the noises of his own body! What a salutary self-disgust it breeds!

One would use every trick one's brain could furnish to nourish that body, and yet there was no trick to be found. One could only wait, like an animal, in fear and eagerness, thinking of the basket that would descend, wondering whether, by chance, the bit of bread would not be bigger than it was yesterday. Oh, the wines, deep garnet-coloured or golden, the clear spring water, water springing and running and wasting itself in vain, one filled one's helmet full and drank two mouthfuls and threw away the rest, what madness! Madness, too, all the meals eaten hastily, so much meat left on the bones, or thrown to the dogs! So many grapes culled in passing, never more than one at a time, when one was free to have taken a dozen! So much clear water wasted, so many lovely hours in the sunshine and blue sky, so many good log fires in hearths as big as this cell! Lord, when I am out of here, how good life will be!

"Hey, there, comrade, hey there! Haven't you got a mug of wine to give me? I'll pay you with all the lice you want!" It was not ill-temper which made Roger want to jeer at the keeper, but simply the need to hear a human voice. It's not possible, is he really deaf? Was there ever a more surly fellow? "Hey, there! If you want payment I have things on me that will bring you a good price!" No answer. That fellow could not lack comrades to gossip with.

The hours passed. Stretched out on the straw, legs and thighs wrapped in his cloak, arms crossed and hands thrust under his armpits, Roger forced himself to shut his eyes in order to stop his endless watching for the appearance of the light above his head. He had selected a particular stone, and after each meal he made a scratch on it, half an inch long, with the point of a pin. He

319

thought: "So many meals, so many days." He realised he was losing all sense of time, and that but for these scratches he would have imagined he had been there for months, when in fact it was only ten days, or alternatively, that the whole thing was merely a dream, and the day before yesterday he had still been addressing the Brothers of the tribunal. One thing was certain: the time when he was still a free man, free to walk the streets and talk to whom he pleased, was nearly as distant as the time of his youth. He said to himself: "What, was *I* that man?" and it was certain that that time was gone for ever. It was as if someone had told him that he had once worn a Count's coronet and owned ten castles. "And I never knew."

For a long time, about fifteen days, he lived in a state of pointless agitation, attempting to talk to the gaolers, and tapping the sides of his cell in all directions to see if other prisoners would answer—but the walls must have been too thick. He tried to enlarge the gap between the flagstones by scratching along the cracks with pins, buckles, and earrings, every hard object he had on him, but it was a futile task because the huge quarry stones might easily have been as much as three feet thick and would hardly have yielded to a pickaxe. Next he made a rope, using his belt, the braid on his cloak and his laces, which he flung in the air, weighted by his belt buckle, in the hope that it would catch on the grating. Unfortunately, after hours and hours of repeated attempts, he realised that it was impossible to make the rope catch fast without a stout hook. It was not easy to aim in the dark, there was not enough room to cast properly; and several times the buckle hit the metal and slipped between the bars, only to fall back again.

"Lord, am I here to be taught patience? They will tell me: 'Your brother has lived like this for a year. . . . Your brother and many others.' Patience? Lord, I would as lief never learn it. Lord Jesus, these people who claim to speak in your name should be made to listen to this parable: *A certain man went down from Jerusalem to Jericho.* . . . Was he a just man? No, he was rich: robbers do not bother to attack beggars. *He fell among thieves which stripped him of his raiment, and wounded him, and departed leaving him half dead.* Who were these thieves? It does not matter, because he had deserved it for his sins. And the Levite passed by, and the priest, and still the man lay there, naked and unable to move. And then came the good Samaritan and said: '*I could take you on my ass, and*

320

pour oil and wine on your wounds, and take you to an inn. But this would not be charity. It would be much better for you to stay here, naked and alone before God, to meditate on your sins; you will then be brought to self-knowledge by excessive pain and fear.'

"Brothers, I do not say this to mock you, because perhaps you honestly believe I am a heretic. But even if I am a Catholic, you tell me: 'Jesus Christ suffered for you, and do you reject suffering, when the life you have led has been rotten with sin? When will you learn patience?' And there is truth in that, Brothers, I acknowledge it. By God and the Virgin I acknowledge that there is truth in that, and that every man would deserve to be used as I am, if his sins against God were to be held against him! Why then did the good Samaritan interfere?"

In his mind Roger often addressed such speeches to his judges, less from piety than to take his mind off his troubles. "You answer me: *'Your story of the good Samaritan comes directly from the heretic teaching. For the oil and wine in the Parable, and the inn, and the money given to the innkeeper, should not be taken grossly at their face value. They refer to spiritual remedies and the sacraments of the Eucharist and Confirmation; the inn is the Church herself, and the good Samaritan, who is Jesus, does indeed wish to save you by taking you, wounded as you are by your sins, into this holy Inn.'* You see, I am not so ignorant since I myself have found that answer for you. How then shall I answer you again, Brothers? That hitherto I have always believed that, since these are spiritual remedies, the sinner received them, as it were, spiritually, by practising contrition in his heart and taking communion with a pious spirit, and honouring God's Holy Church, and that healing was granted him according to his sincerity, according to the mercy of Christ Jesus and the blessed saints. But your remedies are far from spiritual; you seize the sinners by force and make them live in cells with no light, and groan with hunger and thirst."

See how small is your understanding of the Church's wisdom: when a doctor bleeds his patient, is he a man thirsting for blood? He does let blood, but the patient's body is comforted thereby. It is the same with the soul. It will take much bleeding before your body will be cleansed of the poisons which a guilty life has allowed to invade your soul.

"The thing that you cannot understand, Brothers, is that although your way of thinking seems good to you, and to the Pope and to many other churchmen, it is not so to all Catholics. The faithful are greatly shocked that you claim to represent the

321

Church, for judge for yourselves: a heretic who is maltreated becomes more firmly heretic than before, since he says to himself: *Surely this is the Whore of Babylon, drinking the blood of God's martyrs,* while a Catholic can come to doubt the Church's holiness, because no man can love those who maltreat him. This brings scandal on the Church, Brothers, when so many people are seen going to Mass and to communion, and blaspheming in their hearts, merely through fear of being put in prison."

By such futile speeches one strives to allay the thirst for another human face! It is thirst which becomes crueller than the body's thirst, or the cold and the lice crawling on a skin tanned in its own filth!

Far from taking the mind off evil thoughts, the body's wretchedness makes them stronger than ever, because bodily exhaustion saps the spirit. Roger thought: "What shall I look like when they haul me out of here? How shall I talk to them? I must stink like three litters of foxes and I no longer even feel it. I must be a fearful sight with my matted beard and my face covered with hair." There were times when his mind was not strong enough to dominate his body's weakness. Cold, pain in his chest and back, pain in his joints, a constant search for a position where it would finally be possible, if not to sleep, at least not to be in too much pain. Ah, no! He is a wretch indeed who can get used to this life. Lord, if this is what they call doing penance! It makes a man in all things like a beast.

They must all be thinking: "*Why didn't he take flight, or refuse to appear?*" as though I did not say it to myself a thousand times a day! One pays more dearly for a blunder than a crime. They can keep me here for months and no one will call them to account; their files are secret, and they conduct their enquiries as they like.

They have brought false witnesses against me, Rigueur, and slander, and truth more false than lies, because to justify herself the miserable creature who has betrayed me can say: "*What I have testified is the truth, and I have done what the Church commands me to do*", as though the Church could command our wives to deeds so vile that any robber's trull would blush for them! My only true judge, before you I have no sins, but I know what you would tell me: "*You see, Roger, you see! What have you to gain by remaining faithful to the Great Whore? You too are now called to account, like your brother and so many others, for what were really your good deeds!*"

I tell you, truly, you will not be freed until you have paid to the last obol.

Are you sick? They do not care, it was not for the good of your health they put you here. Now, I would not be able to climb a ladder even if they were to give me one. Roger crouched in a corner trying to prevent his recurrent cough, muffled in his cloak, his hands and feet well wrapped up, and his head nestled in the corner resting on what was left of his hat. He could hardly breathe, and from time to time picked up the pitcher to drink a mouthful of water. But as the hours passed the pitcher seemed heavier, the hot sweat became icy cold, and he lost hope that his shirt would ever dry.

But his fever made the time seem less long—sometimes the light appeared on the ceiling, he closed his eyes, and there it was again, he could see it without raising his eyes, and it called out of the walls horses' heads and painted banners and flowering trees, and naked women in alluring postures, and faces, or rather heads, disembodied but alive, unknown heads, that was the most infuriating thing, they were always strangers. "If only," he would think, "there was one that I could recognise. . . ." Once a great bird descended from the light above and alighted almost at his feet, and Roger screamed with fright. Then he realised it was the basket with his bread and water. He was seeing double and his hands failed to grasp the pitcher. He heard a strange noise above him, like neighing, or barking. A voice? Even if these were words they had no meaning.

This time he was drawn out of his delirium by the best and most powerful of remedies: bread. He ate only a few mouthfuls, having learned to make do with a little at a time. Then he thought: "Man is the craziest of the animals: here I am glad to find myself in this stinking black hole! Alone with my sweat and my excrement and the cold stone. And my lice. For how long? One day I shall die here, and they will forget me and I shall rot on this straw until I am nothing but a mass of worms. Lord Jesus, is there any forgiveness for those who die unabsolved when it is not their fault? . . . Then they will say that I let myself die of my own free will, and that I am a heretic, and they will burn my body and forbid all Christians to pray for me! And they will publish my name in the Cathedral of Toulouse, and in all the churches in the diocese, as a recreant, excommunicate and delivered up to the eternal fire, and they will

323

be absolved before God and men for my death! Lord, is this just? "I have sinned, but not enough to deserve that."

Either by chance or an effect of divine mercy, Roger felt his fever abate and his cough become less painful. He was quite determined not to let himself die, and to hold out for another year if he had to. He was no longer counting the days. He had stopped thinking—for the clumsy, formless thoughts which invaded his brain were a worse torment than the lice; and to avoid thought—because even prayers would not drive it away—he finally found a task within his strength. He began carving the letters of Rigueur's name on a flagstone with his belt buckle, in letters an inch long which he could read with his fingers in the dark. The stone was hard; he carved and scratched away gently, concentrating on making the lines straight. The work absorbed him to such a degree that when he had finished the first R, he barely stopped for a second to take a breath before going on to the next letter, which he had already sketched in—he devoted himself to his task with such extraordinary concentration that he might have been engaged on an urgent command for which he had too little time, for at any moment he might be sent for and taken out of his cell, and when that moment came it was important for the name to be completed.

He sometimes wondered why he had not at least chosen the name of Jesus, or Mary, but had preferred instead the name of a woman who had been—to put it crudely—his partner in lust. (Once in prison and compelled to think of his soul, he could not help but realise that the love which is most honourable in the eyes of the world is a mortal sin before God.)

But the more he recalled Rigueur, the better he understood how much she deserved his affection, and how deeply he had wronged her. In order to satisfy his own desires, he had led a chaste creature into the perils of a carnal union, and had purified himself (since he had renounced a dissolute life for her sake) by defiling a pure woman. Though she had renounced sin, she must none the less look back with sorrow to the time when she had been subject to the Devil. He thought that he could never honour her enough for that. . . . *Ah! She had been more loving than many a light o' love, an ardent and submissive mistress who had never known false modesty. Can any man be such an ingrate as to forget that?*

By working away at his letters, Roger killed time and also

324

killed some of the pain in his body; the task gradually became an obligation to him, and he would not relinquish it through a superstitious fear of attracting disaster—all his thoughts were on forming the letters and ways of carving them more deeply in the stone. When he had finished the first *Rigueur* he began on a second, with some half-conscious thought in his mind that if he carved three he might be released and his trial end with a light penance.

He had reached, not peace, but a measure of indifference, when one day, as he was lying face downwards with his cheek pressed against the flags scratching away at the stone, he heard the trap open and looked up. A ladder was being let down to him and he had to fling himself back into the corner before it landed on his back. A voice from above asked if he was in fact Roger de Montbrun, knight. As always happens, the thing he had dreamed of for so long came at an untoward moment; he did not at first understand, and thought: "*Alas, I have not had time to finish.*" (Three letters of the third *Rigueur* were still to be carved.) While as for answering the question, the devil if he wanted to. The voice which he had so pined to hear now seemed as hideous to him as the howling of a wolf.

The question was repeated. Whoever it was up there said that the prisoner Roger de Montbrun was summoned for interrogation by the tribunal and must answer if he was able. At this Roger blinked and thought: "Lucky, then, that my name is Roger de Montbrun; now I can be let out."

He was not strong enough to climb the ladder and they threw down a rope which he fastened under his arms. They were calling to him: "*Shut your eyes! Shut your eyes!*" But even through closed lids he felt an intolerable red light scorching his pupils. A hood was put over his head, but in spite of that, the air in the passage was so different from that in the cell that on breathing it in Roger fell to the ground in a faint.

He came to himself in a room which seemed to him immense; a lantern covered with a wire mesh stood on the floor, a few steps away from him, searing his eyes so that he had to hide his face in his hands. "*Don't be afraid, you'll get used to it in a moment. Drink this.*" Roger felt something hard and warm pressed against his lips and liquid trickled into his mouth; he tried to swallow and spat, the liquid was warm, like blood, and its taste and smell were

325

choking him—though it was only water coloured with a little red wine. "Water," he said. All the same he finally drank two or three sips and felt better.

Two men were supporting him, sponging his face and shearing off the stiff, matted tufts of his beard and hair, lacing up his shoes and the sides of his gown with string, commenting as they did so: "*This was good cloth once, ten sous an ell, at least!*" These gaolers were brawny fellows, with red unshaven faces, and dirty, calloused hands, but they seemed to be experts at the job of nursing. They busied themselves about the prisoner like soldiers caring for a wounded comrade.

"There now," they would say, "stretch that leg, bend the knee, don't be afraid, your hamstrings are still all right, you won't need crutches this evening. You must have had some fat to spare! Don't worry about your eyes, only try not to look at the candles." Roger had become so completely unused to seeing live men that even their kindness hurt him. He could not answer them. His ears were coming to life again, serving a new apprenticeship to the sound of voices, which was as painful as having infected scabs ripped off a wound.

"Is he ready at last?"

"Er, well, just a moment to shake the lice off his cloak into the fire, we've got enough of them of our own! This fellow may be as tough as oak, but he still needs a minute to get his breath back."

"He'll have to get it back a bit quicker, curse it! We've had word that the Brothers of the tribunal have already arrived, and whose fault is it if they are kept waiting?"

"Come on," said one of the gaolers, "lean on my shoulder and by the time we're out of the room you'll be walking like a lad of twenty."

In a small room with grey walls and a low, vaulted ceiling, Roger found the Brothers Alberic and Guillaume once more. They were sitting at a plain wooden table, on which were two metal candlesticks, and Roger could not see the men's faces for the bright light of the candles. They made him sit on a stool two steps away from the table, and he held his head down because the light was hurting his eyes. At that moment he felt as meek as a lamb, all faces and all words were alike, nothing to do with him. They asked him to give his name, age and titles, and the effort of speaking revived him a little. "Now they expect to have me," he thought.

326

Brother Alberic said that before leaving for Comminges on a mission for the Inquisition, Brother Peter Seila had remembered Roger de Montbrun and given orders for his interrogation to be reopened. As he was occupied elsewhere himself, he, Brother Alberic, had been delegated to collect the accused's confessions. However, Roger must realise that on this occasion the tribunal had very little time to spare for him and that if he allowed the interrogation to drag out too long he would be returned to his cell the next day to await Brother Peter's return. Brother Guillaume asked whether the accused understood what was being said to him. "Yes," said Roger, "I understand. Brothers, this is a sin. I am like a wounded man."

Brother Alberic said: "Since you are in a fit state to speak you are also in a state to think of your salvation. It appears from your previous interrogations that you deny ever having confessed to the heretic errors, either Cathar or Vaudois, and that you say you are a good Catholic."

"Yes."

"Therefore you should be able to tell us about your faith."

"I believe all the teachings of the Catholic Church."

"Can you recite the *Credo* to us?"

"I can." Roger began to say the words; he was not afraid of making a mistake, but he was afraid that his faltering voice might make them think he was stumbling.

". . . You claim to adhere with all your heart, without reserve or pretence, to every one of the articles of the *Credo* which you have just recited to us?"

"Yes." Roger was leaning forward, his elbows on his knees and his chin on his clasped hands, staring at the wooden table and the monks' spare, brown hands. Brother Guillaume had a rosary wound round his left wrist. "*That was what I needed in prison, it's more use there than anywhere else.*"

"To which of the Three Persons of the Trinity do you usually address your prayers, when you yourself call on God?"

"To the Son."

"Why? When you pray to God, then, do you always say: Lord Jesus, or merely 'Lord'? Or 'Lord God'? Do you never say: 'Our Father' or 'Father'?"

"I recite the *Pater*, naturally."

"So you consider it of no use to pray to God the Father, apart from the Lord's Prayer?"

327

"I don't know."

"Should the Father be honoured less than the Son?"

"No."

"Should He not rather be honoured more?"

"No."

"Yet, do you not believe that there was a time when the Son did not exist, and when the Father was alone?"

"No. It is said: *Genitum ante omnia saecula*. There was never such a time."

"But, before all the ages, was there never a time when the Father, by His will, created the Son, as He did all the other blessed spirits?"

"*Non factum*," said Roger, with a faint smile. "They shall not catch me in that trap," he thought, "I am not yet altogether a fool."

"Yet, in your heart, you can believe that He who engenders is greater than He who is engendered and that, to some extent, He creates him."

"No. The Son existed through all eternity and there was never a moment when He did not exist."

"So the Father gave birth to someone who already existed? That is a contradiction."

"Ah! You are trying to make me say that which I cannot say!" exclaimed Roger. "I am no scholar, but if you want to make me out an Arian you will not succeed."

"For a layman you seem to me very well informed," said Brother Alberic. "Why do you defend yourself so eagerly if you are not conscious of guilt? It is possible for good Catholics to confess in all ignorance that the Father is greater than the Son. You have anticipated the questions in advance and have prepared your answers."

"Ever since I was a child," said Roger, "I have listened to people arguing about the manner in which we must believe in God. It would be astonishing if at my age I could not distinguish between Catholic and heretic doctrine."

"Yet you know the Church forbids laymen to discuss matters of faith."

"Short of being a mindless beast one is bound to reflect upon such questions."

"Not so, since all that can come of your reflections can be the smoke of error and the poison of doubt."

328

Roger felt so exhausted and so dazed by the light, air and noise that he wanted to close his eyes and lie down on the floor. He himself was astonished at the agility of his mind, which managed to find adequate answers to fairly difficult questions. It was as if there were two men inside him: one speaking and taking in what was said, the other listening without understanding; this second man was still in the cell, wondering whether he would ever leave it, if he would ever speak to men again. While the one who was speaking persisted stubbornly in a painful struggle where the main thing was not to yield at all costs. Yet he was incapable of thought and could not even tell whether there was anything to be gained by fighting.

"Why are you questioning me about my faith if, according to you, I am not even permitted to discuss it?"

"Know," said Brother Alberic, "that not every man who says 'Lord, Lord,' enters into the kingdom of heaven. Your theoretical knowledge tells us nothing of your faith."

"Then how will you find out whether I believe as I ought?"

"What are the prayers you usually recite on waking and when you commend yourself to God before you go to sleep?"

"The same as everyone else: the *Pater*, the *Ave Maria*, the psalms of contrition, the litany to the Virgin, and prayers to the saints according to the day."

"Do you say them regularly?"

"No. Only whenever possible. Except for the *Pater* and the *Ave Maria*."

"You have been alone for forty days in fasting and mortification of the flesh. Have you had no leisure to pray?"

"I did pray."

"Can you say to us the prayers you were accustomed to address to God during your confinement?"

Roger felt himself blushing to the roots of his hair. "No," he said. "I can't."

"Suppose I command you?" asked Brother Alberic.

"Only in confession. It should be enough for you to know what the prayers were."

"If they were those you say, why do you refuse to repeat them to us, so that we may be convinced of your innocence?"

Roger looked up at the man who had spoken with a hard, contemptuous expression.

"I am not in a proper state of mind for prayer."

"And supposing we take your refusal for proof of obstinate perversity?"

"Take it for what you like."

"Roger de Montbrun," said Brother Guillaume, who of the two was the more well disposed to the prisoner, more from a worldly liking than for any other reason, "you must understand that the Church would not have accused you without strong evidence. It is up to you to prove that we are wrong about you."

"The Church has not accused me. And you are holding me in prison unjustly, so that I cannot appeal to the Pope."

"These are all subterfuges and evasions," said Brother Alberic, "we know that. Since you refuse to repeat your prayers to us, we are within our rights to believe they are heretic prayers."

"Oh! If he would only be quiet!" thought Roger. "They should have kept me chained up. . . ." In spite of his weakness, he was itching to strike out, to strike out wildly, until he thought he would go mad with the temptation.

"Have pity, Brothers," he said at last. "I am so weary that if I had anything to confess, I would confess it. Put it down in writing that I did in fact give the key of the underground passage to the heretic Guiraud de Montauban, and that I myself conducted him and his companion Arnaud into the cellars of Layrac. I did not do it for love of their faith but out of my friendship for a man who had asked this service of me."

The scribe wrote down the deposition impassively.

"This man's name?"

"Bérenger d'Aspremont."

"Were any other men involved in this?"

"No. And Jean-Rigaud de Marcillac knows nothing. My wife knew because I had to ask her for the key."

"How could the man in charge of the castle be unaware of such a thing?"

"I have told him nothing. I merely told him not to cause trouble for any heretics he might find in my domain."

"He has been charged at Montauban and has said nothing like this."

"How should I know what he said?"

"He said that the passage no longer existed and that he had never heard of any heretics at Layrac. Now, judge for yourself, how can we believe you, since you admit that, until now, you have been lying? Especially as you managed to take us in so

330

cleverly that we were actually beginning to think you were not lying on this point."

"This time," Roger said in an expressionless tone, "I have told you everything. I did it for Bérenger d'Aspremont because I saw that he was greatly afflicted by the death of a relative; I could not refuse him this service. Now, you know the whole truth, and I will tell you, too, that three times in my life I have prostrated myself before heretics in the manner of the believers. I did not do this to honour their faith but in simple courtesy and because my friends were doing so."

"Which friends?"

"Brothers, I have told you everything. Supposing I told you these friends belonged to the Aspremont, Layrac, Mirepoix and Rabastens families, you would not be learning anything new."

"How can we believe you? All the people you mention are already condemned or beyond our reach. These people were not the only ones present at the sermons you heard?"

"I don't know."

"Roger de Montbrun," said Brother Alberic, in such a solemn voice that one might have thought the interrogation was only just beginning, "we have sufficient proof of your bad faith to be justified in not believing the rest of your story. Do you persist, against all probability, in denying that you are a heretic at heart? If your repentance had been sincere, you would have admitted that in the past you had been led into error."

"Neither now nor in the past. I do deny it."

The two men began examining him again about his faith, asking questions in turn, until Roger no longer knew who was interrogating him and which of them to answer, he felt as though ten different men were talking to him. He was now so weak that he could think of nothing, beyond struggling to prevent himself bursting into sobs. The cramp in his stomach and the pain in his back prevented him from understanding what was being said to him; and his distress grew with every minute that passed because he had an hour, or two hours, left and if he did not confess now, it would be the dungeon. The more he felt light and air and sounds around him, the more amazed he was at the terrible speed with which his body was becoming accustomed to them.

His heart was beating like that of a man about to be buried alive in an hour's time.

331

At last he said: "Mercy. I can no longer follow your questions. Give me an hour's respite."

"We could not, even if we wished," said Brother Guillaume, "because we are leaving Toulouse after second Mass. If before then our investigations have not reached satisfactory conclusions, Brother Peter will not be able to pronounce judgment and your case will be deferred until our return."

"I am not a heretic."

"But you have been one?"

"I have never been one."

"How long," Brother Guillaume asked gently, "will you go on denying the evidence? Your own behaviour is sufficient proof against you."

"Then condemn me on this proof."

"We cannot, because that would mean giving you up to the secular arm as an obdurate heretic, and we do not desire your death."

"I have admitted everything. If I said I was a heretic it would be like denying my faith."

"It would not be denying your faith if you showed a sincere desire to be reconciled with the Church."

"I have a sincere desire to be at peace with the Church. But I will not perjure myself."

"Given the high esteem in which you hold certain heretic believers, such an admission should not strike you as shameful."

"For *them* it would not be shameful. For me, yes."

"There is nothing to be got out of this man," said Brother Alberic. "Why do we persist in trying to save him? Let him be returned to his cell, he has made fools of us for long enough."

Roger wanted to fling himself on his knees and scream for mercy; but his knees would not obey him. He stood up and the two gaolers bound his hands and led him out of the room. He thought: "Rather die than go back to that cell," but he had never had less intention of dying. The hopeless longing to stay in the fresh air made the blood drum so strongly in his head that he no longer heard or saw anything. He found himself in a square chamber where a torch was burning in a ring in the wall; a number of soldiers were sitting on the ground throwing dice, their spears propped up against the wall. "All this, I have seen it all before," Roger thought, "so often . . . in so many castles. That loophole gives on to the street. Lord, and I thought I was

332

so far away from everything!" But how could he escape? His hands were tied and he was weaker than an old man of ninety. But they did not take him back to his cell. He was left in the room, near the soldiers, and lay down on the ground and went to sleep.

Roger would have been considerably surprised had he known that he had very nearly succeeded in convincing his judges. They both argued: "This man is certainly not lying. But Brother Peter is very set against him, and will be even more so after this evening's admissions. He will never let him escape with a canonical penance."

The two monks did not like one another and it was on this account, to test their patience, that the Father Superior had yoked them together as the Inquisitor's assistants; justice, he said, must surely benefit by it. But since Brother Alberic came from Montpellier, he was the stronger of the two, in Toulouse at least, and it was easy for him to accuse his companion of lenience towards fellow-citizens. He was a man of forty, endowed with a great hatred of evil, and the austerity of his life could be read in one glance at his long, stern face. The heavy eyebrows, the deep creases in his cheeks, the clear, penetrating eyes and chiselled mouth, every feature of this monastic face seemed to have been moulded by long years of prayer and fasting. Brother Guillaume, on the other hand, though he led a most exemplary life, was afflicted with a lively, mobile countenance that might easily have belonged to any tradesman, and this made him jealous of the involuntary respect which laymen accorded his companion.

They had still two women to interrogate that evening, or rather that night, and when dealing with women, especially if they were still young, both vied with one another in severity, as their natural dislike of the impure sex was reinforced by the fear of finding themselves accused of undue lenience. Where the men were concerned it was quite different: a prisoner had only to please Brother Alberic to displease Brother Guillaume, while as soon as Brother Guillaume seemed inclined to be lenient, Brother Alberic redoubled his severity; on occasions they even went so far as to accuse one another, by implication, of the basest motives. It was no small test for monks to be exposed every day to the temptation of seeing their fellows at their mercy. (And who knows what inadmissible tenderness may be roused by the face of

333

a once handsome man whose ravaged features still retain traces of the inconceivable seduction which makes the beauty of the flesh so dangerous?)

"What shall we do?" said Brother Alberic. "If he confesses nothing more before matins we shall have to send him back to his cell, and he is not a man of twenty any more."

"In any case we must call him back to sign his confession before we leave the prison. If the recantation is drawn up in advance perhaps he'll sign it."

"You will see," said Brother Alberic grimly. "He'll say again that he is a good Catholic and talk of appealing to the Pope."

"In that case, Brother Alberic, do you believe it is permissible to drive a Catholic to a false confession? He has said enough to deserve a fairly severe penance, he'll be only too glad to escape with five years at St. John of Acre."

"You know how it is with the Count's courtiers: he'll find a thousand excuses to put off the voyage. And we shall see him strutting about Toulouse, and riding from Provence to Aragon and Aragon to Carcassès, sowing hatred of our Order and a spirit of rebellion everywhere. Such intriguers are worse than the real heretics."

"That, Brother Alberic, does not concern the tribunal of the Holy Office. It is only too true that this man's conduct is very bad in all aspects, but if he is a Catholic we cannot condemn him for heresy. There is a great gulf between a man guilty of abetting heresy and a believer."

"Not a gulf, exactly, only a small ditch that is easily crossed. Figuratively speaking, this man is only clinging to the Church by a single hair; and by letting him go we shall infallibly precipitate him into the abyss of error. That is what Brother Peter will tell you, even if we venture to assert that we have discovered the man really is a Catholic."

"I should be troubled in my conscience, if I drove a Catholic to a false confession; on the day he admits he is a heretic he may perhaps be inclined to become one altogether."

"This man is an accomplished liar and the truth has to be dragged out of him by blows, threats and cunning, and yet you are afraid of making him tell another lie? You see before you a man who, for years, has been abusing the Church, spilling the blood of Christ's soldiers, robbing the poor, committing a hundred adulterous acts, and because he has lost his fine clothes and the

334

arrogant confidence of this world's wealth, you hasten to return them to him. Hasn't he publicly proclaimed his longing to drink our blood before now?"

"If we had to take everyone's drunken words into account . . . we should be immune to insults by now! Must it be said that our tribunal condemns men merely because they do not belong to our party? This man is accused of toleration and lenience by many witnesses but no one has said anything against him which could lead us to question his orthodoxy."

"You sound as though you were pleading for him," said Brother Alberic. "If his faith is good but his conduct in all things belies it, is he to be judged by his secret thoughts rather than his behaviour? It is right and proper to remove the wolf's teeth and claws."

Roger was awakened at dawn and taken back to his judges; this time he could barely stand and felt much worse than on the previous day. His confession was read aloud to him and he signed without a word. Brother Alberic announced that if he were willing to sign a paper acknowledging himself guilty of heresy and asking to be reconciled to the Church, there would be every chance of his trial being over that very day; all that would be needed was the Brother Inquisitor's decision. "Roger de Montbrun, understand that we are asking you to sign this paper out of pity for you, because you have placed yourself in such a position that if you refuse to sign we cannot answer for the consequences. Brother Peter can declare you a heretic merely on the evidence of the confession you have already signed, and you know the danger you are in."

Roger shook his head slowly. "No. I will not put the rope around my own neck. I know the Count will not let me burn."

"Is that your final word, Roger de Montbrun?"

"No. But for the respect I owe to your cloth, I should have said another not fit for your ears."

"Well!" said Brother Alberic, when the accused had been taken away. "The fellow is tougher than I thought. It was not forty days he needed, but three months."

However, the two monks knew from experience that a prisoner who was put back in the dungeons after such a short interval was often liable to lose his reason. They decided to ask their superior for permission to have the prisoner transferred to a lighted cell if there was one empty: he could not be put in the

335

communal prison as he was a fluent speaker and therefore in need of solitude.

Contrary to what might have been imagined, Roger experienced no feeling of gratitude towards the worthy monks, though they wished him more good than harm. After enduring the dark cell with a proper enough Christian meekness, he now looked on an infinitely better prison as an unbearable torment.

There was a door to the cell. This meant that prisoners confined there were invariably fettered by uncomfortably short chains on their feet, while those on their wrists were barely long enough to allow the man to stretch his arms. In this cell Roger could take three steps lengthwise and two across; he had a wooden bucket and a stool, and by climbing on to this and raising his arms he could reach the narrow, barred window, fitted with one upright iron bar and four horizontal. By looking straight at them it was possible to see a patch of sky with a six-branched, black cross outlined against it. Could these eight, small segments of sky really be a source of great happiness? At times they were. In the early morning, when the rosy light was cold and clean, and also a little before noon, when the sun, which for the rest of the day was hidden behind some invisible building, cast a small wedge of light on to the paving stone near the door.

Every day the gaoler would come and throw open the door, to bring a bowl of soup and some bread and empty the bucket. This gaoler showed no inclination to talk: he was forbidden to enter into conversation with prisoners suspected of heresy, and Roger had nothing to bribe him with beyond a few trinkets, somewhat the worse for wear and now worth little more than the weight of the silver. "What should I do with them, anyway?" said the man. "My sentence is twenty years, and so far I've only done seven."

"You can't make me believe you have no comrades who can get wine and other things in to you." The man dropped a wink and agreed, then claimed that these 'comrades' were not to be trusted and refused to perform the services asked of them. "What do you expect? They are frightened of hell fire."

"Do you think I was born yesterday? You'd go to hell yourself for ten crowns. You know I am lord of the manor of Layrac. Once out of here, I'll help you to escape."

The man gave a derisive shrug. "That's what they all say. I

336

stay where I am. I'm better off here than in some stinking sewer."

What help was to be expected from a thief? The man, Raimbert, was a former wool seller, convicted of giving short measure and of appropriating seven thirty-pound bales himself—and too poor, naturally, ever to pay back such a debt. Roger flattered him outrageously and did his utmost to keep him in his cell as long as he could. The man was certainly reluctant to leave, and would say as he went: "Watch out for Père Cornu!" This was his nickname for the warder in charge of that floor, whose real name was Raymond Cornille.

When the gaoler had gone, Roger found himself alone again for the rest of the day, except for the invisible sun which travelled across the sky and sometimes, towards evening, reflected a rosy light off the clouds and between the bars before it disappeared, leaving the window to turn paler and paler and finally to blue— while on cold, clear nights a few stars shone in it, though it was hard to tell to which constellation they belonged.

A good prison. There was even enough water to wash his face and hands, and on Sundays the soup smelled distinctly of pork. He could hear the church bells ringing. Occasionally, sparrows and turtle-doves would come and settle on the bars of the window, poking small, inquisitive heads inside and apparently watching the man who lay motionless on his mattress of straw. Roger spread crumbs of bread on the ground to encourage them, and also set himself to learn to imitate the doves' cooing. He became so proficient at this that one fine morning an unsuspecting bird slipped through the bars and alighted on his chest. For a few seconds he lay without moving, holding his breath, while the dove regarded him, unseeing, with her little, round, bright eyes, turning her head this way and that with an air of innocent surprise. No long able to control his yearning tenderness, Roger grabbed at her suddenly with his chained hand, holding her prisoner: she fluttered her silky plumage under the pressure of his fingers and then was still. He only wanted to stroke her, but his heart was beating furiously and his hand tightened. Even if he had tried, he could not have stopped himself gripping her harder, and he heard the fragile bones cracking in his palm. Afterwards he wept. Wept not for pity, but out of impotent rage and tenderness, because he could easily have crushed a hundred doves in the same way, or rather, he would have liked to see this one come back to life again a hundred times. But he never tried to attract

337

birds again. He told himself: "Even in prison does our natural wickedness make us kill?" It seemed to him that the death of this innocent creature would bring him bad luck.

In this good prison Roger felt his hatred and anger growing to such a degree that there were times when he would fling himself at the door and batter the wood with the iron rings on his wrists. He screamed that he was innocent and was being held there without cause, and that those responsible for it should pay dearly. In the end he was deprived of food for three days for causing a disturbance. Since he was not the only one to make a noise he discovered that his neighbour in the next cell was called Roger Guillaume and was accused of harbouring heretics. But they had to shout to make themselves heard and then the keeper would come with his cudgel.

"... *Obviously, if they have put me in a good prison, then they must be convinced of my innocence. And they want to prevent me from communicating with my friends in case I reveal their perfidy. Therefore,*" thought Roger, "*they are afraid of me. But equally obviously they will not let me out of here of their own accord. Therefore, it is up to me to find a way of escape.*"

At first he had hoped to obtain news of the Count or his friends through Raimbert. But if any of the gaolers did receive letters or gifts for the prisoner Roger de Montbrun he was undoubtedly keeping them for himself or handing them over to the authorities. They never even reached Raimbert.

Roger quickly learned to know the man; he could tell, merely from the way he held his head, whether the gaoler was lying or not. "Of course," he would say, "who would trust a thief like you with a message? Your comrades must say to themselves: it will all go into his own pocket."

"Thief!" Raimbert would say. "Thief! *I* don't wear chains on my hands and feet!"

"But you have brought me nothing, when I know that people come to enquire about me every day! Naturally you must be thought a robber."

"And how do you know," Raimbert would ask, with a nasty jeering smile, "that anyone comes to enquire about you? Did a little bird tell you, or the Holy Ghost?" In fact, Roger knew he was speaking the truth and tormented him on purpose, thinking to himself: "The day he has any news he will be delighted to prove to me that I was wrong." It was humiliating to be so

338

dependent on so base a creature: no doubt it was true that beggars could not be choosers, but it was a wretched business, paying court to this petty gaolbird!

"What were you doing in the wool trade anyway, you old fool? With that face of yours, you'd have been a captain in three years if you'd gone in for soldiering!"

"The devil! Giving false measure for two whole years!—They should have given you a job in the Bishop's treasury instead of putting you in prison! If you weren't more nervous than a scalded cat, I would have put you in charge of collecting the dues of corn on my domain." Raimbert laughed at these friendly jibes, with the conceit of a foolish man glad to find an appreciative audience. Roger spoke to him with a mixture of affected contempt and real good nature that was proper for a knight addressing a man he knew to be his inferior but whom he nevertheless respected. He would sometimes laugh at the crudest jokes while at the same time pointing out their stupidity: "Was there ever such a clown? You were surely cut out to be a mountebank!"

Raimbert was neither tall nor broad, but he could wield a cudgel adroitly when he had to; he had the nature of a bully: he was timid, suspicious, but not as greedy as many others since he was not anxious to leave prison. "I am wasting my time with this devil," thought Roger; and when he saw the gaoler lingering in his cell, shuffling about, turning over the straw and whistling absently, he would sometimes take pleasure in looking the other way, giving a convincing, and indeed perfectly sincere, pantomime of disgust. "Ah, ha! Sir knight has received a letter from the Holy Ghost! That's what makes him preen himself in his fox fur cloak, so fine that even a leper wouldn't take it." Roger let the man go, resisting the temptation to speak, but afterwards he had nothing to do for the rest of the day but torment himself with his loneliness, which he detested more with every hour. He tried to make up songs or letters in his head and gnawed his fingers with fury—what songs, great God! No one would ever hear them. Sometimes the man called Roger Guillaume in the next cell would shout his battle-cry, something like: "Hail to all Christians!" Roger would shout back, "Hail!" Sometimes, by pressing his ear to the door, he could hear shouting. Raimbert had a ready fist. Roger had only felt it twice. Afterwards Raimbert had almost apologised, saying: "I have my orders." He had told Roger how he himself had been beaten and put in the pillory and branded

339

with a red hot iron on the left shoulder, and how the women of his neighbourhood had hurled stones at his head.

"You have no more blood in your body than a stuck pig, and what do you expect to become of you? They won't keep you here when you have done your twenty years. You'll be fifty, and you'll have to beg for your living. Three doors and a guarded moat, you say . . . what is your cudgel for? It's brave work, beating chained men; a woman could do as much."

"You are all the same; you promise wonders, and I have known some who have held the ladder for prisoners, and then they have stayed behind; and flogged, I'll say they were—until their own fathers wouldn't have known them."

"What about you, would *your* father have recognised you as you are now? Would he be proud of you?"

"Think of it! Some of them have promised me a hundred crowns."

"Look me straight in the eye, fellow, and tell me how many people have promised you a hundred crowns. Anyone would think you guarded no one but knights and bankers. You'll grow as proud as an abbot in such good company. Today, in my chains, I am less than the dust, but outside I am lord of a manor. But you, outside you are nothing at all. I am not joking, I will make you a tithe collector on my domain." Raimbert laughed, his usual surly, insolent laugh, but he seemed less sure of himself. Once he said: "In the prison they think you're pretty stupid not to want your case judged."

"How do they know I don't?"

"I'm no fool. You never talk about judgment, you only talk about escaping."

"Have you repeated that to Père Cornu?"

"Maybe. If I were ever fool enough to listen to you, I'd have to make sure that he didn't suspect me, wouldn't I?"

"He'd be wasting his time suspecting a wet hen like you!" said Roger in disgust. "If they gave you a wooden ladder you'd be afraid to climb down it." All the same he thought: "He is tempted, that is something." He had fully made up his mind to confess nothing, since he reasoned, with some justification, that if his enemies were determined to make him confess, then it was in their interests to do so, and he did not want to play their game.

On the Sunday before Easter, Raimbert appeared in the

340

morning looking decidedly gloomy, he put the bowl of soup on the stool without a word, and gave a deep sigh.

"What's troubling you?" asked Roger. "Are you ill or what?"

"Not me. You're the one who may be in for a bad time, if I tell you what I heard."

"Tell me, all the same."

"Your father is dead," said Raimbert. "His funeral was announced yesterday morning."

Roger, who was lying on his straw mattress, his chained hands clasped behind his head, stiffened and closed his eyes, like a man who had been hit. "Get out. But you did well to tell me. Now leave me."

Raimbert sighed again. "It comes to all men," he said, clumsily, because he was not used to showing sympathy. "It can't be helped, sir knight, and he can't have been a young man either."

"Go, leave me. I'd rather be alone."

"*—Roger, if I do not see her again before I die, the sin will be yours....*" "*You are bad sons, both of you, you never tell me anything....*" "*I am becoming senile.*" "*Bad news, Roger?...*" "*What have you done with your brother? I am waiting for you to say*: *Am I my brother's keeper?*" "Bertrand, always Bertrand. Oh, God! Let him tell me a thousand times more that it is my fault Bertrand is still in prison; let him turn his head the other way on his pillow in disgust when he sees me come into the room! Who closed his eyes?"

He saw his father's head again, the cheeks at once hollow and sagging with loose fat, the deep pouches under the eyes and the damp, grey locks sticking to his feverish brow. I knew him, he thought, when he was strong, handsome and proud, and I have seen him humbled thus, and yet I never found him old.

"He died cursing his sons in their maturity because they could not protect his old age. It was not our fault, we were no worse than other sons. We have been destroyed by our country's enemies."

His throat was choked by an unreasoning hatred, and because the mind is more easily swayed by frenzy than by reason, he thought: "*They caused my father's death, they killed my father.*" Pierre-Guillaume had been seventy-six and had made a good end, but it was not so much his death that hurt as the manner of it. He had died thinking of his sons in prison, tortured maybe, perhaps dead; at an age when a man of his rank had a right to universal respect, he had died trembling in case he saw himself

341

thrown out into the street. "You could not protect your old father from this outrage. The house will be inherited by children, and Guillelme has not enough sense to defend their rights."

Roger had already cursed his brother so much that now he no longer bore him any grudge. The fault lay with their country's enemies. "Why shouldn't Bertrand have been a heretic, if he liked? That was his faith, and all men want to live according to their own faith. He was doing no one any harm, quite the reverse, he devoted himself to charitable works more than Catholics much richer than himself do. It is these men who are the real heretics, the ones who say that God beats people into loving Him. . . . Liars and hypocrites that you are, you who set yourselves up to judge things that cannot be judged by men. You tell me: 'Your father was a sinner who devoured the goods of the poor; he did not die of cold or hunger, then why do you blame us?' That is their way of thinking, they forget that God permitted the bad, rich man to live and did not judge him until after his death. What God dare not do, you are doing, and you torture folk not in order to steal their goods but from pride and perversity and the desire for power."

Roger wept bitterly for his father, and it seemed to him that he had not suffered so much even on the day he had buried his son. Now he was the head of the household: a prisoner, chained, so securely confined that his friends could not even get a letter through to him; he, the eldest and the head of his family, was reduced to begging the help of a gaoler.

The next day he spoke to Raimbert, with a sadness that was not feigned. "For once you bring me some news," he said, "and it is to kill me. Have you been given orders to torment me? Perhaps you were lying to me."

"I wish I had been lying," said Raimbert, "and your noble father were still alive."

"It becomes you well to utter pious words."

"Just when I was going to tell you something," said Raimbert.

"What could you tell me? With a coward like you, they could leave the door wide open and I shouldn't escape."

Roger shut his eyes and turned to the wall so that the other could not see his eagerness, and Raimbert went away. He came back half an hour later on the pretext of searching the cell. "Can't you see, then, you fool, that I am mourning for my father and don't want to be disturbed?"

342

"Anyone would think you were still a great lord sitting in state in your castle hall! I shouldn't be talking to you at all."

"So much the better. Be quiet. You'll be doing me a service."

"A comrade of mine," said Raimbert, "has been promised forty crowns for you. He told me. But with Père Cornu, nothing doing."

"Suppose he were promised a thousand crowns? Even if you had the guts to climb down the walls on a rope, where would you find the rope? What are you? A prisoner like myself, except that no one would pay ten sous to get you out."

Raimbert sat down on the stool, chin in hand, and contemplated his prisoner with a mixture of insolence and apprehension. "Now then, sir knight, that is all well and good, but you would gladly sell your soul to the Devil to get out of here. Only don't think I am a fool. You promise me this and that, but you are a nobleman, and do you expect me to believe that you want to keep a fellow with you who has thumped you with a cudgel?"

Roger raised himself on his elbow, and whistled, his eyes crinkling with amusement. "Not so bad," he said. "Not so bad, faith. But what's to be done? It's quite true, of course, that it's not fitting to let oneself be thumped without some thoughts of revenge."

"There you are: once the danger's over, it's goodbye to the saint. Why should I be that saint?"

"Listen to me, Raimbert. As for the shame; since I have been in prison I have suffered more than my share of that. And as for the blows, devil take you, I'll probably give you a buffet or two one day when I'm rid of my chains. Only, if you help me to get out of here, it will be life and death between us, you have my word as a knight for that."

Then Raimbert told him that his comrade promised to steal the keys from Père Cornu that night, and smuggle fifty feet of knotted rope into the prison. "Only, if I get caught," he said, "I'm a dead man, to say nothing of the flogging."

"Good, let's not talk about that. Anyway, you'll let go of the rope, I can tell that from here."

"Maybe you're the one who will let go. Look how thin and worn you are. I am younger than you!"

"That is different. I am a soldier. And what about the keys for the chains, eh? Père Cornu doesn't have those."

Raimbert laughed slyly, and said that he had long ago manufactured a hook capable of opening the lock on any chain: he

343

hadn't wasted his time in prison. "I wouldn't do it for anyone but you. It's because you aren't proud."

For four days Roger prepared for departure, massaging his muscles, limbering up his body, stiffened by four months of inaction. He felt feverish and happy and had to fight against the temptation to shout out to the man called Roger Guillaume: "Goodbye. I'm off! Wish me a good journey!" Raimbert had succeeded in picking the locks on his chains and Roger exercised himself by walking about and swinging his arms, having some difficulty in getting used to the strange lightness of his limbs; he was to leave on the night of Good Friday.

A few days later Roger was lying on a woollen mattress in a dark, but reasonably clean room which he shared with five other invalids, struggling to find a reason for the agonising sensation of wretchedness which chilled his heart. It seemed to him that he could feel the presence of something huge and black close by him, in front of him, a foggy mass, black and heavy as lead, which prevented him from breathing.

He had a faint recollection of a few seconds of delirious happiness: of a fine, clear night, the roofs and spires of the town gleaming in the moonlight, towers lit by flambeaux. . . . There had been two of them there, tense and shivering with excitement, fastening the rope to a stanchion in the wall. The sentinel paced slowly towards them, without seeing them. It was impossible to hit him noiselessly from behind because of the helmet, nothing for it but to slit his throat before he had time to cry out. And because that fool had taken fright and started running, everything had gone wrong.

How badly injured he was he did not know; his left hand was bandaged, and his head (a good pint of blood seemed to have flowed down his face from the wound on his scalp). Stupefied by pain and brandy he had somehow endured three days of hell as he was carried on a stretcher from room to room and from building to building.

"Where have I see you before, Brother?"

"You have a short memory. You have seen me here in this seminary; we had a long talk together one night, three days before Our Lord's Nativity." Yes, Roger thought, the man of the fifty strokes of the lash. The doctor.

"Yes, by God! I know you now. Have they taken me out of prison for interrogation?"

344

"You were in a bad way, and our Father Superior permitted Brother Peter to have you brought to the prison hospital."

Roger looked about him, frowning, still trying to understand the reason for the weight which oppressed him, since this was not caused by his injuries. At last he said: "Raimbert?"

"I don't know who you mean, my friend."

"Raimbert, Raimbert Maillan, the gaoler."

"I believe I heard that he was already dead when they got him out of the moat."

Ah, so that was it. He jumped. He was afraid of the cudgels. He left me alone to face two soldiers, and he jumped. Dead. . . . To think that for two and a half months he was the only person I had to talk to; and now I shall never talk to him again.

I got away with it, he didn't.

But the foggy black mass was still there, close to him, invisible, and yet he knew it was there. Heavy, heavy and sad, a black hole of sadness, fallen from goodness knows where; a fragment of the other world suddenly breaking into the air breathed by living men.

Do they even know what a man is, he wondered, a man with a body, a voice, eyes, this man and no other? This man, who yesterday was my only friend (where are the others?), drowned in a mud-filled ditch. It is soon forgotten. Who will remember? If I were ever fool enough to listen to you . . . You fool, why the devil did you listen to me?

"Brother, I should like to make my confession."

"That is not exactly a reasonable request, my friend."

"I am sick and injured and it is more than six months now since I have attended confession, more than five months since I heard Mass. They have no right to deprive me of the consolations of religion."

"You have deprived yourself of them, by your obduracy. While the Church considers you a heretic she cannot grant you the right to confession."

"Brother, tell those who are my judges in this matter that if they find me guilty of any sin which I have not admitted, I will admit to that sin also. But they cannot refuse me the right to confession."

Thus, in return for a promise of sincere repentance, Roger de Montbrun was granted the right to receive absolution for his sins before his trial was concluded.

Carried into the monastery chapel on a stretcher, between

345

vespers and compline, Roger endeavoured to drag himself as close as possible to the grille dividing him from the priest, so that he would not have to speak too loudly. Ten paces away from him monks were at their prayers, kneeling on the bare flagstones and telling over their beads. Thirty candles were burning before the altar, and the white pillars and the lecterns were decorated with the young leaves and flowers, still fresh, which had adorned them for Easter Sunday. There was such an air of rustic innocence in these humble decorations that Roger was amazed at his own hardened worldly thoughts. THIS IS A HOLY PLACE. What does it matter what men enter it, and what they do elsewhere? Let God be their judge.

"*Confiteor Deo omnipotenti, beatae Mariae semper Virgini, beato Michaelo archangelo . . . et tibi Pater,*

"*Quia peccavi nimis cogitatione, verbo, et opere. Mea culpa mea culpa mea maxima culpa.*"

"Very well. Say what you have to say."

"Father, I have sinned. Father, I have committed an ugly deed, one I can never undo, though I were to spend twenty years lamenting it."

"Speak boldly, my son. There is no sin so great that God's mercy cannot wipe it away."

"Father, can even God make the evil we do as though it had never been? A man has paid for my folly with his life. And his soul is still so near to the place where he lived that I feel it always at my side. He died, like a dog, without the sacraments."

"You have been a soldier. At your age you must have more than one death on your conscience. The sin is great, certainly, but it was unintentional. This man took the risk himself, just as you did."

"Much good it has done him now to have taken the risk. It is true, I have killed, but they were men who were trying to kill me too."

"By birth, and perhaps by inclination, you have been led to follow an ungodly profession and to shed your neighbour's blood. All the same, you know that neither God nor the Church have condemned this profession beyond all appeal."

Roger saw again the wooden palisade along the moat at Auterive, and a tune, at once sad and powerful, echoed in his head, a song in a language no one could understand; the Basques were marching along the ditch, in their scarlet finery, their maces over

346

their shoulders, already somewhat drunk and, not exactly happy, but indifferent. All round them men were rushing screaming into the attack, dragging rams and scaling ladders. They had no armour, helmets or greaves, and where Roger was leading them they had not one chance in ten of earning their silver marks. "You don't know what it is like, Father, you regret the men you have killed much less than the men you have led to their deaths. There will be many who will say to me at the Day of Judgment: 'We sold our lives to you, for an oath or a piece of silver.' But even so, they were soldiers. I sinned more gravely against this man, because it was not his job to run risks."

"Then you have no graver sins to confess?"

"I say I am guilty of a man's death: can any sin be greater than that?"

"You stand accused of a culpable toleration of heresy, are you unaware that the Church considers that a mortal sin?"

"Father, there are some things which are considered sins one day and good deeds a year later. For twelve years I was excommunicated, like all the rest of my party, for actions which I believed, in all sincerity, to be right, and which I can never recant. Do you think I am justifying myself, instead of proclaiming my guilt? I do sincerely repent the blood I have spilled and the evil I have done to my neighbour, and my offences against God. I accuse myself of not having honoured my father as I should. And I accuse myself of having neglected my duties towards my wife and, through that, of having driven her to debauchery and bitterness of heart. And I accuse myself of having committed the sin of lust with a number of women, with married women too. And I accuse myself of excessive fondness for money, not for its own sake but out of worldly vanity; and in my greed I have not always taken proper note of the wretchedness of the poor on the lands under my care. And I accuse myself of having lied frequently, and flattered many men, and of having blasphemed and broken fasts. Pray to God that He may forgive me and open my heart to the knowledge of His will."

"I would gladly do so, if you had less pride. For the sins you confess are venial, but of the offences against the faith of which you stand accused you say nothing and appear to take pride in them."

"Father, I know that a priest of any other Order than the Dominican would not have refused me absolution. Are you not judging me according to the interests of your own party?"

347

"May God forgive you, my son. We do not take sides. Only bad Catholics and envious spirits can say that we are moved by the desire to take sides."

Thus Roger failed to receive his promised absolution; but when he was taken back to his hospital room he found Raimbert's ghost no longer there—though this might have been the effect of his contrition or simply of a change of mood. His mortal anguish had given way to a flat, resigned bitterness: the penalty for an unsuccessful attempt to escape is a cumulative one. Only a madman still persists in his denial when faced with a choice between confession and the grave. Raimbert had leaped to his grave, for him there was no other way out. "I too," thought Roger. "I was stupid not to have taken advantage of the one chance left for me. . . . They are only tending my wounds today so that I shall be in a fit state to appear in the cathedral on Ascension Day for the next *Act of Faith*."

His neighbours in the other beds were ordinary citizens, of varying heretical convictions; two had fevers and the other three were recovering from the effects of interrogation; they were well looked after. However, the lay Brothers who attended the patients imposed a rule of silence, which was hardly broken except by groans, curses or invocations addressed to Jesus and Mary. Half an hour was allowed for recreation in the middle of the day, and the sick men made the most of this, though they kept their voices down. The man in the next bed to Roger was a master mason, aged about thirty, tall and strong; he had, quite literally, gone through fire and water, his arms were burned all over and he said that even so he preferred the red-hot iron, because with the water torture he had believed his entrails would burst: it was the water which had made him talk. His stomach was still slightly swollen from it and he had a nervous hiccup. But he had held out for a long time, he said, and after two months' solitary confinement they had been compelled to feed him with meat and wine before he was in a fit state to bear interrogation. "The whip," he would say, "that's a nasty business, too. I passed out after forty-three strokes. But don't wait for them to try the water on you before you confess."

"I have nothing more to confess."

"Are you by any chance," asked the mason, "a nephew of Bertrand de Montbrun?"

"A nephew? I'm his brother! Have you seen him?"

348

"Before my last interrogation. He's a proud man. They put him back in the dungeon because he wouldn't recant. He was a man of importance in his district, they'll never dare burn him; that's why they can't bring him to trial." Roger was breathing very hard, to stop the sobs bursting out of him. "How is he? . . ."

"*For a man of his age he's standing up to it very well. His mind is hardly affected.*"

"Of his age? He is not forty-five yet!"

The mason shook his head. "*It can't be the same one. This is an old man, bent and white-haired, with no more teeth in his mouth than there are on my hand.*" Roger blinked, wondering if he was still in his right mind.

"But there is no other Bertrand de Montbrun in Toulouse. They must have told you the wrong name."

"I am quite sure of the name, because the gaolers were saying: 'That's Bertrand de Montbrun, you've heard of him. He was the son-in-law of that famous Jew who used to write heretical treatises in Hebrew to corrupt the Jews themselves.' "

Roger wept bitterly. He was conscious of more terror even than sadness, as if these accursed devils had made a sacrilegious alliance with the forces of evil and possessed the power to violate even nature and the course of time. Was this the body which was like an extension of his own, and which once no one would have dared to touch without inflicting an affront on him, Roger. . . . "His back bent, his hair white, his teeth fallen out: could they do that to him? And I was content to make petitions and haunt the chancelleries and the prison gates! I, his elder brother!"

"I wore out the Count's patience with my entreaties."

Bertrand: there was he, Roger, swinging on a trapeze, a trapeze fastened to the branch of an oak tree, he was standing up on it, and flying through the air with his feet pointing skywards and the grass beneath his head. While on the grass a fair child sat watching him, his eyes popping, overflowing with admiration, envy and fear, fear above all. "*Roger, Roger! Not so high! Come down, you'll fall!*" He hid his eyes in his tiny hands, tiny hands that their mother still used to kiss. And Roger swung harder and harder, laughing with all the scorn of the elder brother for the little one's terror. The little one: despite his eight children, his arrogance, his grave airs. Roger saw again, in the eyes of the man clinging to the cloister grille, the same eyes that had belonged to the frightened child of the days when Roger had been a head

349

taller than his brother and could carry him in his arms. . . .
"Don't have anything to do with me. You have always been a traitor."
(That was like him too. Putting a face on it to the end: You see,
I'm still the one who protects you.) How ridiculously bashful he
was, the way he blushed at the lightest word; at fifteen a woman
had only to smile at him to put him in a fury, he believed they
were all after his virtue. How had they done this to him? He
was sound enough physically with the ordered life he led, he was
never drunk—and God knew he was no scapegrace, they didn't
call him a Pharisee for nothing—a man in his prime. . . .

Roger fell asleep and had a dream of ill-omen. He dreamed
that his little son Pierre's tomb was opened and the child was still
alive, but his hair was white and a white beard covered his chin.
Roger came close to screaming with fright; so they did not even
respect children now. What had they done to him? "He was not
yet fourteen, you have no right to burn him. He received extreme
unction. I know, I was there! Look how his body is already humiliated. . . . His mother is not in her right mind, if you burn him she
will go quite mad." But Brother Alberic said: "You will not
deceive me with your tricks; how can a man with white hair not
have reached an age of discretion? Isn't it clear that he died in a
state of heresy? He has been more than a year underground and
he is still alive." Roger wanted to stop the gaolers from taking
away the little white-haired body, but his hands and feet were
tied, and he said: "Curse you, curse you, you respect nothing!"
But his tongue turned to putty and with the effort of shouting he
awoke.

He lay there thinking: the dream could not concern Pierre, his
age was known—twelve—and therefore no one was entitled to
disinter him. Who then? The dream indicated a close relation,
surely it must mean a man connected with him by a similar bond?
It was clear. Hadn't he two heretic sons and a dubious past?
They had waited for him to die before instigating proceedings
against him because they dared not attack old men, especially
those belonging to noble families, during their lifetime. . . . "But
who will defend a dead man when Bertrand and I are in prison,
and my uncle washes his hands of the matter, and the house is
kept by brainless youths who are already notorious heretics?

"Good God, if they do that while his body is still only beginning
to decay, what state will they find him in?" Roger could not tell
himself that this dream might easily mean something quite

350

different, he was restless and anxious, wondering how he could get news of his family. The lay Brothers would not talk, they were good, simple lads, with a tendency to look on the sick men as instruments of the Devil—but their rough compassion was quite genuine. From time to time the doctor came to see him and he was willing to talk. "Brother, do you know how hard it is to live like this, without even knowing if my friends and relatives are still alive? But for that poor fellow who perished through my fault, I should not even have known that my father was dead. He was a bad man, yet he showed me more pity than you."

"Friend, I am only obeying the orders I have been given. Believe me, my life is harder than yours: if the Father Superior pleases to leave me all my life in ignorance of the deaths of all my kin, then I shall never know. Even in prison, you speak and think like a free man, able to dispose of his own person as he likes. But as for me, even my thoughts are no longer my own. And I rejoice because I have made this sacrifice to God of my own free will, but do not imagine that the human nature in me is not mortified much more than it is in you."

"Nevertheless, Brother, consider that I am a layman, and it is a condition of my state that I should be anxious and grieved for my kinsfolk. I have not been allowed to communicate with anyone for five months. The greatest criminals are not so harshly treated."

"Many are treated more harshly. Think of the people who die of hunger in the streets, and the lepers, and the maimed and those in the galleys, and prisoners sold as slaves by the infidels, are they not more to be pitied? Does anyone think of taking them news? Does one single man in the whole world talk to them as I am talking to you? Yet there are thousands of them, and tens of thousands. Are you not infinitely less deserving of pity than they are?"

"Brother, to every man his own troubles. And even if mine are not great, can I sleep in peace when I think that my old father's ashes are in danger of being violated, and my children and my nephews are perhaps thrown out into the street?"

"Do you, then, doubt your father's honour? Wasn't he a good Catholic?"

"By the Virgin he was! But so was I, and hasn't slander fallen on me? When one hears no news one imagines the worst. My brother has been in prison for a year and a half, and I know nothing

351

of him. Could I not, for charity's sake, be allowed to see him?"

"My friend, I am going beyond my authority in speaking to you of this, but you must know that, for your own safety, you would be better never to see that unhappy man again, for it is now well established that the enemy has taken possession of his soul."

"Have you seen him then, Brother? Only tell me whether you really believe him to be mad?"

"No. Men possessed by the Devil are immune to human madness."

"Brother, I cannot bear to hear such words! I am listening to you because I am compelled to, but I would as lief you spoke to me no more."

The doctor did not speak to him any more. Later, Roger was to regret this moment's anger; the man was talkative and with a little skill it was possible to make him tell at least part of what he knew. What could they have done to Bertrand to make him seem like a man possessed? That he had endured a year and a half in a cell and not become a raving madman, that was their miracle of the Devil. So he would not recant—surprising indeed! Perhaps they expected him to thank them?

After three weeks in hospital Roger's bandages were removed and he was washed, shaved and even dressed in a clean shirt (nothing remained of his own but rags); his tunic had been washed and mended by hands that were clumsy, to be sure— man's hands—but zealous. He looked at himself for the first time for five months, in a bucket of water, and felt inclined to laugh: he was not so bad looking, despite his wasted cheeks and the lines beneath his eyes, but quite unlike himself. This was chiefly on account of his hair, which was cropped short and shaved round the big, black scar in the centre of his scalp. The absence of his head's chief ornament made his features appear heavier, and severe for all the still deceptively gentle expression in his eyes. "A monk," he thought. "It looks exactly as if they have turned me into a monk! They have their own ways of teaching a man poverty and chastity."

The judgment which he had once feared now seemed to him like a release. He thought: "I behaved like a fool. With men like this the only honourable course is to be rid of them as quickly as possible."

But that is what one says when alone. When one is seated facing the three lenten countenances, and the crucifix directly over the judge's chair, and must speak and answer, as a man to men, it is not pleasant to allow oneself to be taken for an idiot.

Brother Peter did not so much as raise his eyes; his white face was wrinkled and corpse-like. The Brothers Alberic and Guillaume took it in turn to speak. "You admit having been a believer in the heretic faith?"

"I admit it."

"At what period of your life?"

"At the time when I was excommunicated. And later, also."

"Who encouraged you to give your heart to such a damnable error?"

"My brother."

"Yet you said you were not on good terms with your brother?"

"I was lying. I have always been fond of my brother."

"Were you never influenced by other persons?"

"Yes. By Bérenger d'Aspremont and his friends."

"Who were the heretics with whom you discussed matters of faith?"

"Guiraud de Montauban and his companion."

"Did you visit the fortress of Montségur in order to pay homage to the heretics?"

"Yes."

"So you admit that you were still a believer in the heretic faith as late as last year?"

"I admit it."

"Were you at the time when you were summoned to appear before this tribunal?"

"I was."

"Yet you maintained, stubbornly and at great length, that you had always been a Catholic?"

"I was lying, for fear of the penalty."

"How can we tell that you are not lying at this very moment, in claiming to repent of your errors?"

"I am bearing witness against myself, isn't that a sign of repentance?"

"How can we tell whether you are not inspired by the hope of being dealt with leniently, or by fear of the fire?"

"Why do you threaten to send people to the stake, unless you

353

hope to make them repent? Fear forced me to meditate and I saw the truth."

"So, it is in the fear of death that you claim to have repented?"

"No."

"What are the reasons which led you to realise the falsity of the heretic faith?"

"I realised that the Catholic faith was the only true one."

"That is not a good answer."

"I turned to the cross of Christ Jesus and I remembered the faith of my youth. And I longed for the sacraments."

"What then were the reasons which formerly made you turn away from the faith of your youth?"

"The war. And the severity of the late Pope Innocent and the excommunication of many good Catholics, beginning with the Count."

"It appears, then, that you are now accusing the Church?"

"No. I am telling you what I thought then."

"Nevertheless, you did not renounce your errors when the sentence of excommunication was lifted. Why not?"

"From habit."

"Good. Now describe to us the manner in which you practised this false religion, what were your prayers, your personal devotions, and your intimate thoughts?"

Roger thought: "I am like a dog to be teased on purpose until it bites, and then pronounced mad. It can't be possible that they desire my death. They will never make an end of their questions until I have lost my temper." In his desperate state he really believed that they wished to bring him to the stake and not to reconciliation. The cruel humiliation he had imposed on himself confused his mind to such an extent that he no longer knew whether he was lying or telling the truth. Ah! Better to be an idiot, an illiterate unable to put three words together!

"My very reverend lords," he said, "why are you trying to force me to remember things I would rather forget? You are imperilling my soul!"

Brother Alberic turned to Brother Peter and said in an undertone: "Must we go on?" The old man looked up slowly and stared at the accused. Roger met his eyes for a second and flushed. In the shrewd eyes of the Inquisitor he read a boundless contempt.

"Let the accused," said Brother Peter, "prove his sincerity to us by revealing all the secrets he knows about heretic believers

354

with whom he has come into contact. God is the sole judge of his soul, and we should be wasting our time in demanding sincerity of heart from a man who has proved to us only too well that he is an accomplished liar."

Roger swallowed the insult without flinching, telling himself, "Let them call me all the names they like so long as they make an end of this!" His whole body ached and he was shivering with fever. *"Could I know that lying, too, was a torture? A lie extracted by force, not by my own will?"* He named many people from among those he already knew to have been compromised long before, all notorious believers. His judges certainly knew much more about these people than he did. There would merely be fifty-nine witnesses against that particular suspect, instead of fifty-eight. . . . "Who denounced *me*?" he wondered. "People, perhaps, who had not spent five months in prison." Yet it was like a bad dream, because sometimes, remembering the names and faces of people he had seen at sermons, he would think: "What am I doing? Perhaps my judges have never heard that name? *I* know he is a heretic, and the whole town knows it, but they may not?"

In the face of his visible reluctance to give evidence, Brother Alberic suggested that his sincerity appeared suspect: he seemed more like a man attempting to impede the workings of the court. Roger said quietly: "I am telling what I know. I should be damning my soul if I named people I have never suspected."

"Have you never suspected so-and-so? And so-and-so? The Cissacs? They were your close friends."

"I have never suspected them!"

"Yet Raymond-Jourdain's wife, Arsen de Miradoux, herself came and confessed to having attended heretic sermons."

"I did not know that."

"It is strange that you should be so ill-informed precisely about your close friends."

"Are you chiding me now for having Catholic friends?"

"No. But you lead us to believe that you are naming all these persons in the hope of earning our clemency rather than by a sincere desire to work for the good of the Church."

"That is my desire," said Roger, at the end of his strength. "I am telling you what I know. I have told you everything."

". . . Have you yourself not testified against your wife, Guillelme de Layrac, saying that she had been a heretic believer from childhood?"

355

"So far as I can see, she came to confess that herself. I know nothing else about her. She is no longer a believer. I was speaking in anger."

"How can we know whether you are not accusing certain persons 'in anger', or if you are not protecting others out of friendship?"

"You will learn nothing more from me," said Roger—he was feeling so weak that everything seemed to be dissolving before his eyes, and he was forced to rest his forehead on both hands to prevent his head falling forward on to his knees. "I have already said much more than I should have done."

It was a fine, mild spring day; the sun was filtering through the grey and white, diamond-shaped panes of the small windows in long, transparent shafts of light in which shone motes of delicate pink and green dust. The windows looked on to a cloister, a clean, light newly-built cloister where white-clad novices were walking with bent heads and rosaries in their hands. As he looked at the window Roger thought of that cloister: "They have sunshine. They have small plants they cultivate in baskets full of earth. They have a well with a gleaming brand new bucket.... O Lord, what prison will they put me in now?" He wondered if he had spoken aloud or whether Brother Peter had read his thoughts, because he heard him saying: "Roger de Montbrun, the tribunal of the Holy Office of the Inquisition, whose agent I am, is prepared to regard your conversion as sincere. But if, taking into account the gravity of your faults, the Church imposes on you, as a penance, perpetual incarceration in a dungeon with no light, beneath the prison moat, will you accept this penance with respectful submission, and will you persist, even at this price, in your desire to be reconciled to the Church?"

Roger could not tell whether this was a trap or a real threat. What? *That* or the fire? What man with any sense would not prefer a swift, though cruel death? He glanced round him like an animal at bay. "You would not have the right," he said.

"God alone is your judge," said Brother Peter slowly. "Never let it be said that conversion is a bargain. Will you submit yourself, unconditionally and without protest, to the decisions of the Church?"

Roger had risen to his feet and was regarding the man sitting opposite him from his full height, making a desperate effort to keep a clear head. *"Don't be afraid, this is a game. He wants to test you, don't flinch, only cowards let go a chance of escape."*

356

"I surrender myself unconditionally to the Church," he said. "I am ready to undergo joyfully whatever penance may be imposed on me."

"Very well," said Brother Peter. "You will sign your deposition and your formal recantation. You will be informed of the sentence later."

The sentence of the tribunal of the Holy Office declared Roger de Montbrun, knight, believer, guilty of aiding, sheltering and protecting heretics, wholly and sincerely penitent for his past errors, forgiven and reconciled to the Church and received again into the communion of the faithful. As a penance for his past faults and as a precaution against his relapse into error, the Church sentenced the said Roger to incarceration in the prisons of the Church until the end of his life; the cost of supporting him to be raised from the property of which the said Roger was formerly possessed in Toulouse and in the region of Toulouse. All these goods were legally forfeit to the Church. Nevertheless, taking into consideration that the said Roger de Montbrun possessed nothing in his own right, having been disinherited by his father in favour of his young children, the expenses of the prisoner's upkeep should fall on his lawful wife, Guillelme de Layrac, legal guardian of the said minors, Raymond-Guillaume and Bernard; and on the same Raymond-Guillaume and Bernard, when they attained their majority and entered into the enjoyment of their estates.

The said Roger de Montbrun, knight, was further sentenced to do penance in the Cathedral of St. Stephen, on Ascension Day, there to make public confession of his faults, and to receive correction by the rod at the hands of the Lord Bishop's deputy as a sign that he submitted of his will to the Church. He was to repeat his formal recantation publicly and renew his oath of allegiance to the Catholic Church. After which the Church would consider him definitively absolved, but if the accused were ever in future to fall back into his errors the Church would consider him relapsed and unworthy of forgiveness and would abandon him and surrender his person to the secular arm.

Roger was taken back to the hospital; and three days later found himself once again in the cell which he had left four weeks earlier, on the night of Good Friday, in the company of Raimbert Maillan. His new gaoler, a massive devil, as black as a Moor,

357

might as well have been deaf and dumb. Still barely recovered from his fever, Roger asked nothing more than to be left in peace. He thought: "After that shame there is nothing for me but death."

What had he lost that was so precious, what had he left to lose, that day? He had sold his soul in the hope of escaping more lightly, in order to save himself from this hell of ignorance and loneliness—but now he no longer even thought of the sacraments which he had so ardently desired on the day after his attempt to escape. "And when I have gone through this shame they have imposed on me, on top of everything else, a shame I am not sure I can bear—for they have robbed me of half my strength already—when I have knelt barefoot in my breeches in the cathedral before the whole assembled chivalry of Toulouse, and been scourged and heard myself proclaimed a heretic when everyone knows I have never been one, who then will ensure me an easy prison from which my friends can help me escape? Because I corrupted a keeper and tried to escape I shall be watched more closely than the rest."

While Roger was indulging in these desperate and depressing thoughts, the gaoler came and announced that he had a visitor, whereupon he told himself, "Perhaps I didn't do so badly after all." True, the visitor was none other than Guillelme. She came into the cell, as stiff and haughty as ever, dressed in a severe, grey cloak with her head swathed in mourning veils. When she lifted the veil, Roger saw that her face was drawn and marred by spots of red, while her eyes seemed made of glass. She was frightened. Too frightened even to look at him. "Oh, God!" thought Roger, "is she still thinking of that? It is clear that she has not spent her time in prison—for myself, I had almost forgotten the piece of foolishness she committed." Yet he felt the remnants of his former anger still clouding his mind—oh, the stupidity of the woman, lacking either honour or understanding!

He remained standing in the middle of the cell, his arms folded and his back to the woman. "Speak," he said at last. "You must have come to tell me something?"

She began to explain that she was the only person allowed to see him, that his friends had been anxious about him since Christmas, but had been able to learn nothing; that judgment had finally been pronounced and she had been allowed, as a favour. . . She added that her father-in-law, God rest his soul, had died the

Sunday before Easter, and that she was having some difficulties about the inheritance, but that, thank God, she had made the Bishop's court acknowledge the validity of the will, because her father-in-law had died decently in the presence of two priests.

"Ah! God be praised," exclaimed Roger, "I feared the worst. What else? Our sons are well?"

"Yes, thank God."

"What about Guillaume and Jean-Bernard? At least they haven't been molested?"

"Oh, don't mention them to me!" Guillelme said irritably. She explained how they had left Toulouse three weeks after Christmas, with Hersen and Azémar, after forcing her with a knife at her throat to pledge the oakwood and the large vineyard at Layrac. "The authorities tried to hold me responsible. I told everything. How they threatened me and took the property and everything. Your father had to get out of bed and go to the Preaching Friars himself to stand surety for me. Their case was tried after the first Sunday in Lent and they were all four condemned *in absentia*."

"The fools!" said Roger. "Why couldn't they have waited at least until father was dead? After all, Guillelme, at their age one wants to live." All the same he was saddened. He thought of the old knight's grief, all the trouble and fear these imbeciles had caused him, of the old man's loneliness once he was deprived of his favourite grandsons, and left at the mercy of a woman like Guillelme. "At least you have been good to him?" She shrugged. "I did what I could. He never loved me. He only swore by Rachel. I tried to get permission for her to come to him when he was dying . . . they told me, 'If he were even her own father'." She added that perhaps it was for the best. "You know she has changed a great deal, Rachel."

"Changed?" repeated Roger, with a stern smile. "And what about me, and you? I wonder if anyone has not changed. If you knew all I have been through, Guillelme! The fact that I am glad to see you says enough."

"Yes," said Guillelme, without looking at him. "You have changed. No one else would have recognised you."

"Tell me then, what about the little nephew you were expecting to present me with at Lent?" She met his sardonic, almost conspiratorial gaze without flinching. "It's a little girl. I have called her Guillelme. She is very well."

359

Roger turned away and spat on the ground more in sadness than scorn. "If you are in trouble again you can always say I lay with you today. They have to admit wives into the prisons to give legitimate fathers to all the little bastards with which the new laws are populating Toulouse. Guillelme, was it because I reviled you that you did this thing?"

"What thing?" She drew herself up as if he were about to strike her.

"You know perfectly well."

"No," she said. "It was not because you reviled me."

"All the same," he said, "don't you think there are cleaner ways of revenging yourself on someone?"

"For me, there was not."

"Guillelme, but for you I might perhaps have been released with a canonical penance. Because of your stupid chatter, there is now no way I can extricate myself. Yet you are not a fool, you must have known that it was serious."

"Perhaps I am a fool."

"Very well," he said, "let's leave it at that. After all, perhaps anyone else would have done the same in your position. What do they say about my case in Toulouse? My friends must have spoken of it to you? Raymond-Jourdain, and Gaillard de Miradoux, and the Roquevidals? At least they have not been molested?"

"Do you really believe anyone else would have done the same in my position?"

"Good God! Think no more of it! Am I putting you on trial? My case, if I ever bring it, will not be against you, or pleaded in words."

She said again, her voice more cracked than ever: "Why do you say that anyone else would have done the same in my position?"

"I don't know," he said wearily. "Listen, sit down on the stool, there are bugs in the bed. We must talk. I do not blame you. I did wrong. It is not decent to ask forgiveness when one is no longer in a position to mend anything. If I behaved badly, God has punished me. But there are our sons and the house. When the Count has suppressed the new laws my case will be reconsidered; you have nothing to gain by treating me as an enemy. Tell me what advice my friends gave you for me."

"I have nothing to gain from anything any more. Layrac and your father's house belong to my sons."

"Listen, even if I escape, Layrac is ours; they will not come to look for us there. Jean-Rigaud isn't in prison?"

"He was let off with three years in the Holy Land, and they gave him a respite because he was ill. He is asking me for money to equip himself, but as your fine nephews have taken everything, I told him to wait until harvest time. You don't imagine I am going to Layrac to be sentenced in my absence, when we can't afford to pay twenty soldiers?"

"You see, if I had been there—— You have never understood that, Guillelme. It is your own domain you are ruining by injuring me."

"Curses on my domain! It was the reason they abandoned me to you. I was not worse than other women. You made a sport of my youth, you seduced me and deserted me like some backstairs harlot. May I be called a coward if I ever do you a service; even if I had letters or news from your friends, I should not tell you!"

"So it's true," said Roger, his eyes lighting up; "you have got letters——?"

She said "No" but at the same time her hand went to her breast and he guessed the letter was hidden there. "Stop this foolishness," he said, "and give it to me at once." She stood up and he moved to place himself between her and the door. "Don't call out," he said. "My chains won't stop me."

"I shall say you tried to kill me."

"Believe me, I'd like to!"

He forced her back against the wall, crushing her with all his weight, and began to undo the neck of her shift, above the stiff, braided edge of her gown—she said nothing, but pressed her lips together and kept her glassy eyes fixed on him. Suddenly Roger ceased to be sure whether what he was seeking was the roll of paper or the smooth, round breast, softer to the touch than the dove's body, and desire was stronger in him than shame or anger, so that he was on the point of begging the woman to grant him a taste of the pleasure that had been so long denied him.

Then contempt for her and for himself mastered him and he took the letter and tucked it into his sleeve, saying: "You can go." Her voice broke suddenly and she said in a hoarse whisper: *"Roger, when I have loved you so——"*

"So you have shown me. There are still plenty of young pages in the house. My father is no longer there, nor is Bertrand or myself: you can do what you please." She looked at him, her eyes heavy with anger, like an animal at bay. She said softly: "I shall tell the gaoler about the letter. He'll take it away from you."

"Never let me see you here again." He rapped on the door and the gaoler came to open it and let out the visitor.

Left alone, Roger flung himself on the bed, bitterly sorry he had not taken advantage of the situation; that was all the crazy woman had wanted. He did not even hate her any more, he did not even despise her—he felt despicable enough himself, worthy of such a mate, and worse than her—she at least had some excuse. Ah, her body had not been violated by the Crusaders, but her heart had, ten times over! He should have thought of that before he married her.

"And to think what I should have gained from it: news, help to escape, and pleasure into the bargain. So young," he thought, "her breasts are still so young—while I have plenty of grey hairs already, and a ten days' beard."

He waited, on tenterhooks, wondering whether the gaoler would come and demand the letter. . . . God be praised, she had been merciful, she was not as bad as she said. He drew the crumpled roll of paper from his sleeve and unfolded it: his hands were shaking badly, making his chains rattle. The letter was from Raymond-Jourdain. Not a conspicuously warm letter, but it contained much reference to a 'person you know of' who was at present across the Rhône, but who was much concerned about Roger's fate. *"Be patient,"* wrote Raymond-Jourdain, *"now that you are, as we hear, reconciled to the Church we have good hope that your troubles will soon be at an end. All of us, and our mutual friend also, are unsparing in our prayers to God, and in gifts to churches and to the poor, that your soul will be out of danger and God will forgive you your sins at last. You can count on us. We are arranging to have a solemn Mass said for you, on the Feast of the Assumption of the Blessed Virgin Mary, from which you should receive much comfort.* . . . The whole letter was couched in similar terms. "At last," Roger thought, "at last! What I have had to endure to receive this message at last! Since the Count is taking the matter in hand it will be the devil if they can't help me escape. Even if it is not until Assumption Day—three months to wait, but at least I can count the days.

"There are some words which, once the lips have uttered them, corrupt the soul—I endured torture and the dungeon in order not

362

to say those words; on the night of Good Friday I fought, un-armed, on the wall, against two soldiers, one five-inch knife against two halberds, and, Lord God, I had the strength and the fury that night to hurl them both over the edge . . . if only that imbecile had not kept the cudgel for himself! He didn't even use it.

"One lie more or less? Brothers, this lie is not one of those one can utter with a light heart. I swear to you that until this day I never knew how much I cleaved to my faith. *Surely I must cleave to it.* And I sold it for a wretched mess of pottage, sold it, yes, since I stripped it away from fifteen years of my past life, a life in which I committed every sin except the one I have confessed to."

Now hunger gnawed at him all day long, although the soup was thick and greasy, the piece of bread three hands' breadth across, and sometimes sprinkled with salt. But not dysentery, fever or his cough could prevent him suffering more from hunger than from all his other miseries. For want of anything better, he tried to appease this insatiable hunger of his body by chewing on a piece of tough fat, but it went on growing until it seemed to him as if the blood was fermenting in his veins and his nerves were being stretched as though with pincers. He knew the cause of this malady: it came from anticipating the day, already close at hand, when he would change his prison, and the fear of seeing that day put off. There was fear of the day itself, too, because he did not know, weakened by sickness and the terror of solitude, how he would stand up to the hours in the open air, in the crowded cathedral square, waiting for the cruel humiliation which he must endure without flinching. "How many of us will be reconciled to the Church? Lord, that I should have come to long for Raimbert, who at least deigned to speak to me; that I should have come to long for my dungeon where I endured such a stupid martyrdom, thinking: Rather die than give in! That dungeon where time went so slowly that I almost grew ac-customed to the life. Rigueur. Who is now there in the dark, feeling Rigueur's name on the flagstone with the tips of blind fingers? Carved twice in its entirety and half of a third time—*Rigueur, Rigueur, Rig*—— Who knows? Perhaps if they had given me time to finish I should not have been caught in this infernal circle? I have left my beloved in the dungeon; she will bring luck to the man who has taken my place."

The great Act of Faith took place on Ascension Day in the cathedral of St. Stephen in Toulouse. The bells were ringing and all the interior of the cathedral was decked with banners and hangings of gold and silver, while red and white wax candles were burning all the way from the great door to the high altar and in the side chapels; such a rich harvest of flames was never before seen, and a thousand oxen might have been purchased for the cost of so much wax. Stands had been erected round the cathedral square on the day before, and people had been crowding into them since before dawn; soldiers armed with halberds were keeping order and thrusting back the beggars who tried to collect along the carpeted avenue which had been kept clear for the Countess and the barons. Those convicted of heresy stood on the left of the square, in front of the stands, surrounded by a hedge of men-at-arms and divided from the burghers by a rope stretched between two posts.

They had been brought there, under heavy escort, before daybreak, for fear of a riot. There were thirty-five of them that day: six heretics and twenty-nine who had recanted and were to be reconciled to the Church, besides two hundred free persons subjected to canonical penances which were to be formally imposed on them. (Rather than expose themselves unnecessarily to the stares of the crowd, these people, who were to be called first, arrived in small groups, a little before first Mass, and came and took up their position in front of the row of soldiers. In their penitential garb, consisting of grey robes, sackcloth or long white shifts, they looked like people who had mistaken Ascension Day for Good Friday.) As for the thirty-five prisoners, already dying of exhaustion even before the ceremony had begun, they took turns to kneel or sit on the ground as discreetly as they could, and talked little; as soon as they raised their voices the soldiers menaced them with their halberds, though the noise of the bells and the incessant, rising murmur of the crowd in the square would have drowned the voice of the Archangel Michael himself, and the prisoners had no thoughts of shouting for help: they had not let themselves be brought there simply to risk the whip and the dungeon. Only the six heretics had nothing more to lose and they had nothing to gain either. Standing apart from the rest, dressed in long frieze shifts, and already prepared, their heads shaved and crowned with mitres made of paper on which their crimes were written in scarlet letters, they waited for their death agony with the patience of well-bred people compelled to remain standing on a boat for lack of room. They seemed at the end of their strength, but were smiling and talking together in low voices, with an air of detachment that made the soldiers say: "Look at them: quite happy because they are going to sup with the Devil." (The guards felt this calm courtesy like a personal affront: what is a soldier whose prisoner is not afraid of him?) These two men and four women (it was almost impossible to guess their sex, all six had the same faces: bare, white, terribly emaciated and rather stern) had been captured quite recently and were still unmarked by imprisonment. They seemed rather happy to be together than horrified by what was in store for them. Occasionally they threw curious and compassionate glances at the other prisoners, possibly looking for any among them who had formerly been believers. The others did their best not to look at them.

These others—the twenty-nine—were for the most part true believers; only seven or eight were Catholics accused in error because they had been friends or relatives of notorious believers. But all of them, whether their apostasy was real or false, felt themselves as contemptible in the eyes of the heretics as of the Catholics: not that the fact of recantation was contemptible in itself, since all men cling to their lives—but it is hard not to feel an object of contempt when one sees oneself as it were exposed on the pillory before the eyes of the whole city.

The processions wound slowly on while the chanting of the choirs was taken up by the crowd. The Bishop, wearing his mitre and purple cloak, crusted with gold embroidery, and surrounded by the clerks of his chapter, blessed the people and entered the cathedral through the doors flung wide to receive him. Next the Friars of St. Dominic advanced, their Prior at their head, stiff and stern in their long white robes, black cloaks flowing in ample pleats down their backs—then came the monks, priests and nuns, followed by the consuls and city magistrates in their red cloaks, knights and ladies dressed for a holiday, young girls in light silk dresses, and burghers in good cloth gowns trimmed with fur—and there was no man, however sad, but rejoiced in his heart at the sight of the cathedral resplendent with candles, and gold and bright colours. The Bishop sat enthroned on his gilded chair on the right of the high altar.

Two of the Bishop's clerks stood before an altar draped in black and silver on the cathedral steps and read out the sentences and the names of persons convicted of heresy: many citizens of Toulouse received gracious forgiveness at the hands of their bishop on that glorious day. As their names were called, the penitents mounted the steps and kneeled to hear their sentences proclaimed and receive absolution, so that they could enter the church. Since there were more than two hundred of them, they were received at the door by three Preaching Friars and three Brothers of the Order of St. Francis who read out the penances assigned to them—fines or pilgrimages—after which the reconciled sinners entered the church in groups of fifteen or twenty (some on their knees), men on the right and women on the left, and went to their places in the far sides of the nave. This ceremony lasted a good hour.

When it came to the twenty-nine repentant believers, Brother Alberic of Montpellier, as Deputy Inquisitor, read aloud the sentence of the tribunal of the Holy Office, declaring the said believers, guilty of abetting, sheltering and acting as agents of the heretics, in consideration of their sincere and complete repentance admitted once more into the bosom of the Church. In expiation of their past faults and to avoid the danger of a relapse into error, the Church commanded them to do lifelong penance, and forbade them to leave their prisons upon pain of excommunication and delivery to the secular arm. Then the twenty-nine prisoners were led by the soldiers to the foot of the church steps, where they knelt, waiting for their names to be called.

There were several noble ladies among them, two knights, three noble-born squires, and two wealthy burghers, while the remainder were townsfolk from outlying districts. Nearly all of them were so weakened by months of imprisonment that they could barely stand upright, and when they kneeled were continually falling backwards or forwards: they were all fasting, since they were to take communion later in the day.

Slowly, with two guards holding their hands, the prisoners advanced towards the monk who was reading, then to the clerk who held the rods in his right hand, and removed their clothes, which were unfastened above the waist in readiness. Roger de

366

Montbrun was the first to be called, and this honour was also something of a disadvantage since it was he who received the main volley of blows, administered by a firm, zealous hand: after that the others, and the women especially, were scourged merely for form's sake and without enthusiasm. Those among the people crowded into the square who knew Roger de Montbrun said to themselves: "Either the Brothers have made a mistake or he must have sent someone else to be scourged in his place," because the man who bore this name, with his grizzled closely shaven head, gaunt, putty-coloured face and cracked lips, bore only a vague resemblance to Roger de Montbrun; but when the other reconciled believers, several of whom were people very well known in the city, had been called, they saw that there was no mistake: all their faces were the same, at once livid and congested, with the same troubled gaze and hang-dog look. They tried in vain to hold themselves straight and maintain their pride because a man brought out of prison is like a man wounded or drunk. All of them were thinking of one thing only: to be taken back to their cells or anywhere else as quickly as possible. But they were led into the church.

There many of them might perhaps have experienced feelings of joy at the sight of the thousands of lighted candles, the gold and purple, the brilliantly painted vaults and arches, at the cheerful singing that rose from the nave and galleries—since even the believers had been Catholic in their youth. But now even this beauty was hateful to them, not because of the humiliation they had endured, but by reason of their extreme physical exhaustion. The women were weeping, lying prostrate on the ground, at the foot of the first pillar; the men, still guarded by the soldiers, were adjusting their garments and tightening their lips to stop their teeth from chattering.

Outside, the judgment of God was still going on: the six obdurate heretics were solemnly excommunicated, cut off from the communion of the faithful and delivered over to the secular arm: from the hands of the ecclesiastical guards they passed into those of the provost, who when the service was over was to conduct the condemned persons to the Pré-du-Comte, where the pyre with its six stakes had been waiting for them since dawn.

After Mass, the excommunicated persons were led to the place where they were to suffer death. They held candles in their hands, and were escorted by two files of soldiers, while a herald and two

Preaching Friars, followed by clerks and cantors, went before them. Behind walked the twenty-nine who had received absolution, led by their guards, then the two hundred penitents, and all along the streets the procession was joined by common people, some inspired by fear, some by curiosity (in the end some morbid souls developed a taste for watching folks burned, and still others were looking for miracles). Meanwhile, Brother Alberic and two monks of his Order went to the cemetery with twenty soldiers to see that the sentences pronounced against the dead were implemented, because nine corpses were to follow the living on the same pyre, and the faggots intended to revive the flames were already piled up ten yards from the stakes.

One after another the six heretics climbed the narrow ladder placed before the heap of faggots, and the executioner chained them to the stakes. Then, from the foot of the ladder, the monk who was acting for the absent Inquisitor raised his cross and, calling each of the condemned persons by his name, asked them whether they would not earn their salvation by a sincere conversion. Twice he exhorted them, and they said nothing, but began to sing one of their hymns. Then the monk moved away and said to the provost: *"Do your duty."* The provost made a sign to the executioner's assistants, who moved forward with long lighted torches and set fire to the large bundles of straw arranged at the four corners of the pyre. The fire crackled slowly, then the straw flared up and it spread quickly to the smaller twigs in the faggots. In the noontide heat, the dry wood cracked and groaned as it caught fire, and the six doomed people saw a wall of flames suddenly envelop their legs up to the knee, first licking and then devouring their frieze shifts—and they sang on, very loudly, louder and louder; then the singing turned to screaming. The women were screaming: "Jesus! Jesus! Jesus!" in heartrending voices as though they were crying for help.

What followed was dreadful to see and hear, because their garments burned fast and the fire devoured the bodies slowly, gnawing at the scorched flesh, and sputtering in the blood; while the inhuman voices howled, and wailed and croaked, rising above the chanting of the monks and the roll of drums.

The penitents and the absolved prisoners were standing in the front row of the spectators, immediately behind the hedge of soldiers, and though they could close their eyes to avoid seeing, they were still forced to listen to the screams and feel the heat of the fire; and they saw much besides, blinking because of the increasingly acrid smoke and the brightness of the flames which hurt their eyes. They saw the bloody, contorted bodies, writhing like snakes on poles—the raw heads, the faces blistered and bursting, and still screaming. It was ugly, never had human faces been so ugly; glimpsed momentarily through the flickering, transparent curtain of flames and blackish smoke, they were nothing but howling and pain without end.

The procession of the dead was approaching the pyre with Brother Alberic at its head, followed by cantors and criers, and the ranks of the crowd parted and pressed back against the walls and barriers, the women screaming with terror. The corpses were piled, two by two, on to hurdles, and men, harnessed like oxen, were dragging the strange chariots. Hair hung down from lolling heads with the flesh half rotted from their skulls, and from the torn or disintegrating shrouds, marked with brown stains, an arm or a foot emerged at random, putrefying, black with flies, or already decomposed, with earth clinging to the yellowed, fleshless bone; and for a while it seemed as though the charnel smell would overcome the stench of burnt flesh. Even the soldiers drew back hastily, jostling the prisoners, to escape the pestilential odour that spread through the place. People in the crowd were screaming: "Run for your lives! Hell has come upon us!"

But, as someone had to make an end of the corpses and the soldiers were still hanging back, Brother Alberic himself, breathing hard, his white robe all smudged with dirt, seized the first pitchfork, crying out: "*With God's help!*" and the soldiers followed his example. One after another the nine corpses were hoisted up like bales of hay on the prongs of the forks and tossed into the fire among the fresh faggots and lumps of pitch and resin.

This made the fire burn up so fiercely that the soldiers who were standing twenty yards from the blaze could feel their helmets burning their cheeks, and the provost gave orders for the place to be evacuated. The heat, the smoke, and screaming and stench in the meadow were now more than any living creature could bear: it was as though the sun had fallen out of the sky and turned into one vast, fiery spider. All eyes were filled with smoke, every throat was parched and people were crying out: "Are we all going to choke to death?" Everyone was running: children and old men fell and were trampled underfoot. A woman ran towards the pyre shrieking: "Me too! Burn me too!"

369

The prisoners were taken away hurriedly, but it was necessary to tie their hands to prevent them escaping, since three of the men had attempted to take advantage of the uproar and the panic among their guards to mingle with a group of free penitents (these three were Roger de Montbrun, Bernard Ribeyre and Imbert de Caussade); however, the people behind whom they tried to hide were afraid of being charged with abetting them and gave them up. Only twenty-seven prisoners in all were taken to the Dominican priory, where they were to spend the remainder of the day, because two women, both very old and ill, had died at the Pré-du-Comte, whether from exhaustion or terror was not known; however, as they had just received absolution and Holy Communion their case was submitted to the Bishop, who decreed that they were to be buried in consecrated ground.

Great feast days rarely passed without fatal accidents caused either by people being crushed in the crowds or through fights, sunstroke or exhaustion, but in the last two years these accidents had become so numerous as a result of the disorders occasioned by public executions that the consuls repeatedly petitioned the Count and the Bishop, insisting that such dangerous and likewise unedifying spectacles should be forbidden. There were growing murmurs against these Acts of Faith among the people, who were saying that they brought bad luck on the city, and also that the Preaching Friars were exhuming the bodies of good Catholics who had died decently, in the presence of priests, from motives of spite and on insufficient evidence. Moreover, once the body was burned and the ashes mingled with lime and cast into the public sewers, it was no good revising the case: they could never put the dead person back into Christian earth.

At last the twenty-seven who were condemned to perpetual penance were allowed a few hours' rest. Because of the two women who had died, the three men who had tried to escape were not treated too severely: they said that they had been overcome by the smoke and flames and had thought of nothing beyond getting away from the pyre, but they had not meant to escape. A meal was served to the repentant sinners in the refectory generally reserved for the poor, but they had little strength to eat, though the meal included plenty of meat and spices. They drank the wine which the lay Brothers brought them with gentleness and humility, bowing to them as before honoured guests.

They had been placed at the bottom end of the refectory, the men at one table and the women at another, separated by a rope from the other diners, paupers and beggars from the locality, who looked at them with a mingled pity and terror because the prisoners' eyes were still red and their faces flushed from standing too close to the fire and their voices were hoarse with coughing. "Ah, what a day this has been my friends! What a day! What cruel mercifulness! Surely we have expiated many sins today."

Brother Alberic was truly a man inspired by a more than human zeal, for after all the fatigues of the cathedral and the cemetery and the pyre, he still held himself upright and spoke with a loud voice, while his face, with its swollen eyelids and burning cheeks, was reminiscent of a captain on the evening after a victorious battle. "Brothers," he said to the repentant heretics, gathered outside the porch of the new priory church, "brothers, I bless God for the grace He has shown you this day. Jesus Christ is my witness that there is no man in this city who should not envy you, for there is more joy in heaven over one sinner that repenteth than for ten just persons which need no repentance. You are here, clad in nuptial garments, guests at the feast, forgiven and redeemed; and let the memory of this day's salvation be engraved for ever in your hearts! For verily the joy of God and the peace of God passeth all understanding: today, before our very eyes, have they not taken on the appearance of terror and destruction? Your flesh has quivered under the rod, your heart has quaked with terror before the fire, and by this fire which consumed God's enemies you have been as though baptised anew. For by the horror of the punishment you have been shown the ugliness of the crime, verily, God's mercy is infinite, which has this day permitted us to triumph over the forces of Evil. Brothers, the flesh you have seen burning was guilty of no earthly crime, but belonged to damned creatures, the visible incarnations of Satan; our land was sullied by their crimes, and this day justice has been done by fire before God and before men! The fire has consumed and purified, it has destroyed and regenerated, destroyed the infidel and regenerated the faithful, annihilated pride and exalted faith, borne witness to the Truth and broken the chains of Hell!

"Your limbs have been seized by trembling and your bowels have quivered with anguish, with your fleshly eyes you have beheld a living flame, lighted by men but consecrated to God! For these false shepherds who have led you into error have been

371

destroyed like Sodom and Gomorrah, swallowed up in the fiery furnace like Korah, Dathan and Abiram, devoured by the fire called down from heaven by Elijah on the prophets of Baal, and the pestilence of their flesh has been proclaimed and made manifest to all.

"You have witnessed this truth, and the fire has come close to you: nay, even at twenty paces were you not almost overcome by the heat of it? For Our Lord has said: 'Thus shall perish all those who do not repent.' You have repented, do not relapse into error, you have been saved, do not rush to your destruction, know that from this day the hand of God is upon you. God judges no one; but the heart's perfidy reveals itself and renders itself manifest: henceforth your eyes and your words will be your judges.

"Know that henceforth he whose eyes and words betray the perfidy of his soul will be held as a relapsed heretic; and whoever, witnessing impious words and acts, shall neglect to inform the servants of the Church will be held as abetting heresy and as relapsed himself; for woe to the guest at the feast who sullies the nuptial garments, woe to the man healed of a palsy who speaks ill of his Saviour, woe to the barren fig tree and woe to Judas! For them there will be no second pardon.

"For God does not give with reservations: today He has given Himself whole and entire to each one of you. Rest in Him. Remain faithful to Him in suffering as in joy, for the Church does not deprive you of your illusory freedom in order to afflict you, but to keep you out of danger and to strengthen your faith. Rest in Him, for by the loss of a tallow candle that reeks and smokes you are gaining the Sun of Truth!"

As Brother Alberic spoke he himself was trembling and panting, less from fatigue than from a sincere desire to touch their souls; and a few of the women listening to him burst into sobs, though this was due more to physical exhaustion than to piety or bitterness. The prisoners' hearts and heads were still on fire from having been too close to the pyre, for whoever is not threatened with burning may talk as he pleases, he does not know what it means to his own flesh.

Roger de Montbrun believed that day that he had lost his faith for good. Why had they been forced to endure this Communion service in the cathedral—as though God could not forgive sinners more discreetly? True, tears of shame and bitterness taste the same as tears of repentance, and a broken body leaves the soul naked, while the chant of the *Agnus Dei*, the glittering candles and the golden chalice, the smell of incense and the pure whiteness of the Host proffered by a hand which though it may be loathed is consecrated—all this pierces the heart with a more than human love, a love you want to die of. But this is not love of God, this is the supreme temptation of the Devil. And two hours later the Host had been vomited up into the foul water of a kennel, together with a good half-pint of bile.

"Oh, Lord, Lord, the peace they have flung at us is the peace of a prison in Hell, all day long burning ashes have rained on us, from the cruel morning sun to this damned man's insensate words."

They sang hymns and cried: "Jesus!" And the Devil mocked them: because a fire of ordinary, dry wood is much stronger than Jesus.

There were seven men in a room fifteen feet long, all from noble or wealthy burgher families. Only three of them were new, the rest had been there since Christmas. Their feet were fettered, but they could go out of the room and walk along the passage as far as the square chamber inhabited by the guards and gaolers. They could go into neighbouring cells and, on Sundays, visit the women's prison. It was not a bad life. Once a week friends were allowed to come and see them and stay until nightfall. Life, in fact, was so sweet that it was almost possible to imagine oneself a prisoner on parole, since with money one might have nearly everything, even paper and ink. After three days they grew accustomed to it and began to make friends.

Roger was so certain of making his escape when Assumption Day came that to begin with he thought of nothing but his physical well-being: there was no point in getting out of prison only to succumb to dysentery a week later. Guillelme had sent him clean clothes and Raymond-Jourdain a purse containing three marks in silver, and Roger felt like a great lord again. He could buy water for a bath each week, and Spanish wine, and peppers and fruit—and he needed a great deal of this, since it was the custom, in prison, to take food to impoverished inmates. On Sundays after Mass they would take gifts to the ladies, and there was considerable competition as to who could find the most graceful mode of presenting a pomegranate or a pot of ginger,

373

tied up with a silken ribbon and accompanied by a letter in rhyme or simply by a sprig of lavender or laurel. Those who could play the viol or cittern arranged the words of well-known songs, slipping in the names of imprisoned ladies, and covertly wishing them a speedy release and the end of their troubles. Altogether, among those reconciled to the Church (those, at least, who had money), worldly vanity reigned to such a degree that their rooms were like inns on the eve of a tourney. They drank and played at dice and told stories of love and war; but as for faith, no one so much as mentioned it, even in their cups.

After two weeks of this life, Roger felt as if he were drunk; he was in love with all his room-mates and with the ladies he saw on Sundays, and strangely enough he found news from the outside world more tiresome than exciting. When Raymond-Jourdain came to see him (his other friends either for lack of time or for fear of compromising themselves were content with writing), he welcomed him without enthusiasm. "You will never know how it is. So long as I am in prison, Raymond, we shall be like two strangers. Maybe it's because I envy you too much."

"You know I am doing all I can. The Count is at war and your case has already caused him so much trouble that he looks the other way whenever he sees me. He advises me to wait, because in his opinion the Preaching Friars will not stay in Toulouse for long, and once they are gone he will have a free hand. He says that you have escaped the worst, thank God, and now you are treated no worse than a prisoner of war."

"Raymond, you can't understand: it is paradise, here. But in the end I think I shall have worn chains on my feet for so long that I shall never be able to walk like normal men."

"Roger, oh, Roger! If only my will could change all this!" Raymond-Jourdain wrung his hands and Roger, looking at the pale, fine-drawn face, once so deeply loved, thought that the friend of his youth was on the other side of a triple-locked door, and though they kissed each other's cheeks and clasped hands, they were as different as a rich man from a poor one, and that not every beggar received alms with a grateful heart.

"Raymond, every morning I tell myself that I shall not stay here one more day, because I am becoming like a child who thinks he can get everything he wants by crying for it. Have I not served the Count well enough to deserve that he should do what he can?"

374

Raymond-Jourdain explained that the provost of the prison had been appealed to continuously, but he was unable to allow more than two or three escapes a month and many highly respected people had been waiting their turn for over a year. "I know that this is all a plot arranged by the Count's enemies," he said, "because it is the very men who have served him best that the Inquisition has attacked first—and God knows, Roger, I myself am not safe—but the Count is having such difficulty in making the Pope and the King listen to him that he does not want to be accused of helping people to escape from his own prisons; as it is, he gets himself excommunicated twice a year because of his wars in Provence, and there is not a Preacher or a Frenchman murdered in the land but they attempt to pin it on him."

"I know," said Roger, with more sorrow than bitterness, "once exiled I am no longer good for anything, to the Count at least. Yet, he ought to know that wherever I am, I shall serve him faithfully to the best of my ability, and a man does not change his allegiance at my age. But as for the subject I asked you about, Raymond, think it over, it means a lot to me. And as far as the actual escape goes, one is less suspect in a woman's company."

Raymond-Jourdain twisted his gloves round and round in his hands in embarrassment. Roger had taken it into his head to arrange for his sister-in-law's escape and Raymond-Jourdain was afraid that, if he refused, his friend would think it was a matter of money (which was, in point of fact, perfectly true). "She is converted," he said. "She is in no danger. All those who are reconciled to the Church will soon be released on parole because if they have to keep every repentant heretic for life there will never be enough room in the prisons."

"Soon: that's easy for you to say. Can't my brother's friends make some effort? They managed to help Jacques Tanneur's widow to escape last month."

"Roger, to be honest with you, I can't let myself be seen in the company of your brother's friends. My daughter's nurse goes to see them, and even then in secret. God knows, they are rich, but they need their money for other things. They call it pruning the sound branches so that they will bear more fruit."

Roger hung his head, thinking that Rachel could no longer be called a sound branch; they knew that.

He had seen Rachel again two days before Pentecost and at

375

the time he had still been suffering from the after-effects of the great day of forgiveness. He had hardly entered the room, with two other prisoners, before Rachel came and flung her arms round his neck. "Ah, dearest brother! It is weeks since I saw you! Do you spend all your life warring in Provence?" Roger very nearly burst into tears of rage and shame.

"Look at my feet, sister. Is it possible you have not heard?" She saw the chains and nodded her head with an apologetic smile. "Ah, yes, yes, Roger, they did tell me, I had forgotten. . . . Holy Virgin, what a head I have! What a head! They treat the men more harshly than us; they say the chains hurt your ankles." She made him sit down on her bed, which stood in a corner beneath the window. It was the neatest of all the beds, little squares of silk had been pinned up above the bedhead, adorned with crosses and the names of Jesus and Mary embroidered in gold letters. As she spoke Rachel had picked up her embroidery frame and her needle. She was still pretty, though her face was the colour of a white turnip and tears shone in her black eyes—the shift she wore under her rather faded purple gown was white and her veil had been carefully darned. "Ah, tell me everything! Roger, how you must have suffered! And they have cut your hair—what a shame! Not so long ago you were still the best-looking man in the city."

"Father?" she said. "Yes, I know, they told me too. Ever since Easter I always say an extra rosary for him. Yes, he did love me, Roger, may God keep him in His paradise, they told me that he was calling for me when he died. . . . Oh! Don't blame Guillelme, Roger, she is kind to me, she is a poor child, yes, a poor child."

"I have said nothing against Guillelme."

"Roger, always tell yourself: They know not what they do. Truly, men never know what they do. I myself, do I know what I do? I have already hurt you twice in a quarter of an hour."

"No, Rachel!"

"Roger, you take me for a poor sacrificial lamb, and I am more guilty than the executioners, because I saw in their faces that they knew not what they did."

"Yes, yes," Roger said, "they do not know."

". . . Bertrand?"

"Oh! Brother, do not talk of him, he is the thorn in my flesh. How can you expect me to forget him, when we slept in the same bed for twenty-two years? Because he was a good husband,

376

Roger, a real husband, although it is not proper for a woman to say so. . . . Apart from secrets which were not his to share, he never hid anything from me."

"If this hurts you, sister, do not talk about it."

"No, I want to reassure you, Roger. He will not suffer much longer, he told me so. He told me: 'My dear, my cup is almost empty, my torment is at an end, and soon you will no longer need to pray for me.' "

"Do you pray for him, then, Rachel?" She shuddered and pressed her hand to her mouth.

"Ah! Did I say that? Do not repeat it, Roger, I don't know how I came to say it."

"Are you sure he is still alive, or was this a dream?" She had let her work drop on to her lap and was pressing both hands against her heart. She said in a broken voice: "He is still alive, Roger, because I cannot sleep. Yes, I do not tell my companions, but I cannot sleep. It is not surprising if they think I am mad. Roger, was there ever such a strong, healthy man? He was never ill in his life. Tell me, how can I get used to it? When you have lived for more than twenty years as one soul, and one flesh . . . rather than recant, he would let them roast me over a slow fire." She was sobbing like a child and Roger did not know how to comfort her. In the end he said: "Rachel, can you swear to keep a secret?"

"Yes," she said, "if it is a secret that might harm others if it were revealed." Then Roger told her that he was thinking of escaping and of taking her with him so that she could see her children again. "Never," she said, "never would I wish to remove myself from the mercy of the Church." Roger answered that she ought to do so for Bertrand, that if Bertrand knew she were free it would make him happy and that he, Roger, would never leave without her.

"I do not wish to leave here ever again," she said. "I want to stay where I can do and cause the least harm."

"But you have never done anyone any harm!"

"What do you know about it? Neither do they know the harm they do. What a hell this would be if all men knew what they did! Roger, Roger, you have killed men who had wives and mothers, do you know how many tears that caused? No, thank God! Enemies? They were enemies? We have only one enemy, Roger, one and one only, apart from Him whom our eyes cannot

377

see! Ourselves. I am my only enemy, and if you could only know how I hate myself!" She buried her head in her brother-in-law's shoulder and sobbed, more and more violently. Her companions were used to these outbursts and went on chatting to their visitors without even turning round. That evening Roger remembered the imprudent words which pity had torn from him and told himself that it was his duty not to leave his brother's wife in this intolerable state of humiliation.

It was a crazy idea, he was to see that clearly enough later, but at that moment he felt in a chivalrous mood because after months of solitude the sight of so many companions in misfortune easily moved him to pity. He was ready to swear eternal friendship to his room-mates: at sunset they would drink together, to the health of the Lady they never named but whose beauties they took turns to praise, sometimes in a bold and loverlike fashion (she must be generous since they all hoped one day to hold her in their arms), and sometimes with respectful devotion, for she was hard to win. All of them were dedicated so completely to that love that they were bound to assist any man who tried to conquer her, without jealousy or dissimulation. It is easier for a prisoner to speak of a Lady, and to assuage his unsatisfied passion with the meagre repast of words and songs, than it is for him to hold her in his arms.

(It was a fact that among the wealthy prisoners, of good family, none really believed themselves sentenced for life. Some were counting on escape, others on the revision of their sentences, since all said: "These laws cannot last, and our friends will not desert us." Many were even reluctant to expose themselves to the risks of escape and, bearing their cross with patience, concentrated on amorous intrigues and the various games and occupations which prisoners invent to pass the time.)

On the day of the feast of St. Dominic (the saint's first anniversary since his canonisation), there were to be great festivities in Toulouse, because the saint had worked great marvels in the city and in the whole diocese, and although he was not born in the country might, with some justice, have been called its adoptive child since it was there that he had taken his first steps as an apostle against the heretics. In the prison, where people condemned for heresy were now considerably more numerous than criminals, the doors of all the cells had to be locked and the number of guards doubled. Every feast day developed into an excuse for brawling, and on this particular day, according to

378

the spies, the prisoners were going to be more troublesome than usual. Wine unlocks tongues and the new feast day provoked angry outbursts among some of the men, who were saying: "They have made this man a saint on purpose to mock us." In fact if all those who made insulting remarks about the new saint were to be regarded as relapsed it would have been necessary to burn half the prisoners.

That day the men paced in circles in their locked cells, all but bumping into one another, as though their bodies had grown suddenly larger and lacked air and space. Because the iron-barred door leading into the passage was locked they became acutely aware of how small, dark and foul-smelling the cell really was, and on such days even the best of friends felt ready to come to blows. Outside, in the big, square courtyard, surrounded by walls pierced by small, barred windows, about twenty soldiers, armed with pikes and wearing red cloaks in honour of the feast, were marching up and down, occasionally shouting at the prisoners not to show themselves at their windows—hands and coloured veils, and a few women's sleeves, were waving through the bars, while from inside came the noise of children crying, because it was a hot, sultry day and quarrels broke out at the slightest word.

Were they going to change the rules and keep the doors shut for good? The prisoners asked themselves the same question every time the portcullis of the great gate was lowered and visiting forbidden. On these days they would keep anxious watch from the windows, imagining they could hear shouts and calls to arms in the distance—what if the prison were surrounded, if the consuls' forces were coming to take it by storm? They called out to the soldiers: "Hey, comrades! What news? What news?" The soldiers swore coarsely and the prisoners returned their curses. "You dogs, you'll see what will happen to you the day we're let out!" The bells were ringing on and on all over the city. Then towards evening the portcullis was raised and the courtyard filled with soldiers and visitors, but visitors brought there against their will, because they were wringing their hands and the women were crying and clinging to the soldiers' spears. Gaolers were running up and down the passages, shouting to one another and calling orders. "Hey, there! What's going on?"

"Pack up your traps, and quick about it! Your cells are being changed."

379

"All of us?"

"Good God, get a move on there! You'll be just as well off next door. They're bringing us over a hundred more." Their belongings were quickly got together, and soldiers armed with halberds let the men out one by one and pushed them into the neighbouring cell. The initial occupants of this chamber swore that there was already too little room, and the new arrivals, not knowing where to put their bundles, stood by the closed door and shouted through the bars that no one had the right to treat them like that, that they were living there at their own expense and would appeal to the prison governor. "If they haven't room to put people, then they shouldn't arrest them. This is a prison, not a poor-house!"

Other detainees passed in the corridor, carrying their hastily bundled up bedding, crockery and clothes, and pulling at the chains on their ankles to help them walk faster. "Hey, what's going on? Have there been riots in the town?" Roger and his companions, determined not to accept their change of cell quietly, hung on to the door shouting to the passing gaolers. "Ten sous for you, Jacques, if you tell us what's going on. Have we been moved out for long?"

"For as long as need be. And be ready to welcome a few more new friends." There were already sixteen men in the cell.

There was said to have been a rising in the town: the heretics had prepared a great plot for that day, and some consuls were involved in it, they meant to encircle the Dominican priory and throw them all out, including the Bishop, who was in the priory celebrating Mass. A traitor had made the plot miscarry. Then they learned from the gaolers that none of this was true, but that someone had been burned without trial, dragged from her bed, or very nearly, and cast into the fire; and that this lady's relations had tried to resort to violence—and the Prior of the seminary had preached a great sermon, threatening to burn all the heretics in the city without trial if the citizens persisted in protecting them. Then the whole city was thrown into such a panic that hundreds of people were thronging round the doors of all the seminaries and all the churches to tell what they knew about the heretics. Soon they would have to put as many as five or six people apiece in the dungeons.

Ah! Lord, Lord, they must be strong if they are beginning to burn folks without trial! They have used such intrigues with the

Pope in order to get their Saint, and told such slanderous tales against our country, that now they are not ashamed to treat us worse than mad dogs before the eyes of all Christendom. . . . No one slept that night; from the women's floor came the sound of children crying, and the voices of their mothers trying to quiet them, or weeping themselves. It was a night of grief and despair. It seemed as though the door would never open again, that there was no more safety in the law, since, if they were burning people who were living at liberty in their own houses, what would they do to those in prison?

Two weeks after this memorable feast of St. Dominic, the trial of Bertrand de Montbrun was begun at last. The two Brother Inquisitors, who were back in Toulouse for a short spell, and much incensed by the slanders about them which were rife throughout the country, said that an end must be made to the plague which was infecting the prisons, and by that they meant the obdurate believers whom they dared not bring to trial out of respect for the consuls and the people. The Holy Office had neglected the interests of justice through timidity and over-scrupulousness; and the Bishop himself had set the example and paved the way for them: he had had the courage to defy public opinion on the feast of St. Dominic when he had burned the mother-in-law of Boursier, who was one of the greatest believers in the neighbourhood of La Daurade, and good rather than harm had come of it. Furthermore, extravagant rumours were already circulating among the believers about such men as Bertrand de Montbrun: they were said to be still alive because God fed and protected them with celestial manna; they were being compared to Daniel in the lions' den.

However, Bertrand, when he was brought out of his dungeon, did not look like a man fed by angels. Brother Guillaume Arnaud had to go to the prison himself with his assistants, in order to be able to interrogate him, because the man was not in a fit state to be moved. A high-backed chair had to be placed in the room where the interrogation was to take place since the accused could not sit upright on a stool, and even in the chair his head was continually drooping forward on to his knees and he had to lean on his crutches to prevent himself falling to the ground.

How can one judge such a wreck? The gaolers had done their best, they would have had to tear off the skin in order to clean up his body, which was one mass of sores. They had cut his beard

381

and hair after a fashion, and washed his face in which cheeks, nose and jaw were reduced to grey skin stretched over the bone, but his eyes and mouth were dreadfully swollen. The man's speech was very bad; he had lost his teeth and, as well as mumbling and dribbling, he was unable at first to utter a coherent sentence because he had been a good three months without speaking to anyone. Brother Guillaume Arnaud's assistant, Brother Jean, said: "How can we judge him, he is no longer in his right mind?"

But when they asked the accused man whether he understood what they were saying to him, he answered 'yes' immediately and stared round him anxiously, as though to assure himself that he was not mad. In fact, being a man of amazing resistance, he was not.

The indictment, which was comparatively brief, contained the statements of two hundred and fifty-three witnesses, the majority of whom denounced Bertrand de Montbrun as a heretic believer from his youth and as the agent, collector of funds and treasurer of all the heretics in his district. He had still confessed to nothing. He was asked whether he was still a believer and said yes. For the rest he would say nothing at all. He scratched his head and chest with one fleshless hand, paying more attention to the lice which infested his person than to his judges. At every movement his body exuded a corpse-like smell.

When asked whether he persisted in calling himself a heretic believer, he raised his head and said in a hoarse, whistling voice that seemed to be coming from a cracked pipe: "I have always served the Church."

"Do not try to prevaricate. To which Church do you refer?"

"To the Church of God. There is only one Church."

By reason of his strange voice, and also because he could not help speaking slowly, the three monks, and the scribe, were hanging on his words as if they expected him to utter a prophecy (they knew well enough that this could only be a prophecy of the Devil, but it was not every day they saw a man keep his presence of mind after a year and a half in an underground dungeon, and all of them were convinced that he had been trafficking with the Devil).

"This Church you speak of, is it the Roman Catholic Church?"

"There is only one Church."

"Then it is the Catholic Church?"

The man's voice was still only a hoarse, coughing whisper: "I do not know that Church."

"But you know that you are being judged by the Church's judges?"

"No, by Antichrist. He will seduce many of the faithful."

"Then you hold to the belief that the Roman Catholic Church is the Church of Antichrist?"

Bertrand looked at them with half-closed eyes which he tried in vain to open fully. "It is not a Church. It is Antichrist. It has taken on the face of the Beast."

"Bertrand de Montbrun, tell us the truth: have you been initiated by the heretics in their baptism which they call the Consolamentum?"

"No."

"Does your faith not say that a man who has not received this baptism before his death in the flesh is surely damned?"

"No, my faith does not say that."

"Yet, you hold it a great misfortune to die without having received that baptism?"

Bertrand did not answer. Brother Jean asked him: "Do you know that once you are convicted of heresy, you become unworthy of the Church's mercy, unless you repent and renounce your errors?"

As the accused still did not answer, Brother Guillaume Arnaud remarked that as a simple believer he was wrong to persist in an error which, even according to his own faith (false and perfidious though it was), would not win him paradise; he would find himself rejected by the Catholic Church without having the smallest chance of receiving this baptism so coveted by the heretics.

Bertrand was only listening with half an ear, but at the word 'baptism' his eyes brightened and he raised his head once more.

"The Church is praying for me."

"Do you understand," asked Brother Jean, "that you have now been judged, and that if you do not repent now the Church can do nothing more for you?"

Bertrand said nothing, and the soldiers of the guard helped him to rise and support himself on his crutches and led him to the scribe's table. He took the pen to sign, but his stiffened fingers would not obey him. "What are you making me sign?" he said. "I do not see very well, I cannot read."

"You are not being tricked into signing anything. You are signing your own confessions."

Suddenly he seemed afraid. "I have confessed nothing. I have betrayed no one."

"You have betrayed yourself, Bertrand de Montbrun. But if you will renounce the heretic errors, you will be put into a good prison and you will win the Church's forgiveness."

"*Forgiveness,*" repeated Bertrand. "*Forgiveness.*" He raised his left arm, which was nothing more than bone covered with cracked and blackened skin, and stretched it across the table towards his judges. "Burn what is left," he croaked, slowly. "Eat, gorge yourselves. Carrion crows that you are. My forgiveness. Shall *you* have my forgiveness? Shall you have my forgiveness? I shall see you all burst like chestnuts in the fire, your tongues sticking out, and squealing like pigs, before you have my forgiveness; I shall see you roasting in hell before you have my forgiveness. I shall become a devil myself and burn you as you have burned and mangled me, you servants of Herod, dogs of Satan, hypocrites, Pharisees." The cavernous, chanting voice seemed rather to be reciting a Litany than uttering curses, and his clouded eyes were staring into vacancy.

"Brother, this man's wits have gone," said Brother Jean. "He does not know what he is saying."

Bertrand shuddered, as though he had been found fault with, and gripped his crutches with both hands. "I have my wits about me," he said, in terror. "I know what I am saying. What did I say?"

"You shall be delivered to the secular arm this very day if you do not recant."

For an instant the man appeared to wake up, his eyes flashed with terror, he staggered, and clutched at his crutches again. "Today?" he repeated. "Today?"

"Perhaps he will sign," said Brother Jean in an undertone. Bertrand had not heard; he let his head fall forward again as though his emaciated neck could no longer bear its weight. "Ah! Satan!" he murmured, "Satan! Satan! *Ah! Realm of Satan!*"

The sentence was signed by the judges, and Brother Guillaume Arnaud gave the order to summon the Provost. It was cruel and pointless to prolong this man's agony any longer.

It was decided that Bertrand de Montbrun should be led to the stake, supported by two soldiers, as the sight of his crutches was too likely to excite the people's sympathy. He was clothed in a frieze shift and a paper mitre daubed with pitch set on his head. He submitted, almost indifferently. But when they led him out to the courtyard he came to himself and asked, as a last favour, permission to see his wife again. It seemed as though the approach of death had cleared his mind; he still spoke with difficulty but was perfectly lucid. "Since my last hour has finally come," he said, "will you refuse me this boon? I am a man, and I was baptised a Catholic, will you deny me the right to say farewell to my lawful spouse? You do not refuse the worst criminals that." The Provost, who had known Bertrand when he was young and strong, so short a time before, took pity on him, and said that he would ask the prison governor for permission to have the Lady Rachel brought down, but that it was hardly reasonable to ask the poor woman to be subjected to such a test. "What's that?" said Bertrand. "I am going to die, and she could not bear to see me?"

The prison governor, out of respect for the condemned man's good reputation, gave the order for Rachel and Roger de Montbrun to be brought down, but only for a few minutes, since word of the execution was already going about the city and it could not be delayed. When Rachel appeared in the courtyard leaning on her brother-in-law's arm and escorted by three soldiers, Bertrand almost dropped his crutches and supported himself against the wall, while the paper mitre with the words 'Obdurate heretic' slipped from his head and fell to the ground. The condemned man stared at his wife and brother with bewilderment and something like gladness. "What, Roger, you too? You too? With chains on your feet? Have they done this to you because of me?"

"No, no, Bertrand, for my own sins." Both Rachel and Roger were trembling badly; but this was not due to the condemned man's aged and frightful appearance or to the fact that he was about to die; it was the simple effect of their emotion at seeing him again alive and talking to him. The three of them embraced as though they were meeting after a long journey. "Bertrand," said Rachel, "Bertrand, see, they have been kind, they have let me see you again!"

"Rachel, my dearest, forgive me. Through my folly, I have ruined my family and brought misfortune on our children! I have been the cause of your ruin, my dove. If I had known they would attack you I should not have done what I have done."

"You have done well, Bertrand. Oh, yes! You have done what you had to do, and I am honoured by all my companions because of you."

"Forgive all the anguish I have caused you, Rachel, I shall have killed you."

Rachel cradled her husband's head against her shoulder and caressed the short white hair and emaciated neck with both hands. "Fear nothing, do not torment yourself, don't cry any more, my dear. God will have mercy on us, it will not be so hard, it will not take long. . . ." She was speaking in a small, cracked, sing-song voice, softly, as though comforting a child. "You will see, Bertrand, it will be all right. We shall meet again, it will not be long, Bertrand." He raised his head and leaned back to look at his wife's face.

"How lovely you still are, Rachel! It was not living, down there in the darkness, it is better so, you will tell our children it is better. Yet I should have liked to see them again too. But they are young, I should frighten them."

Seeing the domestic scene showed no signs of concluding, the Provost approached Roger and told him that it was time to take the lady back to her cell. Rachel turned to him with a little smile of entreaty: "Oh, no! Master Durand. Just a little while longer! I have hardly seen him!" The two brothers looked at one another, not knowing what to say: they had quarrelled so often, and for the secret, dumb friendship between them they had no words.

"Have you been here for long, Roger?"

"Since Christmas."

"Father is dead, have they told you?"

"Yes."

"At least he won't have seen this—you'll take care of her, Roger? If they let you . . ."

Here the soldiers pushed Rachel and her brother-in-law aside, somewhat roughly, replaced the paper mitre on the condemned man's head and dragged him towards the main gateway. Rachel lifted her arms to heaven and uttered a piercing shriek, then fell on her knees sobbing and moaning, her black veil trailing in the dust of the courtyard. Roger thought of the heretics he had seen burned and could not believe that this thing was really happening to his brother; he felt as though it were another bad dream, that he should have said to Bertrand: "Don't go, you don't know what

386

it's like, recant while there is still time! *For once in your life, listen to me. . . .*" Oh, Lord, if one cannot prevent this, if one can never prevent anything, then as well be a beast! As well be mad, like Rachel. She was still weeping as they dragged her back up the stairs, weeping as a woman weeps over her ailing husband who has just received the last sacrament. "Ah, my dear, my dear, must we be parted in this life? My sweet friend, must you leave me. . . ?"

Eight days later, Rachel Abrahamide, widow of Bertrand de Montbrun, was burned as a relapsed heretic. On the day after her husband's death her mind had begun to wander, she said that she was a criminal who had murdered her father, and Bertrand, and many Christians and righteous men. She beat her breast and tore her hair and rent her garments until the flesh could be seen as far as her navel; and at night she wept so loudly that it became a nuisance to her companions, who, although they pitied her, could do nothing for her, while two of them had small children who were frightened by Rachel's frenzy. Roger was allowed to visit her but did not succeed in calming her. He could only hold her hands to prevent her from hurting herself.

"Sister, would Bertrand have liked to see you in this condition?"

"Dearest brother, you don't understand. I killed him. I worshipped the Beast through fear of the fire. I prostituted myself, I soiled myself with the cross and the prayers of Satan, and Satan has rewarded me by bringing about the deaths of my father and Bertrand! Satan always answers our prayers, and gives us the thing we most fear. Roger, they stripped me and beat me with a whip, did you know that? And Satan entered into me that day. I said: I shall adore the Beast, and perhaps he may have mercy on me . . . because Bertrand never had mercy, he never had mercy on me! He let me die over a slow fire, with anguish in my heart for him."

One of Rachel's companions, Lady Braïda Rigaude, told Roger: "Sir knight, there are no spies or traitors here that I know of, and the wardresses are good women. Moreover, your poor sister-in-law says many things which are in all our minds, but if she goes on shouting them so loudly, it will be known. Make her understand that she is endangering her companions, and yourself in particular."

387

Roger tried to explain this to Rachel; she seemed to understand and wept. But that very day she begged the wardress to inform the governor of the prison that she had some information to disclose and requested an interrogation by the tribunal of the Holy Office.

She was flogged—not very severely, since even the executioners took pity on her—in an effort to find out who were the persons who had led her to relapse into her previous errors. She answered that she had never renounced her faith, that she had only feigned repentance, though this was not entirely true. Under the lash, and when she had been hung up by her wrists, she wept a great deal more than she talked, but she talked too: she said she had thought to escape, that she had been urged to escape, but that she wanted to drink of the same cup as her husband and her father (in her derangement she thought that her father, old Master Isaac, had been burned too). Beyond this, she gave no names, and with a cunning which the strongest might have envied, she feigned madness, loss of memory, and a paralysing fear, and gave wildly improbable names, such as the Emperor of Germany or Brother Guillaume Arnaud himself, or the Holy Virgin. She said too that she accused no one, and forgave them all, but that she would not serve the Beast, and that her Church, the Church which she and her husband and friends had served, was the only true Church. She was therefore condemned and led to the stake at the same time as a female heretic who had recently been captured in the woods near Sorèze: she cried out for a long time amid the flames, calling her children and screaming: *"Don't look, my darlings, don't look! Don't be afraid, my lambs! I shall come back!"* The soldiers who had escorted her there were saying among themselves: "This is a sin, the woman was mad." "No, not mad, but possessed of a devil." "Well, then, it's a devil who could not frighten anyone, but inspire pity, more likely." "What do you know about devils? There are some that take on pitiful voices just to make folks sorry for them. Listen, when you go past a graveyard at night." "They are souls who died without absolution." "But, tell me, don't they say the souls of people who have been burned can never come back to earth? It is as if they had been exorcised." They had to believe that, since otherwise the Pré-du-Comte, where the burnings took place, would have been the most haunted spot in the city: superstitious women would come out there in the evenings after executions to glean

388

the remains of the ashes, which they sometimes scattered under their doorsteps to show the souls of the martyrs that here were people who honoured them and sought their protection. Many people, indeed, were more afraid of the spirits than of the living men.

After his sister-in-law's trial, Roger de Montbrun was again summoned to appear before the tribunal of the Holy Office and his interrogation was conducted by Brother Alberic of Montpellier. He was suspected of having attempted to escape, and also of having urged the woman Rachel Abrahamide to apostasy. In fact Roger did not know what Rachel could have said, but he was sure that she had betrayed him. He asserted his fidelity to the Catholic Church and his horror of the heresy which had led to the downfall of his brother and many other honest citizens.

"After your rehabilitation, were you not heard to utter abominable insults to the Order of Preaching Friars, and to St. Dominic and our Holy Father, the Pope?"

"Those who told you that of me were lying."

"Do you mean to say that you have felt no bitterness against those who condemned your brother?"

"What are you trying to make me say? I was grieved by my brother's death, but he alone was to blame."

"You did not utter blasphemies against the Church in order to comfort your sister-in-law?"

"No. I exhorted her to remain calm and resign herself."

"Do you suspect any of her companions? Could they have incited her to renounce the Catholic faith?"

"Quite the reverse, they all gave her good advice."

"Yet the women Braïda Rigaude, Hersen de Lantar and Bernarde Sellier were formerly great believers. Seeing that the late Rachel Abrahamide herself, who gave such proofs of sincere devotion, relapsed into her lamentable errors, is it likely that they should hold no opinions hostile to the Church?"

"These persons have repented and been reconciled to the Church. I have never heard them utter the opinions you suggest."

"Do you know that in seeking to protect persons suspected of apostasy you are rendering yourself liable to suspicion?"

"Would you have me invent lies?"

"Why, on the day your sister-in-law began to vomit up these abominable blasphemies against the Church, did you not at once inform the prison governor? Why did her companions not do so?"

"I took my sister-in-law's words for the ravings of madness; and her companions and wardresses thought as I did."

"It is for the tribunal to interpret such opinions, not for you. You should have reported them as you heard them."

At that, Roger lost patience and said: "I have not been taught to spy."

"You had been warned," said Brother Alberic. "Your duty as a Catholic was to inform the Holy Office of all opinions and actions contrary to religion of which you were a witness."

Roger shrugged scornfully and crossed his legs, to show that he did not consider himself to be dealing with men in a higher position than himself. He was tired. Not tired enough to give up the struggle, but tired of humiliating himself, of controlling his voice, weighing his words. . . .

"Is it not known," added Brother Alberic, "that, in violation of your oath, you were considering corrupting the keepers and escaping?"

"I have never entertained such a thought."

"We have this information from your sister-in-law."

"You should have confronted me with her. She did not know what she was saying." Roger felt his lips trembling with a sudden attack of pity—senseless pity for a woman who was dead. "I did speak of it to her," he said quietly, "she was not lying to you. I cheered her with false hopes of escape, hoping they would comfort her. She was like a child."

"Why should we believe you lied to your sister-in-law? We might just as well believe you are lying now."

"Why do you question me? What new evidence have you against me?"

"Have you not just admitted to us that you made suggestions to your sister-in-law which were contrary to your sworn oath?"

Roger stood up, seized his cloak and flung it over his left shoulder.

"Brothers," he said, "all I have told you is the truth. I have been acknowledged a Catholic, absolved and reconciled to the Church. If this is an attempt to make me undergo a fresh trial, I claim my right to appeal to the Pope. I see that in Toulouse I am suspect whatever I do or say, and I must believe that I have hidden enemies who are working for my destruction."

390

"And who," asked Brother Alberic, "authorises you to declare the present tribunal incompetent? If you are to have a retrial, be sure that the Holy Father has confidence in us and will defer to our judgment."

Roger said: "My case has been tried. No man can be tried twice for the same crime."

"You speak like an ignorant man," said Brother Alberic. "Take care you do not make yourself an object of mockery. You are well aware, certainly, that once convicted of the grave crime of which you have been accused, you are in fact absolved, but only upon conditions. The judge who pronounced a sentence for heresy has every right to revoke his sentence."

"My conscience is clear. I wish my case to be taken to the court of Rome, where I shall have judges who know neither my friends nor my enemies."

"You must be in collusion with great personages in the city to speak with such arrogance, and think yourself above the law. Men of your kind have not yet understood that there are no rich and poor in the eyes of the Church in matters of faith."

"Then why do you attack me for my wealth, Brother?" asked Roger, finally losing his temper. "To begin with, I haven't a penny to speak of, I am dependent on my young sons. And then you boast of having no regard for rich men, but you have none for the poor, either. If a poor man answers you boldly, you say to him: 'You, miserable ignorant wretch, are you teaching us?' While if a rich man does the same, you accuse him of pride and arrogance. I have paid dearly for the knowledge that I am not above the law, but quote me a law forbidding men, whether they are rich or poor, to appeal in matters of faith to the Pope's justice?"

"We have no authority," said Brother Alberic, "to importune the Holy Father with such trifles. Do you think the sun revolves around you? We cannot judge you again in Brother Peter's absence, but as you are accused of attempting to escape and of insolent and equivocal words we can change your prison, and put you down into an underground dungeon so that you shall not be a cause of scandal to your reconciled companions."

How describe a man's terror when he sees himself reduced to the status of an inanimate object? When he has nothing to sell, nothing to give away—and at that moment Roger told himself that he would have sold father and mother for the right to go

391

back to the large prison. (This was easy to say since he had neither father nor mother to sell, and would have sold no one else. . . .) He stared stupidly at Brother Alberic and his assistant (this was no longer Brother Guillaume but a thin young monk with the face of a famished wolf), racking his brains to guess what kind of words might touch these men. It had to be done quickly.

"My reverend Brothers, you are killing me," he said. "For trifles, as you yourself call them, you would reduce a man to despair. Shall I be punished for having loyally submitted myself to the Church? May God requite those who have accused me to you, I am innocent! Never have I thought of escape! If you deny me the right of appeal, you must at least hear me out! How can you accuse me of trying to escape when my only wish is to do penance! And when, for a long time, without daring to admit it, I have secretly aspired to be admitted as a penitent into your holy house, and there to be put to the most menial tasks, wearing chains on my feet and a hair-shirt on my body! So that I only had the right to pray, sometimes, in your church where the most merciful Jesus spoke to me when I was injured! You can see that I have no pride, and that if I speak of appealing to the Pope it is out of my despair in seeing you doubt my faith, and in the hope of being entirely reinstated and obtaining my desire. Ought the Church to reject a repentant sinner? At my age, with my body racked by sickness, can I have any other wishes than my soul's salvation?"

"You talked in another key half an hour ago," said the young monk.

"Ah! Brother, you yourself, would *you* not be angered if someone were to suspect your faith? And do you think that after having seen my only brother perish so wretchedly I have not desired God's presence still more ardently? I beseech you, let your Father Prior question me, your doctors, and your scholars, they will see the extent to which my faith is real. Is it in a dungeon or a prison cell, delivered over to the temptations which fill us ceaselessly, that I shall be able to save my soul? I am a weak, light-minded man and surely I shall be damned. Have you not admitted repentant sinners before now even as Brothers into your monastery? I do not ask so much, only that I be granted the right to do penance and to weep over my sins in a place of prayer and not in a profane place. Would my life there be less harsh, if I am put to work that disgusts the meanest servant? I should

392

endure it joyfully, provided only that I am granted the right to pray in that church where the Lord Jesus calls me to him!"

Brother Alberic and his assistant looked at one another, frowned in some perplexity—this scene had been witnessed by the scribe and the two soldiers of the guard. Certainly, the Brother investigators did not often hear such speeches; they would have to make an exact report to their superior and to Brother Peter because the matter could not be passed over in silence. Brother Alberic ordered the soldiers to take the prisoner away and leave him in one of the cells in the monastery which were reserved for suspects, keeping a watch to see that he was not able to talk to anyone. Roger told himself that this was the first victory; now he had to construct a plan of campaign. His eyes were still wet with the tears which his passionate plea had wrung from him and he thought: "Now, if I have to weep some more, I know how to do it. If they send Guillaume Arnaud to me in person I shall kiss his feet!"

Brother Alberic, feeling distinctly put out, examined Roger de Montbrun's latest dossier: it contained very little—only the depositions of the gaolers, which in any case accused Roger no more than any of the other prisoners, and that of a spy placed in the cell where Rachel had been confined. Roger, this testimony said, had several times told his sister-in-law that he would not escape without her. The young monk said: "That proves nothing, he thought she was mad."

"You still don't know these people, Brother Bérenger. I have followed this man from the beginning of his case. Such spirits are no more capable of being touched by God's grace than a pig of learning to fly. If ever such a miracle occurred it would be enough to set all the bells of Toulouse ringing from noon to midnight." The young man said: "Do not God and St. Dominic work miracles every day? You saw, the man had tears in his eyes."

"Yes, tears of anger and fear, which he was clever enough to make out were tears of piety."

Brother Bérenger, an ardent young man with a vivid imagination, could not forget what the prisoner had said on the subject of the church where Jesus had spoken to him. "Will you deny that the spirit of St. Dominic is really present in our church? If a man uttered such words in deceit would his tongue not wither away?"

393

"Oh, Brother, the whole city of Toulouse and the whole country are peopled with withered tongues of that sort!" Nevertheless, rather than appear to doubt the miraculous powers of the new church, Brother Alberic made a report to the Father Superior which tended to favour the accused: the said Roger de Montbrun, he said, must be examined by monks who were expert in faith and dogma. If the man were really sincere, his conversion could be turned to the Church's advantage in the country.

"God!" thought Roger, "can I carry this new test through to the end? Until now they have always been stronger than I. But by dicing with the Devil one comes to know him: perhaps he is not as cunning as he's said to be. Am I a fool?"

The cell—a small vaulted chamber with a little round window looking on to the monastery stables—was clean and newly whitewashed, with a black wrought-iron cross nailed to the wall opposite the window. On the ground beside the bare, stone bed was a pitcher of water and a whip, its three tails studded with nails and the leather, though still new, blackened with dried blood. Roger examined this instrument curiously, thinking that one of the monks, shut up there for some infringement of the rule, must have been disciplining himself and had forgotten the whip. "If that's what is needed to convince them of my sincere repentance, I'll beat myself until I take all the skin off my back, that won't frighten me!" It was getting dark. The bells of the monastery church were ringing for vespers, so close by that they seemed to make the wall vibrate—lovely booming sounds, like huge hearts beating, great tranquil hearts. . . . "Ah! what a sin these people commit when they make such beautiful, holy things serve their treacherous purposes! The need for prayer remains fixed in our bodies, like hunger. *Lord, have mercy on me a sinner!* If I had to weep over my sins it would take me to the end of my life. Lord, first release me from the hand of my enemies!"

The key ground in the lock. Roger knelt before the black crucifix, now scarcely discernible in the shadows. The door opened, a yellowish light illuminated the wall and Roger saw his shadow sweep slowly over the flagstones of the cell. He turned, blinking at the candle, and nearly cried out: the man who had come to see him was his doctor from the torture chamber. God knew why, but this man's face, already familiar, was at that moment more hateful to him than any other.

394

"I see," said the monk, "that I interrupted your prayers. The Father Superior has sent me to you, since he was informed that you were demanding a doctor, and in truth a doctor for the soul rather than the body. But as I have had many opportunities of speaking with you, perhaps you will confide in me more willingly than in any other. You must know that you are quite wrong in thinking we are your enemies."

"Ah, Brother," said Roger, with a surge of something approaching sincerity, "what do you expect me to think? I have always been frank with you, and I shall continue to be. I made a bad bargain on your account, because in order to earn forgiveness and the right to take communion, I accused myself of more sins than I had committed; I was promised complete forgiveness if I repented, and I hoped thus to deserve some day the favour I desired, but I see that it is hopeless."

"And do you claim," said the monk, seating himself on the bed and folding his hands on his lap, "that this favour you desire is the right to be admitted to live as a penitent in a monastery of our Order? You have never spoken of it before today."

"How could I have dared? It has been my secret wish, ever since the time I was cared for in your hospital, when I was able to make my confession in your church: for the sanctity of the place pierced my heart with love and an ineffable peace and I desired nothing more than to be able to pray there every day, even in the meanest place, by the door with the beggars!"

"That is a pious wish," said the monk, with a calm, melancholy smile, "but don't you think you are asking a great deal? Haven't men of holy and goodly lives joyfully given up their possessions for the right to pray in this place? If we only had room enough to receive all those who wish to come to us!"

"But, Brother, didn't Jesus Christ say that sinners had more need of forgiveness than righteous men? I am willing to submit to every test, but not those that destroy the soul. Shall I find my soul's salvation at the bottom of a dungeon, far from all aid, human or divine? As God sees me, I ask no other right than to pray with God's servants, to hear the offices and sermons and attend Mass, and lead a life which may bring me to salvation: that much I have the right to claim."

"Are you sincere in saying that you hold the Brothers of our Order for the servants of God? Formerly, you had nothing but bitter words for them."

395

"My heart has changed, and you know it, and you know where and when. And to tell you the truth, your own words on the day you spoke to me of the monk's state, how he renounced even freedom of thought and will for God, have been like a pilgrim's staff to me. I have meditated a great deal on those words, Brother, and the harder they seemed to me, the more deeply they penetrated my heart. I am weary of my roving thoughts, and my perverse will, and only long for God, through the prayers of the Church, to release me from them!"

The monk did not answer. He had taken his rosary and was letting the beads slip slowly through his fingers which were as lean and smooth as twigs. He kept his eyes lowered and Roger, sitting on the ground at his feet, watched him keenly, thinking: I must go on talking. I mustn't let him pray for too long.

"Brother, what should I do? If you have come to visit me as a friend and not as an enemy, at least you owe me some advice. You were once good to me. If your Brothers, whom our Holy Father the Pope has set as judges over us, would only speak to us with gentleness, instead of seeing lies in every word we utter! If only I were allowed to speak with some of the Brothers of your Order who are charged with the direction of souls, and not only with the investigation of crimes! It is from such men that I look for the cure of my disease. Can I be accused of pride? Perhaps, because you have always led a pious life, you cannot understand the anguish a man feels when he sees himself in danger of damnation! The few years I have left to live, I need to spend in prayer, and in a place consecrated by prayer! Moreover, the Lord tells us to knock, to be importunate, and not to weary, and no one has the right to shut the mouth of a man who asks for grace for his soul!"

Roger stopped for his voice was breaking and he felt ready to burst into sobs. "I must be mad," he thought.

Slowly the monk looked down at the prisoner, and his cold features, starkly illuminated by the candle, seemed suddenly younger and keener. "My friend, do you think I have a stone in place of a heart? Do you think I have not been struggling against myself for twenty-five years—pitiful athlete that I am!—forcing myself to bring to those I served, not merely an impotent, human pity, but the charity of Jesus Christ? You aspire to salvation. And you are pleading with me, me, the least of all men! You hope to find peace of mind by placing yourself beneath the edge of the sword.

"For this sword which Our Lord has brought into the world and which he will not cease to hold in His hand until the Day of Judgment, it is to us that He has entrusted it in these troubled times, yes, to our weak hands and our idle and lukewarm hearts! Through the apostolate of His servant Dominic, the Lord has placed in our hands the Sword of Truth which cuts through the flesh of error. The saint has not called us to peace, but has said to us, as the Lord said to His disciples: 'You shall be reviled and persecuted for my name's sake.' For in these lying times Truth becomes a sword and inspires terror—to the body also, not merely to souls, for souls have become blind and deaf, only the body's terror can awaken them. I am speaking to you, my friend, as I would speak to a brother, for I have remembered this of your words: that you aspire to penitence, and that had your commitments permitted you would have wished to embrace the monastic life; and that this desire came to you in our church. This is a praiseworthy desire. But you know little of the spirit which inspires our Order and you do not know what you desire to obtain."

Roger said that he asked nothing more than to learn; and that, of all religious orders, that of the Preaching Friars seemed to him the one which had the hardest rule and the most burning piety. "And since you admit that your Order appeared, in our time, as the sword to destroy sin, is it not right that I should expose myself to the edge of this sword, so that my sins may be cut away from me? My marriage has never been lawful and for that reason it has never borne anything but evil fruit. And I hope one day to win my case. Am I asking to end my days in a richly-furnished cell, like a Benedictine canon? I want rough toil, dry bread, mortification and contempt, and my shame as a repentant heretic besides, as well as my prisoner's chains."

"It seems to me," said the monk, not unkindly, "that you have more natural piety than understanding—although advanced in years, you are an infant in grace. And yet, even the very first day I saw you, I felt a kind of joy in my heart that I then took for an impulse of wordly attraction; but perhaps, on the contrary, it was a sign sent by God, bringing me a foreboding that I should one day be one of the instruments—the meanest of instruments—of your salvation. It seems to me that you are asking something

397

almost impossible—and yet, I cannot but encourage you to persevere in your desire, for the desire itself is good. Only consider, even if you were admitted to be one of the monastery servants, even if you were free, it is only after long years of hardship that you might—if God wills—make your request to enter your noviciate. In order to be rehabilitated by the court of Rome, you must give your judges proof of a lasting and flawless repentance."

"Haven't I implored my judges to let me appeal to the court of Rome? And if I had to wait ten years—so long as my bodily strength does not fail me! I am no longer a young man."

"Truly, you know nothing except what you desire. You are a self-willed and determined man. And it is self-will which you must kill in yourself, because we are dependent on our superiors, as a stick on the hand which holds it. In our Order much more than in any other. As I told you, the sword which the Church has placed in our hands is not a mockery of a sword, a phantom sword, an object of mirth for God's enemies! In our corrupt and degenerate days, neither sacred words nor miracles have the power to awaken souls any longer. But the Lord has shown us, through His servant Dominic, the way to salvation. You know well enough how we are hated and persecuted for Truth's sake: that is why I do not find it easy to believe that you really aspire to climb Calvary with us."

"You know, Brother," said Roger, "that I have been attached to the Count from my youth, and my family and friends have always disapproved of the conduct of Monseigneur Foulques; while before the war we held that Monseigneur Raymond de Rabastens had been unjustly deposed, and that he was still our lawful bishop. All men think as their friends think. It is only in prison that I have had the leisure to ponder the matter impartially. I have seen that I was mistaken. I accused the Preaching Brothers as a sick man accuses his doctor who causes him pain in order to cure his hurts. Truly, even in my judges, I have seen only sincere piety and the desire to serve God with austerity and a spirit of justice. This I cannot deny."

"See," said the monk, in a voice that was almost friendly—he seemed to take real pleasure in talking to Roger—"see how in the times in which we live men are divided by heresy and the corruption of hearts: we are two men of approximately the same age, born citizens of the same town, yet it seems as though we have lived in two different worlds. And it has been possible for you, a sincere Catholic (I have always believed that), to remain, until the age of forty-five, a prisoner of the errors into which your worldly passions have cast you. If I were to tell you how God showed me the true way, you would see that the Spirit bloweth where it listeth, and that neither friends nor family nor even sin can prevent us from following Jesus Christ on the day when He calls us by our name."

Roger listened to the man gladly, thinking: "If he confides in me in this way, he will be my ally."

The doctor monk told his story with the rather ponderous simplicity common in people unused to talking about themselves; he seemed to be bearing witness in all good faith. By the light of the half-burned candle, his eyes were shining with a youthful, almost joyous, brilliance.

"Let me tell you," he said, "that my father was Pierre Audiart, the cloth merchant. He was ruined by the war, as you probably know, but at the time when I was growing up he was still chartering one boat at Bordeaux and another at Marseilles, and there were over five hundred workers employed in his clothworks. I was my parents' fourth son, and they treated me with extreme indulgence, so much so that by the time I was fifteen I had lost all taste for thoroughbred horses, fine clothes and gaming. I gave myself up, with the enthusiasm of that age, to the study of the sciences, attending all the schools in our city in the hope that in one or the other I would glean nourishment for my eager spirit. It was then that I met my first mistress, I mean medicine. To this mistress, whose beauty seemed to me surpassing that of women, I gave myself absolutely. I followed her into brothels and places of ill fame, by which I mean the schools where she is prostituted to men who are to all appearance wise, but in their souls more ignorant than the humblest porters: I gave the name of master to Arab and even Jewish doctors, and I went as far as Avignon to hear the famous Solomon ben Levi teach!

"My parents, perceiving my excessive ardour for an art which they held in small esteem, and grieved at seeing me embrace a profession which seemed to them unworthy of me, tried to dissuade me with threats, prayers and even blows, and in the end even stopped my allowance. What more can I say? Since I no

399

longer possessed the means to pay for my studies, or even to buy food, I set the seal on my errors by accepting the hospitality of a prominent heretic, because my great enthusiasm and modest talent brought me to the notice of a deacon of Toulouse who was already reputed to be among the finest doctors in the Count's domains—Guillaume d'Ayros.

"You, even though you have been accused of conniving at heresy, you cannot know the attraction of that subtle poison when it is offered to us by hands seemingly pure in a cup sparkling with the diamonds of science and eloquence! I was not an initiate, or even a postulant, but I took part in their feasts and their prayers, I saluted those I called my masters and I revered them for their knowledge and the sanctity of their lives. But God's mercy towards me was great: by the grace of Providence my heart was too firmly attached to a profane art and was thus able to avoid the traps of a religion so much the more perfidious in that it gave itself all the appearance of extreme piety. What did I tell you? My wishes were entirely turned towards the acquisition of a science which for the ignorant and presumptuous young man that I was, represented Truth itself, when I had the good fortune to come into contact with Monseigneur Foulques, who at that time had just been elected Bishop of our city.

"How those of your party were mistaken in that worthy man! How many vile slanders they have heaped upon him, condemning the old man for the errors of his youth. And yet, even when he was in the world, was his past life not always worthy and blameless? When he gave up riches and honour to become a simple monk, he was far from thinking that one day his virtues would lead him to the height of the episcopal throne of Toulouse. And if you remember (you must have been little more than a boy at that time, proud of shaving your first moustache), it was no sinecure, or even glory, to be the Bishop of our city. Monseigneur Raymond de Rabastens had ruined the diocese to such an extent by his incessant wars that it could barely afford to feed the clerks of the chapter, and there was nothing but debts in the treasury. Besides, the Church was held in such contempt by our citizens that I myself never thought of removing my hat when the Bishop passed by.

"But now comes an extraordinary coincidence, or rather the unlooked-for grace of Providence. My father, who was greatly grieved by what he justly called my folly, had, in his youth, been well known to Monseigneur Foulques' father, a cloth merchant like himself, and had on several occasions been his guest at Marseilles. Recalling this former friendship and, in his paternal anxiety for me, clinging to the faintest glimmer of hope that might bring the strayed sheep back to the fold, he came to find me, in my den of iniquity, and begged me to go with him to visit the new Bishop, who, he said, out of kindness for himself, had consented to see me.

"I did see him, and he talked to me. How deeply I must pity the most hardened sinners, I who, but for this providential meeting, would surely have sunk lower than they. Did you know him? No, you can only have seen him from a distance because the late Count Raymond bore him an implacable hatred: he cleaved to Bishop Raymond like the malefactor to his accomplice and the debauchee to his pimp. When the papal court had finally deposed Raymond de Rabastens, the Count, as you know, did not spare his taunts and gibes at his successor, all of which the venerable Foulques bore with a noble serenity. You, then, and your like, blinded by a misplaced loyalty, saw only an overweening upstart in the man the Lord had sent us to be the regeneration of our city. I saw him, in his palace—poor then, and as bare as the home of a ruined man—and spoke to him at his table where he dined on dry bread in the company of three clerks. How can I describe him to you? He shone in his penury with a royal majesty; he sat in those rooms with their peeling walls, before that bare table, lighted by tallow candles, with the gracious smile that marks the born ruler. He was nearly sixty at that time, but his face and presence were still handsome, for his great spirit added to the natural nobility of his countenance. His voice was especially wonderful, strong and vibrant, going straight to the heart. He spoke to me in a manner that was lively and yet full of dignity, with the kindness of a father. He asked me whether I preferred to be wise among men, or mad with God, because he himself, he said, was a great madman to have come to bury himself, for obedience' sake, in a See where all he met with was poverty, trouble and abuse, and where, though he was the greatest lord in the city, he had barely enough to eat.

"I can still see the silvered locks on his brow, his eagle eyes and the inimitable grace of his smile. God spoke to me that day, through His faithful servant: through his angelic simplicity, and his unshakeable faith. Monseigneur Foulques made me ashamed

401

of my hazy and uncertain speculations, of my callow, student's conceit in my intelligence (I was twenty, and I thought myself as wise as the wisest).

"I told him that I was living in a heretic seminary: it did not even disturb him, so great already was his trust in God on my account. But he deigned to speak to me at length about heresy, explaining that it was like the Pharisee and, while pretending to serve God, was in fact serving Mammon, and its arrogance and success was largely due to the Jews and other unbelievers who were glad to sow discord among Christians. Unfortunately, the Church in our land at that time, he said, was like the publican who, knowing himself a sinner, humbly beats his breast and trusts himself to God's mercy, but that God would redeem the Church, as he had the Apostle Matthew and Mary Magdalene, and that the harvest to come was great and lovely, and the harvesters few in number. What more can I tell you? On the day after that meeting I quitted my former masters and went back to live in my father's house, and he, following Monseigneur Foulques' advice, no longer opposed my leaning towards medicine. Moreover, Monseigneur Foulques gave me to understand that I might one day, while still continuing to exercise my profession, to the glory of God and the service of my neighbours, take orders and be admitted into a Cistercian monastery. It was he, too, who introduced me to the Blessed Dominic, in the house of Brother Peter Seila, who was then still living in the world, though on the point of taking the habit of a postulant.

"As goodness is cumulative, and after one excellent thing we discover another, yet more admirable, so our Bishop,—of blessed memory—was for my soul a kind of John the Baptist, preparing for the coming of the Saviour (I still call him the Blessed Dominic though I should have said the Saint, but the first title is familiar to us, and has become dear from many years of habit). Oh, the invincible blindness of men who judge everything by opposites! You presume to judge the actions of the saint, and when they are not to your liking you say: 'This was not a man of God, he was only canonised through the intrigues of his friends.' But we, who knew him, we know the real worth of these actions which the world condemns; for the Truth was in him, and it is the mystery of his holiness which serves us as a guide. For he was the sword of the Lord, the sword of gentleness and love, of truth and justice, and because you saw him in his humble garment of flesh, you

402

speak of him as of a man subject to the common passions and weaknesses. Just so did the Jews mistake Jesus Christ.

"How can I in my unworthiness describe him to you? I bear witness to the Truth: I have seen him, heard him, touched him with my own hands. From his eyes, from his countenance, from his whole body, there emanated such an inner brightness that it captivated the spirit at once. I have seen him weep tears of blood over the obduracy of the men of this land. I have seen him shaken and trembling all over with divine love, like a frail sapling when it catches fire. The cries of agony which our sins and our wretchedness would tear from him were like the moans of Christ crucified! And for you, such a man was an object of scandal.

"In your false pride and self-interest you fell into mortal sin, by fighting against God's saint at the same time as the soldiers of the Church. And God has triumphed, leaving you desolate and ashamed; though you fought three against one, exceeding in your rage and cruelty the fiercest of the Saracens.

"A year after my meeting with Monseigneur Foulques, then, I quitted the world. Life was becoming difficult for me in Toulouse, since my conversion had provoked the anger of my former friends. One day the man who had formerly been my teacher, or rather seducer, the deacon Guillaume, who was walking in Capitol square among his disciples, took me publicly on one side and cried shame on me for what he called my ingratitude. I had only two friends at my side, but I answered boldly that I had not been seduced by the lure of wealth and honour, but had obeyed the call of Truth, and that it was worthier to obey God than men, and I did not fear the judgment of the Sanhedrin. Guillaume d'Ayros told me: 'It is you who have gone over to the Sanhedrin, and now you are serving the Synagogue of Satan. I neither judge nor condemn you, but your new masters are seeking to seize me and burn me.' (This he said at a time when the heretic bishop was richer and more revered than Monseigneur Foulques himself, and when no one dared lay hands on a heretic in the open street: and this man, Guillaume d'Ayros, I mean, is still alive and practising his perfidious apostolate at Mirepoix, saving bodies the better to damn souls.) As he said these words, his disciples, my former friends, were all for falling upon me, and I and my friends were already preparing to defend ourselves with our fists, but Guillaume said: 'Do not touch this wretch. Let shame be his only punishment.' Then they spat at me, and abused me, and shouted at me to go and collect my thirty pieces of silver, calling me a weakling who was seduced by the fine words of the Troubadour (that was the name they called Monseigneur Foulques). And the common people who were in the square jeered at me too. . . .

"Not long afterwards the country was devastated by the war. . . . But the saint was more intrepid than St. George and St. Theodore, and he continued to preach in the countryside and in the public squares, armed only with his courage and the cross of Jesus Christ. We had to beg him with tears not to expose himself, but he never heeded our prayers. And the insults he suffered! The wretched peasants heaped abuse on him, and flung stones as he passed by and rotten eggs and filth that for very decency I cannot name. They even refused him the bread he begged so humbly. His life was threatened several times and we still do not know all the dangers to which he exposed himself, since in his humility he preferred not to speak of them. He bore this treatment patiently, and more than patiently, joyfully, because no insult offered to his body ever disturbed him. In his own eyes he was nought and less than nought. But unknown to himself, the fire of God was in him and shone through his body."

The candle had gone out and now the monk was talking in darkness, his voice growing increasingly fervent. "Consider," he said, "wouldn't anyone give cartloads and cartloads of common pebbles for one diamond? Do not thousands of men go to their deaths to save their prince? For all men are mortal flesh and destined to rot, but the worth of a saint is a treasure which sanctifies and redeems a whole nation. Do you presume to mourn for your past riches? Do you presume to regret the loss of money, lands and friends, when, by God's will, it is in our land and through this very war that the powerful athlete has appeared who, with one heave of his shoulder, has shifted the chariot of the Church from the muddy slough in which it was stuck fast? The chariot moves forward slowly for the mud is still deep, but the good road is not far off and our courage is continually drawing new friends to our side. . . . Could you understand, deep down in your heart, the nature of the blessed work to which the Church has called us! It is a work of healing, of purgation and of peace: a work, not of punishment, but of true charity, not of discord but of reconciliation! A work of Truth made flesh and not an affliction of the flesh. If, in our church which is dedicated to the saint, you heard the call of Jesus Christ, is this not a sign telling you clearly in what spirit you ought to live henceforth?"

The monk stopped speaking. Roger could just make out his white robe in the darkness, and heard the click of the rosary in his fingers. He himself remained still and watchful, his arms hugging his knees, afraid to open his mouth because the sound of so many words had left him half-drunk and unsure of his voice. But hearts can speak when lips are dumb, and he knew that in the end his silence would betray him. He began, clumsily: "Brother, I don't know what to say," and immediately sensed that his voice, broken with emotion, was pleading in his favour. He gathered courage. "I don't know what to say, you see me crushed as much by envy as by shame: you were able to approach a man filled with the Spirit of God, and yet you had advanced much further along the road of error than I have ever done! And you were treated with gentleness; neither my lord Bishop nor the Blessed Dominic suspected you of being converted through fear or self-interest. . . . Why is it that today when a man turns towards God he should be repulsed by God's servants?"

"Have I repulsed you, my friend, have I shown you distrust?"

"No, not you, Brother, but those who have been my judges. Did not Brother Peter Seila himself turn to God when he was no longer a young man? Why will they not believe me? Is it because I hesitated at first to compromise people who had done me no harm? Would to God that I, like you, could come near to holy and pious men who might guide me to the way of Truth! If your blessed master were still among us, do you believe that he would have rejected a repentant sinner?"

"While he was amongst us, we walked in the light. . . ." said the monk in a voice throbbing with sadness. "Wretches that we are! The torch is out, when it was scarcely lit. Only consider, he would have been sixty-six now, if he had lived, an age at which others still accomplish great things. God had more need of him in heaven than we upon earth, and yet our hearts will not cease from bleeding. Without him, hearts are possessed by a spirit of discouragement, anger and distrust; our task is too heavy for our weak shoulders and (though every day countless harvesters come to aid our efforts) we are still too few. But Satan, whose sport it is to overthrow the works of God, no longer permits us to show to postulants the same wonderful trust which reigned among us in the first years of our Order. I make you no promises. If the Father

Superior condescends to listen to me, perhaps he will consent to see you and examine your case for himself."

Left alone, Roger lay down on the stone bed, and tried to sleep. He did not succeed; his head was on fire and his whole body shaken by inner trembling. He thought: "Lord Jesus, give me strength to know how to speak to them! When a thing is desired so much, surely it is just that it should be won! You will not deny me this." With the irrational optimism which possesses the imprisoned, he envisaged open doors, sleeping guards, and walls that were easy to climb, all over the monastery. The chain? Lord, if they will put me to work in their forge, or let me chop wood, one blow of an axe will be enough to break a link.

Such a faint hope and so many obstacles! Have *they* ever desired anything as much as this? If the longing ever came upon them to throw aside their habits, they would find an excuse to leave the monastery and never return. The fools, it is only their will which keeps them! They do not even know what it is to have your will annihilated by a chain on your feet.

They come and go, they talk, they are incessantly fabricating imaginary desires and false duties, because free men do not know their own happiness, they live only in pictures. These monks believe themselves the captives of an iron rule, but what if they had to submit to a chain which never allowed them to take one step bigger than another!

You think you are strong because you succeeded in touching that man who is probably more susceptible than others; but what if they bring you face to face tomorrow with some 'man of God' expert at reading thoughts? What words will you find to convince him? How will you speak to him about their saint, whom you have never seen; what praises will you make up that will not sound either cold or forced? *"While he was amongst us we walked in the light. . . ."* Roger tried to remember the monk's words, he saw the burning love that was in them and said to himself: "God! Why hadn't I, too, the chance of knowing this blessed man? But no, they would say to me: could you see him, and never show any love for him? Oh, the madness of a too passionate longing! I am banging my head against a portcullis spiked with steel."

Occasionally in his youth when, as a member of the Count's retinue, Roger had travelled like a pilgrim through all the nations in Christendom, he would fall passionately in love with some proud lady, and since he had little time, and desire, in those days, could drive him to deeds of reckless daring, he would build up an edifice of lies, oaths, threats and entreaties and behave to all appearance like a lover mad with passion; yet however wild his talk he meant every word because his desire was as true as the sun. Then he had obtained his ends, not thanks to his lies and false pretences, but simply because of the passion which breathed through them. Now that state of diabolical inspiration came back to him, though it was keener and more desperate because the lady whose favours were to be won was no mortal woman. Moreover it was not even the lady herself who was to be won over, but jealous guardians, suspicious husbands, whose cruel and cunning hearts he had to conquer, while at the same time making them believe that he did not desire the lady at all, that he was even fleeing her. . . .

"But I love her with such passion that I would gladly feign for her executioners all the love which burns in my heart for her, so that I might only reach her; and truly, love I have in plenty, only the words are not the same—whether I call it a vocation, or devotion to their holy house, or St. Dominic, God, or salvation! If they will only let me enter their cloisters, if they will only be merciful and remove my chains (I will wound my ankles until my condition is pitiful to see), then, thank God, I know the way to the door, and the door is often left open, because people are coming in all day to accuse themselves. Once in the street I can run straight to La Daurade and from there to the market place. Oh, Lord, how can I think of it without my heart breaking? Can it be possible that at this moment I am twenty yards from that street, where there are men walking by who are free to go back to their own homes? Twenty yards, and this stupid man talks to me about his Blessed Dominic and his conversion and the chariot of the Church! How dare he take me for a man like himself, when I have chains on my feet?

"Good Brother, if Jesus Christ had put all the Jews in prison, and had chained and beaten them, all, or nearly all, of them would have been miraculously converted, and maybe the hope of getting out of prison would have made them all sing such hosannas to Him that they could have been heard as far as Rome! He was God, and stronger than you, methinks, but not so clever, since He never thought of it. Not so charitable either, since He let them be damned and bring on themselves an everlasting curse;

407

He brought them no sword but words and sermons, a ghostly sword and truly an object of ridicule! Indeed, it appears that He had no desire to address men in chains, and cared little for such a flock. Jesus Christ, Brothers, is an honest fisherman who does not poison the water in order to catch fish, since that is to get one's miraculous draught of fishes a little too cheap.

"Brothers, the love I bear you is so great that I would damn myself to please you! Speak to me, teach me, let me know how to win your favour, I who have no friends to sell, nor great secrets to betray, nor honour to lose, who have only my soul, my soul, for I swear to you that I have one, and my soul is consumed with longing for God. Teach me your truth, since in truth I am already converted and one with you. Do not damn my soul by making me doubt your mercy!"

The Father Superior and the Father Prior had little time to waste on a dubious convert; yet Roger de Montbrun succeeded in astonishing them by his extreme ardour and humility, if not altogether in convincing them. His case was unimportant in itself, but the man was worthy of attention on account of his birth and reputation, and, all things considered, more useful in the monastery than in prison. The Preaching Friars of Toulouse were experiencing considerable difficulties at that time, on account of the special authority for this office of the Inquisition conferred on them by the Pope. Brother Peter Seila and Brother Guillaume Arnaud were performing their task with admirable thoroughness, but as a result of the obduracy of the people of Toulouse and the laxity of the civil authorities,, this task, taken up in obedience, was causing endless trouble to all the Dominican priories in the land and especially to the one in Toulouse. Altogether, in the last two years the Preachers had achieved many forced conversions but had made more enemies than friends. It was for this reason that the Prior wrote to Brother Peter Seila requesting authority to keep Roger de Montbrun in the monastery as a penitent: six months previously, four other prisoners had been adjudged worthy of this favour, in view of their sincere repentance, and they were progressing in humility and obedience.

After a week of prayer and fasting Roger de Montbrun was therefore admitted to the monastery as a guest and a prisoner on parole, since his fervour was so great and apparently sincere that it seemed cruel to send him back to prison, and furthermore his example could be an edifying one to visitors and even for the novices. He was still chained and was put to the task of cleaning out the latrines. (He had humbly asked for this himself, but another reason, it must be admitted, was the shortage of labour: through hard work, fasting and mortification, many of the monks fell ill.)

The cesspit had to be cleaned out every day and fresh straw and lime thrown into it, while the dung was loaded on to barrows —and how Roger envied the lay Brothers who twice a week drove the putrid, black and stinking carts as far as the Garonne. They went out of the great gate in the courtyard holding by the bridle a little bald, grey, half-blind donkey that in Roger's eyes was finer than any king's mount. He had thought to find life easier on the day when he could see with his own eyes men who were free to cross the blessed threshold which led out into the world of the living, but the mere sight of that door made him mad with grief. His work was hard because the weather was hot, and at times the smell from the ditch was so strong it made him reel, while big black flies would settle on his face and on the sores round his ankles. But instead of daunting his spirits all these miseries only raised them higher. "Even if I perish, even if I kill myself, I shall never beg for mercy: they shall see how far I am sincere!" Roger's companion in his work was another convertite, also chained, but younger than himself and of a ferocious temper. He was a former blacksmith from the district of St. Cyprien who had once been a believer but was now afire with a holy detestation of heresy. This man sometimes talked to Roger during the hour allowed them for recreation.

"I was led astray by my wife," he would say, "but when I was in prison I saw what these 'Christians' were like: thieves who sought only to rob us of our money for their own Church. I had to sell my shop and go and work for strangers in order to pay for my father's Consolamentum. But afterwards, I realised that this was all false, that my father had damned himself, because they dug him up and burned him, and the Christians who gave him consolation have fled into the region of Lantarès. . . . It was Brother Alberic of Montpellier who made me see the truth, and showed me how Jesus Christ suffered for us, and how He redeemed us by giving His true blood and His true tears for us; and I took communion in the cathedral of St. Stephen, on Ascension Day, and on that day was I set aflame with the love of God."

Sometimes this man managed to spill filth or lime on his

companion's injured feet, purposely intending to mortify him by so doing. The next day he would tell Roger: "You should do the same to me, because we are here to help one another learn patience and humility."

"I had rather learn first to control myself," Roger answered with some asperity. "I might be capable of taking pleasure in mortifying you." Then the erstwhile blacksmith—whose name was Bernard—said that true charity lay in self-forgetfulness and in thinking only of the salvation of others. In fact, Roger certainly did learn lessons of patience and humility through this man, and yet more from the work to which he was put. He stank so that in the refectory and in church he was obliged to stand apart from the rest, close to the door, and dared not touch the holy water stoup with his hand. For fifteen days he bore this existence with such meekness that Brother Ricord, under whose supervision he was placed, said: "This man has really been touched by grace, if after the worldly life filled with honours which he has led he does not murmur against such a penance." And on Assumption Day Roger prayed in the monastery church, kneeling near the door and prostrating himself and weeping, for his heart was breaking with grief at the thought that on that very day, but for Rachel's imprudence (or rather but for his own imprudence), he would have been able to escape from prison.

That day there were numerous visitors praying in the new church; clerks, canons, and wealthy laymen, as well as relatives and friends of the Brothers of the Order, and Roger saw more than one face he knew pass by, though he himself was not over-anxious to be recognised. However, after Mass the Prior sent for him to go to the parlour where his friend the canon Raymond de Cahuzac wished to see him. "Father, will you expose me to temptation? I no longer wish to see anything which may remind me of the crimes of my past life." Nevertheless, he had to obey. Dressed in a clean habit, but with chapped hands and his feet swollen from the chain round his ankles, Roger hardly dared lift his head in his friend's presence. His short hair was grey and dirty, and his face so thin that there seemed nothing of it but nose, eyes and mouth. Raymond was unchanged: the same strong, rather stout figure, and high-coloured cheeks.

"Ah, Roger, what a pretty state I find you in! What news shall I give your friends of you?"

"I have no more friends according to this world's usage," said

Roger. "And there is nothing pitiful about the state in which you find me: I am not like the wicked rich man, I have no wish to receive my reward in this world."

"How can they leave a man like you in this wretched condition?" exclaimed the canon.

Roger made an effort not to turn and look at the Brother porter who was listening to them. "I can never pay dearly enough for the sins of my life. This you speak of is a favour, not a punishment."

"I should certainly praise God for filling you with so sincere a repentance. But must they break the instrument which can be useful? Who would not pity you, seeing you in this condition?"

"I do not ask for pity," said Roger. "Why should I not be privileged to share the burden of God's poor?"

"What shall I tell your friends, Roger?"

"What you please. I have found peace. May they too find it one day."

The day after the feast of the Assumption, no doubt as a result of the canon's complaints, Roger de Montbrun was released from his chains. The sores on his ankles were so infected that it was becoming dangerous to leave the iron rings on them.

But it can happen that by attempting to aim too high one breaks the bowstring. Roger found the fearful joy which he experienced at the moment of this second victory transformed into bitterness. It may have been the result of excitement, or because the wounds on his ankles were in actual fact extremely serious, but that same evening Roger fell into such a high fever that his life was feared for. The strange thing was that while he was still wearing his chains, these wounds, though they caused him exquisite suffering, were a source of pure rejoicing, and he almost cursed his body's amazing resistance. "Anyone else," he thought, "would have developed gangrene from this." Yet now, on the day the gyves which encircled his red and swollen ankles were finally unlocked and his feet became as light as feathers, the pain came galloping up and seized hold on his flesh until he could almost watch the sores growing worse before his eyes. He told himself: "It is nothing. It does not matter any more," and he forced himself to walk without limping. All day long he kept an impassive face at his work, in the refectory and at prayers, but the pain was mounting to his head and his whole body was on fire.

Then he found himself lying on a bed with a mattress in the monastery infirmary, with a wet cloth on his head and a tourniquet on his right arm, and could see a dark trickle of blood dripping into a bowl from the vein in his elbow. The monastery barber was grinning at him silently, showing huge, yellow teeth, and in the light from the candle the man's gigantic shadow wavered on the low, limewashed arches. "What dormitory is this?"

"The infirmary." At this point Roger experienced a few seconds of anguished lucidity.

"What if I am delirious?" he thought, "suppose I give myself away? I don't even know how I was brought here, so how can I answer for what I may say? Cursed life! When I thought I was at least master of my thoughts. May I be deservedly called a coward if I betray myself!" Pretending to be half-delirious (his mind was, in fact, extremely confused) he said that he wanted to see St. Dominic. After that he was well and truly delirious for three hours and went on calling out and invoking the saint, saying over and over again: "St. Dominic. St. Dominic," with the persistence of a man under torture repeatedly asserting his innocence. The five sick monks and the attendant listened to him, shaking their heads, and saying: "How can he call on the saint like that if he has never seen him? Has he appeared to him in a dream?" Deaths were frequent in the monastery in the hot weather because the monks, exhausted by fasting, fell an easy prey to dysentery and other malignant fevers. Prayers were said for the sick man with no bitterness or sadness, but rather in admiration of the divine mercy which had permitted the sinner to repent in time.

In the morning the fever abated, and since in a monastery boasting a new saint the monks were looking eagerly for miracles, the barber, and Brother Peter, the doctor, saw a miracle in this. When Roger opened his eyes he found himself looking at his two bandaged feet which were resting on a cushion placed on the frame of the wooden bed, while the doctor, whom he knew all too well, was holding his wrist and counting his heartbeats. In the morning light his eyes were bright and full of a strange solicitude.

"Give thanks to him who has given you back your life," he said. "I believe you are out of danger."

"I have every reason to thank God," said Roger.

"Yes, God, whose will it has been to glorify His servant

Dominic once more. These are not light words, I know my art well enough to bear witness that if you had not invoked the saint this night you might perhaps not be here speaking to me now."

"I have no doubts of your art or of the virtues of the saint," said Roger, "but why should I have deserved a special favour?" Brother Peter said that divine favours were never deserved, and began to explain why Roger owed the saint a special gratitude. "We must keep ourselves," he said, "from falling, by excessive modesty, into the sin of incredulity and failure to recognise the gifts of God." Roger, who felt in a mood to hang himself, said that if he had a miracle to thank for all the serious wounds he had received and recovered from, then he had had a dozen miraculous escapes already. Brother Peter did him too much honour, he said, and he did not remember having invoked St. Dominic. For once he was sincere, for, sensing obscurely that he was being spoken to with respect, he began to feel arrogant in spite of himself, and he was too weak to control what he said. But his very frankness stood him in better stead than an affectation of piety would have done, since the doctor (who was fond of him) told himself: "Surely if this man was trying to please us he would have leaped upon the opportunity to praise the saint? But in his humility he prefers to be taken for an ingrate."

Roger thought: "What do they expect of me? Am I in a fit state to argue with them? What further admissions are they asking of me?" Aloud he said: "As soon as my feet are better I wish to resume my chains and my work in the yard."

"We shall see about that," said Brother Peter. "Do not think about your chains; as a doctor I cannot allow you to resume them. Be vigilant and pray. We are praying for you."

Roger let his head fall back on the pillow and closed his eyes: someone put a rosary into his hands. "Lord, how good it is to rest in a real bed! This man knows his job, and since it appears he is so set on curing me, he will cure me." Deep down inside him, in spite of his bitterness, Roger felt some stupid, animal gratitude to the man: "*I never let them go beyond fifty strokes. . . .*" Sometimes he caught himself dreaming, like a child, of the day when, free and armed, he would meet this man somewhere in a defile at Rouergue or Mirepoix, with some other Brothers on a mission for the Inquisition, and he, Roger, would say to his companions: "Do what you like with the others, but let this one go. Merely beat him with an oxhide whip, for such treatment is not prejudicial to the health—fifty strokes, no more, not one more. . . . Afterwards let him go where he will."

Roger dared not give way too much to these thoughts; they were like a heady wine which at first intoxicates and then weakens and irritates. "Get yourself out of this first," he told himself, "only cowards are content with imaginary revenge. Don't let things slide. If they will not 'allow' you to resume your chain, it is in order to watch you more closely, and that is why they have invented this story about a miracle. They are going to watch you to see if you are sincere."

Thinking this over, Roger told himself it was unlikely that six monks (there were six of them, including the infirmary Brother) had invented a concerted lie, and he must really have invoked the saint of the monastery in his delirium. His first thought was: "Thank God! Better to rave about that than something else," and then he was afraid: what if this Blessed Dominic, who had been a man of prayer and strong in spirit, had really appeared to him in his hour of anguish? What if he really possessed the gift of miracles? "If I, who pray only with my lips, have been able to address myself to him in my delirium, is that the effect of my cunning or his power? And what if he really is a saint, and if these men who claim to be his disciples are really God's servants, and if I were, as they say I am, blinded by partisan passions to the point of mistaking the truth of the Church?" Turning these problems over in his mind, Roger fell asleep and saw in a dream St. Dominic, just as the Brothers had described him, in the shape of a thin, upright monk with a handsome face, fair hair and brilliant, shining blue eyes and rays like sword blades encircling his head. When he awoke Roger's head felt heavy and his heart was pounding, and he knew that this was not a good dream, for the joy he had felt in contemplating the saint was a joy like that he had felt in taking communion in the cathedral on the day of his reconciliation. It was not really the saint (assuming the man to have been a saint) who had appeared to him in his dream, but his devilish opposite, made to tempt feeble hearts. And Roger was not yet stupid enough to succumb to such temptations.

That day Roger really feared for his reason. His body was broken and drained of all desires and he almost believed that he was fighting for nothing, that he would never leave his particular hell. He was fed, watched over and cared for by Brother Peter and the infirmary Brother and responded to their kindness with

414

shamefaced gratitude, as a dog which has been beaten by its master responds to that master's caresses. For six days he lived in this way, and on the seventh was able to get up. He was taken to the church, where the Father Superior himself examined his mended ankles and concluded that gangrene had been averted by a miracle. Roger made a solemn vow to devote himself particularly to the service of St. Dominic; he was also given permission to place a request with the See of Toulouse for the annulment of his marriage since he had, he said, stolen Guillelme de Layrac away from her lawful husband, André de Vitry, and this André was still living. Once free of his marriage ties in this way, he hoped he might be admitted to the honour of a noviciate in the monastery of the Preaching Friars if ever his condemnation was quashed by the court of Rome. But on the way from the church to the refectory he was already thinking of ways to reach the main gate of the monastery. Lord God, he had still got nowhere! It is hard to fight for something you have to pretend you do not want.

At night, as he lay struggling against the fleas whose biting he had to endure without scratching for fear of disturbing his sleeping companions, Roger racked his brains to find some way of gaining admission to the paupers' refectory, from which there was a door leading directly into the street. He dared not solicit the favour of serving the beggars' meals for fear of attracting suspicion. (How could he know that the monks were not, like himself, obsessed day and night by the image of open doorways leading to the street? They believed him to be a sincerely pious man.) His neighbour in the dormitory, a young lay Brother named Bertrand (the name endeared him to Roger), brought an appalling number of bugs and fleas from the paupers' refectory every day on his clothes. The monastery as a whole was extremely clean, but the paupers' refectory, and also the hospital where they were cared for, was a veritable citadel of vermin, as young Bertrand complained: "For the honour of serving God's poor," Roger told him one day, "I would put up with much worse troubles!" He regretted this confidence which had escaped him in a careless moment.

Weeks passed and the days grew shorter; the October rains filled the tanks to overflowing, and the covered rear courtyards became a sea of yellow mud, forcing the monks to tuck up their robes almost to the knee as they walked. Warm, wet winds blew away tiles, and rattled the wooden scaffolding around the new

415

church, on which work had come to a standstill. Brother Peter Seila and Brother Guillaume Arnaud came back to the monastery after the wine harvest and announced to the assembled chapter that they intended to pursue the heretics in Toulouse with increased severity, since their insolence was now beyond all bounds and turning to open rebellion. They said that numerous powerful personages would be compromised, and the tyrant (by which they meant the Count) covered with confusion, because his connivance with the heretics would at last be proved. "We must prepare ourselves to face hard times, and if we fail we shall at least have earned the martyr's crown, for truly the hatred of our enemies for those who labour in the Lord's vineyard passeth all understanding."

One cold October morning, Roger begged his director for the favour of taking Bertrand's place in the paupers' refectory as the youth was ill and could barely stand on his feet. Brother Ricord, himself weary and preoccupied, made no objection.

Roger entered the huge, dark refectory, carrying a pannier full of new bread on his back and a big basket on his left arm. There were four lay Brothers and two postulants to a hundred or so beggars, each of whom had to be served quickly in his turn, and the beggars, who were not remarkable for sense or cultivation, pushed and shoved and quarrelled over the biggest pieces, over-turning the benches and often enough hurling their wooden bowls, the property of the monastery, at one another's heads. After every meal there were some bowls missing and others broken. The beggars felt so much at home in the refectory that they had no fear of the Brothers who served them; they were treated with honour because they had to be served as Jesus Christ Himself should be served. Yet these ragged, stinking paupers, who sprawled over the tables and squatted on the ground, scratching their sores, called to mind the Devil much rather than Jesus Christ.

Roger was trembling so violently as he made his way down the tables, distributing slices of bread and handfuls of nuts, that the lay Brother who accompanied him asked: "Have you a fever?" "Yes, I think so." He scarcely saw the hands stretched out to-wards him, the thin, bearded faces, the gleaming eyes: a deathly languor invaded his legs. The door was open, wide open, but two legless cripples were sitting on the step holding their crutches, arguing with the Brother porter. Roger went up to the two men

and bent down to offer them bread, one piece between the two—
he noticed that one of the men had thrown his cloak on the ground
the better to scratch himself. As the two cripples snatched at the
piece of bread, Roger jerked his arm and sent the basket of nuts
flying, scattering its contents over the flags with a cheerful clatter.
At once pandemonium broke out. The men sitting on the benches
were determined not to be outstripped by those on the floor,
while the two cripples propelled themselves forward, using their
crutches to scoop up the nuts, and almost knocked Roger over.
All at once he found himself in the doorway. The Brother porter
said: "Now look what you've done!" and went into the refectory
to separate the struggling men. Roger picked up the cloak
belonging to the beggar, flung it over his head and stepped outside, almost fainting with the effort it cost him not to run. *"Lord,
Lord, what have I done? All is lost."*

He did not see the kennel, or the monastery walls, or the
passers-by who drew aside saying: "Look at these beggars: they
ask for alms at the monastery gates and yet still manage to be
drunk so early in the morning!"

Roger had no idea where he was going any longer; he rounded
the corner of the monastery wall, went down an alley and hid
in a gateway behind a pile of wood. For five minutes he huddled
there, clutching his filthy cloak feverishly around him, as though
it were a magic cape which could make him invisible. Shouts
were ringing in his head and he realised with terror that he could
not tell whether the cries were real or not. "Stop thief! Stop
thief!" But the alley was empty.

Roger stood up, shivering as though he had been tortured,
and walked on slowly, keeping close to the walls; he had to make
a terrible effort to remember the plans of escape that for six
months had been ripening so carefully in his head. The square of
La Daurade, then the covered market: everything hung on
reaching the market; once there, they might as well look for a
needle in a haystack. But he could not seem to recognise the streets
any more; bells were ringing for the end of Mass and the good
people were coming out of church. Shambling and hobbling,
Roger managed to drag himself as far as the square in front of
La Daurade, where he mingled with the crowd of beggars
huddled in rows along the steps. "Hey, there! You, stranger,
back where you came from."

"Maybe he comes from St. Sernin. He's not blind or crippled

417

and here he comes eating the bread of folk who belong here!"

"Mercy, brothers," said Roger, "I am sick." He was so sure he could really hear those cries of 'Stop thief!' that the chiming bells and the voices of those speaking to him seemed to come from a very long way off. But he did as the others were doing and held out a hand from beneath his flea-ridden cloak. It was thin enough, but, he noticed with terror, much too clean and well-shaped. (Ah, why didn't they let me go on working in the latrines!) He was sure the eyes of the whole city were staring at him. He could see no soldiers or monastery guards and thought: "What are they doing? Is this some trick to capture me?"

All day long he wandered about the market place, lingering in front of displays of fresh fish and cheese: he was not hungry, on the contrary the very smell of food sickened him, but he instinctively sought out places where the crowd was thickest and the people most poorly clad. Housewives jostled him roughly, banging their baskets against his arms, and saying: "That one looks to me like a pickpocket." However, one woman took a small tench, which she had just bought, out of her basket and gave it to him. "Here, poor fellow, I'll swear you've had nothing to eat for two days at least." Roger wept. He felt as though he were seeing a human being for the first time in ten months, and, had he dared, he would have kissed the woman's feet. He did not know what it was, this savage joy, the joy of being treated, not like a man in prison or hunted, but like a free man whose only misfortune was to be hungry. He hid the cold, slippery fish inside his shirt (lacking the energy to eat it) and wandered off again, allowing his body's trembling to calm down a little. They were certainly not on his track, and either they were not hunting for him, or they were looking elsewhere.

At nightfall he went and knocked on the main gate of the Cissac mansion. The porter, who was already beginning to draw the locks and bolts for the night, opened the judas a crack and said: "On your way before the curfew sounds."

"I have come to see the Lord Raymond-Jourdain, I have a message for him."

"Give it to me, I belong here."

"I promised to give the message to Lord Raymond-Jourdain himself. It comes from his brother-in-law in Milan."

"Speak softly, you fool. Do you think you're in Milan now?"

The door was opened. Raymond-Jourdain was not anxious to

418

have it known that his sister and brother-in-law were in Lombardy. Roger entered the courtyard, keeping his head down to avoid being recognised by the stable-lads who were crowding round, inquisitive and suspicious, ready to resort to fisticuffs.

"Well, say what you have to."

"I must see Lord Raymond-Jourdain."

"At this time of night? He is at prayers and has given orders he is not to be disturbed. You'll pay dearly if you are a spy; we've had trouble enough today already."

"If you don't believe me, go and say this to Lord Raymond-Jourdain: 'Blithe springtime in Toulouse.' If he won't see me after that you can throw me out." (These words were the first line of a song which the two friends had composed together long before.)

Five minutes later, Raymond-Jourdain received his friend in the little turret room which he used as an oratory; he seemed worried and irritable. "Roger, what are you doing here? They have already been here from the monastery, at midday, to see if you were at my house. They will be back again tomorrow with a warrant to search the house."

More bewildered than angry, Roger let his beggar's cloak fall to the floor and took a step backwards. "Is this the way you welcome me? This is the last straw."

"Roger, I don't know what's the matter with me. You can see for yourself: I am expecting a summons from the Holy Office any day now and today these two monks called me a heretic and a rebel, accused me of harbouring heretics, and God knows what else, while you had given me no warning of this. Those who helped you escape might have found you a refuge for the first night."

Roger sank down on to a cushioned chest near the door and dropped his head on his hands. He had dreamed so much of this first meeting. "Now then," he said to himself, "am I going to weep in front of him?" He sat up. "Raymond, I shall not stir from here. If they find me here you will be the one compromised, because as far as I am concerned if I am captured or not it is all one. . . . It is up to you to give me up or hide me."

Raymond-Jourdain was wringing his hands and biting his lip. "Ah, that you should say such a thing to me, Roger! May God forgive you. If you had only warned me, if I could have prepared." He paced backwards and forwards between the chest and

419

the prie-dieu, then suddenly he turned and flung both arms round Roger, gripping him by the shoulder and kissing him on both cheeks. "What a way to welcome you! Look, what a way to welcome you! Only yesterday, would I ever have believed it?"

Roger returned his kisses, giving way easily to an emotion that, even so, was not without a tinge of bitterness. "You didn't think I'd get away with it? Neither did I! But what did you think then? That I really had turned traitor?"

Raymond-Jourdain said no, but in his shy, almost nervous expression Roger thought he glimpsed a shadow of regret. "You did think that, didn't you, Raymond? You said to yourself: so much the better, he is at peace, he is saving his soul?"

"Roger, no one knows me like you, so what is the use of my lying to you? I don't know what I believed, so many people are losing their heads these days. I have never thought ill of you, but in matters of faith, who can judge? I heard through friends that you were supposed to have repented, and it gave me no pleasure, no, because I thought: they must have made him suffer!"

"Raymond, you know that if I let them catch me now, it means the stake without any form of trial; and I promise you I shall not let them take me alive."

"Now what? Are you threatening me? Me, who would hide you if it were to mean the loss of half I own? I'll help you to leave Toulouse with some of my cousin Guillaume de Brissac's people, as we had arranged. The main thing is to find you a good hiding place for two or three days in case they search the house. I cannot count on all my servants."

Thereupon, Raymond-Jourdain summoned his eldest son and the two of them led Roger down to the cellars, made him up a bed from a bearskin behind a pile of barrels and brought him the remains of their own dinner. In order not to attract suspicion they retired to bed in their own rooms and Roger was left alone, almost as much a prisoner as he had been the day before, but infinitely more weary and anxious.

"Ah, all perfect and too much desired lady, how hard it is to win you. Shall I ever find the way to your bed? Like a madman I believed that it was enough to cross a threshold to possess You, and now fresh doors are shutting in my face on all sides, and I know You who elude me still are behind all the doors. Cruel and fickle lady, you scorn those who have once lost you."

420

"A free man, you who now shake at every glance, at every sound? You did not tremble so much in the monastery. Now see what a sad state you are in because you thought to win me: your enemies are searching for you, your friends fear you, and death dogs your every step." Ah, he had been mad enough to think that he would find his freedom in Raymond-Jourdain's house—yet now she had flown from there across the Garonne and into the mountains; he still had to cross the threshold of the Cissac house, and the barricades at the main gate of the city and how many other doors? How many bridges? How many crossroads?

The next day the house was searched and Roger had to hide in an enormous vat which was almost empty but still contained enough wine to marinade his arms and legs unpleasantly as he crouched uncomfortably inside on all fours. Raymond-Jourdain hauled him out half-stifled and drunk from the smell of wine, staggering, soaked through and plastered with lees. They looked at one another for a moment in the light of the candle which Raymond-Jourdain had set down on the ground, and both of them burst out laughing, wild laughter which echoed for a long time in the hollow cellar. "This is madness, Raymond! Where else must we hide to escape them?"

"Next time it will be in a mousehole. They won't come back in a hurry. I followed them to the door with so many complaints and recriminations that they couldn't think how to get rid of me. Don't be afraid: I have the cellar keys at my belt. I'll bring you some clothes and some ink to darken your hair and a mirror. Once you've dyed your hair the Devil himself wouldn't know you. Wait, I'll ask my wife for some black and red paints and you can see what you can do with them. Even I won't know who you are."

"This is excellent," Roger said, almost happily. "Why can't I change my body too and be reborn in a new flesh? The heretics claim that that happens to the souls of sinners. Raymond, have you ever thought about it?"

"How can we tell? As you get older you think about it more and more. And if we were certain of using up all our chances of salvation in a single lifetime it would be enough to make one lock oneself up in a monastery without delay. . . . It's not much, a single lifetime." The two friends sat on the beansacks, with the big candlestick standing on the ground in front of them, talking of faith and salvation, as in days gone by, and wondering what

421

consciousness the soul retained of its past life. Roger said that he would still prefer to weep over his sins for all eternity if at that price he could also remember the joys of his earthly life: surely the worst hell would be to forget everything? "How would that be hell? You can't suffer from what you don't remember. Supposing we had already forgotten a dozen fathers and mothers, and a dozen mistresses? Supposing we were once Saracens or Germans?"

"*You* really have such thoughts?" exclaimed Roger, "Since when?"

Raymond bit his lip and looked the other way. "Does he think," Roger wondered, "does he think that perhaps, if they recaptured me, I might tell them he had spoken to me about such things?" He did not feel like talking any more.

Left to himself, he set about darkening his hair and eyebrows with the paint brush which Raymond-Jourdain had brought him—feeling a childish regret for his still red locks and the copper-coloured hairs of his eyebrows: he certainly looked younger once he was dark-haired but he found his appearance a trifle sinister. It was like a mask, a clown's head from a carnival. "I am fated never to be done with disguises. What is left now of the man I once was? For me, everything, but for others, not much." He did not know how truly he spoke.

In the evening, Raymond-Jourdain came to see him, bringing a haunch of venison, some pepper, some white bread and a candle in his sleeve. He seemed depressed and scarcely commented on the changed appearance, of which, in spite of everything, Roger was considerably vain. "Yes, yes," he said, "you look very funny. It's much better like that, much better. Give me that goblet and I'll draw you some wine."

"Is something worrying you, Raymond?"

Raymond-Jourdain came back with the full goblet, took a sip himself and held it out to his friend. "The Brissacs," he said. "There are some people who say 'yes' one day and 'no' the next. Don't worry about it, I'll send my son with you, but we'll have to wait a few more days, because I'm still under suspicion."

"Yes, I know. People are frightened," said Roger. "As though the Preaching Friars were the Devil incarnate. But, good God, the Preachers are scared too! Only they have the sense not to show it."

As his friend still said nothing he did not like to drink. "You've heard something else that you don't want to tell me?"

"No, but frankly, Roger, you don't know what they are saying in the city and how difficult it is to escape calumny these days. Perhaps it would be better if I warned you that certain of our friends wish you ill."

Suddenly Roger no longer felt at all thirsty, and he put the goblet down on the ground.

"Who wishes me ill? Why? What do they believe?"

"How do I know...?"

"I will tell you: they think the Preachers wouldn't have received me into their seminary unless I had given them firm proof of my goodwill? Is that what they think?"

"Exactly."

"It's not true, Raymond! What could I have said? I did not mention the names of any of my friends or people who were concealing their faith. Everything I could 'reveal' the whole city has known for a long time."

"Some people say you could have learned names from your brother, because two months ago some secret believers were accused, and when people knew that you were doing penance in the monastery rumour had it that this was through you."

"Listen, Raymond, who accuses me? The Brissacs? I will tell you something. People who have given away more names than they need in order to escape imprisonment are the first to accuse others in order to divert suspicion from themselves! Bertrand said nothing to anyone, not even his wife, and much less to me. You must look among his own friends for people who could have given away secrets that Bertrand might have known."

"That's what I told them."

"But I could not have done so, even if I had wanted to, Raymond! I knew nothing. It is the people who are spreading such rumours about me who should be suspected. Why daren't you tell me their names?"

"What is the use of stirring up dirt? The Preachers have done well with their secret courts: anyone can accuse you without proof. People distrust their own children, and strangers much more so. As long as we have this plague within our walls, we shall not be able to live like men. . . . And besides, what need had you, Roger, to consort with such people in order to regain your freedom? You should have foreseen what people would say, and known that you were risking your reputation."

"Me? Much good my reputation would have done me in my

grave! Had I any choice? Bertrand had a good reputation when he was in prison. And others too. Much joy my reputation would have brought me in a place where I had nothing but rats and spiders to keep me company. According to you I would be better off in a dungeon, would I? Perhaps you are right, because I can see that there is no more freedom for me: or at least, only one kind of freedom: to stand face to face with those good Friars and tell them what I think of them, and hit them, right and left, and send them all to the gibbet, one after another. That is freedom! Nothing else. And to think you believed me capable of loving men of their kind!"

"I said nothing of the sort, so don't lose your temper like that! Considering the laws we have now, is it surprising that people should spread malicious gossip?"

"But you could really think I had recanted!" Roger returned continually to this idea, finding it more and more intolerable. "You believed that of *me*? When I have seen people burned— and stood twenty paces from the pyre. And when they took Bertrand, and first they made all his teeth drop out and his hair turn white and his legs rot away . . . and then they took Rachel away too, and roasted her alive—they made her mad first and then roasted her afterwards. And I know what the underground dungeons are like, and how they torture people, and how they drive them to betray themselves and betray others, and I know the torture by words, and how they dig your grave under your feet, inch by inch; and after all that you could believe that I was capable of loving them!"

"Yes, you did well, Roger, you did well. I am not blaming you." To his surprise Roger suddenly noticed how much his friend had aged—as though the eternal youth which, for every man, lingers on the faces of the friends of his youth had deserted these features, making them suddenly those of a stranger. Here was no longer anything but a man like other men, like thousands of others, any man, no longer very young or very handsome, heavier, dull . . . and what made me love him so dearly? For twenty years we fought side by side; now that time is gone for ever, and we are no longer comrades.

And who knows whether tomorrow he will not be in my place? "Raymond, I ask nothing more of you than a little money for the journey and a horse. I don't want to expose you, or your son, to danger. All he need do is let me follow him as far as the market square, and there give me the horse to hold and leave me. When I have re-established my honour I will come back to see you. We will raise our goblets at the Count's table that day, and he will return my possessions to me and I shall be able to revenge myself on my enemies."

"May that day come! May our children, Roger, live in a land where there is respect for the law. How can men live without law? They become like beasts. May not one of these people who are making a mockery of the laws be left in Toulouse!"

They emptied a cup of wine to this wish, and then Raymond went away, double locking the cellar door. "Another prison," thought Roger, "what difference does it make that he does it to protect me? It is still another lock and key. Who will be watching for me in the street when he lets me out at dawn? What man will run all the way to the monastery tomorrow to tell them Pierre-Bernard de Cissac has left his house in the company of a suspicious-looking man?" He amused himself for an hour with smothering his face in paint, and by dint of rubbing it in all directions finally achieved a ruddy, rather dirty complexion. "Lots of drunkards have that sort of colouring. Who would believe I have come out of prison?" he said to himself. But it was an unpleasant experience, not to recognise himself at all any more, as if another man were watching him from the other side of the mirror.

That night, Roger tried in vain to get some sleep; he kept thinking he heard knocking at the door and voices; he imagined Brother Alberic himself keeping watch in the street outside the house. . . . "It would be madness to go out! It would mean the stake for sure."

But the thought of having to live even one more day in confinement terrified him even more; he even began to suspect Raymond-Jourdain of meaning to keep him cloistered up for ever in his cellar, for fear of the Preaching Friars, and also so that his cousins should not say that he had helped a traitor to escape (who knows, perhaps these people believe I have been released on purpose, that I am being used as a spy?). Lord God! To have escaped from one's enemies only to find one's best friend become one's gaoler, that was an unforeseen situation! Surely if he had been honest he would have trusted me with the key? Didn't he say himself that you can't trust anyone? I have nothing to lose (except my life) but what about him? He has his reputation, his fortune, his wife, his children and grandchildren. (Yes, two grandchildren already. How old we are getting.)

Roger passed such a bad night that he almost regretted the monastery. The candle sputtered dismally round the edges of the candlestick and then died. Nothing but darkness. Ah, what madness! Why hadn't he taken advantage of the flame while he had it, and set fire to the cellar! "They would have seen the smoke coming out of the ventilators, they would have come with buckets of water, and I could have taken advantage of the uproar to escape. . . ." In the midst of such stupid thoughts Roger at last fell asleep and was woken by Raymond-Jourdain shaking his shoulder and saying: "It's dawn, let's go. My son is waiting for you." Roger flung himself into his friend's arms and wept unashamedly for a long time. "Raymond, may God reward you in paradise. May I never bring trouble on you, and forgive that which I have caused you. Forgive all my offences during the thirty years we have been friends. God knows when we shall meet again."

"Soon," said Raymond-Jourdain, weeping himself. "Soon, God willing, Roger. Come, quickly."

Roger went out into the street, holding the reins of young Pierre-Bernard's horse. It was a dark, rainy morning, and the streets were already crowded with the carts of water-carriers and sellers of vegetables, so that they had to keep close to the walls. At the intersections of roads a small, cold wind lashed their faces with rain. The bells were ringing for terce. "This is the time they open the city gates," said Pierre-Bernard. "You will get through easily. There are a group of pilgrims come from Montauban waiting in the square of La Dalbade ready to set out as soon as the portcullis is raised."

There were a good thirty pilgrims, more than ten of them on horseback. The young man dismounted and held his companion's stirrup, though Roger was so tired and shivering with cold and excitement, and with fear more than either, that he had to make three attempts before he succeeded in mounting. Raymond-Jourdain had not let him down: the animal was in perfect condition. "Gee up! Farewell, Pierre-Bernard, farewell. One day, if God wills, I will give you two pure-bred arabs in return for this horse, and I shall not have paid you a tenth of his value."

Roger passed through the gate in the wake of the pilgrims and rode a good three leagues along the Garonne in their company.

It was a dreary day and there was a thick mist; on the watch-towers and castle keeps along the river lights were flickering on and off, and the barges crawled slowly forward, hung about with lanterns, and hooting incessantly; as they passed, the small boats moored along the banks bobbed and rose on the water with a dull slapping sound.

For eight days, Roger pursued his pilgrimage towards freedom. He was plunged into a state of intense desolation, resulting from a vast weariness which left him unable to understand why he had tried so hard to escape from prison.

He slept in pilgrim inns or in barns made of wattle and daub which the local lords of the manor put at the disposal of the poorest travellers. Since the war, travellers of all sorts had been much too numerous, especially in the autumn, when people from the north went southwards and people from the south north, in the hope that in another place there would be bread and work, and then in yet another place. . . . Since Roger had no wish to spend his money before he was out of the region of Toulouse, he journeyed with the poor pilgrims, sometimes allowing one or two of them to mount pillion behind him. He had settled on the town of Foix as his guiding star, and there he intended to rest and equip himself.

Strangely enough, though he was a naturally talkative person, he could not manage to produce three consecutive words in answer to the questions and greetings of his travelling com-panions: every phrase cost him such an effort that he thought: "God, why aren't I still in the dungeon?" He felt that he was cut off from other men by a thick grating, and would forget their faces, names and voices from one moment to the next.

In the mornings, before they set off, crouching near the fire and dipping his bread in a bowl of pea soup, he would watch the others eating and forget his own hunger, and truth to tell, his hunger turned to nausea at the first mouthful. "Why can they enjoy their food, when, as for me, every morsel I swallow and every step I take costs me an effort? There was a time when I would have given anything to see so many men who were free to go where they pleased."

But the invisible grating was there, dimming his sight. He was happier in the convent, among men he hated, men he had to lie to—these, he could not hate, or even lie to (if he had told them

427

he was the son of the Emperor of Germany, the lie would have been as harmless as sneezing). He could not lie, and neither could he tell the truth, because it was hardly possible to leap suddenly on to the table shouting: "Brothers, let us draw our knives and cut the throats of every Preaching Friar we can find!" Anything of the kind, and he would speedily be taken before the local magistrates and from there to Toulouse with his feet in chains. Before he could give himself the pleasure of saying such things he must first reach a region where they could be said with impunity at every cross-roads—and then, though the pleasure would still be great, the Preachers would be far away. There was not much satisfaction to be had from slitting men's throats at a distance of thirty leagues.

Roger felt his very hatred turning to a corpse. He had squeezed it for so long in the bottom of his heart that he had suffocated it. "Patience, my friend, soon you will come out into the open, and grow and spread your wings and make heaven deaf with your cries!" There had been a time when it had beaten there, under his ribs, deep inside his heart, a solid weight that threshed and gnawed, and he could not let it cry out, no, nor even breathe. "Patience, my heart. Your hour is near." Now the hour has come but my beautiful hate stays like a heavy stone in my heart and cannot come out. Ah, it was back there, when you were face to face with your enemies, that you should have shouted it! Fool that you were, to think there was a cure for this ill, it was at the moment when you were their victim that you should have become their executioner. If I saw them, now—now!—chained and bloody and quivering, I should feel joy, yes, great joy, but it would be only dying embers beside the longing I had then.

There can never be a fair fight with them, because as they strike men when they are down, so they too must be struck when they are down, and their defenceless bodies pierced with swords and spears. Lift your arms to heaven and pray, Brothers, and thank us because we wish to make you expiate your sins on earth! Be martyrs: we want no absolution for that sin, we are quite willing to answer for it to the peril of our souls. Long may you suffer, suffer for every innocent you have destroyed, for it needs not a sword of words to pierce your hearts, but a real sword of steel. May God grant you the time to repent!

At night Roger revelled in the intoxication of thoughts like these, but in the daytime he knew they were hopeless and insane.

428

There is nothing to be done against them, he thought, the Pope has sold us to the King and the King to the Pope, and the Pope is sold to our enemies. Their power is so great that two unarmed monks can destroy the law throughout the land; and for fear of a new war we are letting them destroy the laws of our land!

If I cried my innocence to the whole world, who would believe me? When courts are secret, so are the crimes, and to whom can I prove that I have committed no secret crimes?

At Foix, Roger bought arms: a travelling spear, a sword, a small shirt of mail, spurs, greaves and gauntlets. These purchases kept him busy for a whole day. Then he wondered how to set about finding a lodging: at one time he would have found friends or the relatives of friends in every town, or, failing these, a courteous welcome from any knight as soon as he uttered his name. He was not used to roaming the streets in this way, like a stranger who had disembarked from some unknown foreign country. He could always try and pass himself off as some wandering knight in the Count of Foix's castle, but there was a danger that he would be recognised, because nothing remained of his painted complexion and the dye was beginning to fade from his black hair. He thought, too: "What if my enemies (for surely I should call those who suspect me wrongly my enemies?) have carried the story that I am a traitor and a spy as far as the Count of Foix's domains? In that case I should risk some unpleasantness, however I presented myself." It seemed to him that the whole world must be aware of his situation. Taking his courage in both hands, he got into conversation with a squire who was watering his horse at the drinking trough in the castle square. The young man told him that master Jean Barbaira, the goldsmith, was a God-fearing man who would gladly give shelter to anyone who had suffered for the faith. Roger thanked him, and left him his new gauntlets by way of thanks, and then set off in search of Jean Barbaira's house.

His reception in that house was better than he had dared to hope: the goldsmith knew enough of the world to see that he was dealing with a man of the court. He was full of the most sinister ideas about what was going on in Toulouse: they were burning folk there by the dozen, he said, innocent people, married men and the fathers of families. (Roger was actually vexed for his country's sake.) And all this to take their possessions. Even in Limoux and at Mirepoix, people were not free to pray to God as

429

they liked, since they could expect no justice from Crusader lords. These were acting in collusion with the Preaching Friars to divide the condemned persons' property. "Here, sir knight, you can attend a sermon, tonight, in the masons' house. You must have greater need of that than of bread and wine!" Finding himself thus transformed into a believer, Roger said that indeed he had never needed anything so much. Yet, as he sat at the goldsmith's table, on the right hand of the master of the house, he felt a much greater yearning for the pink cheeks of Master Jean's daughter. The goldsmith served his guest with quails and partridges, pheasant pâtés, peppers, ginger, cloves, as much as he could eat. The wines were old and strong and thick as oil. Roger took care not to disappoint his hosts by eating too sparingly. Very soon he was drunk, but it was a melancholy drunkenness; he wanted to weep and to say: "Friends, pray for me, a sinner!" Then he found himself in a good feather bed, surrounded by heavy woollen curtains. "Is this repose?" he wondered. "I should sleep better on the ground. What pleasure does it give men to eat and drink like pigs?" His heart ached and his head ached, and a strange terror beset him: he still had the feeling that he had merely changed his prison, that it was only in appearance he was free to go where he liked and do what he pleased. It did not please him at all to be in this place, nor to pretend falsely that he was a believer, nor to talk with strangers for whom he felt no friendship and even no gratitude. (This was ugly, but there was nothing he could do about it.) Their eyes are like the eyes of dead people, he thought, and their faces transparent as ghosts, ever since I have been free I have felt like the only living man among shadows.

"Rigueur? But how can I prepare myself to be worthy to see again the woman who is the only creature able to cure me of this evil? What retreat, what repose can do that?" Thinking that physical rest might cure him of his continual dizziness, Roger claimed to be ill and in need of solitude and prayer. He spent one interminable day lying in the curtained bed in the little chamber with its painted walls and thick glass panes in the windows. It was cold in there and smelled of rank perfume and damp wool. What a paradise compared to the prison! But it saddened him to be out of prison and find his body still the same as it had been in prison, and this body wallowed in the feather cushions, yet for all that it did not turn into the miraculous body of one raised from the dead.

Can any man live without action? But who can act when he

has neither house, nor goods, name, friends or money? And you thought: "Once outside, I shall be the richest man alive, I shall have won Her after whom we all yearn." Ah, it was a poor and shameful delight to take her as I took her, violently, while she slept. I should have gone to meet her dressed in scarlet with a crown of roses on my head, to the sound of trumpets and before the eyes of the whole city. Wretches that we are to believe freedom dwells in the stones of the road: that is the freedom of rabbits and partridges, not of men.

By these and similar thoughts, Roger tried to explain to himself why the joy he much desired seemed to be going further and further away from him, as the summit of a mountain grows higher and retreats the nearer one gets to it. Before he had it the violence of his longing had made him weep tears of exultation. Once, hymns of triumph had risen in his heart at the mere thought of freedom. "Oh, that day," he thought, "that day when the heavens will be mine and the road, and the mountains and rivers! Oh, if that day is a winter's day I will kiss the snow, I will roll in it like an injured wolf. Oh, if the first free man I meet that day is a leper I will kiss his cheeks!"

Where is that day? None of these things have come to pass: it is as though the heart were still in prison.

Roger left Foix and the hospitable goldsmith without having succeeded in breaking the spell, the invisible barrier which divided him from men and objects seemed to grow larger with every hour; and at night he dreamed of Raimbert: he was waiting for Raimbert, listening for his step in the passage, Raimbert with his overlong nose and his receding chin and the limp black hair falling over his eyes. . . . The two of us were crawling along the parapet, dragging the rolled-up skein of rope—his hands were shaking so badly he could not hook the rope on to the stanchion—he must have been badly bitten by the desire to abscond to have dared it in spite of everything! He jumped, because it is better to drown than be beaten to death. A poor accomplice. But it is harder still to escape alone. There were two of us that night.

He told himself: "*While I have not spoken to Rigueur . . .*" He had not thought of her much in prison, and even now he experienced some difficulty in remembering what she looked like—not that he thought he did not love her. Nor was he sufficiently dejected to believe himself unworthy to think of her. Only he was afraid.

431

He was almost hoping to hear that she too had been in prison and had managed to escape—if that were true, how much I should have to say to her, how I should be able to comfort and console her—for women (even she) are more delicate than we are, and more cruelly hurt by such experiences. (Surely this was the height of madness, to wish such a thing on someone one loves?) He was afraid of seeing her again and finding there was nothing he could tell her. "God!" he thought, "I used to love her so much!" He felt as though nothing were left of the man who had loved Rigueur but a few scattered fragments.

The little watchtower of Montgeil emerged from behind the clumps of bare, black trees on which the last brown leaves were shivering in the west wind. As he climbed up the muddy little path leading to the tower, Roger was not expecting to find any-one there; he merely wanted to rest for a few hours in a place which, he thought, should bring him luck. He had learned in the village that Bérenger d'Aspremont and his family were in the region, but were not living in the house at Montgeil.

As he came nearer he saw a thread of blue smoke rising from a heap of stones at the threshold of the tower. "It is some shepherd or vagabond," he told himself. A man dressed in a plain brown coat was busy broiling some trout which were spitted on a small iron bar over the wood fire. Roger was struck by the man's height and movements: it seemed to him that here was someone very close to him, but he did not know who; someone he had known in days of peace and happiness.

Afterwards he was amazed that he had not recognised Bérenger at once—for he it was, and there was nothing strange about his presence in this spot. Besides, he had not changed. His black curls, escaping from beneath a hat of grey lamb's fur, were still thick, and covered his ears and eyebrows. He raised his head and a big, delighted smile outlined deep creases in his worn cheeks. He sprang up. "Roger! God be praised! You managed to escape, then!" At that moment Roger told himself he would gladly have died for this man.

They shared the scalding hot trout, covered with shreds of blackened skin, and a piece of very dry, grey bread, which they had to dip in their wine in order to make it palatable. Bérenger asked one question after another. How? When? Who else knew? When did Roger intend to take up arms again? In whose service? Money? He must not worry about that too much: a thousand crowns wouldn't make a soldier out of a citizen, but a good man was always sure of finding arms and men. . . . "And you should imagine what soldiers we have now, and how many! They come to us from the plains every day, lads who can just about wield a pitchfork, but as sharp as any others, and even a pitchfork can serve its turn."

"I have been as good as deaf and blind for ten months," said Roger, "and I know nothing about what is going on here. Is it true, as they say, that we have already more than a thousand knights in Aragon and in the mountains?"

"I would say more than two thousand even," answered Bérenger, and his high spirits now appeared somewhat forced. "More than two thousand, but these days a knight is a cut-price commodity—you see, we equip ourselves as best we can, and we say whatever we like (which is a great deal!) and share out the booty in advance, and we wait. Waiting is not a good occupation for a soldier. You can see the way I am living. I ask for no one's charity, but I have already sold everything except my weapons, and these are all the clothes I have to appear in at a castle on a feast day. For myself, I don't care, but it is different for my sons. They are not treated according to their rank."

Roger asked his friend the whereabouts of his family, and Bérenger told him the boys—Ricord, the two bastards (Guillaume, and Saurine's son) and his son-in-law ("My daughter has just married, did you know?") were out hunting somewhere in the vicinity and that he was waiting for them there, because he had promised never again to spill the blood of any creature other than God's enemies. The women were in retreat at the convent of Lavelanet. "They have to pray for us in two senses," he said, "because we are kept busier thinking about food and lodging than about our salvation." He then said that his cousin, Lady de Miraval, had died at Foix, three weeks after Easter, and that he had also lost his mistress, though he dared not grieve too deeply over this because she had died a Christian death, such as he would have wished to die himself, and he had buried her at the foot of the rock of Montségur. "I should make myself ridiculous if at the age of fifty I looked for another concubine," he said, "and it is better so. This life is becoming too hard even for my wife."

"Is she ill then?" Roger asked anxiously.

"No, but her soul is in mourning, because I have not told you the worst: last month my cousin Béatrix died at Narbonne:

hers was a martyr's death. We who are left are too weak to accept such violent partings without a murmur."

Roger bit his lip as he pictured the noble creature, her delicate features bloody and eaten alive by the flames. "Ah, Rachel," he thought, "Rachel, Rachel, poor Rachel!" and he wept. His tears fell, copious, warm, almost peaceful; he wiped them away with the back of his hand. Seeing him weep so much, Bérenger believed his friend had really been in love with the Lady Béatrix; he did not know that they were tears of pity for all burned women, for all the innocent, proud flesh so shamefully destroyed.

"Are we men," said Roger at last, "and can we bear this? May we be damned if we die without our revenge."

"You talk like a young man," said Bérenger bitterly. "Revenge on whom? On the executioners, the judges, or on him who has sent these judges to us? He is the most guilty. Yet princes, counts and kings think only of flattering him."

"As for him," Roger said slowly and hoarsely, "our Holy Father who has betrayed and sold us, and has spat on us for our patience, if I had him in my hands I should roast him over a slow fire. But I have not got him, and that is why it is better to begin with the others. With all the liars, Bérenger, with all those who bear cross and tonsure and say: We are God's Church. They are cowards and traitors, tolerating evil to further their own ends. Why should we blame the Preaching Friars alone? The whole Church acquiesces and says *amen*. For more than forty years I have believed in that Church, Bérenger, and here I am now, like some brigand, believing neither in God nor the Devil."

Not without some surprise, Bérenger told him that since the true Church was there, made manifest by so many preachers and martyrs, no one was obliged to live like a brigand, believing neither in God nor the Devil. "Rather than be reduced to such a woeful condition," he said, "it would be better to be a Jew or a Muslim."

"Would to God," Roger exclaimed, "that I had been born a Jew or a Saracen, or any pagan in some unknown land!" He was sorry for these strange and discourteous words, and added: "Your faith is so great and so high that I do not believe I shall be ever worthy to know it."

"To hear you talk, you'd think a man could reject a thing because he thinks it is too good."

"I tell you, honestly, Bérenger: we have been damned because

434

of this faith. Because of it we shall never have peace. If a brick falls from a scaffolding and kills your brother or your son, you will never love that brick, even if it were made of pure gold. Haven't I thought this over a thousand times in prison? Shall I become converted now, like a child saying: Peter slapped me, I want to be friends with James? Once our country is free we can think of these things, not before."

Roger reached Lavelanet before evening and presented himself at the heretic convent, where he gave his name and asked whether Lady d'Aspremont would receive him. The convent was in actual fact a seamstresses' workshop, but the local people were well aware who the women and girls who worked there from morning to night bent over their embroidery frames really were. Noble lords, sick people, and pilgrims from all lands, stopped in the town to visit these workers whose candles burned late into the night and who sang hymns as they sewed.

"Are you a relative or a friend of this lady?" asked the old portress who received Roger in the parlour. "She is in mourning and is receiving no visitors."

Roger said that he was a friend who had just escaped from prison in Toulouse. "Then if you are from Toulouse," said the old lady, "you must be the brother of Bertrand de Montbrun. I will tell Lady d'Aspremont you are here, and she may perhaps wish to come down and speak with you here before evening prayers."

Roger told himself that he had not expected so much, because the thought of this meeting filled him with more fear than joy. He was so pale that the portress asked him if he was feeling ill, and entreated him to sit down on a bench close to the fire. There were several visitors there, warming their hands and drying their shoes, and they too had come to see friends or relatives. They were men of the locality, poorly dressed and speaking with the rough, mountain accent, but they knew one another and this fact too made Roger feel once more desperately alone. His heart was pounding in his breast like that of a man sentenced to torture. Pain must surely have become second nature to me, he thought, if, at the moment when I am about to see again the woman who was all my joy, I can feel nothing but suffering? How many times I have thought it would be enough merely to see her face for me to fear nothing more, whatever might come. How many times I have told myself that she was a creature so noble her very anger would be like true nourishment to me. . . .

The portress came to tell him that Lady d'Aspremont was ready to receive him. In this pious house the women, even mere visitors, only spoke to men through a grilled doorway which led from the inner courtyard to the workrooms. (In this way it was possible to allow the visits of husbands and lovers without risk of scandal.) Roger saw his beloved, therefore, behind a diamond-patterned grille; he saw her sitting stiffly upright on a bench, her hands clasped in her lap. An oil lamp set on a tall wrought iron stand was burning beside her.

Slowly Roger walked along the covered cloister towards the grille, feeling as though some terrible force were preventing him from advancing; he was being thrust back by the breath of a silent, unseen tempest.

When I carved her name on the flagstones of my dungeon, I loved her with a love that does not visit a man twice. Down there in the cold and the darkness, I needed her!

For a second he was crushed by a brutal agony of desire. He could no longer see, there was a roaring in his ears, and his knees were trembling so that he had to cling to the grille for support. He pressed his living, burning body to the iron barrier which divided him from her, like St. Lawrence chained to his grid-iron—she, his mistress, his beloved, was so near and yet beyond his reach, how was it that his body had not the strength to break that prison? He said in a hoarse voice: *"Rigueur."*

She raised her head and looked at him. He saw her thin face, the brown circles round her eyes and her quivering lips: except for the burning eyes, her face, in age, seemed carved out of brown stone.

"Oh, my life!" Roger cried. "My life!"

That the eyes of a living creature should have such power: that glance tore out his heart as though with hooks! Because of her great heart her own suffering was so fierce that nothing could live in its presence. What was the use of bruising his forehead against the grille? But he stayed there, like a halfwit, and could only say: "Rigueur, my life."

Abruptly she stood up and threw herself at the grille, and the flame of the lamp flickered and then became straight as a spear-head once more. It was already dark in the cloister, and man-servants were crossing the courtyard carrying torches.

"My life, my soul."

436

"Roger, what has become of you?"

"How do I know?"

Their faces were two inches apart and the diamond-latticed grille was between them. "Is there no other way we can see each other?"

"No, Roger."

"I can't speak, my heart is too full. Rigueur, God's curse on those who have brought this grief on you!"

She was terribly changed. Tight-lipped, her chin and cheekbones standing out sharply, and greying hairs showing under the kerchief which was bound tightly round her smooth brow—oh, the long sinewy neck, the bony shoulders clad in worn, grey cloth, the shoulders of a common woman! Her expression, at once calm and sorrowful, spoke of an instinctive peasant toughness, a long familiarity with suffering. "Rigueur, how you must have suffered!"

"What does it matter?" she said. "Why do you call me Rigueur? There was a woman called so, but she is dead. What have you come to me for?"

"Speak to me, I need to listen to you."

"I can't speak to you any more. I have nothing left of the friendship I bore you but an empty void; burned out. How can you still remember me?"

He told her how much he had suffered in prison, and how he had realised that she was the only creature worthy of love that he had met in his life; he said that he came to her like a brother to a dearly beloved sister. "If I felt a stirring of carnal passion when I saw you again, the blame lies only with my weariness and disordered senses. That which you have wished to forget, I wish to forget also. It is scarcely a fortnight since I left prison, and it seems to me that there is no place on earth where I wish to be! You, Rigueur, you are the only thing in the world I have never betrayed in word or thought."

She drew herself up, like a watchful animal, and said abruptly: "Why do you talk of treachery and betrayal?"

He thought: "Lord, what have I done? What have I said? What treachery did I talk of?" At that moment he had the sensation that if she suspected him he would believe he really had turned traitor. How and to whom?

"For pity's sake, Rigueur! Should there be such thoughts between us? Has anyone told you that in order to obtain better

437

treatment I betrayed secrets about which I should have kept silent?"

She stood facing him, her face expressionless, her eyes on the ground. "I am not in the habit of listening to slander."

"You know that I am incapable of base treachery. Was I speaking of that?"

"Roger, it is already too much that we should both have been able to entertain such an idea. What can we say to each other now?"

"Your friendship for me is gone, and mine for you is not. Rigueur, in prison a man loses count of time, and I had such faith in your goodness that I thought a look from you would absolve me from all my sins."

She sat down on the bench and folded her hands in her lap. She stared unblinking at the lamp, and, as he watched the thin face with its dark shadows, Roger felt his former love petrifying in his heart until it was like an image in stone. Once love had made him give the name Rigueur to a loving and tender mistress; because rigour was necessary to her, this granite hardness was necessary; in her simple heart love passed like the flowers on a cherry tree. Now the season was ended, ended the springtime, and the summer, and this proud, stern face was the face of a mother of grown-up children.

Because she is humble she does not remember now, because her own life was never dear to her. A lover's rights have turned to smoke—this burnt-out heart, this wasted body do not remember now. "Nothing, Rigueur, do you really feel nothing of what we once were?"

"I am surprised at *you*, Roger, for still remembering. You took the reflection of a candle in a mirror for the sun. We have moved apart, even our sorrows are no longer the same."

"I am talking to you here as though through prison bars. From now on, must I see nothing but prisons all my life?"

"I wish there was some comfort I could give you, Roger, but I have already said too many words of love to you in the past—what can I say to you now that will not strike you as cold as ice? There is only one thing to say now: may we be revenged on our enemies, and may we win back our freedom! May you have the strength, Roger, and the courage and faith and luck that are needed never to flinch from this task! And may you forget your prison, for now it is as though the whole land were in prison. Let us not lay down

438

our arms until not even the least of our brothers remains in prison without just cause."

"Tell me if you really doubted me!"

She drew herself up and looked him straight in the eyes.

"Roger, it would be easy for me to say no. I have not endured what you have endured. If you want the truth, I will tell you: I don't know. I know that these accursed men have broken stronger men than you by their tortures and their tricks; and perhaps I have doubted, without blaming you. Now I believe you are not lying. But I know that, if you had done things you wished to hide from me, you would die rather than tell me."

"Oh, yes, I would tell you!" cried Roger. "And I'm only sorry I can't tell you I betrayed a hundred people! I have never lied to you. What a thing to say to me!"

"I told you the truth. I make no boast of it."

"You should have lied. You should have told me I was the light of your eyes and the sunshine of your life!"

It was quite dark now, except round the lamp, and only the woman's head emerged from the shadowy room, craning forward, thrust out from the gaunt shoulders that were at once tremulous and still. Her lips were parted and her eyes so heavy with life that Roger could feel her gaze boring remorselessly into his own. Then he thanked God for the grille between them, for at such moments love turns to madness. At that instant he would gladly have taken her by force or killed her.

"May God forgive you," he said. "I hoped you would cure my wounds, but now I know that there can be no cure for me in this world. Tell me, at least, whether you love Bérenger and your children?"

"I love them as much as it is permitted us to love, perhaps more."

"God grant you may long keep them with you! God keep you from prison! Farewell, Rigueur."

She got up and acknowledged this with a brief, courteous bow.

"Farewell, Roger. Thank you, and forgive me for the great love you have borne me."

There were lights in all the windows giving on to the courtyard, and the cloisters were filling with visitors, who were strolling under the arches, talking in low voices, while they waited for evening prayers. They looked at the woman behind the grille, beside the

439

small glimmering lamp, and at the man's tall figure silhouetted against the black latticework—lovers, brothers, sons, often stayed like that for hours. To those who had lost everything, women were like a banner and a blessed relic and their birthplace, the last remaining thing of which they could be proud.

Good news spreads fast and the next day was a great occasion, celebrated at the castle of Lavelanet by a banquet with music and singing. Joyful bonfires were lighted in one castle after another, and could be seen twinkling through the cold, misty mountains from turret tops, like beacons lost amid immense, black petrified waves. That day they thought release was on its way (they had thought that so many times!), now that the Count and the consuls had ejected all the Preaching Friars from Toulouse to a man, and forbidden all trials for heresy in the region. The Bishop of Toulouse and the Inquisitors had gone to Carcassonne, but people were saying: "Soon they will be in Montpellier, in Rome or where God wills—we shall not see them again, the Pope will be forced to yield."

(It would be hard to say how many similar days of rejoicing they lived through: exiles are greedy for joy, and their hearts are sick of hope. The castles were poor and the ladies dressed in gowns that were five years old, the wine was sour, the goblets battered, and they were richer in songs than gifts. But when the ladies had left them, the men drank deep.)

More than one faggot of broom was flung upon the hearth, making the pale, crackling flames blaze up, lighting the hall better than torches. The cup was drained and filled again, passed from hand to hand as the knights took turns to plunge into it the rings given them by their sweethearts to solemnise the pledges they made as they drank. And if all these splendid toasts had come true there would not have been a man in the land crazy enough to wish for paradise. They practically wished for the resurrection of the dead. They drank to the Viscount's return, to the defeat of the King's seneschals, to Count Raymond's remarriage and the birth of a legitimate heir. They drank to the downfall of the Pope, to the siege of Rome by the Emperor's armies, to the heretic bishops installed at Milan and Cremona, and honoured at Carcassonne, at Toulouse and Albi, and to the return of all exiles. They drank, too, to the return of their lands and their fair share of the plundered possessions of the monasteries and churches; and to the burning of all the sentences and files of the Inquisition so that no man in the land should ever again be persecuted for his faith.

No one so much as talked of vengeance: there were so many outrages to be avenged that that thirst would never be slaked. If we went on killing them for ten years on end, they would never be requited for the evil they have done! He is a craven who can ever be consoled for so many lives destroyed, so many lives ruined for ever. Until the day of justice comes, those who have lost too much will never cease from crying and crying again—By what right have they done this to us? They have laid waste the land by hunger and fear, they have caused the deaths of young and old, of women and little children!

Under the influence of the wine, their mood changed from sadness to gaiety, from friendship to anger, from anger to defiance and a wish to set the whole town ablaze. Roger was drunk that evening as he had not been for a year, and he left Lavelanet in the middle of the night, with a torch in his hand, swearing to make it daylight before dawn. He was followed by two knights, Guillaume de Frémiac and Hugues de Carmaux, and three squires, all of them eager to show that there was no love for traitors in their land. They fastened bundles of straw and faggots to their saddle bows and rode full tilt through the town, brandishing their torches. That night they set fire to two churches near Mirepoix. "Good people of the land, we bear you no malice, it is traitors we seek, and if your houses burn the fault will be theirs, so let none of you be bold enough to speak for them." (The soldiers in these towns gladly admitted any who cried the names of the Viscount and the former lords of Mirepoix; if they were attacked by ten men they would claim to have seen a hundred.) Flames poured out of the smashed doors and windows of the little church and reddish smoke mounted from the slit windows in the tower; with a roar of shattered stone and metal, the great bell crashed on to the flagged floor, drowning the sounds of cracking wood and people screaming. Women armed with pokers, their hair falling over their faces, pursued the priest with shrieks of "Death to the traitor!" Naked and bleeding, he staggered round the square, from one door to another, until the baillie took pity on him and let him into his house.

Under a whitening sky, in which the last stars and a small, pale half moon gleamed sadly, the knights rode along the valley of the

441

Hers, sobered and shivering in garments that were drenched with sweat. There had been six of them when they left; now they were nine, because they had been joined by three soldiers from the town. In that part of the country it was more dangerous to be a priest than a thatcher. "That's one bell," the people said, "that won't call folk to the Devil's sabbath any more: and one traitor who will go and play the spy elsewhere after the fright he had last night. If we could only do the same to the churches of Carcassonne and Albi!" With a light heart and a head on fire, Roger de Montbrun took leave of his companions, promising to meet them again before long under the walls of Carcassonne. "Our enemies' backs have been broken in the region of Toulouse," he said. "I am going back to my own land to take possession of my castle and my men." He set off at a canter along the muddy roads, overtaking little groups of travellers on foot and peasants dragging cartloads of stones, harnessed to the long shafts in teams of ten. Their lips were foaming, their eyes glassy, their breath coming in hoarse gasps—the ropes over their shoulders were wrapped in filthy wadding, stained with blood. Oh, the senseless courage of men who will submit to being tortured to death and never even ask the reason why! A beast would have dropped to its knees, but these marched on, yesterday, today, tomorrow. What church or castle were those stones destined for? Churches and castles were burned and it all began again.

"Layrac," thought Roger. "At Layrac I have enough faithful friends to welcome me, even without money or letter from the Count. My judges have fled and I am a condemned man no longer; their sentences have fled with them to Carcassonne and Montpellier. Lord, and to think when I saw them they were as strong as God and the Devil! If I could only laugh at it (and perhaps if my brother and so many others had not lost their lives I should laugh aloud), I would laugh with all my heart, Brothers, for here is your famous sword become a phantom, and the butt for laughter. Go, spiritual sword, excommunicate others, put out the candles, veil the churches in black, we shall enjoy the sight.

"Glory be to God! The first step has been taken, and, by patience, cunning or force, we shall lay them low. But to what tribunals can we go to cry justice for that which cannot be repaired, which cannot be forgotten, which cannot be forgotten for all eternity? To God? The evil has been done before men, among men, to men, and the liars who send us back to God are using false scales, and they always will be false.

"If we burned the Body of the Lord the other night, in that church, is that my fault? The fault is theirs who have taken our faith from us and violated it, as brigands violate mothers before the eyes of their sons. Lord help me! I shall never be anything but their enemy.

"It is their fault that my beloved doubted me, and I her, and what bliss should God provide to balance the payment of that shame, the payment of that bitterness? There is a great lie between us now, though we have never lied to one another in anything, and where it comes from, who will ever know?"

What new joys are there which can drown that grief? That wordless grief, without face or name, like a huge, black gulf. My soul? A pitch-black, gaping, empty soul: ah, what joy it is to live, how great is the desire for happiness!

AND THAT, TOO, WAS A TIME OF HAPPINESS.

The great gate of Layrac was flung wide open for Roger to enter, and he was followed by a troop of peasants armed with scythes and axes; his squires ran to meet him and led his horse by the bridle: women were crying for joy on the ramparts and the vassals waited in the courtyard, dressed in their best clothes, with their hands on their swords, ready to renew their oaths of allegiance. He was the lawful master coming into his own again.

Jean-Rigaud de Marcillac walked out to meet him and their eyes met in a long glance before they fell into one another's arms. "God grant we may long keep you, Lord Roger! Better to take up arms again than to live so." (In every castle men were gathering, and repairing their equipment as they waited for the exiles to come home, and saying: in the spring the Count will march on Carcassonne!) Surrounded by his men, Roger entered the hall and took his seat beneath the shields of Layrac and Montbrun, and he raised his sword, and swore that he had been dispossessed in contempt of the laws, and now he claimed his sons' inheritance for his own again and the Count would deal him justice.

(And the Devil was waiting there, in the shape of an innocent creature, but one who would not remain so for long—often enough a girl's natural guardian becomes her lover, too, but this passion would be cruel and violent as autumn floods.) His niece, Colombe de Montbrun, stepped forward, with her younger

443

sister and her two small brothers, and she bowed the knee before him, like a man, and asked his protection before them all. After their parents' death the children had escaped from Toulouse on foot and after enduring much hardship had taken refuge at Layrac. "God save you, good uncle, we know that you will not desert us! Our elder brothers have betrayed us, and they have taken our sister Hersen with them. It is for you to avenge our father and our mother! I ask you the favour of staying with you always. On the day you see our enemies' blood, may I be at your side!"

Roger embraced the four children, delighted to see his nephews and nieces once more, and took Colombe's hand to seat her beside him under the shield of Montbrun. That evening the orphan presided over the meal on her uncle's right hand, trembling all over with excitement, her pale, delicate cheeks still marred by the scars her nails had torn in them as a sign of mourning, because she had wept for her parents until she made herself ill. More than one cup of Layrac wine was drained to the Count's health and the destruction of the Preaching Friars. The vassals of Layrac had three of their people in the prisons of Montauban.

As he drank, Roger felt like a man who has sold his soul to the Devil upon receiving the rewards promised him in exchange—a great happiness, a sense of giddiness and bodily well-being—freed of his invisible and unwanted guest, a great giddiness, dancing and singing amid red fires, fire and blood, let us drink blood!

Ah! The desire is enough! Everything is at my feet. Here I am in my own castle, honoured and obeyed. And we shall win back that which we have lost, the Count has kept his promises. Before spring comes, I shall re-enter Toulouse with my men, and take possession of my father's house again. I shall settle accounts with all my enemies. What enemies, and where are they? Secret enemies, everything is secret; let the Preachers settle happily in seminaries in France or Italy, and we will give them our blessing, so long as they never come back!

So long as they never come back! . . .

Ours is a lame revenge. When shall I show you the blood of our enemies, Colombe? What do the affairs of the country mean to her—to this tall, lovely child, with her trembling mouth and her big black eyes, scorched with tears? Her father and her mother, whom she loved so dearly. She was drinking too, though

444

she had never learned to drink; she drank *to the death of our enemies*, thinking by so doing to hasten the vengeance, and her cheeks were flushed scarlet, and her long, dark gold hair fell over her face and shoulders as she stood there, wild-eyed and shivering, like a girl who had just been raped. Drunk. "For my father! For my mother! For all our people! Long live the Count!" The noble dames of Layrac watched her with an affectionate sadness; she was so lovely, and her anger was so savage and so innocent. Jean-Rigaud's wife tried to take her away, and she clung to Roger's arm. "Tomorrow, Colombe, I will see you again tomorrow."

"My friends, it is for us to re-establish justice in this domain, and let everyone understand that the time of the Preaching Friars is over! And let the Pope never dare to send them back, let him know that the Inquisitors have done more harm in this land in two years than the Crusaders in ten. If there are any spies or traitors on our lands, let their names be given to me and I will see that justice is done. I take all on myself, I am already under attainder, I have nothing to lose and everything to gain!"

... "Jean-Rigaud, what questions did they ask you about the secret passage?" The two men were alone in Roger's chamber; the old man scratched his chin, with a harsh smile, and his eyes were hard. "It was my lady Guillelme who accused me."

"How do you know?"

"Because they described the key to me. The four notches on the ring. She was the only person who knew."

"You didn't think it was me? She could have told me."

The old man shook his head. "No. They interrogated me over and over again until in the end they believed that you knew nothing, and neither did I. But tell me, Lord Roger, is it true what they said: that you showed Guiraud de Montauban the passage?" Roger shrugged.

"What's the use of lying to you?"

"*Seigneur* Roger, until your sons are of age, we are your men. Rather than go to the Holy Land, I would prefer to flee to the Corbières if things go badly."

The next day Roger had the church at Magnanac burned and the priest hanged. Hatred of his faith was tormenting him like a burning fever, and he was on fire with so many desires that he felt as though a single body would never be enough to satisfy them all—desires for blood, fire, wine, meat and lighted candles,

445

and singing and hunting horns and dancing—he wanted grey skies and blue, and wind and snow, and riding for hours on end on horseback in pursuit of deer—and the delights of that other chase, in the turret chamber, by the glow of the red brazier set on its tripod, the delights of the chase on a white bed, mouth against mouth and heart against heart.

"My desire for your young body is like a poison burning in my blood, daughter of my own burned blood, let the Devil take us into his flames, let us engender vengeance together, and new joy!" (Colombe gave herself to love as a girl does at fourteen, with all the ardour of a young animal and the passion of an adolescent. In height and stature she was a child no longer, but the loveliest of women.) So, in a few days, through the torment of a new desire, does one forget a love that was too bitter.

Six months of feasting at Layrac were followed by a melancholy summer, heavy with menace. There was talk of so many inquisitions, at Narbonne and Carcassonne and in other royal fiefs, that in the region of Toulouse men were beginning to say: "If they are going to come back, then let them come quickly, because the later they are recalled the more they will want vengeance!" (Roger did not dare even to show his face in Toulouse in those days: he was a publicly proclaimed rebel and heretic: and when the Inquisition was set up again in Toulouse and the Preaching Friars back in their monastery, he left the land with his vassals who were, like himself, compromised by deeds of vengeance. This was how the Devil had deceived him, and instead of being exiled alone, he took with him into exile a dozen men he had not the means to support—and people, moreover, who were attached to their lands and not used to living off pay. It was then Roger began to lead the life of a soldier, paid by the month, or the week: a hard life for an ageing man, and one in which in three months he had more adventures than could all be told. But to the old warhorse all music is the same: travelling and fighting, plots and intrigues, pillage, quarrels, revenge, sickness, journeying from Perpignan to Saragossa, and from Barcelona to Foix—all names, faces and countries soon forgotten.)

Looking back through the years, as one leafs through a book from back to front, one wonders which was the moment when life ought to have stopped. There had been no lack of occasions. Happy days when one said: "It would be a pity to die!" and days, black as ink, when one said: "Let us take our revenge first!" The heart never lays down its arms.

Later on, one said: "What, could I live on after *that*?" Hoping to win at every throw of the dice, you lose, you throw again, and the greater the loss, the greater the hope of winning, the frenzy to win the next throw. You go away as naked as the day you were born, pursued by the laughter of wiser and more cautious players. . . . You go away, to beg, borrow or steal, and then back to the gaming table and take up the dice again! "If this throw is no good, I'll give up." The worst, and most treacherous, part of it is that you don't always lose.

Yes, for eight whole months there were no Inquisitors in the domains of the Count of Toulouse: true, Brother Peter Seila and Brother Guillaume Arnaud fell back on the districts of Quercy and Comminges and Razès, but the Count stood firm for eight months —only to see, at the end of it, Brother Peter Seila returning with the title of Prior of the monastery of St. Dominic, and the trials begin again with such ferocity that one might have thought there was ten years of absence to be made up for. In Toulouse alone, enough dead and living were burned that year to help all the Preachers of the realm win through to paradise, and they burned three times as many on paper. Many people had to take the road for Spain or Italy in the hope of returning before long—the more so as in twenty years they had grown accustomed to such goings and comings.

But in those days it was nothing yet; they thought: "Very well. The Preaching Friars are having their revenge for the insult they suffered, they will calm down." They had suffered violence at the hands of the citizens in many towns, and not the Preaching Friars alone, but monks and clerks who had nothing to do with the Order of St. Dominic. Moreover, the people were waiting with great hopes, and plenty of false joys, for the death of the Pope, who was now past ninety. "How can a man of that age act in a reasonable manner? The next Pope will lend a more attentive ear to our complaints." They dared not hope either for justice or kindness, but they believed that the Church's interests in the land, and fear for the lives and property of churchmen, would force the Pope to abolish illegal practices.

There was no petty knight, burgher, merchant or craftsman who could not have presented the Pope with a well-argued case showing him quite clearly how he ought to act. Never were there

447

such numbers of eloquent lawyers in any land, or with so little influence. Even the complaints of the Count himself received no more attention than the whining of a child with the toothache. Moreover, when, thanks to the support of the Count of Provence and the King of Aragon, and somewhat also to his own intriguing, the Count finally won his divorce petition, they might well say: "Now his hands are free: what good would a fresh war have done us if the Count were still without an heir?" The Count was still young—only forty—and noble enough for a king's daughter (at least so his subjects thought: the kings were to think otherwise). But the exiled men of Toulouse—and there were enough of them in those days to raise an army of three hundred knights— drank to the Count's remarriage, and to the confusion of his son-in-law, Alphonse de Poitiers, and of King Louis. As though a boy-child from a countess's womb would be enough to make the fallow fields yield good harvests and turn the coarse linen in the coffers into silk, and copper pennies into gold pieces. Indeed, perhaps if that child had been born, if he only had been born, even greater miracles might have occurred. What changes that child's birth might have wrought in men's hearts, who can say? Men talked of his rights and titles and how to assure his inheritance, when his father was still not married or betrothed. Then he was betrothed and not married. But men deprived of their rights cling hard to the belief in justice and good sense. Undoubtedly, if they had been listened to, the world would be a paradise.

And yet we were not mad. We had almost won our victory. At Carcassonne, the Viscount of Béziers and his followers already held the outskirts of the city, and in the town itself the Count had more friends than opponents; if the siege had lasted one more week they would have taken the place and the Seneschal, Guillaume des Ormes, and all the garrison with it. The fall of Carcassonne would have brought the whole land up in arms, because we already held the districts of Razès and Carcassès, and Limoux and Montréal. . . . All was regained and lost again more quickly still, in the time it took to see the fields burn, cities open their gates, new banners replace the old, and to hang traitors and slaughter monks and priests. As for the number of burghers who paid for these murders, the number of houses burned and the length of walls razed, and the number of hanged and mutilated bodies which adorned the roads that summer, whoever wished to count them would have to get up early in the morning. Old soldiers thought themselves thirty years younger and back in the time of the Crusade. The Viscount withdrew into the Corbières with his knights and what was left of the foot-soldiers, and to tell the truth he was not greeted with blessings. He said: "If the Count of Toulouse had come to my assistance . . ." And the Count said: "If the Viscount had chosen a better moment . . ." The result was that both were right in the eyes of their friends. But since Olivier de Termes had made his peace with the King, it was becoming awkward for men under sentence of excommunication, and condemned by every tribunal in the land, to serve in his army.

Moreover, if this were merely a preliminary attempt it was an expensive one—but two years later the Count appeared in Narbonne in person and received back his ducal coronet from the hands of the old Viscount Aimery of Narbonne. Then they thought the time had almost come when the whole land, from Razès to the Albigeois, would repudiate their oaths of obedience to the King and swear fealty to him, because the King was at that time fighting against the English in the province of Saintonge. But this king, who was a knight as valiant as Roland and Alexander, had undone his enemies so rapidly that the Count's friends, in the region of Toulouse, accepted defeat before they had even joined battle, and placed themselves at Louis' mercy, swearing that they had never been a party to Count Raymond's treachery. All the Count could do was go to Paris and beg forgiveness for his brief spell of happiness at the cost of fresh concessions in land and promises. Was it really all over? Men were thinking: "How much longer will he live?" He was ailing and exhausted, and they knew he would not live to the same age as his father, but surely another ten, or fifteen, years would not be too much?

Who to fight against now, that was the question, and who for? In Roussillon, and Cerdagne, and in the Sabarthès and Corbières and in the districts of Sault and Tarrascon, there were too many thousands of men (and women too), thousands of people who possessed no rights in any land. Excommunicate, heretics and rebels, they were almost resigned to the permanent loss of the honours they had once known. The Preaching Friars had good memories and had condemned so many people, living and dead, that it might have been thought that only animals could still escape being charged with heresy. After the business of

449

Montségur, people thought their fury might abate, but it was quite the reverse. The Seneschal had taken the castle and destroyed it so completely that the heretics could never again gather there to pray, and then, as the woods were beaten and the Inquisition set up in the mountain towns, life became harder than ever.

I. Brother Alberic of Montpellier

"Roger de Montbrun, knight, son of Pierre-Guillaume de Montbrun and of Alazaïs de Miradoux, formerly Lord of Layrac in the region of Toulouse, by right of his wife Guillelme, formerly Lady of Layrac.

"Captured in the woods about Castres in company with the heretics Bernard de Foix and Othon Vidal, and believers Jacques de Luscan, knight, and Séverin Maurel, squire (both of these, like the aforementioned Roger, offering armed resistance and causing the death of two of the Count's men-at-arms).

"Accused of having in his youth secretly honoured the depraved heretical doctrine known as Cathar or Albigensian, a fact testified to by numerous witnesses, from whose evidence it appears that heretics were still given an honourable welcome in the house of his father, Pierre-Guillaume de Montbrun, during the period of the said Roger's childhood, a fact which the accused has never mentioned in his declarations.

"Item, the accused at all times tolerated the guilty conduct of his brother Bertrand, a notorious believer (and burned as such in the year 1235), by refraining from bringing this to the notice of the ecclesiastical authorities. Beneath an appearance of false piety, the said Roger, by his own admission, honoured the heretic faith in his heart, attending heretic sermons and doing adoration to ministers of this sect after the heretic fashion, both in the Count of Montfort's day and during the years when the city of Toulouse was under the interdict; and continued in these practices after the raising of the interdict.

"Item, summoned to the tribunal of the Holy Office of the Inquisition by Brother Peter Seila, the accused persisted for a long time in trying to mislead the court by denying the offences of which he was accused. And when reconciled to the Church after a feigned conversion, the said Roger set the seal on his perfidy by conspiring to escape from the Dominican friary in

Toulouse, to which, in their charity and confidence in his repentance, the Brothers had admitted him as a penitent.

"Item, having by this act rendered himself unworthy of forgiveness, the said Roger did with his own hands set fire to the church of Roumengoux in Mirepoix, in the company of Guillaume de Frémiac and Hugues de Carmaux, believers both since killed in the Fenouilledès. Item, the said Roger, after this heinous crime, did return to his domain of Layrac, taking advantage of the exile of the Preaching Friars and the disorders in the land which had resulted therefrom, and did upon false pretences and in contempt of the law make himself master of it. The accused had all ecclesiastical persons in this domain of Layrac driven out and ordered the church at Magnanac to be set on fire and the priest hanged. Item, with his men-at-arms and ten Basques, the said Roger did break into the church at Semalens, near Castres, and give orders for the priest and the sacristan to be locked up in the belfry, and all precious objects found in the said church removed; after which he had a meal served there and presided over it in company with the young woman Colombe de Montbrun, his niece and concubine, with whom he committed adultery in the sacristy of the same church.

"Item, the said Roger de Montbrun did invade the village of Saint-Martin, belonging to the monastery of the same name, with his men, and plundered cellars and granaries and took away one hundred and thirty sheep and ten horses.

"Item, the said Roger, having entered the service of the Lord of Termes, continued to maintain relations with notorious heretics, and persons condemned as such, and to frequent heretic seminaries and places of assembly, notably the castle of Montségur. Furthermore, numerous witnesses attest that at this time the said Roger frequently uttered the most abominable slanders against the Church of Rome and our Holy Father the Pope and the tribunal of the Holy Office. Other witnesses testify having seen him enter the church at Sonnac, near Chalabre, in the company of Sicart de Montgeil, squire and free lance, and a band of armed men, and interrupt the celebration of Mass in sacrilegious fashion, snatching the chalice from the hands of the officiating priest, and himself drinking the wine already consecrated; after which the said Roger had mounted the pulpit, and declared that he had a better knowledge of religion than this same priest, that all laymen should be authorised to preach from the pulpit and

452

denounce the falsehoods of clerics, and that by their lies the priests of Rome were attempting to deprive the land of its freedom.

"Item, the said Roger is accused by numerous witnesses of a leaning towards the Leonist heresy (otherwise known as Waldensian); he has been seen on many occasions in the company of ministers of this sect, and in particular the deacon Arnald Marcabru, to whom he acted as bodyguard from before the siege of Carcassonne. Item, during this siege and the campaign of the Viscount, Roger de Montbrun did fight with great fury against the army of the seneschal and was seen engaged in the directing of missiles. Item, in the course of the same campaign the accused did not prevent the massacre of the garrison of Montoulieu but did utter words of encouragement. Item, he was seen to rejoice at the murder of priests in Carcassonne. Item, after the destruction of the city of Limoux, the said Roger, in company with Bérenger d'Aspremont, knight and believer (burned in the year 1246), and of Guiraud de Lavelanet, knight and believer, did plunder and burn the village of Montferrier, held in fief by the marshal Guy de Lévis. Item, the said Roger, then taken by surprise, with the deacon Arnald Marcabru and five men-at-arms, did murder the escort which was to conduct himself and his companions to Carcassonne.

"Item, after the capture of the castle of Montségur, the accused did act as guide and bodyguard to the heretic Sicart de Chalabre, and was seen with the said heretic on many occasions; item, the accused did salute the woman Braïda de Bélesta, an ordained heretic well known in the land of Foix, after the fashion of the heretics; item, the accused and the young woman Colombe de Montbrun, his niece, did accompany the said female heretic into the districts of Lantarès and Mirepoix, giving her the protection of ten men-at-arms (including the squire Séverin Maurel) and compelling the inhabitants of divers villages to do great honour to the said heretic.

"Item, the said Roger and his companion, the above-named Colombe, not content with following heretics and offering them protection, did visit many castles in the district of Lantarès, with the object of persuading the lords of the said castles to pledge them loans of money and weapons, claiming that they were defending heretics; moreover, they did say on many occasions that every citizen who was not a traitor should pledge

453

his property to defend such men, since all those who honoured the Catholic Church, whether outwardly or in their hearts, were in danger of damnation, and were nothing but a flock of sheep destined to be sheared and skinned.

"Item, the said Roger did act as bodyguard to the heretics Bernard of Foix and Othon Vidal, and did force the bailiff of Carmaux to give them shelter in his house and to summon the citizens of the town to their sermon; which sermon he attended in company with Jacques de Luscan and Séverin Maurel and Colombe de Montbrun, all of them armed with swords and daggers; item, when surprised by the Count's men-at-arms, the said Roger and his accomplices did fall upon these men-at-arms furiously, uttering the most abominable curses, and wounding several of them (two unto death); and they further declared that these men were traitors, executing the orders not of the Count but of the Count's enemies.

"In consequence of these accusations, and many others, Roger de Montbrun, here present, should be considered by the tribunal of the Holy Office as a heretic believer, abetter of heresy, rebel, relapsed and unrepentant."

There were two men interrogating the accused; and one of them was Brother Alberic of Montpellier. Brother Alberic's hair was grey now, he had deep lines down his cheeks, wrinkles round his eyes and brown lips. He was worn out by fasting and ill-health; his former ardour had turned to bitterness and his zeal for God into disgust for men. As he listened to the scribe reading out the indictment he closed his big, grey eyes, letting the beads of his rosary slip through his fingers. Can any man listen repeatedly to the recital of such unspeakable depravity and escape contamination? After fifteen years as a member of the Holy Office, Brother Alberic had now only one ambition: to rest in silence and prayer. He had gone beyond the temptations of anger and the desire to humble the enemy, who in his chains was often contemptible, sometimes dangerous, always repulsive: he knew they all lied, lied even in their confessions, even in their bluster. One man would come with a bold face and declare himself a 'Christian' and boast of his crimes, and formerly Brother Alberic had preferred suspects of this temper; he had humbled several. Now, he knew that this apparent strength was merely pride and lightness of spirit; and that, beneath a semblance of humanity, the rare ordained heretics were only empty husks inhabited by the Evil One. (Brother Alberic had long since learned to distinguish their true nature by the icy-cold sensation which pervaded his heart in their presence. A burning cold. Their thin faces, their grave, level voices, their calm, all revealed to those who could see that they were already living in another world, the world of black fire and everlasting ice—for terrible indeed is the passion which the Enemy of the human race can rouse in the hearts of his elect! In our land, O Lord, and in our time! Slight are the flames, and the screams of pain a little thing, compared to the yawning gulf of fire and ice that is a soul possessed by Lucifer!)

After a close acquaintance with creatures of this kind, how mean and pitiful these petty victims seem; they are legion, more contemptible indeed than the herd of swine which were possessed by the Devil and plunged into the sea. The ignorant and craven herd who flock to the monastery gates to confess their sins do so not from repentance but basely, out of fear. The herd may be caught in the act, abetting and sheltering heretics, but whether they admit or deny it, sorrow that they have offended God never enters their minds. If they pretend to be sorry, it is merely in the hope of pleasing their judges. . . . Has the faith of Jesus Christ ever been so despised in any land? Time and again, men confess to having betrayed it, as though it were a venial fault for which it would be unfair to blame them!

"The said Roger de Montbrun, not content with uttering the most abominable abuse of the Catholic Church in divers places, and with indulging in violent threats to the persons of clerics and the property of the Church, did, in his impudence, venture to maintain that he was an obedient son of the Church, and complain in letters addressed to the Count, to the Bishop of Toulouse and to the Archbishop of Narbonne of wrongs done to him by the tribunal of the Inquisition; and protest against his condemnation and the confiscation of his property, and against the posthumous trial of his father, requesting authority to appeal to have his case tried by the court of Rome.

"Item, his perfidy being revealed and made manifest, the said Roger did continue to deny his faults and refuse to repent."

"A bad business," thought Brother Alberic. Nothing provoked him more than these brazen liars who claimed to be Catholics against all probability. The man in question was apparently quite incapable of having committed the crimes of which he was

455

accused. He sat on the bench placed for the accused, in an attitude of considerable detachment, legs crossed and head held high, listening with assumed indifference to the reading of the charges against him, his lips drawn back in a strained smile, his eyelids quivering slightly. He was dressed shabbily: his leather jerkin, torn in the affray, had been raggedly cobbled but was still bloodstained, his fine linen shirt was extremely dirty and his red cloth breeches blackened at the knees. He was by no means an old man and might have passed as easily for forty as sixty; his long hair was sparse and grizzled, and his chin hidden by a short, slightly reddish beard. His tired face, with the big, darkly shadowed eyes and long, aquiline nose, still retained that suggestion of deceptive and appealing sweetness which Brother Alberic had found so antipathetic thirteen years before.

Thirteen years: the man had already passed through that very room in the days when the Preaching Friars of Toulouse were so cruelly persecuted by the Count and the civil authorities and when the enemies of Christ were openly flouting the laws of the Church. At that time this man, trusting in his impunity, had appeared of his own accord to answer his indictment, and had found his cunning foiled. Then by a still more abominable trick he had succeeded in escaping. Now, Brother Alberic had forgotten even the anger and disgust which this creature had formerly aroused in him.

When asked what he had to say he denied everything. He had never ceased to be a Catholic, all the evidence was false. *He had been captured, with weapons in his hands, acting as bodyguard to heretics?* That was his only crime: he owed a debt to the heretic Othon Vidal. *How was that? Did he borrow money from heretics, and render them services for money?* He had to find a living for his men and horses. He was not the only one to sell his services so; the Reverend Brothers knew that he had been dispossessed of his property. He was blaming no one, except the personal enemies who had wrongfully accused him.

"Which enemies?"

"Supposing I knew! I have not been informed of the names of my accusers."

"Roger de Montbrun, do you take us for children?"

"God forbid! But I am innocent."

"You have heard the charges against you."

He said that none of them were true; and that the people said

456

to have been his accomplices in this or that action against the faith were either dead—like Guillaume de Frémiac and Bérenger d'Aspremont—or in Spain, like Sicart de Montgeil and the Waldensian, Arnald Marcabru. His father, he said, had always been a Catholic, and had been exhumed and burned wrongfully. He himself had never given the order for the burning of the church at Magnanac or for the hanging of the priest: this priest had long been known for a spy, and matters had chanced to come to a head at a time when Roger was at Layrac. He had never plundered the church at Semalens, or committed adultery in the sacristy, or lived in concubinage with his niece; neither had he drunk the communion wine at Sonnac, or compelled anyone to attend sermons; he had only met the deacon Arnald Marcabru by accident and without knowing who he was, and had fought with the people who arrested him merely because they had offered him violence. Moreover, all the speeches attributed to him were false, and no one could prove that he had ever uttered them. He said that it was easy to accuse a man in his absence, especially if he were a stranger in the land (because they knew well enough he came neither from Lantarès, nor Mirepoix, nor from Castres, nor Corbières, and it was in these districts that his accusers dwelled. No one had said anything about things he had done in Toulouse).

"Why," asked Brother Alberic, without animosity, indeed with a hint of pity, "do you persist in such a clumsy defence? The number of witnesses and the nature of the deeds of which you are accused show that this is no longer a matter of personal accusations, but of flagrant offences and widely-known facts."

"My good reputation," said Roger de Montbrun, "was also a widely known fact on the day I was charged, thirteen years ago. And I was condemned on secret evidence. I maintain that I have always been a good Catholic, and I will never confess to faults which I have not committed."

"Enough of this game," said Brother Alberic, coldly, "your words are an insult to religion, and nothing more."

The accused leaned forward, resting his chin on his hand, and stared at the black and white tiled floor. It seemed as though the effort of too much talking had left him drained, and his drawn features expressed nothing beyond exhaustion. Still barely recovered from his wounds, and worn out by two months in prison, the man was only defending himself by fits and starts, more from stubbornness than conviction. What was to be done with him? Send him to the stake for his obduracy, or force him into making some admissions, which would be truthful undoubtedly, but would not prove his repentance? Brother Alberic inclined somewhat towards the second solution: so do cunning men abuse the gentleness of the judges of the Church, since although they have merited death a thousand times over, we are reluctant to expose to it souls that are ill-prepared.

What further motives were driving this man, ageing, ruined and dishonoured as he was, to flee the grace of repentance? What was it he still hoped to gain? A minor sentence, exile to the Holy Land? Was he counting on the friends he had once had in Toulouse? What did he hope to save? The wretched remainder of his life . . . a woman, a child? Brother Alberic had interrogated the abject creature who served this man's lust: the daughter of a twice renegade Jewess who had been burned as a heretic, and bearing in her face the stigmata of the fallen race—the hooked nose, concupiscent lips, and long black eyes, at once impudent and cringing, to which her youth gave a semblance of beauty. Questioned for two days on end, she had answered insolently at first and then had collapsed and admitted everything, more than was asked of her. She had even admitted to being the mother of the bastard whom Roger de Montbrun took everywhere with him and who was in prison, like his father and Séverin Maurel. She had not denied the acts of pillage and violence of which she had been a witness. She said she had consented to them, 'through ignorance'. However, she persisted in denying the miscreance of her uncle, and also of Séverin Maurel. She stated that they were not heretics, but, so to speak, 'in waiting', and that they had been 'Waldensians in their hearts' but were so no longer. She said that her uncle sincerely believed that the bread and the wine of the Mass were the body and blood of Jesus Christ and was sorry that he could not take communion. Asked whether it was true that he had drunk the consecrated wine at Sonnac, and taken the chalice into his own hand, she said yes, he had done so. It was because of the great longing in his heart, not in derision. *Yet he knew that it was sacrilege?* Yes, he knew. *He spoke ill of the Pope and the Church?* Yes, but that was 'in bitterness and grief', because of the new laws and because he had been deprived of his possessions. *Was it true that he followed the heretics?* Yes, he talked to them a great deal on the subject of faith. *Did he venerate them?* Yes, he did

458

venerate them. *So he believed that their faith could bring them to salvation?* Yes, he believed that. *He was of their faith, then?* No, she, Colombe, did not think so. He said he was a Catholic. *In that case why did the heretics accept his presence among them?* They accepted him out of friendship, and because they thought that one day he would know the truth. *Then the accused thought that the heretic faith was the true one?* She did not know. It had been her parents' faith. . . . *Had her grandfather, Pierre-Guillaume de Montbrun, been a heretic believer?* She had never thought so; but since he had been condemned and exhumed, then he must have been.

She was very ignorant, and scarcely able to recite the *Pater* in Latin. Questioned about her faith, she answered that she had taken her first communion and taken the oath when she was twelve, because it was necessary, and that was the law; her father and mother were then in prison, and her grandfather, Pierre-Guillaume, told her that the Catholic faith was good, and the Count and many noble and worthy men had always believed in it. . . . Yes, she believed her grandfather was a Catholic: he always said that her own father had been mad. *Was it true that her uncle had corrupted her at Layrac when she was little more than a child?* He had been trying to comfort her in the great grief she felt after the death of her parents. Upon Brother Alberic's assistant's remarking that the heretics had an odd way of comforting their relatives (a question not entered in the records) she said that her uncle was not a heretic. *Did she then reckon that the Catholic faith permitted such abominations?* No. *But she meant, then, that if her uncle had been a heretic he would not have seduced her?* She did not know. It was not a matter of faith. *Had she been taught to regard incest as a mortal sin?* Yes. *How was it, then, that she had lived for so long in a state of mortal sin?* Many people lived in sin. *Nevertheless, she had been admitted to the presence of heretic ministers despite her unlawful union with a close relative?* It was a secret union. *Was Roger de Montbrun not said to have lain with her before witnesses in the sacristy of the church at Semalens?* At that she blushed violently and said that it was not before witnesses, that she had never done such a thing before witnesses, and that they had no right to insult her. Some people lived in sin all their lives and no one shamed them before a tribunal, and if they were rich they confessed and paid a fine for the poor of the Church. She was quite willing to answer for her faith, but not for things which men should not ask a woman.

She had had a child by Roger de Montbrun; had he been baptised?

459

Yes, Roger himself had baptised him an hour after his birth, in rainwater. *Did she consider he had the right to perform baptism?* He had told her so. She did not know. *He was excommunicated and therefore had no right.* He had never considered his excommunication valid. *Had the child been brought up in the Catholic faith?* No. *Had he already saluted heretics?* Yes. *How many times?* She did not know. Many times. *If his father was a Catholic, why did he allow it?* He saw no harm in it. *Did he not know, then, that he was incurring damnation by so doing?* He thought he would repent before he died.

Had he never been in danger of death, then, in the twelve years the accused had lived with him? He had been wounded twice, once in the head and once in the left side. And before the Viscount's war he had almost died of dysentery. *What state of mind had he been in on the last occasion?* He was in great affliction. *At seeing himself deprived of the comforts of religion?* He was afraid of death. *Had he called for a Catholic priest?* Yes, he had done so. And Séverin had brought the priest from Sonnac by force. *Had this priest confessed the sick man?* Yes, but without giving him absolution, because he said that he had no right to. And Séverin had threatened him with a knife and Uncle Roger had said: 'Let be, I don't need it.' *He did not believe himself in need of absolution?* No, he thought that given in that way it would have no value. *Did he not also ask for the heretic baptism?* No. He hesitated a great deal. Then he got better. *If he was hesitating he must believe in their faith?* I don't think so. *Why don't you think so?* He told me so. And he often used to pray in the Catholic way. *In what way?* He made the sign of the cross and recited the *Ave Maria. Perhaps he did that in pretence?* I don't think so. He was accustomed to do it at night before he went to bed. *None the less, did he not frequently utter blasphemous and sacrilegious speeches?* Yes. *Was he sorry for this?* No. He liked to talk.

"One learns ten times more from a woman than from the most talkative man," thought Brother Alberic, "for a man, even if he confesses, thinks of nothing but turning the truth to his own advantage, and he is generally lying. While once a woman has decided to talk, she warms to her own theme and distorts little." This one had been neither beaten nor threatened with death, but she seemed very much weakened by imprisonment; so much so that after two days' interrogation she had begun to cry and said that she could not go on; then she was taken before Brother Alberic and he had only to look at her to realise that she would

460

talk as though in the confessional. More sincere than their men-folk, why were these creatures so infinitely more repulsive? Much of the reason lay in their bodies, those lasciviously rounded bodies, which their lay garments made more emphatic rather than concealing (moreover, the present creature was young and displayed breasts as round as balls). To these natural blemishes, was added the stale and acrid smell of unwashed flesh, a more pungent odour than that of a man; their flesh, fecund in humours and secretions, their features so easily bathed in tears and mucus, their long snake-like hair, all this, viewed at close quarters, aroused more contempt than pity. Yet, for the sake of bestial lust, men will deliver up to these creatures the secrets of their hearts, and talk to them of faith and God. Such is the sad condition of men who live in the world. If women would only talk from sincere repentance, or at least out of hatred for men! But for the most part they were trying to protect a husband or a lover, and confessed in spite of themselves, because of their weakness. This one wished no harm to her accomplice. At first she had spoken of him with the proper respect of a girl for her father's elder brother. Then Brother Alberic had looked her straight in the eyes and asked her whether she was going back on her promise to speak the whole truth, and she had started to cry again, like a whipped child. Well, yes, it was all true, and young Phoenix was her own son. Roger had made her swear not to tell. She had lost her virtue when she was fourteen.

When a woman reaches this point one is sure of the man too. For they are more perceptive than a father confessor and can guess at secret thoughts and unspoken designs. How many apparently innocent men have been convicted of heresy thus! In bed, they deliver themselves up, bound hand and foot, to the enemy.

Was it true, they asked, that Roger de Montbrun had given her a piece of red silk with gold threads, that had once served as an altar cloth? Yes. He was very much in love with her at the time, and gave her many presents. . . . (A number of witnesses had drawn attention to this woman's rare beauty—a pitiful beauty that was so easily destroyed by tears, hunger and lice! And this lewd body had been decked in fabric woven by pious hands to the glory of the Lord.) *That was sacrilege. Did she know that?* She did not think so then. She had been brought up in the heretic faith. (In fact, she was certainly more of a heretic than

461

the man, but less culpable, because such young people, brought up by impious parents, were paying for others' faults; it was a consequence of the troubled times, and another generation, perhaps two, would be needed before the poison poured into innocent souls would cease to act.) *What did she think of her father?* Her father had always been more concerned about the affairs of the Church than about his family. *Which Church?* That of the heretics. *Yet she had honoured him?* Yes. *Did she honour him at the present time, did she remember him with respect?* She did not know. *Did she consider he had been condemned unjustly?* She did not know. *Did she believe in his salvation?* She did not know. *Did she believe that by his death he had become one of God's martyrs?* She had often been told so. *Did she then believe it?* She did not know. *Did she feel any hatred for those who had condemned him?* She had hated them very much, for his sake and for her mother's. *Did she hate them now?* She did not know. . . . *Wasn't Roger de Montbrun cherishing plans for revenge against the Preaching Friars of Toulouse?* Yes. *Did he hate them?* Yes, very much. *Yet he knew they held their authority from our Holy Father the Pope?* He hated the Pope too. *In that case how could he call himself a Catholic?* He wished the Church of Rome a better pope. *What did he mean by that?* She did not know. *What kind of pope would he have wished for?* A pope who would not wrong innocent people. *Then he considered the heretics innocent people?* She did not know. He said that the new laws were doing more harm to Catholics than to the heretics. *What did he mean?* He said that it was a shame for the Catholics. *Did he believe, then, that the heretics should be allowed to preach in public and corrupt the faithful?* He did believe it. *Was that not a heresy?* She did not know.

"Roger de Montbrun, it is vain for you to persist in denying the facts. Your niece has confirmed her statements on oath."

"She must have done so through fear, or under constraint. I know nothing of what she may have told you."

The man was at the end of his strength. Asked whether he was ready to undergo a harsher interrogation, he replied that he did not know. What did they want of him? A confession of heresy? He was innocent. He had fought side by side with heretic believers, but he was not the only one. He had been trying to win back his possessions. That was not heresy but the natural desire of every man. . . .

He continued to deny it under the whip, with a wearying persistence; he was extremely weak, they could not beat him for long. To threaten him with torture was useless: he was an old fox who knew very well that his case did not justify such measures, that they required special authorisation. Besides, perhaps he would confess. As he dressed again he was trembling violently and seemed about to collapse in sobs. He asked whether he was going to be questioned again in the same manner. Brother Alberic told him that on account of the absence of confessions the interrogation was only adjourned, not finished. The man gazed round him wearily, his eyes pausing on the pillar with the chains suspended from it, on the torturer's assistant who was wiping his hands, chest and neck which shone with sweat. He asked: "Where is Brother Pierre Audiart?" This was the name of the Brother who, owing to his knowledge of medicine, had formerly been present when a man was to be flogged. He was no longer fulfilling this duty, having imprudently allowed an old man to die under the whip; he was a gentle man, performing his office with the most admirable charity, as harsh on himself as he was patient with his Brothers.

Brother Alberic looked at the broken man, slumped on a stone bench with his head in his hands, an eloquent picture of desolation and helplessness. He marvelled at the divine justice which could thus bring all proud, presumptuous men to nought. Where now were his fine clothes, his splendid armour, banqueting halls, tourneys and battles! The smiles of women, the intoxication of profane music, the pomp of courts and the friendship of the great! *Behold the man*, as wretched as the meanest porter, more wretched, since he had never known the virtue of humility which is taught by poverty. Blessed be Thy name, O Lord! You have sent back to us the prodigal son (these, much more than the poor, have need of repentance). "Unnatural son, acknowledge the wisdom, love and mercy of your Mother! When will you cease to strive against Her?"

"What do you want of me?" the man said, lifting his head. "Am I striving now?"

"In your heart you are striving against Her who seeks only to stretch out Her arms to you."

"I swear before God that I am innocent."

"What do you hope to gain by such statements?"

The man stood up and opened his mouth to answer but his face became the colour of clay, he bit his lips and turned away precipitately, retching, with his head down and hands clutching

463

at his chest. It seemed odd that a man who had not eaten since the previous day could still vomit, but he threw up nothing beyond large quantities of bile, phlegm and blood. He retched, painfully, violently, with choking sobs, and finally dropped to his knees in his own vomit, and leaned his head against the bench. He was gasping and trembling, and wiped his mouth on the back of his hand, but was unable to stop spitting. The guards helped him to his feet. His knees were covered in filth and he rubbed them with his hand, then rubbed his hands on his shirt sleeves, blinked and looked at no one.

Brother Alberic had seen this before; he thought it possible the man was ripe for repentance. "Roger de Montbrun, speak!"

The man muttered: "I am in no condition to speak."

"You can speak and you ought to. You are being asked for the truth, nothing more."

"There is no truth."

"Are you a heretic believer?"

"No."

"Have you ever been?"

"No."

As he asked, one after another, the questions he had asked a thousand times before of so many different men, Brother Alberic himself felt a sense of vertigo; he was almost as tired as the man he was interrogating. In the end he was no longer sure who was the hunter and who the victim: the other, whose short-sighted eyes never looked at him, seemed to be deliberately flouting him with his perpetual: "No. I don't know. That is false. I deny it. I deny it, I deny it, I deny it." What then? What had he to deny or not deny? The greatest of all his faults was the refusal to repent. "The Brother Inquisitor would not have dealt as gently with you as I am doing. He has entrusted me with your case, because he knew that I have met you before. You know what awaits you if I do not obtain your repentance."

"I would prefer to die."

"Greater persons than you have been condemned on the grounds of their obdurate perversity."

"I am innocent."

Never had man deserved less to be called innocent; Brother Alberic was beyond relenting at the sight of a drawn, grey face, or traces of vomit in a beard: there was something vile in the degraded body's refusal to acknowledge its wretchedness; as

464

though a little vanity in a little clay were rising in puny, selfish revolt against the Creator, presuming to hoard its poor pride like some unimaginable treasure! There seemed more excuse for a heretic (Brother Alberic had arrived at a measure of tolerance with age), more excuse for his madness, than for these creatures who cleaved solely to their fleshly pride. (They go on counting on their friends, believing they have something to hope for—hence their rage against a court they know to be incorruptible.) "*What have you been promised in return for your silence?*" The accused failed to understand the question. His head flung back against the wall, nostrils quivering, he ran the tip of his tongue over dry lips. This was familiar to Brother Alberic: sometimes thirst made even ordained heretics speak. "What have you been promised in return for your silence?"

"Who could have promised me anything?"

"Count Raymond, for example."

"He has made me no promises."

"You know very well that he has no power to quash a sentence."

"I expect nothing from him. I am innocent."

Ah, why is a monk not permitted to hit that insolent, suffering face, to smash it with his fists? Brother Alberic would have done it not in anger but to arouse, in a last effort to shake this tardy soul which could no longer be touched by words. Is it just that the Church court, which has to elucidate matters of faith— matters touching the gravest offences—should not be permitted to use the means which civil justice employs to convict common felons? The whip was certainly not enough (and even the rack and thumb-screws, which were applied in exceptional cases, and even then frowned on by the Bishop, were frequently unsatisfactory, for the simple reason that the investigator was a cleric and therefore unable to be present during the torture, and ask the right questions at the moment when the victim would be disposed to talk).

"I am thirsty."

"Can't you see that you are torturing yourself by your refusal to repent?"

"I will speak, but give me something to drink first."

"Can I take it that you confess your crimes?"

"No."

"Surely it is madness to destroy yourself like this when you wish to be saved?"

465

"What do you want with me? What have I done to you?"

"To me, nothing. You yourself know what you have done to the Church."

"For pity's sake," said the man, "for pity's sake."

Ah, that was an unworthy trick, invoking pity thus, the shepherd's pity for the wolf! When he could obtain that pity with one word. . . . "Shame on you, demanding pity for bare-faced lies! Look into yourself. What do you hope to gain by lying?" Can this man, beaten, sick, and dying of thirst, still keep the strength to persist, and shall *I* weary of my quest? Brother Alberic pulled himself together and gave orders for a cup of water to be brought. "As soon as you have shown your willingness to repent, you will be allowed to drink, even before you are taken back to prison. Take heart, it will not be long now." The man closed his eyes.

"Why are you doing this to me?" he said.

"Admit that you have been lying."

"It is not right."

"It is always right to tell the truth."

The man was gnawing his wrists, staring, fascinated, at the mess of vomit on the ground at his feet. It was horrible. Less than a beast. The cup had been placed on the ground, four yards away from him; a pewter cup full of clear water, reflecting the light from the candle. He leaped to his feet and was forced back by the two guards.

"I will talk," he said.

"So the things you are accused of are true?"

"Yes. Now give it to me."

"When we are back in the audience chamber and you have signed your confession."

"No."

"You are going back on your confession?"

"I have confessed nothing."

"So, it was a trick?"

"Yes. A trick."

"We shall be here all night," Brother Alberic said to himself. "He is not yet as far gone as I thought." In his irritation, he seized the cup and drank deeply, because he too was thirsty. "Torturer," hissed the other. They stared at one another. They might have been two prisoners locked up together, quarrelling over a cup of water.

"—It would sicken me to drink from it after you!"

466

Brother Alberic emptied the rest of the water in the cup on to the flagged floor. "Roger de Montbrun, you have made a mockery of this court for long enough. You will go back to your dungeon and there you shall stay until you howl for mercy."

The man was taken back to the prison and Brother Alberic returned to his cell to await the hour for matins. His mouth was dry and he seemed to be still thirsty. He did not lie down, for fear of giving way to the temptation of anger, and instead remained on his knees before the crucifix fastened to the wall, but his body's weariness made it impossible for him to pray with a tranquil mind.

Happy the Brothers who spend their lives in perpetual prayer, happy those who go from village to village preaching, happy those who expose themselves to the glory of martyrdom in a pagan land! Yet I may not murmur against my lot, for surely ours is the better part: we whom our obedience forces to cure souls of most hideous leprosy? We are the surgeons of the soul, persecuted and reviled for Christ's sake. (Oh, do not give way to the temptation of pride; have you not seen long since how cheap are these souls, and how flimsy their repentance?) Is it just that an adulterous brigand can make a mockery of our court with impunity, because his body is strong enough to bear thirst? What excuse can he claim? What excuse? Great is the power of words: the felon who proclaims his innocence offers an insult to the truly innocent, and when a thousand witnesses accuse him, his lies are a blow in the face to his judges. God's work in this land suffers because we are too gentle with men like this, who are encouraged by the secret support of the people. "I am innocent." God be thanked, the trials do not take place before witnesses, but if we deliver this man to the secular arm, no doubt he will go to the stake, through the streets of his own city, crying out: "I am innocent and a good Catholic." Besides, Brother Alberic did not desire the man's death.

A soul. His aim was to awaken the soul in all these bodies abandoned to debauchery and self-love. At the moment when a man is reduced to nothing, when he lies there in his own vomit and urine, humbled, stripped of his illusions at last, with the last glimmer of defiance driven from his eyes, it is then that the soul appears, naked, innocent, if only for an instant, abandoned, trusting, no longer even begging for mercy but yielding itself unreservedly to those who have brought it to this abject condition.

467

There is beauty in this moment. (This very man, long ago—this man had feigned a conversion, with such fervour that he had succeeded in convincing Brothers of great experience, even the Father Prior himself—he, Brother Alberic, had never believed in him—he had wept real tears, he had succeeded in touching them, finding words that seemed inspired by a true love of God. . . . How justly hated are men's words and voices, and even the expression in their eyes, as long as a man is still master of his expression!)

"Innocent." Men like this have the insolence of Saul and Ahab, and it is for this reason that unrestricted use of the torture should be permitted, because only women and children are afraid of the whip. He will talk—after all, he is an ageing man, nearer sixty than fifty, ageing and worn out by a dissolute life (the girl's words, when she was asked if the accused often sinned with her, had been: "No, seldom more than twice a week"), exhausted by imprisonment, driven beyond endurance. "Innocent", only guilty men speak so, since the souls of those who are really innocent are not hardened, and they are easily led to remorse. Sacrilege, plunder and blasphemy—common enough crimes for a soldier; but this man was one of the Count's agents, and beyond all doubt the things the Count could do, and in secret had done, to thwart the justice of the Church were only too well known—like a latter-day Judas, the Count pretended to pursue the enemies of the Church with zeal but secretly accorded them his protection, so long as they did not admit to being heretics.

This man would be hard put to it to prove his innocence; the Montbrun mansion had been destroyed after the posthumous trial of Pierre-Guillaume de Montbrun (a dubious trial that, they had never proved that the old man had received the Consolamentum on his deathbed), and the family was notoriously gangrenous with heresy. The woman Guillelme de Layrac (a most dangerous female) had been in prison for three years, following a complete confession. Her sons were living on their domain—and were, moreover, irreproachable Catholics. At her trial the Lady of Layrac had displayed such animosity towards them that she had succeeded in convincing Brother Peter Seila. (Men are stronger than women, and the ordained heretic stronger than the believer; but mothers of this kind are stronger even than heretics, and are more cunning in protecting the issue of their bodies than the Devil himself.) Young Raymond-Guillaume de

Montbrun and Bernard de Montbrun could not be accused of acting in collusion with their father: they were among the first to accuse him, as also were their cousins, the youngest sons of the notorious Bertrand. There was no cause for self-congratulation in this: the young people were acting purely from motives of fear and cupidity. The Church was reaping a field of tares and would have to wait a long time yet before the good corn began to appear: these people were corrupted to the marrow of their bones. This fellow calls himself a Catholic because he is able to bear arms and command a company: in these degenerate times, we are compelled to employ men of all sorts in defence of the Holy Sepulchre. The Holy Father in his laudable zeal for the cause of the Holy Land hides crimes against the faith beneath a Crusader's cross, and Louis of France, who is young and ambitious, will grant amnesty to the worst enemies of the faith if they are prepared to make a show of swearing allegiance to the Church by taking the cross! While men of the Church, blinded by their personal friendships or animosity towards the mendicant orders, are all prepared to testify in favour of men accused of a thousand crimes. . . .

"Confessions. Coward that I was to lose patience. Another hour and he would have confessed."

Another hour. Brother Alberic pictured that fierce hour which he had so stupidly denied himself at the moment when the accused man's need for water had aroused the same thirsty contraction in his own body. They were panting, their tongues hanging out like dogs', and trembling violently. "*As the hart panteth after the water brooks.*" Oh, if the soul only desired God with such a longing! God would flow into it like a waterspout into a gaping hole. The entire man is all one gaping hole, a gaping void—there is no more shame or thought in him, he is nothing but insatiate longing.

Moreover, one is free to satisfy this longing or not.

Others have been known to talk when they saw their wives or mothers scourged; this man would not talk for the woman, but perhaps for the child? The boy was a trifle young (eleven or twelve) and Brother Alberic had a weakness for children. Little Phoenix was a sweet, attractive child, like a flower grown on a dungheap: huge hazel eyes, a small innocent mouth, and a trustful air, that was still trustful despite his fear and two months' imprisonment. His parents must have taught him well because he would say nothing beyond: "No, my lord", and: "I don't know, my lord." "And what if we beat you?" He looked down and did not answer. (He thought his mother was dead and called his mother 'Cousin Colombe'. They could take him into the monastery orphanage and so turn his parents' sin to the benefit of God. Such is the Lord's infinite goodness that he does not despise the fruit of an unlawful, even sacrilegious union! Bastards were known to have attained the highest Orders and set examples by their saintly lives.)

The sight of his child being given a beating easily touches any father, and one who is getting on in years especially. It was not customary to chastise boys below the age of fourteen, in court procedure, at least, although it seemed strangely inconsistent that what parents and schoolmasters were permitted to do, the Church's court should not be. As though a child were not as well able to tell the truth at eleven as at fourteen.

It was a nice piece of calculation: there was no need for the child even to undress. When the boy was brought into the torture chamber (his father was there already, waiting to be flogged himself), he submitted, docilely, as they led him up to the pillar: he had been told that he was naughty and deserved a beating. He drew himself up, gnawing his small, much-bitten lips. But when he saw his father he changed, reddened and struck at the soldiers who held him with his hands. It was curious to see how the mere sight of his father had turned a sensible boy into a baby: his features had suddenly softened and drooped, his eyes filled with tears and sought his father's as if to ask: "Where am I? What is happening?" Roger de Montbrun gave in with a fairly good grace and declared himself ready to bear witness to the truth.

His capitulation, indeed, seemed somewhat too easy, since it was evident that he was mainly anxious to reassure the child. He winked at him, and even made pathetic attempts to smile, while his voice was level and, if not altogether cheerful (that would have been too much to ask), at least not harsh. Returned to the audience chamber, where he and his son were seated, each between two guards, on the bench set for the accused, he declared that, having always been faithful to the Church, he was prepared to acknowledge his faults and respectfully desired to satisfy the Brethren of the Holy Office in everything, and would be ready to repeat his confessions in the presence of the Father Inquisitor. All the charges against him were true. Altogether, he said much the same as any accused man who had been touched by repentance, with, in addition, a kind of gentle courtesy which gave his confessions an indefinable air of urbanity that was more than a little irritating. Only the day before he appeared to have reached the last stages of exhaustion. (Even now Brother Alberic was too well acquainted with the little nervous twitches, the quivering nostrils and eyelids, and the smile which had less to do with real gaiety than the grin on the face of a corpse, not to know that he was very little stronger. A man driven to that condition sometimes fell into paroxysms of demoniacal laughter or into convulsions.)

Roger de Montbrun, do you repent? Completely. He repented that he had followed the heretics. *Did he belong to their faith?* Yes, since the reverend Brother Alberic had found him guilty of heresy. *That was not a sufficient answer. Did he feel in his heart that he was guilty of heresy?* No doubt he did. The Church knew better than he did what was or was not heresy. *By what means did he intend to prove his devotion to the Church?* By a complete submission. *What had he to say about the secret intrigues of the heretics in the districts of Lantarès and Razès?* That he detested these intrigues. *What did he know of people who sheltered heretics?* Many people sheltered them. Never having stayed for long in the same place he did not remember any names. *If he did not know names, then presumably he knew their rank or occupation?* People who attended sermons did not always say whether they were blacksmiths, carpenters or masons. *Yes, but what of those who received heretics into their houses?* We usually came at night: people are wary and distrust everybody. *It seems to me that you are mocking us. You know that we cannot believe in your repentance unless you give us reliable proofs.*

The child seemed to be half-asleep, leaning forward with his elbows on his knees and his face in his hands, though from time to time he blinked and opened large, terrified eyes. As the father was being taken into the next room, he looked at the boy with an affectionate smile that seemed to say: "Be patient, I shall come back for you." Such is the false power of carnal affections! This child had been enveloped in falsehood from his cradle; waking was hard! It would certainly be better for the boy, who was still almost innocent, if he were never again exposed to the pernicious sweetness of such affections.

Flogged expertly, this time (for the torturer was a deft workman who did not allow his victims to lose consciousness), Roger

471

de Montbrun uttered enough names for his repentance to appear plausible. The scribe wrote them down as he said them, since it was essential that the man could be reminded of them at the moment when he was taken down and might attempt, as prisoners often did, to repudiate his words. Roger lay on a hurdle, looking about him with the indifference which often characterises men exhausted by pain. No, he was not trying to repudiate his admissions. *Such a one?* Yes. *Such a one?* Yes. *The priest of Villemaur? His sister-in-law? The Lord of Sennazac's equerry? His son's wife? The son of the late Jean-Rigaud de Marcillac, Agnes de Magnanac, wife of your son Raymond?* . . . *Rixende, daughter of Raymond-Jourdain de Cissac?* Yes, yes, yes. Admittedly, most of these names were already on the lists. *Had Count Raymond entrusted him with any secret mission?* No, never. *When the said count was treasonably styling himself Duke of Narbonne, had the accused not solicited an audience with the Count in a private house in Narbonne?* Yes. *With what object?* In the hope of obtaining my pardon, and that he would intercede for me with my lord Bishop of Toulouse. *Had the Count promised him this?* Yes, if things went well for him. *Was the Count not encouraging rebellion in the land by abetting the heretics?* He had done, yes. Not any more. . . .

When the accused was taken back to the audience chamber to sign his confession, the child, who had fallen asleep on the bench, awoke with a start and almost fell to the ground in his horror. Then he ran to the hurdle and had to be held back by force as he struggled and wept. *"But I wanted to be beaten! I wanted to!* . . . *I wanted to, as well! I want to stay with him."* His father looked at the child, a lingering, exhausted look, and made an attempt to smile, but this time his smile held only a bitter unhappiness.

II. The Last Prison

Thus Roger de Montbrun, knight, obtained the Church's forgiveness a second time for sins which in other times and in another land would have merited death. But human justice is an inconsistent thing, and even the most appalling acts of sacrilege, when they have become more or less common offences, do not receive their due punishment; moreover, justice should be merciful towards those who have repented. Roger de Montbrun was convicted under ecclesiastical law, as a believer and abetter

472

of heresy; he was judged sincerely penitent and condemned to perpetual incarceration in a dungeon of the Alemans prison. As he was advanced in years, and noted for his devotion to the Count's person, he was eligible for a fairly clean cell with a window high up in the wall giving on to the moat, and chains an ell in length.

On the day the chains were gyved about his ankles, Roger had said to himself: "Rest, at last." That day he asked nothing better than to be left in peace. The prison governor had informed him that a diocesan ruling authorised prisoners who had been sentenced to share a cell with their lawful wives (so as not to separate those whom God had joined together), a matter which was the simpler in this case because the said wife was already in the same prison. Roger answered that he would have been delighted with the company of any other lady, even of a common whore, but that particular lady he would not have at any price, and he did not imagine she would insist upon the favour; many people, he added, would find small comfort in being locked up for the rest of their days with their lawful wives. In fact he was not interested in any wife, lawful or otherwise; he wanted to be alone.

Solitude and a good prison, and the knowledge that he would be dragged through no more interrogations. It was an enviable fate and many prisoners dreamed of nothing more: a good prison with light, a bed of straw, and a gutter in the middle of the cell to drain away the ordures. The two chains were fastened to a ring stapled into the wall; they were not long enough to allow him to reach the door, but he could take one large step or two small ones, and touch the opposite wall. All the prisoners feared the short chain: they were careful to keep quiet on that account, because the prison smith would shorten the chain of any man who made trouble so that he was obliged to perform all his physical functions in one place, and had to lie on the ground and stretch out his arms in order to reach his bread and pitcher of water. (The door was never opened. It was made of criss-crossed iron bars and the gaoler merely pushed food and drink through it on to the floor.)

On the first day, Roger paced up and down his cell, as far as his good chain permitted, exploring with the palm of his hand every bit of the wall within his reach, and measuring the window embrasure with his eye. This was situated at just below ceiling level and by putting his arms up above his head he could reach

473

the sill. The wall was so thick that he would have had to jump as high as the ceiling to glimpse a patch of sky; he could see nothing but stone, sometimes grey and sometimes tinged with yellow by the sun: rays of sunlight penetrated as far as the topmost bars of the door. It was July, and the heat brought a noisome stench from the moat, which, as the cell was on one of the lower floors, immediately above those actually underground, could not have been very far away. The prison had never been so full and anyone who fell into the moat would have been drowned in three feet of sewage—the product of saints and brigands alike, since in this, more than anything, all men were created equal; it is one brotherhood which even popes and kings have never escaped.

"Many people," thought Roger, "would gladly be in my place." He had been in prison for three months (the lilacs were in flower on the day he was captured, and the grass was still green and fresh), and in those three months he had become a good judge of prison life. He had been in the hospital, in the communal prison, in antechambers and audience chambers, and in the evil dungeons where, for lack of room, people were confined three and four at a time, in a space hardly big enough for one man. In such surroundings a man would come to hate his best friend—assuming they locked you up with your friends! It was a relief to be taken for interrogation. But once before the judges, even the cell was preferable. Men deprived of food and sleep and tormented by vermin soon begin to lose all their faculties—how could you blame those who talked? Degrade a man to that extent and a few strokes of the lash were enough to make the words pour of their own accord, like tears or urine. Suppose they had beaten her? Parbleu! They would be fools to think twice when they could see breasts like hers and not a penny to pay for it. She was no coward. (Disguised as a boy, with her braids wound round her head underneath her red bonnet, at the siege of Carcassonne, she had been such a boy that men had turned round in the middle of a battle to point her out. "God! Have you ever seen such beauty, even in a woman?" While dressed in women's clothes, she inspired love even in men like the Count of Foix and the Viscount of Béziers who might have had their pick elsewhere.) Yet she was faithful, that was the most astonishing thing, faithful to a man who could not marry her; because he was the first. Rachel must have turned in her grave—if she had a grave. Somewhere on the banks of the Garonne a few fragments of charred

474

bone, buried in the mud, turn over. . . . *"Roger, this is not well done. Ah, Roger, she is a child, a child who doesn't understand yet, Roger. . . ."*

"And I? Do I understand? What good did your virtue do you, Rachel? Your faithful husband, your daughters brought up in the fear of sin? Colombe has had nothing to complain of from me, I guarded and protected her, and drew my sword against anyone who impugned her honour. She turned informer of her own accord—God keep her! They got everything out of her: she said so much that she could not have let out one more word even if she had wanted to." Gutted like a chicken—he had seen her at the trial, at the *Act of Faith*, looking pale and sallow, with grey shadows round her long eyes, her back bent, her head drooping. He imagined—since carnal thoughts give a man no rest in prison —that more than one gaoler must have had his pleasure of her, perhaps even, who knew, Brother Alberic himself. (He would merely have to lock her up and come to interrogate her in private, he could still be sprightly enough with such a lovely girl in his power. . . .) So lovely—oh, the tiny, ringlike curls on her temples and the nape of her neck, her dark golden braids, her alabaster nose. Her mouth was softer than a ripe peach. Her slender waist and fair, damask belly would have damned an angel, her tender round breasts, like two small snowballs, and her young arms so round and smooth.

What had they done to her? Yet it was still better for her to be in the common prison with other honest women; better that, Colombe, than the feather beds of a brothel where men would have made you ill and ugly in a year. What is freedom for girls like you, dispossessed and condemned for heresy, without men to defend you? Even your brothers would not take you back: the elder ones are in Spain, and the younger good Catholics.

Good Catholics, thank God, and my two legitimate boys are Catholics too, beyond reproach, no doubt they gave as many names as they could, beginning with their mother. (Mothers are like that: *"Accuse me as much as you can, my darlings, I shall not escape in any case and so at least you may as well profit by it."* That is the new way of bringing up children.) Could they doubt the faith of a boy who would denounce his mother? My good Guillelme, let them put her in here with me (whom God has joined together. . .), she can't be more than forty anyway, we could still breed legitimate offspring and have them live here, between the bars of the door, my chain and this window where there is no sky. My son born in sin is no true son (why did she have to mention him, the poor fool?), not even a real bastard, he has neither father nor mother any more.

They will take him into their orphanage out of charity, and will he be safe from the birch there? You betrayed yourself rather than see him beaten; did you spare him one thrashing only to have him suffer two a day, perhaps, in future? Madmen that we are, raving madmen, able to think of nothing beyond the present. A wise man would have said: "Let my child die under the lash, here and now; it's the best thing that could happen to him." (No, they would not have beaten him to death, the Father Inquisitor would not have stood for it, it would have been a grave irregularity. . . .) No, not to death, but even so? Should I have stood by and watched? There you are, Brothers, it was fear, not piety, made me yield. I saw that there was no way out for me because you were set on extracting a confession. (And who knows, maybe I had made up my mind to die rather than submit?) Besides, the things you set such store by are of little value, my confessions are of little value; they are not worth your taking off a child's shirt and breeches and you shall not touch him in my presence. There are many things which I cannot prevent, but at least my son shall know his father still had the power to stop you beating him.

You will teach him many things: that all he had been told before was lies, and the people he had lived amongst were damned; that he was the fruit of sin and must thank you for your kindness, but, whether he believes it or not, my Fathers, he shall know what a real father is. I have never beaten him in my life.

Supposing you live for another ten years, and they bring him to you one day, your son, become a lay Brother in their seminary, a real monk, dressed in grey frieze, with hard eyes, tight lips and pinched nostrils, proud of being able to confound the 'heretics', and blessing those who have raised him in the fear of God? An arrogant young monk, ardent and stern, because he is not Bertrand's grandson for nothing. "Phoenix . . ." "*Brother Phoenix.*" "Phoenix, do you remember this, or that?" "*Since I have seen the light I have forgotten everything. I pray for your sins.*" "Pray rather for the sins of those who have put me in prison." "*Shame on you for those words! May the Lord grant you the grace of repentance.*"

"Even so, Phoenix, would I wish to see you live? Alas, yes. Am I God? *Even so!*"

476

Roger sniffed and realised that there were tears in his eyes and his nose was running. He sat on his palliasse, leaning against the wall, and stared at the barred door, imagining he could see, already, behind the bars, the figure of the child in a monk's habit. Then the sobs rose in his throat and shook his chest: so do men break their hearts over evils to come, when they have had more than their share of evils past and present. And the future seems more real because the past is already dead and nothing can change it.

He was such a pretty child: gay and affectionate, and with such a lively intelligence for his age. A brave little man already; even when he was ill he did not cry. We had not hardened him to blows and rough words. Now he is all alone in a house where he will be grudged every morsel of bread: without furs in winter or shoes in summer, with dry bread to eat and the mattresses in the dormitory stuffed with bugs. Three of his grandparents burned—one dead and two alive—and his father and mother imprisoned for life, all these things must be paid for. How much piety will it take to wipe them out? Otherwise, you will get nothing but blows all your life. God save you.

Yet what does his life mean to you, his and so many others, when you can no longer do anything for anyone? Are you, by any chance, hoping times will change? Are you hoping the Count will drive them out again, the King of France ban them from the realm, the Pope condemn them? Ah, we have talked of it so often! We could have taught all the kings in Christendom a lesson—even the Pope himself! What a pity; a pity we only talked among ourselves and neither kings nor popes ever heard a word of what we had to say. Outlaws can talk of justice and charity, it costs them nothing. But only the strong can truly display these qualities, and they know neither charity nor justice.

I am not strong, then spit on me, and when you no longer do so, I shall know you are not strong enough to do it. That is all the justice there will ever be in this world.

From tears, Roger passed to bitter laughter, telling himself: "What have you done? You, with your grey hairs, for twelve years you have been behaving like a child—twelve years, did I say? All your life, because even in the days when your hair was red, hadn't you a head on your shoulders? Didn't you see which way the wind was blowing? But, my God, when and how could I have been more Catholic than I was? Had we any choice? As a

477

man of Toulouse, could I have betrayed the Count? Once exiled
and condemned, what traitorous action would have redeemed
me? Because at least," he thought, "whatever else men may
reproach me with, I have never been false. . . . But are you not
like the nun who permits her lover every favour except that of
kissing her mouth, in order to keep intact the lips which pronounced her vows? The jibe is fair, but not altogether, because
the magnitude of the sin varies with time and circumstance.

"You let yourself be captured, stupidly, with weapons in your
hands. And you defended yourself, stupidly, like a poor fool,
instead of telling them: 'I know the place where ten heretics are
hiding. I will take you there at once if I am promised a light
sentence for myself and my family.' But I did not do it. So what
am I complaining of?

"O Lord, I did not do it, and a fine piece of folly it was!
Brothers, tell me how you have managed to turn treachery into a
good deed, and how Jesus Christ loves men who sell their brothers
and their friends? Shame on you, Brothers, because, from all the
holy apostles, martyrs and confessors, you have given us Judas
Iscariot for our pattern and our model. God forbid that I should
ever pray to that saint, though you preach his virtues to me until
Christmas, until the end of time!"

That night, Roger de Montbrun fell asleep with a tranquil
mind, or at least as well satisfied with himself as he could be.
What is the use of weeping over ills you cannot prevent?

He woke in the morning to the noise of the pitcher of water on
the flagstones by the door. He leaped up and dashed to the door,
hoping to catch a glimpse of the gaoler, but the man had already
gone. "Ah, God!" thought Roger. "What is the matter with me?
What was I thinking of? What does it matter to me whether the
gaoler is called Jean or Pierre? Yet, perhaps if I watch I shall see
him pass again and can call to him." It seemed, then, that the
love of men was incurable. What other man could he see there?

He stood there, still haggard with sleep, holding his breath and
listening to the clatter of the man's shoes in the flagged passage.
There was the sound of a bucket being put down, the chink of the
pewter jug against the edge of the bucket. He was quite close,
would he say anything?

The footsteps receded. Roger picked up the pitcher of water
and the piece of bread. A good ration. They were not mean. From

habit he made the sign of the cross and said grace as he broke the bread. He always did this for the first meal of the day. He drank some water: the water was cloudy and tasted slightly of metal, but Roger could not forget the days when he had been thirsty, and he felt very rich. If they give me as much every day, I shall have nothing to complain of.

Having quenched his thirst, he took a step towards the door, dragging his chains: he could touch the bars with his hand. They were a good two fingers thick, how could he think of sawing through them, and what with? Even the links of the chain were much too big. Roger realised that he was thinking idle, stupid, impossible thoughts, like a child dreaming of a voyage among the stars. He would never break out of prison with only his own physical strength: everything there was iron and stone, beside which the toughest flesh was soft and tender and could only bruise itself.

It would be possible, with a long chain and a good deal of effort, to strangle himself; it would also be possible to hurl himself head foremost against the wall, but strangulation was more certain and less painful. Roger was not tempted to try. Instead he sat down on his bed of straw, chin in hand, and tried to understand. "Man's life is made up of the joys and sorrows of the day, and of tomorrow, and he fashions himself a future according to his own hopes and fears. But when he must tell himself: 'The future is all there, now, and nothing will change, nothing different will ever happen to you'—when he says that, there is a blockage somewhere in the back of his mind, thought cannot go on because that is something as hard to conceive of as a wall behind which there is *nothing*—not earth or water or town or forest or precipice, but simply nothing."

Only the previous day he had been thinking his fate an enviable one, as though his confinement were to last no more than three days. "Well, my lad, after those three there will be three more, and if the first three days are good, why should those that follow be any worse? They will be the same day, the same day, endlessly repeated. The same day, but if they told you that it was your last, you would wish for a thousand more. It is not the last, then why are you complaining?

"Never again to see anything except these walls? What's that, you are fifty-seven years old and you have seen more than many people would see in ten lives, isn't that enough for you? Instead

479

of thanking God for the fine things you have seen, you are wishing for more. You have seen such evils come upon your country that another man would have plucked out his eyes for grief. Is it Brother Alberic's face you lack, or the cathedral of St. Stephen full of enforced penitents, or the city streets where so many splendid houses (including your own father's) have been pulled down, or do you want the communal dungeons where bodies are crawling with lice and faces distorted with fear? Or the torture chamber, and the shame of speaking, vomiting up the words because you can no longer control what you are saying? You are at peace. They will set no more cups of water in front of you, and then drink them themselves. Here is a pitcher still almost full, take it, drink, you are the master.

"Lord, if they only told me that once a week I should be entitled to see the prison courtyard, to walk as far as the chapel and hear Mass! If I could see other prisoners, even though I could not speak to them."

As he went over his trial once again in his mind, Roger told himself that after all he was not a lamb, and he had been guilty of more than one blunder which he could have avoided. But for the suspicion that he was attached to the heretics, he would have been put in the communal prison and not chained to the wall; he would have been able to keep Séverin with him, perhaps even the child. . . . But then can a man not be led astray by passion even when he is fifty? Can he not desire vengeance and wish to help his friends? How many men should be in prison if these were crimes? You went too far. Lord, did we think of that then? Who thinks about going too far when he is fighting to recover his rights and his country's liberty?

Do not evade the issue. You worked for the heretics, you defended their faith. Rigueur's faith. The heart is a strange creature: it can happen that it loves more strongly when love is over, and where it no longer aspires to gain anything, it is there it aspires to give. God knew, his friendship for that woman was sincere.

There are some crimes which can send a man mad, or at least turn his brain, and on the day Roger had learned of Rigueur's death he had promised himself to attend on those she loved and spill the last drop of his blood for them. He was out in his calculations, but he had, in fact, spilled a good two or three pints.

He had been in St. Bertrand-de-Comminges, in the house of

Bernard de Luscan, when he heard the news. It was the Nativity of the Virgin, and the bells were ringing until the air in the streets and above the rooftops shuddered and vibrated with the endless, all-pervading *ding-dong-dong*. There was a procession round the cathedral and the cloister, and gold-embroidered canopies surmounted by glass cabochons shone in the sun. Banners glittered with golden fringes and light glinted from gold crosses encrusted with opals and amethysts. Everywhere windows and turret gables were decked with red curtains and shields. But only madmen rejoice to see good things they cannot have. Bernard de Luscan was a courtly man, somewhat of a heretic, and instead of following the procession he chose to remain at home, on the excuse of illness, watching from the window and drinking cooled wine. So Roger stood beside him, leaning on the window frame, and watched too. That was life! To think that I too could have lorded it in Toulouse, dressed in scarlet among the Count's knights in the procession! In Toulouse, also, the bells are ringing and they are bearing aloft the crosses and banners and relics, and singing *Salve Regina*.

It seemed as though he would only have to open his eyes to find himself twenty or thirty years younger—here, in Comminges, the bells are ringing just the same, there are the same psalms, the same feasts come round again every year. Distant swelling voices take up the same chant: *Regina Coeli, Redemptoris Mater*. They are chanting in Rome, and in Paris, and in Constantinople. Very good, and what then? To all eternity.

A fortnight later, Bérenger d'Aspremont and his wife were burnt alive, in Toulouse, with two other believers.

How had they come to be captured? They were doing no more harm to anyone: they were living like vagabonds. An old couple; an old man and a woman no longer young, going through towns and villages, working for a little bread. Bérenger was ailing, wounded in the leg; his soldiering days were over.

They had not taken their vows and were therefore burnt as obdurate and unrepentant. Imprisonment for life or the stake? They had preferred the stake. Less from fear of imprisonment than because they were unwilling to deny their faith. Their faith was all they had left. Their children were in Spain, their hopes dead and buried.

If we had fought better, Lord, if we had been able to defend ourselves better. . . . This man was the flower of the chivalry of

481

Toulouse, and, in other times, he would have lived in his own mansion, with his children and grandchildren around him, respected by the Count, the arbiter in all matters of honour and the sponsor of more than one young knight. He would have been consul, and not merely once, but five times, while his voice would have carried more weight in the Parliament than a dozen others. *In other times.* We would have given our lives and our souls for the return of those times, when we were masters in our own house, and when honour was valued at its rightful price!

They took Rigueur for a wooden doll and put her in the fire— when she spoke to them and looked at them with living eyes. It was still only a few days ago that her eyes were living and her heart beating. Now all the warmth of a generous heart is wasted, such a warmth that across mountains and valleys this silent, jaded, hardened heart warmed to it again. Her ashes will warm no one any more. Her pitiful ashes, a little heap of blackened bone and offal; what though we knew it was fated, that she was not alone, what though we have forged our hearts of iron? Rusted, rusted to the quick, they are hearts of rust.

Rigueur let them burn her, and her soul—pray God—dwells in paradise (and those who tell us differently are our enemies). There is no more Rigueur in this world, no more Rigueur than there are grapes in a devastated vineyard, no more Rigueur than water in a dried-up well. Nothing any more. She no longer hates, nor fears, nor prays. She has no eyes now to see the young moon climbing over the mountain, no longer huddles in her cloak to keep out the cold, she will never be hungry again. Was there, then, too much warmth left in this world? No more Rigueur than sun at midnight, no more Rigueur than justice in this world.

It was she who wished it so, this proud woman who could not recant. The Church offers them a pardon which costs nothing: it is easy to forgive those who lie down flat and lick your feet. Bérenger had never licked anyone's feet and he was not going to begin when he was sixty.

There was one folly Roger had committed: he had gone on a pilgrimage to Montgeil, to be again in the place where Rigueur had passed her childhood and see again the tower where once they used to meet. Rigueur's soul lay heavy on his soul at that moment, and instead of shutting his heart to regrets, he called them to him. Late as it was. A man still young had loved her, what was left of that man now? Old age strides to meet us, and

482

still we have said nothing, found nothing: age leads us not to wisdom but to an ever more fruitless perturbation. In a worn-out heart the memories fade, one after another, and one fine day a spark ignites and all flares up—burnt, the poor sweetheart, the wasted, ageing woman, like a boxwood branch thrown on the fire.

Here, except for the house of Montgeil, which had been destroyed, all was almost as before. The young trees had grown and nut trees had sprung up around the threshold of the watch-tower; but the outcrops of stone still protruded from among the undergrowth on the hillside and the big oak was still standing, with only a few more dead branches.

The bright blue sky and the hillside which stretched on the far side of the stream—covered with trees, black, purple, green or yellowing, a tapestry of many colours—seemed to have been washed in sorrow and shone with a purer brilliance than ever. So does a mother put all her jewels in her dead child's coffin. The dead child, decked in all the glory of a fine October day, clothed in crystal and gold and azure, lamented her unburied body through the cries of the wild hawks, Shuddering still, and bleeding, shattered by the horror of the thing that had happened to her, but gallant as always, she struggled to tear herself from earth towards heaven; and by a thousand griefs and a thousand joys the earth held her prisoner. Shall I haul a scrap of red cloth up to the dead branch of this oak again? Do not tempt her disembodied spirit, stripped of its garment of flesh. She is close at your side, like the betrothed girl who put the ring of invisibility on her finger, and she can see and hear; but the ring of death is welded to her finger so that she cannot take it off.

Perhaps there, at the foot of the oak tree, or beside this rock rising out of the tall, yellowed grass and the faded foxgloves, her soul is waiting, an invisible bundle of light, at once powerful and poor, a pure resonant voice singing in a house of the deaf. She is certainly here, Roger thought; my heart returns incessantly to the time when we were lovers. She was strong and steady as this grey stone against which I press my forehead, the doorstep of our tower—then what is this pain, Lord? The pain of seeing stones crumble to dust, melt into water. Oh to be able to think, if only for an instant: *"She is thirty, or fifty, leagues from here, she sees the sky through the bars of her prison."* They stripped her of her body as one flays an animal.

483

You are here, before me, Rigueur, living and bodiless, living and apart, living and tall as the sky and divided from your poor, human voice which is silent for ever.

You are here, before me, Rigueur, for ever mute, when there is so much left unsaid. Your soul, flayed alive, beats its wings, on and on, and cries its endless lament to God. I stay here, lying on the stone threshold, as though deaf, dumb and blind, pleading my cause before my silent Judge. The fire has devoured her lips.

Is there a law which says that children should not be slaughtered, nor women raped, nor the poor starve? Is there a law, human or divine, which says that people who will not renounce their faith should not be burned? Where have you ever seen such a law?

She was pure and innocent. "That is not for you to judge. We know better than you what she was. A heretic and damned."

Slowly, Roger got up from the doorstep of the tower and started down the slope towards the spring: his head was on fire and his eyes burning until he no longer knew if he was hot or cold. In the days when he used to come here to meet Rigueur he had been twenty years younger and never went hungry. "What, twenty years already? We used to think we would have won our peace in twenty years. Many things have happened since then, but that year was longer than the rest."

At the spring he cleared away the moss and rampant grasses from the trickle of water and drank from the hollow of his hand. It was like ice, it was fresh and clean and hurt his lips and numbed his hand. The cold was so exhilarating that Roger threw back his head and drank from the rock itself, and the water ran down inside his collar and soaked the hair on the nape of his neck. He went on drinking until his chest and stomach were frozen and his throat hurt. Then he stood up, blinking, his head whirling and his eyes burning more than ever.

He could no longer tell whether he was thirsty, but that water must have been the water of forgetfulness. His head was empty of all thoughts. He lay down on the dry grass and watched the trickle of water threading gently between tufts of moss and stones. A big sapphire-blue dragon-fly with green wings was darting and hovering over the spring, occasionally coming to rest on the black beads of an elderberry. A little further off, on a rock which jutted out from among the tall grass, Roger saw a bed of moss and on that bed a couple lay embraced. They were naked yet untroubled by the cool breeze, because they lay in the full heat of mid-July; all around them hung a strong scent of warm mint, pine resin, sweat and earth. Roger could not make out their faces very clearly, but he saw the two gleaming bodies: the man's lighter and brighter in colour, the woman's like the husk of a ripe hazel nut. They were embracing with a kind of peaceful frenzy and their sighs of love were like the cries of the wild hawks. The woman's black hair was spread, snake-like, around her, while the man's hair was red, a bright, glaring red like maple leaves in autumn. Before this vision Roger felt his own body become frail and insubstantial. He knew that he was looking at his own image, the image of his soul in another time, a truer time. (Man is a lute not easily tuned, and one whose sound is more often false than true.)

The blue and green dragon-fly swooped over the lovers and they vanished. "Here too, then?" Roger thought. "Not quite naked surely: she had on her shift of raw linen, and the water crept from the spring drop by drop when I collected some in the hollow of my hand to cool her cheeks and her breasts. . . . "Roger, I too remember our happiness, but why have you come to disturb my grief? The man you were then is almost as I am.

"Roger, what a face is this? You have wrinkles under your eyes, and hollow cheeks, your nose is longer and your lips wasted, your head is partly bald and the colour gone from your hair. It is strange that I can still recognise you, I who came here to find our joys again!"

Ah, her soul is here, walled up within her thoughts just as I in mine! . . . How well she used to sing; and how she could laugh; her laughter was like a proud, quick wild foal rushing through a mountain stream. When she was thoughtful it was as though the flies stopped flying and the leaves quivering. Out of so many men who knew and honoured her, I am the only one to mourn her body.

(How proud and chaste and pure this woman was, this he had not learned all at once, but she had shown herself to him in the course of long years and grown in his sight, revealing ever more and more the excellence of her soul, so that as he came to desire nothing for himself he had loved her better still, for the memory of their past joys.)

He had seen her, five years earlier, below Montségur, and times were good then. The Count was at Narbonne and in every town and castle, from Comminges as far as Roussillon, the news was being read and proclaimed: how Count Raymond, compelled and constrained by the numerous vexations, injustices, acts of treachery which the King and the seneschals had perpetrated against him in violation of treaties they had made, did solemnly break the pledge he had made at Meaux in the year 1229, to his sovereign lord the King. A day good enough to make you kiss the lips of your worst enemies! Many barons were gathered below Montségur, both the landed from those parts and those who were landless. There was talk of weapons. In the castle of Montségur alone, there were sufficient reserves to equip every able-bodied man for ten leagues around. The time was coming to descend on the plain otherwise than in small bands.

But there was something like surprise in the men's eyes: what, all to begin again, was it possible? Are we being deceived? Has the day we have been waiting for come at last? *Like a lightning flash from East to West.* . . . We have not seen it, are we really ready? (By being in continual readiness they were never ready, and *besides they were deceived*. But they did not know that yet.) Rigueur was gay that day as she sat with the ladies of Bélesta and Montferrier in the hall of the hospice, now transformed into an armoury. She was mending the battle tunics belonging to her menfolk—her husband, her son and her son-in-law. Under her swift fingers the needle flashed through the stuff in time to the rhythm of the song. The women were singing in chorus, and now it was a song of battle. . . . A month before, the Inquisitor Guillaume Arnaud and his companions had received their payment: twenty or thirty mortal blows apiece; and those who did the good work were men of Montségur. Now songs about Guillaume Arnaud were being sung throughout the land from Montauban to Perpignan. (That, too, was a joy to be remembered, as a bright star in the night. When good days are few they are more highly prized.) After that blow, they thought, the Pope will recall the Preaching Friars, and we shall have no more inquisitions beyond the regular courts. All cases will have to be tried again. Among the men present in the hall, there was not one who had not been sentenced at least once. Nearly all the women were. Rigueur was not thinking of herself or of Bérenger, but she hoped to see her children's trials revised.

The days are so long in prison that ten years of life are quickly relived in thought between morning and night. Ten years,

486

twenty years, thirty. . . . The days are so long that there is time to study every stone in the wall, every flagstone in the floor, to take one big step thirty times and two small steps thirty times, and yet still not to have succeeded in killing one hour. Thoughts, memories: you get drunk on memories and believe the night will fall soon, and the rays of the sun slip straight and rainbow-coloured through the window and play on the bars of the door. You watch them move. By moving towards the door, tugging hard on the chain and lifting your hand, you can catch a little sunlight on the tips of your fingers.

On the wall above the ring to which the chains were fastened, one Jean Saunier had carved his name, and announced that he had been in prison since Christmas of the year 1234, making in all—here the stone had been much scratched. Jean Saunier must have changed the figure every year, and he had remained in that cell for eight years. "So he was imprisoned at the same time that I was," thought Roger, "and he did not escape. Lord Jesus! To think that I might not have escaped—twelve years of life, I gained twelve years of life and while this poor fellow was scratching on the wall, year after year, *I* was living! And such a life! My head held high, with horses, weapons, a young mistress, friends, freedom and so many hopes and projects that it would take more than two months to reckon them all up." Jean Saunier had also carved a dozen square crosses, recommending his brethren to be patient and trust in God. *Brothers, patience, God will deliver us. In the sixty-second year of my age.*

Some worthy burgher, no doubt. He was a neat hand at carving letters. Two other men had written on the stone beside the bed, but this had been a bad idea: the letters were almost worn away by people walking on them. Next to Jean Saunier's pious words someone had written: *The short chain is a whore.* After a few obscenities the same prisoner had added: *I am thirty. Death to traitors.* There were other, much older inscriptions too. *A.D. 1199. Guiraud Peytavi, master dyer. To the M. H. and B. Virgin Mary.* (Most Holy and Blessed?) Anyone would have thought the dyer was short of time or space! Or perhaps he was hoping to be released before long? Roger already knew by heart everything there was to be read on the walls.

"I am thirty. Death to traitors." He wondered whether the man who was thirty had died here, on his short chain, or whether he had been transferred elsewhere. There was a strong chance

487

that Jean Saunier had died after his eight years. They did not treat you badly here: a whole loaf, fresh air, a man might live for a long time, it was not the dungeon. A long time? And it was only three days as yet!

In three days he had gone over his pilgrimage to Rigueur's native country, and had lost himself so completely in the joys and sorrows of his past life that he had almost forgotten his prison. He had had time to weep and curse, and plead a dozen cases against his enemies, and still it was only three days. He longed for night and sleep, and sleep did come, sweeter than a mistress' arms. But waking was cruel, waking before the dawn, in a cold grey half-light. There was the whitish ceiling, the black bars of the door standing out against grey walls, the pitcher of water, like a round stone bullet with a handle and a long spout added, and the chains wound round his legs and his numbed feet.

At the moment of waking, Roger remembered nothing at all about his life; it seemed to him that he was a great criminal, justly condemned, one of those from whom men turn away, one cursed by God. He was uglier than the toad, more forlorn than the forgotten stone at the bottom of a well, alone, drowned beneath oceans of crime and shame. God, what crimes? So great was his self-loathing that he believed he had killed his father and mother, slaughtered children, and, although he knew it was not true, found himself even more repulsive than if he had committed those crimes. The slime of a soul left to itself, ugly, craven, spongy as the body of a man ten days drowned. . . . Gradually memory would come back. "What have I done? What could I have done? I have lived a long time. Lord, I have killed. . ." There the impulse to defend himself would return, in spite of himself: "It was in battle, it was to punish traitors, it was in self-defence. No, not that, not that at all, your lawyer is pleading another's cause; *your* judgment has not begun yet, you know nothing of yourself. . . ."

These black hours of undirected remorse dragged by with appalling slowness, but with daylight the Devil went away. Roger began watching for the arrival of the gaoler. The mere hope of seeing a living man drove away fear and self-disgust; he waited: the man appeared behind the bars. He was a bent old man with a whitish stubble on his chin and naked arms that were a mass of freckles. "Greetings, friend! What news?"

"Greetings."

"Stay a while. Have you been doing this job for long?" The old man was not talkative; he put down the bread and the pitcher and went away. "Hey! At least tell me . . ." Roger shouted. He did not know what to ask; he heard the gaoler serving the man next to him, a believer named Azémar de Villemaur.

From time to time it was possible to exchange a few words with this man Azémar, but this could not be done without shouting. Old men remember in the chimney corner, but at least they have someone to tell their stories to! Telling them to oneself is no joke. With Azémar de Villemaur, Roger exchanged such remarks as "Greetings! God give you long life!" *"Long life to the Count!"* "Honour to the ladies of Toulouse!" *"Shame on all traitors!"* "It will make two years at All Saints!" *"What about the man before me?"* "Bernard-Jean de Belvèze." *"Dead?"* "Yes!" *"Long live the Preaching Friars!"* "Beware the short chain!" (Roger learned later that the gaoler complained about the men who shouted too much. He was well and truly threatened with the short chain and did not shout so much. They communicated by chanting prayers out loud in Latin and slipping in a word ingeniously here and there that was not part of the prayer. The prison priest, who came to confess the prisoners on the eve of feast days, said that it was sacrilegious to use prayers in this way and that in order to pray there was no need to shout like a bear-leader in a fairground.)

Instead of thinking of God and his soul's salvation, therefore (though he had plenty of opportunity), Roger spent his time listening for the sounds that came from the street and the prison, and pacing up and down like a caged beast; he explored the walls of his cell as though he hoped to find some new inscriptions or hidden signs.

The strange thing was that in those first days he had made a firm resolve to put his enforced inaction to good use and make his peace with God. At all events he had to die, and now at least he had the chance not to do so in a grave state of sin; he had only a few hard years to endure and eternity to gain. The restless life he led had left him little time to pray and he had often been sorry for it. Now you have all your time, time for a thousand *Paters* and a thousand *Aves* every day—nay, five thousand if you like! You are free to wear out your arms with making the sign of the cross, to wear out your knees with prostrating yourself. Like a Carthusian monk. Free to repudiate the Devil for ever, his pomps and his works, to repent of all your sins, from first to last, to meditate on the excellence of Jesus Christ, the Virgin, saints and angels. Free—so free it makes the head spin!

After all, aren't I a good Catholic? He no longer knew. A man cannot pluck out the faith of his youth from his heart as he would pluck an arrow from a wound. He had tried in vain; faith, for many men, is like their mother tongue and their native land, a thing that cannot be undone, that must be borne.

But no sooner had he finished his morning prayer and wished to plunge deep into pious thoughts, than the Devil showed him obscene pictures; or then the fleas and bugs would irritate him to such a degree that he was obliged to stop and hunt them, or he was simply overtaken by an unconquerable disgust and his piety seemed to him cowardly and hypocritical: he had no more love for God than for the old gaoler who brought him his bread. "And certainly," he thought, "I must first purge myself of the sins of my past life, I must re-examine myself, all the way from childhood to old age, without sparing myself, before I can offer myself up to God with a regenerate soul." But the examination was long, and tedious, and, above all, pointless. There were two men: one, Roger de Montbrun, son of Pierre-Guillaume de Montbrun, knight attendant on Count Raymond, and so forth, had led a life no better and no worse than many others and would die at last (God willing) with all the comforts of religion, and receive the just reward for his good and bad deeds. The other, the other was himself, a man in chains, alone, nameless and with no past, a thing, in short, endowed with eyes, ears and bowels but senselessly, horribly, useless.

It was not fear of the fire, or fear of hell. No, it was the crazy desire to be revenged, one day—but which, great God?—revenged, so as not to think one has been a fool to the end. Live long enough to see their accursed laws abolished? Ah, not even that! Long enough to find peace of mind? Not even that.

The day will come, Roger, when you are white as lamb's-wool, bowed, toothless, wrinkled, sluggish, whimpering, when they will open this door, they will take off your chains, they will carry you through the streets of Toulouse on a litter covered with red cloth and you will stretch out your arms to the crowd. "Behold the worthy knight who has suffered so greatly through the fault of traitors! Honour him too, good people, because he fought for our freedom while there was strength left in his arms. He was never a heretic, but because he was faithful to the Count they put him in prison!" *In the great hall of the Capitol, before the whole Parliament, the prisoners would show their ankles, wasted by the chains, their emaciated arms and flowing beards; great furred mantles would be placed over their shoulders. How many of them would wear the consular purple that year? Votes are taken, and the names announced. "Know, good old men, that of all the citizens you should be the most honoured, because you have moistened your bread with tears and cursed the walls of your dungeons. You were condemned by treachery and great injustice."*

"Thank you, brothers! You have acted as befitted men of Toulouse! For those who are no longer here, we thank you. Where their souls dwell there will be joy this day. Let us pray for them! For all those who died in prison, and for those, also, who were burnt in contempt of the laws!"

With one accord, Parliament decides to raze the new prison to the ground, and to take the stones from it to rebuild the city walls. Let every man who can handle a spade, from three leagues around, hurry to Toulouse and let work begin! The citizens will give the boarders lodging for nothing. Ah, in the fine streets there is more than one house missing, and in the outlying streets too, and weeds grow in their place. "Friends, brothers! My great-grandfather, Roger de Montbrun, built this house in the time of Count Alphonse-Jourdain; my grandfather, Bérenger, added the galleries, my father, Pierre-Guillaume, raised it another storey and flanked it with two turrets; now not one stone is left upon another, they have all been taken to build churches and prisons! My father's aged bones have been torn out of Christian earth and cast into the fire. Those of you who are over forty will still remember my brother, Bertrand, who was so ready to help poor folk, and his good lady, Rachel! I do not ask for the stones of my house back, nor the flags, the columns or the iron grilles! I do not ask for my father's tomb, and as for my brother's tomb—how could I speak of that? In this day my house has been restored to me, the burnt bones find the peace of the grave because our city welcomes them, and re-establishes their honour for ever."

No more houses will be pulled down, no more graves profaned, fathers need fear their children no longer, nor masters their servants, nor women their husbands! None shall be judged, except for real offences. There will be witnesses and advocates at every trial, and informers shall be bound to give their names in public. We shall behead the serpent of treachery!

So Roger passed the long winter evenings, lying on his straw mattress, letting his thoughts wander, attempting to console himself with the idea that his sufferings might not be useless. If ever he saw that day—he who had seen so many black days, and so many days of rejoicing—he would be able to tell the newcomers the price that had been paid in blood for every stone and

491

every plot of ground. Ah, he would be able to tell what things were like in a time when men did not live in fear. *And to think that day might come.*

To think . . . who better than a prisoner can conclude alliances, celebrate the marriage of princes, order battles, capture fortresses? *He will never remarry.* What great baron would want him for a son-in-law, sick and weary as he is? He is fifty years old. Who will defend us, since the Count's heir, Prince Alphonse, has never visited Toulouse and does not even speak our language? The Countess Jeanne is twenty-seven and childless (unquestionably they are giving her potions to make her sterile, so that there will never be a legitimate Count in Toulouse). . . . And yet, if the Count were to find a wife of noble birth, the swords would start from their sheaths even for an infant in swaddling clothes! In twenty years that child would be a young man fit to bear arms, and the rights of Alphonse would be so much smoke beside his. If the Countess Jeanne is sterile who will fight for her? Our fate lies in a woman's loins; beggars and poor labourers have more children than they need, and the Count, in order to take a wife, must needs intrigue and supplicate like a man trying to obtain another's goods by false pretences. Is it to Count Alphonse, Louis' own brother, that we must look for mercy?

Brothers, see how we are treated by our Count's heir: Prince Alphonse holds us in such contempt that he has never come to our city, never paid a visit to his father-in-law. Toulouse is a free city. Let us not swear fealty to him until he has pledged himself to respect the customs of our land! And if he will not be a true count to us, then let him never receive our homage. Let him make the people love him by throwing open the prisons and putting an end to the Inquisition. He is King Louis' brother, he will obtain this favour from the Pope more easily than Count Raymond could. . . .

Roger set these speeches in the Capitol (occasionally putting them in the mouth of one consul or another). He shouted them in the square, from up on the balcony, while the crowd applauded. "What's this?" he thought. "Am I burying the Count already? God grant him long life! Without him we are all lost because no good will ever come to us from Alphonse, he is our enemy. . . .

Louis the Ninth is killed on a crusade, the Regent, Blanche, dies of an illness, a little child is king. . . The Duke of Brittany and the Count of la Marche form an alliance with the King of England, while the Emperor Frederick crosses the Rhône and takes possession of Provence. Carcassonne

492

*is liberated and we swear fealty to the Emperor! The Count recovers his
cities and receives the King of Aragon's daughter in marriage.*

O Lord, the craziest dreams are not so crazy as the thing that
has happened to us! Was there ever such a thing before as a
game in which you lose at every throw, even though you never
miss once? This is the most piercing thought: that this thing
should not be, it should have been *possible* for it not to be. How
did we make a mistake? When? What alliances did we neglect,
what promises did we fail to make? Always, at each moment, the
margin was so small, at every throw of the dice we played a
losing game, *but it was not a game*, IT WAS NOT A GAME. We played
honestly against people who cheated, who had agreed among
themselves beforehand that they would cheat and had decided
once and for all that their dice should always be loaded. The
Church. Thieves have possessed themselves of the seamless
garment of Jesus Christ.

The days passed, and weeks and months, and Roger no longer
found the time so long. He learned to think little, to occupy his
hands, either carving on the stone with the edge of one of the
links in his chain, or writing on the walls with a lead button, or
by plaiting fringes with hairs and threads of cloth. But as there
was no foreseeable end to his imprisonment these occupations
seemed a senseless game and he put little enthusiasm into them.

He carved his name. He carved: A.D. 1247. He carved: *Sancta
Maria Mater Dei ora pro nobis.* And also: DE PROFUNDIS CLAMAVI
AD TE. ET IPSE REDIMET ISRAEL. This psalm struck him as highly
appropriate to his situation and plunged him into edifying
thoughts. In thinking of 'Israel' he could not help thinking of
Toulouse, and the psalm roused in the depths of his being a trust
in God forgotten since his childhood, and very sweet. Sometimes
he felt as though he had only to close his eyes to find again the
soul that had been his as a child. "The Lord shall redeem His
Israel after all her sufferings, out of the depths have I cried unto
thee, O Lord. . . . From the morning watch until night—Let
Israel hope in the Lord. . . . And he shall redeem Israel—from all
his iniquities. *Ex omnibus iniquitatibus eius.*"

"And their tears shall be dried and their groans changed into
songs of cheerfulness." O strange error, worthy of a child, or of a
man in second childhood! Is Toulouse Israel? In point of fact
it is more often compared to Sodom and Gomorrah, and God has

493

never made it any promises. Who ever said that 'redeem Israel' meant: throw open the prisons of Toulouse, who ever said that it matters to the Lord of Heaven whether we are delivered from our enemies?

He has promised us the heavenly Jerusalem. Lord Jesus, Holy Mary, if you give no one justice in this world, will not men say: the heretics are right? Roger consoled himself for hours at a time with these innocent reveries, but they brought, not peace of mind, but a numbing of all thought. When all memories become nausea, regret or remorse, then one remembers God and the time when it was as simple to reach for God as for a bowl of milk. Ah, God and the saints protect you very well as long as you stand stock still, but as soon as you take one step they desert you. The spirit scours the country like a battle charger that has lost its rider. Forty years of struggle and hope, of love and hate, stampeding away, forty years' thought, calculation, cunning and plans—so many discourses, speeches, oaths, songs and soft words! Forty years of a man's life, not counting his first youth. So many sorrows for a single life! The dead at Béziers, piled high in the squares with rivers of blood flowing from severed hands and feet, the bodies of little children floating in baths of reddened water. It will be forty years soon. We have forgotten that blood, and so much besides. . . .

What a glorious life I could have led in any other time!

Et ipse redimet Israel. How easy it is to pray in silence. Thought, like a thread of water, loses itself in the great river of the psalm. There all is resolved for ever, no more doubts and torments, life is forgotten, forgotten all the injustices ever perpetrated: not one word of this psalm or of any other psalm will ever be changed. . . .

After Pentecost there was smallpox in the prison and the inmates shouted the names of the dead from one cell to the next. In this way Roger learned of Colombe's death. He suffered less than he might have done: she was so far away, at the other end of the prison, in the communal cells. Another world. And of this, the last and longest of all his love affairs, he retained only a vague, scarcely tender, memory. His heart was not in it any more. He had come to her too old. Yet, God knew, he had never thought that she would die before him (he was almost proud of that).

Yet she had been his pride, none the less, his last ornament, the bouquet of flowers on his lance. Never—however madly in love they were—had he allowed her to lack honour in the eyes of the world; she was his niece first and foremost. Who could tell? With another man perhaps she would have escaped prison? Young bodies, so full of life and energy, more readily fall a prey to the violence of the disease. Dead, without a message for him, with no other message than her name, shouted from door to door.

Dead, the poor girl-mother, the proud little sinner who had been so thoroughly stripped of her pride. (What had they done to her to make her talk so much?) *"Your niece has admitted to us . . . your niece accuses you of this and that. . . ."* They were not lying, they could not have learned those things from anyone but her. Séverin is not a talker, and none of the things he knew have been brought up against me.

Roger realised with surprise that he was regretting those days: the trial, the underground dungeon, the interrogations and the whip, and the cup which Brother Alberic had drunk from in front of him, and Brother Alberic himself, they were old friends! He was already there, on Brother Peter Seila's right, on the first day that I was deprived of my freedom and my rights, on the very first day, the last I really lived as a man. He was already there, watching me with his big eyes, like a hunter; we were both young in those days, and both of us had much innocence left to lose. On the day of the burnings, when he was hoisting up the bodies on the end of a pitchfork, he looked like a soldier rushing in to the attack. "With God's help!" He was red and panting and his robe was splashed with mud, his eyes smarting from the smoke, but burning and merciless. Ah, it was like another world! They roared like lions, they hurled flames.

It was a hot fight, they still were not sure they were the masters. Ah, *in my time* even the prison had a different smell. Raimbert used to come and hover round me. *"I am not such a fool as to listen to you."* (But he was *such a fool*, and he paid dearly for it.)

They have buried Colombe in the paupers' graveyard with the other women who died of the smallpox; they will not even have told her brothers, because Layrac is a long way off. When I die, who will bury me? My sons will certainly not buy a gravestone for me, at the most they will have one or two Masses sung for me. What sort of 'father' am I? Moreover the domain is so heavily mortgaged and let out to tenant farmers that they live little better than peasants. The thought of dying in prison hardly frightens me any more. The time he had left to live now seemed to Roger neither long nor short; he lived one day and then another. He even got used to the cold in winter, even to the pain in his joints, his cough and the pain in his bowels. There are few troubles which, in the end, do not become a distraction.

The day the Count's death was proclaimed in Toulouse, the knell was rung for him in all the churches, and it was still ringing late into the night. The gaoler went his rounds at an unaccustomed hour, round about noon, stopping outside every cell to say: "*The Count is dead!*" His voice was hoarse and his eyes red. The prisoners did not call out to one another and exchange remarks; they were all listening to the bell.

Miserere mei Deus, secundum misericordiam tuam—O useless tears, O grief that will not be comforted, may God have mercy on him at least, though He had no mercy on us! *Requiem in aeternam dona ei, Domine—Et lux perpetua* . . . May He take no more heed of his sins, may He give him crown and realm in heaven. Lord, You have taken away our hope, surely You owe him that! The knell beat against the walls, and tolled out the great sorrows of the dead Count. Now we have no one, we are delivered up for ever to a foreign count.

The good olive branch has not flowered, the branch is withered.

Non intres in judicium cum servo tuo Domine, Lord do not sit in judgment on Your servant! For Your servant, Raymond de Saint-Gilles, has suffered such persecution that his soul will come to judgment panting and hounded like a stag at bay: have mercy on a soul hounded to death.

He has left us in order to find peace at last; You abandoned him on earth, Lord, do not abandon him now.

What! He lacked nothing, he did not want for attention, or nourishment, or good beds or flowering borders, or music or good company. He was still not much past the prime of life, could he not have guarded his body better? Old men last longer, chained and sick and starved: yet he, whose life was of such value, lets it slip between his fingers!

The next day the prisoners were given white bread and water reddened with a fair amount of wine, so that they might the better pray for the Count's soul, and be comforted in their grief, because even those who bore their chains by the Count's will were mourning in their hearts. The knell was sounding for the end of the glory of Toulouse. Now we have no lawful *seigneur* any more, but a foreign master instead. The city has lost her crown.

For the first time for two years, Roger forgot that he was in prison. His chains no longer weighed him down, and the cell was as large as a banqueting hall. Even supposing I were in a fine house, in a cool, green garden filled with birds, he thought, would the Count be any the less dead? Happy the man who drinks the wine of sorrow in a place which suits his grief. Day after day, for twenty years, we have watched our land become a prison.

Surely prisoners should be envied? They have no need to tremble any more, they will never be betrayed by anyone again. They will not eat their hearts out with false hopes again, nor will they bow their heads any more. Alphonse de Poitiers will make his entry into Toulouse to the sound of bells and the lily banners will fly from the Capitol and all the towers. The people will go to greet him, the knights will swear allegiance to him. He will be accorded the honours which are his rightful due, he will distribute bread to the poor and have the squares strewn with copper coins. Rejoice in your celebrations, Count Alphonse, the heritage you have so despised was the lifeblood of our hearts.

A face can be seen, looking up from the bottom of the pitcher, a thin face with eyes drowned in shadow—a straight, over-long nose, a brow hidden under locks of grey hair, the mouth lost under a drooping, yellowish moustache—the whole face can never be seen at once, so one makes up for it by moving the head. It is drained of colour, like a ghost on the black surface of the water. Watching himself so, Roger felt more curiosity than sadness. The weary, pensive gaze of those black eyes was the look of a friend. Drowned in a pint of water. Look well at this face, try and realise what five years of solitude have done for you. Azémar de Villemaur has gone; they opened the door for him, they struck off his chains. He had howled and screamed for six days, and for six days and nights his neighbours could not sleep. The priest had come, bearing the cross and the chalice. Then they had taken the body away, and Roger had seen him for the first time: a little wizened old man, his skin almost black, lying on a hurdle; his lips were tight and proud, his head hanging down. "*Azémar de Villemaur, squire, son of Pierre-Othon de Villemaur, of Toulouse. Pray for his soul.*" Roger's new neighbour, Jacques Roubaud, a candle-maker, was not yet forty. He kept shouting: "Let me out of here,

I have done nothing!" It was not pleasant to hear him. When you have done five years, you do not like new names. You do not like changes. The old gaoler was dead, and the new one had a brutish face and a wart under his nose.

"Strange," thought Roger, "strange to see that there was some good in the cruellest of the past. Because he is no longer here to torment us, we are prepared to love him."

He knew he was ill. The mere sight of food made him feel sick, but he ate none the less. The retching and the pain in his bowels left him no peace, and in two weeks he had lost so much weight that his arms and legs were no more than skin and bone. When he looked at his reflection in the pitcher, he saw enormous, dark-rimmed eyes, huge cheekbones jutting above hollow cheeks. He altered every day. He thought: "It is the hot weather, it will pass." He would not complain from a superstitious fear of hearing himself say: "It's not a doctor you want, it's a priest." He felt less than ever ready to die and told himself: "I have lived five years already; the worst is over, surely one day I shall find peace." He felt as though he had not even begun to look for it.

At nightfall, when his aches and pains allowed him some respite, he lay without moving, his eyes closed, his arms behind his head, and succeeded in controlling his body to the point of forgetting fear: that fear of the return of the sickness which all day forced him to remain alert, like a hare trapped in his earth by a dog.

To feel no fear: that, in itself, was repose. He thought over his life. A life so completely cut in two that it seemed to belong to two different men: the man of the last five years thought of the other with the indulgent fondness of an elder brother. There had been many sins, but even more bad luck. Errors, crimes perhaps, but what a span! He had commanded men, borne a sword, lain with the loveliest of girls right up to the last! He had escaped from one prison, after he had earned an indictment ten pages long . . . and before the first prison—God!—it had been the life of a king: the court, Paris, Rome, London, and the finest battles and the highest love. To think . . . *just to think that that was me.* . . .

But he could not succeed in fixing his thoughts on the man of today, the man who needed to make his soul, and prepare himself to render his account to God. This aged, bearded man, with the melancholy expression, he knew little of him and was weary of his company: the chain, the pain in his bowels, his

498

aching head, the lice, the horror of waking in the dawn. Sick, yes. Old? . . . It could not be. Old, yes, over sixty and therefore old. Innocent or guilty? In the end he had come to the conclusion that he was guilty after all, that he must be, that men's laws were a game of dice and whoever allows himself to be beaten is guilty, since the offence is nothing in itself and all that matters is the punishment.

If we had not had this war, he thought, the land would never have endured such laws. Because they have slaughtered and ruined and degraded us, we are guilty. The defeated are judged. Their turn will come.

Who will judge Pope Gregory (may God not have his soul!) and Brother Peter Seila? They will be called blessed. But whoever is put in prison is guilty, otherwise what are prisons for?

Their turn will come, but we shall never know it, unless such things are remembered in Heaven or Hell.

Your soul is naked before God—since nothing but a shadow is left of your body—naked before God, and are you still arguing? *De profundis clamavi ad te, Domine.* . . . Lord, Lord, I have been subjected to a nameless outrage: avenge me!

A long delirium. The door is wide open, I shall not pass through it alive. There are two of them, they have white habits, black cloaks and tonsured heads. They have had a stool brought in, covered with a black cloth, to put the chalice on.

One is at my head, the other at my feet, their eyes are lowered and they are reciting prayers. They are not men, they are not my brothers, they have no chains on their feet. Their chins are clean shaven, their hands clean and smooth; they are not men. *Confiteor* and *mea culpa.* "Am I dying? Who told you to come?"

"You have been unconscious for two days, my son. God has brought you to yourself again so that you may have time to repent and be comforted by the sacraments."

He is a little old man with brown eyes outlined with triangular brown shadows. "Brother Peter Audiart?"

"Father Peter, my son. Our Father Abbot, in his goodness, has given me permission to attend the sick in the prisons."

"I owe you fifty strokes of the lash, Father."

"Control yourself, my son, you are wandering."

"I will not make my confession to you."

"My son, do not waste precious time. The respite will be short."

499

"I should be damned if I received the Body of the Lord from your hands."

"My son, banish all hatred and bitterness from your heart. This is the great day. Whatever the hands which offer it to you, God's sacrament is the same, always and everywhere, to all eternity."

"May God have mercy on me, but I will take nothing from your hands! Do you flay the beast and then expect him to lick your feet?"

"My son, it is hard for you to speak, you have little breath left and you are wasting your strength in idle talk."

"You are troubling me with idle talk."

"Why are you trying to damn your soul?"

"It is you who have damned it. You will never be absolved from the blood that has been spilled. Jesus Christ Himself cannot grant absolution for innocent blood."

"You are blaming me," said the old man, "for an involuntary offence, painfully expiated, and from which the Holy Father himself has willingly absolved me. Otherwise, should I have been judged worthy of the priesthood? I bring you the Lord, so that He may comfort you, what are your harsh words to me? Have I not heard others? You blame me, because you see in me the friend of your enemies. But at this present hour, my son, you have no more friends or enemies in this world. Know that my bowels are burning with pity for you. God does not send us here to judge, but to heal. Hate the man, he is hateful indeed and the meanest of sinners, but then forget your hatred in the love of God. The Lord did not lie to me when he told me that one day I should be the instrument of your salvation. Your hours are numbered, shall I pray for you in vain?"

Roger turned away his head. He was burning with fever so that he was no longer sure that he was seeing or hearing clearly; his whole body was filled with small red flames, each drop of blood was a flame, he seemed to be able to see them. His mind was clearer than it had ever been, or so at least he thought, so clear and sharp that he could have talked endlessly and made them understand everything, everything, show them that they were not men but living corpses, real corpses, vain, tinkling bells. . . . This man's voice was a bell, a feeble, never-ending tinkle, all on the same note. . . .

Is a man said to be raving because he talks a language fools do not understand? In point of fact he was not talking at all, the raging fever had stiffened his jaws. Yet he was sure that in a moment the new language, the true language, would be born and burn this man with his grief-reddened eyes. The silver pyx, covered with a square of red silk, was the dwelling place of the suffering Body, the pure white Body, the true God. He had entered this very cell, weak and defenceless, borne by impure hands, for impure lips. Broken, transpierced and eaten everywhere through all the ages. You willed it so, Lord, You gave Yourself to the executioners for ever. This is the Church You have chosen for Yourself: Herod, Pilate, Caiaphas and Judas, the four beasts of the Apocalypse. The lion, Herod; the eagle, Pilate; the bull, Caiaphas; the man, Judas. In order that the lamb shall be the only innocent, that it shall be known that there is no other innocence in this world, the four Beasts are covered with wings and eyes in heaven but on earth their image is in the four horsemen.

Here is the innocent body, delivered up by Caiaphas, spurned by Herod, transpierced by Pilate, sullied by the kiss of Judas. Merely a little flour and a drop of water, this is the true Body of Him who created the universe, this is true love, torn and humiliated throughout the ages. They are Your true servants, Lord, they who are such expert executioners. Who else would have dared to crucify You?

I have desired You so in vain. I have received You so many times unworthily. I have betrayed You so many times. You come into this cell as a beggar, brought by impure hands, and shall I sully You with my kiss? Here is the Cross; You are alone with the crown of thorns, the nails and the spear, and the vinegar and gall, and the cruel mockery. If You are God, let this Chalice glow like the sun and burst asunder the prison walls!

"My son, you have only to repeat the words of the *Confiteor* after me, if you can still speak. Can you hear me, my son?" I can hear him. Why is this man tormenting himself? Am I his relative, or friend? Oh, his is an impure pity, the perverse tears of a man who wants to be at the same time the executioners' accomplice and the servant of God, and so win all joys!

"Can you still hear me?"

"What do you want of me?"

"My son, forget all hatred, do not let me see you depart in a state of mortal sin!"

501

"I am a heretic," said Roger. "I have always been. I want to die as a heretic. Leave me."

"Why slander yourself? Do I not know what you are?"

"You know nothing of me."

The man in the black cloak stood up slowly, without looking at Roger, and knelt before the chalice. He left the cell without another word: the stool, covered with black cloth, stood out against the grey wall like a small catafalque. Empty. "It is all over," Roger told himself, "they will let me die alone." There was no doubt now, he was alone in the cell and the door was open.

Why had they left it like that? Wide open, I shall not see my iron bars again. For a moment, fear seized him: were they going to find the farrier and some soldiers at once, take him out of prison and fling him, still living, into the fire? "Your hours are numbered," they had said. But I am not in so much pain. My head is still clear. And what if this were a trick, if . . .?

His eyes were blurred by the fever and now the stool looked to him like a great coffin, surrounded by candles. An empty coffin. The Body of the Lord had lain in it, and was there no longer. WHY ARE YOU WEEPING? WHEREFORE SEEK YE THE LIVING AMONG THE DEAD? The angel sitting on the edge of the coffin turned on Roger a look of stern surprise.

The angel was no longer there. The shroud was lying on the ground, trampled and bloody. Wherefore seek ye the living among the dead? They have all risen from the churches and the squares which were running with their blood; they were still bleeding, naked and mutilated, and they ran about waving their arms, mothers holding up their little children. It was June, and the fire took hold so fast that in an hour the whole city was burning, and the great church flamed and roared, and its windows burst like chestnuts in the fire, while three thousand dead were burning inside, fresh corpses, with their hair and their clothes. . . . God have mercy on us, it is better to be burned dead than alive!

The door was still open. Had they done it on purpose? Roger's brain was so confused that he forgot his chains, he no longer felt them; he leaped up from the bed and flung himself at the door, but the chains jerked him backwards suddenly and he collapsed in the doorway. His head and arms were projecting forwards into the passage and he thought how strange it was to see so far, to see the passage and the other barred doors, and the window at the end; a real window, long and covered with an iron grille—if he could only see what was behind it—with a reflected, reddish light.

A man was there, kicking him and dragging at the chains to get him back into the cell. He was being dragged along, and it seemed to go on for hours, he was fastened by the feet to a horse's tail.

Men were shouting, raining blows on him, hurling stones. Punished, like a traitor. Why? . . . There was blood on his face, he was vomiting blood. Why have they done this to me? . . . Rigueur. Sweet Rigueur. Gentle Rigueur.